Robert Cameron is a retired professor of evolutionary biology, living in Sheffield. His professional expertise relates to slugs and snails, and studying these have taken him around the world. While he has written many scientific papers and books, his interests in dystopian fiction, SF and fantasy have seduced him into his own, distinctive pattern of storytelling.

To all my colleagues and friends who worked together for the Department of Extramural Studies at the University of Birmingham, 1973–1994.
"Those were the days, my friends."

Robert Cameron

GROUND

AUSTIN MACAULEY PUBLISHERS™

LONDON * CAMBRIDGE * NEW YORK * SHARJAH

A CIP catalogue record for this title is available from the British Library.

ISBN 9781398481367 (Paperback)
ISBN 9781398481374 (ePub e-book)

www.austinmacauley.com

First Published 2022
Austin Macauley Publishers Ltd®
1 Canada Square
Canary Wharf
London
E14 5AA

My debt to my colleague and friend, Ann Hurman, cannot be overstated. A writer herself, her pertinent comments and constant encouragement sustained me through the rough patches. Julia MacDonald Ogilvie also sharpened my wits, even from her sickbed, and Beata Pokryszko gave me much encouragement. Our son, Alexander Cameron, provided the necessary details at a critical point in the narrative.

Table of Contents

Part 1 Catalyst

Mark

Hue and Cry

Beyond the Bounds

Part 2 Reaction

The Royal Domain

Eden and Beyond

Things Fall Apart

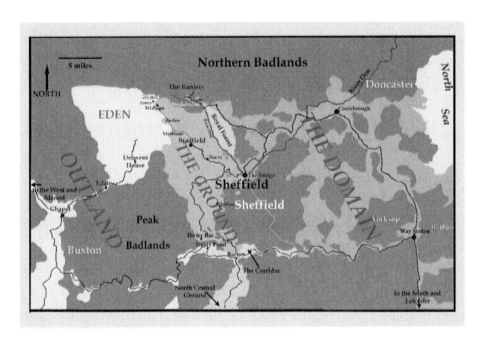

Part 1
Catalyst

Mark

1. By the River

Mark and the others watched as Jamie swam across the river and scrambled up the bank. He untied the sealed pack, took out his clothes, dressed and turned to give them a salute. Then he crossed the bankside path and disappeared into the scrubby woodland. A few minutes later, they heard his whistle. Mark replied with a single note, and Julie honked once on a bullhorn.

Jamie's whistle sounded once every two or three minutes, getting the same reply each time. Eventually, the whistle became faint. Mark and Julie sounded twice. No further, Jamie. Two whistles came back, and the next one was louder, though Jamie was still out of sight. Mark and the others kept their eyes on the path along the opposite bank and on the open track down the hillside from which the Rangers and their dogs might come. *They'd been lucky this time*, thought Mark; there was an east wind and the Rangers would have to lead their dogs down to the bank to pick up any scent. The horses could not get into the scrub in any case, and the Rangers would have to dismount if the dogs picked up a scent earlier.

Ten, fifteen, twenty, thirty minutes passed. Jamie sounded as though he had stopped. Then he came closer, but still out of sight. Forty minutes, fifty, an hour. Of the Rangers, there was no sign. *Enough was enough*, Mark thought, *now we know*. Of course, Jamie had wanted to go further in. But if the Rangers came, they could give no warning and Jamie would be caught. He *might* be returned via the bridge, with bruises like some of the squatters trying it in the city. He *might* just be thrown back in the river, and watched till he reached the other side. That had happened with Stan, but what happened after was not so good, as Jamie knew very well. Equally, though, they *might* never see him again, as with David, or with Steve, for that matter. They had proved David's point and that was enough. He blew his own whistle three times and Julie honked the bullhorn. Jamie replied, and very soon reappeared on the bank, repacked his clothes and swam back to them.

"Why call me back?" he asked, while dressing again. "There were no Rangers. When they came, I could have beaten them to the bank easy, and they'd not cross the river. They don't have the gear."

"You would not have heard our warning, or heard it too late if you had gone further in. They'd be between you and the river. The dogs would sniff you out. We've proved the point," said Mark. "In an hour, you could be miles away. It's all to the good if they never know anyone's crossed, or who. We don't want more patrols or suited Kingsmen crossing the river."

He turned to the group. "Right, let's get out of sight in case the Rangers do turn up. Seeing a bunch of us on the bank and the dogs picking up the scent, and they'll put two and two together."

They walked away from the path and found shelter behind a large ruined building. They still had a view of the track down the hill opposite. No Rangers came. The city kids, Jack and Sue, were questioning Jamie, a Jamie still aggrieved at his recall. Yes, there were ruins in the wood. No sign of recent digging. He'd poked about, but nothing obvious except heavy iron machinery. The three Rivelin girls were whispering together. Only young Peter stood quietly by Mark, who remained silent and thoughtful.

Mark knew his companions; this gap, this entry into forbidden territory, would be a temptation. The Rivelin girls might sneak out on their own just for the sake of breaking the record now set by Jamie. Left to his own devices, Jamie would be a mile or more inside. Peter, the youngest, would not act without Mark, but Jack and Sue would be weighing up the prospects for the more serious business of salvage, of Relic-hunting. He broke into the muttered conversations.

"Look, we've done it, we know David was right. The boundary is not guarded here. If we're lucky, the breach will not be discovered. If the Rangers had come, they would not cross, but they would step up patrols and the mayor would be told to get a grip. There'd be Proctors up and down the path our side every Kingsday. No, absolutely no, testing the limits on your own. Another chase and we'll be blocked for good, even if you escape or just get thrown back in the river. Remember what happened to Stan? And his family? And David? You might disappear with no trace."

He turned to Jack and Sue.

"I think the bailiff would say the same. We need to see how far the breaches go. Together, with watchers. We'll be drafted for the summer, anyway. Let's let it lie until autumn and have a think."

No one said anything more and the group dispersed, down the bankside path towards the city or, like Mark and Jamie, heading westwards towards home. Mark hoped that he had persuaded them all; any more disappearances, and the place would be out of bounds forever.

***

It had started with simple curiosity. Their side of the river, the west, was not farmed. It was just a strip of scrubby woodland enveloping a few ruins. It was part of the Ground, and both city folk and those uphill and close by would scour it for firewood, often with some bad-tempered clashes. But the east bank was forested, at least this far north of the city. Indeed, the map on every classroom wall labelled it the King's Forest. True, woodsmen from the Domain would fell a few trees each year, but it was, for the most part, lush and undisturbed. Undisturbed by law. The lessons, the sermons from the mayor, the admonishments of parents all said the same: this is Royal property; Grounders are forbidden to enter.

They all knew the bounds of the Ground. There was the Outie boundary to the west, not obviously contaminated, but clearly marked. Go beyond it, and you might be snatched away by monsters, Outies, partial to human flesh. Outies, though, that none had ever seen, even when working on the boundary farms. To the east, apart from the forest, there was only the bridge to the Domain. Contaminated beyond? Who knew? City kids might be returned after a brief trespass; for all others in the Ground it was a one-way crossing to the Domain. Elsewhere, and especially in the city, the boundaries were made clear by the signs of contamination, contamination that served as a warning more effective than any fence. Signs that were learnt at an early age, and were backed up not only by stern parental warnings, but by the drummed-in need to avoid destroying fertility, that cardinal virtue. The older children soon learnt that those few who ignored them brought down yet more intrusive tests by the hygienists, and often resulted in a whole family being transferred out. The dreaded word *unchosen* was often muttered.

But this forest? All could see that it was clean; clean and unused. For swimmers, the crossing was easy. Easy and very tempting. Of course, it was patrolled. The impressive Rangers with their plumed helmets would ride along the bankside path on the east side, always in pairs, with dogs alongside. Summer Kingsdays would see kids swimming and resting on the west bank, partly to see the Rangers pass. More stirring and spectacular than the dull, suited Kingsmen who appeared alongside the Visitor, or the rather sinister but rarely seen Security men in their black uniforms.

The Rangers had paid no attention to the kids on the other bank or in the water. Then a kind of sport had developed. Good swimmers would cross the river and sit on the opposite bank until the others shouted 'Rangers' or they heard the horns blowing and dogs barking. Stay the longest time after the shout before plunging into the river, and you were the temporary champion. Illegal, of course, but if you stayed on the bank, you had plenty of time to swim back. The dogs sniffed around for a bit, then the Rangers went on or returned the way they had come. They said nothing, even when those on the other side were still in sight.

It was not long before the more adventurous strayed away from the bank and into the forest. It soon became obvious that doing that usually triggered some kind of alarm. You could sit on the bank for hours with no Rangers in sight, but venture more than a few tens of yards away, and a Ranger patrol was galloping towards you within ten minutes or quarter of an hour. Horns always blew, and there was time to rush back to the river. A new game developed; go out of sight into the scrub, and stay until that last rush was needed.

It was during one of these games that they had been accosted by a gang of city kids, squatters. An intimidating bunch, extending their search for Relics northwards. A gang who did not take kindly to a bunch of pampered uphill kids on their patch. The gang had taken a lot of persuading that Mark and the others were not in the same business as themselves. Packs had been inspected. Towels and sandwiches rather than coins or rusted gadgets had lowered the temperature.

City folk had traditionally supplemented basic allowances by finding Relics of all sorts, and exchanging them for credit with the Receiver. The supply among the city ruins had largely dried up, and the search for smaller items had become a casual teenage occupation. Inevitably, it became a cause for disputes and fighting. This gang had chosen to do some prospecting upriver, away from their older and more aggressive rivals. When told about the uphill children's game, they were at first contemptuous. But the possibility of finding places to cross grabbed their attention.

"Haven't you tried lower down?" Mark had asked. "There are far more ruins in towards the city."

"There's fewer clean patches there. Where there are, we get caught within minutes. Damned Tadgies grab us, beat us and send us back across the bridge. Then our fathers usually give us another thumping. Not to mention the beating we get from those Hillsborough louts on the way if they see us. Not that they have had any more luck."

"Tadgies?"

The gang looked contemptuous.

"Security. Truth and Justice, their bosses, Tadgies. Right bastards."

Spoilt brats, harmless, but useful, was the verdict of the squatters. An agreement was reached. Uphill would not nick Relics, and two of the gang would join them to find crossings. So, Jack and Sue had been with them on most Kingsdays.

The year after this meeting, they got a nasty shock. Stan Rogers was well into the forest when the Rangers came. He would have made it, but tripped and fell. A Ranger picked him up, grabbed and read his tag, clouted him around the face and threw him in the river. Much like the Tadgies, they had all thought, and laughed on the way home. It had not been the end of the matter. The following Monday, two black-clad Security troopers had come right into school and removed Stan by force. School over, and they learnt that Stan's parents had been removed. *Unchosen* or merely transferred? Nobody knew.

The headteacher had delivered a homily on the crime of trespass; the mayor had preached on the sanctity of the Royal Domain three Kingsdays in a row, and a hygienist had addressed the school on the dangers of contamination and their duty to keep clean. The inference that Stan was contaminated was baffling to the children, but the shock of the family's disappearance was enough to put an end to the game for a while, the more so as anxious parents reinforced the message. The squatter kids were equally baffled; Tadgies just give you a hiding and that's that. You don't get disappeared.

The event had made Mark think back. Very rarely, his father told him, a child went missing and was never found, despite searches. After a while, the mayor might hint that they had been carried off by Outies. Usually, the whole family would disappear soon after, escorted by Security. These were the rare occasions when those from uphill saw the black uniforms all too familiar to those in the city. Transferred to another Ground was the standard story, but the dreaded word *unchosen* was sometimes whispered.

Usually, yes, that happened, but not always. The year before Stan was caught, Jamie's older brother, Steve, had disappeared. Both had joined in the early river games, but often went out without the others. Steve had simply disappeared on one such visit. Jamie told his parents, and everybody else, that they had been Relic hunting up river on the west side. They had separated and he had lost his brother and eventually returned home. There had been the usual hunt. His parents had been as much angry as saddened. They were of the highest status, with four children already Chosen and over the bridge. There would be more to come, for Muss had three young ones and was pregnant with a fourth. They pestered the mayor incessantly.

Nothing had happened. No transfer out, no sermons or prohibitions. A fortnight after the disappearance, the parents suddenly ceased their complaining. They resumed the high and mighty airs of those who had made such a notable contribution to Royal Service. There were mutterings about friends in high places. Mark's father grunted about *one family Arkell couldn't afford to lose,* but said no more. Jamie himself became withdrawn and uncommunicative, staying away from the river. The others, though, had thought little of it; it had no obvious connection to their games.

The shock of Stan's later removal wore off. The challenge, the itch to find crossings, remained. The following spring, though, David Reynolds also disappeared. David was weird. He could not swim, and never made the crossing. Nevertheless, he was among the keenest at turning up at the riverbank on Kingsdays to watch others cross. After Steve disappeared, David had followed Jamie's example for a while, and kept away from the river. Or so it had seemed. Then he started returning, but without Jamie. He watched the swimmers, and the Rangers. He had, so the others said later, a little notebook and wrote in it. After a while, he seemed to wander off, not part of the gang. Occasionally, he would encourage them to try new places, usually further north, and often with no view of the tracks down which the Rangers came to the river. He was usually ignored. Just before Stan's capture, though, the three Rivelin girls had often tagged along with him. They still hankered after records.

David was Jamie's best friend. The family, with a history of successful Relic retrieval, were the official Receivers of Relic and Reward. They were up and down between the city warehouses at the bridge and their house in Bradfield. A privileged family, and one regarded with envy, for David's work stints in the school holidays were always with his father, an unheard-of arrangement otherwise. Jamie, likewise, had done two stints in a row alongside David, an aberration that did not go unnoticed.

Then one Monday in spring, nearly a year after Stan's misadventure, David was not in school. Mr Barndee, the headteacher, told them at Assembly that he had gone missing, never having come home on Kingsday night nor on Sunday. A Proctor standing beside him then asked: had anyone seen him on Kingsday after the Service? Or Sunday? Silence. When they went into the first lesson, Mark and Jamie went to their own desks, side by side. Chronicles, damned Chronicles, Mark had thought, as he opened the desk to take out the rather dog-eared *Book of the King* that was the only text used. Mr Arkwright fussed around the high desk in front and cast his eye over the class.

"Today is the anniversary of what…Perkins?" jabbing his finger at a boy at the back, noted for his abilities with sums, but not much else.

"Er…The Battle of the Peak, sir. Fifth of May, KY 16."

"And what happened there, Perkins?"

"The King's forces won a glorious victory, sir. Lord Edmund was slain, but six renegade nobles fell and their forces fled to the west."

"Very good, Perkins." Even Mr Arkwright sounded slightly bored. Almost every one of many anniversaries they learnt by rote related to glorious victories for the King. The Battle of the Peak was the last. Mark, who tended to drift away in Chronicles, had wondered for some time, why, with so many glorious victories, the Deceiver seemed to be as much or as little of a threat as always, at least as far as he could see. He had asked his father about the Peak. It's to the west, he was told, but it's not in the Domain, that's for certain. Badlands for the most part. The Outland boundary had remained the same for at least 200 years. Maybe the hill farmers suffered from the Outies' livestock raids, but that seemed to have been going on forever, and no one was short of food. There were tales of kidnap and murder, even of cannibalism, but nobody could point to a particular case. The day's lesson was about a more recent time than that.

"Where were we last week? Morris?"

"The plague of 113, sir, and how it started."

"Very well. So, we will learn what happened after that. Chapter ten; we were at page 177."

Arkwright had looked down at his own copy of the Book, then started talking about population, death-rates and the necessary injections that had been provided. The origin of hygienists, now an honoured occupation. The spread from the south and, of course, the whole thing a product of the wicked Deceiver and his Outie servants.

It had sent Mark into a reverie. His great-grandparents had lived through the plague as children. The family story was not that told in the *Book*. Here, the plague had started in the hill farms by the Outie boundary. There had been an attempt to isolate them, but the disease had moved downhill. There had been an army of suited Kingsmen and real doctors giving injections that cured. The hygienists came later. Rumour had it that many had died in the King's Domain too, even some of the nobility. The *Book* said nothing of that. Mark's grandfather had been told the tale when a child, and once when he paid a visit, he had told Mark and the others about it. He relished describing the symptoms. Of course, it was a vile weapon of the Deceiver. But never mind, the King looked after his own. Mark's father had been rather sharp.

"It's always said so, Father. I always wondered how they knew for sure. Wouldn't it have got them too? I always thought, and they'd not have medicine like ours was then."

"Maybe they'd more than we knew of," Grandfather had said. "But look where it started, up against the Boundary. There's farmers there get closer to the Outies than they ought, so we heard, and not in a fight either."

Mark's father had scowled at Grandfather, said nothing and turned back to his desk. The children started mimicking the symptoms while Grandfather laughed.

As his mind snapped back to the present, Mark glanced sideways at Jamie. He was sitting perfectly still, looking blankly ahead. On his open copy of the *Book* was a letter. By the look of it, several pages. Arkwright was at the blackboard, droning on with his back to the class. Mark leaned over and poked Jamie, signing desperately for Jamie to hide it. Jamie turned and looked at him blankly. For a moment, Mark wondered if Jamie had understood. Then, to his relief, Jamie looked down at the letter, folded it and slipped it between pages of the book.

At the end of the lesson, Mark saw Jamie slip the letter into his pocket. After school was over, he scrambled to be outside the gates. He had a feeling that his friend would slip off. As Jamie came out, he grabbed him by the arm.

"What was that you were reading, Jamie?" he asked, "Arkwright would have taken it if he'd seen you. You looked awful."

Jamie said nothing. He turned away, and started off for home. Mark followed him.

"For Majesty's sake, Jamie, what was it? Tell me something!"

Jamie stopped, still looking away.

"It's from David. It was in the book. Just at the page he knew Arkwright would start off on. He must have put it there on Friday, after we'd left the last class. Here, I can't explain, just read it."

He handed the letter to Mark. There were several pages of it, neatly written; not done in a hurry.

Jamie, the reason I'm writing this is that I know something about the river and I think it tells us what happened to Steve. You told me that he simply didn't come back. No Rangers. After that, I stayed away from the river for a while like you.

"What's this about Steve?" he asked. "You never told me you knew where he'd gone."

Jamie looked away again. His words came out in a mumble.

"I was scared. I'd not told my parents the truth, nor the Proctors. Even more reason to keep quiet later after what happened to Stan. I didn't mean to tell David, but I let something slip when he was going on about how was it the Rangers always knew people had crossed. He jumped on it, and so I had to tell him all about it. I knew he'd not blab."

"And you thought I might?" Mark was indignant.

"No, no not that, Mark, please! There seemed no reason to tell anyone. Steve was gone, and when Mum and Dad gave up on complaining, well, I sort of gave up too, especially when they got cross if I mentioned it."

Mark read on:

Then I saw that a few were still trying, so I hung about for a bit again, and I worked something out. You know that the time it took for the Rangers to appear varied. It seemed to me that times got longer further north, though it didn't always work out that way. I tried nudging a few to try further and further from the city. The only ones who were really interested were the Rivelin Farms girls, the twins and Julie. They'd been knocked off the top spot by Arthur and wanted to win again.

So, three Kingsdays ago, I went with them as far north as we could go and still get home without questions. I'd seen a few good places with a view. I would be their timekeeper and witness. Well, we found a good spot, with good views north and south, and opposite one of the tracks downhill to the bank, so that I could see there as well. They all swam across together, and went a little way uphill, but in sight of me. We waited, and nothing happened, and it went way past ten minutes, then twenty, then thirty and there wasn't a sound. Forty, well past the record.

Then Jane started up the Ranger's track for about 200 yards. Then she turned and ran back. Get too far away and she'd not have made it to the river if they appeared. Still nothing. Then they shouted across to me to pick up their packs and set off down the bankside path downstream. I kept pace with them on our side. We were fools. There was no clear view up a trail, and a bend in the river. Suddenly, we could hear horns and barking from the south, very close. We had all got too cocky. Well, all the girls jumped in and swam like mad, and they were safely on our side and hidden before the Rangers came round the bend. I was too, behind an old alder. At first, they behaved just as normal, letting the dogs sniff around.

But the dogs picked up the scent upstream. Then one of them dismounted and peered at the ground. He started walking upstream, stopped and he spoke. We've never heard a sound from them before. It was more of a shout, really. The other one rode up to him and dismounted, also looking at the ground. They had seen the girls' footprints extending northwards. One continued up the path with the dogs, and the other waited with the horses. I did not dare to move, and hoped the girls were well hidden. The one who had gone upstream returned. They talked to each other, but of course, I couldn't hear. One mounted and galloped off, but the other stayed there.

Now, I wondered what to do. Something told me I shouldn't come out. But I couldn't stay there forever. Unless the girls were already on their way, we would be out of time, with some explaining to do back home. Then there was the noise of an engine and a Security man appeared, riding a small mobile, a two-wheeler like the ones they keep near the bridge. They talked together, then the man got off his mobile and went back upstream with one of the Rangers. They soon came back. Then the Rangers mounted and went off downstream. He undressed and *crossed the river. He swam well. It's as well we had all moved from the path, because he could find only a mish-mash where the girls had landed and my prints coming from the north and ending at the same place.*

He scuffled around for a bit, then swam back over the river. He got dressed, mounted the mobile and disappeared northwards. I came out and ran fast down the path and caught up with the girls. They'd not seen the Security man, but had seen a way to escape behind a set of ruins. We agreed that this was one record we would keep to ourselves, at least for a while. They got home just in time. I had to make a lame excuse of getting lost, but did not get questioned.

Jamie, what we found was a real gap. What if there are others? When Steve went in and did not reappear, you heard no horns or hounds. Did he find a gap like this? I'm going to find out. I remember a squatter kid telling me how they taught the younger ones to swim, using floats of wood or oiled cloth bags. There are pools in the city, so no Kingsmen could see. I've made a large one, so I can put clothes and food on it. I've stashed it far upstream, as far as I can go and get back in time. I'll take it further when I go, so about a mile further on from where I was with the Rivelin girls.

It's near the Stocksbridge Clearance to the west. It can't be far from the Barriers. I'll float myself across, and land still north of where we were before. I'll go as far in as I can, and when the food runs out, I'll return. Of course, I'll be missing, but if I get back, I've thought of a story to tell. Jamie, I know I should have told you all this, not just do it. But you have avoided the river ever since Steve went, and I didn't want to involve anyone, nor to have you try to stop me. It should be Monday when you find this if I'm not back. At least, you will know where I went. Burn this as soon as you can, or rip it into shreds. David.

Mark folded the letter up and gave it back to Jamie. His first, mean thought was that David was a complete idiot. It was far too dangerous and particularly stupid to try on your own, especially for a non-swimmer. And the letter! Such a risk for Jamie had it been found.

"He's crazy," was the best he could manage to say. "And for all we know, he could have drowned."

Jamie did not reply. He put the letter in his bag and stood silently by the road. *At least, he looks a bit more normal now,* Mark thought. Then Jamie hunched up his shoulders, turned and set off in the direction of home. Mark wondered whether to follow him, decided not, and himself headed off in the opposite direction.

When he got home, Mark told his mother that David had gone missing and that it had been announced in school. He said nothing about the letter.

"When was he last seen?" she asked Mark.

"I don't know," he replied, evasively. "He was in school on Friday, and I suppose he was at the Kingsday service. No one at school seemed to know anything."

When his father returned from the mayor's office where he worked, it turned out that he already knew.

"We had Proctors in and out of the office this morning. But this afternoon they told me the search was off. Arkell had had words across the bridge."

"King's Peace! I hope he isn't dead and they've found his body," exclaimed his mother. "They'd maybe not want to tell folk that right away, at least till they've seen the parents. Or something worse."

Days went by. There was no news, no corpse retrieved from the river. David's family were not removed, another cause of puzzlement. Later, though, Jack had told Mark that the Tadgies had been all over the warehouses by the bridge, and had been asking round the city. But nobody had seen David. He was a loner; he was weird. Mark and Jamie said nothing. At Mark's insistence, Jamie burnt the letter. The affair fizzled out.

Then came a bombshell. Jamie had felt queasy on a Kingsday morning. The occasional absence from Service attracted little criticism, and the family had marched off, leaving him behind, just in case. With the walk, and the usual long exhortation from Deputy Markham, they would be away at least two hours. At a loose end, Jamie had mooched around the house. Purely out of curiosity, he had opened a cupboard in the hall, a cupboard that his mother had repeatedly said she needed to clear out. It was full of junk, but among the odds and ends was a folder made from old packing and loosely tied with a piece of ribbon. Curious, he undid the ribbon. Inside was something wrapped in an old towel. He could feel a frame. A picture? A concealed Relic?

No. He recognised it at once: a Certificate of Service, like the others proudly displayed on the living room wall. A Certificate in the name of Steven Mallory. Steve had been Chosen! So why had his proud and patriotic parents not displayed it with the others? Two months ahead of the normal selection. He looked at the date; it was about two weeks after Steve had disappeared, just when his parents

26

had gone quiet and discouraged him from asking more questions. Why? Why? Why? He looked at the hall clock. 90 minutes had gone by since the family left. He wrapped the Certificate up, placed it in the folder and tied the ribbon. He put it back as much as possible where he found it, and closed the door. As an afterthought, he mopped up some dust that had fallen on the hall floor. He was still at it when the family returned, getting a pat on the back for thoughtfulness.

Mark and Jamie often got together on Kingsday afternoons, though no longer at the riverbank. Announcing that he felt fine, which was true only as far as his earlier queasiness was concerned, he walked off up to the broken dam above Stacey, a frequent rendezvous. Mark was already there sitting on an old chunk of masonry. Steve had been Chosen! But in secret. He had been found, after all. Why did his parents not tell everybody with pride? Boasting was almost obligatory when it happened. How far had he gone beforehand? Why no sound of Rangers?

David must be right; there were places where you could cross the river and not be found, at least for far longer than ever before. Could they find such a place? And still be safe from the Rangers? They would try with those they could trust: the Rivelin girls, Jack and Sue from the squats, and Peter, who although younger, had been on most of the river excursions. They made a plan. There was plenty of time before they were due home. Jamie went down towards the city to find Jack and Sue. Mark went westwards to find the girls and Peter. The next Kingsday, they had assembled at Stacey. They had agreed to try the following week, and the test was on. The test that had confirmed what David said.

Somehow, the proposed autumn adventures never happened. Jack and Sue were hauled in front of the bailiff, and told in no uncertain terms to lay off. As Jack said to Jamie, when passing the message on, the bailiff had been much fiercer than usual. He knows something we don't, was Jack's opinion, something bad and dangerous. Mark had other things on his mind. His summer stint had turned his world upside down. There was something wrong, something concealed in the small world in which he had grown up.

2. The Education of a Groundling

Mark's mind had churned as he returned home from that last successful expedition to the riverbank in late June. He had never had the simple, competitive desire for acquisition mixed with adventure that had lured Jack and Sue. Nor had the more sporting, more innocent motives of the Rivelin girls appealed. Most certainly, he did not have the personal, half guilty, half angry drive that had fired Jamie. It was Jamie's revelation and David's letter and disappearance that had reinforced his sense that things were not as they seemed, nor as he had been brought up to believe.

His doubts had an uncertain ancestry. His earliest clear memory was of sitting on his father's shoulders as a procession assembled and departed with much clapping and cheering. There were Kingsmen, mobiles, and even the noble Visitor in person. Later, and when in the creche, he came to realise that he was seeing the finale of a Choosing Ceremony, with the Chosen departing for service in the Domain. The boys and girls involved were much older than him; to all intents and purposes they were adults. Other ceremonies had followed, of course, and by then, he was aware of their significance.

To be born, like Mark Norman, in the Ground, to be born healthy and well-formed, and most importantly, to be found fertile later, placed future obligations on these babies that would take years to assimilate. Obligations that would be reinforced at home, at school and at all public occasions. Icons of the King hung over cots. Toys would include Rangers in their plumed helmets, Kingsmen with guns, and their dreaded foes, the demonic Outies, misshapen, sometimes grotesquely oversized. In the creches, childish voices would sing to the glory of the King and his children, the eternal ones who gave up parenthood for the good of all. Not much penetrated, but it was a message that would be reinforced throughout childhood, and, little did they know it, policed with vigour among adults.

He had barely grasped the characters of his parents, his two older brothers and his sister, when another woman entered the household. She was to be addressed as Muss. He associated her only with sadness and confusion. Less than a year after her arrival, she had been confined to bed for some days, and no explanation was given him. A year later, she was again confined, but there was a greater commotion. Older women and his mother were in and out of her room. For the first time, he saw one in the uniform of a hygienist. Shooed away by his brothers, he nevertheless saw her bringing down bloodstained cloths and a small wrapped bundle. Later, Muss' own body, well-shrouded, had followed. His mother did her best to explain. Muss had had a baby. But it was not really a baby, but an abomination of the Deceiver's making. It had killed her. There had been mourning, but young though he was, he sensed anger as well as sorrow in his father's face.

That September, he was sent to a creche, and his sister Lisa started school. While he was happy, singing songs and reciting words he scarcely understood, she became rather solemn and uncommunicative. Her elder brothers were often angry with her, and there were tearful arguments with her parents. Words like *attitude* and *reputation* were frequent, and lodged, scarce half understood, in Mark's mind.

Two years later, Mark himself started school. An occasion marked by ceremony, with the Visitor and his suited Kingsmen in attendance. The new intake recited in childish sing-song the Declaration and Oath collectively, but were called individually to swear on the Good Book, *The Book of the King*. Writing was as yet beyond them. The words came easily, learnt without understanding in the years of the creche.

I acknowledge the King, our Sovereign Lord, our master and protector, the one and ever-living authority over us.

Who, in his goodness and mercy, preserved the Domain and our Ground from Chaos and the Great Catastrophe.

Who for our sake, and for our salvation, sacrificed his fertility that ours might be saved.

Who, with his royal sons and daughter, and all the company of nobles defied the Great Deceiver and his rebel traitors.

We abominate the Deceiver, his forces and corruptions.

We abominate all false gods, the invention of the foul Deceiver for our confusion.

We dedicate ourselves to his Royal Service, according to his will.

When Chosen, our lives are his, all else forsaken.

May the King live forever.

That same evening, though when he told of his day at the supper table, Lisa had rather sourly said that we might as well have recited *Mary had a little lamb* for all the use it had. There was a row, a frightening row. Before either parent could speak, both John and Max had shouted at her. It was Max, only one class above her, who turned to Father.

"You see, Father. She says this kind of thing in the yard, and she cheeks the teachers. Now we get called Outie-lovers."

Lisa had cried, and was obliged to give a grudging apology. No more was said at table, but afterwards Lisa was closeted with Father in his study for a long time. That same evening, Mr Norman had summoned Mark.

"You will learn soon enough why Max is upset. Lisa says things that are misunderstood, things better left unsaid. There are many that see the work of the Deceiver in such things. It makes trouble for all of us. Be obedient, Mark. There are things you don't say at school. If something worries you, speak to me, not to the teachers or the children. Never question what is said about our duty to our Sovereign."

It had not occurred to Mark to do so, and his lessons in the early years instilled both meaning and reverence to the once parroted words. Lisa had hidden whatever heretical thoughts she might have had, and the slur of Outie-lover was never hurled at him. Family life was tranquil; he was a quick learner in the less contentious matters of reading, writing and arithmetic. Life was not merely tranquil; he absorbed almost unconsciously the fact that his family were among the favoured and respected despite none having yet been Chosen. His father, the senior clerk to the mayor, was a man of importance.

Then on one bright day in May just after his own seventh birthday, Father returned with John and the momentous news. Selection had taken place, and John was Chosen. Come Kingsday, he would be across the bridge and into the Domain. He would be gone from their lives for ever. At once a shock and an honour, the family reaction lodged in Mark's mind. His mother, struggling to hold back tears, went upstairs to their bedroom. Father gathered the younger children around him.

"This is a moment when it is good to be sad and proud at the same time. We will lose John, but the King must be served, and it is an honour for the family, a great honour. The kingdom depends on us in the Ground to provide the Service that protects us all. We will remember John, and he will remember us."

Remember. Remember but never see again, unless by luck you met in the Domain when both had been Chosen, as Mark later understood. John was so much older that no special bond held him close. His first feelings were of pride. Pride, and the lively appreciation of the prestige and rewards that fell to the families of the Chosen. Lisa, of course, felt differently.

"Why is it so, Father? We get stories of bringing infection or contamination into the Ground, but I heard that Security troopers go about the city with no protection. Could not the Chosen wear suits like the Kingsmen or Doctors? Or at the least, letters. They surely cannot carry contamination."

Mr Norman looked a little disconcerted, and his reply sounded strained even to Mark.

"The Oath, child, and the Declaration: *all else forsaken.* They could make some such arrangements. But think: Some serve far away. There are never enough for the King's Service. Suppose some were allowed a visit and others not? The same rule applies to all. There is contamination in the Domain. They wish to protect us. We can send letters, and we will, but we are warned that they may take many months to reach them, since those at the bridge will not know where the Chosen have been sent. Replying is a security risk. The Deceiver's agents are among those in the Domain."

Lisa subsided into a rebellious silence. Max, like Mark was enthusiastic. Their image of Service was of the Kingsmen seen at Ceremonies or with the noble Visitor when he made other, less formal, journeys to see the mayor, or to address the school. Or maybe the magnificently uniformed Rangers many had seen across the bridge or along the riverbank. Maybe, also, the mariners who explored land beyond the seas, land uninhabited, so they were told, but ripe for new, uncontaminated additions to the Royal Domain. The yard games of Kingsmen and Outies, the latter disfigured by mud, and by make-believe defects, only added to the sense that John was set for a life of adventure and gallantry.

In the few days that followed, his mother was remarkably silent. Neighbours came around to offer congratulations. But even Mark could sense that her responses were somehow not what was expected. When the day came, she had breakfast alone upstairs, carried up by Father. When she descended, ready for the ceremony, she was holding tightly to his arm. They sat in the places allocated for families. All went smoothly. At the formal parting, it was Father who embraced his son, while Lisa held her mother tightly by the arm. When Mark looked up at his mother's face, he saw only a stony stare. When the convoy departed, it was only Mark, Max and Father who did the shaking of hands, the exchanges of congratulations.

As they walked home, Mark had questioned his father about another of the Chosen, his classmate Veronica, the girl who always came top in every test. There had been a famous occasion when she had corrected a teacher. Her Selection had given him a chill; to be Chosen was an honour, but one for the distant future. Her family's pride, if present, Mark had thought later, was hidden in tears that earned no rebuke.

"She is no older than me, Father. I thought it was sixteen or more before you were Chosen? Might I, or Max, or Lisa be called before then?"

"Children like her are called prodigies; the ones with such talents that they need training in the Domain. She's beyond what your teachers can do. They get special teachers, and move to important positions in the Service. But it's hard to part with one so young, and it's not unpatriotic to show it."

So quietly that Mark almost missed it, he muttered, "And triple credits can dull even the worst of pains for some."

***

Mark settled into school easily enough. His teachers in the first two years were local people, often those who had never left the Ground, but had learnt on the job from those coming before them. Beyond that, however, all had been trained elsewhere and posted to Bradfield. Most, native to the Ground or posted from elsewhere, had attended the college in Leicester. By no means did all have families, and it became known, though never openly acknowledged, that some of the childless men and women that taught them were themselves Chosen and allocated to this task. Chosen, and thereby likely to be rendered sterile by their stay in the Domain. That had required some explanation when Mark heard of it.

"I thought all who were Chosen went to the Domain for ever," he had said to his father.

"Well," his father had said, "you know that some come here for a short time, like the Kingsmen, the soldiers and the Visitor, of course. There are some stay for longer."

"Don't they bring contamination with them? The Kingsmen wear those suits."

Mr Norman had paused before giving him an answer. He knew that the danger in allowing those from the Domain to enter the Ground was slight, and the Kingsmen's suits something of a token gesture. Security did not bother with such niceties. But even a short stay in the Domain was likely, though not certain, to cause impaired fertility. Only rarely did the hygienists allow an incomer to marry a local, and from what he had gathered, those few had been exposed to the Domain for very short periods.

"The contamination is mainly in the soil, and little is carried on the person. That's why we must stay in our Ground. The really clean places in the Domain are few, and they are small, so small that you could not get anyone to stay in one for the whole of their lives."

***

The school curriculum to which Mark was subjected was laid out very rigidly. Reading and writing were given the greatest attention. The reading material, besides the basic primers, was not calculated to induce enthusiasm. The Kings Print books, all that were allowed, were meticulous as regards grammar and spelling, but distinctly lacking in range. There was, of course, The Book of the King *that featured not only in Chronicles, but as a set text for copying and the parsing of sentences. In fiction, there was no hint of romance, just war stories, accounts of prodigies of reproductive contribution to service and tales of reclamation or exploration. There was no history beyond the description of chaos before the time of the King. To call geography rudimentary was inadequate; beyond the details of their Ground, and the skimpiest account of Britain, there was just the vague 'overseas', so far as known unfit for occupation. The map pinned up in each classroom displayed only the Ground and the land immediately around it. Land polluted, even within the Domain, land contaminated into utter sterility, land occupied by ferocious Outies.*

What the classroom left out, however, rumour and parental lectures supplied. Mark heard more about the *unchosen,* those who left the Ground not for honourable Service, but for work in reclamation, and in particular at the Barriers to the north. To most uphill, even his father, the term meant disgrace, a ticket to a harsh menial life with no reprieve. To Jack and Sue, though, it was to be dreaded. It is a death sentence, they told him, a painful degrading death from contaminants in areas of clearance. Jack had elaborated a bit.

"It's the Tadgies' delight, bastards that they are. They grab folk at night with no warning, and they are gone for good. Clever with it, too. Be unchosen and you'll be sent far from home. Chances are you won't even know where you are. Nowhere to escape to. Our Barriers? They are part of it, but it's folk from down south mostly that get sent there. Once or twice one of ours escapes to a city down south. We get messages. It's a good trick, though. I bet even you lot uphill shiver a little when those Barriers are mentioned."

Which was true enough, Mark had thought. Barring transfers to or from other Grounds, and the very few sent to Leicester and returning, you lived out your life in the Ground, or left it for ever, honourably or otherwise. The idea of escape, a shameful escape, belonged to fantasy.

Science and mathematics, added as the children got older, were better treated. Those with a marked talent for the latter were often Chosen as prodigies, and it was one of the few guides to the likelihood of being Chosen. Science served three functions. Perhaps the most important was sex education, more properly, perhaps, reproductive biology. The paramount importance of good breeding, of the consequence of not following the rules to ensure good progeny, and the deference to expert instruction as a patriotic duty were all drummed in with vigour. Lurid illustrations of the misbegotten were backed up by none-too-subtle references to the unchosen fate of transgressors.

An added deterrent to any unofficial liaisons was provided by the always unpopular hygienists. Nearly always sterile themselves, and always originating from outside the Ground, it was they, with supervision from the higher authorities of the Domain, who made matches, kept pedigree records of fertility and health, and also subjected girls to intrusive and embarrassing examinations. Penalties could be severe, though their application was by no means standard; expelling a piece of choice heredity when no pregnancy had resulted from an indiscretion was too wasteful. Unplanned pregnancy almost always meant expulsion to an unknown fate in the Domain. For the boys, there was just one, very embarrassing test, the need for a sperm count, where ancient but well-maintained microscopes from pre-war days were unpacked for use. No result was divulged, but it followed that the likely infertile were to be Chosen when their age was right. Not only the infertile, though; the needs of the Domain were great.

Rather surprisingly, the system worked quite well. Teenagers only too well primed with the consequences of accidental pregnancy developed codes that strongly deterred pairs on their own. Mark shared with his contemporaries a mixture of prudery, caution and knowledge.

The remaining science split two ways. The basics of chemistry, electricity and mechanics, the science of everyday life and of the most basic industries formed one branch. Of particular importance was the distillation of alcohol, the scarce, expensive fuel that powered the mobiles. The other was a form of applied botany and chemistry: the many signs of the different kinds of contamination and their strength. It was always popular, for much was out of doors, and led to exploration up and down the Ground. It was Mark's favourite.

The overwhelming problem for the teachers of this strange curriculum was the issue of how what was taught had been discovered. With the exception of a few basic mathematical primers, all material was not merely in Kings Print, but edited to the point of rewriting. All avoiding any reference to the process of discovery or the history of any idea. Questions along these lines were frowned upon. This in turn created problems when those at home, relying on oral transmission, contradicted what had been learnt at school, or added touches of knowledge that lay outside the covers of Kings Print books. Pre-war books, printed matter of any kind, were most definitely Relics. To be found in possession was a certain passage unchosen across the bridge, probably to the Barriers or worse. As time passed, of course, the issue had become less pressing, but the hidden transmission of family knowledge, degraded, perhaps, but remarkably persistent, caused a steady flow of complaints, interrogations, and in extreme cases transfer or expulsion.

Of the remaining subjects Chronicles was both the most straightforward, the most boring, and the hardest within which to have any sense of progression once the book had been gone through once and basic literacy achieved. Once again, the problem was not merely the absence, but the consciously denied provision of any background. More contentious and difficult to handle was the subject that in *any other time and place might have been called religious studies. Civics had been suggested, and even adopted for a while, but in Bradfield it became simply Our Beliefs and Our Duty, inevitably degenerating to OBOD.*

For many, including Mark, OBOD often became little more than the recitation of the Declaration and the most basic examples illustrating its application. There were, though, a few things that attracted more attention. Evasion, the fleeing from Service when selected, was the crime of crimes, the ultimate treason. In fact, no one Mark talked to had ever heard of a case, and when it was discussed in solemn terms outside, it was Mark himself who pointed out that there was nowhere to flee to. There had been a suicide. Almost as bad, and the family had disappeared across the bridge, fate unknown.

Other matters also became clearer. Other Grounds, never clearly located, were not as successful in untarnished fertility as their own. Our contribution, the teachers told them, was of special value to the King, and we are blessed with more rewards. It is our duty to fulfil all the demands that are made on us. It was a message underlined by the noble Visitor on every occasion he came to Bradfield. They also learnt that life in the Domain was not completely sterile. Land is improving, so the teachers said. In time, but a long way off, the whole Domain might become like their Ground, populated by their descendants.

Inevitably, there were awkward questions asked by the cleverest, like Lisa. They soon learnt to keep these to themselves, after stern interviews with the headteacher or mayor Arkell. Mark was monitored closely by his father, and kept his silence from an early age. More terrifying were the very rare cases of what the teachers called heresy, the expressions of belief that ran flat contrary to the Declaration. They involved God, *A false god* the teacher would shout, *a device of the Deceiver.* Most quickly learnt to hide these heresies, but in two families, things reached the point of defiance. The families, martyrs in other ages, merely disappeared among the ranks of the unchosen. Rumours of pre-war *Holy Books* found in their houses remained just that, but the searches were the only occasions on which most uphill had seen the black-uniformed Security troopers. Much later, recalling his father's words, Mark had wondered at their lack of protective gear that was supposed to shield Grounders from contamination.

At Bradfield, the only school outside the city, other than a few creches, this regime was followed pretty much to the letter. Mark learnt that both the Chosen and those transferred to a Technical College in another Ground would learn

36

more. All knew that there were many older books, books kept in the great libraries of the Domain. Dangerous books, available only to the best of the Chosen after they had entered Service. Books that must be declared as Relics if found.

The city was something else. Mark, along with the other children 'uphill', learnt to despise, but also to fear, the squatters, the inhabitants of the scattered nests among the ruins of those parts of the city that had escaped contamination. This prejudice was reinforced by an incident the winter before John's Selection and departure. John had grown up. He was roaming free with friends in the evenings and on Kingsdays. One evening, there was a knock on the door, and two Proctors brought in John bleeding, with a black eye, and with torn clothes. Mark, frightened by the blood and tatters, had then been unable to make sense of words like *squatter scum, our side of the line, Mr Norman,* and mention of *a few Relics.* It was much later that he learnt of the rival gangs that searched through the unoccupied ruins for Relics and the Credits they earnt.

Later, when both he and Max began to go roving away from home, their father had warned them not to go beyond the unmarked but well-known dividing line between uphill and city. There had been an explanation. Uphill was privileged, and therefore resented.

"We are carefully selected to provide those most fit for Service. We provide not only the cream of the Chosen, but also the fertile stock and crops that sustain the Domain," Mr Norman had told them. "The city merely provides labour. They need feeding and more, where we can sustain ourselves. They live poorly."

It was later still, and after his first meeting with Jack and Sue, that he learnt a little more. The two schools there had, notionally, the same curriculum as that at Bradfield. The practice was rather different. Not all births were to couples or polygamous unions arranged by the hygienists, but all crammed into the large, rowdy classes. There were unregistered children; there were even adults that had evaded the hygienists' attention. It was only after Max had been Chosen and out of their lives, that he really understood the city.

There had been no reason why Max should not be Chosen, but the announcement still came as a shock. Only three years older than Mark, he was far closer to him than John had ever been. The family had changed. Only two years before, another Muss had joined the household. She already had one healthy boy, and was pregnant with another. An immigrant from another Ground, a transferee, she had been delighted with her place, and full of patriotic zeal. She was delighted with the news, and baffled by the subdued reaction in the others. The Ceremony passed off; Max was gone, over the bridge and out of their lives. Miss, Mark's mother, became more and more withdrawn from then on, and the atmosphere at home became strained with the chirpy enthusiasm of the much younger Muss.

After the event, Mr Norman was more open with his remaining children than he had been when John had gone. The mayor's office held a few files that a more efficient mayor or a patriotic clerk would have destroyed. There had been a time, decades ago, when correspondence was thought to benefit morale. Visits had even been contemplated. But not all Service was glorious; some was dangerous, some was degrading, and some who broke under it were unchosen. Censorship had been tried, but had proven too demanding. His predecessor had inserted a marginal comment on instructions for letters sent across the bridge: *and where do they go from there?* Somehow, his urge to write had faded away after that. He said as much to Lisa and Mark, and Lisa's complaints were dealt with not with argument as before, but with a blunt warning of the consequences for them all if she made her feelings known.

Already shaken in his sense that to be Chosen was not, at least in the eyes of his parents, the ultimate honour, the wished-for end to childhood, his passing on the news to Jack and Sue further disturbed his mind.

"Bad luck," Jack had said, "it's often families that get picked on. We manage to hide a few. The hygienists can't really keep track. But if they suspect, the damned Tadgies will break in at night and whisk people away. No ceremony for them, and often the whole family will be over the bridge. For sure, they don't all end up in Windsor." He spat.

"You've a sister, haven't you, Mark," asked Sue, "older than you? She's not been Chosen?"

"No, we already know Lisa will be married when she's eighteen. No news of the match, but there's a good chance she'll stay local."

"She's the lucky one then, and to wait till eighteen. Back home, there's mothers of fifteen, all legit and hygienist approved. Still better than being Chosen. We hear things about them that I'd not want to talk about. I suppose it's different for your prodgies though."

There was a mixture of the ghoulish and envious in her tone. Innocent as Mark was, it did not take him long to catch the meaning. The Domain must have two, even three times as many men as women.

38

"Have a healthy sprog, even unregistered, and you'll likely not be across the bridge," she went on, a malicious grin on her face. "And to make sure, we sometimes use the services of those uphill. Not hard to get some co-operation."

Mark blushed. Already, he had heard the stories of those who had been lured downhill, and the boasting about their exploits. Exploits not without risk, since a beating by rivals, and a further beating at home when detected had often followed. But the contrast with his heavily supervised community was stark.

***

For the Domain, starved of labour, and still facing a slow decline in population, this issue of reproduction had dominated policy. Other than in the Grounds and the parts of cities within them, successful reproduction was rare; sterility or misbegotten monsters were the norm. Even those recently Chosen often acquired genetic damage within days or weeks. Those born physically normal were often slow of mind, a consequence not so much of the Catastrophe as of the war with the Outland that had followed, a war marked by the desire to breed docile servants for the near-eternal nobility.

Motherhood among the healthy was the supreme virtue. It was not to be left to the whims of mere romance, but to be carefully managed with the tracking of pedigrees. That, at least, had been the intention. The cities, though, were impossible to regulate thoroughly, and since much labour required little brains, they were left more to themselves. In the last resort, brute force was always available. In the rural Grounds, the source not only of labour, intelligent labour at that, but also of livestock and uncontaminated seeds, more subtlety was needed.

That need for a certain quality in a minority of those Chosen for Service had given to the Northernmost Ground, Mark's Ground, a uniquely privileged position. Of them all, it was the least contaminated. Successive noble Visitors responsible for its management had fought off both excessive demands for Service, and the tendency, based on experience in the cities and less fruitful Grounds to treat the inhabitants as mere breeding stock. They had argued successfully for the benefits of organised family life, and an education fitted to the likely status of those to be chosen. Arguments that were coming under increasing pressure from those at Court concerned more with the train of servants to maintain their status, or driven by the need, the lethal need, to clear new areas for occupation.

Thus this, the Northernmost Division, was known, not always in a friendly manner, as the Queen of Grounds. Its maintenance required much effort, surrounded as it was by mostly sterile or dangerous land. Unknown to all but a few of its inhabitants, the Division's management, indeed its very sustaining, were a subject of contention among the highest in the land. For the nobles managing it, this meant a degree of dissimulation when the issue was raised at Court or in Council.

The issue of gender was a more general one. Those whose lives were extended by the doses awarded by the King, the nobility, lost not only fertility, but also all traces of sexual desire. Those rendered sterile by mere contamination or unfortunately matched parents most certainly did not. Within the male-dominated Domain, the fate of infertile women, especially those lacking the talents to become doctors, hygienists or teachers was almost predetermined. City folk were well aware of this, as of the likely fate of the unchosen, male and female alike.

***

Mark learnt more from his city companions. He knew that the city had a bailiff, a man supposedly subordinated to the mayor at Bradfield. A man accorded great respect by both the city children, certainly far more than that given to mayor Arkell. Not only that; he was born and bred in the city, as were his parents and grandparents before him. Unheard of for a mayor. A man who was openly unpatriotic in a way that would be unthinkable uphill, and whose views were widely held in the city.

In the end, though, it was his father that had brought Mark to his confused and doubting state. In his ninth year at school, the year of Max's Choosing, his aptitude for maths was prompting praise. Miss Spooner had sent him home with a glowing report. But his father's reaction, and even more, his mother's, had surprised him. They'd said well done and all that, but his mother had looked almost tearful, and it wasn't for joy. His father had taken him for a walk and a talk, "Man-to-man, now you are 14," he had said, and suggested quietly that it didn't always do to show all your talents, and he'd be happiest to see Mark somewhere comfortably in the middle. Of course, Mark had asked why, and got no very clear answer, but there was something in his father's manner that made him take note. But he'd started off making silly mistakes, and Miss Spooner had accused him of doing it deliberately: "Such things get reported," she had said.

Being reported from school was a matter for concern to the family, as Mr Norman knew very well. They could suffer for any lack of patriotism; families were supposed to report any child showing anything less than enthusiasm over Selection. And while the criteria for Selection were, to put it mildly, obscure to both children and their parents, mathematical ability was prized in the Domain, and accounted for most of the early departures across the bridge. A child under suspicion would be counselled and questioned. Too many doubts, and there was the horrible, ultimate sanction of being sent over the bridge without being chosen; work on the Barriers, or worse. In the worst cases, known more from the city than uphill, a whole family might be taken. Even without that, the families were split, with some being transferred to other Grounds and the kids being fostered by those with unblemished records of patriotic service.

There was more; children talked more freely among themselves, and a report might come from a classmate, a Patriot, and such gained Credits. Not all such children were easily spotted, and Mr Norman had seen from his position how anonymous reports of this sort had led to families being brought in and questioned closely. It paid to be pre-emptive to avoid trouble.

It was all mysterious to Mark. His father had coached him to make less obvious errors, and he soon relished the game. Nothing more was said, though Miss Spooner often frowned when returning his work. He knew about the other anonymous reports that had you up for interrogation. Some Patriots, like John Gregory, were a bit of a pain, and Mark and others tended instinctively to avoid them or watch what they said in their hearing. When they were all younger, there was a lot of summoning to interview: "We heard that you said this; do you not realise?" etc. Even the mildest of remarks, such as sorrow when a sibling was Chosen, and vanished from family life, tended to find its way up to the authorities. In a few cases, a classmate had disappeared, and the family transferred. Lisa, he realised later, had had some lucky escapes. It paid to be in the Norman family, as he soon discovered.

The things his father said, and did not say, his attitude and that of his mother, were all given weight by the peculiarity of his father's job. Mark soon realised that the mayor, Mr Arkell, was out of his depth most of the time, and that it was his father who really made decisions, along with the two Deputies, who treated his father as an equal. The respect extended to the family, and Mark realised that many were turning to his father or mother to deal with accusations and complaints that Arkell was not trusted to manage.

Two occasions lodged in his mind. The most important was that when his father came home to announce that Lisa had been selected for marriage at eighteen, and not among the Chosen. She had been happy enough, but when she left, leaving Mark alone with his parents, his mother had said,

"So those reports, you got rid of them?"

"Yes. Easily enough. Arkell never reads them until just before the Visitor comes. He never knew they were there. Even with them, a good fertility report is usually enough. The one I found was far too poor, but Arkell would be too dense to see it. Thank God for Amelia. I told her, and she went through the hygienists' original records, as she is entitled to; just as well, they told a different story. She made a copy of the original and it was the one in the file for the Visitor."

"I wonder which of them did that? Could she tell by handwriting?"

"She didn't say, and I didn't ask. They may be surprised by the decision, but they'll not challenge it. By her account, there's a gang of them, hygienists and a few teachers sniffing out those they think best out of the Ground. Childless, all of them, surely Chosen, but not saying so. Patriots all."

Mark had stayed silent, pleased that Lisa would be around. Later, he realised it was a conversation he had been meant to hear, even including the heretical calling on God. By Amelia, he recognised the elderly Deputy, Muss Franklin, a rather formidable lady who had taught him advanced writing for one term.

The second occasion involved the Visitor in one of his periodic visits aside from the Chosen ceremony and the opening of the school year. It happened that Mark, fresh out of school, had called in at the Council Hall, expecting to find his father about to return home. He arrived as a meeting of the Visitor with the mayor and his deputies was ending. Seeing the party with his father in attendance, he had hung back a bit in the hall, overawed by the Visitor. It was the Visitor himself who recognised the situation, and asked for an introduction.

"Has this young man ever travelled in a mobile, Mr Norman?" he had asked his father. "No? Well, let us indulge him, and yourself as well."

They were driven a short way out of Bradfield to the west. The Visitor stopped the mobile and turned to his driver.

"Ernest, entertain this young man for a while. Mr Norman and I are off for a little walk."

The driver, a Kingsman, was friendly enough. While he tried to teach Mark the basic mechanics, the time passed. The talking pair did not go far, stopping to sit on a rock only a few hundred yards away. Mark was actually behind the wheel, and Ernest preparing to start the motor when they returned. The journey back to Bradfield was silent, and when his father and the Visitor parted, it seemed almost a parting of equals. As they walked down the hill to home, Mark had asked about the conversation. His father had been gruff.

"Things our simple-minded mayor would not understand, and is better off not knowing."

There was a finality in his voice that deterred Mark from any further questions.

3. The Stint

The June after the last river crossing drifted lazily into July. It was the time for draft placements over the summer. There was just the weekend after the last day of school, then the notices would go up in the Square outside the Council Hall. Mark knew the routine. Since age eleven, he had done four of these eight-week summer stints, all on the outfield farms. Most placements were out there, haymaking, harvesting, repairing old walls and buildings, helping with all the less-skilled jobs while the farmers did what only they knew how. In all probability, it would be the same again; reports on previous years were read by farmers and bids put in. His had all been good. He had never understood, though, why it was never to the same farm. His father had been rather vague, even evasive, when he asked. Just something about not allowing particular attachments to make efficient allocation at Selection more difficult, or raising 'unrealistic expectations'.

It would be his last summer draft. Come next May, there would be Selection: the future laid out for adult life. He might be Chosen, or it might even be a farm apprenticeship, with a prospect of first marriage when a farm fell vacant, or transfer south to the Technical College. His father had often talked about farming with a degree of enthusiasm that Mark found odd. A clerk who knew nothing of crops, beasts or pests other than the rats that had to be rooted out. Get a skill we really need, he would say, get a skill and you will be fine. Farming is the best of all.

So, it was with few worries that he went to inspect the notices on Allocation Day. There was a crush around the notice. Working his way to the front, yes, there he was, along with four others, allocated to Mr Pickless of Midhope. He studied the names. All boys, which was usual, but he pulled a face at one name, his classmate John Gregory. John, the ostentatious patriot; John, the teacher's pet; John, the sniffer-out of notionally subversive remarks. It was not just Mark who disliked him; he was widely suspected of telling tales on those who had kept trivial Relics and were foolish enough to show them off. The family were all the same, incomers brought in for the father's skills as an electrician. Mr Norman had snorted derisively when Mark had brought back tales from school.

"Living *in sure and certain hope of Selection,*" he had said, his tone recalling a part of the Kingsday Service. "Serve him right if he were sent to breed in some hellhole of a Ground down south."

The other three on the list were all younger; Peter and Simon were the year below, He knew Simon by sight, and Peter had been on the river bank. Tom was only 12, second assignment. As he moved away, he saw John a fair distance behind in the crowd, avoided him and went back home to tell his parents and sisters. Both parents seemed delighted. He got mock punches from his father, and a hug from his mother. Even Muss smiled. Lisa, two years older and waiting for her marriage order, smiled too, but looked from him to their father and back, with a slight shake of the head.

The draftees had the rest of the week to prepare, before going to the mayor's office on Friday to collect certificates and assembly instructions. The time passed quickly enough. Friends swapped stories of their previous stints, and sought out those who had worked for their new employer in past years. Mark found a couple who had worked for Pickless. No problems, nice bloke, good food. One, Robin Ware, did make an odd comment; six boys had been Chosen over the years from that family. The certificates were on the wall, but the Picklesses never mentioned them. Families in Bradfield and elsewhere usually drew attention to the certificates, and six from one family was exceptional. There were no children at home, just the three of them, all at least 50.

"I congratulated them, as expected," said Robin. "I got a grunt in return. Nothing more was said, and I got a feeling it was not something to mention again."

Friday came round. Mark acquired his documents, uniquely from his own father, whose job it was to prepare and deliver them. Kingsday had its traditional sending off after Service, an outdoor banquet that was blessed with sunshine. The Visitor himself, resplendent in the trappings of nobility, attended both, his mobile and those of his escort attracting the children's interest. Mark noticed that John hovered around the Visitor. His father, freed from official duties, rolled his eyes at Mark at a particular bout of John's toadying; Mark had to contain his laughter; it was he, not John, who had ridden in the Visitor's mobile.

Sunday was the day for family alone. At one point, his father drew him aside.

"I don't think you need the warning, but be on your guard when that Gregory boy is around. Last year, we had to deal with his reports on his gang and on his employer. Never amounted to anything, mind, but those reports get filed."

On Monday morning, he walked to the assembly point outside the inn on Down Street. He was the first. Peter and Simon came together. John rolled up with five minutes to spare, and with a very smart backpack, undoubtedly from the special stores of the Domain, bought on Credits. Tom came last, looking nervous but brave. They set off up the old road north. After they passed Mortimer, where he had worked in his second draft for Mr Pye, the road skirted the moors. It was a sunny day, but to their left the moors still held a feeling of threat. Here, the moors were notionally in the Outland, marked with poles painted black with pitch. Mark had seen these on previous drafts, but for Peter, Simon and Tom it was their first sight. In practice, they were in front of a kind of no-man's land, which farmers on the bounds would use as pasture. Mr Pye had sometimes taken cattle up there with folk to keep an eye on them and bring them back infield at dusk. He'd grumbled about it, too. His predecessor had built a wall further west, quite a job, it seemed. Outies had not only broken through and carried off some cattle, but actually demolished the wall too. Usually, you could get a special draft to do a major project, but when he asked for help to rebuild it, there was a lot of mumbling and delay. Then he was told it was not policy, and he was advised not to try it himself. He had left a rather bitter note for Mr Pye in the farm log.

However, the hillside was bright green with fresh grass and young heather. Someone, presumably Mr Pye, must have burnt it recently, though there were no cattle to be seen. The cleanness of the land did a little to diminish the vague sense of unease at being so close to the bounds. They did not talk much as they walked, though Peter and Simon chatted to each other a little, more or less out of earshot. It was about six miles altogether, so no distance to walk, but the furthest he had been drafted away from home. The furthest north too, not far from the Barriers, and the northernmost point of their Ground.

Down the steep twisting track to Ewden Dale. There were several farms here. His third draft had been in one of them with another Mr Pickless, a cousin. There were some woods, and plenty of cattle. It was altogether more friendly, and they were waved at by a couple of elderly women already stacking hay in the meadows alongside. No doubt they too would be getting a draft. Up again, and much grimmer moors again on the left. This really was on the bounds. The boys closed up, though there was, according to the adults, no real danger. There were burnt patches, but small clumps of gorse and young birches, and some stumps and felled small timber. Keeping the bounds clear was the task all the farmers hated; no real gain, and firing required skill and good timing. Not a task for draftees, nor one for the summer.

To the right, though, the contrast was great. There were many farms, and even a track that went down to the Midhopestones village. They kept straight on, though, a managed copse on their right, but the same bleak moorland on the left. The remains of old walls were visible, running straight up the hillside. Only the wall along the track was in good order, and every 200 yards or so there was a tall post, standing out black with its coating of pitch, the official marks of the boundary. Unspoken, they closed in on each other. Now there was only one destination, theirs. The road dipped a bit, crossing a stream by means of a very rough causeway of rocks. To their right were reclaimed pastures, and in the distance the two ends of the pre-war dam. Ahead was a cluster of overgrown ruins bar one house, lower and to the east. Smoke came from a chimney, and the roof was intact. That was it. A few minutes later they were crossing the yard to the south of the house.

As they crossed towards the front door, it opened, and a tall and strongly built man opened it and came out. Mr Pickless. Under a cap was a disordered mass of white hair. His trousers and boots were what Mark recognised as standard issue for farmers, but he had on a long, oiled jacket that would not have been locally made, not standard issue. Credits had been earned and spent. He did not smile as they approached, but neither did he appear unwelcoming; *deadpan*, Mark thought. John was quick off the mark.

"King's blessings on you, sir, we are your draft for the summer."

"And to you, boys, I'm sure," said Mr Pickless, with a grin on his face that was a touch sardonic. "Well now, I guess you must be John, by all accounts. Mark, I have heard of from my cousin, and you must be Tom, but which is Peter and which is Simon?"

The introductions were made, and they entered the house. There was a hallway with rooms off on either side. The stone walls were panelled with wood, not in the style of the mayor's office, but simply. He ushered them into a room on the left. There was a table in the centre, with simple wooden chairs around it. A window on the same wall as the front door looked out over the yard. Two women stood beyond the table.

"Boys, there's Miss, and there's Muss. Ladies, this is Mark…and John…and Peter…and Simon, and the youngster is Tom." The women advanced, and shook each boy by the hand.

"Right, boys, there's a big room upstairs with pallets, and that's yours for the duration. Miss will look in when you're out in the fields, so you'd best keep it tidy. This here is where we eat, and you'll be hungry, no doubt. Midday meal here in half an hour, so get your things upstairs. Muss will show you where the washing and the necessities are when you come down."

They settled in. After the meal, Pickless marched them round the bounds, or at least those that bordered on the boundary with the Outland. That was marked by a strong drystone wall and with the pitch covered posts they had seen earlier. Only to the north was the boundary unclear.

"You don't go beyond that, ever, other than with me, and if you see anything other than sheep and the bull out there beyond the wall, you drop whatever you're at and come back straight to the farm, unless you know where I am, then to me. You'll have no cause to go north, either."

He did not need to spell out the danger. All had seen the illustrations of Outies in school or in the Kings Print books that some had at home. And yet, the land looked unharmed. Moorland, to be sure, but evidently burnt and grazed by Pickless' livestock. John's wondering aloud about why such land was left to monsters got a sharp put down from the farmer.

"It's the law, that's why. And I don't question what the King's officers have decided."

It was a statement that confused them all. The Treaties signed with the Outland were certainly not in *The Book of the King,* which was their only source of information. Only Mark had picked up from his father that the boundaries had been a matter of negotiation. For the rest, they were just there. John might well have asked more questions, but mention of the King's officers was an effective silencer.

The first week flew by. Mark was set to repairing drystone walls away from the boundary, and got Tom attached to him to learn. He'd learnt the knack on previous drafts. The others went with Pickless down to the meadows for haymaking. Early mornings and evenings were busy too: helping the women attend to the hens, feeding and mucking out the pig, an old sow who would be slaughtered before winter set in. Milking, cheesemaking and the brewhouse were reserved to the women. Only on Kingsday were they free of all but the most basic chores, and when it came round, they were sufficiently worn out to hang around the farm.

Even Mark and John, with the most placements behind them, had never before stayed in such isolation. Thursday, a man came up with a trap to collect eggs and cheese, using the other track down to the village, but they were out and about and did not see him. Otherwise, Pickless told them, he, or one of the women, would go the same way from time to time, down to the village, or even to Bradfield itself, sometimes with livestock on the hoof for slaughter or transfer. But not that week, and the boys saw nobody other than their employers. They did not see much of the house other than their own quarters, the scullery, the outhouses and the room in which they ate. It seemed to be used for little else, and had a rather formal air. And, yes, there were the six Certificates of Service, framed and on the inner wall. Mark looked at the dates. Only 5 years between them, the years they were 16, presumably, three each mothered by Miss and Muss. Even John had refrained from comment; somehow, without words spoken, Pickless gave the signal that it would be unwelcome.

The Tuesday of the second week brought a surprise. They were sat around the table in the evening, waiting for Muss to come in with the pot. Mark had a view out of the window looking out across the flagstone yard. It was still light and he could see the old byre. It was dilapidated, with slates missing from the roof, but well built in the old style, a pre-war relic. As he stared, rather vacantly, a movement caught his eye, and a figure with a wide-brimmed hat appeared briefly, passing out of sight almost at once. He started up in his chair.

"Someone just crossed the yard, sir. I thought you were on your own? Do you get thieves or Outies? Do you want us to go after him?"

"Sit, sit, boy. What did he look like?" asked Pickless.

"I couldn't see his face, sir; just a big hat."

Pickless cursed inwardly. *Damn the man for a fool*, he thought, the idiot knew I had a draft in the house. He should have waited till it was properly dark. Now I have to say something, and not have the lads talking about him; most particularly not John.

"No, let him be. It's only Old Jones," said the farmer. He hesitated. A calculating look passed across his face. Finally, he said, "He came here from somewhere down south. Across the moors."

For a moment, the boys were silent. It was John who jumped to a conclusion.

"You know him, sir? Is he a vagrant without a certificate? Shouldn't you have reported him to the Proctors? He could be an evader."

"So many questions! And you so keen to do the right thing." There was an acid tone in the farmer's voice. "Well, now, he does the odd job for me, and no, he doesn't have a certificate. There's always something needs doing, and he knows to turn up in daytime only when there are no gangs like you lot on the job. And if I expect a visitor, or see one coming, I leave a signal and he stays out of sight. And we leave him food, beer and cast-off clothes, though I think he's a smart hunter too. Never seen him looking like he's starving. But he'll have come for his parcel no doubt. He should have waited till it was properly dark. The dogs know him."

He looked directly at John.

"As to the Proctors, or thinking of reporting me back in Bradfield, do you think they don't know he's around? He's the only one I know around here, but I'll bet there are others further south. Off the books, as it were. Report him, or me, back home, well, it'll be like this: You'll find the mayor or the Proctors mighty hard to interest. Oh, they'll make show of it and the mayor will thank you kindly for being a good law-abiding boy. Nothing will happen. Make more fuss, and you'll find that there is an 'emergency' up north or somewhere, and the lot of you will be out of here, over the bridge and on the Barriers or worse before you have time to turn around or talk to anyone. And you'll not come back, leastways not back home. Even if they've had their eye on you, you'll not be Chosen. If not the Barriers, then some clearance elsewhere, maybe even overseas."

He gave John another hard look at the end, but the others looked at him with amazement. Was this an evader? They were almost mythical. None of them had heard of one directly, but only by rumour. John could not contain himself.

"That must be wrong! They'd surely come! It's downright treason! He must be an evader."

"If they did come, well, you can be sure Jones would be out of sight. And they could put questions to me any which-way, and it would do them no good, because I don't know where he goes when he's not here. I take trouble not to find out, either. And they'd not go far beyond the bounds anyway, they'd be fair game for the Westrons. It's not allowed. As for taking me in, I think you'd find they put more value on a good farmer than that. I've earned that mayor more credits than he deserves, and they don't jump too readily on one who has contributed so much to Service."

For the first time since their arrival, he nodded his head at the six Certificates adorning the wall behind him. Mark was thinking furiously. Westrons? Was that their name? You talked about Outies, simply evil monsters; deformed monsters from over the moor, who stole sheep and cows, and even, it was said, people, and carried them off to the west. It was never spelt out what happened to the captives, and, indeed, Mark had never heard of anybody who had actually vanished, though the losses of livestock were real enough. It seemed obvious that the latter would be eaten, and that made the fate of any captive seem grim. None of the boys spoke.

"As to why, well, think for a bit." Pickless went on. "There's me, Miss and Muss to run this place, and you've learnt the hard way that there's plenty to do to keep it going. It's the same for all of us up here on the hills. Yet folk downhill, and the Domain, and the cities, you all need our meat and potatoes. Our breeding-stock. Our children."

At the last, he turned again slightly towards the certificates.

"Jones does more than lend a hand; I don't know how he does it but we get much less stolen or spoilt than our neighbours. No Outies, or as near as none. You think those in the offices in Bradfield don't know it? They turn a blind eye just as long as the sinners are out of sight. There are quotas to be met, quotas that would fail often enough it were not for us up here."

He turned to John.

"Still feel like earning an honest Credit or ten, lad?" he asked. "Hoping to be Chosen?"

John said nothing. His cheeks reddened a bit. Muss came in with the meal, followed by Miss. The boys were usually too hungry to talk much over a meal, but this one was exceptionally silent. When it was over, John and Peter cleared the dishes and left to wash up. The others also had chores to do before bed, but Mark lingered.

"Excuse me, Mr Pickless," he began, "but Westrons? Is that what they call themselves, the Outies, I mean?"

"Yes, so it seems. It was Jones called them that. Mind you, he talks of Outlanders more often. I was on the moor once with him, years ago, and we saw a gang of the things, a long way off, thank goodness, and they saw us and halted. Half a dozen of them. Jones told me to move back towards the boundary, and so

I did. He walked towards them and they vanished over the hill. I've not seen any since. He told me not to go so far in in future. When the sheep go further, it's thanks to him, and the dogs, of course. How he knows that's the name they use, I don't know, and I didn't choose to find out. He must have talked to some. There's a lot of things he knows that others don't."

"He can't live that far away, can he, if he comes to the farm so often?" asked Mark.

"Well, I guess not, but I have never asked or tried to find out. Ask no questions, get told no lies. But over the hill and you are just about on the bounds. The markers are down there, as I told you, and I think there was an argument about placing it. There are old quarries and shafts there, lots of them, and old pre-war buildings too, beyond the broken dam. Only a mile or so away. I only step over those bounds, not that they are clear, mind, in broad daylight and a good view in all directions. There's things lurk among those ruins, or in the scrub. Not saying I'd be got at, mind, never heard of someone going missing, but its spooky all the same, and they say you can get contaminated. Not that I believe it. The land is healthy enough."

While he spoke, Miss was glowering, and Muss looked flustered.

"That's enough," said Miss. "The boy shouldn't think of such things, especially when it's getting dark. And the time you saw them was ages ago; we don't get any trouble now."

Mark got up and left to round up the hens. No trouble from Outies, Pickless had said, and then there was Mr Jones. On the other farms he had done service on, like Mr Smith, or the other Mr Pickless over by Ewden, the farmers had been loud in their complaints about losses from over the hill, especially in the autumn. Mr Smith had even written a letter to the mayor to ask for 'something to be done', though he admitted going to a schoolmaster in Bradfield, to have it, as he put it, 'tidied up and made official looking'. He'd had a reply, too, eventually, and not from the mayor, but from the Royal Visitor, assuring him that His Majesty's Forces were doing all in their power to destroy the monsters. Mr Smith had shown Mark the letter; it was on very thick paper, with an elaborate crest at the top. A crowned tree, as Mark remembered. Both the farmers had said how old Pickless at Midhope seemed to be the lucky one, and grumbled that he must have friends in high places, though nobody had heard of any Kingsmen passing through the Ground. Not that it would have been any use unless they camped out there for ever.

Nothing more was said about Jones or Westrons for the rest of the week. Kingsday was approaching. Back home, attending Service was, more or less, an obligation, but out here, it seemed, the Proctors were satisfied with the occasional appearance from the farming families, and the gangs of boys doing their stint on the farms were included. Their first Kingsday, everyone had remained on the farm. This time, the Picklesses wanted to make their way downhill for the service and to visit their cousins in Ewden. They would eat with them, and not be back till late. The boys would be left on their own, with only a few chores before a free day stretched before them. Somehow, everybody had been too busy the day before to decide what to do. At breakfast, there was a lot of chatter, but it was Mr Pickless who suggested they might like to go fishing in the pools a mile or so from the farm.

"But one should stay behind to mind the farm. The dogs have taken a liking to you, Mark, and they'll do as bid. The rest of you might find some Relics alongside the old dam, too. That would earn you a few Credits," he said, giving John a glance. He rummaged about in a tall cupboard in the hall, and produced a couple of rods, a net and a bag. Soon after breakfast the trap rattled off southwards.

While doing the odd jobs, Mark took Peter aside.

"You remember the night Mr Pickless was talking about Old Jones?" he asked. "The man I saw through the window? I want to go and find where he lives if I can. But I don't want John or the others to know what I am doing. River business. Just in case, you'll know what I've done."

"But Mr Pickless said he wasn't to be disturbed. You'll be on your own over the boundary. There could be Outies waiting to catch you. Anything goes wrong and both of us will be in trouble."

Peter did not like this at all. All the farmers insisted that no one should go on the moors by themselves even in broad daylight, and when the work took them there it was almost always as a gang, with the farmer in charge. 'River business', though. No time to find out what Mark meant. There was something about Mark that commanded consent. Peter nodded, and they returned to go back to the yard.

"Try to keep them down there as long as possible," said Mark.

4. The Evader

The four boys soon set off down the road. When they were out of sight, Mark stood where he was for a moment, then went round the back of the farm, and cut off westwards towards the cliff, and along the top until he could see the broken dam and the ruins beyond. He scrambled across the valley bottom towards them. Among others, a couple of roofless buildings emerged from behind a tall crumbling wall that ended in the hillsides at both ends. There seemed be a cliff or old quarry face cut into the hill behind it. Relic hunting on the edge of the city and around had taught him to recognise the wall and most of the buildings as the earliest After-the-Catastrophe type, cobbled together, it appeared, anyhow with no great skill. He walked to the wall. The place was silent. There was no sign of Old Jones, indeed, no sign of any life at all. There was a faint track in the sparse grass that fronted it. Outies? He looked around anxiously. As he walked along the track, he could see that the base of the wall was pre-war, mortared blocks, neatly cut. It was the top that was ragged, made up of rocks and pieces of old masonry, taking it about ten feet high. He passed the two ruined buildings he had seen, but then found what he had not seen: a gateway with a fallen arch and rubble in the entrance. The rubble was no obstacle. As Mark climbed over the debris in the entrance, his foot dislodged a stout stick. It dislodged some stones, and there was a brief clatter.

He paused, but the silence returned. Nothing moved. He climbed down into the walled enclosure. It was still; no sound could be heard. It was level, mostly gravel with the same stunted, greyish grasses in small patches. A cliff had been carved out of the hillside, and against it was a more solid building. It had clearly been built right into the cliff, and was made of pre-war concrete, the material Mark had seen so much of near the old city. You couldn't see it from above. There were windows, in two stories, but the lower ones were tiny and at least fifteen feet from the ground. There was a door, too, a very large one, but that had been roughly walled up. The place seemed not much deserted as sealed up. He turned around to look back at the roofless sheds, and around the compound for any signs of life. There was none, and no signs either that it had been a quarry. He was starting to cross towards the building itself when he heard a door creak behind him. He turned. There, unmistakably, was Old Jones, who had come, not out of the walled-up door, but from the far end of the concrete building. He held a crossbow, but it was pointing down, and not at him.

The temptation to run was nearly irresistible. Jones was not between him and the gateway, and he didn't look as if he could run far or fast. But the old man showed no sign of anger. He had stopped when Mark turned, but easily, as though inviting Mark to look. He had not crept up. He approached Mark, crossbow held loosely in one hand.

"I…I was just looking round," said Mark, feeling very foolish, rather than frightened.

The old man came up to him and grinned. Some teeth were missing. Dark eyes looked at him from a long, brown and wrinkled face. There was a ragged beard. He was thin, but certainly not gaunt or starved-looking.

"All by yourself? Out here? Didn't your parents and teachers and all tell you about Outies up here, what takes boys like you away and eats them? You are way over the boundary, boy, and you know it." There was something mocking in his tone, rather than anger.

"Well, yes, sir, but all the farmers say that Mr Pickless never gets bothered with them, and he said that when you and he saw some…" Mark stopped. He'd grasped that Mr Pickless, and for that matter, Miss and Muss Pickless, were afraid of Old Jones' leaving, and that if Mr Pickless knew that he had come here and told him that Pickless had talked about him, there would be even more trouble.

"You? So, you know who I am, don't you?"

His tone was neutral, not angry, and there was something about the way he said it that made Mark want to talk.

"Yes, sir, you're Mr Jones."

"I'll bet it wasn't Mr he called me."

"No, sir," said Mark.

"Well, sir will do for now. And how about your name?"

"Mark, sir, Mark Norman."

Jones visibly relaxed, as though he recognised the name.

"But you were saying, Mark?"

"He said that when you saw some they stopped and waited till you'd moved towards the boundary. Or went away. And when I was with Mr Smith, and with the other Mr Pickless at Ewden, they complained all the time about Outies taking their sheep, but they never seemed to be frightened about going up on the moors alone, specially Mr Smith. And they didn't have swords, or shotguns or anything like that."

"Did you go up on the moors with them and see these fearsome beasts then?"

"No, sir. I did ask once, Mr Smith it was. He said it was far too dangerous for the likes of me, and he'd never get any lads working for him if one got took. And when we were walling up in the outfield together, there was never any sign."

"And you didn't sneak out on your own, like today, and have a look for yourself?" said Jones. He had a peculiar expression on his face, more grimace than grin.

Mark was taken aback. He had thought of doing just that at the Smiths', but he must have shown something in his face, because Mr Smith had then supervised the remaining three Kingsdays remarkably closely, even sending Mark with his wives and two remaining daughters by trap to the Service in Bradfield, staying behind himself. Nothing had been said, but there had been no room for argument either. The Misses Smith had taken this for granted, for Smith himself normally made the most of his farmer's licence for himself, but was happy enough to pack the family off by themselves.

"No," he said, and then added to his own surprise, "I thought of it, but I think Mr Smith guessed, and he didn't give me the chance."

"No, I don't suppose he would." Jones' face was now rather stony. "So, you've not seen Westrons?" he continued.

"No," said Mark. In fact, when he came to think about it, the only people he had met who had seen them, Outies or Westrons, were the farmers near the moors for whom he'd worked, and then only from a distance. Of course, he'd heard lots about them, not by name, both at home, and even more at school, but, facing Old Jones, who had seen them, he sensed that Mr Arkwright, the Chronicles teacher, who made them learn all about the Great War and what happened since, had not. There were pictures, of course; there had been some in the *Chronicles in Colour* book that Jamie had once shown him. They had looked terrifying enough, but the pictures in those books had never seemed realistic to Mark. And the farmers up here, though angry enough after a raid, did not seem to be frightened for themselves.

"How long were you working for Smith?" the old man asked. "The usual eight weeks, was it?"

"Yes, that's right, sir, it was last summer."

"And you were by yourself?"

"Yes, sir. Mr Smith had had a big gang the previous summer, to patch up all his walls and dykes, and he didn't have the work for more than one, was what he said."

"Out alone on the moor a lot by himself, was he?" asked Jones.

Mark thought back. He'd been on the moor with Mr Smith quite often, working on the high wall that separated the outfields from the moor proper, but it was true that Mr Smith had often disappeared up into the hills when Mark had been set to working near the farm, or in the lower fields.

"I suppose so," he said, a bit uncertainly.

"Hmph." Old Jones said nothing for a while, and Mark wondered what was going to happen next. After the shock of being found, he had expected a roasting for trespass, and a promise to tell Pickless, not a whole lot of questions about his previous stint-master.

The old man seemed to guess his thoughts.

"It's only Pickless knows I live around here, and when he let it slip, he'd have told you to leave me be, isn't it so?"

"Yes, sir. I saw someone in the yard, when we were waiting for supper the other night. I knew Mr Pickless didn't have any hands, and I thought it might be an intruder, one of those types from the edge of the city who go about stealing hens and such. So, I said that I'd seen someone in the yard, and he seemed to know that it was you, and then he said a few things about you and Westrons. Then he wasn't that keen to carry on, and I think his wives felt the same. And, yes, he told me not to come bothering you, sir, sorry."

"There's quite a gang of you with Pickless, aren't there? Do you all know about me? Where are the other lads?"

"Yes, sir, but he told us all not to mention it to anyone, or it would be trouble for us, not you or him. It was only me got told about Westrons. The others are down by the pools on the track to the Stones and Ewden, sir, fishing and looking for Relics. Mr Pickless said some turned up by the old dam. I was told to stay by the farm. There's one I trust, and I told him, but the rest don't know. I need to be back before them and the family. They have gone to their cousin in Ewden, and they'll not be back till dusk. I'll not say a word to anyone, nor will my friend."

Old Jones was looking angry and thoughtful in turn, the creases in his brown face deepening. Mark heard something like, "fool Pickless, and more fool I..." muttered under the old man's breath. There was a long pause after that, and Mark wondered if he should ask if he could leave. He was about to open his mouth when the old man started again.

"So, you came looking for me, and knew where to find me too?"

"Not exactly, sir. Mr Pickless let slip that it was this direction, but he had never known where you went when not on the farm. This was just the first place I reached."

"And what was the attraction in coming to dig out an old man in his home, then? The other lads had more sense and manners, so it seems."

Mark didn't know how to answer that. Why had he come up here? At best, he now realised, he would have seen nothing and nobody, and just missed the opportunity of a Relic. At worst, which was what seemed to have happened, he would find Old Jones, and there would just be a whole lot of trouble. There had just been that sense of something hidden, something that was connected in some way to events on the riverbank. The uneasy feeling that things were not as the teachers told it. He hesitated.

"Well, boy? Did Pickless tell you some fantastic tale, that fired you up, eh?"

"No, sir. But...but there was something odd, sir. Everyone is accounted for, but not you. He said you were not local and he did not know where you came from. But it was obvious that you must live close by, but he did not know where, or so he said."

"True enough, he doesn't know, and for good reason. But that was enough to set you off, beyond the bounds by yourself? Heard of the saying, curiosity killed the cat?"

Jones was looking at him intently, a frown on his face. It dawned on Mark that the man was not so much angry as puzzled. But the man was an outlaw; tell him the truth, and it would surely not get back to the Proctors or the Domain.

"Friends of mine went missing, sir, and we knew that they'd gone over the bounds into the Domain. There were searches, and we were told the Outies must have caught them, though it seemed unlikely. And here you were, sir, and the Outies had not taken you. I got thinking that there were things happening beyond the bounds that we were not told about."

"Ah, so you're one of those kids that been messing with the Rangers on the riverbank? And found a way or two into the forest?"

Jones' face relaxed, but Mark was shaken. How could Jones possibly know? All of them had kept the secret ever since the big row over David, knowing that parents and teachers alike would react by banning visits to the riverbank altogether. The mayor had preached about trespass after that, but nothing else happened. How did this old man living in the hills know about them? He could think of nothing to say.

There was a strong, sudden gust of wind. Both looked up, and saw the squall crossing to them from the west, off the bleak moors that held all the menace of the enemy to a Grounder like Mark.

"You'd best come inside with me," said Jones, "It'll not last long, and you and I have things to talk about. Seems I'm not the only one with things they'd rather others kept their noses out of."

He led the way back around the side of the building, where there was a small door in the wall joining the front to the cliff face behind. Beside the door, there was a strange construction of boards nailed together, but roughly, as though just stacked. There was a prong in the middle, sticking right out from the boards. After Mark had entered, into the gloom of the space inside, the man picked up the construction and propped it against the outside wall, so that it covered the whole open doorway. Then he closed the door from inside, and Mark saw that a small hole had been cut in it, through which the prong slid. Jones bent down and picked up a small vice, pulled hard on the prong, and tightened the vice around its shaft, close against the door. Then he bolted the door, and turned to face Mark.

Mark's eyes were adjusting to the gloom. The tiny windows gave just enough light to see by. There was, though, an old table just by the door, with a candle and a box of matches, the same kind as Mr Pickless used in the farm. Without thinking, he said,

"If someone came around, like me, and tried to move that cover, and discovered the prong, wouldn't they know someone was inside?"

"Yes, that's so. But I've not been expecting anyone to come looking for me, see, just that maybe some of the lads like you, working for Pickless, might get the idea of exploring. I doubt if you would have tried, if I hadn't come out."

"No, sir, I wouldn't. Why did you come out, then, sir?"

"Did you stumble coming through the gateway? I know you did. I've a set of triggers that tip stones off in here, then I know someone's around. More often than not, it's a stupid sheep. I've had a few Outers a while back. The stupid ones. They should know to stay away. There's an agreement of sorts, see. They stay clear, and I don't go more than a mile west. You have seen my crossbow. I've fired off a few bolts, and they've got the message. There's nothing for them here. I watched you from a window upstairs."

"I had that bow ready, mind, when I came out, but have a Grounder go missing would cause no end of trouble; for Pickless most of all. So, I watched, and hoped you'd go away. You might have been after Relics, seen nothing, and gone away. Then you were alongside the building, and I thought even if he doesn't find me, he'll be back, or he'll say something, and I can't be spending all my time hiding."

Jones walked across the room towards the opposite end. The ground floor was a single, large space, with a concrete floor. It was strewn with old boxes, and there were two quite tidy woodpiles. The back wall was the cliff. There was a door set into it, a massive one about fifteen feet wide and just as high. It was obviously made of metal, and, equally obviously, it had not been opened for ages, perhaps not since the War itself. The sheer quantity of the metal took Mark by surprise; here was a Relic, all right, and one for which there would be huge reward. Not ordinary iron, either, since although tarnished, it was not really rusty. Of course, you'd have to take a salvage party to it, rather than the other way round, and it was hard to see how they would break it into small enough pieces to carry away and send over the bridge. Maybe Kingsmen would come with special tools.

At the corner of the far wall running from the front to the cliff was a metal ladder, rising perhaps twenty feet to the ceiling. There was a closed trapdoor at the top. Jones led the way, and after Mark had scrambled through, he closed and bolted the door. The bolts were loose. There was a hook in the middle of it, to which Jones hooked a string attached to small brass bell suspended from a little wooden frame held to the floor with a few lumps of concrete.

"I expect visitors to ring politely," he said with a grin. Now he was inside, he seemed more at ease.

The upper floor was brighter. Mark could see that the windows were made of the pre-war security glass, with wire inside it, another Relic with value, if you could find a large enough unbroken piece. One of the windows had been broken, and was boarded up very thoroughly. There were only three windows to be seen here, for, unlike the ground floor, this had a kind of hall, with the trap door, and then a rather gloomy corridor running the length of the building. Mark saw that what light there was there came from three doors, obviously left open, which, presumably led to three rooms facing the outside. There were doors on the other side, too. These were shut.

Jones led the way down the corridor, passing the first open door, through which Mark got a glimpse of a bed, a chair and table, and a number of cupboards. On the table was another crossbow. He stopped at the second, and waited for Mark to go in ahead of him.

Mark entered. The room was more-or-less square, perhaps 20 feet in each direction. It had a single, large window, letting in plenty of light. He gasped as he took in what the room contained.

Relics! Relics in quantities and of a kind that he had never seen. Enough relics to give their finder a certificate and Credits that would, in theory, keep them in idleness and wealth for a lifetime. Relics that if not handed over immediately, and their source shown to Receiver's officers, would get you sent away to who knew where. Metal shelves, cabinets and cupboards; a variety of small metal objects whose purpose was obscure; and books, hundreds of pre-war books. On a large table, more books, together with papers, ink, and the whole paraphernalia of writing. Mark had heard of Relic hunters in the city making finds like this way back, though not on this scale; the finders had been reticent enough, even after they had received their payment.

"Sit," said Jones, pointing to one of two ordinary, wooden chairs by the window. Mark did as he was told, too amazed to exclaim. Jones took the other chair, more-or-less facing Mark. At that moment, the squall hit, and the noise of the rain against the window brought Mark out of his blankness.

"Well, boy, what do you see?"

"Relics, sir, more than I've ever seen."

"Enough to make your fortune, eh?"

"Enough to have you sent away for ever, sir. But you could not declare it," replied Mark.

The rules about Relics were very clear, and dinned into everyone, at home, at school and in frequent homilies at Kingsday services. They must be handed over at once at the Receiver of Relics' office. For stuff that had an obvious use, especially some metals, there was a payment, determined by the Receiver. Or stuff like the ceramics John had found, but lost to a squatter gang all those years ago. When you presented it, or took the Receiver or his deputy to see it, if it was too big to carry, your find was registered. If you found a lot, you had a chance to have 'Relic-hunter' added to your certificate, and it could become a full time and recognised occupation. In practice, it was only people in the city squats who had ever found enough to get such status; outsiders prowling in the ruins were likely to get a beating as with John. In any case, valuable Relics were getting harder and harder to find.

In practice, pre-war coins, and other small metal objects were kept as souvenirs; they had little value to the Receiver, being made of base metal, and no one got punished for having them. The real offence was to keep anything like a book, anything with writing or pictures. Even those who presented them to the Receiver were questioned closely, and the site was then searched thoroughly by his men, sometimes, in the city, by Security. Mark did not know of anyone who had hidden such a relic, but Jamie had told him that a city girl, known to David through his parents' Relic-hunter days, had hidden a book, been caught with it, and had been held for three days. After that, she had been taken to the bridge, handed over to Security, and was never seen again. Her parents, and her sister and brothers had been sent further south, still in a Ground, just as labourers. This had been widely advertised.

Such things were very rare. Finds were made, but nowadays mostly in such a state that they were scarcely recognisable, never mind readable. Mr Arkwright had told them that most had been retrieved a long time ago; useful ones were in the King's libraries and colleges, mostly down south, but with some in Conisbrough and elsewhere in the Kingdom. A few had been reprinted for the Civic Colleges to the south. All their school books, and those kept at home were King's print. The teachers told them that many pre-war books were full of 'moral poison', or held material which could aid the King's enemies. Some might have instructions about weapons, or other things that might aid the King's Forces in their struggle. There were three on display in the antechamber of the Council Hall in Bradfield, in a glass-lidded cabinet, itself pre-war. All were open at the title page, and two had intelligible titles, though the first had needed explaining:

INSECTIVOROUS PLANTS. By CHARLES DARWIN, M.A., F.R.S,
THE TRUTH Terry Pratchett.

The third had an unintelligible title, which seemed not to have proper letters at all.

There was no label or explanatory notice, but one of the Visitor's secretaries, Richard Dean, had told Mark's class that they were part of a large find made 40 *or more years ago in the city; a cache which had been stored in boxes in a cellar. Mark could understand the nature of the first, when it was explained, though he found it hard to imagine how a whole book could be written about the little sundews and butterworts growing on the moors. He was astonished to be told that the second, with its portentous title, was, as Mr Dean said, 'just a story'. The opposite page of this was covered with modern paper, evidently glued on, unlike the first, where the page was blank but obviously original. The third, so Mr Dean said, was written in a very distant country where they used different letters, and a completely different language; it was about snails, judging by the pictures, which he had been allowed to see during one of the Visitor's official visits.*

Jones merely nodded at Mark's words. He seemed still to be uncertain what to do or say, but he was clearly not frightened by the half-implied threat. Then he got up, went to one of the bookshelves, and took a book. Opening it at the title page, he handed it to Mark.

"Read to me what it says there," he said.

"The Holy Bible, containing the old and new," Mark paused, 'testaments' and then the rest, haltingly, because many of the words were long and unfamiliar.

"Ever heard of it?" asked Jones.

"No, sir. But I don't think I have ever heard of the names of any pre-war books, except for the ones in the council hall at Bradfield."

"Know what Holy Bible means?"

"Well, Holy is to do with the King and his laws, of course, but I haven't heard of Bible. And testament is what they say after they bury the dead: *Now hear the last will and testament.* Oh, is it the will of the King? No, that can't be right, he hadn't started his reign. Is it to do with an ancestor?"

Mark paused. Instead of telling him anything, Jones said,

"Turn over the page." Mark did so. He read:

To the most high and mighty Prince JAMES, by the Grace of God, King of Great Britain, France and Ireland, Defender of the Faith &c.

He was reading silently, and with increasing difficulty, because the language was difficult, and the meaning worse. It seemed some kind of nonsense. The King was just the King, he had no name, though he could be given descriptions, like Saviour of the People, or Ever-Watchful. Britain, he had heard of, though, but only as the island in which England lay. The King certainly could not be a prince as well, though Princes did have names; there had even been a Prince James, who had died driving back the enemy in the south, 'Battle of Upton, December 23rd, 15 KY' slipped into Mark's head reflexively from Chronicles. He had never been clear where that was.

And who was God? There was only the King. *I acknowledge the King, our Lord, who banished for us, and for our salvation, the worship of imaginary gods, the creation of the Deceiver for our confusion.* Mark quoted silently the familiar words from the longer form of the Declaration. Then he remembered, this was a pre-war book, the king was not reigning. He looked up, to see Jones watching him intently.

"What is this?" he asked, "It is pre-war, so who was God? The enemy?"

"Food for thought, boy, that's what it is. There's no time to start explanations, and it would be near a lifetime if I tried to tell you a tenth of what I've learnt. What I'll tell you though, is that that book was written more than 600 years ago, though this copy is much younger. And it was based on even older books in strange languages."

600 years? Chronicles dealt with anything more than a few years before the birth of the King in the skimpiest way. Mark had not even bothered to think if books were known that long ago. Except for the prelude to the War, the Noble Births, the ennobling of the righteous and the Great Deceit, the past was given to you as:

"And we are here, as on a darkling plain
Swept with confused alarms of struggle and flight,
Where ignorant armies clash by night."

It was one of the rare pieces from the pre-war period that they had to learn by heart. When it was written, and by whom, was not revealed. Darkling and alarms also needed a bit of explanation. The only other ancient text they learnt on the matter was:

It is a tale told by an idiot,
Full of sound and fury
Signifying nothing

Both were used to show that the past was a jumble of meaningless chaos which provoked nothing but despair in even the best. The King had delivered us from darkness, and probing it was dangerous; an unhealthy and potentially criminal activity. The Deceiver was always looking for entry to your mind.

"You will need to get back in good time before the others return," said Jones, interrupting Mark's reverie, "but there's time to show you one other thing." He got up and went to a set of very wide and shallow drawers, opened one and pulled out a huge sheet of paper, which he placed on the table.

"Come and look at this," he said, "but look, don't touch. These things are getting fragile."

Mark got up and looked. He could see at once that it was a map. But like no map he had ever seen. The maps they used in school had a fixed purpose: this is your Division, your Ground. This is where you belong, and these are the boundaries. You do not go beyond them. What *is* beyond them is not your concern, and is not shown in any detail. You knew only that to the north were the Barriers and vast Badlands, to the East, the King's Domain, to the south the Royal Corridor and beyond it more Divisions of the Ground, to which you might be deployed. To the west, the lands of the enemy, blighted, twisted and inhabited by rapacious monsters. He knew, and was made to feel proud, that theirs was the northernmost of all Grounds, and that clearing the Barriers would move it further north still.

This map, though, was intricate, and very detailed. And the details went right to each edge. At first sight, there were no boundaries. He grasped roads, but there were many of them, shown in different colours. And there were markings that must be buildings or representations of towns and villages. There was a river. Before he had started on the writing, Jones asked,

"You can see it's a map. Do you recognise of where?"

Mark looked more closely. Suddenly, the names came into focus. That huge mass of roads and grey colouring, Sheffield! They knew the name of course, but to them it was just the city, the ruins from which nearly all Relics had been stripped. As he peered there was more: Bradfield, Ewden, even Midhope. There were others too. He noticed that someone had inked in lines. He traced them. Some seemed to mark out the Ground, but others meant nothing to him. Handwritten notes were written on some, but not whole words. Roads, villages, even towns, now he could recognise them, extending in all directions. Here was the river. Where there was now the Kings Forest, blank beyond the river to him, more roads, more houses, and only a scattering of green, which he recognised as woodland, for that, at least, was also the case in the maps on the schoolroom wall.

"It's here," he said, "but not like it is really. There are even roads and houses to the west, and more cities north of the Barriers."

"More food for thought, eh, boy," said Jones wryly. "From what I can work out, that's what 'here' was like sometime before the war; before the Catastrophe. Not much left, is there, at least what we know of."

Mark's head reeled. Surely, they had been taught that the war was terrible, but this? And why was their little enclave still there, when destruction and pollution had been so great all around them?

"Have a closer look. See the lines drawn in? I think someone knew what was clean and what was polluted. They are marked but I don't understand the letters. I can make some guesses, though. There are others like this."

Jones picked up the map carefully, and returned it to the cabinet. He looked directly at Mark.

"I'm taking the chance with you, lad. I can see you have doubts about what you've been taught. You don't know the half of it. Times are changing, but not for the better if the Domain gets its way. I guessed it was you when I saw you outside. Pickless was always looking for an apprentice and successor he could share with. He was wondering about one he could trust, and he mentioned your name. You seeing me will settle it, unless you turn us in. Not a word to him, though, leave that to me. If that works, you'll be the only one who knows what's here, and you've seen just a fraction. It'll take time to work out what it means. And what to do with it. I'd have got the Westrons to take it, but the locals are not that clever. The ones around here, most of them can't read, and the stuff that matters is fragile. And they've reasons not be around much. I've kept them away, and I'll carry on like that until I've worked out what matters and what doesn't."

Mark was overwhelmed. Everything the old man said reinforced his feelings that things were not as they had been told. But he was being invited into an actual conspiracy against the King's rule. Information to help the Outies.

"I'll not turn you in, sir. I'm not sure about the others. There's one very patriotic, as we say. I think they'll stay quiet. I was hoping for a farm posting anyway, and my father has encouraged me. Mr Pickless could ask for me next year. But there's no certainty when it comes to selection or posting. I might be transferred, or even Chosen."

"Thank you, Mark. I'm taking more than one chance here. I'm getting old, and there's not much I can do if I'm sick or have a fall. I can't march into Bradfield to see the hygienist. Muss Pickless had some training, and she's patched me up more than once. If you get back to the farm, and there's no message, I'm probably dead. If you are transferred or, God help us, Chosen, Pickless will need to find another, if he's spared. Whichever, what to do will be up to you, with no one the wiser if you just do what you are told. I know a little about the costs, believe me."

The oath hit Mark. Jones got to his feet.

"You'd best be on your way, now. I don't want any questions to Pickless or Kingsmen starting an incursion because you've been caught out. Posted here or not, you never come nearer here than the farm again without I say so through Pickless. Get there, and I'll find ways to see you. As long as Pickless is around, you'd be safe enough."

Jones went to the window to view the yard. Satisfied, he led Mark down and out. When Mark had climbed over the rubble at the gate and been gone five minutes or so, he went to the gate, shifted some rubble and went back inside, closing the screen and door behind him. Insurance was the next item, and half an hour later, he set off west with a heavy pack. An hour or so later, a notional watcher would have seen him return, and he had made three such trips before going back inside for good. At the end of the corridor furthest from the hall, there was a strong metal door. He swung it to and fro, greasing the hinges and the bolts on both sides with fat from his cooking.

Mark was soon back at the farm. The dogs greeted him, but no one had returned while he was away. The boys were back first, about three hours later. Back, and also tired and grumpy. No Relics, and no fish. After the hubbub of news, or the lack of it, John went up to their attic quarters. After sitting a while on a stone bench in the yard, Peter muttered something to Simon, who went with Tom to see if the hens had laid. Peter had brightened up on seeing Mark when they returned. Left alone, the conversation was predictable.

"Well?"

"I found him, Peter. He talked to me. I've seen too much to take in."

"What, for King's sake! Wasn't he angry? Will he tell Mr Pickless?"

"Yes, he'll tell Pickless sooner or later, I'm sure, but that's the point, Peter, he trusts Pickless to take it no further. Think about that. And he trusted me too.

Yes, he was angry at first, but in a funny way. I think you are better off not knowing any more. I'm back here, no explaining needed from you."

Mark sought to change the subject.

"Sounds like you had a dull day."

"Yes. Those pools were pretty barren, and you could see that folk had scoured the place for Relics. Piles of rubble where they'd searched for cellars. Old piles at that. It's a long way out, but I'd have said squatters' work."

"John? Was he behaving?"

"Yes, pretty much. We all stayed together, and I think he was keeping an eye to see we didn't hide any Relics. Fat chance. Actually, he was all for giving up and returning at lunchtime. I managed to keep finding another ruin to check, and even led everyone some way downstream."

"Thanks, Peter."

He was about to say more, when they heard the rattle of the trap's wheels, and the Pickless family entered the yard. Conventional chatter followed. No, nothing untoward at the farm, Mr Pickless. No, no luck with fishing or Relics. A different plan for next Kingsday? Miss and Muss indoors to prepare the evening meal, Mr Pickless to stable the horses. A few small tasks to be seen to by the boys.

The rest of the stint passed almost without incident. Pickless made a point of using Mark to help with the book-keeping and showed him how the stud book worked. But most work, for all of them, was out of doors. Most Kingsdays, they hung around the farm, but on the sixth, Pickless packed them all off with presents for his cousins at Ewden, while Miss and Muss took the trap to Service. He remained at home.

It was in their last week, on Wednesday, that Pickless sent four of them off to the meadows, and kept Mark in the yard and byres. Mid-morning, he asked Mark to come to the farm office.

"Sit. Mark, I've some things to say that'll not come as a surprise, I think. I've had words with Jones, and I know you've found him, and at home too. How, I don't know, he's a clever one when it comes to invisibility. No, don't tell me, I don't want to know. What I do know, he trusts you, and so I must do the same, earlier than I had planned for. We are at your mercy, lad, much more than from that patriotic bag of wind."

"I'll not say a word, sir, on my heart. My brothers were both Chosen. We were all supposed to feel the honour, but I could see something more than sorrow at parting from my parents. More like anger. And Father has been encouraging me to get a reputation for farm work, like here. Then there were things that a few of us were finding didn't fit what we learnt in school. Things about the inner boundary. Mr Jones showed me things that shook me, sir."

Pickless sat silent, head in hands. Mark was a golden opportunity, better than they could have hoped for. But he'd learnt too much, too early, far too early. He'd sized up stint gangs for a potential apprentice for a few years, with the notion of probing their thoughts, and always had enough doubts not to request an apprentice from among any of them. It wasn't discovering Jones as such, the mayor knew very well that there was an evader, but knowing what he knew and could prove was what mattered. And could be passed on.

His cousin, completely in the dark, had given Mark a conventional, but praising reference. The women had done sterling work after Service and when shopping or delivering; innocent gossip including a little about the river adventures that made Mark more and more of a mark. Pickless groaned inwardly at his own pun. Now, Mark knew too much, but was not yet secured. He might be given a different job, he might be transferred out of Division, or, worst of all Chosen. And who knew what life behind the bounds was like. For all the glory in Service, stories from the squats made it clear that those caught out of bounds were questioned and beaten in ways that would have shocked the lumbering Proctors. One slip of the tongue, one lead from elsewhere that pointed to Mark, and for all his promises now, the pressure and the threats would probably overwhelm a sixteen-year-old. Pickless grimaced as he braced himself to tell the boy the substance of his thoughts.

5. Selection

Mark's return home from the stint caused no stir among the family, at least at first. Of course, he said nothing about Jones, nor about the talks with Mr Pickless that followed. His father and mother were delighted at his enthusiasm, and the signs that Pickless had singled him out for special treatment. It was only after school started again in early September that certain tensions appeared.

That final year was always a matter for worry and speculation. At its end, there would be Selection, with all the consequences that followed. Some would remain in the Ground. For boys, and a very few girls, this meant an apprenticeship. For the girls, it would imply marriage in the near future, with a variety of jobs to do beforehand. But the decision on marriage did not, in itself, mean remaining in the Ground when it took place. Lisa, indeed, was still awaiting the decision as to who her husband would be, where he was, and whether she was to be Miss or Muss. She had been working in a creche, and also in a mill in the time since school.

Still others would be sent away for further training, but in a Ground, rather than into the Domain as a Chosen one. It was rare, but not unknown for one trained elsewhere to return, fertility undamaged more often than not. Letters, even visits, were possible, though the latter were rare and hard to arrange. Chosen, though? That was goodbye for ever, with all the mixed emotions that went with it. As the school year advanced, the mix soon came to dominate mealtimes, with Muss not merely hoping for Mark's selection, but badgering him and his father about how the choice was made, and what steps Mark was taking to improve his chances. Mr Norman tried hard to give out a fatalistic explanation.

"Nobody knows, Muss. Fertility is one point against, but none of us get to know how the hygienists assess it. There'll be many fertile boys cross the bridge, though, that's certain. Then there's the skills needed in the Domain, and we don't know that, either. Someone in the Domain, in the Visitor's Office, has to balance it all out. Think a bit. Suppose there's a family producing prodigies. Like Mark's classmate Veronica, chosen at only eight, before your time. They say gifts like that run in families, so if you whipped all the children across the bridge, you've cut off the supply. Best just to wait and see."

Of course, Muss was not satisfied. She had taken in that both her husband and Miss were less enthusiastic than she thought proper, while Lisa was beyond the pale; a downright heretic, that one, was her private thought. Only the knowledge that guilt for any misdemeanour was visited on whole families had prevented her making a report. Settled in a family with prestige both from Service and Mr Norman's position suited her very nicely. With that in mind, she cast a sour glance at her stepdaughter when she asked:

"But what about attitude? Don't they want the most enthusiastic, the most patriotic? I'm sure Mark could show more enthusiasm."

Lisa got up and left the room to avoid an outburst. Mark grimaced, and looked to his father for help.

"Not that simple," said Mr Norman. "Put on a show, and they wonder why, and balance it against what they actually need. Fertile but untalented, and they'd likely transfer you to a city where the life might be harder than in the Domain. There are patriots sure they were headed for Royal Service bitterly disappointed when they ended up in the Leicester squats."

Mr Norman had explained the process of selection accurately enough as far as the young men and women were concerned. He did not add the less celebrated Choosing of adults, that happened when a match proved infertile. Technically an honour, such adult selection was, nevertheless, widely seen as a mark of failure. Had his first Muss survived her second miscarriage, she would certainly have been across the bridge. This Muss was safe. Safe from a choosing that she knew, as well as did he, was not a passport to health, wealth and happiness, an outcome reserved only for those girls or women with special talents.

Things were easier when Muss was not around. Mr Norman was delighted with the avidity with which Mark now warmed to the idea of being a farmer. School in that last year sent the children around many trades. Employers were required to submit reports on their aptitudes to the Mayor's Office. Time with the hygienists; time at the bridge, at the mills, even with John Gregory's father dealing with electricity. The Proctors gave time to every boy too, as did the mayor's office, though Mark worked besides a junior clerk, well away from his father. But it was at the farm placements that Mark put in the effort to impress. As he soon discovered, it was practice not to use any farmer where the boy had done a stint; no chance of his meeting again with Mr Pickless.

It did not trouble the mayor that it was Mark's father who collated and filed all the reports. Mr Norman was uniquely placed to see the growing files and the messages they were delivering. He saw things moving in the right direction. With Muss mothering two boys already, neither with any complications or defects, the Domain had plenty of prospects for more Service without calling on Mark, the more so since he had surreptitiously obtained evidence that Mark was fertile.

Here, he had needed to be devious. Hygienist's reports went straight to the Visitor's Office, and only the senior Deputy, Muss Amelia Franklin, was authorised to inspect them. A stern and rather formidable woman of sixty, long since widowed, and with children all grown up, her part-time role as Deputy meshed with work as a teacher of language. Her demand for precision intimidated most of her pupils, but Mark had enjoyed the brief period in her classes. Much cleverer than either Arkell or the other, younger Deputy, John Markham, there was a mostly unspoken bond of respect between her and Mark's father; a bond displayed by raised eyebrows at each Arkell nonsense.

Mr Norman had merely hinted that it would be good to know Mark's status. Amelia had understood without further words being spoken, and it was not long before he found a short note among his papers. It remained only to get Pickless to put in a request for Mark as an apprentice. Again, it was done indirectly, by Miss Norman talking informally to Miss Pickless after Service one Kingsday. The request was duly in the mayor's hands before the Visitor's assistants passed the information to Conisbrough.

When Selection came round, therefore, Mr Norman was confident. The families of all school leavers and others who were interested crowded into the Council Hall. The Chosen were named first. The list ran down the alphabet.

"...Henry Masters; Alex Minshull; David Namier; Alice Nightingale; Mark Norman..."

Mr Norman sat paralysed. Mark was shocked. Everything that could be done had been, all for nought. As they all left the Hall, both had to endure the applause and the slapping on the back. Mark soon turned his thoughts to Mr Pickless. Mr Pickless, who had asked for him by name. Despite the age of all three of them at Midhope, Pickless had never asked for an apprentice before. Of course, Mark knew why: another man on the spot all the time would inevitably find out about

Jones. And he'd get a wife, then another. Kids would go to school. Silencing a draft had worked; keeping the secret then would be impossible. The authorities would not be able to hide it, and would have to act.

As all dispersed, he saw John Gregory in the distance, in animated conversation with Muss Norman. John turned as Mark went by. There was a look in his eyes, a look that conveyed more than satisfaction at his own selection, which they had all regarded as inevitable. Mark managed a grin and a nod. Muss left John and his family, joining Mark and his father, gushing with enthusiasm. Miss had avoided the ceremony; Lisa had come, but now stood apart. There was more backslapping, more congratulations. Three Chosen in the family, not that unusual, but rewarded with Credits and status. His father was attempting to accept the praise with good grace, but Mark could see the mixture of fury and despair in his eyes. All that work, all those hints to Mark, the cultivation of skills needed in the Ground, the concealing of talents that were commonly associated with being Chosen, all to no purpose. Mark's meeting with Jones and talk with Pickless had made him wake up to his father's purpose; a purpose innocent of the knowledge that Mark had gained; a purpose turned to dust and ashes.

They started downhill for home together, Lisa dragging behind. Smiles faded, and the party walked on in silence. All knew the routine, with two gone before. There would be just three days in which the Chosen would visit friends and relatives to say goodbye. There would be a party at home. The minimal list of things that could be taken would be assembled. Then the special Kingsday ceremony, where they would sign the Oath, take the shilling, and travel in procession to the bridge, escorted by Kingsmen. Families did not follow; final waves were limited to the space in front of the hall.

As they sat down to the evening meal, only Muss was in good spirits. Ben and Johnny were far too young to be Chosen in the normal way, but she regarded Mark's selection as a good sign. Mark, however, was in turmoil. He responded as well as he could to Muss' repeated, overstated congratulations to both him and his parents. Would they rearrange the other Certificates to make a neat line on the wall? What would father do with the Credits? Did this increase his chances of being a Deputy Mayor? Mr Norman said little in response, and Miss nothing at all.

Mark could not stand any more, and left for a walk as soon as he could. There was something about Muss' enthusiasm that was smug, a hint of satisfaction that was not accounted for simply by her thirst for status. She had been talking to

John, he recalled. And for weeks beforehand she had been particularly friendly with the Gregory family. A nasty thought entered his mind. Everybody knew that guessing who would be chosen was, as Mr Norman had explained to Muss, futile. Certainly, some very bright kids were always on the lists, but not all of them. Some families seemed to have a Chosen one more often than not, when the boy, or more rarely the girl, were the right age. Pickless had parted with six.

And yet, he thought, *what might have influenced the final decision?* His father had hinted at the correction of the hygienists' report for Lisa. The Gregory family were friendly with several hygienists. But, for certain, nothing would be proven, and even if it were, Selection decisions were never challenged. There were other puzzles too; Simon and Peter had both been Chosen, a year earlier than usual, but not unheard of. Bar young Tom, certainly no prodigy, all of them who had done their stint with Pickless had been Chosen. Mark could see nothing but that in common between them. And Jamie too. That family had been remarkably favoured; considering Steve, even more so than would be known to the world at large. And why Julie? Again, a year early, and the twins passed over. They would both be married very soon. Had she also been thought infertile?

He returned home, thankfully finding that Muss was engaged in putting her children to bed. There was little to say to his parents or Lisa. He went upstairs to the room he had once shared with Max. It was a sleepless night. In the morning, he left the house immediately after breakfast, almost running down to Jamie's house in the hope of catching him before he started the ritual visits and goodbyes. He was there, and they headed out to Stacey. Others would be unlikely to come there, and they could talk without interruption. Jamie's family had not shown the same reserve as Mark's. There had been a sense, almost, of relief, as Jamie felt it. Steve's disappearance would normally have had bad effects on the family's status. It had not, and Jamie knew why. His own attitude was one of resignation.

"Steve must have had something they really wanted, unlike poor Stan," said Jamie. "They'd not waste a talent on reclamation. So, I can at least hope they want me for something important, not just labour."

Neither of them could work out the reason for Mark's Choosing. They might suspect John's hand in it, but it scarcely mattered. Baffled, they parted, being careful to say what in all probability would be a final goodbye other than in the formal departure. While it was never said that Royal Service would always separate friends, it was made clear that many would serve in distant parts of the King's Domain, possibly even in overseas exploration. Mark left to carry on down to the squats to tell Jack and Sue. There would have been a separate ceremony in a hall within the old city, and it took time for news to travel between the city and the mayor's bounds. Neither had been Chosen, though both, rather oddly, had had sisters called, to their dismay.

"So, that's you, and Jamie, and Peter, and Julie all called," said Jack. "That leaves just us two and the twins, and they are likely to be married before the autumn." He was thinking of all those that knew the river's weak spots. "And among us down here we get more Chosen than most, so it might be that there's none to explore further. Not that the bailiff would allow it; he's got proper cranky."

Mark thought that Jack was thinking of Relics. He could think of nothing to say. Had there been several of them, Jack and Sue could rummage in areas they had found where no alarms were triggered. Others would be keeping watch. On their own, it would be hard. And if caught? What had happened to Stan was a warning, and the squatters had already started to wonder about the few from way back that had simply disappeared. Almost certainly, they would not have been Chosen.

Friends and families had been told little, as part of the deal. Even the bailiff, they thought, knew only enough to warn them off. Even evidence of past adventures could be dangerous. Tadgies were always around, and there were those willing to sell them information, or score a point in a feud. Trouble could find you unchosen and shipped out immediately. Shipped to unpleasant and possibly dangerous work elsewhere. The Barriers featured in the list of potential destinations. It would be goodbye forever, that was sure. Jack and Sue could be trusted to keep their mouths shut, but if one of them were taken, Tadgies had a powerful lever when interrogating others. Would the twins be called in? Would messages be sent to the Domain to call in those who were Chosen?

These thoughts went largely unsaid. Jack and Sue were ahead of him here; life in the city taught lessons that those uphill and notionally respectable did not need. Mark would be gone anyway, as would Jamie, and the girls would have no influence, and might have been transferred for marriage. It was up to them: use what they knew or give up. Mark said his goodbyes and returned uphill towards home.

Home was tense. Muss' enthusiasm was trying everybody else's patience. There was an element of triumph in her babbling. Mr Norman and his mother were remarkably taciturn. Muss had been around other families with Chosen, who had shown more positive spirit, and she recalled her parent's delight when her older brother had been chosen and Credits had been awarded. Mark himself tried hard to respond positively. Yes, it was a great honour. No, he had no idea what he would be called to. Would it be military? He felt like shrugging. No one knew in advance. He had no high scores on anything technical other than farming. Might he go overseas? Might he even see the King? Eventually, Mark pleaded tiredness, and went upstairs to his room.

His dealings with Muss were a sham, and those with the rest of the family scarcely less so. From the moment his name was read out, there had been no real choice in his mind; he must run. But he must run without exposing others, Jones and Pickless in particular. The consequences for his family, he could not avoid. Muss, of course, would be spared, though her next marriage might take her down a peg. For the rest, at best, they would be demoted and transferred, at worst, across the bridge unchosen. Only his conviction that his parents and Lisa would accept that sustained him. Should he tell his father? If so, when? Or maybe Lisa? He could see she shared his father's fury. No; better that their innocence was genuine, not feigned. Ask them, he had enough sense to reject; the burden was on him alone. He slept little that night.

The following morning, he made his way to the Rivelin Farms. Julie was out, saying her goodbyes and receiving congratulations, but the twins were at home, working in the dairy. They had not heard that Jack and Sue had escaped selection, and Mark relayed his conversation with them. With marriage upon them before the year's end, they would be in no position to continue their visits to the river. But if any trouble arose from the capture of a squatter, they would be forearmed.

Back home that afternoon, he started to think about practicalities. The items that the Chosen could take with them were tightly prescribed, and certainly did not include food or bad weather clothing. The recruits would be kitted out in the reception centres. Equally, no weapon, no matches, not even water. He would need to pack all these things without attracting attention, and particularly attention from Muss. His parents and his sister worked regular hours, but Muss and the youngsters were at home part of the day, disappearing each afternoon to the creche where Muss helped out. She had a habit of inspecting all rooms for tidiness in the mornings too.

In his room, he assembled two piles on what had been Max's bed: the sparse collection that would fit into his school bag, as prescribed, and the rather larger pile that would go into his bigger backpack, the one used to carry stuff on drafts each summer. This he packed, then put it in a cupboard, behind Max's pack which was the same design. He wondered for a bit that it had not simply been passed on. The small pack, and the things to go in it, he left out on the bed.

The evening passed much as the previous one. Muss in high spirits, Miss saying nothing, and Father attempting to respond appropriately to Muss' gushing. Lisa had absented herself with friends until late. Mark gave an edited account of his visit to Rivelin. The last day was tomorrow.

"What will you do, Mark?" asked Muss, "anyone left to see before you go?"

"Yes. But I have a few coupons left. I'll buy a few things in Bradfield as presents for some friends, in the morning, then go around in the afternoon to give them away. I'll maybe still be out when you get back from creche, but not to worry, I'll be back before mealtime."

His father looked up at that. "That's good, son." He got up from his chair and went to the desk where he kept the spill-over from work and the various family documents. He rummaged in a drawer and returned, handing Mark a bunch of Credit tokens. The family earned more than the average, what with his father's work and their contribution to the Kingdom. "Get them something to remember you by, don't stint."

The following morning, Mark was all around the village. His purchases did not arouse any odd looks, though he was praised for his generosity. Mostly, it was stuff that made up the standard equipment for a stint, "For the young ones later, I know how expensive it can be," he explained. The odd items, like matches and some food: "Mother asked me to get these while I was about it." The expense was certainly greater than normal, but aroused nothing but admiration.

He carefully returned home after Muss had gone to the creche. Gifts for the family, he left on his bed. The rest was loaded into his backpack. Looking to see no one in sight, he set off, skirting around the south of the village. Soon, he was at one end of the burst dam. There were ruins there, and he carefully hid the pack, first taking out of it a cloth bag with a knife and water bottle in it. He calculated. He'd not been long gone. He could return via the creche in time to catch Muss and the kids.

And, indeed, they were wrapping up as he entered. He started towards home with them.

"What's in the bag, Mark?" said Muss.

He opened it to show her. "They're for a friend down in the city. I knew I would not have time to go there again. He's a good friend, and they don't have much credit. I was going to ask someone to take them down after I've gone,"

Muss sniffed. As the junior she had said nothing when Mark had talked of his friends in the city, since neither Mr Norman nor Miss seemed to think anything of it. She wanted nothing to do with squatters.

"I saw that you are all prepared for tomorrow," she said after a pause. Mark just nodded. As expected, she had looked in at his room.

They reached home. Muss started preparing the meal. Mark went to wash, then up to his room. He collected the presents for the family and went downstairs. He laid them out on the table: first stint kits for the kids were the big item. For his parents, notebooks with his inscription inside the cover. Paper was expensive, and notebooks were the traditional present for those that could afford it. For Lisa, a recipe book, again traditional for those who would be married soon. For Muss, he had racked his brains. Clothing was difficult. She was not one for reading or writing. In the end, he had chosen a clasp with the Royal Sigil enamelled on it. A shrewd choice; Muss flushed with pleasure.

Much appreciation. His father looked a bit thoughtful. The coupons he had given Mark would have covered all this, and to spare. Then Muss spoke up.

"And he has something for a city boy, too, that he could not deliver. Perhaps you could arrange for it to be delivered," she said to Father. Mark retrieved the bag from his room and handed it to his father, giving him the name, a name Muss did not catch.

Muss' two were put to bed. Later, the rest retired also. Mark sat on his bed. He could still abandon his flight, go to the Council Hall with the others, and across the bridge to the Kingdom. No one would miss his pack. His family would be saved the inevitable interrogations and penalties. But his experiences at Midhope were decisive. There was something of the prison here, worse for certain in the Kingdom. There was something that would nag at him for ever, this side of the river or the other. An hour passed, then two, then three. He peered into the landing. No lights under the doors. He put on his boots and an outdoor coat, opened his window and climbed out. Holding the window-sill he dropped to the soft ground below. Picking himself up, he opened the back gate to the fields and set off for the dam to retrieve his pack.

***

Mr Pickless had heard, made sure he had heard, of the Selection and Choosing. Miss had gone to town that day, openly to buy and deliver, and had learnt that Mark was among the chosen. She made sure that she did not speak to Mark's parents directly. She did see John's family, and congratulated them at length. John had looked downright smug. The news plunged the Pickless household into gloom, not only on Mark's behalf, but because the time would come, soon enough, when they would have to accept another apprentice, with all that meant for dealings with Jones. Gloom, and also much anxiety about what John might say when outside the Ground.

Pickless left a signal. Nothing happened that night, but the following evening there was a tap on the window. He left the house, and walked with Jones to the barn, the building where for so many years he had left packages and received messages.

"Mark's been chosen."

"Shit! How the hell? Coming here was more or less certain, wasn't it?"

"I've no idea. It makes no sense at all. Good reports for farming, good breeding stock, the Normans." Here, he pulled a wry face. "It stinks, Jones, it stinks. There's more to this than just their manpower requirements. And John's over the bridge too, he'll have no reason to keep quiet about you once he knows it's not the mayor makes the decisions. Earn a few more credits or whatever they use the other side, no doubt. Peter and Simon too. Only Tom was spared from my last stint, and he's young yet."

"So, I'll have to be ready to move, then. I'd come to that in my mind straight after Mark left me, so I've taken some steps. It's not my safety that bothers me, though, it's the material I have. There's far too much of it to move, bar a little that I've already parked. I've never shown you where I live, and you've never asked, and we both know why. Maybe they'll search hard, or not at all. I can only hope they don't find it."

Jones was silent for a moment. Pickless' face was in the shadows.

"I've to confess something, David. I had only a short time with the lad, but I could see the way he was thinking. There may be worse to come for you. I put in the boy's head that if he were Chosen, he might Evade. Not that he was to come anywhere near here if he did, but if he scarpers, then Kingsmen and Security are going to be all over this place. When it comes to it, there's no

79

knowing what the other lads will say. They'll be following every lead, unless the poor sod is caught. I'd not rely on Arkell either. That one will look to save his own skin."

Pickless did not reply immediately. The boy was not stupid. He would know the consequences for his family if he ran. He would guess what might happen up here. An expression he had picked up way back from his father sprang to mind: it's a cross we have to bear. It had puzzled him at the time. His father had explained the meaning, but not the origin, which he did not know. When he had used it in front of a teacher, though, he was hauled up and told not to use it again. But Mark's cross was certainly heavy. Over the bridge as expected, and the worst would be John talking. Mark's family would be fine, and at worst there would be a search up here, and it would be easy to concoct a story provided Jones was not found. Evade, though, and they would be much more thorough, and age would not protect them from unchosen service. He had put the idea from his mind. Indeed, he had not really faced the possibility of Mark being chosen, because having him as an apprentice was so good as to drown out all else. He tried to be practical.

"The departure's on Kingsday. I've not been to the ceremony for years, having nothing else to contribute. They can't hide it if he's missing, but they'll likely put out a story. I'd best be there with Miss and Muss. We'll all ride. If he's gone, I'll slip out straight away, and they'll say I was taken poorly. I'll be right back here and leave the signal. You keep an eye, and get well away. And stay away a week at least. If he's gone with the others, though, I'll leave the all clear."

He thought for a bit.

"Your stuff. You never told me much. If you can't move it, what happens if they find it? I imagine they'd send out a working party to remove it, though they might burn stuff that has no value."

"The metal and the machinery and stuff like that, don't matter much. Most of it never worked, and half of it, well, I don't even know what it's supposed to do. It's the documents, and some pictures that bother me. I'd wondered about sending them west, but there's few as could make sense of them, least of all the Outies that hang around the boundary. I tried talking to one once when I had him cornered; thick as hell. He could hardly speak properly. Now they avoid me with good reason. I'm still trying to put it in order in my head. I've taken a few things I do understand, and I can take a few more in the next few days. I'll take the risk, I think. I could burn the lot, but when I think of it, they'd not do the Kingdom much good. I reckon they must have the same and more in the Royal archives. They may miss the spot.

Here's an idea though. You come back from the ceremony early whether the lad's gone or not. Either way, drive a few cows into the outer field. I'll take them and stake them along towards the end of my route. The Outies will see them; they keep an eye on me. They'll be suspicious, but they'll not resist coming for them. They've a powerful pong, most of them, and it'll maybe mask my scent. And they are none too fussy when it comes to emptying their bowels either."

"Jones, I'll maybe not see you again, and anyway we'll be out of reach for a while. Provisions? I can load up a pony. It's an idea anyway, that if I've had some losses, you were long gone and I lost my protection."

Jones nodded. Pickless fetched the pony and put it to harness and saddlebags. Bags of dried peas and beans, salt, beef jerky and biscuit were loaded, together with matches, candles, tallow and two leather flagons of beer. Jones disappeared uphill with the pony as the light faded. Pickless returned to the house. One thing at least was good: his complete confidence in Miss and Muss. All your children across the bridge, isolation, and Jones, and there was complete honesty between them. Now they must be told.

The following morning, Jones got busy. He had long prepared for evacuation. Using only the back entrance opening on the hillside above, he moved as much as possible to his new hideaway. On his last visit, he laid his false markers. On the ground floor, he lit a small fire, kept going long enough to create a smoky atmosphere. Burnt out, he added more ash and charred timber. Bones, broken and charred, were scattered nearby. The logs were put in a disorderly pile at the end, the youngest hidden under the oldest. Bags of dried Outie shit were opened and tipped into corners. He removed the vice and spike from his small door, and left it unbolted. The camouflage cover was dismantled. Finally, its bolts removed at the base, and loosened at the top, he climbed the ladder and heaved it up through the trap door. He left it unbolted and removed the bell. Out through the back for what might be the last time, he caved in the sides of the entrance, and filled it with sods dug previously, still with dead heather and bilberry. It was dry. He set light to it and to the moor around. Previous burnt areas contained its spread, which took in the vent through which his cooking fire smoke had risen. This he also filled before the fire reached it.

Come Kingsday he was stationed with the pony in sight of the farm. Seeing the signal, he rode to the south-west for about a mile, over what had once been the lake behind the dam. He tethered the pony to a stunted birch and continued westwards. Then he backed north, waded along a small stream, and reached his hideaway.

6. On the Run

It was a cloudy night. It was as well Mark knew the layout of the fields to the south of home. It was not long before he was at the end of the dam, and after some tumbles and grazed knees, he found his pack. Now what? He could not go to Pickless or Jones. They would be first in line for the Proctors, perhaps even Kingsmen, when his absence was reported. The Proctors would have dogs, and his trail from home would be picked up unless it rained heavily. He had always known the answer, but had blacked it out of his mind. He would have to cross the boundary, and keep going until the pursuit itself would venture no further. Outie land. Westron land.

While it was still dark, he picked his way through the rubble-strewn valley down which a huge wave must have passed when the dam broke. The other side was farmed. It would be about a mile to the boundary, following an old track where the fields at least had gates. The clouds lifted. And in the moonlight, he could see a little distance ahead. Eventually, he saw ahead a bigger wall, and sure enough, the blackened posts that marked the boundary. He remembered Jones' map. This was once Bradfield Moor. A small valley faced him. He clambered over the wall, and made his way slowly upwards, using the stream to keep his bearings. It was slow going, and he stumbled often.

He reached a small waterfall. By then, a dim dawn was breaking. All around him was a monochrome desolation. There were the stumps of felled birch and the remains of fires where the brash had been burnt. Burnt patches of bare ground were interspersed with straggly heather and grey tussocks of mat grass. When he climbed northwards out of the small valley to get a view, he saw to his dismay the tall wall and posts of the boundary barely two hundred yards away on the other side. He would have to turn northwards, across what looked more like bog than moor. He trudged uphill. Soon, his boots were soaked through. He crossed another small stream, and up another gentle and very boggy slope. It was eerily silent. Once, he disturbed a grouse, that clattered off south. No burning here, just the wet moss and clumps of withered grass and sedges through which new growth was emerging. As it warmed up, he was tempted to strip off his coat, but now there were swarms of midges landing on every exposed surface. He had no clear idea of time, and clouds concealed the sun completely.

Then it started to rain. Not hard, but a misty drizzle that narrowed his view to twenty or thirty yards ahead. The midges at least disappeared. He ploughed on in what he hoped was a north-westerly direction. The slopes were very gentle; he could scarcely tell whether or not he was going uphill. He began to feel hungry. There was absolutely no shelter of any kind, nor, indeed, any stone to sit on. In a brief spell of better vision, he saw ahead of him an area with flowering cotton grass and moss. Already wet enough, he nevertheless turned away to the left, where the ground was more stable. The mist came down again. Stumbling in what he hoped was uphill and westerly, he was forced to turn away from boggy patches again and again. His pack weighed heavily on him. He fell several times, and was soon muddy and wet through. He lost all sense of direction.

Suddenly, he came upon a track that ran across his path. There were hoofprints and footprints going in both directions. An Outie track, for sure. The ground was a bit firmer here. He turned right and followed it a short distance. Very soon, he found cowpats and sheep droppings. There was more wind here, and in a brief moment of clearing he saw that there was a steep downward slope to his left, with rocks at the crest, no distance from his path. He made for the nearest rocks, stopped, removed his pack, and pulled out some bread and cheese. As he ate in this silent wilderness, the rain stopped. The clouds lifted. Below him, a view emerged. Below the steep slope on which he sat was another much flatter area, and a plunge below that again. He was wondering whether to descend or to continue along the path behind him, when he saw movement below him to the right. Cattle, or what looked at that distance to be cattle, were emerging from a valley onto the flat ground before him. Then behind them came three people, or at least something resembling people, and a dog. He dropped out of sight, and peered out from behind a rock. The cattle dispersed over the flat ground, and the people sat down together with the dog beside them.

He could not move without being seen, at least if they had been looking that way. The wind, slight though it was, was blowing into his face, and the dog lay quiet. He watched. Some of the cattle got closer. Most looked normal to him, but some were lame, and the proportions of others looked out of kilter in a way that eluded him. There were few calves. He turned his attention to the men. All were heavily clothed, and wore wide-brimmed hats. At such a distance, he could see no features. After a while, though, two got up, one to take something from his bag, the other to walk away a bit to piss, facing Mark. The contrast in height was huge. The one feeling in his bag was much smaller than the other, maybe only half the height. Soon, they were all seated again.

So, these were Outies, Mark thought. Despite Jones and Pickless, the stories of what happened to those found by Outies went through his head, and he hunkered down even more, wet though he was. Right now, they appeared to behave as ordinary folk. A few cattle wandered towards the foot of the slope below him. One of the men stood up, and bent to the dog, who raced off towards Mark, but only to get between him and the cattle, which were herded back towards the men. The clouds cleared. The sun warmed him a little, and he could see that it was now well into the afternoon. He expected them to go when it was dark, but that was a long time to wait. He had time, too much time, to start thinking about what he was to do. In the agony of decision, he had planned the escape *from,* but not escape *to,* other than the need to find Jones, but also not to betray him. He had seen no shelter, he had food only for a few days, and he had only the vaguest idea of where he was in relation to Midhope. He was a fool. Late spring it might be, but he could die here of exposure or starvation, or be found by the Outies, with who knew what consequences.

Only when the sun was low in the sky did the men stand up. The dog was sent out. One man blew a whistle from time to time, and the cattle were assembled and driven away the way they had come. The whole party disappeared down a valley to what Mark could now see was the north. He was alone. He looked around. To the north, the ridge continued, but beyond it was nothing but high moors. He picked up his pack, returned to the path, and headed southwards. After a slight rise, the track and the ridge dipped slightly. He went to the edge and looked down. Another valley led away to the south-west. There were hills beyond, but a deeper valley lay hidden. He had to find shelter, Outies or not. He climbed down the steep slope and towards the valley.

The sides steepened and the valley turned west. There was a track, and signs of animals again. It became wooded, and with the sinking sun it darkened rapidly. Mark moved slowly and nervously, ready to plunge into the woodland at any sound. He arrived at a small clearing. At the far end was a crude shelter; it had drystone walls and a turf roof. Mark moved behind a tree and watched. No sign of life. He moved a bit closer. It was open in front, where the ground was bare and trampled. A byre, post-war for certain. It was empty.

He entered. The earthen floor was dry and clean except towards the front. A small ring of stones surrounded a long dead fire. The ashes were even slightly damp. Against one wall were three shovels, traces of dung still adhering. Nearby was a wooden bench and a small table on which there were some pots. One had a spider's web across it. At the back, two crude racks, one with a few branches and logs, the other empty bar a few remnants of hay at the bottom. Mark was now exhausted. Outies or not, here at least was shelter. He dropped his pack and sat on the bench, elbows on the table. After a while, he slowly unpacked. He lit the field cooker and prepared a stew of sorts in his own pot. A drink from his own water bottle, then he spread his waterproof cloak on the ground near the racks, and collapsed into sleep.

He woke to a dry but overcast dawn. Aching and cold, he left the byre and looked up and down the track. Below the byre, the woods closed in again. No sounds. He returned to the byre, ate a little, and repacked his belongings. Going around the byre, he passed a midden. Well-rotted. Nobody had been here for some time. Going a little way into the woodland, he found a heap of boulders in which he hid the pack. Returning to the track, he moved slowly downhill, ready to jump for cover if he heard or saw anything. But nothing stirred; It was not long before the valley opened out and he had a view downhill and across to woods and moorland on the other side of a much larger valley. The bottom was clear of trees and a set of drystone walls enclosed fields in which there were cattle; cattle with a few calves.

A little further, and his track joined a larger and well-used track that ran along the side of the larger valley. The path was freshly churned. There were animal droppings. Moving quickly into the woods, he took in the view. To the south, at least half a mile away, the larger valley was partially blocked on both sides by high, sloping walls, while the centre held rubble. A familiar sight to all Grounders in the Division: yet another breached dam from the pre-war era.

He was still in concealment when a party advanced up the larger track from the south. Three ponies, loaded down with packs, each led by a man. Each man was dressed much as the ones he had seen yesterday, and like them, they differed greatly in size. One had a limp. Although he was much closer than he had been on the ridge, their faces were hidden by wide-brimmed hats. Compared to the ponies he had worked with at Midhope, these were scrawny. They looked old.

They passed on north out of his sight. Mark remained by the tree he had hidden behind. That track was not safe, except, perhaps, by night, and where, in any case, did it go? Northwards, perhaps, to wherever the men he had seen yesterday kept their cattle. Did Outies have villages? He had no idea. Outies were just marauders across the boundary. Here, though, there were clearly farms.

It was now warm and sunny. Mark found himself disinclined to move. What was he to do? Too early to attempt to find Jones, and only the vaguest idea of how to find him anyway. North and east, he supposed, but there were bogs in his way. To be sure, he would have to retrace his steps to the boundary and move northwards along it. Could he retrace his steps?

He was about to move off, when another person appeared on the track below, from the north. A solitary rider this time, and on a healthier-looking pony. Better-dressed too, and with what looked more like a helmet than a hat, less flashy than those of the Rangers. This time, Mark got a glimpse of his face. Browned skin, and a thick beard. But, to all appearances at the distance, completely normal, a face that would be unremarkable in Bradfield. Not remotely like the fierce, deformed faces of Outies shown in the illustrated history that Jamie had shown him. The man continued towards the south, and out of sight. Mark carefully returned to his own track and back towards the byre.

He retrieved his pack and went back inside. Not yet midday. Several days at least before it would be safe to find Jones. He made himself a meal and sat for a while on the bench. Bored, he went back outside. Jones had hunted, he knew, but Jones had crossbows, maybe traps too. All he had was a knife, well, two knives just in case. He wandered carefully in the woods around the byre. Oaks, birch, hawthorn he recognised. The larger trees were gnarled, but looked healthy enough. A foul smell drew him to a deer carcase, far too far gone to be edible, and covered in a buzzing swarm of large flies. Something small scuttled away as he approached, and two indignant crows cawed in the trees above his head.

Eventually, he returned to the byre. As evening drew on, it got noticeably colder, and the sky clouded over. Still damp, he started shivering. Much of his kit was damp too. Only the matches, wrapped in oilskin, were completely dry. He took the risk; collecting wood from the rack and a handful of dry hay from the other, he lit a fire. Soon, he warmed up, and bit by bit, everything was dried out. Wrapped up in many clothes, he retreated to a corner to sleep.

He woke to a thick mist, and drizzle. He had intended to hide his pack as before, and retrace the last part of his descent from the ridge the evening before last, perhaps getting some landmarks. Despite the potential risk, he remained inside, sat on the bench, peering out. He searched the whole building and found nothing of interest. He cooked some more stew. He rearranged the stones around the fire. Occasionally, he went briefly outside to look at the sky. No change. Never had a day passed so slowly. Once, a fox trotted past the building, stopping briefly to look at him and then moving on. Chilled and depressed, it had only started to darken when he lit another fire. It would be the last of the wood in the rack.

It burnt out. Wrapping himself up as best he could, he retired to the corner. Thoughts, painful thoughts, flooded his mind. Father, Mother, Sister, Muss and the young ones? In the hands of Kingsmen. Pickless and Jones? There was no direct connection, but the mayor was feeble, and if they got to John, a raid would be certain. Catch Jones, and he was done for; nowhere to go, no food, soon, and no shelter. Surrender or death. Surrender, and who knew what he might be forced to say. The thoughts went round in circles. And yet, the thought of crossing the bridge, Chosen, had been impossible then, and even more so now for different reasons. Eventually, he fell asleep.

A crash woke him suddenly. It was pitch dark. Something large made a grunt. There was a silence, then the sound of breathing nearby. Stretching for the candle and matches beside him, he struck a match. Two glowing eyes retreated a little and stopped. The candle lit, a huge shape turned and left, padding into the darkness outside. Mark staggered to his feet. He held the candle up. The table was tipped over, the pots, including his own, lying on the floor. He looked around. His pack was ripped, some of its contents scattered on the ground. The stew left for morning, a tin plate over the top, was all over the floor, the pot on its side. What kind of monster was that? Surely not an Outie?

He did his best to assemble what was left in the feeble candlelight, a task made harder by the shaking of his hands. A few loaves of dry and now dirty bread lay on the ground. The jerky and the cheese were gone. Clothes were intact. A few small oddments, including the spare knife were still in the pack. He righted the table, and placed his possessions on it. He sat on the bench, head in his hands. Most of his food, gone. The refuge, now unsafe. He thought enviously of the secure building in which Jones lived.

Gradually, it got lighter. The weather was the same. He went out. The track was visible for only about a hundred yards in each direction. No sounds. He went back inside. He put what was left of his water in his pot on his cooker, with an onion and a potato, sliced. He did his best to wipe off a loaf and started nibbling it. He inspected the pack. The top and one side were ripped, but it could be held together with a shirt tied round it. Seeing the route or not, he would have to retrace his steps. While the pot was boiling, he started to pack the remainder of his possessions. He was bent over his pack when he heard a noise outside. Grabbing a knife, he turned to face the open.

Six Outies stood in a line before him. Three huge ones carried long spears, and axes hung at their waists. Two much smaller ones held dogs on the leash. The one in the middle, more or less of human height, held a rifle. He was dressed as the solitary rider Mark had seen on the road. There were two feathers in what Mark could see was a leather helmet. They did not move. Neither the gun nor the spears were pointed at him. Mark stared at them, knife in hand.

"It's a long way from home you are, young Grounder," said the feathered one, not moving forward. The voice was slow and drawling. "What brings the likes of you to such a place, I'm wondering? Aren't you taught that us beyond the bounds are cannibals and worse? And, by the by, you can put that knife down, no harm will come to you."

Mark put the knife on the table. He was too overcome to speak, simply staring open-mouthed at the man. And with a jolt, he realised that he had thought man, not Outie. He looked at the others. They too were recognisably human, though with irregular features. One dog handler had one arm shorter than the other; one spearman appeared to have no nose and another no ears. They looked back at him impassively.

The feathered one, obviously in charge, spoke to his men.

"Ian, you stay with me. The rest of you, onto the trail. Down to the dam house with or without by sunset. Anyone had firearms practice?" A spearman nodded. The officer, as Mark was already thinking of him, handed over his rifle and dug in a pouch for some bullets. The group left.

"Sit down, boy. Now tell me, did you have an unwelcome visitor in the night?"

Mark nodded. He was able to recover his voice. "Yes, some huge animal. I think it would have eaten me if I had not struck a match. But how did you know?"

"Indeed, it's lucky you are not be breakfast. Did you not recognise the beast?"

"No, sir. I thought it a monster devised by the Deceiver." No sooner spoken than regretted. He was in the hands of the Deceiver's servant. He expected a blow, but none came. Instead, the man laughed out loud.

"For the love of God! What tales you get told by the Domain. You had a bear as your visitor, as natural a creature as yourself, but not one to meet face to face. That's why we're here at all, to track it down and kill it before it kills any of us or our wretched animals."

"A bear, sir? I've never heard of such a creature."

"I'm not surprised, now I come to think on it. I'm thinking you are from the northern extremity of the Grounds, but beyond you is sterile, yes?" Mark nodded. The man continued.

"This side we suspected that there were patches untouched in the far north after the Catastrophe and the war, but nobody left there. No people, that is, but certainly wild animals. It must be true, because as things have cleaned themselves up, the creatures have been moving south. God only knows what they have picked up on their journey, but the last thing we want is a breeding infestation. We've been on the trail of this one two days already. Then here, the dogs picked up a different scent, yours. Let those animals reach your precious breeding grounds, and you'll have the soldiery all over you."

There was a pause. Mark realised he had started talking to this man as a man, not as monster. He did not feel that he was about to become anyone's breakfast. The officer looked at him intently.

"So, bears apart, why are you here? And by the look of it," he glanced at the cooker and the rest of Mark's gear, "not on a whim or a panic. Wanted for something?"

"I was called for Service, and I was unwilling. I ran, and this was the only direction, sir."

The hunter's mind spun. An Evader, by God. Rare enough, and in our hands. In just the wrong place, though, if there's a chase. This must go higher. The occasional idiot that strayed had his uses, but this one? And one prepared to come our way? And no kidnap or breach of the treaties. No comeback.

"A big decision, for sure. Would it not affect your family or friends? Did anyone else know you were going," he paused, "to reject the duty you owed to his ever-loving majesty? What did you expect here, in the name of all that's holy?"

At this, Mark collapsed. Tears in his eyes, the consequences for others forced themselves once again to the front. Consequences that he would never hear about, but could vividly imagine. True or not, tales of the Barriers were frightening enough, and maybe there was worse overseas. The hunter waited. Eventually, Mark spoke.

"Yes, sir. Because we were being lied to. And I found out by meeting another Evader and what he told me and showed me. I came this way to try to reach him, but I dared not be too close for fear he'd be taken. There're others that doubt what the Domain is doing is for the best, and he opened my eyes. I lost my way and ended up here. Yes, sir, my family will suffer and to no good purpose unless I can find him. My father most of all, but he taught me to doubt."

Way above me, thought the hunter, *far beyond me*. He'd travelled here before, and further east, even into the Domain, a while back. He'd heard of an evader that seemingly got help from the Ground, and was left alone. Now he was only here to eliminate bears and anything else that might appear as things loosened up. He'd take the boy to the Derwent House and get orders. But there were other things to think about first.

"You have nothing to fear now, young man. I will take you back to the Derwent House just a short march away. You'll get to talk to someone better equipped to handle this than a hunter like myself. Oh, that's Mr O'Neill, by the way. And your name?"

"Mark, sir, Mark Norman."

"Well, Mark, it may be a while before that's arranged. No danger as such," the hunter paused, "but I need to ask you a few rather personal questions. Are you ready?"

Mystified, Mark nodded.

"How old are you?"

"Sixteen, sir."

"Ever been with a girl?"

Mark blushed. "No, sir, it is forbidden. Only when you are assigned a wife."

"And if you had? The temptation must be there on both sides."

"The girls are inspected, sir, or so they say. Any evidence, and they are likely sent across the bridge unchosen, unless they name the boy; then he is the one to be discharged. We would never condemn a girl to that. We have a code, sir, to be in groups when both boys and girls are together."

"Unchosen? Across the bridge?"

"Sorry, sir, I suppose there are different words elsewhere. Across the bridge is the Royal Domain. We never go there unless for ever, either as Chosen for Service, or unchosen. It is always a disgrace to leave unchosen, and it means work on the Barriers or worse. We never hear exactly, sir, but it seems life there is short and painful."

"Your parents, they have many children?"

"My mother and father have four, sir. His first Muss had two that miscarried. The last one killed her. My two brothers were both Chosen and my sister will be married soon. Father and his second Muss have two young ones already, and she is pregnant."

Will be married soon, Mark thought, *but now?* Certainly, she would be far from the Division, at best.

Polygamy, or at least bigamy, thought O'Neill. Quite mild compared to stories he heard about other Royal practices.

"Things are rather different here. Thanks to your royal master, it's few men that are fertile and free of defect. Grounder men are quite a prize. A prize to be grabbed sooner rather than later, as contamination often creeps in. Let me put it this way; you will be in demand as the news spreads, and I'll have moved on. You've been warned, if that's the right word."

Mark was speechless. The farms had taught him about putting out to stud, most particularly taking Pickless rams and bulls to neighbouring farms. He'd learnt to read the stud books too.

"Right, get what you want together, and we'll be off."

Thus, a few minutes later Mark was on his way. On his way into the hands of the Deceiver, the evil one. But for some purposes that he had never dreamed of.

Hue and Cry

7. Consequences

The household stirred. At first, nobody noticed the absence of Mark as they washed and dressed, in their best for this day. But the silence penetrated. Muss was about to go upstairs to knock on Mark's door, But Mr Norman beat her to it, telling her to wait. He knocked. No answer. He went in to the empty room. The bed was unused, the small pack was on Max's bed, the window swinging loose. He opened the cupboard. Max's empty pack was there, but not Mark's. He stood by the open cupboard, heart racing. Mark had run, and it was no last-minute panic. Consternation was followed by anger, which was followed by a kind of release. He had half expected this, though not so late. He looked round the room. There was no note to be seen.

"What's the matter?" Muss called up from below, "hasn't Mark got dressed yet?"

Mr Norman said nothing, but left the room, shutting the door behind him. He walked to the top of the stairs. Muss was in the hall, looking up at him. No one else was in sight. Muss saw the expression on his face. There had been a Selection suicide years ago, a tale still told in hushed voices when she had arrived. She was about to scream, but he pre-empted her.

"Everybody in the dining room, now," he shouted, coming slowly down stairs. "Now!" he repeated. Muss stifled her scream and turned towards the dining room. Lisa was already there, laying the table; Miss emerged from the kitchen, clutching a very frightened child in each hand. Father never shouted.

"Sit down, everyone," said Mr Norman. They sat, Lisa still clutching a handful of knives and forks. The small ones moved to Muss, holding her hands tightly.

"Listen to me, and keep quiet," Mr Norman said. "Mark has gone. He was not taken. It was not in panic. He is an evader."

The words caused all to stiffen, Muss let out a scream.

"He can't have! Why would he? Evade? What was in his head?"

The children started crying. Miss was expressionless, rigid. Lisa let go the cutlery, which clattered on the table.

"Rebecca," he said, turning to Miss, "You and I can talk in a bit. Take the children out, or we will get nowhere. Lisa, you and Muss stay here, and for the love of Majesty don't say a word until I've finished." Miss rose, and having detached the hysterical children from Muss, led them out of the room.

"Mark's bed was not slept in. His big backpack and working boots have gone. He left through the window. The Selection kit, including his best clothes, were on Max's bed. King only knows where he has gone, or when he left. He has evaded. Not kidnapped, not had a last look round, meaning to return. Evaded."

Muss was about to speak. He glared at her.

"None of us has ever seen an evasion. I'm not sure there's been one here in living memory, just the suicide at the George's all those years ago. Folk go missing, yes, especially in the city, but not just before they're due to cross the bridge. We get warned and instructed at school and at Service, and that's it. But in the mayor's office there are books of instructions and orders. I've had the chance to read them. Here's what happens. The moment it's known, the office notifies the bridge. The search starts immediately, not just Proctors and their dogs, but Kingsmen in their gear too. They'll will be all over this house, and you will be questioned. They'll be looking for any collusion."

At this point, Muss could not contain herself.

"Collusion? This is a patriotic family. We've contributed nobly. How could he do this to us?" she wailed, "how could he reject Service? He gave no sign. Was he mad? Did you have no idea?"

Mr Norman raised his hand. "Mary," he said, unusually using her name rather than status. "Save that for the Proctors and Security. No, I had no idea, and I am sure no one else in the house did either. It is important that you say that and nothing else. Any hint that you thought that others might be involved and did not report it, any blame other than for Mark, and things will get much worse."

He was half-lying to himself. Not that he had any evidence; Mark's disappearance was a genuine shock. And yet, not wholly a surprise, and the consequences for him and the others notwithstanding, there was a glimmer of pride and hope. But now he must prepare them for the ordeal to come.

"The Ceremony is at noon. You will stay here. Change into working clothes. No one is to go to Mark's room, and I am going to paste some paper over the handle. Miss will stay here too. When I have spoken to Miss, I am going to go up to the mayor's office to tell them that Mark is missing. They will have their hands full with preparations, so I do not know how long it will be before they come here. They will certainly detain me out of sight until the procession has departed and folk have dispersed. You will be questioned one at a time. There is no reason to say anything but the truth." Here, he turned to Lisa, "And just the facts. No suspicions or afterthoughts, nothing other than shock."

"I don't know what they will do. They might try to pass it off as a kidnap by Outies, but it'd not be believed this far in, so I doubt it. But if they do, it's important that you have not said anything to others about what I have told you. Stay here. It's unlikely any neighbour will visit on this day. They will make an official statement; you will stick to it. But more likely, they will say openly that he evaded. They'll want to make an example. Whether they catch him or not, it is certain that I will lose my job. If I am lucky, I'll be transferred elsewhere and downgraded, if not, I'll be unchosen but over the bridge. Lisa, play it straight, and you'll still be married, though certainly transferred. We are good stock," here, he grimaced, "and they'll not want to waste the potential these days."

Muss was now sobbing, but there was a look of anger in her eyes too. Life had been good. It was a good match for her. Two young sons, and with luck, the one she was carrying. There was so much to look forward to. And Mark, crazy, selfish or both, had ruined it.

"Mary, listen carefully. You are a good patriotic woman. We have two good kids. Mark was never your responsibility. The truth is that you had no idea this would happen. Just stick to that. Don't be tempted to elaborate or give them any afterthoughts. So long as they believe you, they'll find you another husband, as they would if you were widowed. Probably elsewhere, but you'll likely lose no status. Any doubts, and you'll be transferred, and the kids fostered. But whatever the outcome, this family is finished, and living in this house too. When I leave, that's the last you'll see of me."

"What about Mother?" Lisa asked, "will she be sent over the bridge with you?"

"That's for me and her to sort," said Mr Norman. "We'll be parted for sure, as will you. I will say whatever I can to avoid her going over the bridge. Now all of you, go and get changed. Muss, get the children. I'm going to talk to Miss then I'll be off. Eat some breakfast, if you've a mind. Regular meals may be hard to come by soon."

Muss made her way to the kitchen, and grabbed her children. Lisa left for the front door. She needed air. Miss came into the dining room, tears in her eyes, but silent and composed. Twenty-seven years together. She knew it would end now. With little spoken, as though walls had ears, they had shared a sorrow rather than the expected pride when first John and then Max had been Chosen. The threat to Lisa had been averted. With few words spoken between them, Rebecca had seen her husband directing Mark towards talents and experiences that would keep him in the Ground. Both had thought it settled.

They hugged. Both knew that whatever the outcome, they would be parted. Past childbearing, she might be allocated as housekeeper/stepmother to a widower with young children, surely elsewhere. He would certainly leave, either downgraded and far from her, or, even worse, be across the bridge. Neither would see Lisa again.

He managed to repeat what he had said to the others. Then he started to apologise, but she put her finger to his lips.

"No, David, no. We've had what we've had. We've said little, but Mark being Chosen was the last straw for us both. I felt it, and I know you did. And ever since the last stint, I could see that he had changed. We can only pray he's not caught, though where he will be if not, I fear to think. Now go. I'll see that the others think what to take with them when they are moved. It'll be little enough."

He did not change his clothes. He would be seen walking to the mayor's office, but that would arouse no comment. Families usually travelled together, but as a clerk, others might assume he had work to do before the ceremony. It was not long before he was at the office. Since most things were already prepared, there were few people around, and no sign of the mayor. He went to the door at the back and upstairs to Arkell's home. He knocked.

It was Arkell himself who opened the door, still in his shirtsleeves.

"David! What are you doing? It's three hours early. You weren't needed, you know that." Then he took in the look on Mr Norman's face. "Come in, come in."

He called down the hall, "I've a messenger. We'll be in my study. It'll not be long."

He hustled Mr Norman into the room. He knew only that it would be bad news. Sometimes, a mother broke down, and would be left behind, with the excuse of illness. And he had had to deal with that suicide, only months after his arrival. Surely not that?

"Well, what is it? What's happened?"

"Mark has run. He's an Evader."

"What? When? How do you know?"

"He was gone this morning. His pack's missing, and the window was swinging. The Selection kit and clothes were on the other bed."

The mayor was struck silent. A rather odd conversation with the King's Visitor sprung into his mind. When he had been presented with the list of the Chosen, he'd expressed surprise to see Mark's name among them; he'd been sure that Mark would stay on as a farmer. Not that he had any rights in the matter, but the Visitor had looked a little uncomfortable, and muttered something about confidential reports, and turned to the next on the list. Eventually, he managed to speak.

"And you had no idea? No signs? Surely you noticed something? If you'd mentioned anything, we would have had him in for counselling, even pushed forward his selection. It's been done before."

As he spoke, he looked directly at Mr Norman, looking and feeling angrier as he spoke. One of his own clerks. Another black mark. A bigger one, for this was no mere disappearance, though that was bad enough. He'd had warnings enough, almost reprimands, over Steve, Stan and David. The bailiff in the city had had worse to deal with, so he heard, with Security all over his patch.

"Of course not. Do you think I don't know the consequences for all of us, never mind Mark?"

His face was steely and unrevealing. He doubted the mayor believed him, but it was not going to matter much either way. The others were his to save from the worst if he could.

Like Mr Norman, the mayor had never had to deal with a real case of evasion. Learnt about it in training, yes, a long time ago, and the files for Procedure and Administration were on the shelves in his public office. He stared at his clerk. The ceremony must run smoothly. A known Evasion beforehand would provoke chaos.

"I take it you all know what's happened?" he asked, eventually.

"Yes. How could they not? I sealed the door of his room, and told them all to stay put and speak to no one."

The mayor's mind raced. Could this be concealed? There was no body. He toyed, as Mr Norman had said he would, with a story of Outie abduction, but dismissed it rapidly without a word: too far from the boundary, no tracks or scents, no surety that one or other of the family would say the wrong thing. This had to be by the book. And by the book when all would be occupied with the Ceremony.

"You will stay here with me. I'll call Andrew to fetch a Proctor and a sergeant. When they arrive, you will go with the Proctor to the back door, and to their Station. You will appear to be dealing with official business, not being escorted. Nod to anyone who recognises you. Any trouble, and it will be the worse for your family. You know what can happen."

Mr Norman nodded. The mayor left the room, closing the door behind him. There were muffled sounds of conversation, then footsteps in the corridor. The outer door closed, and the mayor returned. His anger was mounting, but there seemed nothing worth saying. They sat in silence for about ten minutes. There was a knock on the outer door, more footsteps, and another knock on the study door. Sergeant Baines entered with a Proctor Mr Norman did not know. Both were clad in their ceremonial rather than working clothes.

"This man's son," the mayor said, with a rather forced look of contempt at his captive, "has evaded Service. Proctor, you will take him to a cell. You will tell the Station that he is detained on the King's Writ; that it is Royal business. No one is to talk to him, and no questions are to be asked. Outside, you and he will behave as though just together. You will stay in the station with the prisoner until otherwise instructed. Any trouble, and you let me know. Dismissed." Mr Norman moved towards the Proctor, who saluted and turned to the door. They left.

"Of course, you know him, sergeant?"

"Yes, sir, Mr Norman from below the town, your senior clerk, sir. It'll be Mark that's gone missing, I assume. A great surprise, sir."

Arkell winced; yes, his own clerk, and one without whom life was going to get very difficult. Damn the man, and double damn the brat.

"Yes. Do you know the procedure, sergeant?"

"With a disappearance, we'd start a search, sir. But right now we are all lined up for the ceremony."

"Right, listen carefully. Whatever happens, the ceremony must not be disrupted. We can spare two Proctors and their dogs. As soon as you are out of here, you will send them to the house. They are to be told that there is suspected contamination associated with the disappearance. They are to make sure the family stay indoors. There must be no physical contact unless someone tries to leave, and then only with dogs if possible. One should see if the dogs can pick up a scent, but stop them leaving the property. Tell them that Kingsmen and a doctor will be on their way. They are not to ask questions, nor to answer any from the family. No one, including themselves, is to go into the boy's room. There must be clothes of the boy elsewhere for the dogs."

"Very good, sir. The family will be missing at the ceremony, though, as well as the boy. There'll be questions asked."

"Just so, well done, sergeant. The story of suspected contamination will be relayed to all the Proctors, and they are to say that I will announce that at the beginning. In the meantime, I will be ringing across the bridge and getting more Kingsmen and a doctor for show. Once the procession has left, the Proctors will be free. I want them all here by half one, bar those at the house, and the one with the prisoner. Understood?"

"Yes, sir." The sergeant rose, saluted and left. The mayor followed him to the hall, and then to the public office upstairs, where the telephone resided. It was not a happy call. Once the nature of the call was clear, he was transferred to a major, whose tone was decidedly unpleasant. However, the mayor's plan was sound, and he got credit for it. Across the bridge, the Kingsmen for the procession were already assembling around three large mobiles that would carry them to the hall. The major would come immediately with a team in smaller mobiles including Security and a doctor. He would carry the labelled testing kit. The mayor was to wait in his public office.

Arkell returned home, finished dressing and returned to his office. Half an hour later, there was the sound of motors outside, then silence. Four men in heavy gear marched through the hall, leaving others outside. They went up to the mayor's office. One turned and left, closing the door behind him. Two of the others removed their outer gear. The mayor noticed the rank insignia of one; indeed, it was the major he had spoken to.

"Sit," said that officer, remaining standing on the other side of the room. "I am Major Cornwallis. This is Security Commandant Hope." He did not introduce the third. "First, tell me how to reach the Norman house."

The mayor gave directions. The unknown man saluted the Major, and left the room. Soon, a mobile could be heard starting up and moving off.

"Now, Mr Mayor," the major said, with an emphasis on the Mr, "we have another sorry tale, don't we? And this one's the worst. One of your own staff, and a real Evader at that. And the Visitor had told you there were problems, but we've seen no action."

Arkell started to speak.

"No, no, just shut up and listen. You've done the right thing just now, and I'm sure the ceremony will pass off all right. The important thing is to catch the stupid little sod. Once we've done that, it's over to the commandant here to find out what's behind it. Then the Visitor will no doubt be talking to you about admin efficiency in this Division. We'll see to the father soon. Meantime, any idea of anyone else might have influenced the boy? A list of his classmates will be in the commandant's hands by a quarter past one. No problem, right?"

The mayor nodded.

"More urgently, do you know of his close associates? We know there was a group messing us up on the river, and that he knew David Reynolds."

"Oh, you found David then?" said the mayor. It had remained an unexplained loss. He had been told of Steve's Choosing, but also ordered to silence.

"Not your business," said the commandant, speaking for the first time. "We have more than one source of information. If it is appropriate, we'll let you know about him. Probably never. Your Proctors aren't up to much."

They don't know, thought Arkell. The riverbank? It had involved others, and it did not sound as though David had headed towards the Outie boundary.

"The only one I know is Steve Mallory's brother, Jamie. Jamie's Chosen too, and I have no reason to think he won't be here with his family any time now. Mark's father would know more."

"Right. Are you finished in here? Got your lists and all the regalia?" The mayor nodded.

"Off you go then, and do your duty when the time comes. Mind that list, and if something else occurs to you, you will be sure to tell us, won't you?"

Arkell took his robes and hat from the rack, grabbed his notes and departed.

"Right, Mac," the major said, "looks clear to me. I'll toddle down to the house and see what's going on. That bunch of women won't need your gentle touch. But I may be some time if there's a trail. He'll have been gone several hours. First, use the phone and get the Rangers alerted. They're to look in depth our side of the river, and work northwards towards the Barriers. Then get down to the Proctors' Station and see the father. He may be tough, but working here he'll have more notion than most of what happens to those who cross the bridge unchosen. You can dismiss the Proctor, but keep him in the station till the ceremony's over. You'll have time enough with Norman before the shenanigans are over, and the rest come back. Be back by half one. The Proctors will have assembled here. You will tell them this is not contamination but an evasion. The mayor will give you list of his classmates. Any that are Chosen, notify Reception and get them to detain them at the bridge. Don't let them move on to Conisbrough unless we say. The remainder can wait; they're not going anywhere. Get the Proctors searching within the bounds. Especially up river. I may be a while: it depends where the trail leads."

He got up to leave. A thought struck him. There was a fuss over the boy's performance at school. Raised by a classmate.

"Mac, you read the Domain files. Who was the child that prompted an enquiry into the Norman boy's schoolwork?"

"John Gregory. A good patriot. Chosen now, I think?"

The Major nodded.

"Right. I think there was more later. Tell Reception to keep him and Jamie Mallory apart from the rest and each other. Let them be told it is potential contamination."

He left, and walked up to the remaining mobile crews hanging about outside. Taking one and its crew, he made his way to the Norman house. A Kingsman was standing in the yard, while the doctor, services not needed, sat in the mobile.

"Where are the others?"

"The lieutenant and Kingsman Francis are inside, sir, keeping an eye on the family. Their Muss is hysterical and the kids are in tears. Lance-Kingsman Troth is round the side under the lad's window with the Proctor and his dogs. There's a scent all right and it goes to the wall along the south, sir." The major and his men went round the side. They all went to the wall where the trail left the property.

"Right. We will follow the Proctor and his dogs. It's unlikely, but if we see the boy this side of the boundary, we catch him. The dogs will outrun him. On no account is anyone to harm him."

They set off. The dogs could follow the trail, but it was erratic and slow. Always, though, the trail led to a gate or a low place on a wall. Once, they found freshly fallen stones. The boy had been moving at night. Soon, they were at the dam. Stones had been moved. The trail got faint, and the dogs were let loose to roam. They soon picked it up across the valley. Twenty minutes along an old track, and they were at the boundary. The boy had crossed into the Outland.

The Proctor climbed on the wall and peered about. Nothing. He turned to the major.

"It's Outie land, sir. I've no protection."

"Not to worry. It's clean. We know so," said the major. Just as he knew the soldiers' gear was more for show, and a damned nuisance. Just to impress the natives. The Proctor remained worried.

"You'll get a check from the hygienist when we return. You'll be clean as a whistle. Service does not go unrewarded, either."

Hesitantly, the Proctor sat astride the wall, had both dogs passed over, then jumped himself. The rest followed. The trail started up the little valley Mark had climbed only ten hours previously. The major was worried. There was no view from the bottom.

"Listen up. The Proctor and the dogs will follow the trail. Sergeant, you and marksman Phelps will follow the Proctor. Keep fifty yards behind him. The rest of us will be in line along the hillside to the north, always in line of sight to the next man, and so to you."

He turned to the Proctor.

"Any sight of Outies, without the boy, turn and start walking back. The rest of us will do the same. If they try to rush you, you run and over the wall. If they get too close, we'll open fire. But they will most likely keep their distance. The rest, standard retreat with cover. No shooting unless I say so. Understood? If you see the boy alone. Let the dogs catch him. Collect him as before. But if he is with a gang of Outies, and they try to run with him, then he must be taken out. Ignore the Outies. Phelps?"

"Sir."

"Phelps, have you ever killed a person? I don't mean Outies."

"No, sir, only Outies in Sherwood."

"If you see the boy in the hands of Outies, and they are in range, you are to shoot the boy, not the Outies. If they've not seen you, try to close the range. Get him down. If the Outies run, then wait, give us a signal and go to the boy. If he's alive, try to keep him that way. We'll be with you, fast. But if you miss, or they move towards you, then run like hell back towards the boundary. We'll cover you. But they'll likely run."

The marksman was not the only one to look stunned. Outies, no problem. They had all seen combat, usually while herding Outies for the Great Hunt. But a person? Even criminals were only unchosen and sent into danger. People were precious. Especially, Groundlings were precious. Another thought, though, went through many of their minds. Who knew what the Outies might do to a captive?

"That's an order. Believe me, it's an act of mercy. Proctor, keep your eyes peeled for a signal on your right. Turn back if you get it. We'll have a view to your left as well. Go."

The Proctor set off. He had only crossed the boundary before where it was unmarked, and in ignorance. It was forbidden without special orders, though none who had overstepped had come to harm. Only the suited Kingsmen had ever been any distance, and that very rarely; major raids were almost unheard of. The men waited a bit, then formed a line up the hillside. They had something of a view. No sign of life. Then the Proctor stopped and pointed uphill to the north-west. He started climbing. They turned to stay in line. At a scarcely perceptible ridge, the Proctor stopped. He did not turn, but signalled for them to join him. There before them was a wet desolation reaching to the distance. It started to rain.

"The trail seems to go straight on, sir," the Proctor said. "None of us has ever been as far as this beyond the bounds, but we know its treacherous ground. We heard that a King's patrol nearly lost one a bit north of here. Pulled out of a bog up to his waist."

The Major looked ahead. Nothing moved. The boy was drowned, captured, or at least two miles away. Then a distant movement caught his eye.

"Drop!" he commanded. He brought out his antique pocket telescope, a Relic reward for gallantry. More than a mile away were two people. They walked side by side. One had an odd, slightly limping gait. Their path seemed to be at right angles to their own. If they waited, the pair would get no nearer. They showed no sign of having seen the party. He edged his men back down behind the ridge.

"Two Outies, for sure," he said, "not the boy. I don't think they've seen us, but that's it. He's so far west, most likely, that it's a lost cause. Back home."

They returned to the house, rather faster than they had set out.

"Sergeant. One man to drive the Proctor back to Bradfield. He's to be left with a hygienist for a check-up. He can go if he gets the all-clear."

He turned to the Proctor. "No worries, man. I'd be obliged if you keep this little excursion to yourself. Understood? Very well, off you go."

He entered the house. The family were all in the dining room with one guard. Ignoring them for now, he went upstairs. There was the paper stuck across the door. It appeared untouched. The room was as Mr Norman had told Arkell. There was a small set of drawers by the bed without the kit. Must be Mark's. He tipped the contents onto the bed. Nothing of note. He put two school exercise books aside. Cupboard and wardrobe, the same. No outdoor clothes, no boots. He removed a shoe that looked well-worn. The shelf held a few books. He ruffled the pages. Nothing fell out. A quick riff found no writing or underlining. Just schoolbooks and the normal war stories from the Royal Press. He picked up the exercise books and left the room.

Then the interrogations, one by one. Miss, then Lisa. No, they had no idea. No signs? No. Had Mr Norman said anything? No. Had Mark altered his behaviour? No. Had he been associating with anybody new? Not that they knew of. He'd gone around saying the traditional goodbyes, and left traditional presents the previous evening. On the face of it, he felt, he had been given honest answers. And yet, there was something missing. The shock and expressions of shame, had a forced feel to them. There was no time to apply pressure, pressure that in any case was the commandant's speciality, not his. He summoned Muss; maybe there was more to learn from her.

But no. Her distress and anger were unconstrained, but she also had noticed nothing unusual. What will happen to us was the repeated refrain. What will happen to us? He had almost given up, when she spoke again.

"Oh, there is one thing, sir. Something I did not approve of. He seemed to have friends in the squats. Not that they were ever here, of course, and I did not catch the names. I think we were talking about Relics. But it was months ago. He had a present for one of them that he had not delivered, and he asked his father to do it for him. A knife and a water bottle, sir, he showed me when he met me at the creche yesterday."

"Name?"

"He did not tell me, and I did not catch what he said to his father when he brought it down last night, sir."

"Did Mr Norman take anything with him when he left?"

"I don't know, sir. He sent us away while he talked to Miss, and then he left."

Muss was dismissed and a search found the bag. No note or label. A knife and water bottle as Muss had said. Almost certainly for a boy. *Useful, possibly*, thought the major, *but a pain in the backside*. The commandant would have to get a name out of Norman first. But they were a devious lot, the city folk, and clannish with it. Bribes rather than threats might work. It seemed unlikely that he had doubled back to the city to hide, as he'd have to pass through the Ground in broad daylight.

Then a doubt gripped him. If Mark had planned his evasion, he would surely realise that there was no way Mr Norman would be able to deliver the bag. A mistake? A ruse to confuse? Whatever, it did not alter the picture. He called for the lieutenant.

"We cannot move this lot until tomorrow at the earliest. You're to stay here with two men and see they stay inside. I'll see you are relieved at midnight. Any callers, and the place is sealed for suspected contamination. Got it?"

"Sir."

The major sent those that could not squeeze into the mobile back to Bradfield on foot. He drove ahead with the rest, having added the school notebooks and shoe to the bag.

***

Calls completed, Commandant Hope walked down to the Proctor station with one of his men. Sending the Proctor to the outer office, he unlocked the cell, ordered Norman out and made him sit facing the guardroom desk. The Security man stood behind him.

"Now tell me where the little traitor's gone, *Mr* Norman."

"I don't kno—" began Norman. Before he had a chance to speak further, the commandant nodded. Norman received a heavy blow to his head that knocked him off his chair.

"Pick him up, Bates."

"Let's start again, shall we, *Mr* Norman. You'll have read the manuals. You are no fool by all the records. Never mind that there is plenty more where that came from, you have a family. You know what we can do to them. There's those that want to keep good stock in the pool. I have a different belief in what constitutes good stock, and a family with an Evader isn't among them. Co-operate to my satisfaction, and maybe they will not get what I would give them."

Mr Norman's head was still ringing. There was blood on his cheek where Bates' gauntlet had hit him. He tried to collect his thoughts.

"He did not tell me, sir," Norman started. The trooper raised his arm. "But I can make a guess, sir,"

The commandant signalled; the trooper lowered his arm.

"Do go on."

"Well, sir, he said things about crossing the river. I think you know that kids had been messing about. He stopped that though, a while back after the mayor warned them all."

He was taking a chance, he knew. He reckoned Mark would not head anywhere near the Royal Domain. And he had not been there for a while, as far as he knew. The kids would know nothing.

The commandant pondered. He knew about the breaches and the missing Reynolds boy. That was planned too. The chosen one, the Mallory boy, had done the same. So, alerting the Rangers was the first step. The major was right.

"Of course, you had no idea, eh. Shocked to the core like the good citizen you are, naturally."

The trooper moved closer and raised his arm again.

"That he would run, no."

He was hit again, though not so hard, and remained in his chair.

"Try harder, *Mr* Norman. Your son planned this. You seriously expect me to believe you saw no signs, no preparations?"

"Last night, he had the usual presents for all of us. He'd been round the shops getting presents for others, too, and delivering them. The kit for today was laid out on the other bed, and it had been there earlier; Muss saw it."

The commandant made a note. Stories would need to be checked, but Norman would know that. Probably telling the truth. He backtracked.

"That he would run? No, you say. What was his attitude, though, and yours, come to that? Third to be Chosen from the family, it would have been, quite an honour, no?" He looked down at the file.

"There seems to be a bit of confusion about his abilities two years back. A sudden set of failings in mathematics, then a partial improvement. A few later doubts about the boy too. If I had a suspicious mind, *Mr* Norman, I might wonder if he was already hoping to avoid being Chosen, and rather overdid it. I wonder who might be advising him here. Well, actually I'm not wondering at all, it's plain enough. You wanted him here, didn't you, and took steps to increase the chances?"

"He went through a bad patch, yes. It was in his reports, and I told him to try harder. Things got a bit better."

"Got a bit better? Just enough? And how would he know? You are a lying bastard. Enough."

The commandant's voice rose as he spoke, his cheeks flushing. He signalled to the guard, who knocked Norman off his chair. The Commandant rose and stood over Norman and kicked him in the face. Norman tried to protect his face, but another kick fractured his arm.

"And when he was chosen, you helped him plan an evasion." Kick to the stomach. Norman, mouth full of blood, could not speak. Kick, again and again.

"You're a stinking, lying traitor." Kick. "I'll be back." Kick. "You can think about consequences. I don't mean for you, and you know it." A final kick, delivered with force.

"Drag this piece of shit back to the cell and lock him in," he said to the guard, "and lock yourself in here. You open up only for me or Major Cornwallis, understood?"

The commandant made his way back to the mayor's office. After a few calls across the river, he summoned a couple of Security men.

"You are to visit every damned shop or store in this stinking village. You are to ask if Mark Norman visited them in the last couple of days. Explain that we are tracing contacts of a possible infection. Ask what he bought. They'll probably be shut till after the ceremony, but hammer on the door and shout King's business. Any you can't reach, report to me after the ceremony."

He found some of the mayor's paper, and started drafting a report. The major was not back. Half an hour before the ceremony was due to start, a Kingsman knocked.

"Major Cornwallis left instructions that if he had not returned to the house by eleven, sir, I was to tell you the he was on a trail."

"Do you know where they were headed?"

"Only that they started off south, sir. It's all fields that I could see."

The commandant sent the man back to the house. He pocketed his report and headed for the Council Hall.

8. To the Bridge

As noon approached, the Chosen assembled in a side room to the left of the stage in the Council Hall. Only forty-one of them this time. A Proctor and a Kingsman were with them. With about five minutes to go, another Proctor closed the outer door and stood outside. As most were the same age as Mark, and some in the same class, his absence was noticed, and there was a rising sound of questionings. The Proctor banged a table.

"Listen to me. You can see that Mark Norman is absent. There is a suspected infection or contamination at the Norman house, and the whole family is quarantined. A doctor is at the house. We think it is a false alarm, but we take no chances. The ceremony will proceed as normal, and the mayor will explain things to your families before it opens."

The muttered questioning subsided. Infections or contaminations were rare, but much feared, as even a doctor, never mind the hygienists, could often do little, and whole households would be isolated until death or recovery had brought things to a conclusion. The main hall was filling up. On the stage, but at the rear, sat twelve Kingsmen, their gear covered by ceremonial cloaks. Behind them on the wall hung the Royal Ensign, the sign that the Visitor was present. A row of six chairs was laid out in front of them; the outer pair on either side had tables in front of them, the middle pair, more ornate than the others, had in front of them a lectern and a small table on which a large, leather-bound book, the *King's Mandate*, was placed. Proctors stood at each corner of the room, and at the main entrance and the side doors by the stage.

Families of the Chosen occupied the frontmost rows of chairs facing the stage. Others crowded in behind. As with the Chosen themselves, the absence of the Normans was noted. There was a whispering and shaking of heads. But the clock struck the hour, and the Kingsmen rose, standing to attention. The hall fell silent. Escorted by a Kingsman, the Chosen made their way from the left to the block of seats reserved for them. The Visitor's procession then entered from the right: the two mayor's deputies, The Visitor and the mayor, and finally two King's Officers. Bowing to the audience, they took their seats.

The routine was familiar. The Visitor would rise and make a patriotic speech. The mayor would rise and stand beside him when he had finished, and call each name in turn. Each would hand a certificate or a school discharge to the deputies, sign the letter of release, advance to the centre and recite the oath of loyalty, hand on the book. The Visitor would shake their hand. Each would then sign the pledge for one officer, and receive the King's shilling from the other, then move to a block of empty seats to the right. It was therefore a surprise when not the Visitor, but the mayor who stepped up to the lectern.

"I have something to say before we commence. Most of you will know that one of my clerk's sons, Mark Norman, was among the Chosen. Early this morning, his father told me that he had been taken ill in the night. His father has been isolated here, and the rest confined to their house. A doctor is with the family. Mark is therefore not here today. After the ceremony, anyone who has been in contact with Mark in the last two days and feels unwell should stay at home after this ceremony and a report be made to the hygienists. No one is to approach the Norman's house."

He paused. There were murmurs around the hall, and a shifting in seats. At the back, near the exit, Mr Pickless nodded to his wives and left unnoticed.

"The doctor has told us that this is probably a false alarm, or a case of non-infectious contamination. On advice," he turned to the Visitor, "we will continue in the normal way with this sacred ceremony, rather than delay." He turned again and bowed.

"Your Excellency,"

The Visitor rose. The ceremony started. To many who had children Chosen in previous years, his words had a familiar ring. The Chosen came forward in order of declining age, most fifteen or sixteen. At the end, however, came the Prodigies, the eleven or twelve-year olds whose talents had been spotted early. Sometimes as young as eight or nine. There were but three of them this year. Here, tears were allowed, both in the Chosen and their parents. When the last had been called and seated, the Kingsmen descended from the stage and lined the central gangway. The mayor and his deputies led the procession outside, the Chosen next, and the Visitor and officers last. The rest followed after them.

Outside, the mobiles and their drivers were waiting. Proctors kept the space around them clear. The Chosen lined up. As the Mayor called each name, the family entered the space for a final farewell, a brief hug only. Each Chosen then got into a mobile. When the last had boarded, the convoy set off slowly towards the city and the bridge, flanked by Kingsmen on either side and behind. No one followed. Proctors kept the space clear until the Visitor and his attendants entered a smaller vehicle and drove off. There was a similar ceremony to attend to in the city before dusk. The crowd dispersed.

It was already past half past one. When the square had cleared, the Proctors returned to the hall. Sitting in the chairs used for the ceremony were the mayor, the Proctor captain, the commandant and three of his men in their unfamiliar black uniforms. The commandant stood up, and the room fell silent.

"I have something to say to you. You will be aware that one of the Chosen, Mark Norman, and his family were not at the ceremony today. You will have been told that this was due to a suspected infection. This was false, and deliberately so, to avoid disrupting the ceremony. We have conclusive evidence that Mark Norman evaded Service. He has absconded."

There was a communal gasp; an Evasion, a thing that none of them had experienced.

"It is your duty to apprehend the absconder. When I and my men leave, Captain Phelps will give you detailed orders. These will involve a thorough search of the Ground. You are now to make it clear to all that we are dealing with an Evasion, and not an infection. There are severe penalties for concealing such a traitor."

The commandant, his men and the mayor left, retiring to the mayor's public office. Two Security men were waiting outside the door. The commandant marched straight to the mayor's chair, leaving the mayor to stand or sit elsewhere as he chose. The two by the door were summoned in, while the three who had come with him from the hall left and waited outside the door.

"Well?"

"There's a couple of shops or stores where nobody answered, sir, but we've interrogated the others. We've put a list of purchases together, sir."

He handed the commandant a paper. He ran his eyes over the list; many identical items bought at different places. Mostly just what you would expect as goodbye presents, but also food, matches and clothing as repeat items. Even one purchase of a field cooker and pan. That needed a fair few credits. Where would the boy get those but from his father?

"Any comments made?"

"Most thought he was uncommon generous, sir. We did ask about the food, sir. He told each of them he was shopping for his mother, but we got repeat purchases in different places."

The boy was planning, and devious with it. They'd check what was in the house, of course, but the picture was crystal clear. What was not clear was where the hell he thought he would go. He sent the men off to find the missing vendors, though it would add little. He browsed through the boy's files again. But the mayoral files were not very revealing: school reports, stint reports, final year reports and the concluding entry, Chosen, with no further remark. There was that sudden failure in maths, dutifully recorded. The Selection Board files had only been reported to him before he set out. He had not seen them himself. It seemed that the boy had been thought to have priority talents, and that an informal report had suggested they were being concealed. *Bloody Board of Heredity*, he thought, *why did they not notify us and we would have had this idiot of a mayor bring him in for analysis.*

The 'idiot' mayor, meanwhile, had remained standing, not choosing to demean himself to sit facing his desk.

"Any idea why the boy was chosen, Mr Mayor? It looks like he was cut out to be a farmer, and you'd have been a bit sorry to lose him."

"No. It was a shock, and I asked the Visitor. Seems he had something, some ability wanted across the bridge, though it was not specified. Not my business to follow it up. And you are right. We would certainly have allocated him as a farm apprentice if he'd not been Chosen. In fact, the farmer where he served his last stint put in a bid, as he was very impressed."

"Name and farm?"

"Oh, Mr Pickless at Midhope. He's a cousin at Agden, where the boy had worked previously. Good reports from both."

The commandant made a note. These requests should be on the child's file.

"Tell me about this Mr Pickless. Anything out of the ordinary?"

Arkell was dismayed. He saw a gaping hole ahead. Jones, though not known by name, had been quietly ignored in the interests of meeting quotas, where the Pickless team had excelled. No one under his present command were aware, and he had subtly diverted attention away from the farm. If the commandant discovered, he'd be for the Barriers or worse.

"Very reliable. Seven sons between them, and six Chosen. Almost a record. The other died young. Very creditworthy and very productive, for all there's only the three of them now. We always send them four or five for each stint."

All chosen, and all boys, thought Hope. And no child left at home. Bloody Board again. He'd been given a briefing on selection policy, but not thought much of it at the time. Only experience had taught him that there were limits to patriotism, and that a sequence of Chosen offspring led often enough to a dull resentment. In the cities, it was not unknown for notionally accidental miscarriages to occur when two or more from a family were across the bridge. Not to mention disappearances. Could the boy have gone there? Stocking up food made it seem unlikely. But maybe the boy was thinking to hang around until things had quietened down. A thought struck him.

"Where will your Proctor captain be now?"

"He'll have gone to the Station to arrange the search parties."

"Find him. If any Proctors are going towards Midhope, they are to be called off. I want a Proctor who knows the way to be here now. He'll be taken out by one of my men on a mobile. That should be in time to call them off. Just orders, no explanation."

The mayor left. Hope called in one of the men outside and briefed him. Still no Cornwallis, and he needed the manpower and the authority to make a rapid descent on the farm. Perhaps they had found the boy already, and the need for all this searching would be ended, and the real job of rooting out of deviancy could begin properly; his job, not the major's.

He rang Reception across the bridge. Yes, the Chosen had arrived. Yes, the Gregory and Mallory boys had been isolated. There were four others in the boy's class that had been chosen. *Too many things happening at once*, he thought. Those boys might be useful; he had not finished, not nearly, with the father, and now there was that damned farmer. And the major might well turn the rest of the family over to him. The father, he could take across the bridge, the rest not, if he knew Cornwallis; Soft, those bloody soldiers. He made up his mind. The other classmates could be found if needed. They'd be at Conisbrough for a few days anyway. Release them with the others, he told Reception. Hang on to the two boys and carry on with the infection story.

Where the hell was Cornwallis? He sat in the mayor's chair for some time, drumming his fingers, and wondering if he should have another session with Norman, when there was a clatter outside, and the major entered. He was anything but smart, with mud on his uniform trousers and boots. He sat down, shaking his head.

"No luck. There was a trail all right, straight off to the west. We were too far in to risk following further. Either he's taking his chance with the Outies, or he'll be thinking to double back, though the Proctor told me that people drown in the bogs there."

They swapped all that they had learnt. What to do next? The boy had clearly planned carefully; was he simply alone? Why head for the Outies' land? What hope did he imagine he had of returning undetected? Eventually, they drew up a plan. Hope would take Norman across the bridge. His team would interrogate him and the two boys. The mayor would be told to get the Proctors patrolling the Outie boundary, and the Kingsmen would rush the Pickless farm at dawn with as many men as possible. That left the family. The commandant wanted them sent across the bridge; he could deal with them later. As expected, the major demurred.

"No, Mac, I don't think so. There's good breeding stock there. Standing orders. They'll have to leave, of course. The mother is too old for the kind of service you know will be wanted across the bridge." Here he pulled a face. "But there's housekeepers needed elsewhere. The sister will be married out of division and Muss and her children likewise, but elsewhere. They are to stay until I've finished at Pickless's, then I'll get redeployment orders and send them south."

"As you say, major." The commandant's face was stony. Too much concern for recruitment, not nearly enough for the rooting out of doubts before they spread more widely. The boy *might* have acted alone, but where did the thought come from? There was Evasion in thought as well as deed. Well, he would make it clear that he was obeying orders in his report. He rose and left to arrange to take Norman back across the bridge. The major went down to the hall to brief his men.

***

Pickless had left the ceremony unquestioned. Mounting his pony, he rode quickly back home and hung out the agreed message for Jones. He led a few cows up to the boundary, opened a gate to let them through then shut it behind him. He poked around the farm, checking for any signs of Jones' visits. A few hours later, Miss and Muss trotted into the yard. They had a tale to tell. After setting off back home, they had been overtaken by a posse of Proctors, and feared for the worst. Then a mobile had driven past them, frightening the ponies. Just before they reached Agden, the mobile returned past them, followed a while later by the Proctors, who saluted but did not speak. To find out more, they rode into their cousin's yard. There was a commotion. Did they know that Mark Norman had evaded? The search was on all over. And a Security man had driven up, and they had all departed back towards Bradfield. All of them? Yes, two were about to go up towards you, but they didn't. Perhaps they've found him? That certainly sounded likely.

Poor lad, thought Pickless. He can't have got far, and he's certainly not here. Nevertheless, he briefed his wives; the apparent losses due to Outies, including the pony, were to have been discovered when he returned. He would go down in the morning to report them. An anxious evening followed, with Pickless leaving the house repeatedly to scan the surrounds until the light faded. They went to bed in no happy mood.

Just before dawn, a fleet of mobiles departed from Bradfield. Stopping a mile from Pickless' farm, the men dismounted and spread out. Flares showing that all were in place, the Major advanced rapidly on the farm. The dogs barked, but he rushed to the front door; it was unlocked and he stormed in with three men. Others guarded each outhouse and doorway. The three Picklesses were dragged from their rooms still in nightclothes and hustled downstairs. The house and outbuildings were searched. The major himself rifled through Pickless' desk. Behind him sat the family, shocked into silence. Eventually, the major turned to them.

"You know why we are here." It was a statement rather than a question.

"No, sir, we don't." It was Miss who spoke. "Nor why you drag us from our beds. This is an esteemed family, not a bunch of criminals."

"Very well. One name, Mark Norman. Any trace of him, or the boy himself, and that remark will see you all out of here unchosen, esteemed or not."

"But he was missing from the ceremony, sir, and the mayor said—"

The major broke in, "—that the family had an infection, yes. You knew that was not true, didn't you? You knew that the boy had evaded."

"No, sir, we did not." Pickless himself this time. "We were sorry to hear of the isolation. He was a good worker here; I'd asked for him as an apprentice. But he was Chosen, and that was that. We went to the ceremony just to wave at him. Has he disappeared?"

Cornwallis did not answer. Had they seen the boy? Unlikely. There were more questions, certainly, but unless they found evidence, there was nothing to point to collusion. The boy had vanished westward far from Midhope. They'd last have met months ago. Telling them to go upstairs and get dressed and return, he went out. No sign in the house or buildings. After about half an hour, reports came in from the boundary. Again nothing. It would be a waiting game. He'd need Proctors and their dogs to go further. He ought to have thought of that. Orders went out; those on the boundary were to stay hidden. A mobile was sent to fetch Proctors and dogs. He returned to the house.

"We have work to do, sir, work that won't wait," said Pickless, when he returned to the room, "and I need to check the boundary. There must have been an Outie raid while we were at the ceremony. We're missing five cows and a pony. I would have reported it this morning after the rounds were done. Only discovered it when I returned yesterday. It's rare that there's no one here, some of them must have been watching yesterday."

"An Outie raid? I'd heard that you'd been luckier than most with them. Very well. You will do your normal tasks, but one of my men will be with each of you at all times. The Proctors will pick up scents soon enough when they get here."

The family went out to do their work. The major retired to the dining room, sat at the table, and pulled out the school exercise books he had retrieved from Mark's room. He looked up at the wall opposite before opening either. Six certificates of Service. Even in Divisions milked more thoroughly, this was outstanding. Necessarily childless himself, he nevertheless recalled the mixed feelings of his parents when he had been Chosen. And he had been the only one, with two older sisters married and one pregnant when he left, and Muss's youngsters. Well, not his to reason why. He turned to one of the books. Maths. He opened the other: the same. His own maths had not been strong, and some of the scribbled formulae and equations provoked recognition but not understanding. There were lots of crossings out and a succession of what might be answers, often several to the same question. Only one handwriting. No marks or comments. These had not been shown to any teacher. He recalled that the boy had been accused of masking his talent; it seemed that he was indeed working out how to appear less able than he was.

He was still ruminating over the books when there was a clatter outside. A Proctor sergeant knocked on the door. He had a team of six and three dogs. The major gave them the shoe. Together with three troopers, they started to search.

No trace around the farm, and they set off for the boundary. Over the wall they went, and up and down the boundary. No trace again. As they worked away from the edge, a Proctor called out. Cowpats. There were other smells here too, and a cattle trail heading north-west. The Proctors looked anxiously at the major. Few had been any further, and their orders were strict.

"Right. I can assure you that there is no danger of contamination in this sector. I want a volunteer with two dogs. There is Credit involved. Any sign of Outies, and we are armed and will be here to protect you."

The Proctors glanced at one another. Then one stepped forward. "Sir."

"Good man," said the Major. "The rest of you, back behind the boundary. Find my men and replace them, tell them to return to the farm." He fished out two tokens. "They'll recognise these as my authority. I'll see you are relieved before nightfall."

The five set off. Soon, they were at the wall around Jones' refuge. There were more cowpats, and a pile of excrement that had the dogs retreating and whining.

"Outie shit," said the Proctor. "We train them to tell us when there's traces, sir." He pulled the dogs away and set them to sniff around. The cattle trail went due west. There was a view, but no signs. Scarcely surprising; they'd have been gone at least ten hours, perhaps more. He peered over the rubble in the gateway into Jones' compound. No Outie traces there, and no sign of life. So far, the farmer's story held good. He gave the signal, and they returned the way they came, the troopers glancing anxiously to either side and behind as they went.

Back at the farm, the major briefed the sergeant and then walked down to the mobiles with their drivers. The watch had been set; now, he needed reinforcements to rotate it, and he needed to make arrangements for the rest of the Normans. He needed the telephone.

***

The commandant wanted to depart at once. Norman, however, had become unconscious. Afraid he might croak, Hope sent for a hygienist. Another that would need to be transferred out. Not just the arm, was the verdict, but a cracked skull, a broken jaw and many broken ribs. Possibly some internal injuries. No, he could not be moved, at least not today. In the hope that his prisoner would come round and talk, he reluctantly returned to the office and telephoned out. John and Jamie were to be given places to sleep.

Two of his men knocked on the door. The last shopkeepers had been found, but Mark's purchases merely confirmed what they already knew, food that would keep, water bottles etc. The boy was planning to survive out of sight for a long time, but towards the Outies? Across the river, he might have managed until his food ran out. Try thieving on his own side, and the Proctors would pick up the scent. Hiding in the city having cut back? Planning to cut south and back onto the Ground in the next Division? That prompted another telephone call. Tedious, because it meant dictating a message to be passed on. *Time was when we had better comms*, he thought, *and more resources too*. The Proctors there were probably as dim-witted as those he had seen here.

Late afternoon dragged into evening. He was about to return to the Station to see how his prisoner was doing, when the Proctor captain knocked and entered.

"No trace, sir. I've left patrols out, but with shifts there'll be patches unseen for several hours. Any hope of help from the King' forces, sir?"

"Not my business, Captain, you must find the major, and I don't know where he is. He'll be needing all the men he has tonight. The patrols *will* be maintained, Captain, reinforcements or not. Your men have some ground to make up with me and the Visitor, if you get my meaning."

The captain saluted and turned to leave.

"Oh, by the way, Captain, where is the mayor, do you know?"

"In his home, sir. He looked unwell, and there was not much for him to do."

"On your way out, go upstairs and tell him to stay there. Either the major or I will be using his office here till further notice. We'll send for him if he's needed."

He returned to the station. Yes, Norman was breathing more evenly. No, he can't be moved, wait a few more hours. He went in to look at his prisoner, now on a bed brought in by the hygienist. The man was on his back, head propped up, bandaged and with a drip. His arm had been splinted. As he looked, Norman briefly opened his eyes. There was a single look, one of open defiance. Then, a lapse into unconsciousness.

"Hygienist. You are to keep him under observation all the time. If he becomes conscious, you are to send the Proctor out there to tell me at the mayor's office. He may attempt suicide. It is to be prevented. I expect to find him alive when I return."

He left, frustrated, wondering what to do. Cornwallis would be uphill, disposing his forces for the dawn raid. He wandered through the town. There was a hard core of pre-war houses, variously patched up and extended. Then there were the more recent dwellings, cruder, but functional enough, he supposed. Nobody was about. The news of an evasion was now universal, and people had hunkered down with their families to wonder what would happen next. He did not like the place. In other postings, groundlings had been given both less respect and less pampering, as he saw it. Gently does it, he'd been told, the Commission has a high regard for this Division. A message reinforced by the Visitor when he had taken up his command, just after the Reynolds boy's disappearance. He had worked in places little better than baby farms, places where the abnormal outnumbered the healthy. Places in which abortion, both medically sanctioned and otherwise was commonplace, and a steady recruitment to the unchosen followed on. Here, they were smug, that was the word, smug; too damned conscious of their value. The squats were different. Them, he could understand, as they could understand him.

Darkness fell. After an hour, he returned to the station. No change, the hygienist said. No response to questions, no opening of the eyes. Hope took a chair from the guardroom and sat beside the bandaged body.

"I think you can hear me, you pile of dung," he said in a low voice. "I need some answers. You can go easy or hard, your family can go the same way, up to you. Nod if you understand."

No response. The temptation to shake the bastard nearly overwhelmed him. He turned to the hygienist.

"Is there any way you can bring this wretch to consciousness? Whether he dies or not as a result is immaterial. This is King's business, Mr Hygienist, King's business."

The hygienist made a pretence at deference. He had not told the truth. Norman had spoken, and asked him in a whisper to make sure he did not leave the cell alive. The hygienist had already come to the conclusion that his patient was not long for the world in any case. But dying before the commandant returned would condemn him to who knew what. Certainly not a hygienist any longer, and certainly not here, where life was much easier than in the Division in which he grew up. He was quick-witted.

"There is a drug, sir. We use it sometimes when there has been a heart attack. It might waken him, but it might kill him. We keep it in the clinic, locked up. We are only allowed to use it with explicit permission from above, and there is always an autopsy if the patient dies. It would be detected, and I would lose my job unless I could show I was told to do it. Give me a written order, sir, and I'll go and fetch it."

Hope impatiently pulled out a notebook, tore out a page, asked the name of the drug, and signed the order. The hygienist left. *Easy*, thought Hope, any problems with doctors can be dealt with. Ten minutes later, the hygienist returned with a vial. Filling a syringe in front of the commandant, he bared the uninjured arm.

"Ready, sir?" he asked. The commandant nodded. In went the syringe. Norman jerked. His eyes opened. Colour flushed his cheeks. He gasped and looked straight at the commandant, triumph in his eyes. One more gasp, and he went limp. He was dead.

"I did warn you, sir. There will be an autopsy, of course. All deaths have to be reported."

Something about the hygienist's tone nagged at the commandant, even as his mind clouded with anger. Had he been tricked? Was this yet more treason? Was the killing deliberate? He summoned up enough composure to reply.

"Of course. We must be sure that the right drug has been administered, mustn't we? So, we will leave the vial with my man outside. The cell will remain locked and the keys left with him. You will notify the doctors in the usual way, and follow their instructions."

If the hygienist had anything to fear, he did not show it.

"Cause of death, sir? I can account for the drug, but it's my opinion he'd not have lasted many hours with those injuries. They'll be noted, obviously."

"Injuries inflicted while resisting arrest by His Majesty's Security Corps. Questions to be directed to Commandant Hope."

The commandant was seething. Hours wasted to no good purpose. He returned to the Council Hall, and started up a mobile. Ages since he had driven one himself, but his patience was at end. He drove off towards the bridge. The lights were feeble, but until the outskirts of the squats, the road was clear and straight. Then through a mixture of ruins, squatter's homes and vegetable gardens, the cleared roads were twisty and branched. He hit a couple of dead ends and had to turn with difficulty. Occasionally, a curtain would be flicked aside as his engine's noise reverberated around the semi-derelict streets. In the next, there was a loud bang. The mobile swerved and hit a building. A lump of concrete in the road, breaking a wheel. Cursing, the commandant left the vehicle. He would have to walk to the bridge. Then it struck him that he had no idea of exactly where he was. To his disgust, he would have to ask for help. He walked along the street until he found a curtained window with a flicker of light behind it. He knocked on the door. It was not answered immediately but a curtain in a bay window was pulled aside, and someone peered out. The curtain fell back, and a moment later the door opened a fraction on a chain. An old and croaky voice spoke out.

"Who's that? Who's about at this hour?" Behind the silhouetted figure was a very dim electric light.

"Royal Security, open up." The commandant held his warrant card up to where the face would be.

The door was opened fully, and in the better light, he could see that he had been answered by an old lady. As she let him in, she called out.

"Bert, there's a Tad—a policeman here. An officer. Come and see what he wants."

A man of similar age emerged from one of the rooms. He took in the uniform and rank. Here was a senior officer, by himself, in the middle of the night. Not a raid, then, though Majesty knows, they'd done nothing to deserve one.

"Good evening, Commandant. How can we help you?"

"I have urgent King's business across the bridge. Unfortunately, I have had an accident, and I must walk. I need a guide to the bridge."

"At this time of night, Commandant? It's a brave man goes through these streets except he's known for his swagger. Even the young go around in groups."

"I think my uniform offers sufficient protection, Mr?"

"Jackson, sir. And begging your pardon, but I'm not that fast on my feet these days, and there are those will see us and make a big to-do about what I was doing with an officer."

The commandant recognised the ploy.

"I have a pocketful of Credits here. Get a group of younger men here in fifteen minutes, and there's good rewards for them, and for yourself." He pulled out an envelope and waved its contents around.

It had the desired effect. The old man did indeed move slowly, but after a couple of knocks and conversations others took over, and soon there were four men assembled. He paid Jackson, making sure the others could see the size of the reward. Then they were off. In about thirty minutes, they were at the bridge.

He turned and paid the men, adding that if the mobile was intact when a retrieval gang came for it, there would be more to come. Then over the bridge and into Reception. There was just one guard, asleep on a bench outside the entrance. The door was locked. Sheer frustration overtook him,

"Trooper!" he yelled in the man's ear. The guard woke with a start, and struggled to attention.

"This place is to be opened up immediately. There are two boys in custody. They are to be woken and told to get dressed, but to remain in their rooms. There are to be guards with them. I am going to the Security Office. I will be back in half an hour. Understood? Good, get to it."

He walked across to the Security Office. To his pleasure, the door opened, and there were two men who sprang to attention as he entered. He explained the situation as briefly as possible. The mobile would need retrieval in the morning. No, he did not know exactly where it was, but about thirty minutes northward on the other side. They were to offer credits to any who guided them correctly, and to those around it if nothing was missing. There was an officer's apartment upstairs, an apartment that he had occupied ever since David Reynolds had disappeared. He washed, changed his uniform, and crossed the street again. There were now two men behind the open door, and others in the corridor leading to small rooms. Which first? The easy one, the young patriot.

John stood up and saluted as he entered.

"Sit down, lad. I've some news for you. Your classmate Norman is not sick, he's absconded, he's evaded. We are searching for him now, the little bastard. So, you need not worry on that score, you are clean and ready to go. We kept up the pretence so as not to spoil the departure. But we could do with some help. I gather that you were in the same class, but not close to the traitor, right?"

"No, sir, we had little in common. I found him lacking in patriotic spirit, sir. Almost as though he was trying to look unsuited for Service, sir."

"Did you say anything about it?"

"I mentioned it to a teacher, sir. She just thanked me, and I heard nothing more. I tried later, too. Even Muss Norman was not happy with his attitude. I was pleased he was chosen, and I thought that was the end of it."

The commandant groaned inwardly. Yes, it had been noted, but the idiots had not acted on it. Rather, they had alerted the boy without reporting upwards, and he had changed his behaviour. He changed tack.

"Your last stint was with him, yes? At the Pickless farm at Midhope? Anything out of the ordinary there? He seemed to be all set to be apprenticed there until he was Chosen."

"Yes, sir. He did seem to be hoping for that, and not to be Chosen. Mr Pickless certainly favoured him, sir. He was put to the farm books and did things that the rest of us were not allowed. And left him at the farm when the family went to Service and the rest of us went fishing. I did think it odd, sir, that he left one of us alone for that."

John paused. How safe was he here? He'd taken Pickless' advice and said nothing about the evader that Pickless used.

"May I ask a question, sir?"

"Go ahead, lad."

"Suppose the mayor or the Proctors were told that there was an evader around, they'd be bound to catch him and report it here, wouldn't they?"

"Of course. That's what's happened, except that we did not catch him. We've traced him, and he's headed west beyond our reach. Just a pity they lacked the sense to call him in before, after the kind of warning you gave them."

"But if they were told and did not want it known, could they get those that knew out of the way, sir?"

"What are you on about, lad? It would be a crime not acting. The mayor knows his duty. The father reported it and the mayor acted correctly. Just too late."

"I mean, sir, could the mayor order an expulsion on his own, without consulting you?"

It dawned on Hope that John was not talking about Mark. There was more going on here; that did not surprise him in the least.

"No, lad, he could not. Chosen or unchosen, those who cross the bridge are the King's, and we decide what is to become of them. And we'd not accept an unchosen without good cause, well attested. So, if anyone made that claim, they're wrong, and treasonous with it."

He looked straight at John.

"But if a good patriotic lad like yourself, for example, were fooled in believing it until he learnt better, you can be sure it would not be held against him when he did, and told us."

And so, the story was told. There was even a name, Jones. One for the clerks, that, as he did not recognise the name. Damn and blast. This Division was riddled with treason right to the top. Now not only bloody Pickless, but the mayor too, who else besides, and all the other lads on that stint. Peter and Simon could wait. They'd be at Conisbrough for a few days at least. He'd have to refer upwards for Tom, though. He reassured John, told him to wait and left the room. Straight back to Bradfield it was, and with more men.

"I've finished here," he told the duty officers now at the desk. "Get both of these to join the others as soon as possible." No time for Jamie Mallory now. If needed, he could easily be found later. He went back to the Security Office across the road. He telephoned his DC with a brief report, collected three more men and headed back across the bridge. Dawn was already past. The mobile met with no accidents, and they drew up outside the Council Hall.

9. Mayhem

The commandant and his men entered the hall. It was barely six in the morning. Bar the guard at the entrance, a Kingsman, not Security, and another of his own outside the Mayor's Office, there was no one visible. His squad behind him, he went straight to the mayor's apartment. The door was not locked, and they stormed in.

"Where are you, you vile traitor?" he shouted, as doors banged and the men looked into every room. Arkell was in bed with Miss. Still groggy, he was hauled out of bed and hit hard across the face. He fell. Miss started screaming and was slapped. Children started yelling; Muss, silent and shocked, was held by a trooper.

"Get him dressed and bring him to the office. Get the rest of them dressed too, and keep them in the living room. No one is to leave."

He went back into the hall. Men of both services asleep in side rooms had been woken, and were trickling into the Hall still struggling into uniforms. He went up to the office to be ready for his prisoner, leaving the door open. A few minutes later, a racket broke out below. There were shouts, then silence. He went downstairs.

It was as though all were frozen. By the door leading to the mayor's apartment stood the mayor, a Security man holding each arm. His face was bloody. Facing them, about ten feet away, was the Proctor captain and one of his men. Security men stood on either side of them, pistols drawn and pointing. A few Kingsmen stood to one side, looks of astonishment on their faces.

Captain Phelps had had a trying day. No not a day, a whole day and night. First, Mr Norman delivered to his cells, and the guardroom sealed off from his men. The commandant had been there with him, so the duty officer had said. Then serving at the ceremony. Then the shock of an Evasion, and the sending out of patrols. A message to withdraw from the north-west, with no explanation. His men thinking that the boy was captured, to be told otherwise, and sent out

125

again. Redirecting patrols from the riverside to the Outie bounds and the Corridor. The abrupt instructions from the commandant when he had asked for help, and no sign of the major. The last straw had been returning to the station to be told that he had a corpse in the cells, and that the hygienist had said, briefly, died of his wounds and he would be reporting across the bridge in the morning. The Security guard had point blank refused to let him in. He had gone to the front and dozed in his chair, only to be woken by a messenger requesting men and dogs for the major at Midhope. The next patrol to report back had been despatched with their dogs, turned around immediately on arrival at the station. He'd had enough, and gone to the Hall. No major, no commandant, no mayor. No idea when they will be back, *sir,* was the snarky reply he got from both forces. He had returned to the station, and had just settled back in his chair, only to be nodding off when the roar of a mobile passing had aroused him again.

He did his best to smarten himself up, ordered out the only man he had left at the reception and marched to the Hall. As he had entered, the door at the back had opened, and he saw his bleeding mayor in the hands of Security. Shouting with rage, he had run forward, only to see firearms pointed at him from both sides.

The commandant descended the stairs slowly. He beckoned his men to holster their guns and approached the captain.

"What seems to be the trouble?" he said, without emotion. The captain was reduced to stuttering with rage.

"What have you d-done to the m-mayor?" he spluttered. "Why is there a b-body in my c-cells and not the m-morgue? Died of his w-wounds? Where is the m-major? What the hell is going on?"

"Questions, questions. Just a little presumptuous, perhaps, *Captain* Phelps? And 'sir' would show appropriate respect, don't you think? On whose authority do I act, *Captain,* and on whose do you? The mayor? That lump of treasonous garbage over there? For your information, that creature is about to be charged. As of now, he has no authority. You and your men are under my direct command, *Captain.* You will remain here under guard. I am sure there will be things you want to tell us in relation to this rogue's," he glanced at the mayor, "activities. You will have shared many secrets, to be sure."

He turned to the attending Proctor.

"Who is the second in command of your rabble, man?"

"Lieutenant Briscoe, sir."

"Know where he is?"

"Down south, sir, managing the patrols along and into the Corridor."

"Know when he'll be back?"

"Scheduled for ten o'clock, sir."

"One of my men will accompany you to the station. He will replace the man in the guardhouse who is to return here. The guardhouse and cells remain out of bounds. You will tell all incoming and outgoing patrols that I am in charge, and that any news, or, of course, the evader himself, will be brought directly here. When Briscoe returns, he is to report here immediately. Dismiss."

As the man left, Hope wondered if he should have told him to keep his mouth shut otherwise. But no: anyone coming to the hall on business later would find it full of his men. The mayor would definitely not be available. His chief clerk was dead, the deputies were not to be trusted. A spot of fear in the community might loosen tongues. As for the body, he needed a doctor to get it shifted across the bridge as fast as possible. The hygienist would probably have blabbed too and would need a call made for a doctor. Better do that now. It would be good to pin the death on a bungling or malicious groundling, but he dared not throw his weight about with a doctor.

He turned to his sergeant.

"No one other than a Proctor is to enter the building. Any questions, and the whole office is closed for Security investigations. If a hygienist comes, he's to be told that the medics have been called and are on their way. He's not to go to the station. Hold Phelps in a side room, and keep the mayor here. I'll signal when I want him brought up."

He went back upstairs to telephone. It was a while before a doctor could be found, and the conversation was not easy. Even a criminal grounder was good for something alive. And such a fuss about this Division in particular. A Division that required massive inputs, notionally because the stock was exceptionally pure. Eventually, he got a commitment, but was asked to hold. A minor noble, Lord Bohun, came on the line, a man with connections in heredity and selection. Was the major available? No, he was in the field. He is to ring when he returns. Hold who you must, but no ill-treatment, still less any more deaths. *Snooty bastard*, thought the commandant, *so pleased with himself to have been dosed*.

He put the phone down in exasperation. Two weeks, no, one week with a free hand, and he could get enough evidence to declassify the whole Division. That, or direct rule with no pussyfooting. He decided to change his strategy. A man was sent to summon Phelps rather than the mayor. He would pass right by the mayor on his way up, leaving the latter to guess what was said. The man was brought in. I've to be nice, have I? Well, being physical is not the only way.

"Sit, Mr Phelps." Strike one.

The interrogation that followed was indeed mild by the commandant's standards. There were frequent references to families, transfers and being unchosen or shipped out of the Ground, but, in truth, little was gained. They'd not been asked to patrol the river more frequently, but in any case, trespass had declined after the various warnings from the mayor. Yes, it was true that Pickless made fewer complaints than any others on the boundary. No, he did not know why. Was he co-operative? As much as any. An evader there? We'd heard talk from way back, but the mayor dismissed it, sir. Anyone called Jones go missing? Not in my time. sir. Any night patrols there? No, sir. Elsewhere? Sometimes, sir. Any reason? We're not really equipped to deal with Outies, sir, especially in the dark. Short staffed, too and the mayor suggested we avoid less bothered areas like Midhope. Searching beyond the boundary? Very little, if there was a major raid, they called in Kingsmen. Norman and his family? Highly regarded.

A bit of theatre was called for. Hustling Phelps out into the upstairs corridor with a guard, he beckoned another inside. The door was left slightly ajar. Then those below heard the crash of something against furniture, the smashing of wood, and agonising screams. There would be pauses and repeats. Then a guard came down the stairs and whispered to others. The mayor's guards hustled him into a corner facing the wall. Phelps was then led down the stairs, followed by irregular footsteps, groans and slithering, and gasps from others in the room. Once the procession was out of sight, the mayor was turned around.

To Hope's combined disgust and amusement, the effect on Arkell was a little too dramatic. He fainted and soiled himself simultaneously. He was taken away to be hosed down, while a man went to the apartment to get fresh clothes.

Eventually, the mayor was led up the what had once been his office. He was sat facing his desk. A man stood on either side of him, both swinging truncheons. Another sat to one side with a notebook; this was official.

"Mr Arkell, I have evidence that you have aided and abetted the concealment of an evader in or near your jurisdiction for an unknown period, but certainly several years. Further, you have failed to report or to act on behaviour likely to lead to the avoidance of Service to His Majesty."

Arkell made to speak, a last throw.

"What evidence," he began. The commandant cut him short.

"One word, Mr Arkell, one word: Pickless." He waited.

The mayor collapsed, head in hands. How had they got there? Certainly not Mark, for he had gone by the book there, and if the boy had holed up there, it would not be his fault. But if Pickless had talked, he was done for, Pickless too, of course. Had they caught his evader, whose name he did not even know, while looking for Mark?

The story had echoed in his head for ages, and flashed through it now. There had been just one, oblique conversation soon after his arrival. The need to send stock and seed across the bridge had been great, and the farmers struggled to fulfil the demands. He had noticed that Midhope did better than the other boundary farms nearly every year, with less loss to Outie raids, and that despite a small labour force, which decreased as the sons were Chosen in turn. An old Proctor, dead these fifteen years, had told him that someone not of the family had been seen a couple of times, but not been reported out of laziness as much as anything. There was never any trouble there. So, when he had paid a visit, part of a traditional routine for a new mayor, he had mentioned the Proctor's sightings. Pickless' words had stayed with him.

"Well, Mr Mayor, sometimes there's a bargain to be struck. You know we contribute more than most, and with fewer of us too. And if a stranger not on the books and not from these parts lends a helping hand, and is no drain on your rations, why take an interest? And not just a labouring hand either. I'm sure you'll have noticed we lose near enough nothing to Outies. Ask our neighbours or consult your books. I think you'll find they're losing quite a lot. Now you can take us in, or you can station Proctors here all the time to catch the fellow. But I can tell you what will happen. First this place will lose more to raids. Second, you'll need more labour to get anything like what we do out of this land. Thirdly, there's three already Chosen from this house, and I've a feeling the rest will follow. Be different if we had a girl or two. A credit to your patch, no? So: one patriotic duty against another patriotic duty. Quite a puzzle, eh, for a young man in a good position; one of the best, so I've heard?"

The dreaded word had not been uttered. He had said nothing before leaving. And with each day that passed, it became less and less possible to report or keep watch. Nothing was reported to him; Pickless was careful. The Division met its targets, the Visitor was complimentary, He earned credit over and above the nominal allowance. Gradually, it had dawned on him that Pickless owned his silence.

All of this and more poured out of the mayor. Not as coherently as his private, inner thoughts had developed over the years. The Commandant was happy. He even felt a tinge of pity for the sobbing creature in front of him.

"So that's an admission of guilt, then, on the main charge. Well done. But there's a bit more to come. Let's turn to the Normans. What about the father; did he have any inkling of any of this?"

"He never said or hinted anything, sir, nor I to him. But he was a master at the book-keeping and the reports across the bridge. He'll have seen the figures same as me, and would be quicker on the uptake. If I'm honest, I should have recommended him for a transfer as a Deputy, and he'd have made a fine mayor somewhere in time. But he was a great asset."

Fine indeed, thought the commandant, *spreading disloyalty in more populated Divisions*. The Kingdom's been spared that, at least.

"What about his son? What about those reports on concealing talent? Did he pressure you over stints and allocation?"

"Never sure about the first, sir. The school made a report of a sudden weakness in maths. Not my strong point anyway. I talked to the teacher. She'd thought it but a phase, but a pupil caught her and suggested she investigated."

"A pupil? That wouldn't be John Gregory, would it?"

Arkell was startled out of his abjectness. He almost said, "How did you know?" but bit it back.

"Yes, sir. A very patriotic lad who is over the bridge as he deserves. Mind, he could be a little overzealous, but he seems to have been right on this one. But it went into Mark's reports, and the next year there was an improvement. His father did tell me he was leaning hard on the son to work harder. I trusted that family, and why not; two Chosen and no sign of anything unpatriotic."

And very convenient, thought the commandant. Lose Norman, and you'd have had more work to do, and above your competence at that. Well, that's not your problem anymore.

"And the stints and his future?"

"Nothing odd about the stints, sir. Employers can put in requests, and the youngsters can express preferences for different jobs. That last stint, Pickless did name him, but that's not unusual. The farmers swap stories, and he'd worked for the cousin a few miles down the road two years previously. Good report. It was his father would have drawn up the lists, but I'd have done the same; no reason not to."

"And his future? Be careful now, the whole truth."

"I could see his father wanted him to be a farmer, sir, and I think he wanted the same and showed the right aptitude. And people do put in names for apprenticeships too, but they usually come in a rush after Selection, and they know who's been Chosen. Pickless surprised me a bit with an early bid, the more so since he's never put in a bid at all before, just asked for big gangs for each stint."

"That's the point, isn't it, Arkell," the commandant's voice got harsher. "You knew why Pickless never asked for an apprentice. Living in, he'd be bound to find out about Jones."

Arkell looked up, a frown on his face.

"Jones, sir?"

"Oh, I forgot to tell you. The evader's name was Jones. All the boys on that stint got to know it, but Pickless said things that shut them up."

Convincing enough. Why them and not the mayor, though? I guess John's account explains it. The mayor had never seen the man.

"But more to the point, surely you realised that asking for the Norman boy meant that he was trusted with the secret? That this disease was spreading? You thought it was in the bag, and then the Visitor took it away from you. On good advice, as it turns out."

The mayor said nothing. The commandant had seen all too clearly. The Picklesses were getting older, and he had no idea how old the evader was, but at least the same or older. The time was coming when there would be changes, when he had to impose an apprentice on them for the sake of production.

"So, guilty again, Arkell?" The mayor nodded slightly.

"One last question. What is the position of the Proctors in this? Captain Phelps?"

"As far as I know, sir, they know nothing. We've discussed patrol patterns, but the light touch at Midhope was common sense. We're stretched as it is, and it was the least disturbed part of the boundary."

For once, the commandant relented, partly for amusement. He called a guard.

"Fetch Mr Phelps, and bring him here. He's to stand in the door and say nothing."

The mayor's astonishment at this request was dwarfed by that when he saw Phelps standing in the doorway. No sign of any injury, no blood. Phelps was led away. The commandant laughed.

"Really, Arkell, you did not imagine we are a bunch of barbarians, did you? There are brains in this business as well as muscle. It has certainly paid for you to use what little you have just now. You've earned your family some kind of reprieve. They'll be split, but almost certainly stay in the Ground somewhere. I can't say the same for you, but as unchosen, there's bad and then there's worse. I'll see what I can do."

He turned to the guards. "Find somewhere secure to hold this man. Not with his family, and we can't use the cells until that corpse is removed."

He looked up at the clock; barely past nine. Less than 24 hours since he and the major had arrived in Bradfield. The scribe was putting away his papers. They could be copied, but not here. He sat down and started to compose a list; where had he got to. Let's start with the known guilty.

The brat (unaccounted for)

The father (dead)

The mayor (confessed, in custody)

The Picklesses (all of them, his wives cannot have been unaware).

The evader Jones (unaccounted for)

Probables

Most of the Norman family (especially Miss and her daughter)

Those on the Pickless stint, excluding John (two over the bridge, and young Tom. Low priority)

Jamie Mallory (his brother was chosen, but only after trespass. Also Chosen. Low priority)

Some unknown boy in the Squats.

Improbable, but bad attitude.

The whole bloody corps of Proctors (not his decision, but their cage needs rattling)

The hygienist (see what the doctor says)

Improbable, but need shipping out

The mayor's family

When written out, it did not seem that impressive. But his mind was not at ease. The mayor, just venal. By itself, common enough and understandable. Many folks could turn a blind eye to crime or treason if the incentives were there.

But at the top, or what passed for the top in this backwater, it opened up the possibilities for more serious deviance. And that seemed to have happened to the other two families. Who knew how far the same attitudes had spread? What was it the mayor had said about 'overzealous' in reference to John? What about the school? And as for the squats? That Reynolds boy could be hiding there, though for Majesty himself he could not see why; the brat had not been chosen; no reason to run. The whole place was plain sloppy.

He was lost in thoughts like this, when there was a knock on the door.

"The doctor, sir. Will you see her now?" He nodded. 'Her', unusual but not unknown, particularly where the Ground was concerned. A short slim woman entered the room, gender only visible in her face. A doctor's rig was more protective than most among those that entered the Grounds.

"Please sit down, Dr?"

"MacDonald. Thank you, Commandant."

"You've seen the body, Doctor?"

"Yes, Commandant, and removed it to my mobile. It will not be seen. There will be a full autopsy when I have the right facilities back in Conisbrough. The hygienist was waiting outside the station, and gave me an account of events while the deceased was in his care. At present, it is my opinion that the injuries sustained while," the doctor paused and looked straight at the commandant, "resisting arrest, would have been fatal within a few hours of the actual time of death. I will of course confirm or modify that conclusion in writing after the autopsy."

"And the drug?"

"Was as stated in your order and on the vial. Judging by the size of the vial, a correct dose was given for the symptoms that usually warrant its use. Again, I will confirm this later. There was no indication that the vial was tampered with. I believe you saw the hygienist draw the drug into the syringe yourself, Commandant?"

Hope nodded.

"May I ask, Commandant, why you saw fit to suggest that the hygienist might not have done as you instructed? The man is understandably concerned when someone in your position appears to suspect them of malpractice." Her tone was sharp and uncompromising.

"The prisoner was strongly suspected of aiding and abetting an Evasion of Service, doctor. I needed some answers, but he was unconscious. I had waited several hours in the hope that he would either regain consciousness or be in a fit state to be carried over the bridge. My attention elsewhere in what is clearly a traitorous conspiracy was needed urgently. I asked the hygienist if there was any means of rendering him conscious, and he recommended this course of action. He did indeed regain momentary consciousness, and then died. While the hygienist did warn me of this possibility, I was struck by the possibility that the suspect intended to commit suicide, and that the hygienist had assisted him. It appears that I was mistaken. I will speak to the hygienist and apologise. I might add that I was unaware that the injuries he had sustained were inevitably fatal."

"Very well, do that. I have two observations to make, Commandant. You will know that the Commissions place a very high value on the life of Grounders, and on those with premium reproductive capacity in particular. Leaving aside the drug, this man died a violent death from injuries consistent with being beaten and kicked when on the ground. Of course, other explanations are no doubt possible, but this will, of necessity, be stated in the autopsy report.

Second, it is highly irregular for a person unqualified in medicine, of whatever rank, to oblige a qualified person to carry out any medical treatment. The hygienist received a direct order from you in writing. In fact, there was no drug that could alleviate the condition. It might, and indeed did provoke a very temporary period of consciousness. Again, there may be circumstances in which such an action is warranted, though I have never heard of any such cases. It is only right that I bring these matters to your attention. What, if anything, will follow from this is not for me to decide."

She stood up and walked out. Hope, in fury, kicked a chair so hard that it fell apart. Bloody medics. He would, of course, contest any charges, and his DC would certainly stand by him. But he might be recalled for a hearing before he could sort out this bloody mess, and yet again there would be a failure to deal with what was obvious systemic subversion.

***

By now, a small crowd had gathered around the main entrance to the Hall. Initially, it had been a few needing to do business. They had been faced not with the usual lone Proctor, whom most of them would know, but with a Kingsman and a Security trooper in full gear. No entry was the message. As a consequence of the evasion, the mayor was suspended, and Royal Officers were now responsible. Others gathered to see what was going on. Proctor families among them, and now there was a hubbub of questions. The Proctors could not use their own guardroom. There was a prisoner in the cells. No one had seen Captain Phelps. There had been mobiles roaring through in the early hours. The two guards remained impassive and uncommunicative, but felt increasingly pestered. When they were relieved at ten o'clock, the message went inside, and the commandant came to the door. He shouted for silence.

"In the name of the King, I have declared an emergency in this part of the Division. It is under the direct rule of Royal Officers. Until you have further instructions, that means me. This office will remain closed until further notice. When I have finished speaking, you will disperse, and inform anybody you meet that this is the case."

The crowd was silenced.

"If you do not know already, there has been an Evasion, which is treason. The evader is unaccounted for, but he will be found if he is not already roasting on a spit beyond the bounds."

His voice hardened further.

"This evasion, and other treasonous activity was not the work of one boy. You should know that your mayor has confessed to aiding and abetting evasion, as has his clerk, the boy's father, Norman. We are still holding your Proctor captain. This Division has become a sink of disloyalty and disrespect for the Crown, and the rot has reached the top. You can be sure that we will root out all involved.

You all know the extent to which the Royal Domain gives you preferential treatment. Ask those who have been transferred from elsewhere. It has a right to expect exceptional loyalty and gratitude, and these qualities are manifestly lacking. The Crown will surely be influenced by the degree of enthusiastic co-operation we receive when dealing with this treason when it considers the future. And, of course, patriotic acts are always given due recognition."

The crowd dispersed. He had only just closed the door behind him, when one of the guards opened it to tell him a Proctor lieutenant was approaching. Hope was in no mood to deal with the man and his inevitable questions. The doctor was still getting him riled. He had overstepped his authority on the doorstep, and he knew it. He needed to get reinforcements. He called over a sergeant and told him to deal with the Proctor. Tell the man he was in charge, and to maintain patrols. He would be sent for later. He went upstairs to the office.

Lieutenant Briscoe was exhausted. He had returned to the station after more than 20 hours moving between patrols in the south to no good purpose, only to find no Captain Phelps, indeed, nobody bar the Proctor who had accompanied Phelps to the hall and had returned to his post. Phelps detained, the mayor also, and beaten too. The cells and guardroom locked off, a corpse, and its removal by a doctor. And he was to report to the commandant at the Hall. At least, the guardroom had been freed. When he entered the Hall, he asked for the commandant, and was directed to a Security sergeant. The conversation that followed was brief and icy. The sergeant made the most of his opportunity to snub a mere groundling with notional seniority. Briscoe held his tongue. He would have left, but at that moment, the major and two troopers entered. All inside stood and saluted. The major looked around. No other Proctors, and none of the mayor's staff. He accosted Briscoe.

"Well, Lieutenant, anything to report? Anything from Captain Phelps?"

Briscoe's mouth fell open. What the hell was going on? He made an effort.

"No, sir, nothing. And Captain Phelps is detained here, sir, on Commandant Hope's orders, and I believe the mayor also."

He had not heard the commandant's little speech, and had marched to the Hall oblivious of the rather strange expressions on the faces of those dispersing from the entrance.

Cornwallis hid his astonishment. What the hell had Mac been up to? He looked hard at Briscoe. For all his exhaustion, the Major could see his barely controlled anger.

"Have you been given orders, Lieutenant?"

"I was instructed, sir, by the Security sergeant here, to maintain my patrols."

"Countermanded, Lieutenant. You are recall all patrols. I have six of your men at Midhope. I will arrange to have them recalled too. Bar a duty officer at the station, all are to go home. That includes you, Lieutenant. Arrange to have the officer relieved before nine this evening. Have the force assemble at the station at eight o'clock tomorrow, and I will brief them. By the way, is Mr Norman still in your cells?"

"Mr Norman is dead, sir. A doctor came across the bridge and removed his body. The hygienist had been with him earlier, and by his account, Mr Norman was badly injured, sir. We were excluded from the guardroom while Mr Norman was there."

"You now have full use of your station? Good. That is all, Lieutenant. I will see you tomorrow morning."

Briscoe saluted and left. Cornwallis stood in silence. He now allowed his face to show his feelings. Majesty in a dungheap, what had Mac managed to do in just a few hours? Chasing an evader, nasty but straightforward. Now, the whole damned admin of the Division was out of action. A look at one of his own men, who indicated with his thumb that the commandant was in the office. He must pull rank. He approached the Security sergeant.

"When I have left this room, sergeant, you will go up to your commandant and tell him that I will be talking to Captain Phelps, and I am not to be disturbed. Does my man know where he is held? Good. Please ask the commandant to stay in the office until I return."

The trooper led him down a corridor. At one door, a Security guard stood, and saluted as the major approached. He was dismissed, but the trooper entered after the Major. Phelps stood up and saluted. Like Briscoe, he looked exhausted, but did not appear to have been hit.

"Sit down, Captain. I am going to ask you some questions. I remind you that in the absence of the Visitor or any noble, I am the senior officer in this Division. I am aware that the mayor has been arrested. It follows that all, I mean all, uniformed personnel are now under my command. Do you understand what I am saying, Captain?"

"Sir."

The major then extracted the whole of Phelps' tale. Norman killed, certainly not intentionally, but with a degree of force that was entirely unwarranted. The mayor beaten at the least, and tricked into panic by the theatricals when Phelps was led away. At least, Phelps himself had not been harmed; indeed, the questioning had been a lot softer than that associated with Mac. Just as well. There was no reason to doubt he was telling the truth. Back in the Hall there was only three of his own men, two of whom had returned from Midhope with him. There were at least six Security officers, perhaps more upstairs. Time for a show.

"Thank you, Captain. I am sorry you have been detained. In a moment, I am going to escort you to the main entrance, and you will be free to go home. You are to stay there until I say otherwise. Until any issue related to your detention is formally concluded, the Proctors will be commanded by Lieutenant Briscoe. For your information, the whole force has been stood down until tomorrow morning. You will not join them. You are officially on parole, Captain, understood?"

"Yes, sir, thank you." The three marched back into the Hall. All stood again.

"Pay attention. Captain Phelps is discharged on my authority. No uniformed officer or soldier is to approach or apprehend him other than on my written order."

Phelps left. The Major summoned two troopers and climbed the stairs to the office. He dismissed the Security man at the door, and replaced him with a trooper. He entered the office with the other. Hope started to rise from his chair, but obeyed a gesture to remain where he was.

"First things first, *Commandant*. Where is Arkell being held?"

"Somewhere in this building, Major. The sergeant downstairs will know. But why?"

An abrupt, loud interruption.

"Trooper, you will locate the mayor. You will dismiss the Security guard and take his place. On the way, you will leave instructions for a hygienist to be summoned to examine the mayor. I require a written account of his condition before the hygienist leaves. Dismiss."

The pair were now alone. There was a long silence. The commandant was seething. Notionally, his rank was that of the major's. But both by seniority and the established order that military rank took precedence, Cornwallis was within his rights. He had asserted them in front of a junior in a way that was deliberately, offensively, driving the point home. At last, after a weary look at Hope, the major spoke.

"King's Bollocks, man, what the hell have you been doing? A grounder dead in your custody and removed by the medics. The Proctors driven to exhaustion, their lieutenant demeaned and their captain detained. The mayor apparently assaulted in custody, and the normal conduct of business in the Division halted completely. And all this now known to all, with rumours no doubt making it worse. How does this place function now, in the name of Majesty?"

Silence. *There would be more, soon enough*, thought Hope. The doctor's report, the accident on the way to the bridge, any account of his little speech outside the hall, all would reach the major and the Visitor soon enough. But he had some trump cards.

"I think, Major, that you have found nothing of interest at Midhope? In the meantime, I have a confession of guilt to treason from the mayor, a detailed account that reveals a level of subversion and deceit that goes far beyond the Norman boy. Subversion and deceit that goes back even further than this mayor's term of office. A corruption, Major, a corruption that warrants far stronger measures to dig out and exterminate. I have already given a verbal report to my Deputy Commissioner."

This last was a lie, though he would rectify that as soon as possible, with a guard on a mobile if he could not phone. He had been too worked up in the time the major had been with Phelps to think clearly.

"It is my opinion, Major, that the situation requires a transfer of authority here to Security. My full report will make that very clear."

Impasse, thought Cornwallis. Lord Bohun had made it clear to him that the future of this Division was a key element in a long-standing argument, right up to the King's Council. Give it to Security, and the argument would tilt towards abandonment or under Barrier Command. Minimise the dangers, and the rich, uncontaminated stock would remain available to the Crown.

"Just what is it that Arkell has confessed to, then?"

The scribe was recalled. The commandant sat silent while the Major read the transcript. So, Pickless had been harbouring an evader. Not the only case known, but all the others had been short-lived and motivated by pity. And there were worse things suspected along the boundary, things that involved actual contact with the Outies.

"These boys. Have you talked to any of them?"

"Yes, I went over the bridge late last night and interviewed John Gregory. Far too late, or I would have sent you a messenger. A sound patriot, we need a few more of them. The evader was seen, apparently, by the Norman boy and Pickless said more than he meant to in front of all of them, and then spun them a story that shut them up. There are two more were there that are over the bridge and a youngster. They can wait. They will corroborate John's account. There's Jamie Mallory too, you will remember. He was never at the Pickless farm, but he was a close friend of the Norman boy. He can wait too."

Cornwallis eased up. This mess was beyond them.

"Very well, Mac. What happens long term is above both our heads. I have some calls to make, and I need to get this office working again. I will arrange to take the mayor's family and the Normans to a holding area in the Corridor; I don't want them anywhere near the bridge, and we need transfer consents. They'll still be available, but I don't think you or anyone is going to get anything of use there. We do not take the Pickless lot in for now, but we keep watch; I've got them guarded. I can't see how Mark would reach them, but it seems the only strategy. I am going to call in reinforcements, and we'll have another search beyond the boundary. But Pickless had had an Outie raid just the night before, so that evader, Jones, may have moved on. I will grill him again. Meanwhile, we both need a rest. I am going to call in the Deputies and see how far we can get things back to normal. Get your men out of the main hall, and get some sleep. When I'm done, I'll let you know. You can have this office and the telephone. Then you may want to cross the bridge and interview the boys. I need to get my head down too; I've to brief the Proctors at eight tomorrow."

"Oh, and by the way, do you have any reason to continue Phelps' suspension? No? Well, leave a release with your sergeant before you take off."

The commandant left. Cornwallis turned to the phone. First, reinforcements. Next, arrangements with the Corridor Transfer Station to house the families, and, in reply, get a negative report from there: no fugitive or traces. Troopers in to arrange relief of the Proctors at Midhope. Others to find the Deputies. No direct line to the Corridor, of course, and a protracted set of dictations and reading back. A break for a hurried meal. Then he returned to call Lord Bohun. The phone was dead. Cut off. He rushed down to the hall, where the Security sergeant was about to leave.

"Sergeant, where is your commandant?"

"He took a driver and went to cross the bridge, sir, said he would rest in the office there. I am in charge, sir, until he returns, with orders to remain off duty in quarters."

Damnation. Mac had pre-empted him, and cut the line somehow, he was sure. No time to write a report and send it. He had to go across the bridge himself and now. He dug out his lieutenant, briefed him as best he could and left him to deal with the Deputies. Grabbing a driver, he set off for the bridge.

10. Conisbrough

At the entrance to the bridge, Hope dismissed his driver and mobile, sending them on. He looked up to where the overhead wire left the last post and descended to the bridge. Looking around, and seeing no one, he cut the wire where it descended to the side of the old stone construction that had been part of the original, pre-war bridge. Staples on either side held the wire in place. Satisfied, he marched across to his office. Turning first to the practical and immediate, he summoned a clerk: duplicates to be made of the mayor's confession and notes made after other, less formal interrogations. How many, sir? Six, one to be placed in the safe here. A call to the reception centre for the Chosen: a room to be set aside for interviews. When? For tomorrow, unless he told them otherwise. A quick meal, and he called the DC.

It was a long and increasingly frustrating conversation. Despite the copious and conclusive evidence, despite the obvious need for rapid action, no, the Division would not be placed under Security Administration. No, he was not authorised to bring that farmer and his family over the bridge, nor to go to the farm himself. He was to stay this side of the bridge until a report had been received from Major Cornwallis. No, he could not have the mayor brought over either, yet. Was he aware that a doctor's report on a death in custody meant an inquiry was inevitable? Had he told Major Cornwallis that he should report to Lord Bohun? Finally, yes, come to Conisbrough and interview the Chosen boys, tomorrow. Otherwise, he was to wait where he was until the major had reported to his Lordship.

Something had clearly gone wrong. The DC was usually very supportive, and no friend of those who, in his own words, mollycoddled this extraordinarily demanding Division. Maybe Cornwallis had got his call to Bohun in early? Even so, even if he had had orders, the DC would have had a different tone, surely? Expressed frustration to match his own? It was a stilted and unusually formal exchange.

There was little he could do until tomorrow. He might have been left drumming his fingers in frustration all evening, had a knock and abrupt entry not disturbed his further introspection: the major; a grim-faced major.

"Informalities are over, Commandant. We will find out soon enough where the line was cut. In the meantime, just for your information, Lord Bohun is now fully informed of the situation. As it happens, he was in your DC's office when you rang. Maybe that explains a few things?"

So that's it, thought Hope. The DC had that degenerate nobleman on his back. The bastard had acted remarkably fast. A clever bastard, at that. There are others involved here; Bohun must have been informed, and not by the major. Maybe that damned doctor. We need to alert those with more backbone, outside this corrupt Division. I need to get the DC on his own. Council do not understand the threat. They must, if they value their rule. He stared at Cornwallis.

"Accusation, Major? The DC has yet to receive my full reports. They will not stop at Conisbrough, Major. They will be on their way a lot higher than that."

Cornwallis shrugged. As yet, he had no authority to prevent Hope doing whatever he pleased this side of the boundary. Maybe the formal report from the doctor; maybe the hygienist's report on the mayor; maybe the line cut, would be enough to warrant suspension. Maybe. But he had at least gained one thing. He handed over a neatly typed sheet.

"Please read this, Commandant. It is not formally signed, but the authorised original will be delivered to me within hours. The Northernmost Ground is now under my command. I will return to Bradfield with a complete company in the morning. From now on, nobody crosses the bridge in either direction without express written permission from me. Your men will be ordered to leave tomorrow morning when I arrive. Let me be clear, no Security personnel are to enter the Ground or the city. Engineers will be tracing the cut and repairing it. Any messages from the bridge will be through the receiver in the Visitor's office until the connection is restored. Any doubts, Commandant, please ring your DC."

The major left. *No point in checking the order*, thought Hope, it would be genuine. But this had all the marks of a conspiracy going far higher than the Division. The evidence was clear. The damned mayor, the damned farmers, the whole Norman family should be here and not there. The bloody squatters should be given a good work-over. The existence of the whole sodding mess should be reviewed. A thought struck him, and he phoned back to the DC.

"I have received orders from Major Cornwallis, sir, regarding the Northernmost Division. I take it that you are aware of them?"

"Yes, Mac. Both the Visitor and Bohun approved them. I had no say. When we talked earlier, Bohun was even in the room, and hearing my replies. How had he jumped so fast, Mac? He brought a provisional medical report too; it did not look good. Don't worry, we can fend it off, but something or someone is setting out to frustrate proper security. What's this Major Cornwallis all about?"

"I knew him from way back, sir, in basic training. I'd have put him down as straightforward military, if you get my meaning, competent but not too bright, and more than a bit naïve where Grounders are concerned. Reproductive potential and all that. I think he was briefed for something more than a search and capture mission. Otherwise, I think he got a commendation for actions in the Midlands. Something connected to a Hunt, I think. He did not talk about it. We started off on the right foot for this one, but something changed when my inquiries opened up. He was certainly trying to get his reports in before mine, which is why I returned in haste."

"Know his contacts? Anyone high up?"

"Only the Visitor and Bohun as far as I know, sir. We could find his postings."

"I'll do that. Meanwhile, I'll talk to the Commissioner again, Lane needs to know. You'll be in Conisbrough tomorrow to see the boys. Get there promptly, and be in my office at four when you've finished with them. Bohun left for Leicester an hour ago. We should be undisturbed."

There was not much more to say, but their conversation was broken by a set of whistles and crackling. The DC's telephone went dead. A clerk's voice addressed Hope.

"All calls from your office from now on will be routed through the Visitor's Office. Messages for others will be taken down and transmitted at the Visitor's discretion."

The call ended. It was an angry, even an embittered Commandant Hope who retired to his bed.

***

Hope's drive to Conisbrough the following morning was both familiar and depressing. Notionally within the Domain, much of the area had been blighted by the Catastrophe and then by the War. Fences and warning signs marked heavily contaminated ground, bare soil supporting only a few stunted sedges, thickening round the edges. Only a few miles north, and one was in Barrier country. Recovering, perhaps, but at a glacial pace. And not far to the east the coastline, actually a mass of saline marshes, occasional islands and protruding ruins. Besides a residual coal mining enterprise, maintained mainly to generate electricity, the place was essentially non-productive. It survived mainly as a depot, staging post and command centre for dealings with the Northernmost Ground and the Barrier crews. The road from the bridge was adequate, but slow, winding between fenced off areas.

The Royal Offices were around the base of the castle. Even besides the keep, maintained as an armoury and signal station, to describe the patched-up buildings as pre-war was inadequate. They were far older than most. The largest contained offices and apartments for the Visitor and other senior functionaries, their presence indicated by smaller flags alongside the taller pole with the Royal Standard. As they drove into the precinct, the commandant could see that there was nearly a full house: Visitor, his own Deputy Commissioner, the Barrier Superintendent and the captain of the Ranger company. Only the banners of Bohun and the Master of Transit and Supply were missing. Unusual. Leaving his driver, he walked to a humbler set of buildings, the Reception and Induction centre for the Chosen. He was expected, and a room set aside. First, he had all of them together: John, Jamie, Peter and Simon. He gave the true reason for Mark's absence at Choosing, the reason John had kept to himself. He stressed the serious nature of the crime, and the penalties for hiding any relevant information. Chosen could be unchosen. Perhaps their induction had already taught them something of what that implied? Then he started with John alone, the others waiting outside.

"All right, lad, we've talked already. There are a few things more, but firstly, I want say something personal; those Chosen get assigned duties and training, but we get to make requests. If you've a mind to join us in Security, I'd say you'd go far, and I'd be in a position to make a claim. We try to get the most loyal. I'm sure you have noticed that some are, shall I say, a bit lacking in a sense of duty. Those not afraid to expose it, as yourself, are not as numerous as we'd like."

"Thank you, sir." John flushed slightly.

"Now, I'm going to tell you a few things that you are to keep to yourself. Thanks to you we have a full confession from the mayor. The military are out looking for this Jones, and they should be dealing with Pickless. What we are looking at is not one young criminal, but a conspiracy. It's to be rooted out. Let's go through a few names. Anything strike you about Peter and Simon at that stint?"

"No, sir. I wouldn't say they were very patriotic, but I heard nothing out of the ordinary. I didn't know them before; they are a year younger. They stuck together a lot. I was surprised they got Chosen so early. They stick together here, too, when we are out of briefings. Our tutors seem to encourage it."

"Jamie?"

"In the same class, but I did not know him well. He was a great friend of Mark's; they sat next to each other in class. It is a very respected family." Then a thought struck him. "Of course, his older brother disappeared, sir. Nobody suggested evasion, and there was a hunt. And he was friends with David Reynolds, who disappeared last year. The same happened. We were warned about trespassing across the river, but nothing more was said. The families were close too. Neither were transferred out. They were not evaders, were they?"

"No, that's not bothering us at the moment, but thank you. All right, back to your class, and send Peter and Simon in together. Think on what I said."

Well, well. Three disappearances, all linked to this Jamie. Steve, he knew about; Chosen, much to his surprise when he was told, though the Visitor had been right not to make it known in the Division. And he had crossed the river, as had David. The Rangers had lost David's trail, though, and his disappearance had been planned. He'd never got to the bottom of that either, and had been frustrated by the lack of support from the Visitor. The river must fit somewhere, but that's surely not where the Norman boy went. Let Jamie sweat a bit longer.

Peter and Simon entered. They merely confirmed John's account of events at Midhope. But when asked about Mark being alone at the farm, the commandant noticed a slight tension, a sideways look between the two. Not the time or place to apply pressure. It did not look as though any of them had seen anything other than Pickless grooming the lad as a successor. Worth asking the Visitor why they'd been picked so young.

Jamie entered. Hope told him to sit, and then gave the appearance of reading papers on the desk. He said nothing for several minutes.

"Mark Norman. He was missing at the ceremony. You know why now, don't you? And why you are here with me now?"

"I don't know why I'm here with you, sir. We were told he was ill, but I was given a medical test and I'm clean. I was allowed to join the others. We were friends, and I thought that was why I was isolated. I heard about evasion only when you spoke to us all just now."

"When did you last see him?"

"We met briefly after we both knew we were chosen, sir. It's kind of goodbye in private, because we don't know whether we see each other alone after crossing the bridge."

"And nothing said that prompted you to alert the authorities? Really? Even now you know the disgusting truth? Your family have a good record of Service. It would such a pity if we had to tell them you were unchosen because of association with that traitorous brat."

Jamie was silent. He had not known until their summons that Mark had disappeared. So that was why John was involved. The commandant did not pause long.

"Now here's a thing, master Mallory. Your brother disappears. David Reynolds disappears, the Norman boy disappears, and this time with clear intention to evade. The one thing in common, you. And you were the last to see your brother. Well?"

"My brother, sir? I told the Proctors at the time, we got separated and it was late. I'd called and called and searched around. He was never found."

Despite his efforts, Jamie was looking nervous. The Commandant rose and stood over him.

"Odd, don't you think? Not a big area, is it? No chance you might have seen him cross the river?" He leaned right over Jamie as he spoke.

Jamie flinched. "I just lost him, sir. He could have gone across, I suppose, but wouldn't we be told? We knew it was forbidden."

"Indeed you did. But you and others didn't let that stop you, did it? I have a pile of reports from the Rangers of kids like you breaking the law." He nodded towards the desk. "Not the only disappearing act that sticks to you either, there's that David Reynolds as well."

"David, sir? Yes. I worked for his family on stints. We were friends. He just disappeared, and there was a search and we heard nothing later. Like my brother."

The Commandant felt stymied. Jamie was showing signs of nervousness, even real fear, and there was obviously more to learn. But there was no handle. And too much pressure on a Chosen, and he'd have more to answer for than he had already accumulated. A last throw.

"Tell me about the river. You were up there with your brother. We know there were gangs cheeking the Rangers. Who else was involved? The Norman boy? Who else?"

"A few years ago, there were lots of us, sir, but after my brother disappeared, Mark and I stopped going there. The mayor made it clear, and we heard about the incident with Stan. Mostly, it was kids wanting to see the Rangers."

Hope was about to demand some names, when there was a knock on the door. A Visitor's assistant entered.

"Commandant, you are required to report immediately to the Visitor's office. I am to accompany you." He looked at the boy. "You, boy, will return to whatever activity you left, straight away. Now, Commandant."

The tone was sharp. Scarcely past noon. No chance to speak to the DC. He rose and followed the assistant into the main building. Diminished in front of a kid, and by a mere dogsbody. The assistant led him across the green to the main building. Up a flight of stairs, and after a knock, into a small but very richly furnished office. There was wood panelling on the walls, and pictures clearly of pre-war age; carpets, upholstered chairs and an ornate desk under a leaded window, behind which sat the Visitor himself. To his left sat Bohun, and on the right his DC, looking very uncomfortable. Bohun? Wasn't he supposed to be in Leicester? The commandant saluted, but was not invited to sit. It was the Visitor who spoke. A list of charges was read out. Of these, the treatment of Norman, and the irregular order to the hygienist were the most serious, and appeared incontestable. The doctor's report indicated serious breaches of procedure there. Moreover, there were other matters relating to a failure to ask Major Cornwallis to contact Lord Bohun, the nature of the public remarks at the Council Hall, and the cutting of the telephone wire at the bridge.

"Commandant, as from now you are suspended from duty. You will remain here in the castle in a set of rooms in my quarters reserved for visitors. Lord Bohun and the DC will move as fast as possible to set up a court of enquiry. You will be entitled to representation; it will be arranged."

The Visitor nodded to the assistant, who led Hope away. The door being closed, the Visitor turned to the DC. There was to be no contact with Hope. A defender was to be found and brought to Conisbrough. A complete charge sheet would be delivered when Major Cornwallis had returned and made a full report. In the meantime, all Security Corps personnel will be withdrawn from the Ground. The DC was outraged.

"My Lords, the Commissioner will be told of this. I formally protest. Commandant Hope has done no more than his duty in exposing a Division, a Ground, riddled with subversion. A Ground that in the opinion of many of us is not worth the cost of its maintenance. Further, it would appear that Major Cornwallis has sought to hinder the work of the Corps. His actions will certainly be questioned in any enquiry."

"Duly noted, Deputy Commissioner. I am sure Major Cornwallis will co-operate willingly in any enquiry. That is all? You may leave us. Oh, one other thing: all calls south will be through my office."

The Visitor turned to Bohun.

"This Cornwallis? I've scarcely met him. Just chance that he was here when you got the report of evasion?"

"No. Not that I expected this, but I had asked for him by name a while ago. There are many officers with a way of thinking more like that of Security. We know he is reliable; he has an excellent military record from down south in unassigned territories. Strong on military honour, and with no love for Security. Interesting, though, I never knew till Hope arrived that they knew each other. Getting him here was insurance, really. A damned good thing as it turns out."

"Hope will remain a problem, with the DC clearly behind him. There's no doubt that the other evader, Jones, was it? will be a black mark for me. I did not know about him, but there's plenty that will say that I should. This will not stay local, will it?"

"It's beyond that already." Bohun handed over a paper. "Here's my latest from the Songbird. It's not coded; maybe we should think about that, though my clerk is reliable."

Council met yesterday. Mostly routine, with the usual litany of failings and no proposed actions from the Four. Then, as you will expect, time spent on the Hunt. Fun must be had. But Dundonnell was missing, and Pendennis took a chance at the end to raise manpower issues and the whole reclamation project. But T&J put up the standard defence, which puts Northernmost at risk. We know where Arundel stands, and I think we expected it to be noted and then ignored or stalled either way. Great surprise: Buckingham more or less came out on P's side, and the matter will come back to next Council. Of course, not until after the Hunt, but it seems the Four are split on this, and neither side is backing down.

"The Hunt? I should have guessed. Folk in their hundreds involved when we lack the means to use what we gain up here. Buys us a little time. Actuaries and the heredity lot? We can mount counter-arguments? Very well. Don't go south until the major returns."

11. Contention in Council

The surreptitious report received by Lord Bohun at Conisbrough was only the most recent of many. The proceedings of the Royal Council were not made public. Only rarely were Councillors allowed to retain the documents provided to guide its deliberations, though each would be aware of that submitted for their own area of authority. For those outside, the trend of policy, the everlasting, unresolved contention among the Four, the children of the King, these were crucial matters. Clerks, even Councillors themselves, were variously persuaded to pass information to interested parties. Advanced warning of the direction in which the Four might move might be the key to promotion or even survival. The kind of information received might in turn induce a subtle redaction of that provided to their superiors. Songbird's brief report to Bohun merely scraped the surface; the meeting, expected to be routine, had instead exposed the differences in full view.

Lord Arundel, tall, bearded, and with all the airs of a man in his prime, marched along a long, windowless corridor, his red cloak swirling around him. The ancient stone walls were softened by elaborate wooden panelling, and it was lit by a sequence of dim, buzzing electric lights, one of which fizzled out altogether as he passed. A frown crossed his face at this symbol, as he saw it, of the slow decay that only he could reverse. His march continued; outside a panelled door, a soldier snapped smartly to attention. Without knocking, he entered the room. An old man sat by a leaded window, head on chest. The remains of breakfast lay on the table beside him. A fire burnt brightly in a massive stone fireplace, and the room was uncomfortably hot. An elderly woman rose from her chair in the corner as he entered. Rose and curtsied. At a nod, she resumed her seat.

"And how is His Majesty this morning, Miss Thomas? Any developments?"

"No, my Lord. He slept well, and ate his breakfast without complaint. He has been silent this morning; I have nothing to report to you."

Lord Arundel sat down in a chair opposite the old man.

"Well, Father, how are we this morning? A few words to say to your eldest son?"

The old man raised his head to look at his son. A white, straggly beard hung below a heavily wrinkled face from which two piercing but faded blue eyes stared at his questioner. He said nothing, but the beard concealed a pinching of the lips. Then he turned away, a bony hand on the table clenching into a fist.

"Come, come, Father. It is Council today. We shall need you dressed and present, if only to prove you are still with us. Your assent to our proceedings is all that is required, even just a nod when the question is put. Or just a 'yes', if you will condescend, but no outbursts as in January, if you please. I do not want to cause you more unpleasantness."

There was only a grunt in reply, and the old man gathered his nightgown around him. He did not meet his son's eyes. As satisfied as he could be, Arundel was rising to leave when the door was pushed aside, and a tall, imposing woman swept into the chamber.

"What the hell are you doing here, Alfred? You know the rules; one of each team, at least, always. What have you been putting into his head, hey? Father, what has he been plotting with you? Even you must know that this is forbidden."

The anger burnt fiercely in Lady Buckingham's face. It was not the first such breach, though none had seemed to have affected the passivity of their father, who reacted to her arrival by turning away completely, to stare out of the window. A hint of laughter, a snicker, escaped his lips.

"Calm down, sister dear, calm down. I was merely checking that we could haul the carcass down to give assent to our proceedings. Not a word, anyway, just a nasty scowl. But he's fit enough. I'll send the pages up to get him dressed and brought down in good time."

Lady Buckingham looked at the nurse with raised eyebrows, and received a nod. It was as Lord Arundel had said, the King had said nothing. *At least*, she thought, *these women could be relied on not to take sides, with their doses, and those of their husbands, dependent on unanimity among the four.* She turned to her father.

"Good that you have said nothing, Father. Remember that doses need all four of us. Your beloved son is not the arbiter of life and death. As for you, Alfred, another breach like this and we will have to double the guard and require passwords."

The two left the room, walking in silence until their ways could part. Door closed behind them, the old man leaned forward and spat into the breakfast bowl.

Doses indeed. Doses rationed to keep him in order. Doses whether he wanted them or not. He often felt that he would like them to stop, to die and be free of this domination and conflict. He had, half-heartedly, raised the matter with Miss Thomas, knowing full well that she and the others were as much in thrall as he. It had been reported. He knew that the nurses had been threatened thereafter, and that no opportunity would be granted.

And the struggle that would follow his death? For that, he had nothing but contempt. A struggle, also, in which he found the idea of victory for either side repulsive. A reason, perhaps the only one, to stay alive. Alfred, Arundel? Still an arrogant puppy, enjoying the fruits and trappings of power. He, more than others, had provoked that war and all that followed. Alice, my Lady Buckingham? As lacking in restraint as her brother, though with a trifle more patience. Willing to waste the Domain's substance on the futile search for other lands. The two youngest? Kent in slavish obedience to his sister, Sussex a born ditherer.

Such a mistake, to have had children, and then granted them a life as long as his, probably longer. Not a mistake made again after the war, where children rebelled against their immortal parents. Only a sterile nobility, dosed only if they were childless, had preserved the Domain from collapse. Such a mistake, too, to hope that when a dose expired, fertility would return. Instead, he had aged so rapidly that the next had left him in eternal and disabled old age.

He was still muttering to himself when pages arrived to prepare him for Council.

***

Clerks scurried around the Council Chamber. Once a Royal Chapel, those ecclesiastical fittings not pillaged in the latter days of the Catastrophe had been removed. On a dais at the east end was a throne, flanked on each side by two smaller but ornate chairs and immediately below it a long table, flanked by carved chairs, all pre-war and lovingly restored. A room far too big for the gathering that was to take place, but redolent with a certain symbolism that should not be too openly acknowledged. To the sides, there were smaller tables for secretaries and assistants. The Major-Domo, Lord Hunt, watched as papers were placed by each chair. Waiters assembled glasses and flagons on side tables.

All in order, the servants dismissed, Lord Hunt nodded to the guards at the west door, which they opened. The Councillors entered. Fifteen of them this time, each with a clerk or two to sit behind them. All seated, he nodded again, and a side door was opened to admit the Royal Lords and Lady: Alfred of Arundel, Alice of Buckingham, Michael of Sussex and Denis of Kent. Finally, the King was brought in on a wheelchair. All stood until nurses had him enthroned.

Arundel spoke, facing the assembly rather than his father.

"Your Majesty, will you be pleased to open this meeting of your Council?" The King, scarcely raising his head, took a gavel, and banged on a small metal table set alongside the throne. He then gave every appearance of falling asleep.

As agreed, it was Arundel's turn to preside. Most of the day's business was humdrum indeed, if routinely depressing. Reports from the Divisions and their Grounds; reports from the Commissions. The same stories: difficulties in obtaining quotas of labour and stock from all Grounds; complaints from the Board of Heredity about the drain of reproductive potential when attempts to sustain healthy breeding outside the Grounds yielded little of use; the slow but persistent demographic shortfall that followed.

Arundel yawned through it. The court functioned; his military plans were unhindered, even if frustratingly slow to advance. It needed just a little more force. Commissioners and Visitors to the Grounds were slack, and showed a tendency to go native. Shepherds protecting their flocks, rather than delivering what was needed. Go native. Yes, that was an expression he had used more and more as the litany of complaints grew over the years. Reports? They could keep making them, just as long as no jumped-up Councillor started calling for action. Breach the Outland, and our problems will be over. This year's Hunt should whet appetites, when we come to it.

He paid more attention to the report from Truth and Justice. There was increasing evidence of resistance to recruitment in the cities, the Reproductive Priority Zones. It was impossible to police the scattered dwellings among the acres of ruins in a thorough way. There were certainly unregistered inhabitants.

Hygienists and doctors reported high rates of notional miscarriages among families from which several had been Chosen. There were cases of open defiance, and the numbers sent to the short life of a Reclamation worker were growing. Worse, there was evidence of underground movement of people from one city to another to evade Service or criminal allocation to Reclamation and Recovery. *Surely*, Arundel thought, *they could apply more pressure here.* Too often, Visitors took the path of least resistance. He did not, however, interrupt or question the reports.

A report on heresy that followed provoked some uneasy laughter. A chronic problem, this, the belief that the King was not present in bodily form; that he had died defending his flock from the Deceiver, but overlooked his subjects from the ether. The oldest of the nobility recognised this as a *meme*, a notion that tapped into the remnants of earlier religions. No number of portraits circulated, no amount of sworn testimony (artfully distorted), could entirely eliminate this belief. Truth and Justice, represented by Lord Lane, always wanted to take stern measures, but on this matter both the Four themselves and Council were hesitant. The King might die, and in the near future at that. The succession would be disputed. An aethereal Monarch would at least postpone any showdown. For all Lane's fretting, the problem seemed not to threaten anyone, and it was not growing. The report was noted.

Then, at last, matters became more congenial: the year's Great Hunt. The Lord Chamberlain spoke. The site could be pinpointed with precision. Scouts reported Outies living openly in recovering no-mans-land in the south-west, in Cotswold, where the boundary was the Severn Sea. Fair game. They could be cut off with ease and then there would be some sport. Logistics? Two battalions to seal the inhabitants off, with nowhere to escape to. A train of five hundred to service the camps for the nobility. A holding pen for Outies to be reprogrammed. There would be many, more than usual. Arundel looked at Lane, who nodded. *Reprogrammed: now there was a word from the past*, he thought; it will need his most skilled men and a body of guards for containment. All seemed in order. The more strategic goal, the strike at the Outland itself, was not mentioned.

"Thank you, my Lord Chamberlain. All of you: We will choose who will join us in good time, but please send me names of your most promising young bloods. I think we can manage fifty or sixty to join us. Quickly, please; We will assemble here for the move west. Set out on June 15th, if we can. Take them unawares, as we have been much later for years. A summer surprise."

He grinned. He was about to close the meeting, but Lord Pendennis raised a hand. Notionally responsible for the Boundaries and Grounds, his repeated complaints about pressure on the latter had irritated Arundel for years. A stickler for the damned treaties, too. Assuming he would make the usual, and usually noted but ignored, complaint about the levies on the Grounds, Arundel nodded wearily.

"My Lords, we have yet to hear from Reclamation and Recovery, and Lord Dundonnell is absent. But we have before us both this year's labour statistics and the acreage of successful retrieval. My Lords, I cannot help noticing the increasing amount of labour recruited for recovery, and the appalling wastage that accompanies it. For what, my Lords? For gains in ground scarcely above what is occurring naturally elsewhere."

Lord Lane was quick to rise, anger in his voice.

"Reclamation is the path, the only path, to a future of any sort. The 'appalling wastage' that my Lord Pendennis refers to? Criminals, rebels both actual and potential. The sort to be relied on in honourable Service, my Lords? That we have more is a consequence of laxity in the management of Grounds. Not just the only use for such scum, but a deterrent to yet more disloyalty."

Arundel was at first merely irritated by this exchange. Pendennis was a moaner, another gone native. Lane was sound enough, though his obsession with clearance and the rooting out of treason was tedious. Then he got a surprise. After such an exchange, Council would remain silent, anxious to see how the Four reacted. A Council that would happily accept whatever they decided. Pendennis, however, had not finished.

"Criminals, only criminals? My Lords, I have evidence that some of those Chosen, and not just a few, are allocated to this deadly work. Chosen who might serve us here at Court, Chosen who might make soldiers or craftsmen, Chosen who might be alongside us at the Hunt. We should cease this drain on our resources."

There were gasps as he spoke; none could recall such a direct challenge, one that implied deceit. There was a long silence. Most knew that Pendennis was right. Right in more than one way, for productive labour was lost not only in Reclamation, but in the trappings of the Court, in the expanding military and security forces. A few recognised Pendennis' shrewdness. He attacked only reclamation. Not, at least not directly, the Court or the Hunt. They waited.

Lane's mind was racing. How in damnation does that lazy sod Pendennis know that we siphon off Chosen for our work. City scum anyway. Records are fudged, but how do I know what evidence he has, what affidavits he has in his papers? I dare not challenge him directly, but surely Arundel will just thank all for their advice, and close the meeting. Give him some ammunition; use his own oft-repeated words.

"My Lords, any shortage of labour has entirely other causes, as I have repeatedly told Council. A stricter control of the Priority Zones, the cities, would flush out the unregistered that infest the cities. I would extend that to the Grounds in general, where the evidence is that there is increasing hostility to our quotas. Even," he added, a note of sarcasm in his voice, "in that precious Northernmost Division. A greater Security presence is required on the ground. It is necessary to reconsider the brief we give to Visitors and their staff; if I may, I suggest that there is a disturbing tendency to go native, to regard the comfort of their wards a more sacred duty than the delivery of service to His Majesty."

Arundel did not get the chance to respond. Buckingham was on her feet before Lane had finished. She could not be silenced, not here, not in public.

"My Lords, these are high policy matters indeed. As my Lord Pendennis has observed, Lord Dundonnell is absent. His Majesty," she turned to the King, "will surely wish to consider this matter further, and to receive more detailed and practical advice. May I suggest that we postpone this question until after the Great Hunt, which I am sure will occupy us over the next few weeks? We can then consider the matter again." She glanced at Lane. "A commission of inquiry into the status of those sent to Reclamation is in order. We must ensure that Dundonnell attends."

Arundel controlled his anger. Our division is in the open, then. Kent will be with her, and I cannot be sure of that feeble Sussex. He'll be looking for that blasted Defoe's *via media*. Two on two again, at best. A mere majority of council would not be sufficient, and he could not be confident even of that. Most of them would be scared witless about expressing an opinion, and would back the suggestion, as it put off the evil hour when they had to come off the fence. Lane was useful, but there were more urgent matters on his mind. He would have preferred to let it vanish, but no great harm need be done. Dump that oaf Pendennis before we meet again. He nodded slightly, and nudged the King, who was, under pretence of sleep, very much awake during this brief exchange. The King banged his gavel.

"As it is proposed, so it shall be," a voice more quavering than ever.

All stood as nurses assisted the King to his wheelchair, and then left by a side door. Clerks gathered up their materials and left. Councillors and the Four turned to the tables behind them. Normally, this time was one of rather forced affability, in which each of the Four would circulate, congratulating or commiserating with each councillor, allowing themselves to be lobbied. Not so now. Arundel and Lane conspicuously remained together in conversation, while Buckingham and Kent were likewise engaged with Pendennis. Sussex merely looked lost, often left standing on his own. Remaining Councillors soon pulled away from their companions and one by one bowed to the throne and left. A row was coming; heads down, mouths shut. Lane and Pendennis? One or other was for the chop. See which, and we know the way the wind blows. Soon, after an exchange of looks between Buckingham and Arundel, Lane and Pendennis were dismissed. The Four gathered at the end of the long table at which the Councillors had sat. The servants vanished, followed by the Major-Domo. They were alone.

"So, Sister, a fine trick to play. What have you offered Pendennis in return for that little outburst? He's well dosed up already and I'd not agree to more. A mansion in your gift? Postponement is well and good, but we could have agreed that without having those councillors at each other's throats, in public. Now we will have to dismiss one or the other or both."

"No trick. I offered him nothing. And I doubt I would have got you to agree. Indeed, I would rather he had spoken to me in private, but he knows the rules. No meeting without your representative present. Yes, we could bury it, but the matter will remain. We are shedding capability. Nothing in the reports suggests that will cease, nor is the rate of reclamation anything other than pathetic."

Kent and Sussex said nothing; both edged nearer their elder champion.

"Pendennis must go. Give him something if you must, but we need to put him out of the centre. Maritime Affairs? That would keep him at Dover at the very least. And off Council."

"If he's to go, then Lane must go too. You know why. But that man has an unhealthy taste for rough handling. You heard Pendennis: Chosen fit for our service are wasting away on reclamation. Scale back the hunt, perhaps, instead? You have planned a monster this time. Or the military research?"

The latter was a direct hit; Arundel was forever dreaming of subduing the Outies, but the consumption of labour and materials had little to show there.

"Why? You heard him. More can be extracted from the Grounds. Lane and his subordinates know how to do it. Those damned Visitors have gone native, and you know it."

"I know no such thing; Can I remind you of what happened when Truth and Justice tried direct rule in the North Hampshire Ground. Increased infertility, and a near revolt. A mysterious rise in supposed miscarriages. Even in the cities, a bit of carrot rather than stick would not come amiss. Let them know what is happening to some of the Chosen and all hell will break loose. Evasion will be the least of it. Security will be playing hide and seek in the ruins to no good purpose."

There was a pause. Sussex looked from one to the other. Tied to Arundel, he was, nevertheless, always the one who tried compromise. It was an old argument, not easily resolved. More force, and quality declined; quantity too, soon after. More care, and the costs of provision were high. All depended on the great unknown: how fast will things improve, and how much does that depend on the success of reclamation or overseas plantation? Or on bending Outies to our will?

"Can we not simply tell both to let the matter rest? We lack evidence. Two dismissals will cause talk. And who do you have to replace either?"

This intervention provoked little but contempt, scarcely concealed, from both seniors. They glanced at each other. The Council was not secure. Partisans in either camp would know within days. Both Lane and Pendennis must go. And go publicly, but themselves kept quiet in the meantime. It was a familiar impasse. It was Lady Buckingham who spoke.

"Both to go? Both to be offered a dose three years from now subject to obedience in the meantime?"

"Agreed. Very well, we will summon both tomorrow: Pendennis for Maritime. Lane for military research?"

Nods. To each, their pet project: discovery for Buckingham, conquest for Arundel.

"Can we now turn to the matter of His Majesty?"

This was a matter of regular report, a matter for the younger pair to consult with doctors. The King's dose, one of the first, had been made before its consequences were fully known. Fit and healthy, he had lived unchanged but sterile for seventy years, a time in which he had come to loathe his children, conceived before his treatment. Let the doses lapse, he had mistakenly thought, and fertility would return. A younger brood might be more amenable. The sudden, accelerated aging that followed had taken him by surprise. His children had taken control. Measured doses kept him in the state of debilitated old age. Doses released by the agreement of all four children. Not a single large dose: both Arundel and Buckingham hoped that a death of one of the four would resolve the game provided the King died soon after. The King's muttered remarks, hinting at others who might have access to a hidden cache at his death or before, were not believed. Would he not have used it by now?

Kent reported.

"Physically, little change. There is mental deterioration, but the doctors are of the opinion that this is not some kind of dementia, but a suppressed anger. He has again tried to get a nurse to kill him, but not in any very determined way. There are fits of rage, and the doctors do worry about a stroke."

"So, the risk is greater. We stick by our agreement, yes? Death will not be acknowledged, merely ill-health. Are we sure of the doctors and nurses?"

"As much as we can. All depend on us for repeats."

"Repeats? Yes, that's the last matter, stocks. We need another audit. They are not infinite. We should start rationing doses more strictly. Shorter times, certainly, to keep order, but we will have to devise other rewards sooner rather than later."

Uncontentious but unpalatable. Hopes dashed had led to trouble more than once. The four parted, leaving the one-time chapel empty. A chapel that had seen greater sovereigns come, worship and be interred.

12. Military Rule

Cornwallis' force drew up in impressive array outside the Council Hall at nine o'clock. Seven assorted mobiles and forty men. Forty men, moreover, all visibly armed with rifles. Eight men and a sergeant had been left at the bridge. Grounders, some of whom had again congregated at the main entrance, backed off in astonishment. Ordering the remainder to stand at ease by the mobiles, he entered the Hall with a small squad. A few of his own men rose to attention, along with three Security guards.

"Lieutenant Shorten?"

"Upstairs with the Deputies, sir."

He withdrew papers from his pouch.

"I have here a proclamation of direct Military Rule in this Division, authorised by the Visitor. I am now solely responsible for all civil and security matters. I shall pin one copy in here. See to it that copies are pinned outside the main entrance, and outside the Proctor's station. And some for the bailiff in the city." He turned to the Security sergeant. "How many men do you have in the Ground?"

"Five, sir."

"Are they all here in this building?"

"Yes, sir."

"How many mobiles?"

"Two, sir."

"You will immediately collect your men and any gear, and return across the bridge in both mobiles, and report to whoever is in charge at the bridge. Commandant Hope may not be available."

The sergeant stirred himself. The lieutenant descended and reported. Both Norman and Arkell families had been taken to the Corridor. Now, they were in the care of Jacks, the Warden of the Transfer Station at Barlow. A single guard had been left at each home. The mayor had been transferred to a cell in the

160

Proctor's station, and a single guard left with him. He handed over the hygienist's report. The mayor had been struck once at the moment of arrest. He had contusions on his face consistent with this. No serious damage. There were ten men at Midhope, three shadowing the farmer and his wives, the others hidden near the boundary. Nothing to report. The Deputies were waiting in the mayor's office.

"One other thing, sir. You told the Proctors to assemble at eight. Since you had not returned, I took the liberty of sending all but three back home. They can be summoned?"

"Thank you, Lieutenant. Yes, have them reassemble at eleven. Captain Phelps is also to be there; see that a message gets to him."

The lieutenant left. Cornwallis went upstairs to the office where the deputies were waiting. Introductions were needed. John Markham looked about 40. He had always worked in Supply, in the distribution of essentials to and from the bridge, and his role as Deputy, part-time as it was, was scarcely different, a book-keeping exercise. Short, thin and already stooped, he seemed in awe of the major. One wife, two children: one Chosen, the other transferred south to Civic College at sixteen. *Just two offspring and no Muss*, thought Cornwallis; might be due for transfer.

Amelia Franklin was very different. Seemingly about 60, she had sat still and upright in her chair, eyes, eyes with an appraising look, mostly focused on the major. A Muss in her time, all four children Chosen; husband died 30 years ago. Then a teacher: reading, writing and language. Deputy Head until made Deputy Mayor, when her teaching duties became part-time. Social Service seemed to be the best summary of her role, liaising with the hygienists and teachers. It was she, rather than the mayor or Markham who dealt with the city and its bailiff.

As Cornwallis learnt from them about the way the Ground was run, the more of a puzzle it became. The neat admin chart that he had acquired from the Visitor did not do justice to the extremely informal way in which business was conducted in practice. City folk kept themselves apart. There was the bailiff, notionally subordinate to the mayor, and two other schools not far from the bridge. The transfer of supplies in and stock out was the main business conducted at the bridge. The Reynolds family were the masters there, helped, so Amelia said, by the city folk. 'City folk', the major noted again, not squatters. Mr Norman? Here, the conversation got very interesting and awkward. One conclusion might be that the mayor was *very* good at delegating, since Norman was relied on heavily, but Cornwallis was rapidly coming to a less charitable assessment. The news of his death had, of course, spread.

"Can you tell us anything about Mr Arkell's condition, Major?" asked Amelia, in very pointed way, "I believe that he is now in the cells where Mr Norman was held."

Silently, he handed her the hygienist's report. She grunted and returned it.

"Mr Arkell is now guarded by one of my men, Muss Franklin. As you can see, he is not seriously harmed. He will remain this side of the bridge until I receive instructions. In the meantime, if either of you require information from him, you may ask to see him, in the presence of one of my men. He will be moved from the cells as soon as possible. Ask whoever is here."

"Scarcely necessary, Major," said Amelia.

She gave another grunt, and her rigid posture relaxed. The major continued. They were to assume responsibility for running the Ground. They were to do so full time. His force would need billeting. This office was theirs until the telephone was repaired. There was more, a lot more, to ask and to arrange. By the time they had finished, it was nearly eleven. He went downstairs; more instructions. He made a brief report to be sent over the bridge, and leaving the lieutenant in charge, he walked down to the Proctors' station. The entrance hall and reception were packed, and the assembled Proctors struggled to make a passage. The proclamation of his authority was already pinned to the noticeboard. No need to call out; the men were silent and expectant.

"You will be aware that I am now in charge of this Ground, and you will be aware of why. Captain Phelps, please stand beside me." A pause, and a little shuffling in the crowded room.

"Your captain remains your commanding officer, answerable to me. You will resume normal duties under his command. You will be aware that the mayor is held in your cells on serious charges. No one is to speak to him other than the Deputies, who will be admitted to the cells by my man. Any matters normally referred to him will be raised with the Deputies at the Mayoral office. The captain and I will now be in the guardroom for a few minutes. Feel free to wait outside, if you wish, but do not disperse until you have received orders from the captain."

The two men entered the guardroom. They went to the cell holding the mayor, who rose as they approached.

"Right, Phelps. You can see that Mr Arkell is not seriously harmed. Isn't that so, Arkell?" The mayor nodded. "As soon as possible, he will be moved from here, but not over the bridge for the time being. Now get ready to get your force back into routine. I want patrols along the Outie boundary and the Corridor maintained, but nowhere within a mile of Midhope."

The captain left. Arkell was released from the cell, and sat down on a chair. The major extracted a story that differed in no material way from that given to the Commandant. It was damning, and the mayor knew it well. Head down, he answered questions in a monotone. Pressed, no, no more cases like that of Pickless; yes, he knew Norman wanted his son to stay. The story of his connection with the farmer all those years ago came out in order, as it had not with the Commandant. Eventually, though, a bit of spark entered his soul. He looked up at the major.

"What was expected, Major? I was told, we want so many fit ones for Service. We want so much stock each year, so many seeds, by the bushel. Where I came from, Major, a family were lucky if they had one fit for Service, and many Defectives, defective beyond useful contribution, Chosen or not. Here, fecundity, and two or more routinely chosen, often all the boys. Do you think all the families rejoiced, Major? When all were Chosen, like Pickless' sons? Do you think I did not show my concern to the Visitor? Even the suicide had no effect. And we were expected to maintain output without matching transfers in. Praise, Major, but always with a threat behind it. There were years when without Pickless, I would have been given a talking to, and not an easy one. And the Visitor, Major, the Visitor let drop that there was talk of abandonment if we did not meet demands from the Domain."

And the Visitor, in turn, was pressured by Council, as Bohun had made clear. Cornwallis got someone to collect the mayor and take him to his apartment, under guard. Then outside and a quick walk around the town and back to the Hall, which was filling up with people waiting to see the deputies. The entrance was guarded again by a single, familiar Proctor. A cart rumbled up from the bridge with supplies. What next? Replace the trooper at the Norman's house with a couple of Proctors. Pickless could wait. He was under guard anyway, and the boundary watched. It must be the city. He went upstairs to the office. There was talking inside, and he waited in the corridor. Soon, two women emerged, surprised to see him outside, waiting for them to finish their business.

"Were you asked to send another up?" Nods. "Tell them to wait until I come downstairs." He entered.

"Everything all right here? Good. Arkell is being brought back to his apartment, if you need him later. Muss Franklin, I think you know the bailiff and where he works?"

"Mr Stefan Mysliborski, yes Major, I have frequent visits to his office."

A fancy name, thought the major. Seeing his expression, Amelia explained.

"This city had people from all over before the Catastrophe. Some retained a pride of heritage."

Much to the disgust of Truth and Justice, she left unsaid. Efforts to allocate names and unsettle families in the distant past had caused yield to plummet. It had taken a new Visitor to restore calm.

"You'll find other unfamiliar names here, Major. Some rather unconventional beliefs too. Some topics are best avoided when co-operation is required."

Markham suppressed a snort, duly noted by the major. He said nothing, though.

"Very well, Muss Franklin, we are going to pay a visit. I take it you can manage for a while, Mr Markham?" A nod, and a distinct look of relief.

Their mobile soon entered the fringes of the city. The Major had not really looked at it. Mostly, overgrown ruins, and side streets now impassable to mobiles. The growth was vigorous almost to excess; ivy smothered most remaining walls. Trees. often large, sprung from the abandoned streets. Often, whole stretches were just overgrown rubble. The road was evidently kept clear, with some trunks cut up along its sides. He turned to the deputy.

"I heard that this part of the city was never bombed or contaminated. But some places seem far more damaged than others?"

"Not quite correct, Major. There was plague, but it burnt out. Much of the south was contaminated; it's is still barren and dangerous. The east, the Domain, was not so badly hit, but fertility is very low. The standing ruins here in the north are mostly older houses. The big buildings were bombed, so we were told, but not contaminated. Newer ones held far more metal and were demolished to get the metal across the bridge. Metal and glass. Nearly all gone now, except in the south, but that's still a risky place. There are a few tough ones left up here. Get away from the cleared roads and you'll find gardens and old parks. They grow a lot to eke out the basic rations."

As they approached the centre, she pointed out the small groups of maintained houses, mostly a few next door to each other in a row. The side streets there had been cleared, and a few handcarts stood along the sides. Soon, they turned off the main road, and she started giving instructions to the driver as more cleared side streets went past. Eventually they drew up by a row of well-maintained houses. A central one had a flag hanging limply from its pole. A Proctor stood outside and saluted. The door bore the Declaration of Military Rule. *Good for the lieutenant*, thought the Major; the man was proving more than capable.

The door was slightly open. Inside, they found a gloomy hallway, and no kind of reception. Pinned to one door, though was a handwritten notice saying, simply 'Bailiff'. The Major knocked, and a gruff voice invited them in.

A short, bald, middle-aged man rose from behind a massive but shabby desk, clearly pre-war and thus at least 250 years old. His back was to a window in which cracks were covered in some kind of tape. In front of the desk were an assortment of sofas and chairs. One wall supported a few shelves, on which untidy piles of files rested.

"Welcome, Muss Amelia. And you, sir, must be Major Cornwallis. Once the notice was out, I thought it would not be long before I had a visit or was summoned, so I stayed here to await developments, as it were. Sit down, sit down. Can I get you any refreshments?" The major shook his head.

"You know what has happened, Mr Mysliborski? Good. Now, I have a few questions. The evader, Mark Norman, appears to have left a present for a boy in the city. He left it to his father to deliver. Unfortunately, as you probably know, Mr Norman is dead. We are anxious to speak to any boy who may have known Mark."

"There's not much in common between our lads and those up the hill, Major. They don't mix much. We see any of them down here, and we warn them off as Relic hunters. There are slim pickings as it is. And they give themselves airs, some of them."

"Please ask around, would you? We know he knew someone. There is no penalty here, Mr Bailiff, quite the contrary, if you get my meaning. But another question for you. The boy vanished over the Outie boundary, but we think he's a clever one. Anywhere here someone could hide out, any odd happenings to your knowledge?"

"No sign of any boy or fugitive, Major. You'll have seen that there are plenty of possible hiding places, certainly, but any signs of life or thieving, I'd be told and we'd set a trap. There are few that steal from gardens and plots. We deal with them ourselves, Major. He'd know enough not to stay in the south."

Rather than send them across unchosen, thought Cornwallis. As well that Hope had not learnt of that.

"It's early days, Bailiff, and the boy had food with him." He looked hard at Mysliborski. "Any sign and you are to let us know, and keep him under observation till we arrive. This is no petty theft. Any concealment, and Security will be all over your city. Out of my hands, then, Mr Mysliborski."

The bailiff returned the look, then glanced at Amelia.

"Security, Major? I've had reported some strange happenings last night but one. A commandant, Major, a Security commandant, crashed a mobile in the middle of the night down Wadley Lane. One wheel broken. In a dead end as it happens. By himself, oddly enough, and lost with it. Needed some help. Lucky to be in a nest."

The major frowned.

"A nest is the name for an inhabited street, Major," said Amelia.

"Apologies, Major. No surprise that he was lost. But he knocked on a door and got some to show him to the bridge and dished out a lot of credits for the help. Not looking for the boy by himself, surely? A team came across yesterday to tow the mobile away. More credits. A good haul for us these days, Major, and it's not a source we'd normally look to."

There was little else to be gained. The major passed on the information that Security were, for now, forbidden to enter, a message that caused the bailiff to raise his eyebrows. He rose to leave. Amelia held him by the arm.

"Excuse me, Major, but since I'm here, and driven too, could I beg a few minutes of the bailiff's time? I can save myself another journey. I'll be out in a minute."

Cornwallis nodded and left. He talked for a few minutes to the Proctor outside. The man was keen to be relieved. The city was an unwelcoming place. No Proctor had ever been molested in any way, but all felt uneasy anywhere but at the bridge itself. Patrols were rare, and the mayor had left matters of the law to the bailiff. Soon, Muss Franklin emerged. They drove back in silence, but before they entered the Hall, she drew the major aside.

"Congratulations, Major. It's rarely that man says anything to the purpose to those from the other side, or even to us uphill. It's usually bullying Security following up on a hygienist he has to deal with. Having a commandant begging for help tickled him no end. I took a liberty, Major, and vouched for you telling the truth, about no consequences. City kids did meet with some of those from uphill. He did not give any names. It seems they had found ways of crossing the river, and his lot were thinking of Relics. He called them off a while ago. Give it a day or two, and you'll get some names, but don't press them on anything other than Mark, or they'll clam up on his instructions. Oh, and one other thing, Major. I don't like to say so, but folk in Bradfield and on the farms are a bit prejudiced when it comes to the city. You'll have heard the term squatters. I'd not talk about this in front of Mr Markham. He grumbles about his duties at the bridge, and he dislikes the bailiff."

Astonished, the Major thanked her warmly, and they went inside. There was news. The cut in the line had been found. Easy, really, because the line was on poles all the way to the bridge. It had been repaired. Office swap to follow, with troopers carrying files and furniture between the two. A long call with Bohun. The autopsy was complete. Repeated kicks to head and body. Massive internal injuries. Commandant Hope suspended, but it would not be for long. Permission to hold onto the mayor and the Picklesses. A briefing on city recruitment and investigations to reach him as soon as possible. Finding his assigned quarters, the Major called it a day.

***

Seven o'clock the following morning, and Cornwallis set off for Midhope with three mobiles and 20 men. No need for surprise; the vehicles roared into the yard. While the men waited outside, he interrogated Pickless within. A very different conversation to the last. Presented with the mayor's confession, Pickless had few options. Yes, it was true, there was an evader. Yes, his name was Jones. Yes, he had some power to keep the Outies at bay. Yes (not a betrayal, because it was obvious) his wives knew. Yes, I gave him food and other essentials. Yes, the boys found out, but I gave them cause not to speak out. No, I don't know where he went and I took trouble not to know.

"You took trouble? Why might that be?"

"Jones was not from round here, Major. He didn't say from where. I've only his word for it that his name is Jones. Must be from further south, that's obvious. But he said that Security had ways to force folk to say all they knew, even the most stout-hearted. Didn't sound good for me, Major, but I could see his point.

When we were together just beyond the bounds, he would stay put till I was out of sight down the hill."

"When did you last see Jones, Pickless?"

"Straight after the selection was announced. He made it clear he was off. And we've had the Outie raid since. I think he'll be far away now, Major."

So far, just the truth, more or less; no point else since they had the evidence, he thought. But the major would want more about Mark. To his surprise, though, the next question seemed to go down a side-track.

"Were you not concerned that the boys would say something earlier? You spun them a yarn, but some of them might have known better."

"Ah, yes, the great patriot. Yes, Major, I was prepared for the worst. Jones made himself scarce for a couple of weeks when the stint was finished. At least, he would have escaped if there had been a raid. Nothing happened, at least not until now. Then we heard Mark was Chosen. Jones left, and I have a feeling it's for good."

"Just one more question for now. When we were here, you'd had an Outie raid, and we followed it a bit. Any more?"

"No, but as your men will tell you, I've not taken any stock beyond my walls since, and Outies are smart. You saw none when you went over the Boundary? Be sure they saw you."

Cornwallis turned to go. There was more, especially relating to Mark, but he was anxious to spread the search more widely. Pickless was not going anywhere, and he seemed anything but suicidal. The farmer touched him by the arm.

"When are we to be removed, Major? When I heard the mobiles, I assumed it was Security. There's animals here need tending."

"When I decide, Mr Pickless, when I decide. The news may not have reached you, but the whole Ground is under my command, my complete command. It is likely to stay that way for a while. You will continue operations as normal, but there will always be a trooper at your side. I have more questions. You'll not be moved until there are people to run the farm."

With that, the major left, assembled a squad, and retraced the steps they had taken only three days earlier. It started raining, a steady, depressing drizzle. Spreading out, they searched over about two miles of boundary, and one or more into the west. There were few possible hiding places, most with no sign of life, and offering little shelter. A few had the remains of fires and Outie excrement, all old. There were some recently burnt patches. At noon, he sent a party up the narrowing valley of the stream to the west, which bent round out of sight into woodland, while the rest scoured the north. Here were the remains of many walls. Farms, once. There seemed little consistency in which areas remained in the Ground, and which were abandoned to the Outies. Many potential hiding places, but all roofless, overgrown, or with old traces of Outie use. There was a brief moment of excitement when an entrance leading down was found in a ruined building. But after clearing away a tangle of brambles and nettles, they encountered a massive, rusted metal door. To be noted, surely, for possible retrieval, but it had clearly not been opened for years, indeed, possibly since the last days of the war. No sign of recent occupation anywhere.

Sending two men up the valley to recall the others, he and the remainder waited by the wall where they had looked previously. Rather idly, the major clambered over the debris at the entrance he had noticed previously. Exploring the courtyard, he discovered the side door to the building. Unlocked. He entered, and looked around in the dim light. He saw the old fire, the Outie excrement. But the only door inside was the massive one of metal that had clearly remained shut for ages. To be noted, but valuable though it might be, he could not see how it could be salvaged.

His rather cursory inspection was brought to an abrupt halt when a trooper appeared at the door.

"Shots, sir, from up the valley."

Cornwallis ran out. His men had spread out and taken cover. The rain had stopped, visibility was improving but no movement could be seen. He ordered an advance, one group on each side of the valley. The terrain was far from easy; burnt patches, scrubby birch, open moor, and many old walls. They advanced for about ten minutes. Another shot, and then two troopers appeared, moving towards them, rifles at the ready. One fell. The other stopped and dropped. The original squad emerged behind them, cover and run, cover and run, with a few shots at targets invisible to the major. As they reached the two below them, though, shadowy figures emerged on either side, between the party and the major's line.

Those with the major opened fire. One figure fell. Others, dodging and weaving, retreated fast.

"Hold your fire. Stay put. Fire only if you see any returning."

The valley party now resumed their journey. No more shots were fired, and no one fell. The major went downhill to meet them. One, arms over the shoulders of two others, had a heavy bolt protruding from his thigh. Another had a roughly bandaged arm, and torn gear, but walking. Ordering a staged retreat for the rest, Cornwallis and four men moved carefully forward to where the Outie had fallen. Dead, bullet through the chest. No weapon, but a quiver full of crossbow bolts. His companions must have grabbed the weapon as they fled.

The major inspected the body. Surprisingly normal in height and limbs. Face, not so much; lopsided and with a lower jaw that protruded out of all proportion. Clothes, mostly woollen, but an oiled coat of some other material. He heaved the body to remove the quiver, which he slung over his shoulder. The party then retreated, cautiously, but without incident.

At the farmhouse, he found the injured man flat on the dining room table. Muss Pickless had already cut away his clothing, and was washing the wound.

"Are you not afraid of contamination?" was the major's first, surprised, reaction.

"What, that I might lose my fertility? How old do you take me for, Major? Oh, we know that contact is supposed to contaminate anyone, and to be passed on, and so on. But it's easy to put two and two together. I've some hygienist experience, Major; apprenticed before someone decided to transfer me here. By the way, this one's not lethal. I know how to deal with this, if you'll allow me. Leave one man with me, and we'll get this out."

He nodded. Now he needed a debrief. The valley party had entered a wooded area, and it became hard to see if there were ruins. There was a track near the stream, and with the rain, the ground was muddy. There were several footprints in both directions. Seeing this, they halted. The messengers reached them, and were sent back on the run. The sergeant had been about to order a retreat when a band of Outies had appeared around a bend from the west and fired off arrows. Hence the arm wound, *only a graze, sir, the arrow went past.* They had returned fire. The Outies dropped or hid in the trees on either side. No more firing until they were nearly out of the wood. They had emerged onto the scene facing the major. Any Outies hit? Not sure, sir, they all dropped. Numbers? At least a dozen, sir, likely more.

And more on either side ahead too, thought the major. How many? 30? 40? Even more? And why such determination? Faced with guns, Outies invariably retreated. And their raids were made in small numbers, six or seven at most. What was worth these numbers, and this degree of risk? Surely not the evader, they could simply move him further west if they had him. He was puzzling over this, and about to arrange for billeting and duty turns when the sergeant spoke again.

"Pardon me, sir, but could I ask a question? When we were in that wood, sir, it wasn't like other places where we have moved in to drive Outies away. More like the Royal forests, with big, healthy-looking trees, not the sickly scrub we usually move through." The sergeant remembered encounters in the damaged lands where his company had assisted several Hunts.

"Sorry, sergeant, I've no explanation. You know there are more or less contaminated patches within the Domain. I guess there are a few to the west as well. All these moors look pretty healthy to me. The farmers burn them to improve the grazing."

Arrangements made, the major, a driver and the injured man returned to Bradfield. Bar ten left at the farm, the rest followed. The trooper was cheerful enough. A quick call across the river, and the driver continued on to deliver the wounded man to doctors across the bridge. The major sat down to write a report to go across the river in the morning. A phone call was all very well, but he was not entirely sure that such calls were not listened in to. It was an unusual encounter, one that was best kept from Security until Bohun knew.

***

Come morning, report despatched, Cornwallis dealt with matters in the Office, talked a while to the Deputies who assured him things were returning to normal, and then sat for a while in the main Council Hall, as those with business passed to and fro to see the Deputies. Many gave anxious nods as they passed him on the way in, but looked more friendly on departure. One was the hygienist who had examined the mayor. On a whim, the major called him over on his way out.

"Were you also the one who treated Mr Norman, Mr Hygienist?" A nod, but a look of apprehension crossed the man's face.

"Not to worry, man, the doctor's report casts no doubt on your conduct. Did Commandant Hope reassure you?"

A headshake. To be expected. A question or two about his business with the Deputies, and the hygienist started to relax. To the major's surprise, the fertility of the Ground was not just high, a well-known fact; it was very high indeed. Hard to be sure for the girls, but over 80% of the boys, and a low rate of miscarriages or defectives. So, many that were fertile were across the bridge each Selection? Yes. Unofficially, since selection was beyond his remit, he had matched the names of those selected against his test records. As an apprentice further south, his boss had rarely seen those fertile Chosen, but there were fewer of them.

He would have continued the conversation further, but a trooper summoned him to the telephone. It was Lord Bohun, interspersed with the Visitor. We have your report. Outies killed, or at least one, on their own territory. How far from the Boundary? Why so many? Why were your men so far in?

It dawned on Cornwallis that he had unthinkingly breached the terms of the Treaties, too wrapped up in the search. His men had penetrated deeply, and had exchanged fire. Now Bohun was worried that Outies would make a formal complaint, and attract unwanted Court attention northwards, even to the extent of reversing the order of command. He was told, very firmly, no more crossing of the bounds by his men. Absolutely no more, even if either evader were seen.

It did not rest there. He was able to take the following day to travel around at least the 'uphill' parts of his new command, talking in a relaxed way to farmers, reassuring all that business as usual was resumed, and that the deputy mayors were the ones to turn to. A brief call at the Pickless farm was reassuring. No. no trace of the evader, no signs of Outie activity. He told Phelps to ease off on the intensive patrols. Wherever Mark Norman was, assuming he still lived, it would not be at loose uphill. Back to normal, Captain, and give your men some rest. An evening call upset his plans to return to the city the following day. Present yourself at Conisbrough, Major, by eleven at the latest tomorrow.

***

Just in time, the major's mobile drew up in the castle yard. He was led up to the panelled room that had seen Hope suspended. Only Bohun and the Visitor were present, bar a clerk who sat unobtrusively to one side. No DC, then. While the clerk took notes, Cornwallis found himself giving, again, an account of his actions beyond Midhope. This was carefully redacted by the Visitor, telling the clerk what to write. Then a mass of questions about the operation of the Ground. His reasons for leaving the Picklesses in place. The status of the Norman and Arkell families. The regime of the deputy mayors. Meeting the bailiff. It seemed to him that the questions were almost routine. There was no hint of interrogation, nor any mention of Hope or Security. It took a while. The clerk blotted his final sheet, and offered the whole to be read. A good summary, thought Cornwallis, and was happy to sign it. The other two signed it without even reading.

"Thank you, Mr Brigstocke. The original to my safe as usual. Ten copies, six to Council as usual, and dictate to the clerks at Windsor in the meantime. That is all." Brigstocke gathered his papers and withdrew.

"Very good, Major, we can talk freely. The DC is off the premises. With Hope out of action, he has to stir his backside. Inspecting the Barriers today, we'll not be interrupted. So, what the hell happened at Midhope that brought the Outies out in such numbers? It's trouble if they complain, though it will take ages before we get any protest. We will have some explaining to do if that happens."

"Lots of ruins there, sir, any of them could be a hideout. I'd split the platoon to cover more ground. One lot went further than I thought. When we'd finished elsewhere, I sent a couple to call them back. No sign of Outies up till then. Then the Outies attacked them. There was cover, and we couldn't get good targets. But my men retreated in good order, and we gave them heavy fire when we saw them in the open. Just the one body. They vanished westwards."

"But such numbers, Major. Don't they usually run at the first sign of trouble?"

"Yes, I have never heard of such behaviour, sir, other than a few engagements when the Hunt is closing in, and they are desperate. I wondered if they knew where the evader was, and thought we were getting too close or too thorough. They did run in the end, though, when it was clear we were withdrawing. Why they would take risks to protect him, I don't know. They hold off raiding up there, and the farmer thinks it's down to the evader. I wondered about some kind of deal, and that's the best I can do."

"I'll have to include this in the normal report," said the Visitor, "and you, Charles, will have to do the same. We will minimise it as much as possible. One Outie killed? It's happened before, without any comeback. We can hope it passes by with no complaint. If they do go official on us, though, Major, we'll have to go for overenthusiasm in the search. I doubt if it would have consequences in the way of disciplinary action; the Four excuse keenness, especially Arundel, and you've a good record sheet. It's usually just blood price the Outies want, anyway. Our lot will want to settle and be done; they've the Hunt on their minds just now."

"The worry for me, though, is what T & J and that bastard Lane will make of this. If Hope had not been such a murdering oaf, the DC would have been licenced to occupy the Ground already. Even if it waits till after the Hunt, the list of mishaps here is enough to raise the whole issue again. And whatever happens to Hope, guilty or not, once he's out of isolation here and given a defender, there are things he will say that will be music to Lane's ears. He may not be the Commissioner any more, but he's close to Arundel."

The major, junior though he was, had gained the confidence of both nobles. He knew their fear. A Security takeover to extract even more for Service. Aggravation in the RPZ, labour problems in the rest, and a lessening of the Division's importance to a degree that justified its transfer to Reclamation for good. A baby farm to feed Lane's pet projects; projects that Arundel would tolerate provided he was not in any way inconvenienced. Buckingham would resist, but not in the face of damning statistics.

"Major," said the Visitor, "we must do what we can to fend this off. We need some healthy statistics on stock transfers. It's lucky that Selection is over for the year, but the city may be called on out of season. No mad rush, but we need to get the Grounders to co-operate, at least for a while, and not cut up rough. I have hinted as much before to that mayor of theirs, but the man is under arrest. Not the brightest spark in any case. I always got more sense out of poor Norman. Anyone you can deal with?"

Cornwallis thought, *Amelia had sense, and she was trusted by the bailiff.* Any squeezing would fall mainly on the RPZ, on the city, unless there were many transfers in from further south. That would start a chain reaction of trouble to Security's advantage. City folk were more devious, but cynical too: bargains could be struck.

"Leave it with me, sir. There are a few leads I can follow. But there is another thing, sir. When I was at the boundary, it struck me that the land was pretty clean beyond. One of my sergeants noticed the same. It's theirs, Treaty and all that. But if we last for a year or two, maybe the Outies would trade?"

"Not only there, Major. That forest along the river, where we've had all that trouble? It's clean as can be, as are the moors to the west. There are even patches to the north. We could have asked officially to expand the Ground. It would have attracted attention. Attention we don't want while there are those wanting more forceful management. Talk to the Outies? That's for the future, perhaps. We've never provoked them enough to retaliate, if they still can, so it would be tough talk. We don't want Kingsmen and still less Security all over us. We'll let it lie."

The major was dismissed. A quick meal with the reserve platoon across the yard, and he was on his way back to Bradfield.

Beyond the Bounds

13. A Valuable Prize

The hunter and his companion walked with Mark past the old dam. A couple of miles later, and another came in sight. On their side of the valley was a large but ramshackle building surrounded by other, smaller ones nearby. Widely overhanging eaves sheltered what turned out to be drystone walls rammed with soil. Windows were shuttered and glassless. Three Outies were sitting on benches outside. As they approached, one shouted out, and others emerged from the houses, staring at Mark. More shouts, and a crowd gathered around them. Some reached out to touch Mark's clothes.

"Stand away, all of you, stand away. Yes, this is a Grounder. No, not kidnapped, here of his own accord to avoid the sterile service. Is the Chief of House here?"

The hunter kept a close grip on Mark while speaking. Other than his appearance, he had no authority over these people, whose land he was passing through. But the boy was more than a useful stud; he had information that needed to go higher. Soon, an elderly woman, better dressed than the others, emerged from the house. The crowd parted to let her approach the hunter.

"Rhianna Evans, Chief of this Riding, and certainly of this House. And you are?"

"Michael O'Neill at your service, ma'am, licenced hunter. My team have freedom to traverse in pursuit of game or predators."

Rhianna indeed recognised the insignia, and had heard the name, but the man lacked the precious rifle that hunters carried.

"And where's your gun, Mr O'Neill? And who is this that you've brought with you?"

"My gun? We were tracking a bear, ma'am, moving south. The trail led to an open bothy not three miles from here, and we found this boy; a different scent indeed. Lucky he was not to be killed when the bear entered the bothy. He struck a match and the bear left. This boy is more important than the bear, but we were not far behind. My rifle is with a companion. He knows how to use it. He and the rest are still on its trail. They will be here by sunset, I hope, with a bearskin that is the property of this Riding."

There was a stir in the group around them. They'd heard of bears, and of the slaughtered sheep, and even people, that followed the animals' movements south, but none had seen one. A skin brought in would be a wonder indeed.

"And the boy? More like a man as far as we are concerned, Mr Hunter." There was female laughter. Mark blushed and looked down. More laughter followed. The rare opportunities to acquire Grounder sires was a subject of many a ribald conversation. A few had even seduced farmers straying over the bounds.

"His name is Mark, Ma'am. He's an evader. Does that mean anything to you?" A shaking of heads, though Rhianna merely frowned.

"You know about the Grounds, though, I'll be bound. Where they have bonny babies with no problems?" Nods and more laughter, though now subdued.

"What you may not know is that many of those bonny babies get taken into the Domain." Here, several of those present made signs to avert the evil eye. "Get taken into sterile service when they are this age or even younger, sometimes three or more from the same household. There are a few who reject that and run. Evaders, they call them, and a greater crime cannot be imagined. And there are few of them, because where's to run to? They get taught that we cut them up and eat them."

A ribald voice interrupted. "Waste of good flesh that, isn't it so, ladies?" More laughter.

"And why do you think he risked being for the pot, and was here deep into our land? I'll tell you. Happens he met another like him, but much older, one hidden out just on the bounds and been there for years. One who has knowledge that helps the cause. That one's in more danger than Mark here. And there's others on the Ground that are turning against their sacrifices."

He turned to the Chief, who was now staring at him hard. There were not many outside her Riding that knew about that man. Even within, all were instructed to stay clear.

"Ma'am, I have no authority here, other than free passage in the course of my work. But this one should be moved west. You know why. It's too close for comfort if there's a big push to capture him. Old-timers should talk to him soon, and take action. That means sending a message and moving him where he's needed. Not keeping him hidden here for your own satisfaction. In the meantime, all three of us are in need of a bit of real food. I'll be staying the night, with your consent, but I must move on in the morning, bear or no bear. With luck, there'll be a bearskin here before dark."

Rhianna gave him a long look. Then she nodded. The trio were sat on a bench outside, a table brought and a succession of plates and refills of mugs were provided by young women, and the not so young, giving Mark a close inspection. Mark himself started wondering about what the hunter had said. He clearly knew more about the Ground than the rest. Had he met Jones? Soon, however, the fumes from the ale rising in his head, Mark fell asleep on the hunter's shoulder, who warded off those suggesting a bed indoors. A little later, a young Outie left southwards.

"I've sent him to Edale, Mr O'Neill. There are horses there, and stages beyond. We'll move the boy along the same route, the day after tomorrow, and he'll no doubt get met by someone coming the other way. You don't want him too far from the bounds, after all?"

The hunter nodded. No chance of getting Mark on his way right now, and he had other calls, the more so if his men had not killed the bear. But long before sunset there were cries of excitement. A party came from the south, the four of them carrying a huge animal hung beneath two fresh-cut poles. The hunters deposited their load, the whole bear and not just a skin. O'Neill showed the onlookers the claws and the teeth. Two of his men started skinning. Completed, and the skin pegged out, the four restrung the glistening carcass and marched away to dispose of it. No, not good to eat unless you are really hungry.

Another meal in the dark. Then the Chief showed O'Neill to a small room, and the others to a larger one with many pallets. Mark, she also led to a room at the far end of the building, a room in which she fastened the window shutters with very firm bolts on the inside. Once the building had quietened, she stationed herself by the door. There was to be no free for all here. Rations were to be granted on likely outcomes, not on off chances. She called a name, quietly, and a young woman was let in, and the door closed behind her. Three others in turn, the last giving her a thumbs down; she padlocked the door and left for her own room.

It was a haggard Mark who was released for breakfast. The hunters departed south, and he was left, fortunately enough, with little to do. A herd of remarkably normal cattle were driven down from the north, a few calves among them. The herdsmen stopped for food, while their dogs watched the cows. Then they moved on. He was able to start looking at those around him. Close up, there were few with serious deformities, and all were recognisably human, though varying greatly in physique. At the midday meal, there was a lot of joshing, making Mark blush furiously, to more laughter. Later, though, things quietened down, and a group who had been up at dawn had their leisure time and started to question him. The Ground, and Groundlings were almost mythical to most this far in, though a few had done a spot of raiding in their time. Some were hard to understand, and others seemed to have problems understanding him. After a while, he realised that some, even many, were slow in mind. Only one, taller than most, could read. No school, he discovered, and what was learnt was from parents or the Chief and her husband, a small man, old like her, but bright and better informed than the rest. After a while, the Chief shooed away all but her husband.

They were as greedy for information as he. The arranged polygamy appalled them, as did the whole business of choosing for service, while he was shocked, though rather less so than he might have been the day before, by the apparent promiscuity and the women's right to choose their partners. However, when it came to unchosen transfer, and the reputed dangers of the Barriers, the things that frightened most Grounders, they were less surprised.

"There's places, many of them, so befouled that no one breeds true, if at all, nor livestock. But they are good for growing, and for pasture. We even have some mines, and recover stuff from before the Catastrophe. A few get sent there for downright wickedness, but most go freely, those that have found themselves sterile, or those too badly hit by the Royal Bounty." Rhianna's lip curled with the last two words, and spat afterwards.

As the conversation wound on, Mark was able to get a vague sense of how the Outland worked. As it was back home, there were areas of greater or lesser contamination. Whereas, for the most part, the issue at home was fertile or not, here, it seemed, the problem was not so clear: abortions and serious defects were more frequent than sterility. 'Royal Bounty': the contamination that had wrecked the heredity of so many short of complete sterility. At one point, Rhianna paused and shouted a name. A middle-aged woman came and sat with them. A cloak covered her to below the knee. Her face looked normal enough, surrounded by a shawl.

"Megs, I'd not ask this without good cause. I want this young man from the Ground to see what the Bounty does. Take off your cloak and shawl and turn around."

Mark could not repress a gasp. Both arms too short. Hands with a finger missing on each. Back of the head irregularly swollen and a scalp raised in protuberances. Hair in clumps only.

Megs replaced her clothing. Under Rhianna's prompting, Mark heard her story. Born right here in Derwentdale. Arms notwithstanding, capable and hard working. Slept with a few. One miscarriage, a monster. Wanting a partner, gone south to the semi-Badlands. Met a man 'blessed with the same bounty', though the defects were left unspoken, and partnered. A group of weavers doing great things with water power. Each visited their original homes once a year, which was why she was here.

There were more details. Those in the semi-Badlands were mostly sterile. Nearly all conceptions resulted in monsters, but they had the means to prevent pregnancy if needed. If those failed, an abortion was obtained. They were nearly surrounded by land unfit for anything, but the foulness was declining, ever so slowly, and their patch was expanding year by year. She had never seen Grounders or those from the Domain, separated by miles of land that sounded just like that north of the Barriers, the real Badlands. The Chief started frowning a little as Megs spoke, and eventually thanked her and sent her back inside. This Grounder might be entirely reliable, but there were some things that were best told, if at all, by an Old-timer. Things that she was told, but had not made explicit even to her own House.

Mark's mind whirled. He could see that these Outlanders, not Outies any more, his thoughts were turning respectful, had problems like those of the Ground and the Domain. But the manner of dealing with them was completely alien. No Choosing, no selection determined by the authorities, a free choice of partners. He turned to the Chief.

"If Megs had wanted to stay here, could she have done so?"

The Chief hesitated. One for an Old-timer, really, but she could hardly avoid answering.

"Would she be forced to leave? No. But she'd not have much choice of partner or occupation here. And for all that we are used to the *bounteous gifts* bestowed on some, there is something of a stigma attached. And pity, which may be harder to bear. The only time people get moved by order is if we have a dearth."

She did not elaborate on the not-so-subtle pressures brought to bear here, pressures that, to be fair, included promise of good things elsewhere, a promise seemingly honoured more often than not. The Domain was far more direct, by Mark's account, but she could not understand the basis on which Choosing was done. It seemed that the boy himself, and Grounders in general did not know either.

***

All were sitting to a midday meal, when there was a shout. A large party were coming in from the north, all on foot. There were three stretchers, and several walking with the help of companions, variously bandaged or with arms in slings. They were led by a woman with a helmet like that of the hunter, but with three feathers in it. She was taller than most, with a face that showed no sign of 'bounty'. The party went inside. The Chief told Mark to stay outside, and followed them. After a while, the uninjured emerged. Both men and women, mostly in what Mark had come to recognise as standard Outie clothes. Most had crossbows, but one, with a helmet and a single feather, had a gun. Even to Mark's untutored eye, it looked crude. He did not approach them, and they mostly sat silently, looking occasionally at the main door.

After about an hour, someone beckoned Mark inside. He was led to a small room where the Chief and the helmeted woman were seated. The door was closed behind him.

"Master Norman, this is Captain O'Hanlon. I'm sure you have similar titles the other side. She is a warrior. I think you might say Kingsman or soldier. As you can see, her force has been in combat, and suffered losses. There are dead left behind, besides those being treated. I have explained who you are. She needs to ask you some questions."

O'Hanlon looked at him, a deep stare from a face that showed both tiredness and anger.

"We have just had a battle with the King's forces well inside our lands, and as you can see, we have suffered from it, though they withdrew. We've never been attacked in that way here since the Treaties. Now, I find an escapee from not far away. From what Chief Evans has told me, I'm thinking there is a connection."

Mark's heart sank. They'd come from the north. That could only mean that Kingsmen had been at Midhope. He'd not been there. Either they thought he would go there, or they had found out about Jones and were hunting him. The Picklesses would be taken. He started to explain his own movements and the connection to the Pickless farm. A battery of questions followed: when did you run? Kingsday? Which day is that? When were you at Midhope? Did you meet the evader? Did the authorities know about him?

The captain was making sense of it. May 5th, a report of Kingsmen to the south. The two who had seen them thought the soldiers did not know they had been seen. A scout had later found nothing; they had withdrawn. May 6th, a morning incursion from Midhope, but short-lived. They'd left men not very well hidden their own side of the bounds. But uncomfortably close to the one place where Domainers must be excluded at all costs. The place where it was her job to prevent the locals from offering any provocation, but watch from a distance. Then, yesterday a much larger force searching for something, and a detachment straight where we don't want them. Too late to block them near the boundary, so a scramble to assemble a force. A force that had indeed caused the soldiers to withdraw, but not before the bounds of Eden had been approached. The hostile force had numbers and arms way outside that permitted, and beyond the distance allowed for hot pursuit. A clear breach of the Treaties.

She dismissed Mark. In talking to Rhianna, she was unrestrained. Both knew that just a mile or so further, and the growing sweet spot where stock bred true, where there were rich pastures, would have been discovered. As it was, the Domainers might well have noticed the vegetation, though the whole area east to the boundary was not badly blighted. The cattle had been hustled west to avoid detection. But they had, of necessity, to cross contaminated land, if only for a short time.

"They'll not have been after the boy," said Rhianna, "but I think they must be looking for the other that's been there for years. When I stepped up here, I was told to make sure he was left alone. I did not know he was an evader, as they call them. Maybe they'll give up. Maybe he doesn't know. It's rarely he goes more than a mile or so beyond his refuge. More often, he goes across the boundary or helps the farmer on the periphery. If he did run west, we were to hold him if we could not scare him away. What do we do now?"

"Not up to me," said O'Hanlon. "The Old-timers will have to decide. Let it rest, and just watch and hope, or make a formal protest and the threat of retaliation or the real thing. It might be a deterrent, or they might wonder why the fuss, and probe deeper. If they do move in force, we've nothing to stop them. The harder we try, the more they'll wonder why. Colonel Anson told me their devilish Hunts are getting bolder. March their forces through here, and it's not just Eden at stake."

"As you say. I'll be sending the Grounder to Edale in the morning. Another went yesterday with the news. Do you want to go with him, or send someone with him?"

"No, thank you. I'll be going back north with the fit. Do what you can for the wounded. There's few enough left there, and we need to be right in front to delay any new incursion. Can you spare some that have the use of weapons to come with me? I'll send a senior straight away, and they'll go right through Edale. The Old-timers should get this news before they see the boy, and they'll need to act fast if they invoke the treaty. I think there is a semaphore or fit ponies at Chapel?"

***

Two of the stretcher cases had died; one had been dead on arrival. O'Hanlon briefed her messenger, and he set off for Edale. Mark had been wandering around outside, attracting little attention, as all were discussing the arrival of the war party and what it meant. It was not long after, though, that the captain assembled her troops and a dozen from the House and set off to the north. Shortly after, the Chief went a little way south with a gang armed with picks and spades, while others used the stretchers to carry the bodies, now wrapped completely in dark cloth. Mark followed. A small piece of flat ground served as a graveyard. The diggers were quick. Mark remained out of earshot as the Chief said something as all removed their hats. The bodies were lowered, the graves filled in. Two plain wooden posts were hammered in. The other graves had proper, if crudely shaped headstones. As the party started to return, Mark moved to be beside the Chief.

"Don't they get headstones?"

"Yes, of course. But it is tradition that either families or comrades choose a stone and inscribe what they wish. It's simple here. Further west, they sometimes get a craftsman to do it. They'll be ready in a week or so unless their comrades don't return from the north. We have the names."

There was a rather sombre evening meal, shared with those of the wounded fit enough to do so. Attitudes had changed. Without the specific knowledge of the Chief and the Captain, word had got around that there was some connection between his arrival and the fight to the north. He was not exactly avoided, but there was none of the jollity of the previous evening. Mark's second night was also very different from the first. Another pallet had been placed in his room, which he shared with a wounded warrior who said nothing.

In the morning, Mark was kitted out in Outlander clothes. His pack, deftly repaired, held more clothes and the rest of his kit. The candles and some of the matches he left for them, and at the last minute, he gave his second knife to the Chief. A guide had been chosen, Evan Thomas, a thirty-something looking man, unusually tall, and with a twist in his spine that made his walk seem jerky. But as they set off, Mark found the man's pace hard to match. They crossed by the ruins of the dam, and climbed up the hill beyond. Another valley lay below them. As they descended, Mark saw little difference from the one he had left, but as they skirted a hill and entered a wider valley running west, the vegetation grew sparser and stunted. The hillsides were scarred with landslides, and were largely bare. In the valley, similar bare patches, not burnt, but without grass, crossed the tumbled remains of many walls. His question to his companion elicited a curt response.

"Hit badly, it was. See it ten years ago or more, and it was worse. There's a sweet spot around the House, and a passage to the west. They're banking on it getting better, else there'd be no point."

Indeed, as they walked west, Mark saw a cluster of straggly trees and houses, a small spot of green in a desolate land. As they approached, he felt the reassurance of the familiar: pre-war houses patched and added to, if more crudely than those in Bradfield. This was Edale. Evan called out as he entered, and an elderly man came out to greet them.

"Chief, this is the Grounder for the Old-timers. You'll have had instructions?"

The old man nodded. Evan vanished with rapidity. The man approached Mark and shook his hand.

"Greetings, Mr Grounder. Euan Price's the name. I'm the Chief of this House, such as it is. Follow me." He led Mark into a well-maintained house, and closed and bolted the door behind him.

"Your full name, Grounder?"

"Mark Norman, sir."

"Well, Master Mark, I've instructions. You will spend the night here, and one of mine will be with you on the road to Chapel in the morning. It's not far, but I've no ponies left, what with announcing your passage to the Old-timers out west and then O'Hanlon's man. So, it's another walk. Meanwhile, you don't leave the building bar the outhouse at the back. Chief Evans did well to disguise you, but the word's got around, and there's some have more hope than sense. Not a place for progeny, this isn't, and you'll be more use elsewhere. Meanwhile, you may find a few things in here to pass the time."

Mark could not suppress another blush. He was given a simple meal by a woman he assumed to be Miss Price. Like Megs, she had a shawl over her head, and said nothing. He was shown a room upstairs with a pallet bed, a table, chair and basin of water. He sat down on the bed, and looked around. Shelves with a few books caught his eye, but also a map, pinned to the wall. He got up to look at it. It was hand-drawn, with names hard to make out. Whole areas had been crudely shaded, with some question marks inserted along some boundaries. At first, he could not make any sense of it. It resembled the school map at Bradfield rather than the map he had seen with such amazement at Jones' hideout. Eventually, he realised that it was, like the map in the schoolroom, basically a map of Mr Price's territory. Towards the top right corner, he made out Chief Evans' territory, that he had just left. North-east, that must be. To the south, right up to Edale itself the map was tinted grey with question marks along its border. Mr Price's land seemed to be a narrow strip bending southwards to the east, where a different colour had been painted in. To the west a crude representation of hills separated his patch from the Chapel that Mr Evans had mentioned. Like Jones' map, the colour and names went right to the edge, but none of them made sense to him.

He went to the window. Shuttered like those by the dam, but with a sheet of tailored animal hide on a roller above. He looked out onto what might pass for a street. Within sight were a number of occupied houses, interspersed with ruins. As he looked out, two women passed below him. Women, only by their voices and long skirts, for the typical Outlander broad-brimmed hat obscured much of a view from above. Only when they had passed by did he notice the disproportion in their bodies, and the very short stature.

The books proved a disappointment. They were handwritten on rough paper, or printed even more crudely than the King's print at home. Most were copies of ancient farm management handbooks. Over an account of diseases of sheep, he slumped back on the bed, and was soon asleep. He was woken by the shaking of Chief Price. It was already darkening, but a meal was ready.

It was a gloomy one. Just the Prices and himself, and little said other than related to food. No children, he noted. He tried to ask about the map. Yes, said Price, there's a better one downstairs, and he had copied the basics for visitors to see. Not that there were many such. He became a little more animated when asked about the question marks.

"You saw those grey areas? They are befouled beyond use, the Badlands. But the poison is weakening. Little by little, we reclaim territory, but it's slim pickings. We are here only to maintain a passage, and it won't change much in my lifetime. I'll think you noticed things were healthier around Chief Evans' House?"

Mark nodded.

"I'm the first Chief here at all. Thirty years ago, even this ground was dangerous, and the beasts from her House were driven over the high moors. It's strange all right, that patch that's clean, or cleaner than most, right up to the northern Badlands. She's a lucky woman. Give her credit, she'd admit it too."

The brief conversation stirred him. A bitter tone entered his voice.

"I suppose all this is strange to you, being a Grounder. We hear how everyone has babies, fit and healthy, not to mention livestock and crops. Kept from sharing with us by your Royal masters, no doubt."

"Not so strange, Mr Price. Yes, it's true we can reproduce, but there are still contaminants. There are many who are sterile. And there are Badlands, as you call them, less than ten miles from my home, and they stretch north forever as far as I know. And like Chief Evans, but under compulsion, the beasts we breed are sent to the east, to the Domain. People, too. That's why I'm here, Mr Price. People are not stock, Mr Price. Chief Evans and others before her opened my eyes."

Taken aback, Price grunted, and the conversation dried up. Mark was a little surprised at his own outburst. Soon, he went up to his room and fell asleep very quickly.

The following morning, he was on the road again, this time with a middle-aged woman who introduced herself simply as Megan. As on the previous day, he was put to shame by the pace. The path, no longer a road, went high over the hills. She allowed a rest as they reached a pass, and he had a view to the west. The further from their starting point, the more the landscape became barren. Steeper slopes were scarred with landslips; the soil and rock were often exposed, and bar a narrow strip around the path there was little vegetation. To the west, small patches of green were surrounded by an equally bleak prospect. It was not any great distance, and it was well before noon that they descended into Chapel, the nearest of the green oases seen from the top. To Mark, it resembled a hybrid of Bradfield and what he knew of the city. There were abandoned houses, either stark on the one hand, or swamped in vegetation on the other. At a riverbank, Megan turned sharply north, and soon they encountered a small group of maintained houses. There were grassy enclosures nearby, in which a few ponies grazed, and for the first time since leaving Edale, there were people about. Deformities, if any, were concealed under wide-brimmed, floppy hats and swirling cloaks. The familiar smell of manure suggested that other animals were nearby.

One house had a sign swinging from a post. It featured a crowned head, severed at the neck and dripping blood, with a similarly gory axe painted above it. There was writing: 'The King's Head' at the base. Mark had no difficulty in recognising the meaning. The door was open, and Megan led him in. Passing through a room with a few people, still with their hats and most with mugs, they went through to a corridor behind, and into a small room, sparsely furnished with a few tables and benches.

"Wait here," said Megan, and left. Five, then ten minutes went by. Eventually, a tall man entered. He was hatless, and Mark saw a handsome face, not unlike that of the hunter. Hatless, but holding in his hand a similar helmet to that of the warrior captain, with three feathers. Mark stood up, but was signed to sit. The man went to the door and shouted. Then he sat opposite Mark.

"You can take your hat off; by all accounts you've nothing to hide, master Grounder."

Mark removed his hat. The man stared at him a while. A woman knocked and entered with two mugs of ale and left. The man lifted a pouch off his shoulder, and pulled out a sheet of paper.

"Just humour me for a minute. I've a problem for you here, or rather two. Take your time." He handed over a piece of charcoal and the paper. Mark looked at the paper.

The first was an equation: $2x + 4 = 8$, what is x?

Mark could easily write 2.

The next was a question: when did the Great War end?

Chronicles, thought Mark: KY 16.

He handed the paper back. The man looked at it briefly.

"Easy, wasn't it? But here, only one in a hundred would make sense of the first, and you'd be laughed at for the second by those that know, not many, I grant you. What might you think if I said 2065 AD?"

More than two thousand years recorded before the war's end? It had dawned on Mark that Chronicles had been notably vague about dates before the beginning of the war, but Jones had told him about the old book, that Holy Bible, that he had looked at.

"I saw a book 500 years old, sir, though the man who showed it to me said that that copy was much younger, but pre-war. We never learnt dates for things that happened before the war, except the king's birthday, 48 BK and the period of the war, 13 KY to 16 KY. AD, sir? We never heard of that in Chronicles."

"Chronicles, you call it. We have history, or what's left of it. AD? Anno Domini, the year of Our Lord, meaning the birth of God."

"You mean this God is still alive, sir? We were taught that great Deceiver in the west invented gods. God was mentioned in the book I saw too, the Holy Bible. I did not have time to ask Jones about it, but I suppose he was alive 500 years ago."

"Jones?"

"Another evader, like me, sir, but he had a hiding place near the boundary. There was a farmer shielded him. He had many pre-war books."

"God still alive? Well, that's a question still argued about. There's many say that there never was a God. That Holy Bible? Yes, we have it here, and it's read by those that can. We even manage to print new copies. Those questions you answered were not a test. I put them just to show you that things are different here. You will find stranger things than that; call them a sample of what's to come. Oh, the Deceiver: I am not sure what you've been told, but we have a leader, yes, one of the Old-timers who chose a different path. A bit younger than

188

your king, by all accounts, but he'll not live so long. He may be good for a few decades, God willing; the rest even less."

He got up and opened the door, shouting down the corridor. More ale, and plates of food were brought in. As they ate, the man continued talking.

"Time for formal introductions, I think. The name's Alexander McEnery. Save for Chief of House or Riding, we've little in the way of formal titles. Chief is mine. These three feathers," he pointed to the helmet, "give me a certain authority, because Chapel is a gateway to the east and south, and there's a fair bit of traffic in all directions. Oh, and I'm no renegade noble; I have just the allotted span. I'm a father too, rare enough, but our children are all blessed by your King's Bounty. They'll not be parents."

"Mark Norman, sir. My father was the Clerk to the Mayor of Bradfield in the Ground of the Northernmost Division of the Domain. He will have lost his position due to me running away. My two older brothers were both chosen. They are in the Domain, and we never hear of them. My sister will be married this year, if my action does not result in worse for her. And I have two small half-brothers and another expected."

"Has she a young man, then?"

"Oh no, sir, she'll have a husband chosen for her, to be Miss or Muss as they decide."

"Miss or Muss?"

"First or second wife, sir. Men with good heredity usually have two, the more so as many more boys get chosen for service than girls. My father has a Muss too, she's the mother of the two small ones. And one before, but she died in childbirth when I was small."

McEnery shuddered, but said nothing. He'd heard worse about life in the Domain. Was this the best?

"Very well, to business. I've had instructions. There are two Old-timers coming to talk to you. They've a way to travel, and I don't know when to expect them. You are to stay in Chapel till they come. There's a room upstairs here prepared for you, and they'll give you meals down here. Here's a key; the room can be locked from either side. Leave it unlocked when you are out, and you may find company when you return. Word gets around. Your choice. I'll look in around midday tomorrow to give you any news. You can explore the town, but don't go where there is nothing growing; there are still hot spots of contamination."

189

"Could I have something to read, sir? Are there copies of this Holy Bible? I only got to see the first pages."

"Surely. I'll ask around on the way out, and I'll bring one tomorrow if I can."

***

Mark went out and wandered round the settlement for the afternoon. The place was basically a dilapidated version of Bradfield, larger originally, but with fewer inhabited houses. There were areas of little or no vegetation, which he avoided. The surrounding area was also mostly barren, but the roads certainly carried more traffic than at home. Mostly carts and flocks and herds mostly headed west or south. Everybody seemed busy, and no one accosted him. While dressed the part, his idle ramblings made him self-conscious. He was given an evening meal in the small room where he had first met McEnery. Afterwards, he walked a little as dusk descended. The streets were dark, and inhabited houses appeared to be lit by candles or lamps. He did not go far, and soon returned to the King's Head. A few people were in the lamplit front room, drinking from mugs. They looked at him as he passed through, but no one spoke or called to him.

The following morning was much the same. But the Chief appeared as promised at midday on the first day, bringing a Holy Bible with him. It was similar to the one he had seen at Jones' lair. Yes, it was pre-war and valuable. Not that it would be stolen, no, but such old books were easily damaged. Yes, they did print books, but it was expensive, and there were few printing works. A big book like this was not often printed, the more so since there were more of this one than any other, though there were some slightly different. As expected, there was no news.

"Can I ask you a question, sir? Do you have electricity in the Outland? Last night I saw no signs."

"Ah. You have it back home? Yes, we have it, but it's hard to generate steadily, and expensive where there's no water power. We do generate some to the south of the town, but it's reserved for a few workshops. Uses a lot of metal too. If you get to go further west, you'll find it's used more."

This made sense to Mark. There were watermills at Bradfield and elsewhere, but most houses lacked it. In the city, though, there was a more stable supply

190

from across the bridge, though only enough for dim and short-lived lighting that frequently blacked out. It was never depended on.

That afternoon, it rained steadily. Mark stayed in his room, and in the rather bad light by his window, he examined the Bible. It was hard to understand. It was in English, clearly, but there were many words unfamiliar to him. He struggled through a part of Genesis. So, there was God, who created the Earth. His own education had dismissed God, or gods as the invention of the Deceiver, but the question of origins had never been raised. Before the King, there was just chaos and conflict, of which gods were a part. Indeed, as the quote had been drummed into him: "a tale of sound and fury, signifying nothing." So, was the Deceiver present already? Was he older even than the King? After a while, he abandoned the attempt to read systematically, and flicked through pages. The passages, chosen at random, made little sense. He recognised that it was, at least in part, a history, the word used by Chief McEnery. Indeed, he found a section called Chronicles. It seemed to be little more than a set of family trees, more like Mr Pickless' stud book than an account of events. As the light deteriorated, he gave up. After the evening meal, there was little to do. The rain continued. Mark lay on his bed, thoughts churning in his head. Eventually, he slept.

There was, at least, something new to experience the following day. The rain had stopped, and as he emerged to take a walk, he noticed many walking in the same direction. The shops, which he had not entered, were shut. It seemed to him that nearly everybody was marginally smarter and cleaner than on the previous day. He followed the crowd. It converged on what Mark immediately recognised as a church. There was one in Bradfield, a relic of the past, now roofless because not easily converted to other purposes. There had been talk of using the materials, but it remained as a ruin, surrounded by a graveyard that still retained its original function.

Here, it had been kept in remarkably good repair, though some windows were sealed off with boards, and others held rather irregular glasswork as in Bradfield houses. As the entrants tailed off, Mark took the step of following. Inside, it was mostly a long room with a central path and rows of benches on either side. What he noticed immediately was that all the men had removed their hats, and exposed a variety of heads, from the apparently normal to the bulging and lopsided. Baldness was no surprise; clumps of hair and bare patches brought Megs to his mind. The women had also removed their broad-brimmed hats, but all had headscarves. He had no time to take in anything else, when a man in a black cloak signalled him to sit, pointing to an empty bench at the back.

The building was not full, but his view was somewhat obscured by people in front. He could see, though, that there was a smaller section at the end, with benches running parallel to the gangway in the middle. What might be a table or a large stone beyond was covered in brightly-coloured cloth, a striking contrast to the muted colours he had seen on the streets, and indeed in Bradfield.

Those on the parallel benches rose to their feet. A pair of men rose, and started playing what Mark took to be violins. Back home, these notional Relics were among the few that people were allowed to keep. Post-war versions were said to be inferior. Those at the front started singing, though Mark could not make out the words. All stood, and Mark followed. A small procession passed him and walked towards what Mark now thought of as the front. A man in front, holding a cross, then another, dressed in robes that recalled those of the King's Visitor on ceremonial occasions, flanked by two girls in black and white robes. At the tail end were the Chief, plumed helmet in his hand, and a smartly dressed woman whom he assumed to be Miss. The latter pair stepped sideways into a bench near the front, as did the girls. The robed man stopped at the junction of the main hall with the smaller one and turned. Everyone except him sat down. The music stopped.

The robed man started speaking in a deep voice. Mark did not catch a lot of what was said. Again, he recognised English. He caught, "Dearly beloved brethren, the Scripture moveth us in sundry places," which immediately caused confusion. Scripture? Sundry? He soon gave up, and concentrated on copying those in front of him. There were standings, sittings and kneelings; there was singing and also speaking all together. He could not join in with these, but being at the back, it was not noticed.

As the service progressed, Mark saw more and more clearly that he was seeing something similar to Kingsday Service, but more elaborate, and certainly with more music. Back home, the mayor would lead. Here, though, it was not the Chief, but another. Further, when it came to what Mark recognised as the Sermon, it was the robed man who delivered it. Much shorter than the mayor's usual rambling, and spoken in much simpler words than those that had gone before and came after. He caught the general tenor: through God's mercy, their world was healing; there would be more children, whole in body and mind; we are all brothers and sisters, working together to fulfil God's will. *God, again*, thought Mark, I am still not understanding this.

The service ended rather as it had begun. The little procession left as they had entered, and then people started to leave behind them. In the queue, Mark received a few stares, but no comments. He returned to the King' Head. It was not long before noon, and the Chief appeared on time, this time with his wife. She was full of questions about life in the Ground. Lunch was brought in. Mark managed to answer rather better than at the Derwent House; he was learning what it was that needed explanation. It was well on into the afternoon before he could ask a few questions himself. The answers were confusing. No, God was not the equivalent of the king. He was a supernatural being, not present in the flesh. But those who believed thought that his son, who was also God (no, not another, the same) had been a man born, grown up and had then been executed though innocent. That's what we use for our dates, AD. Yes, more than 2000 years ago. Yes, they had reading and writing even earlier, much earlier. But some did not believe God existed, and others believed different things about him and held their own services. No, that was not treason. No, they were not punished or sent to the semi-badlands. Called to service? If they felt called. Only used for those who became priests. Like the man who led the service. Did they believe? Miss, yes, Chief not sure, and he attended other services or meetings of non-believers too, a part of his duty.

Mark had many more questions, but the Chief was needed elsewhere. Sunday was the day of rest for most, but he had, as he put it, to show the flag. Another explanation needed, then they left him; left him in a state of total confusion. What held people together?

14. Planning and Poison

For Mark, the next two days were filled with soul-sapping boredom. It rained more often than not, and the settlement had been tramped around repeatedly. The few he passed outside were evidently busy, and none approached him. The Bible held few attractions without someone to explain what was written. The Chief would appear at midday, but usually in a hurry, and with the same dreary message, no news. At last, on Wednesday morning, the Chief arrived early with news. A messenger had arrived. The Old-timers and their staff would arrive tomorrow. Mark was to move to the Chief's house, which backed onto a small hall and offices. He was shown a room not much different to that in the King's Head.

Going down to the hall, he discovered a lot of activity. Furniture was being changed. Beds and bedclothes were being brought in and taken to rooms off the side. A fire was lit in the main hall. Men and women scurried around with papers and with plates and cutlery. Mark ended up being both homesick and sardonically amused, recalling the scurrying around at the Council Hall when an official appearance of the Visitor was imminent. There was the same desire to impress, the pride in a good show. Chief McEnery, though, was a far more commanding presence than Mayor Arkell. Feeling superfluous, he left for yet another tour of the small settlement.

***

The Old-timers had travelled fast. Unheeded by the sleeping Mark, their convoy arrived around midnight the same day. Three four-horse carriages drew up in front of the Chief's home and offices. In the lamplight, doors were opened on two, and from each there emerged an elderly, robed person accompanied by assistants. They were led inside. No fewer than twelve riders, all armed with guns, dismounted. Their commander, three feathers on the helmet gave orders in low tones. The horses were led away to be stabled, while the riders were shown to the billets arranged beforehand by Chief McEnery.

The third carriage had more the appearance of a covered wagon. The two men visible on it did not climb down. It was led to the back of the building, and into an enclosed courtyard. They descended, and two others emerged from inside. Six padlocked chests heavy enough to require two men for each were carried in turn to a store built into the courtyard wall. Its door was locked, and two men remained on guard outside it. The horses were stabled in the same yard.

Nearly all the residents of Chapel were in their beds. Only the Chief and a few of his staff were there to witness the greatest show of force seen for well over a hundred years. Only two of the Chief's men were left to help guard the unhitched carriages and the entrance overnight. Silence soon returned. Mark slept through the entire affair, and descended to share a breakfast with excited staff, discussing the arrival in hushed tones. He was told to be ready in his room for a call to come. Back there, he examined his clothes, changing into what seemed to him the least dirty or ragged. After about an hour, he was called for.

He was ushered into a small room off the main hall. It held a long table. At the far end were two imposing figures, a man and a woman, clad in robes of black. No trace of abnormality was to be seen, but both were manifestly old. Mark at once identified them as the Old-timers. To one side, a young man in uniform had in front of him all the paraphernalia for note-taking. Nothing visibly *bounteous* in his appearance either. Next down that side was an older uniformed man, unknown to Mark. A helmet with three feathers lay on the table beside him. Opposite him was the one familiar face, that of Chief McEnery, who signalled him to sit in the chair at the other end of the table, facing the Old-timers. The room was uncomfortably hot, with a log fire burning vigorously.

"Welcome to the Westron lands, Mr Norman, to the Outland," said the man in black, in a slightly quavering voice. "Let me introduce myself and the others you will not have met. I am Archibald Ogilvie. You may hear me referred to as Lord Ogilvie, a relic of times long past. I am, at 264 years of age, what is referred to as an Old-timer. My colleague is Elisabeth Hawkins, likewise Lady Hawkins, another Old-timer. She is of an age not much different from my own. Mr Howell is our secretary. You are participating in history, Mr Norman, and history must be recorded. The officer on your left is Colonel Hunt. I think you know what a colonel is? We do not maintain an army as such. If I say he is one of those entrusted with our security, I do not mean to suggest any relationship to either the purpose or the methods of the Royal Security Corps. Chief McEnery you already know."

Mark had realised that the so-called Old-timers were the nobles who had revolted against the King. The only noble he had seen was the Visitor, who had seemed much younger, though he had been told that he was not much younger than the two facing him. Both Ogilvie and Hawkins looked old by Grounder standards, seventy or more. He understood the fire. Ogilvie pulled himself up a little more erect in his chair.

"We had already started travelling to meet you, when we were told of the surprising attack across the boundary in a place called," he looked down at a paper in front of him, "Midhope, near the northern Badlands. You saw the result of that attack. What you may not know is that ever since the end of the war, peace between us and the Kingdom has been maintained by treaties, treaties that overlook minor transgressions, or arrange for appropriate compensation. An attack on the scale here is a clear breach of those treaties. It appears that there is a connection between that attack and your escape, your evasion, I believe it is called. We are here to decide how to respond, and we have to do so very quickly. What we need from you is the answers to some questions."

Mark nodded. But the questions were all about Jones. Not about the knowledge that Jones might possess that would help the Outland, but about what he knew of the land further west. Jones had said nothing much, was the answer. When he left his home, Mark related, it was to help Mr Pickless or to roam secretly near the Barriers or along the river.

"He kept Outi—Westron people away, sir," Mark concluded. "He had even shot at them if they came too close. Mr Pickless was not raided by your people, and gave credit to Mr Jones for that."

As to why Royal forces should have advanced so far, Mark found that even these Old-timers were as ignorant of the governing of the Ground as he was of the Outland.

"Sir, Mr Jones was an evader, like me, but he had come from another Ground a long time ago, so there was no hue and cry for a missing person. Only the Pickless family and the mayor knew he existed, and the mayor had good reason to tell no one. He helped them out at the Midhope farm, where the family resented the loss of all their children to be among the Chosen. They hid him. But evasion is just about the worst crime in the eyes of the Domain, and aiding an evader was nearly as bad. Their forces would have been looking for him."

"So, how did they find out about him?"

"I saw him by accident, sir, at the farm. Other boys heard about him too. There were five of us knew, besides the farmer and his wives. Later, I found him at his home. When I ran, it was not there. But my running will have had them question the other boys and Mr Pickless. The Domain, Security, will have found out about Mr Jones. One of the other boys was a patriot, devoted to Royal Service. He'd have told them. They'd have been very keen to catch him, perhaps even more than me."

At this point, Mark faltered. For a moment, he was silent, his head in his hands. There were tears in his eyes as he managed to continue.

"I ran. My family will suffer. The Picklesses will suffer. Even Mayor Arkell will suffer, because he knew about Mr Jones and did not report him. They may have caught him by now. It all happened too quickly, sir. It was planned that I would be apprenticed to Mr Pickless, and help Mr Jones to help you. Then I was Chosen. I'd be gone forever into the Domain."

There was a silence. Eventually, the Colonel asked in a very quiet voice,

"Why would your family be punished? Did they know of your plans?"

"No, sir, I was careful not to say anything. My parents wanted me to be a farmer, and not to be Chosen, but I said nothing to them, and gave no one any hint. They were preparing to say goodbye to me after the Ceremony."

"I can see that they would be questioned; but why punished?"

"That's how it works, sir. Suspicion is enough to get you sent to work in the Badlands, the Barriers as we call them. It's deportation to the Domain unchosen. And I think that any bad behaviour raises suspicion that you are not good breeding material, you and your family both. It's like the stud book I worked on at the farm."

Another silence. All had heard something of the practices of the Kingdom, but Mark's account shocked them. Eventually, Lady Hawkins spoke.

"You knew these consequences, then? I don't think you would do this just to avoid being Chosen, where you might have had a good, if sterile, life. What drove you, Mark? There must be more."

"Little things, ma'am, many of them. My father's doubts. What Mr Pickless told me. Mr Jones opened my eyes even more. Many of us knew that there was something wrong, something not true about how the Domain worked. We did not know what. Then, Mr Jones told me that he had, or thought he had, information that would help you, and bring down the Domain. He showed me a few things, but there was a lot more, all pre-war stuff, books and machinery in that place. He was old, ma'am, and worried that he might not make sense of what he had found. If I had gone to the farm officially, I could have helped him, and been able to tell you in the west. But being Chosen, I had to run in a way that led the Kingsmen away from Midhope. Not that that kept them away."

"What did he show you, then?"

Mark thought, *Jones had shown him little enough, and the Bible, he now knew, was not unknown here, though it was in the Ground. But there was the map.*

"There was a map, ma'am, a pre-war map of the area around our Ground. All the roads and towns that were there before the war, including what is now your land. But someone had drawn lines and symbols on it, splitting it up into areas. I made nothing of it, except for the devastation, but when I was in Edale, there was a rough map of the Chief's Riding, with different areas shaded by colour. He told me that it indicated the levels of contamination. Mr Jones had not worked that out, or not properly, but I think it might be the same. He had other maps, perhaps of other areas, but I did not see them."

The silence that followed seemed to Mark to go beyond mere absence of words. All the others stiffened. Looks were exchanged. He was asked a few more questions in a very different, almost casual way; questions about military matters in the Ground. His answers were necessarily vague. He was thanked, and asked to leave.

***

As the door closed behind Mark, the four principals looked from one to the other in astonishment and alarm.

"Maps," said Ogilvie, "maps showing contamination or its absence. And the very one that includes Eden. Who knows what other clean patches are recorded there? They might help us, or not, but in the hands of the Domain?"

He did not need to spell it out. Lady Hawkins turned to the Chief.

"Do you know exactly where this Jones lives, or hides this material?"

"Not personally, ma'am, but the Chief there, Rhianna Evans, does. It's very close to the boundary, less than three miles from Eden. They've been told to offer no provocation there. A few idiot rovers got close to it, but the man himself frightened them off. The Chief has been firmer since. From what the boy says, that farmer and their mayor think it's the man that keeps us away. It suited us. Until now."

"If I may, ma'am," said the Colonel, "we should ask the boy more about what he actually saw there, and what it was like. I suspect that it is a late Catastrophe survival centre, even a strategic reserve."

He crossed himself.

"God knows what might be there. If the Domain knew about it, they'd have stripped it ages ago. The boundary would not be where it is; the land there was marginal."

"We could try to strip it ourselves? It's our side of the boundary," said Ogilvie.

"It's a big risk," said McEnery. "There's not much in the way of force nearby, but if we were seen, they'd be all over us in force soon enough, and no way of stopping them. Nothing to stop them driving us westwards, either. The boy's running has stirred things up there, and the fact that we did not just withdraw when we met Kingsmen will have aroused suspicion."

"Very well," said Lord Ogilvie, "we have to decide how to act. We can do nothing, lie low and keep a guard well out of sight of the boundary. No further actions by them, and we can try to find the man outside, if he's escaped. Have we had any more reports of activity? Any evidence that they have caught him?"

"No, sir," said the Chief, "and no news is good news. But it takes the best part of a day for a message to get here."

"There is a problem with just waiting and hoping, sir," said Hunt. "What happened is a gross breach of the treaty, and they know that as well as us. No official response, and they'll be wondering why. There were fatal casualties. They'll expect us to demand reparations. We've come to the Point for far less in the past. They will wonder at our resistance too."

"Thank you, Colonel. We can protest. I think they will stall if we do. They'll talk about hot pursuit, or delay, or not respond at all and see what happens. We take time, too, to respond without their damned telephones. Breach though it is, they may wonder at the fuss we are making, and even more about the resistance we put up. We need to distract them from the area, not just to deter breaches."

Lord Ogilvie turned to look at Lady Hawkins, raising his eyebrows; she nodded.

"There is another option. We can indeed protest, but in the meantime, we need a show of force. We need to show the Domain that we can harm them, harm them badly. We brought with us canisters of Agent Z. They are ancient, but we have run a test on cattle. It is still active."

The colonel stiffened. Agent Z? He could not remember all the often-distorted accounts of weapons used in the war, but all were abhorrent. Mutagens? Plague? Nuclear, a name he barely understood, but knew only of its long-term effects? He crossed himself again. The Chief had a similar look of revulsion. That accounts for the third carriage and the security around it, he thought. A residue of the past, or had those at Manod or in Dean devised new and more terrible weapons? Ogilvie saw their concern.

"Agent Z is a chemical weapon only, a poison. It kills or injures; it has immediate effects, but it is short-lived once released. Ground is not contaminated; heredity is not damaged. We would not be causing long term damage. We can retaliate far from the place of interest. What I have in mind is a limited strike, a demonstration if you like. Kill stock in areas of the Ground far from where we have an immediate interest."

"How can we use such a weapon, sir?" asked the Chief. "Except for here in the north, there are Badlands between our lands and the Domain, or any Ground that I know of. Our rockets will reach only a few hundred yards. Attack here, and we will draw down their forces where we least want them."

"Just so, Chief. What we have in mind is a limited attack, far from here. We have the means."

Ogilvie turned to the colonel.

"The Montgolfiers at Hereford can be mobilised fast? Their crews are trained, I think. The poison can be dropped from the air over a poor Ground to the east. Dropped on stock rather than people, if possible. Our plan is for Lady Hawkins to go to the Treaty Point with demands. We need to time it so that the blow has been, or is about to be delivered when she makes contact. The Domain, the Court, must know it has happened within one or two days of her mission."

"Yes, sir, they can, at least within a few days of being asked. But it is a suicide mission for the crews. They know that, of course, but they will need to be told why. What if the Domain retaliates and the war is renewed? Do we have the means of defence or offence, or are we bluffing?"

"That is the risk, Colonel. No, frankly, we do not. There is enough in the boxes for a second strike on a larger scale, and that is all. Alfred in Dean has more, but it is in bulk, in the original storage. It would take time and great care to prepare more weapons. Many key targets are out of range, and anyway dependent on the wind. Only a few balloons are needed this time. But lose Eden, and its expansion, and the Domain may overwhelm us with numbers in any case. They have not used powered aircraft or missiles since the war. Montgolfiers? We've never seen any. The winds favour us even if outnumbered. Two strikes, and westerly winds persisting and they may come to terms. They are struggling for manpower as are we, and there is evidence that Grounders resent the increasing demands made upon them. The boy is a symptom."

Lady Hawkins followed on immediately.

"There is more. Chief, I think you have had bears moving south through your Riding?"

"Yes, ma'am, from the north. Hunters have kept the numbers low, but we are losing stock, and even folk that work outside without weapons. We do puzzle as to where they are from."

"Just so. We have interrogated hunters and even had a doctor examine a corpse, and compare it with descriptions in ancient books. No abnormalities, though for all we know, they may be sterile by the time they reach us. It's an irony. They were not in Britain until just before the war, so Defoe and the librarians tell us. After plagues depopulated parts of the north, they were introduced from overseas. Why, I have no idea; the Catastrophe seems to have seen an outpouring of odd ideas. The creatures survived somewhere, somewhere to the north. The numbers show they can breed true there. Gentlemen, Eden may not be the only Eden. Maybe, somewhere north there are others without humans. But to find them, with miles of killing Badlands in between? We have dithered, gentlemen, because the chances were that any parties would die before they found them, never mind returning. The boy said that this Jones had other maps. If they are what he thinks, they might be our passport to finding them. If the Domain hears, they will sacrifice anything to reach them. We will remain confined and increasingly outnumbered."

"Not just confined," added Ogilvie. "Reach Chapel, here, and they have cut us in two, to all intents and purposes. The tracks through Wales are poor and lengthy. And they can get here with few choke points; with no tracts of Badlands to traverse."

The colonel brooded. The Montgolfier crews would do their duty. There was a remote chance that some might find their way back on foot. But life was sacred, however endowed, and wherever it was found. Folk would die on the ground, too, folk who had committed no crime. He glanced at the Chief. The two of them were the arbiters, the real Outlanders, the inheritors, in the eyes of the Old-timers. If they both objected, the Old-timers would not press it. The Chief nodded.

"Very well. With your assigns, I will escort this poison south. I will deliver the cargo to the Montgolfiers. Packhorses, if you please, Chief, there's places a carriage will be a hindrance. And a chit for changing them good for any Riding, please, Lord Ogilvie. They will launch in the first available westerly wind once I am ready, but no earlier than nine days from now. I suggest just three balloons, and instructions to drop over livestock rather than people. There are marginal Grounds there. Lady Hawkins should be at the Treaty Point in eight days too. She should make contact a day after the first westerly after that. We can only hope to get the timing right, because it will take a day at least to send her a message. With their damned telephones, they'll know all about it by then, and it's not far for them to meet and make a response."

"Ma'am? Chief? Very well, Colonel, and thank you. There are some semaphore links, I think, but not complete. A message back as fast as possible when you have launched. We will have your documents ready in an hour. You'll be ready to leave then?"

The colonel rose, bowed slightly to the two at the table's end, and left. The secretary prepared the documents, while the rest remained silent. When they were done, the Chief left with them, and returned a few minutes later with Mark. The boy was put to work with pen and paper while also being questioned about what he had seen in Jones' lair. A rough map and a plan of the inside took shape. He was again dismissed.

"The colonel was right," said Ogilvie. "It must be a military reserve. I think the word they used is bunker. There are doors that Jones could not open. God knows what is behind them, and I doubt that we can open them either, or not without weeks of work. Any contaminant stores might be viable."

"I have a small amount of gunpowder, sir," said the Chief, "we can blow up the building itself as a last resort. Clearing the rubble would delay them a little. We can even blow up some other ruins to set false trails."

"No, or not yet. But move what you have up into the Derwent, with those that know how to use it. Keep them well west or south of Eden itself, though. And keep scouts out of Eden. Chief Rhianna knows who or what is safe. We don't know what has become of this Jones, but if he is seen, we want him safe with us. After the first foray, he may have jumped ship. We have to hope that he'll not fall into their hands."

Lady Hawkins spoke up. "I have a suggestion. It sounds as though the man is not wholly sure of us. He trusts the boy, and would recognise him. Move him back up to Derwent in due course and let him be seen in the right places, where we know the enemy is not watching. And even put him into Eden with some likely mates. He's more use there than anywhere else."

"Agreed. Chief, we need as many extras as we can get up there. Any hunters in your Riding are to be conscripted. Find O'Neill especially and get him here. We'll give you the written authority. And whatever supplies are needed. Also, send the message west. Semaphore, and a written account which Howell will prepare for you. You will stay here with us, so that we can react if necessary. The messenger should also demand people and supplies from the near west to be sent here. We leave it to you."

The Chief stood, and unexpectedly saluted rather than bowing. Somehow, it felt appropriate.

15. The Montgolfiers

The one-time city of Hereford, like so many others, is a scene of desolation, sterile desolation caused by the last, most destructive, but most focused weapons of the Catastrophe. Around it, the region is sparsely vegetated, land that the Westrons call semi-badlands. There are small patches of richer cover, and in some of these, there are dwellings. A visitor, most especially a visitor from the Grounds, would be shocked first by the appearance and later by the comprehension of most, but not all the inhabitants. There would be children, but few of them with intelligence other than in a few, valued, settlements.

In one such patch, just a few miles east of the ruined city, there are large wooden buildings around a grassy square. Smaller houses are scattered nearby. Smoke emerges from the chimneys of those close to the centre. Many cattle, sheep and ponies are pastured in the fields nearby. Observe it for few days, and convoys of pack ponies, heavily laden, will be seen arriving from the south, while unloaded ones return. Fewer will be seen on the north and westerly tracks, the latter skirting the northern limits of devastation in the city.

Coupled with the Forest of Dean to the south, with coal and charcoal, with the capacity to smelt iron, this is the largest and most important industrial centre for all the Westron lands. It is also one of only two Montgolfier stations east of the Irish Sea, and the only one that has a military function; a function that has been endlessly rehearsed, but never used.

It was late in the evening on May 24th when Colonel Hunt and his diminished party arrived at the station. Behind him was a trail of refurbished and freshly staffed semaphores and shielded beacons. An unencumbered rider had preceded them, arriving the previous afternoon, and the place was already busy. Shaped linen sheets, dyed black, were stretched out on racks, some glistening slightly in the evening light, while others were being coated with the peculiar, elastic lacquer that had been developed after years of less than satisfactory experiments.

A coating that would seal them, for a while. To one side, three huge pear-shaped frameworks of very thin struts lay on their sides. Already covered in the sealed linen, one was being slowly rotated as the seams were sealed; another one was half-covered, but the third remained bare.

As he dismounted, the colonel was greeted by a giant of a man, albeit one showing signs of advanced acromegaly. His movements were slow and looked painful.

"Welcome, Colonel. I am Moses Meredith, Aeronaut in Chief. As you see, Colonel, we have moved as fast as possible. The Montgolfiers are never kept assembled, and the fabric needs testing for each flight. We will complete the task tomorrow, weather permitting."

The colonel's forces were shown quarters; the ponies were put out to grass, and their cargo safely locked away in a shed. The Aeronaut led the colonel to a small dwelling built into the side of one of the large, windowless buildings. They sat in a small, simply furnished room. A window in the west let in the last of the evening light.

The colonel handed over his written authority. The Aeronaut read it slowly, occasionally asking for help with some of Lord Ogilvie's more elaborate language.

"So, Colonel, we are at war again? I had hoped never to see our fleet used in such a way, for all that is what we have trained for. Three will be ready for you. We have a further five that can be assembled in a few days. More, and we have to build from scratch, and that would mean weeks."

"We hope not war, Aeronaut, but a reprisal that may deter further incursions. But it is deadly. Deadly for your crews, I am afraid, unless they are very lucky."

"Yes, Colonel. But all our crews know this. A war voyage is one-way. All are volunteers, and most have good reasons to want revenge. They'll not shirk. We do practice survival drill in the open, and they have the means to deny the enemy the satisfaction of slaughter and the risks of interrogation under duress."

Colonel Hunt explained the plan hatched in Chapel. He had the canisters of the poison ready. The Station already had dummies, to rehearse their use. Canisters devised to be hung well below the balloon with a release triggered by the crew. Springs would burst the container and spread the dust. Yes, there was a safety catch. So long as the wind was west or south west, they would be over some Grounds after 20 or 25 miles. Target stock and farms if possible, and not the villages. Would the balloons make the distance?

"Yes, Colonel, they can make the distance if the wind keeps up, but only if. Stay up more than a few hours, and the fuel will be gone. They'll sink. Sunshine, and they'll last a little longer. Any rain, and they are in trouble."

"Second strike, Aeronaut. You have five here. Get them ready the moment we have despatched the first. Can you protect them from weather? Good. We wait for a signal, semaphore or beacon. Burners? No need to light them until five days after first strike."

The next morning was sunny but calm. Outlanders swarmed around the unfinished Montgolfiers. Others were assembling a massive wheeled scaffold, a scaffold with winches, lines and hooks. Still others were attending to charcoal stoves, doing the minimum to keep them alight. The Aeronaut Chief assembled the crews for the colonel's briefing. There were eight people in front of him, most showing the manifest signs of the Royal Bounty. Even the colonel, of necessity exposed to all sorts and conditions in the course of his travels, was shocked by the concentration of malformation on view.

"Eight, Aeronaut? There should be nine."

Crews of three were standard, as the Aeronaut had explained.

"There are nine, colonel. I am the ninth. Do you think I will not go where I send others?"

Seeing the colonel's face, he added, "Do not worry, Colonel, there are three deputies as well equipped as I to do what is necessary here. You see my condition, Colonel. A few years, perhaps months, and I will be unable to fly or to manage. I have trained with these and others these last ten years. Now, we put it into practice."

The briefing was short and to the point. Ride high over the Badlands. Descend when you are over the Ground. Pick your targets. Not villages; go for farms or herds. Use all your canisters, then land as far away from habitation as possible. Burn your balloon. If you can, head west on foot. A rehearsal of dealing with the canisters. Then, the explanation. The prospect of Eden, and the threat from the Domain. Those before the colonel showed no emotion that he could read, certainly not fear or uncertainty. A few technical points from the Aeronaut, the formation of crews, and they were dismissed. The Aeronaut turned to the colonel.

"All in order, Colonel? I forgot to say last night that there is very limited steering on these craft. We will be able to target if the density is good. By the way, since there is no flying today, for sure, I would like to show you something I have worked on for several years. Come with me."

He led the way to one of the big wooden sheds. With rope and pulley, he lowered shutters to let in some light. The vast space was full of benches, racks holding paper and cloth, stone containers and many buckets of water around the whole space. On one bench stood a row of what were clearly miniature Montgolfiers.

"Heard of Chinese Lanterns, Colonel? They were popular as toys, more or less, before the war, so Lord Alfred told me. Unmanned Montgolfiers, Colonel." He went to a chest and withdrew a short, fat candle. He inserted it in a fitting at the base of the tiny balloon. Taking it outside, he invited the colonel to light the candle. Very soon, the miniature balloon lifted and rose higher and higher, drifting very slightly to the north. It was soon invisible.

"It would show up more in the dark, Colonel. Used in the right conditions, they can travel for miles. No steering of course. A bit of a fire risk, too, though we have never started one in our trials."

"Ingenious. It had not occurred to me. But to what practical use?"

The aeronaut fetched a narrower, taller candle. Two pins were inserted on opposite sides, one slightly higher and much shorter than the other. He picked up a small, cylindrical container, to which two short strings ending in loops were attached. One was glued to the side of the cylinder but the other was attached to one side of the base, a side weighted with a blob of resin. The Aeronaut put a small amount of wheat grain in the container, then cut off most of the upper part of the candle, retrieving the wick.

"Take this one outside, colonel, tether it and light the wick. When it strains, let it go." The colonel did so. The tiny balloon rose slowly. It was not long before it rocked suddenly, and a rain of wheat grain was released. The tilt pushed the flame towards the side, and the little balloon caught fire, and flaming fragments descended to earth.

"Colonel, we can make these in the thousands. It needs little training. It would be indiscriminate but scattered in its killing power if you had poison enough in the right form. The distance depends on wind, of course, but also on the size of the candle and the position of the pins. I could release more than two hundred of these within a week. More material, and we could make thousands here alone. We can adjust the candles and pins to spread drops over a large area. We've tested it in east winds with watchers."

The colonel was impressed. Deliver death to the enemy without risking your own. And it did not have to be that effective. Poison did not have to be in all; one in ten might do when the possible consequences were known below. But then: what could safely be put in those little containers, with their open tops and far from completely sealed, hinged bases? Certainly not that contained in the very secure canisters he had brought. And, of course, it would invite retaliation, because the balloon and the method were easily worked out. The wind was not always in the west. Who knew what weapons the Domain possessed?

"Ingenious, Aeronaut. But this poison is lethal. I cannot see how we could place it in these little containers of yours without risk to our own. I do not even know where what we are about to use came from, nor its age. But if you can spare one with the knowledge. I will send him or her north to the Old-timers. Lord Alfred has stocks, I think. Does he know of this?"

"That we have been experimenting, yes. How far we have got, no. He tolerates us, Colonel; he is not a man of war. Ingenious devices, and precision, yes. I am told he is trying to re-create functional steam engines. He is in a hurry, colonel, I think his time is running out."

"Again, can you spare someone to alert him. He is strategically placed in a way we are not in the north. Unless we were lucky with the wind, any Montgolfiers, or these miniatures would move only over Badlands, or over Ground we must protect. He should make as many as he can. If he can devise a useable payload, we can use them. But if we get no response from the Domain, I am afraid any second strike will have to go as planned with what you have here."

Lord Alfred's time running out. The story again and again among the few Old-timers, those who had known life before the war. Only the three of them now, besides Defoe himself. And so hard to pass on skill and knowledge when so many naturals were handicapped in mind or body, and so little remained of the machines and the means of making or even repairing them. Just the slender hope of Eden, and what it might do, sustained the spirits.

***

There was little for Colonel Hunt to do for the rest of the day. The wind remained light, and straight from the south. Outlanders were completing the last of the Montgolfiers, while the first was already upright and tethered to the scaffold. He ate a largely silent meal with the Aeronaut and his deputies, and went to bed.

He woke to the sounds of strong winds and rain. Cursing the latter, he emerged. Certainly, the wind was from the south-west. The tethered Montgolfier was shaking a bit. The other two were firmly pegged down on their sides. The Aeronaut appeared.

"Not to worry, Colonel. This rain will ease off, and the wind speed too, but not too much. Luck is on our side. Give it an hour and we'll launch the first."

He was right. Cloud cover thinned, the sun shone intermittently, and the wind was a steady breeze. What followed was a remarkable demonstration of the Aeronaut's regime. The Montgolfier by the scaffold was raised so that its base was about 10 feet from the ground. A trolley with a stove was run under it. A chimney was raised by men with hooked poles. Others rushed to operate bellows. Soon, the Montgolfier became buoyant, tugging at its moorings. The chimney was lowered, the trolley moved, and another with the basket moved in; a basket already armed with its deadly canisters. In its centre was a smaller stove, ready lit. Ropes hanging from the straining bag were attached to the basket. Three people stepped forward, saluted the Aeronaut and the colonel and climbed aboard. One got to work on a bellows. Another gave a signal, and all tethers were released. The Montgolfier rose rapidly, moving north-east.

It took a little longer to launch the others, as the Montgolfiers themselves had to be brought to the scaffold and winched upright. It was about an hour later that the last was ready to ascend. It carried the Aeronaut and his two crew. He saluted the colonel. The moorings were released, and the craft ascended rapidly, soon being lost to sight.

***

As the Aeronaut looked down, he could see below them the sparsely vegetated semi-badlands of the Hereford Riding. Occasionally, he could see flocks of sheep or herds of cattle and their minders. They would know what the sight meant, war. There were rare patches of richer vegetation, even some planted fields. Soon, however, the vegetation got sparser still; bare and gullied earth became common. They were over the Badlands proper, still ascending.

Ruins now lacked cover; old roads could be made out. No sign of the other craft, which would be trying to veer to the south of his track.

Vegetation returned, and soon there were villages and fields. They were over the Ground. He nodded to a crewman, and the heat was diverted away from the mouth of the balloon. The craft slowly descended. Another nod, and heat was returned upwards. He lowered a canister gently on its line. It was not long before a target appeared, a herd of cattle with two herdsmen. Just before the Montgolfier passed over them, he tugged vigorously on the line which jumped back in his hands. Death delivered. He crossed himself. May we find stock without people, he prayed, while lowering another canister.

The bellows were pumped harder; they rose a little. Small patches of contaminated ground passed beneath them. No targets.

"How much longer have we got, firemaster?"

"Not long, sir, fifteen minutes, if we are lucky, twenty if the sun shines."

Then a village. People gathering and staring upwards. The string was not jerked. Fields below but no beasts. The poison would kill crops, but take longer to act. A farm; the string pulled; another canister lowered. Three left to deliver. A field of ponies. Pull, with no knowledge of the spread. The firemaster gave a thumbs down; the fuel was nearly finished. The two remaining canisters triggered over crops.

Five minutes later, the craft grounded, tipping out the crew. Two chased it and held it, aided by a small bush to which they could tie a loose rope. The other lit a prepared torch from the spilled embers of the stove, and soon the lacquered linen was ablaze. The three looked around them. Semi-badland again, and no-one in sight. They started the long walk west. How far they had gone, they had no idea. For several hours, they tramped over the same barren ground, clearly to the north of where they had flown. The pace was slow; the Aeronaut's disability started to tell. Eventually, as evening wore on, the landscape changed. Small areas bounded by posts held rows of potatoes or young rye. There were tracks in good repair. Larger areas were evidently pasture. In the distance, they could see a village. There was little in the way of cover, but they saw no one.

The Aeronaut could walk no more. They found a small copse in which they could rest out of sight. Night would be good, but not for him. Go, he told them. Go, that is an order. Find a stream. Split, one up-, one down-stream in the water for as long as possible. One of you may save the other. They stared at him for a while. Eric cried openly; Daniel looked away. GO, for the love of God, NOW.

As they left, the Aeronaut lay back. It got colder. Come morning, he might hobble some way, maybe. Sleep did not come to him. Rather, the years of preparation and experiment, preparation for an event they all dreaded and had now happened, circled in his mind. A rain shower chilled him more. He started shivering. In the early hours, he heard them, saw the flaming torches wavering. Hand to his pocket. Shakily, the stopper withdrawn, the quick swallow.

Minutes later, a posse of Proctors and their dogs stood over him. Still warm. The Proctor sergeant turned him over and searched. The bottle beside him and nothing else. The trail ran on, and the party soon moved off, westwards.

***

It was several miles before Eric and Daniel found a stream that they could walk in. Unsure of their direction until dawn, they hugged and parted, with few words. In a world where limited capacities restricted most to the humdrum of agricultural survival, to be aeronauts was something else. To be singled out and trained under the Aeronaut. To work in a place visited by officers and even Old-timers. Ahead of them were who knew how many miles of Badlands, Badlands of unknown capacity for harm. They were soon out of each other's sight or sound.

Dawn broke as the Proctors reached the stream. The sergeant dared not split the party. Who knew what weapons a pair of desperate Outies might have? They went upstream, and found the trail. To no good purpose, as within a few miles it led straight onto Badlands. The dogs were held back.

"We're not going in there, sarge, are we? The buggers will be lucky to survive, and good luck to them if they do."

The sergeant nodded. You could risk a short walk on the edge, especially if you had a mask, and clothes that you could shed afterwards. But there was more to it. The troop had seen the balloon fly over their village. Only later had damage been reported elsewhere. They had realised that the Outies could have killed dozens, and had not done so. Outies stole, they did not destroy or murder. He led the men back to the stream. On a hunch, they moved downstream. The story was repeated. Back home was all that remained.

Hours later, the party arrived at the Proctor's station. The reception was crowded with Proctors. The sergeant was told to go to the mayor's office, alone. Outside it was a single two-wheeled mobile. He was directed to the office room itself. A Kingsman major, the Proctor captain, two other Proctor sergeants and the mayor were inside.

"You are the last to report, Sergeant. Outies accounted for?"

"Not all, sir. One suicide, the other two ran into the Badlands. Ugly brute, the one who topped himself. Feathers in his cap, though, does that mean an Outie bigwig?"

"You did not follow?"

"No, sir. It's a bad patch, and we do not have the benefit of gear, sir. Chances are they'll die before reaching safety, and they'll be none too healthy if they do."

"All reports in, then. Three balloons, all burnt. Seven suicides among the Outies. Two missing. At least a hundred cattle dead, more not expected to survive. Twenty or more ponies, again many very sick too. Twelve dead, eight of them at Godspass farm. Sick, Mr Mayor?"

"Only three, Major, and not badly. The hygienist thinks they will recover." The mayor thought for a bit.

"Major, two of those balloons passed right over villages in daylight. Folk rushed outside to see them. They were low. If they had discharged, we would be talking a hundred or more dead and more incapacitated than we could deal with. Many of our Proctors among them. We can warn people to stay indoors if they see any more, but a more determined attack would still kill many. Do we have any protection? Is this a warning or something?"

"The King looks after his own, Mr Mayor. I am not up to reading Outie minds, and I advise you not to try. I will be using your telephone, and then I will drive wherever I am commanded to brief our rulers. You can be sure that there will not only be reprisals, but the elimination of the threat. There are semi-badlands to your west, I think. Time to think of expansion."

It was not long after noon. The locals trooped out, leaving the major to telephone. In the main hall, The Proctor captain pulled the mayor aside.

"I'm worried, Jonathan, very worried. We could have the Division swarming with Kingsmen with rifles and we'd not prevent the Outies attacking in this way. I've talked to two of the men. The balloon comes in from a height, and swoops low with a box or something hanging. I don't think rifle shots will down it fast enough. Somehow, the box falls apart and the poison is released. It blows with the wind. We might down the balloon as it passes by; too late. They'd likely open all they have at once if they are going down. Z? it's the least of the problems, I think. It was mentioned only in passing in our training, because it does not last long. If the Outies have that, what else do they have?"

"Enough warning and we could get folk to scatter?"

"With Z, yes, if people scatter fast enough, which I doubt. But long-lived mutagens? Unseen and unmarked till we find the consequences?"

The mayor grimaced. Year by year, their Ground had been expanding, mostly by small improvements in the semis. No need for the kind of work used up north. But the numbers of those Chosen rose faster, as did the demand for stock, meat and seeds. A host of balloons discharging over the Ground, even at random, could undo decades of grindingly slow improvement. As he thought about it, it seemed to him that they did not even need balloons. A horde of suicidal Outies carrying devil's brew in their bags could overrun any feasible number of Proctors or even Kingsmen. Enough would cross the Badlands knowing that they would not return. But why would they? For all the tales of Outie kidnaps, there had been none to his knowledge. Nor any attacks like this. What little experience he or anyone had of Outies, they recognised the value of the Grounds, and did no damage. They just stole. His thoughts were interrupted as the major emerged. The pair got a frowning glance, but nothing more. Soon, the major and his driver were on their way east.

***

Colonel Hunt had been told to remain where he was until the second wave had been launched or cancelled. Although far too early, he and many others kept glancing up at the semaphore tower the whole day after launch. And at its next on the line north. Of course, there was no signal. Cursing himself for a fool, he accosted one of the deputies, Martha, a young woman with stunted arms and legs, but a look of intelligence in her face. She led him back to the shed where the Aeronaut had showed him the Chinese lanterns. He knew of no weapon in Westron hands more deadly than Agent Z. God forbid that they had mutagens, and he would have disobeyed orders had he been told to use them. But nothing besides the Z would have any impact by air. All the aeronauts had seen the dummy containers used in training. Many had even released harmless contents in trial runs. With one in his hands, he asked Martha:

"Could we ever have such a device release by itself from such a lantern? The Chief thought not, or rather that we could not load it without killing our own people, or shedding it in dribbles as it was carried. He was hoping some new load could be designed."

Martha turned the dummy canister around in her hands. She operated the release again and again.

"Is all that you have in these canisters, Colonel? If so, we have a problem to begin with. To lift them, the lanterns would need to be much larger than those you see around you. And a more powerful source of heat too. And if we did have smaller containers, how could we safely load them and seal them?"

To that, the colonel had no answer. But Martha continued to turn the device over in her hands. He left her for yet another futile glance at the semaphore tower. The following day was no better. The second wave were being assembled. With one of the other deputies, he spent most of the day rehearsing the drill for the aeronauts selected. The technicalities were not the problem, but the rules of engagement were harder for them to swallow. No mercy this time; be over a village, let fly. If it is big, do so twice. The assent was grudging. After a break, he noticed that a few did not return, being replaced by others. He refrained from comment. Murder, other than in extreme cases, was the worst crime imaginable. This was not combat, but slaughter, and not all could face it.

After dark, though, there was a shout, and the colonel emerged from his quarters. On the tops of Semaphore towers, beacons were blazing. Blazing with interruptions as screens were placed in line. The Kingdom would negotiate. Hold the second wave. There was little cheering, but a sense of relief that swept the compound. Many slept better than for days.

First thing in the morning, Martha led him again to the shed housing the lanterns. Up all night, and with two assistants, she had something to show him. One of the Aeronaut's lanterns had been hooked to a small ceramic pot. A candle was wedged firmly in its mouth. Along one side a thick, corded fuse was held away from the candle's side, disappearing into the pot through a nick made in the candle's base. This candle was short, and the fuse ended not far short of its top.

"Take it outside and light it, Colonel." He did so. There was little wind, and the miniature balloon ascended almost vertically. Moving slightly east as it caught the breeze, there was a sudden bang. The pot disintegrated and shards fell to the ground. The lantern, in tatters, descended more gently.

"It works, Colonel. A pot full of gunpowder. A fragile pot that bursts easily. It would be more powerful if we used a cork or stopper wired down. We could use thicker walls too, and fragments would be scattered more widely. They might cause injury on their own. Give us a way to add poison without killing ourselves in the process, and it will be scattered. Alter the length of the candle or the distance between fuse and flame, and the range and altitude will vary, but not in any very ordered way."

The colonel looked around the shed. Many tiny balloons were there, rigid over their lightweight frames and ready to be attached to their loads. But he saw no pots of the kind Martha has used. The Aeronaut's cylinders had been of a kind of cardboard; scraps, shavings and sawdust mixed with glue and shaped in moulds.

"These pots, are there more of them? Are they easily made?"

"We have a few dozen here. They are used to store the powders and potions of the chemists and doctors. They are mostly in use, though. They are made in Dean and used all over our lands, but I do not know how many they make or how fast."

Time for action. Leaving instructions to his men, the colonel commandeered a pony and set out for Dean, a sample in his bags. Twenty-odd miles, maybe twenty-five. With luck, he would be there by dusk. The road was good, the route that carried the weight of Outlander traffic.

***

Evening was falling over the small settlement of Leysters. Close to the Badlands themselves, its few inhabitants were employed in herding, and tending, as best they might, the stunted orchards and their feeble crop. Too small to have even a formal Head of House, the dozen or so families might have been regarded as a primitive communist community in times long past. But a closer inspection would reveal some features unknown then. Nowhere, was there any notice. No paper would be found. Indeed, there were none who could read or write. In physique, most would pass for normal, but in conversation the slowness of mind would be obvious. The bounty *here had done this. It had not caused sterility, though. Children were at least enough in number to replace often premature losses among adults. It was a child running, screaming, to the cluster of cottages that brought the inhabitants out onto the track that led to the west. And into the wider world in its terrifying complexity.*

"Monster, Mum, Monster, back there, it's coming, it's coming. From the Baddles."

The child ran to her mother, grabbing her legs and hugging them. People stared to the east, from where the child had come. Towards the Badlands, scarcely two miles away. Nothing to be seen.

"What do you mean, a monster, child? There's nothing lives out there. What kind of monster?"

The child remained incoherent, sobbing into her mother's overalls. Nothing or nobody appeared.

"Happen she's had a fit, Miss. Or dreamt up a make-believe beast," one man said to the mother.

The child stamped her feet. Between sobs she shouted. "No, I didn't. It was a real monster, like a man. It had clothes. It was crawling. Its face was all wrong. It was coming this way."

"Did it see you, child?"

"I don't know. It was looking at the ground. It was scary. I ran."

There was a hubbub of conversation. When nothing appeared, three men set off with pitchforks. It did not take them long to find the monster. Lying on his side, gasping, was a man in a bedraggled uniform. His face was indeed hideous, but not in the least frightening to those who had travelled west to market or exchange. Just one product of the *bounty*, one that had passed this community by. They heaved him to his feet, and with one on each side, walked slowly back to the village.

Slow they might be, but all recognised the symptoms of contamination. Bad at that, probably too bad. As gently as possible they cut away his clothes. Buckets of warm water were poured over him, several for his hair alone. He was wrapped up in blankets, and propped up in the bed set aside for the rare visitor. His breathing was heavy and rasping. The naturally disfigured face was further marred with welts and blisters.

"Never seen one that bad. Must have been out there for days, and not just the edge neither."

"Why, for God's sake? Gone crazy? Everyone knows what it's like out there."

The man opened his eyes, and stared at those around him. A spasm of coughing took hold, but it seemed to clear his breathing.

"Eric. Aeronaut. Attacked them. Chief told us to run. Left him behind." His sobs as he spoke provoked another fit of coughing and retching. He lay back, exhausted. His eyes closed.

"What did he say, ayro something? I heard something like that from Fred. Someone go fetch him. He's the travelled one around here. Attacked? Who's them when they're at home? There's only Grounders other side, and they don't harm no one."

Fred arrived. There were muttered conversations. The contaminated clothing was shown to him, gingerly on the end of a stick. He touched the sick man gently on the shoulder. Eric opened his eyes.

"Just nod if I get it right, lad, don't waste your breath. Your name's Eric, yes? You're one of those Ayronouts what lives in Hereford? That has those balloons, what do they call them, Montgoffers? Flew over the Badlands, right to the other side? Chief still there?"

The last got a look of conflict rather than a nod. Eric raised himself a little, and gasped.

"We dropped poison. The Domain is attacking. We landed. Chief can't move, told us to go. Be dead by now." He coughed again, and a trickle of blood came from the corner of his mouth. He collapsed back on the pillow. The group left the room and stood anxiously in the hallway of the guest cottage, waiting for Fred to explain.

"Those balloons, they're weapons. Met an ayronout once, when I drove a herd to Lemster. They're for war, war with the Domain. Last resort, he said, if the bastards come for us. And no return. And that's the uniform, right enough. Looks like there's bad trouble, but we never got told."

There was silence. Some effort had been made to teach them about the Great War. What had sunk in was the horrid fact of murder, murder all the worse for its colossal scale. Death raining from the skies. Poisons that had made the Badlands what they were. A little more had sunk in, transmitted by tales of daring deeds and last stands.

"Reckon this one's a hero, then, Fred, and his boss? Chief he said. Don't that mean three feathers?"

"It does and all, that's right. And deserves respect. This one's mates will want to know. We'd best think about that in the morning. See what state he's in."

But to no one's surprise, Eric did not survive the night. He had not regained consciousness. After much discussion, the body, wrapped in many blankets, was placed on a cart. A pony, led by Fred as the quickest thinker and talker, pulled the sad burden away towards Hereford. One night near Hope summit, where there was a primitive caravanserai, way station as they called it, and the following morning down to the Aeronaut's compound.

Fred led his dismal burden into the compound. There was much activity; frames were being assembled; linen sheets re-lacquered. No one paid him much attention, but he spotted a short woman with two feathers in her helmet. Her manner immediately suggested command, and tethering the pony to a fence, he approached her, touching his traditional wide-brimmed hat.

It was scarcely a conversation. Martha strode swiftly to the cart, and uncovered the ravaged face. A death worse than the poison that all had been given. With an effort, she covered it, and stood mastering her tears. She turned back and barked an order. Two came to her call and carried the concealed body to the centre of the compound. Another order, and all stopped work and gathered round. With Fred's help, she unwrapped the body, laid on some of the blankets that had covered it.

"This is Eric, comrades. He braved the Badlands, and he has paid the price. The Chief is dead, but his mission was fulfilled."

What followed was strange to Fred, but was the tradition. Deaths were frequent enough, though usually from natural causes. This was the first they had witnessed from combat, if indirectly. One by one, each in the compound walked up to the body, removed their helmets and bowed. The body was lifted and carried indoors. Fred was thanked and sent on his way. Act One of that great storm, the storm that would change his small world was over.

16. Treaty Point

A track runs north just below the crest of a ridge to the west. As it starts a descent, what was once a farmhouse marks its end. There are poles beside it carrying a single cable that descends to the house. Beyond it, another old farmhouse is visible a mere 150 yards downhill. A path links the two, but beyond the lower house, the land dips steeply, and any other route to it is hidden. Both houses have high-walled yards. Both have tall and conspicuous flagpoles, usually bare. Around these farms only the tumbled remains of drystone walls reveal an agricultural past. Drystone walls mostly covered in brambles, save where fire has exposed the stones once so neatly laid. A hill rising beyond the lower house is covered in scrubby woodland, the typical cover of areas recovering from severe contamination. What were once fields are now moorland, healthy enough, but with recently burnt patches.

Beyond the crest of the ridge to the west, the land falls away very steeply to a narrow valley. On the opposite side, a gentler slope rises to high moorland with clumps of birch. These are thicker in the valley bottom, concealing a set of posts along the streamside. Red-painted posts here, and no wall. These posts mark, uniquely, the direct boundary between Outland and Domain, a stretch of about two miles south to Hare Edge. Go further, and the full force of contamination is seen in the barren landscape. Behind the scrubby hill to the north, another, smaller barren patch is replaced by the familiar landscape of the Ground and the boundary farm of Owler Bar. To the east, however, there is more barren land.

Less than a mile south of the upper farm, the track and accompanying poles turn sharply east. Further east still, the track skirts more contaminated land, and passes through areas far from healthy, but at least vegetated. Twelve miles in, and it skirts the dead southern half of the city, stark ruins contrasting with the luxuriant growth in its northern parts. The track and its poles mark the narrow, twisting route that connects the Domain proper to the Outland. This is the

Corridor. To its north, patches of barrens give way to a short junction with the extreme south of the Northernmost Ground. Much less free from contamination than the area north of Whirlow, the few farms are mainly for sheep, and for direct export to the Domain rather than for breeding stock. There is a barracks for the Proctors at Woodhouse, and across the boundary and into the Corridor a despatch and transfer station at Barlow. The route south from Barlow is the only one to other Grounds not passing through the Domain proper.

***

To say that duty at the Treaty Point was boring was, to Sergeant Mills, an understatement. A week at a time with bugger all happening, but without any source of entertainment. Someone looking downhill in case there was a signal all through daylight hours. For all he and his men knew, the Outie equivalent was unoccupied altogether. No drink on the premises, a few packs of greasy cards, a few dog-eared books, mostly cheap war stories, all read on previous turns of duty.

The previous detail had at least a little excitement with a message to look out for an absconder from the north. They'd even opened the reception room to talk to a Proctor from the north who had daringly crossed the moor to the west and come up past the Outies' post. No sign of life there, apparently. No absconder either. The poor bugger was probably making a nice roast for an Outie barbeque.

So, it was quite a relief when a trooper entered the house to announce a red flag on the Outie pole. Red: that meant serious. He telephoned. See what they want, sergeant, came the languid tones of a captain at the other end, see what they want and call back. The squad set up the reception room: open the outside door, arrange seating across a wide table, then run up a green flag to say we are ready. The sergeant sat down with a trooper to wait. Another outside yelled, "they're coming, sarge, four of them."

"Any visible weapons?"

"Two have bows, that's all, sarge."

The sergeant and trooper removed their pistols and placed them on the table. A bit nervously, as it was the first time either had actually had to receive an Outie visit. The Outies entered. Two were what the sergeant thought of as bog-standard Outies. The sort you saw dead or in chains at the Hunt. They took chairs at the ends of the row, having placed crossbows on the table. Another was less misshapen, and rather more smartly dressed, but the fourth was something else. Tall, regular and wearing a black robe, she sat after removing a helmet. A *metal* helmet, polished and with plumes. But her face! That of a lady back home, long, thin and with bright eyes that met his from above high cheekbones. Apart from an aged look, she'd pass for a noble in the Domain.

"Is there no one more senior than yourself here, sergeant?"

A toff accent if ever I heard one, thought the sergeant, *though she sounds old as well.*

"No, I am in command, Miss Outlander." He suppressed a gut reaction to say 'ma'am'.

"Very well. I am going to hand you a message. Your telephone is in order, yes? Good. You should read it in full to your superiors the moment I leave. If you can do so safely, you should also send it back with one of your men. There are those who will recognise my handwriting. In the meantime, I would like you to read it out loud, and in full. If there are words you misunderstand or mispronounce, we can make appropriate adjustments."

She passed over a single sheet of paper. It was astonishing to find an Outie who could read and write, but even more so that it was written in a flowing, ornate hand. Evenly spaced and perfectly horizontal lines too.

To My Lord Pendennis
Sir,

On the eighth of this month, a large body of Royal troops entered our territory to a depth of nearly three miles near the northern limits of the inhabited zone. When warned off, they opened fire with rifles. Three Westron men were killed outright and a further two have subsequently died from their injuries.

This blatant breach of the treaties follows two minor incursions by Royal forces in the same area, incursions that were short-lived and involved no contact.

I would make the point that the area in which this outrageous incursion happened is one in which there has been just one, very minor, incident of rustling in the last fifteen years. No warning or complaint about such activities has been received by us. Nor was any hot pursuit involved.

If it is not already known to you, we have made a proportionate military response. We require the presence of a plenipotentiary at the Treaty Point within five days to agree further reparations and guarantees. In the absence of such, we will be entitled under the terms of the treaties to take whatever further defensive measures we think appropriate.

Elisabeth Hawkins

Quondam Countess of Lindisfarne and the Isles

"Westron? Rustling? Pleni-potent-iary, ma...?" the sergeant stopped just in time, to the amusement of the other.

"Westron to us, Outie to you, sergeant. Rustling is removing livestock, usually those foolishly left beyond the bounds unattended. Plenipotentiary? Capable of agreeing terms on behalf of his *Sacred* Majesty on the spot, sergeant, and guaranteeing they are honoured."

"Quondam?"

"From an ancient language, sergeant, 'once upon a time' will do. Yes, sergeant, I am indeed among the nobility, deprived of my title by the fortunes of war and the animosity of your adored sovereign. Older than your great grandfather by quite a margin. When you pass the message on, sergeant, you can also indicate that I will be here for the next five days or within easy reach."

The Outies rose and left. The sergeant and the trooper simply stared at each other in astonishment. Outie nobility! Had they not been killed in the war? The sergeant pulled himself together and made the necessary call. Actually, one call out and two back as confirmation was required higher and higher up. A mobile would be sent to pick up the paper. Nearly three weeks after the claimed attack, the sergeant noted. Of course, Outies did not have telephones.

Back in the Westron post, Lady Hawkins removed her cloak and helmet, and sank wearily into a chair. Her time was coming, and she had near-daily intimations of machinery breaking down. The dose had been second rank. Its expiry time was near. Out of time and the decay moved fast. And a late booster, even if it were possible, would condemn you to a century of enfeebled old age at best. The journeys had been arduous. Even the last stage, merely from Chapel, but riding rather than in a carriage had been draining.

Clearly, she thought, *no news of the Montgolfier attack had reached the Point, or the sergeant would have reacted differently.* Had it failed? Once launched, there would be no way of knowing. She would have to wait. No response, and they would have to launch the second strike, their last throw. A wave of pessimism swept over her. So sure, they had been, that they could break the Royalist cause immediately after the Catastrophe. Then the missiles and drones, ours and theirs, but not for long, and a residue of sterility or impairment that had nearly broken them. The few truly unpolluted areas in their opponent's grasp, as well as most of what was left of pre-war technology. That sergeant could get a message sent 200 miles in as many seconds, damn him, where we would take ten days if we were lucky.

So few of our fertiles with any brains, try as we might, even with a bit of what was euphemistically described as outcrossing. The world was getting cleaner, but so slowly, and she was one of the few of the old nobility left. Most of us were minor only, like herself; many had fallen in the war, and others had run their course a long time ago. The remaining few, like her, were nearing the end, bar, perhaps, Defoe himself, good for another hundred. The Domain knew it too, they had the genealogy and treatment records. The last of them gone, and leadership would be defunct unless Eden worked. Steal Grounders, and there would be legal retaliation. Boundary liaisons achieved little; those seduced were few. Gloomy and exhausted, she went to bed.

***

Later that day, a mobile did indeed arrive at the Point, a simple two-wheeler with a despatch rider, who turned around immediately with the letter. The Outie post flew a green flag, meaning that a negotiator, presumably Hawkins herself, was there. Come nightfall, and with no instructions, the sergeant turned in, leaving a corporal in charge. He was rudely awakened at six the following morning.

"Phone, sarge, there's a flap on. There's been an Outie attack to the south. Balloons. Agent Z, whatever that is."

The sergeant struggled to the telephone. Had they been attacked? No. Was there still an Outie high-up in their post? Yes. Fly the blue flag. Tell them that a Noble would be with them today, but not to conclude any resolution. Might be more than five days before a delegation arrived.

"A flag, my Lady, blue. They will have a message," the Westron observer reported.

The officer who had been with Lady Hawkins the previous day climbed to reception. A nervous sergeant delivered his message. Back home to wait. Around noon, the red flag, and the whole party marched uphill. This time, though, the sergeant and one of his men were seated either side of a smarter pair: a man in major's uniform, and a young-looking male noble, a pair who had been routed out and despatched by mobile.

"I am the Earl of Hastings, Miss Outlander," he started, to be interrupted with vigour.

"That is Lady Hawkins to you, if we are to continue this meeting. You have powers to conclude it? No, as we were told by your man here. Our letter was clear to you, was it not? Why are you here *my Lord,* without any powers? Is Lord Pendennis no longer authorised to deal with us? We were notified of no change."

Hastings? That did not ring any bells. Elevated after the war then, a promoted Grounder. Wonder how much he got. How much more he hopes for? Are they treating the attack seriously or not?

The last question, at least, was answered immediately by Hastings.

"A day ago, *my Lady*, your forces launched a savage attack using Agent Z on our Ground in Worcester Division. It is banned under the treaty. Damage to the Ground is, in the opinion of His Majesty's Council, a wholly disproportionate response to a minor policing operation in the north."

"Wrong, my Lord. Z kills, yes, cripples, yes. So do rifle bullets, my Lord. Neither pollute long term, nor are they mutagens. At best, its status under the treaty is moot. As for minor policing action, five people were killed, on our own territory, my Lord, and others may yet succumb. There was no hot pursuit, no body of stolen cattle to be retrieved, but a considerable armed force that had been offered no provocation. Ask your major here, my Lord, about the rules governing boundaries, if you are unfamiliar with them."

The major looked uncomfortable. He was not clear just why this meeting was taking place at all, when Hastings could agree to nothing. The Outie was right. The best thing, in his view, would have been a retaliatory raid in the south. They could be kitted out, and use unchosen for the real dirty work. Balloon attacks? A new trick, to be sure, but they were very inefficient. Ground forces in gear could target better, even if moving slowly. Few people had been killed. Ignore and retaliate, push the buggers back to the mountains for good. The word was that Lord Arundel himself was warming up for a real war. To his surprise, though, Hastings changed tack and tone.

"My Lady," dragged out again with reluctance. "I am authorised to say that the Council wishes to avoid any further damage to the Ground, a humanitarian concern which I am sure you will share. Without prejudice, therefore, I am pleased to say that a plenipotentiary delegation is willing to meet you, provided no further provocations occur."

"When, my Lord, when? We said five days. Our forces are ready to attack on a far greater scale than that mounted as a proportionate first response. Balloons are not our only means of delivery, nor is Z our only weapon. Lord Pendennis is ill, my Lord? I expected a more empowered representative to meet me, not a messenger. All is ready, my Lord, and will happen unless I signal otherwise."

The advantage of age, she thought, *and the residual respect for rank.* I can bluff with a straight face. Hastings, though, reddened. Stave them off, he was told, buy time. That was official. What was on the grapevine told a different story. Pendennis was out, the Council was divided. The major stepped in.

"May I suggest a short adjournment, Sir? Madam? An hour? I am sure the sergeant can offer our guests some refreshment here."

Lady Hawkins grinned. "Why, of course, Major, an excellent idea. I am sure his Lordship will wish to receive some instructions."

And, indeed, Hastings could see no way to avoid agreeing. Like it or not, he needed instructions. The Domain party withdrew back into the station. The telephone conversations that followed were baffling. After his report, he was asked to hand the instrument to the major. He could then hear only the major's replies.

"Sorry about that, sir, I sent a messenger with a report. I was told to meet with whoever was here, sir. Not near a telephone after that until I got here."

"Yes, sir, Z for certain. We think it was targeted on stock. Villages were overflown and could have been attacked. All over poor Ground. No evidence of anything else, no, though it might take a while to detect anything."

"Three to each balloon, sir. Seven dead, two unaccounted for. No, suicide, when we approached; One crew were all injured on landing. They'd poisoned themselves. Another crew were found on the run, did the same before we caught up with them. Dogs found one other. He heard them coming and did the same. Tracked the others until the Badlands proper."

"The Balloons? They burnt all of them."

"Hard to say, sir, I've no expertise. But I'm told that if they go high to start with, the range is extended. The furthest away reached east of Worcester. Maybe 35–40 miles, sir, we don't know for sure where they launched from."

He put the phone down. Hastings was to wait for another call. The major left the room to talk to the sergeant and his men. The call came. Instructions were given. The party returned to the Reception Room.

"I am authorised to promise a full plenipotentiary meeting here in 14 days' time, during which there will be no hostile action across the boundary on either side."

"Far too long, my Lord. Our forces are not going to stand on alert while you plan counter-attacks. Six days, my Lord."

"Ten?"

"No, my Lord, eight, and subject to conditions. The mobile in which you arrived is to be brought to the back of your station where we can see it. It is not to be removed. No mobile is to approach your station until one arrives with your plenipotentiaries. We can watch. You are to give us warning before their arrival. No more than six persons will meet us in this room, unarmed. Four will be nobles; The party is to include Lord Pendennis. At least, one of the others will be first-born. There will be signed proof of the delegation's powers. The Royal seal, my Lord. Be aware that we are familiar with some of their seals and signatures. Any breach of these conditions, and our attacks will resume. Needless to say, any incursion, anywhere in England, will trigger the same response."

It went beyond the limits he had been given. In particular, the minor conditions were designed to humiliate. But the instructions were clear, for Royalty's sake stall them. He nodded. The officer next to Lady Hawkins wrote out the agreement, twice. Both were signed by all bar the two Outlander guards, who left inky thumbprints. Waiting only to see the mobile manoeuvred behind the station, the Outlanders returned to their own. A messenger was despatched to the south, with a simple signal to the first semaphore reached. Lady Hawkins prepared for the trek back to Chapel next day.

17. More Education

When Colonel Hunt had left, Mark assumed that he would be taken back to the Derwent House. It had been hinted. But it did not happen. Nor did he see Lady Hawkins again. Ogilvie remained in Chapel and kept Mark by his side for a while, and the Chief busied himself with calling in hunters and others, along with supplies to send east. Mark was left kicking his heels in a place that held few attractions. At least, however, Ogilvie produced more reading matter. In particular, he was given a short and crudely printed book entitled *A Short History of our Times*. It was written in very simple language. As Chief McEnery had told him, there were few that could read and write, and information was passed on by a few readers, themselves mostly barely literate.

It told a tale that was partly consonant with what Mark had learnt in Chronicles, but with very different interpretations. Yes, before the Catastrophe, the world had been full of people, people in many different kingdoms or nations. They had fought one another with increasingly destructive weapons: poisons, diseases, mutagens and explosives delivered by millions of small unmanned flying machines called drones. What was worse, so the book said, was the destruction of the systems for communicating and for storing knowledge. This was not at all comprehensible to Mark, though the story of physical destruction was all too familiar. So far, so much like Chronicles, except that the riches and good life led by many before the conflict was never mentioned in the latter. *A few places had survived, and there had been some defences, limited in their scale. Grounds*, thought Mark.

Then it told of the life of a Jonathan Farnham, a very rich man, and how he had taken over a laboratory developing a drug or potion that delayed aging. It had turned into *The Institute*, a name that the book imbued with a significance far greater than the name itself. Certainly, a place that did far more than develop a cure for aging. How he had given that cure to himself and then to his adult children, to the scientists involved, and to other rich people who were his

227

partners. Had done so before all its effects were known. How they had protected themselves from many of the weapons used in the Great Catastrophe, the war, so it seemed to Mark, of all against all. How, as the Catastrophe had ended, it was he and his companions who had re-established some kind of society from the few survivors.

That *Institute* had changed. Most of those with extended lives had nevertheless been killed. Mark found the story of why and how completely impossible to understand; seemingly, children had murdered parents; quarrels had occurred over who might receive such doses, and of what magnitude. As Mark knew from Chronicles, those doses carried with them the penalty of sterility. With the singular exception of Farnham's children, doses thereafter had been given only to the childless, many of whom were already sterilised by contamination.

It then became a story that made better sense. Farnham and his children controlled the supply. It drew others to their service. The Domain was established. His family became Royalty, those dosed a nobility. They alone had the means to preserve order; they alone had maintained a core of medical treatments and technical abilities. It told of how Grounds were identified and protected, but then milked for their reproductive capacity. Despite all efforts, population had continued to fall, and that consequently exactions from the fertile were made more onerous.

When it came to the war, though, the account was radically different from the story that Mark had learnt in Chronicles. The King, as he now was, and his children had determined to create a source of the naturally servile, limited in intelligence. But many of the nobility had defied him, and rallied to the defence of those in the areas chosen as breeding grounds. It had been a one-sided war to start with, a fact that Mark could understand all too well: all those *glorious victories for the King*, the dates of which had been learnt by rote. All but a few of the rebel nobles had been killed. As a last resort, they had used the last of the old weapons of the Catastrophe to destroy a whole Ground, with the threat of more. That had brought a truce. A truce and then a treaty, A treaty which left the largest and cleanest Grounds in Royal hands, but stopped their advance westwards. A treaty that bought survival, but little in the way of fertile territory free of taint to the rebels. A treaty that deprived them of much of what little technological capacity remained intact, capacity locked up securely by the *Institute* turned Kingdom. That destruction of a Ground that the book's writer felt obliged to justify as the last resort. Even later, the Domain had tried to weaken the Outland, the Western Lands, by subterfuge. There had been germ warfare that had backfired. Mark recalled the plague, *KY 113, sir*, and the tales of his grandfather. The King had done that?

There were many other things that he found hard to understand. The slow improvement as time went by was not a surprise, but the clearance of tracks through poisoned land by volunteers, not by unchosen criminals certainly was. There were references to a Royal Hunt that mystified him, tales of slaughter of Westron folk moving into clearing Badlands. There were sections on religion, fertility and choice of partners that were less surprising given his recent experiences. He realised that Lord Defoe, a first-born, had become the rebel leader. But it was totally unclear to him how authority was maintained in the west. No potions, doses, were available as rewards. Those capable of reading, and of thinking clearly seemed to gravitate to positions of leadership. He thought particularly of Chief Rhianna, and the hunter O'Neill. The final message was clear. Old-timers would die sooner or later. The world belonged to naturals, but the King and his servants would do all in their power to prevent it.

After a while, Ogilvie had little time for him or his questions. The old man seemed to Mark to be aging day by day. A Sunday came, but Mark was not minded to return to the Church, merely watching from a window in the Chief's house as people passed by in the rain. But the following day, there was a tall man to meet him after breakfast.

"Do you recognise me, young man?" Mark looked up blankly at him. "No, sir, should I?"

"I did not see you myself, but you attended the service in Church on Sunday last week, so I was told. But not yesterday, when I was hoping to talk to you. I was the priest at that Service." Seeing the blank look on Mark's face, he explained, "The one who led the service, the one in robes. On other days, I dress as others; those robes are mostly from before the Catastrophe. They are precious to us."

Ogilvie had been approached, and had approved the contact, hoping that Mark would learn more from a literate man not involved in preparing for defence. The priest took Mark back to his own house, a house perceptibly better maintained than many. He was led into a front room in which there were many chairs behind rows of tables, and many things pinned to the walls: maps, pictures, writing in many hands ranging from the infant scrawl Mark had started with to writing in an ornate style that was well beyond his abilities. A desk and blackboard at the end enabled Mark to identify it as a schoolroom. Only the cross mounted above the blackboard betrayed the connection to the church he had visited.

"I think you had the impression that we had no schools, Mark? Not quite true, as you can see. Those of us that can be spared do our best to teach those capable of learning, few though they may be. I am one such, and we assemble when we can. A group will arrive soon, though many have been called for other duties since your arrival. With your consent, I would like to introduce you to them. I think that learning might go in both directions."

Mark nodded, and looked around the room. A single large picture caught Mark's eye. Garishly coloured, like the pictures in Jamie's *Chronicles in Colour*, it portrayed a battle scene. Centre-right was a dying nobleman, blood staining his chest, his upper body supported by comrades. Bodies of the slain lay around him. The few Outlanders left standing fought with brightly uniformed soldiers in large numbers. Behind those, a mounted noble waved a sword, on his face an expression of diabolical triumph. Underneath was a simple caption, handwritten in ink: *Death of Lord Stark, Battle of the Peak, AD 2065.*

"A victory for your beloved Monarch, and his devilish son, Arundel," said the priest, drily, standing behind him. "Maybe you were taught about it too? A victory that confined us, but in the end destroyed one of the cleanest places to survive the Catastrophe. Maybe our sin, but also our salvation. The first Treaty followed soon after."

The flashback hit Mark. That time in class before he had seen Jamie gazing blankly, David's letter in front of him. "*The Battle of the Peak, sir. Fifth of May, RY 16.*"

"*Yes. And what happened there, Perkins?*"

"*The King's Forces won a glorious victory, sir. Prince Edmund was slain, but six Renegades fell and their forces fled to the west.*"

"I think so, sir. If it's the same battle. Just before the Great War ended. But most of what we call the Peak is Badlands now. I saw just how bad when I was taken through Edale. It's not part of the Domain, for certain. We heard of no treaty in class, either; the war just stopped as far as we could see, but my father did say there had been some agreement."

"That's our sin and salvation, Mark, as I said. That part was the White Peak. Untouched, by God's grace. In our hands, but we could not hold it. We used our weapons to destroy it, to render it uninhabitable for centuries. That halted their advance, but at such terrible cost. Thousands perished then. That was the lesser evil. The permanent damage was a greater. But as the Old-timers taught us, it *brought them to the table.* They had similar weapons, but we did not offer them such tempting targets. They had a few such, the Grounds as you know them, on which they depended for their survival."

Mark had just moved on to look at a map, when there was a knock on the door. The priest left to open it, and soon the room was filling up with people, though not all chairs were taken. Most were those of his age or younger; a few were clearly adult. The latter, Mark saw, were mostly afflicted with physical deformities. Keeping to one side, Mark did not stand out in his Outlander clothes, but he attracted glances at his unfamiliar face. The priest walked to the desk, pulling Mark with him. There was a brief silence.

"Brothers and sisters, this is Mark Norman. He is the one who has fled from the Royal lands. I think you will know that he was among us."

There was a stir in the class. All had heard of his arrival, and the scurrying that had seized the community ever since; the presence of two Old-timers, Old-timers staying, not passing through, an unheard-of event. Rumours of war. People armed and sent east. Eyes turned to him, eyes that noticed his lack of defects and the intelligence visible in his face. A Grounder.

"Let us carry on as usual for a while. Before we end, though, I will ask Mark show you something of his knowledge, and see what he knows of ours."

What followed was like no lesson Mark had experienced. Some, at the back, were copying letters from card-backed sheets onto slates. Mostly the smallest, but with two crippled adults among them. The priest would walk behind them. At times, he would adjust a grip on a small hand, or speak a few quiet words of praise. Others appeared to have individual tasks, working from books open in front of them, sometimes raising a hand to summon the priest for help. Mark could see that most of this work was mathematical, but he did not move to take a closer look. Those in front were turned towards each other in groups of three, engaged on some testing of each other's knowledge. Mark was quite close, and overheard the quietly asked questions and answers. Some involved pictures of plants and animals. Others, shocking to Mark, showed various deformities of both people and animals. There were books to which they could turn. Some answers provoked laughter, good-humoured enough, and Mark realised that this followed a wrong answer.

A girl in the group saw Mark's interest. Raising her hand, she asked the priest if he might join them. A nod, and another chair was brought up. Introductions were made: Lizzie MacDonald, John Hughes, Martin Baker. The task was to learn the signs of different kinds of contamination, and how to react to them. The books beside them, Mark realised, were similar to those in the Hygienist's centre back home: lists and descriptions of ailments, their causes and treatment. They tested him. On plants, his answers were admired, but for all else he was at a loss, to their astonishment. He heard, in sickening detail, about the different kinds of contamination, and their effects, both immediate and long-term. Their matter-of-fact approach to things that turned his stomach astonished him.

Towards noon, the priest called a halt. Turning his back to the class, he put on the blackboard a set of equations. There were x's and y's. There were groans. Mark grinned, and spat out answers almost without any delay. There were gasps. Giving Mark pen and paper, he asked him to write out a piece from the Bible he opened before him. To Mark's relief, it was more straightforward than the Genesis he had struggled with earlier. He wrote:

"*In the beginning was the word, and the word was with God, and the word was God.*" The priest waved the paper in the air to dry the ink, then passed it around the class. The words themselves were familiar to those who believed and came for instruction, though not all could read them. But Mark's writing was clear. It marched evenly across the page.

"Better writing than yours, sir," said Lizzie, grinning at the priest, who gave her a mock scowl. He turned to Mark.

"Where you come from how many can write like that and at what age?"

"Nearly all, sir, by eight or earlier, but not all as neat as me."

Nearly all! When barely one in five could read anything other than a few words learnt by rote, and one in ten could write legibly. But the priest was not finished.

"When did you first come across the Bible, Mark?"

"In the home of another who escaped, sir, and then here in Chapel. We see no books from before the Catastrophe. What survives are in the King's libraries in the Domain. We are allowed only King's Print, as we call them, those written since the war."

Finally, the priest took from a cupboard a large scroll, hooked it over the blackboard and let it unroll. There were muffled cheers; here was a popular test, unlike the horrible maths that defeated most. It was a map of the world, but lacking any names. In outline only, sea and land were alike white while thinner lines marked the boundaries of nations before the Catastrophe. Mark looked at it blankly; a map, clearly, but of where, he had no idea.

"Mark, can you point out the Atlantic Ocean?" *Atlantic Ocean?* Some remote connection in Mark's mind equated ocean with sea, but it was little help. The brief glance at the wall map, recognisably of the same place, before the class had entered made him realise that blue was sea, as rivers were in the map back home, and even in Jones' map. There was obviously a lot of sea shown. He stood dumb before the class, shaking his head.

Or perhaps Britain? Mark thought furiously. Britain, he knew, was an island, the island containing England. A hush. Mark peered at the map. There were many islands. He examined each, while the class were whispering and nudging each other in amazement. He knew there was 'overseas', a toxic area visited by the King's ships. An overseas mainly to the east and south. North was at the top of all maps he had seen. Eventually he pointed with the stick the priest had given him. He was greeted with an ironic cheer and some clapping. He had got it right.

"It is a map of the world, Mark, all of it, as it was before the Catastrophe. We learn the names of the oceans, the seas, and of the many countries that existed. And we remember that, as far as we know, we survive only in this battered piece of a small island."

He summoned Lizzie to the front, and gave her the pointer. Atlantic Ocean? North Sea? France? America? India? Australia? Nods. Angola? A pause. No, that's Mozambique, other side. Narnia? Lizzie grinned and pointed to the priest's head. The whole class burst out laughing. He dismissed them, saying that Mark might visit them again if he was not needed by the Old-timers. He sat Mark down in a small kitchen, and laid out a simple meal of bread, cheese and fruit. So much to explain. Pre-war books opened before him. An atlas, fast disintegrating. But the priest had other duties, and such classes were not every day. None that afternoon as he went about his duties. He would leave a message with the Chief. He had a final word for Mark.

"You saw that class, Mark. It is the only one in all of Chapel. There are a few get taught by their parents if both are capable, but that's just three families now. For every one of the young ones in that class, there are four or five that cannot learn, and half that come will never reach your level. The kingdom and those that came before it did something very wicked, and we know of no way to right it. Remember that when there are those that seem stupid to you."

There was no message the following day, also wet and miserable. Mark started to inspect the few books the priest had sent him away with. The sun emerged the day after. Wandering a little north of the settlement, he saw in the distance a troop in a field gathered around something he could not see. There was a whoosh of noise, and something hurtled into the sky. High up, it exploded. People rushed forward, inspecting the ground under the blast, then returned. One looked in his direction. Immediately, two ran towards him. Mark was tempted to run, but immediately realised the futility. He waited. They closed in; one was recognisably an officer, with two feathers in her helmet.

"You are the Grounder from the east?" Mark nodded. "You should not be here. Stay in the town. Tell Chief McEnery what you have seen, and do what he tells you thereafter." Her manner was worried rather than angry. Nevertheless, Mark turned without any questions and walked back to the Chief's office. There was a bustle of messengers, and others waiting for orders. He overheard snippets of conversation. He caught 'from Manod' and 'Montgolfiers'. There was talk of ships. Mark had assumed that forces were being assembled to find Jones or his refuge, or to protect it from the King's forces. These words meant nothing to him. Eventually, he was let into the Chief's room, and reported on what he had seen. The Chief was silent, other than to tell Mark to go to his room and wait.

It was not a long wait. A woman summoned him downstairs, and into the room where he had first met the rebel nobles. Sat in the same chair as at his first meeting, he faced only two: Ogilvie and the Chief, no Lady Hawkins. There was no clerk, and no papers lay on the table. As before, the room was stiflingly hot. Ogilvie himself seemed to Mark to have aged even since the last meeting. His hands twitched nervously at his cloak, which was wrapped tightly round him.

"I am sorry, young man, that we have given you neither any information nor useful employment. There are reasons for that. At present, you know only of our interest in Mr Jones, and of the attack near his hiding place. But you have seen the marshalling of forces, and now the testing of one of our weapons. I think you will be familiar with fireworks?"

"Yes, sir, the Visitor fires some on the King's birthday each year. But they are fired after dark, and chemists add some ingredient that makes coloured sparks."

"Just so. But fireworks can be used as weapons too. That is, though, beside the point. You seeing it merely advances a conversation we were bound to have.

There is indeed a danger, a grave danger, of a war. You are," here, Ogilvie's mouth tightened, "what would have been known in old times as a strategic asset."

Mark looked blank.

"I mean that while you are, and already have been, a great asset, a benefit if you like, to us, you are equally if not more so a prize for our enemy. You know a little of our actions, and you know where Jones lives and something of what he has discovered. Alive in their hands. Mark, you would tell what you know. You may be brave enough where pain is concerned, but could you trust yourself when your sister, your mother was tortured before your eyes? We know something of Security, Mark, and that *Truth and Justice* that oversee them. Whatever happens, we cannot let you fall into their hands alive."

Ogilvie saw the look on Mark's face, and shivered. But it was axiomatic that actions were freely chosen, even if the choice deprived others of advantage. Why else the war and what followed?

"No, we are not going to kill you. But there is a choice for you to make. We can ensure your survival beyond doubt by sending you west, west near the deep caves where Lord Defoe and our best brains can be protected. He will, indeed, be delighted to meet you, as he is already aware of your presence. You would be treated with honour there. If that fell, all would be over anyway. If we win, your life will be pleasant indeed.

But there is another choice. There are uses for you, not far from your home. In the long run, your heredity is valuable where there are undamaged partners. I think you are already aware of this. More immediately, Jones knows and trusts you. We have not found him, and assuming he is still alive, he may be unwilling to come to us. So, we can move you back, north of the Derwent House. You would move where Jones might see and recognise you, or leave messages that might be found and bring him out. What he brings may be our saving. In the hands of the enemy, it is our downfall. If we do not find him, we may depend on you to guide us inside his refuge.

If you make that choice, however, there is a condition. You will always have at least two by your side. Any risk of capture, and they will kill you. Even the women who may choose you will have the means to kill in the event of a surprise attack. In addition, you will carry with you a phial of the most potent poison we possess. If your companions are killed, we will, of course, have no means of obliging you to use it. Fail, and we fail with you, and what will follow will be worse."

No choice, really, thought Ogilvie, *but it must be offered, and the risk made clear*. As would have been the case with nearly all Westrons, Mark accepted his task and left. Ogilvie summoned doctors.

***

From then on, Mark was left largely to his own devices. He paid many visits to the priest's classes, and was often asked to stay for a meal and to talk. As time went by, these conversations became more inconsequential, but challenging and tinged with humour. It dawned on him that the priest simply enjoyed conversation with someone able to understand his thoughts. Within the classes, he soon became popular with those struggling with maths, and he was regularly engaged with the middle ranks, and occasionally with those in front. In breaks, and with the priest joining in, he was bombarded with questions about his home, and about the Domain. Knowing only of their own Old-timers, many did not know about the system of doses and the minor nobility. Here, even Mark was not entirely clear, since this information was filtered through his father's private conversations with the mayor and the Visitor. In the Ground at large, it was deliberately kept vague.

Above all, though, it was the element of compulsion that both fascinated and horrified them. That work in Badlands was dangerous, they knew very well. Indeed, as Mark had learnt early on, they were better trained to assess risks than Grounders, for whom much less was needed. But the notion of conscription to work on the Barriers was shocking, as was work in Badlands for anything other than clearing routes to more friendly places. Wait, and God's mercy will do its work, provided the devils in the Kingdom did not frustrate it. Choosing in particular aroused fierce debates. Why were there not many more like Mark, they asked. It was unnatural and cruel. It was hard to explain to them the elements at work. The subtle training in childhood. The glory of respect and the material rewards for families involved, and the simple question of where to run. The dire penalties for Evasion. There was outrage when he told them that fleeing to the Outland was to go to a certain death, and cannibalism. Kill? A human being? One harmless, and of good stock? It reinforced all that they had been told about the evils of the Kingdom and the justification for rebellion, even at the terrible cost endured.

When it came to marriage, polygamy and the rearing of children, Mark became rather reticent. Although he had learnt, in practice, that attitudes here were very different, a certain prudishness from his upbringing held him back. The priest saw this, and on one afternoon dismissed all but those of about Mark's age.

A small group: six only, and with the priest in attendance. You can talk freely, he told Mark. All learn very early. In fact, it was Mark's turn to ask questions. He knew that the Chiefs he had met had husbands or wives. Was marriage universal? Not quite, and often unofficial, especially among the known infertile. Always monogamous? Nearly always. Always by free choice? Yes, yes, yes. Of all the things they had heard from Mark, the arrangement of marriage partners repelled them. Lizzie in particular declared that she would run or kill herself rather than be a Muss. And she gave a kick to a boy who thought that two women in the household was more than any man should bear.

Mark was reluctant to reveal his experiences at Derwent House. So, in a roundabout way, he asked about fertility and compatibility, compatibility in the biological rather than temperamental sense. Here, the tables of embarrassment were turned, and the young turned imploringly to the priest. He called time, and sent them away.

"It's like this, Mark. We value free choice more than anything. But love, even lust, may not be between those with the capacity to give healthy children. Your authorities have one answer, but one we would never accept. It is a source of conflict that is not talked about here, though they are more open about it away from places like this. Our problems seem to affect men more than women. If a marriage seems infertile, or there are monsters or miscarriages, the wife will sleep with others. Often several, but in times and places away from home. Several, so that the actual father is unknown, and the chances of success greater. And it will be repeated if it works. The children are regarded as those of the husband, but there are resentments. Not that any child is ill-treated, but the household may be less than happy. The wife may resent the need, and for the older but fertile men at least, there is, maybe to your surprise, sometimes a reluctance to an impersonal act with no attachment. Some, indeed, prove incapable of it."

Put at ease, Mark told of his experience at the Derwent House. The priest nodded.

"That Chief knows her business well enough, then. It's a Riding with many fertile women, but few men. Your companions will have been young wives, or at least partnered. The men will guess, for sure, but they are more robust about necessities than many here or in the west."

But the unattached? While uphill was strict, things had always seemed to Mark to be less so in the city. Dire penalties could follow detection, and the city had raids from Security. Those embarrassing dates with hygienists to determine fertility.

"It happens. If there are children, they will be loved by any of the infertile couples. Not that it is thought well of, and for my flock notionally sinful. But so is the practice I told you about just now. When each one born and healthy is precious, we do not bear down on such transgressions."

18. Council of War

After these meetings with the priest, Mark's time was spent more happily. The Chief would give him news. To the relief of all, the north remained quiet. He did not meet Lord Ogilvie or Lady Hawkins; he learnt that she had departed. Then, on May 30th the great news came, and had to be explained. The Montgolfier attack had succeeded in its purpose: the Kingdom was willing to negotiate. The second strike, the strike that would be far more deadly, might be averted. Three days later, he was summoned to a full council. Lady Hawkins had returned. Grey faced but upright, she took her place at the table's head. Ogilvie, though, was brought in with a stout helper on each side, and lowered gently into the seat beside her. How long since he had last seen Ogilvie? Little more than a week, but the man had aged even more, and now looked ill as well. The Chief, he knew. He was delighted to see the hunter O'Neill, though rather surprised. Others, he did not know, and there were no introductions. None needed telling who he was.

Lady Hawkins gave them a detailed account. The Kingdom was rattled; they had agreed rather too easily to stiff terms for a meeting.

"There are reasons for that," she said, "but we can explore those later. We must first agree both about our demands, and about those who should return with me."

There was a short debate. It was obvious that Ogilvie was no longer capable. Indeed, his obvious deterioration cast a gloom over proceedings in which, so far, everything was going to plan. Other nobles? Alfred in Dean might be in no better state than Ogilvie for all they knew. Mark himself? No, swiftly dismissed. Any shock effect would be cancelled by focusing attention back to the north. And the Kingdom should not know that he was alive.

Lady Hawkins waited. No further suggestions were put forward.

"I would wish Mr O'Neill to be of the party. With your consent," she nodded at Ogilvie, "he should be promoted to Chief, even if without a Riding. They read our symbols. Colonel Anson," she nodded towards a stout, balding man with a magnificent moustache, "who has enabled many to escape when the Hunt tries its worst. Finally, gentlemen, I require my doctor. She may be concealed in a military helmet. I must appear before them in good shape. She has the means, even if their effects are temporary and debilitating in the longer term."

There was a slight stirring, a wave of doubt. A man unknown to Mark queried O'Neill's selection.

"No offence, my Lady, nor to Mr O'Neill, but someone of more experience?"

A grin appeared on Hawkins' face. The same grin she had shown at Hastings' discomfiture.

"No offence taken. Mr, or I should now say Chief, O'Neill, has rather more experience than might be suggested by his humble title of hunter. He has travelled in many of the Domain's precious Grounds, undetected. He is known to the bailiffs of three cities, cities now simmering with resentment but powerless to express it. With their assistance, he has travelled between them. He has smuggled the wanted to us, where they have improved our stock. He knows the least perilous paths though Badlands. In a word, he is a spy, and the most adroit we have known. We have a plan, gentlemen. If you will approve the team, I will outline it to you."

There was a babble of assent and curiosity. Few had even met O'Neill, and now stared at the man openly. Even Ogilvie managed to raise a smile. He knew, of course, and Hawkins' choice was no surprise to him.

"We do not know for sure who we will meet. But they will be of high rank, and be sure that their warrant will be valid. Valid, but not necessarily honoured. At all costs, we must draw their attention from the north, but not make it show. We will, of course, ask for compensation in stock. There will be haggling but it is secondary, a game we are used to. We will both ask for guarantees of no incursions. They will of course be given, both knowing that the condition may be breached, if it can be breached with impunity. Now, they are very much in doubt of that impunity, but if presented with a target, the north, in their grasp, they may think the losses worthwhile. Arundel is not squeamish.

We will ask for hostages. They will not hand over a first born. These days, it would have to be one of the precious Four themselves; I don't think that there are others left. My guess is that they will offer us Hastings or some other simpleton, and take us for fools when we accept. Indeed, Hastings is entirely expendable. But we must look as though we are in earnest, even if dim-witted.

Now we come to the crux. They will expect us to demand no action in unassigned lands as well, lands where our people move in and raise stock and harvest timber. Places where their devilish Hunts are held. This is not normally the time of year for such a hunt. We have reason to think it will be brought forward. Be sure that Arundel will never abandon the Hunt. It conditions the younger 'bloods' to become complicit in the way the Four rule. They will not be unduly worried by a bit of rustling along the border of Grounds, and will hint as much. It will be all business as usual, why not, never been any fuss till now. So, they will of course reject this condition as lying outside the Treaties. We will insist, they will refuse. It will drag. We will eventually, and with an air of despondency agree, but in such a way that they anticipate our attempting to rescue those we can with more than usual vigour. We may, indeed, hint as much, but they will already be inclined to strengthen the forces that trap our folk. They will bank on us not knowing where the Hunt will be, or when. We never have known until it is too late, and even then, our forces have suffered greatly to rescue a paltry few. As far as that goes, gentlemen, I have news for you, But the honour should go to O'Neill, for he discovered it, and more besides."

"The Hunt will be in Cotswold. It will be very soon. Less than a month from now, possibly within two weeks. Already, preparations are being made. Paths through the Badlands cleared. Camps are set up. Kitted Kingsmen and Security have been driving labour to gain access."

He looked around the room.

"That includes those of our own who were captured last year. They do not last long."

"Cotswold is ours, surely," said Colonel Anson. "There is even a Chief of Riding there."

"Unfortunately, not, Colonel." Ogilvie's wavering voice broke in. "The Treaty bounds are up the Severn Sea. To the east, it was all Badlands, no-man's-land as far as anyone knew then. It was fishermen from the Dean side discovered a pocket of green, way back. It is narrow enough at the coast, but it broadens out a little way inland. It's no Eden, but larger. Plenty *bounteous*."

An attempt at a spit, here, which turned into a fit of feeble coughs. There was a long pause as Ogilvie summoned his strength.

"Bounteous, but fertile enough, and there are many folk living there now. It has been taken for granted. Now the Domain have found it out. We are lucky that O'Neill has alerted us; thousands are at risk. Were it not for the north, we

241

would have told Alfred to evacuate as many as possible. Still a good idea, but we need to do more." He slumped back in his chair.

A voice unrecognised by Mark: "How do you know this, O'Neill? Fugitives?"

"How do I know? Because I am told, told by reliable sources. No, not only fugitives, but from those in the cities. I've not been to Oxford or Swindon, the two nearest that are partly in Grounds, but news travels. After I brought Mark in, I remembered a conversation I had in Leicester not long before. That bailiff was fuming. He'd had evidence of what all city folk in the Grounds have suspected. Notionally Chosen are sent to clear the Badlands, sent for slave labour. A strange boy from the north had seen the Barriers, as they call them, with his own eyes and talked to the victims. What in hell he was doing, I don't know. The Sheffield bailiff passed him down the line, because he'd be recognised on his own patch. For all I know, he's been sent from city to city. Certainly, his account has. It was then I grasped that they have ways of moving people and news without the Domain catching them. They call it the Metro.

There's something else. Cities always get the odd escapee. They are a nuisance, because they have to be hidden and fed, and they are never local. Mostly, they are very ill and don't last long. Some get found by Security, and then their city gets a hammering. Night-time raids, and people removed on mere suspicion and never seen again. When I went back soon after bringing Mark in, I got some pretty startling news from down south. They were getting their own folk turning up with horror stories; folk they thought had been Chosen. Too many of them, as well; the populations are going down. The Domain is getting lazy or, more likely, very short of labour. Moving their labour far away was an efficient tactic up to now. Folk that know roughly where they are will make a break for it."

Mark's heart had jumped as O'Neill spoke. A strange boy from the north, from Sheffield? Surely David. David alive, and with city folk. He was about to ask, but another, unknown to him, took matters further.

"Let them succeed in Cotswold, turn it into Domain, and we have a new frontier. No Treaty cover, and just Severn to separate them from Dean. That estuary is not so wide. They'll be building a fleet and make for Dean in a few years. A few balloons won't deter them."

O'Neill nodded.

"You are right, I think. Have their forces reach Severn shore, and they'll not budge. The north is tempting enough for them, but Dean is more so. They know of its importance. Occupy it, and there are even fewer barriers to further advance than in the north. It has been a blessing that their fleets don't dare brave the Atlantic to reach us."

Lady Hawkins surveyed the room. Tired though she was, she could see that there was fear in many eyes. The west threatened both north and south, with enslavement as its objective. Against which, she could see them thinking, we have what? A few balloons. They had not taken in the full significance of what O'Neill had said.

"Cheer up, ladies and gentlemen, and think for a bit. This is no ordinary hunt. There has never been one for which so much preparation has been made. It is Arundel's doing, and he has driven all to meet his needs; more men, more horses, more mobiles. More people to be sacrificed to clear the path for others. Why else did they agree so readily to negotiate? They want no distractions. He will call in across the Domain. The more they do so, the less there is for any activity in the north. Our intention is to speed things up a little. Make them take even more precautions to prevent its frustration. They are not used to serious resistance. Make them a little nervous. Chief O'Neill has better news yet, though."

"Thank you, ma'am. There's something you may not know here. The Domain has always had trouble policing the cities, the cities in a Ground. Those cities need feeding, but in return, they sacrifice more children to Service. It's not liked, and many evade it. There are too many hiding places, tiny passages through heavy contamination. Try heavy policing, and they get even less. The Domain can't just pick a tame Grounder to run them as they can with mayors. Proctors are laughed at. Their bailiffs are not exactly elected, but one way or another, cities have ended up with bosses who get respect in their own right. These cities are near revolt. Only fear and the bailiffs' authority keep them down. Up to now, they have held their people back, because the price of resistance is too high. They will work with us now, if only to make the Hunt an expensive business so they don't try the same thing again.

It is already agreed. I will give the message today. It will be taken to Leicester, and it will move fast from there. A system of runners, in relays, all through the night. Start on the night of June 9th? The message will be simple: South, light your fires, North, douse the flame. Security will need more men. Trouble only in the south. Swindon may even get a message to the slave labour.

The north, and particularly Sheffield, to behave like little angels. Start even as they are returning to Windsor. Even as they move forces will be diverted, and we draw even more from the north, well before the Hunt starts."

O'Neill glanced at Lady Hawkins, who nodded.

"We also have a message from Hereford. The second wave of Montgolfiers is ready, but it cannot strike at the Hunt directly unless the wind is just right. But the Aeronauts have devised weapons that can. If they can make enough in Dean, they will be deployed when the Hunt reaches their target. We have rockets, too. They do not travel far, but if their forces get near the coast, they can be fired from boats."

An anxious voice, "What weapons? Not those that were used in the Great War, in the name of humanity."

"No, no. Agent Z, yes, but no deliveries of plague or mutagens. Even if we wished, they no longer exist. Just gunpowder and our guns and bows otherwise. As to the methods, we are not quite clear. Long messages along the towers get scrambled. But I will be there before the Hunt commences, and I will be on their side of the river to harass them from the north before they get started. Most of them, even the soldiers, have never encountered an enemy that fights back."

O'Neill had one more thing to say.

"As my Lord Ogilvie and Lady Hawkins know, the Domain is no monolith, no power with but one mind. There are those within it, at the highest level, who would rather leave us alone, at least for now. The failure of the Hunt will strengthen their hand, and weaken that of Arundel. Its success will threaten our existence."

Hawkins looked round the room. Bar Mark, and of course Ogilvie, they ranged from mid-twenties to sixty or more. Except for the colonel, none had been in what might qualify as combat, and even the colonel had been involved in little more than retreating skirmishes. Soon, all too soon, they would be on their own. Excepting Defoe, locked in his caves, all Old-timers might be gone before this battle started, and certainly soon after. And Defoe was no Napoleon.

"Ladies and Gentlemen, this is war. War that none of you have witnessed. It is not only the north that is at stake. The damage done in Cotswold needs to delay their appropriation. They need to fear. Extend the Domain to that coast, build a fleet, and our future is bleak."

There was no further dissension. Duties were allocated. All left except the Old-timers, Mark and the Chief. Hawkins turned to the Chief.

"One request, Chief, and I apologise. That route to the Point will not take a carriage. Riding nearly saw me off last time. A fall would finish me. I fear a litter and spare horses will be needed. Can you arrange that?"

The Chief nodded and left. Hawkins rang a bell and the two attendants returned to help Ogilvie to his bed. Mark and Lady Hawkins were alone.

"You have made a brave decision, but the right one, Mark. Now that you know all, we will see you back at Derwent tomorrow. There will be others with you. Your orders will always be from Chief Rhianna or Captain O'Hanlon. There will be orders for you to deliver. May God go with you." Mark was left alone.

Part 2
Reaction

The Royal Domain

19. Shock

Today, thought Arundel, *today is the day to introduce Lane to the Armouries*. It had been annoying to lose the man from Council, simply in exchange for disposing of that rat Pendennis. But truth be told, Lane, with his obsession for clearance, had begun to irritate him; he did not want a subordinate who fancied himself as possessing the big picture. The wastage was high, and gave Alice ammunition, as that last Council had shown. The agreed replacement for Truth and Justice, Lord Blackstone, was a nonentity who would do as he was told. Meanwhile, there was plenty of work in military research, which, as far as Arundel was concerned, most certainly included the reprogramming of Outie captives, of which there would soon be many. Reprogramming: how he loved the word, redolent of the past in all its glory. Enough of them, and Lane could indulge his little hobby.

All the more so, since his drive to recover, to reconstruct, the weapons and capabilities that had preceded the Catastrophe and the war had stalled. Weapons that were, in his living memory, more than enough to counter any threat that the Outies might represent; weapons that would open up the west as a breeding ground for the obedient servants that the Domain required. Weapons that would justify breaking with the damned Treaties that tied the Domain to what it could extract from the Grounds and the meagre pickings from past Hunts. Damned Defoe again, actually mocking him at the Treaty Point all those years ago: *How are the mighty fallen, and the weapons of war perished!* That damned treaty, the only time he had met Defoe after his defection. We should have killed the bastard then, though the man had not the wit to control their strategy.

Progress had been disappointing. There were books, diagrams, even blueprints in abundance in the Royal Libraries. There were clever recruits among the Prodigies and others among the Chosen from the Grounds. But there was never enough material. Skills had been lost. Anything digital had been lost. Even the brightest seemed to have difficulties with the underlying principles and processes. Mere maintenance of firearms production and the ammunition to go with them sucked up most of the resources he could command. Antiques to be kept functional. Aircraft? A few 'string and sealing wax' prototypes, some of which had fallen out of the sky when engines failed, while others had disintegrated on landing.

The suspicion had entered his restless mind that this workforce was just a bit pampered. The Master-at-Arms could be relied on to report problems, not solutions. Technical problems that he lacked the knowhow to brush aside; problems that invariably required more labour, better materials, more time. When he had briefed Lane shortly after his appointment, a new perspective had opened up. Never one for carrots when a stick was to hand, Lane had said: *There are those, my Lord, who mistake trust for gullibility, those who think of their own comfort ahead of duty. Let me remind them of that duty, my Lord. Not all those Chosen for Service enter it in the spirit of obedience to which you are entitled. I am accustomed to dealing with such.* Well, now he could get to work, on the spot. A taste of Lane might stir their arses. Things could hardly get worse, and he was not minded to wait.

Arriving at the Armouries, he had barely started to introduce Lane to the Master-at-Arms as the new overseer for the Armouries as a whole, when a rather flustered messenger rushed into the courtyard where they were standing.

"May I be pardoned for interrupting, my Lord. There has been a message from the Treaty Point, my Lord. The Outies claim to have launched an attack on the Grounds or the Domain. We have had no report of such. There is a letter on its way, my Lord, from a Lady Hawkins. They allege a breach of the Treaties, seemingly a battle. Your sister and brothers have also been told. They are waiting for you."

Hawkins? Should not she be dead or moribund? Was Arundel's first thought. Do they have more doses? Impossible, the stock had been uncompromisingly protected. And what breach, where? Arundel left Lane and the Master, and returned to the castle, a journey of about thirty minutes. No hurry; he would not appear panting. In the small room where their private meetings happened, his siblings were already assembled, with two clerks.

"Any more details?"

"Yes, brother, and they are strange indeed. The actual letter will be with us soon, but we have a transcript dictated by a sergeant. It is addressed to Pendennis. Here it is. It alleges a major incursion by our forces in the far north. Do you know about this?"

Arundel scanned the paper. "No, I certainly do not. Our problems there have nothing to do with Outies. Lane told me there were problems in the RPZ and with trespass onto the Domain. Security has been strengthened, that is all. Oh, there was some recent fuss about a local officer. 'Exceeding orders', or some such nonsense. Another Visitor gone native, and an inquiry set up. I believe a commandant was suspended. I do not know of any outcome. Lane may know more, but he is at the Armoury. More to the point, Hawkins seems to have been there in person. How many of those supposed nobles are left there? Haven't their doses expired?"

Kent's territory, this.

"By the books, there were about seven who had the same dose within a few years, due to expire any time between twenty years back and up to ten from now. It's not exact, but aging advances rapidly afterwards. Two were killed in the war. It's a while since we saw or heard of any of the others, because there have been few meetings at the Point, and mostly trivial. Attended by some of the cleverer Outies, usually not a noble. Last one seen was Ogilvie, about twenty years ago. Any given lesser doses then will have died long ago. Only Defoe is good for a hundred more before he runs out. He'll be the same as ever, I guess."

Arundel grunted. He had in mind that only Outies would be left soon, bar Defoe, but he was an idealistic idiot who had urged the others on. Certainly, he was no soldier. Ogilvie and Hawkins were another matter. They had brains. He turned back to the matter in hand.

"No reports of any attack from the west?"

"No. But the Outie post is still manned. They seem to be waiting for a response."

"What is this incident? The messenger you sent mentioned a battle? Any information from the Visitor up there or the military?"

"They have been asked. I believe reports will be with us soon."

And, indeed, it was only minutes later that another clerk entered with a rather long transcript. From the north: An evasion; another concealed evasion, military action, and a significant Outie response in Northernmost. Military rule in the Ground. And all about three weeks ago.

Arundel exploded.

"King's Bollocks! That sodding Division again. Those bastards are out of control. Pleased with yourself, still, Alice? Who is this Bohun? Why did we not hear about this at the time?"

"That there had been Outie resistance to a search, yes, we knew, and it was in all the routine reports, if you could be bothered to read them. It was seen off, and we lost no lives. All outside the bounds, but our force was searching for an evader. Looked like nothing of significance. And Bohun, if you remember, was appointed to liaise between the Visitor, the military and ourselves or Council. But the scale certainly comes as a surprise, at least to me. Outies run; they don't fight unless cornered. Shielding the evader, perhaps? No great matter for us."

Sussex had been re-reading the report. Normally almost silent, he now spoke up.

"Alice is right, there is something odd about this fierce resistance. Most minor incursions go without remark. Oh, we get a few complaints, but usually no great harm has been done; Outies have run away. We meet at the Point, mutter about hot pursuit, and the whole thing dies. Usually, it's the Hunt overstepping the mark. At most, we hand over a few cattle. We've not had a threat of retaliation, still less an actual attack. And they would scarcely claim to have made one if they had not."

"Who can read Outie minds, inasmuch as they have any?" said Arundel. "Maybe they had a herd there. More to the point, what does 'appropriate military response' mean? A few Outies perishing as they cross the Badlands with bow and arrow? We've had no reports of any further action in the north or anywhere else. All they could do would be to rush a Ground and contaminate it, but they'd be outgunned even by local Proctors. I say let them stew at the Point until we see just what 'military response' means in practice. A good slaughter as Outies cross the bounds, and they'll not be inclined to try again."

It was not long before they had an answer. Sitting together for a largely silent midday meal, they were interrupted by a clerk: An Outie attack near Worcester; poison dropped from the air. More reports of the same. Arundel and Buckingham went to the telephony centre to get reports at first hand where they could. The messages were frustrating: some necessarily at second hand, others delivered by panicking mayors or Proctor captains.

Only as the day wore on did anything like a clear picture emerge. News of the Montgolfier attack was coming through, piecemeal. Balloons; poisoned cattle and farmers, burnt balloons and Outie suicides. To all appearances, just Agent Z. An officer headed to the Treaty Point to brief any noble authority who was sent there.

So, not a bluff, and with a weapon that we might have thought they lacked, thought Arundel. We have hardly any, and it's not been tested for decades. No targets anyway, and no means of delivery. Sealed stocks? Or had they the means to make more? What else might they have after all these years? The means of delivery? Original, and we could do the same, though whether there were targets worth striking was doubtful, and the mission would, as for the Outies, be suicidal.

For once, Arundel and Buckingham were of one mind. At all costs, we must prevent a more serious attack, until the size of the threat could be determined. The only noble who could reach the Treaty Point quickly was Hastings. More calls.

***

The following day, the weakness of their position was demonstrated by their conversations with the humiliated Hastings. One first-born? When there were only the four of them left to claim that title? No way. Sussex was too feeble to match Kent. Arundel and Buckingham would have to go. And Pendennis?

"That's absurd," said Arundel. "The man's a disgrace. Gone native more than the Visitors, for Kingdom's sake. He'd surrender anything to preserve his precious Grounds. Present them with someone else, and see what they do. Chances are it's a bluff."

"And if it is not?" asked Buckingham. "Those balloons may be crude, but we do not know how many they have, nor what weapons. There is intelligence behind this, brother. Defoe may be a starry-eyed nincompoop, Hawkins is not, nor Ogilvie if he's still alive. Michael told you: there will soon be Defoe alone. No leadership then, and that is the time for force if it's needed at all. Pendennis must be there, and summoned now from Dover. Play the long game, brother, or you will scrape the barrel for labour and food. Serious damage to any Ground and we are screwed."

Arundel grunted. He could see that even Sussex nodded as Buckingham spoke.

"If Pendennis, then Lane too. I will have balance. And there will be unanimity before we agree to anything."

"Two men known throughout the Kingdom to be in some disgrace? And one known to be your pet? Such matters do not remain secret, brother, and you know it. There is a reason for Pendennis. Apart from being named, he at least had a post that was relevant. Outies know about Truth and Justice. There have been enough escapees from Lane's 're-education centres' after each Hunt to make them wary of a Security uniform. Some may even recognise him; I'm told he often interrogates personally. Do you think he will contain himself when face to face with Outies? He will advocate slaughter. Indeed, I would not put it past him to conceal a weapon and try to kill their delegation on the spot. Not Lane, brother, or we will never agree to anything, and it will be obvious to Hawkins. You remember her as well as I; she's no fool."

"Very well. But remember that if I disagree, that's that. We will just face whatever they have, and retaliate as maybe. Who might we take instead?"

Sussex intervened. "I suggest a soldier. Whatever is agreed, they will ask for no incursions, even trivial ones. General Lord Wilkes will command respect among all the regiments. And he can spell out the realistic options in terms of defence or any retaliation on our part."

Arundel nodded. He added a rider.

"No concessions on no-man's-land, though. I will not have the Hunt hindered in any way. Those creatures move in faster than we can cull them. And the dimmest make good servants when Lane has schooled them."

Especially not this Hunt, he thought; a Hunt that will give us the base from which to strike free of Badlands. So, to the details: Pendennis to be summoned from Dover. The general to be briefed. Assembly at the Transfer Station in the Corridor, since Hastings had agreed to no mobiles at the Point until the delegation arrived. Kent and Sussex to deal with logistics, and acquire any who seemed useful as advisors. Buckingham to make sure that Bohun and whoever was in charge of the military up north were summoned.

***

The Transfer Station at Barlow was a simple affair. Patched up pre-war buildings were connected by later, coarser construction, and the whole surrounded by a high wall. A lower wall to one side enclosed barns and stock pens. Bar the Warden and a few permanent staff, it might lie empty for weeks at a time. A small force of Kingsmen had a barracks outside the walls. These provided what little security was needed. Once a year, it might be the temporary resting place for Grounders transferred between Divisions. More frequently, there were transfers of herds or flocks, usually to the south, but sometimes a prize bull or ram might be moved east in yet another attempt to make parts of the Domain self-sufficient. Very rarely, it might house important Grounders appointed to high-status posts like that of mayor, hygienist or Proctor officer. For these, there were rooms set apart from the dormitories that housed routine transfers. Very rarely, a noble and entourage might head to the Treaty Point. Travelling by mobile, however, they almost never spent the night. Occasional social calls by Proctors from north and south enlivened what was a rather dull posting. This rather sleepy atmosphere was about to be disturbed.

There had been just a little excitement in early May. Trouble in the Northernmost Division, an evasion, no less, had Proctors and Kingsmen alike patrolling the Corridor. Rapidly followed by an instruction to accommodate two families, each minus their head. To be kept apart, Mr Warden, but to be treated well. For how long, sir? Until otherwise instructed. So, two of the three decently private apartments taken, who knew for how long. And what families! That of the mayor of Bradfield, no less, and that of his senior clerk, both known to Mr Jacks. They said little, and it was made clear to him that their affairs were none of his business. But gossiping Proctors soon filled in the gaps. Mr Norman's son was the evader; Norman himself: died in custody; the mayor: under house arrest for treason. *House arrest?* thought Jacks; traitors were usually into the Domain and on to reclamation at the speed of light. Well, not his business, as the high and mighty frequently told him about transits through the Station.

The days went past, and he received no more instructions. The mayor's family were subdued and no trouble, but there was much shouting and crying from the Normans. It appeared to be an argument between Miss and her daughter on one side, and Muss on the other. Muss even petitioned to be moved with her young children. Jacks was actually considering this, when there came a call that ruled it out. He was to prepare for a body of nobles preparing to go to the Treaty Point. Not any nobles: Arundel and Buckingham, no less, several others, and a horde of clerks, servants and soldiers. When? Fourth of June. Just five days. For King's Blood, how was he to prepare. No problem, Mr Jacks, a Quartermaster will be with you tomorrow. Just do what he tells you.

Not that simple, thought Jacks. Those families will have to move out. Indeed, I and my family will have to move. Shabby though our house may be, it is the best there is, and it will surely be commandeered by the first-born. Other apartments for lesser nobles, dormitories for the rest. Where do we go? He crossed the road to the Kingsmen's barracks. Set up in more troubled times, it did have space for more than the present force. But the rooms left empty were bare, damp and dirty. Fortunate indeed that the lieutenant in charge had also had a call and had been instructed to assist the Warden. Grumbling troopers and his own staff were put to making them as habitable as could be managed.

To his initial relief, a quartermaster did arrive the following day in a mobile with three assistants. Yes, relax, Mr Jacks, there will be convoys with supplies. Yes, we will bring cooks. Yes, extra lighting. Etcetera, etcetera. He was impatient with Jacks' uncertainty and nerves, and his pomposity and condescension induced a grumbling resentment in the warden. This turned to suppressed anger, as the strutting little man marched around the place, giving instructions to his assistants with scarcely a word to the warden. It soon became apparent that there were more people involved, and of higher rank, than could be accommodated. While his evacuation of his own house, and the move of the families was given grudging approval, *good to see a respectful attitude, Mr Jacks*, it became apparent that there was no room for him, for his staff, or even for the Kingsmen in their barracks. When Jacks pointed it out, the quartermaster waved him aside.

"Come, come, Mr Jacks, I'm sure the Kingsmen have tents, do they not?" entirely without irony, he continued, "Nobility must be served, Mr Jacks."

To add to Jacks' rising fury, it chose that moment to start raining. Turning away, he went to find the Kingsman lieutenant, who had wisely made himself scarce. Tents? I suppose there must be some somewhere. We've never had to camp out, Majesty be thanked. A routing around produced three small tents. When unpacked, they were riddled with holes and mould. The lieutenant shrugged. Further attempts to point out the problem to the quartermaster were waved away.

"You will just have to find somewhere, Mr Jacks. These premises are now under my jurisdiction; You can tell the lieutenant the same. All out by the second."

The quartermaster's assistants smirked openly. One tittered behind a neatly gloved hand. Jacks was left to call in favours from the Proctors in both Divisions.

One family to each with some of his staff. Kingsmen were a problem. In the Grounds themselves, full kit was to be worn. For how long? Further, without them, what security was provided for this plague of cockroaches, as both Jacks and the lieutenant were disloyally thinking of them. Calls up the line did little good. No, Major Craddock had not heard of this movement. No, he could not overrule the quartermaster. In the end, however, two military mobiles did appear on the second with expeditionary gear for a full company. The soldiers gloomily assembled a camp in a steady drizzle. The fancy quartermaster had planned for all comforts, but had forgotten the issue of security completely.

***

The machinery of Court ground into action. Sudden transfer to this dealing with Outies, this stationing in the backwoods, when all had been gearing up for the luxury of the hunting pavilions and the festive spirit that went with it; a mood of more than usual grumpiness prevailed. Rank was asserted by servants of the nobility; more, and better, tents were ordered. Sanitation was inadequate; gloved minions held handkerchiefs to their noses. All in a steady, cold drizzle that belied the season. It took the arrival of General Wilkes and his adjutant to bring order to the increasing chaos.

He was the first of the delegation to arrive. He was swiftly followed by Lane, and then by those summoned from the north: Major Cornwallis, Lord Bohun and Commandant Hope. The latter was quartered with Lane at his request. He was still notionally suspended. Pendennis turned up exhausted; the journey from Dover had been hard, and he had received little information beyond the summons. He had no assistants. Of the first-born, Sussex appeared first. Finally, Arundel, Buckingham and Kent arrived before nightfall on the fourth, along with the Major-Domo and a further flock of servants. As they were settled in, there was more grumbling as some were turfed out of houses to tents. Some had to wait in the hall of the Warden's house while more tents were erected, tents wet inside and out by the end. All because of a bunch of Outies. The mood was one of vengeance.

***

The communal dining room, the only one large enough in the compound, was filled to overflowing the following morning. A table had been placed centrally. Lesser folk, whose advice might be sought, were squeezed around the walls, on the few chairs available, sitting on side tables, even left standing. The select few that sat with the Four took their places. There was a stir around the room. Neither end was manifestly the head, but Arundel and Buckingham took opposites. Sussex and General Wilkes sat alongside Arundel, Kent and Pendennis with Buckingham. Down the sides, there were Lane, Bohun, and to the surprise of all, a major and a commandant known only to a few. Lowly indeed in such a gathering.

All knew by now of the Outie attack and, of course, the call to the Treaty Point. Few, though, had encountered Outies other than as corpses or huddled prisoners at the Hunt. Only Sussex and Pendennis had met them across the table. Arundel nodded to the General; it had seemed to the Four that he was best placed to recount the facts.

"You will know that the Outies claim that we breached the Treaties in the north. It appears that they suffered losses in an engagement with our forces within their boundary. Our forces, led by Major Cornwallis," here he nodded to the unknown figure at the table, "were indeed set upon by a number of Outies. Major, will you outline the events on that occasion, and what led up to them?"

Cornwallis recounted the tale. Knowledge of an old evader within Outie bounds. The search, and the encounter with Outies. The limited casualties, and the Outie retreat. A few questions followed about numbers, distance penetrated, any further events? To the last, the major was able to give a full reply.

"No, sir, no trace of any activity since, at least that we can see from the boundary. My men keep guard there in case the young evader you will have heard of attempts to reach the farm. With so much time passed, though, I think this unlikely."

Commandant Hope had looked increasingly angry during this questioning. Unasked he burst out.

"My Lords, whatever the status of the engagement, I must point out that it was entirely unnecessary. If Security had been allowed control, the hiding place would have been revealed by traitors within that Division. Instead, we have been denied any presence whatsoever."

Buckingham interrupted him with a steely look.

"Mr Hope," a dig at his unresolved suspension, "you are here to answer questions if required. Though I wonder what you might add to our knowledge if you did. Silence, Mr Hope, or we will have you removed."

There was a certain stirring in the room. Cornwallis and Bohun were hard put to it to keep a straight face; they kept their mouths shut. Arundel and Lane glanced at each other. Of course, Hope was out of order, but a point had been made public. A point scored in a game going far beyond this annoying distraction. It was Sussex who brought the meeting to order.

"If we are to reach any agreed position, what has happened rather than why or whether is all that concerns us. We have to consider their claim. There was an evader, though he was not seen. I suggest that we claim hot pursuit, at least as an opening position."

"Not tenable. Too many of our soldiers. At best, we can claim only local over-enthusiasm at junior level," Kent interjected, looking at Cornwallis, "coupled with a failure to alert the Court to the extent of the breach and the numbers involved."

An acid glance at Bohun. A pre-emptive apology and a few cattle might have settled this, was Kent's first unspoken thought. Settled it and left us clear. Now the north is attracting attention again. But then again, it would have needed approval. As for the idea of Arundel agreeing to apologise for anything? He got a surprise, though, when Arundel spoke.

"Look at the terms we have agreed to already. There are good reasons why. In particular, I want no disturbance until the Hunt is done; after that, we can think again. That is why we have taken a degree of humiliation. No mobiles beforehand. Hastings cooped up there rather than take a shameful walk back here. Our delegation defined for us, more or less. Why? Because we do not know if they are bluffing. Agent Z is long-lasting in storage, but we have no idea how much they have. Can Mr Pinkerton make himself known?"

A thin, stooped man stood up and moved to the table. With spectacles on a cord around his neck, a disordered mat of thinning hair, and clothes on the downside of shabby, he was distinctive among the uniforms and fancy garb of the Court. The questioning was straightforward. Agent Z had been stored in many places, but records had got lost. No, it was impossible that they could have made more. Other weapons? Almost certainly no mutagens, they were hard to make even before the war, and crude ones would harm the makers. Nuclear, no chance. Diseases? Possible, but unlikely. They would not have the means to develop selective strains, never mind vaccines. Explosives? Yes, but basic like gunpowder.

A few military and intelligence men were called on in a similar manner. Of those captured or killed in Hunts, few Outies had firearms of any sort, and fewer still had rifles. There was a rudimentary military hierarchy, but any resistance they had encountered seemed disorganised. At that point, however, Wilkes intervened, addressing Cornwallis.

"Major, you seem to the one with the most recent experience of engagement. I believe you have had tussles with resistance on Hunts too, to your credit, I am told. What impressions did you gain?"

"It is a difficult comparison, sir. Resistance on the hunt was out of the ordinary, because we were away from the main action, and greatly outnumbered. They tried to rush us in no very organised way. Brave, certainly, but more or less suicidal. Our experience in the north was very different. They were trained to use cover, and actions were planned. And they retreated once we withdrew from the forward positions. Nothing remotely suicidal. They were seeking to drive us off their patch, sir."

"In which they succeeded, didn't they, Major? Unusual, that."

The Major reddened slightly, but kept his mouth shut. From the moment firing started, he should have known he was at fault, in Treaty terms. His men would have certainly beaten the Outies had he ordered it so. That would have been an incident worth complaining about. Five Outies killed, he had been told, though he had seen only one. It could have been scores by the look of the way they behaved, had he not retreated.

There were a few more questions. But the point had been made. Terms had to be agreed, in the full expectation that they would be dishonoured at some future moment. Nobody was going to argue about blood money in the form of livestock. That was traditional. Hostages? That raised some eyebrows. The Outies had asked for first-born to be there. But the look on both Arundel's and Buckingham's faces answered that.

"Hastings will do, it will be an education," said Arundel. There was nervous laughter. Those of the same status more nervously than others. Minor nobles were expendable. He continued.

"So, a promise of no incursions on either side, a hostage or two, and the blood money. Will they want more? Wilkes, I think you could ensure that none of our forces cross the boundary. I doubt they can do the same, so reverse demands should be agreed. Outies are not the only ones to make mountains out of molehills; when it suits, of course."

Lane whispered to Arundel in the short burst of laughter, laughter that recognised that Arundel had no intention of complying any longer than was convenient. Sussex broke the spell.

"They will make another demand. They will ask for no hostile actions against them in no-man's-land."

"What! Cancel the Hunt? Never," Arundel shouted, cynical amusement turning to anger in an instant. "Attack us for that, and it will be war, proper war. Let them poison a few in the Grounds; we are set to help ourselves to far more elsewhere."

"You are sure of that, Brother," came Lady Buckingham's cool response, "sure that they cannot do more harm? Pendennis knows of these things. He has kept silent. Tell us, my Lord, what the Outies know, and what they can do."

"I know nothing of their capacity for harm, my Lady. But they are well informed about the place and size of each Ground. Not only that, but a shrewd idea of their relative productivity in people and stock. The rebels took with them a lot of intelligence briefs when they fled. Some had fulfilled the role we would now assign to Visitors. There are Grounds that are very near, even on the boundary with the Badlands that separate us. I think of the northernmost in particular, about which we have heard already. No real Badlands there. They are not afraid to die. Balloons would not be needed there."

He paused.

"But until now I would have doubted that they would do it. Consider; the attack that has been made was directed with intelligence, and, pardon me, with humanity. Stock was targeted, not people. I cannot tell what they might do in desperation, but," here his voice wavered, "I have found that they value human life rather more than us."

There were gasps. Lane scowled, and Arundel was disgusted. Gone native? Gone right over the edge more like. The little bastard would be straight for reclamation if he was not named by bloody Hawkins. And he knows it. Get this sorted, and it's up to the Barriers unless there is something worse available. If Sister dear gets in my way, then a discreet accident will be arranged.

It was time to call a halt. They had as much information as they could get. Both Arundel and Buckingham had agreed that such a large gathering was needed; without hearing what had been said, the fact of agreeing to terms would in itself have nibbled at their authority. It would have worked too, but for that rat Pendennis.

A telephone call to the Treaty Point; tell the Outies that the delegation would arrive tomorrow. Three mobiles to bring servants and clerks as well as the team. A set of journeys up and down the hill between the posts. Down to two mobiles. No more than four in the room with one clerk. Arundel fumed. Lane suggested a kidnap or massacre, firmly resisted by all others. He could come to the Point, but was to remain with the garrison. It was an angry and frustrated delegation that prepared for the morning.

20. When Princes Meet

At the Outland post of the Treaty Point, the doctor fussed around Lady Hawkins. The journey had not been kind to her. It had also done nothing for her temper, a fact she realised was to be dealt with firmly. *They will watch as we climb to their station. Stumble or be carried, and they have every incentive to prolong the meeting, even to ask for adjournments.* Only at the last moment, when the red flag was raised uphill, did she consent to swallow the stimulant prescribed. The doctor herself carried more, knowing, as did Hawkins herself, that each dose carried with it the risk of seizure, even of death on the spot.

To assist her, an escort of Outlanders to the front shielded her from view, a view that would otherwise have revealed the support of the doctor herself on one side, and O'Neill on the other. In through the door to Reception, there was only a clerk at one end of the table, who rose as they entered. He waited until they had sat down, then knocked on the interior door, opened it and stood aside. The Domain delegation entered.

First, Pendennis, who nodded briefly, stationing himself at one end. A military man unknown to Hawkins, who took the other. Then to her shock, Arundel and Buckingham themselves. *It is as well I am sat down*, she thought, *I might have fallen else.* Unchanged since she had last seen either, more than two hundred years previously. *More than can be said for me, and they will notice.* No word was spoken till all were seated. Not to her surprise, Arundel got the dig in.

"My, my, Elisabeth, you have aged well. We feared that the grim reaper had an earlier appointment with you. No companions of your class, I see. Should we offer condolences?"

"Honoured by your presence and concern, Alfred, and delighted also to see you, Alice. I wonder at the need for both at our meeting. Only one first-born was needed. Never one without the other when there is business to attend to? It speaks well to the importance you give to this meeting."

Buckingham visibly poked Arundel. "Enough pleasantries, I think. And a proper respect for titles from now on. Lady Hawkins, you are familiar with Lord Pendennis. On my right is General Lord Wilkes, after your time, I believe."

The General, taking his lead from Buckingham, nodded in a respectful way. Hawkins introduced her fellows.

"All military people, Lady Buckingham. Colonel Anson, Major Briggs, and Chief O'Neill. You will, I am sure, understand that their precise roles in our lands is irrelevant here."

General Wilkes gave a start at the introductions. A female major? Not that she looked especially fierce. Buckingham and Arundel, equally surprised, were better practiced at controlling their expressions. They looked to the General to open on their behalf.

"Lady Hawkins, as we are all, surely, concerned to protect human life, it is a matter of regret to us that a minor incident has provoked such a disproportionate response. To our knowledge, it has done more damage than was caused by our troops. We are, however, prepared to put that to one side, and to settle the blood debt in the normal way. I am sure we can also agree to respect boundaries more rigorously than before, and to agree mechanisms to secure it."

Rubbish, and they know it, thought Hawkins. But there is a turn of the screw to make first.

"Before we talk about any agreement, General, there is one requirement made by us that has not yet been met. We asked for written evidence that your plenipotentiary status is guaranteed. You have such a document? His Majesty consents?"

Arundel reddened, though he kept his mouth shut. So much for the power of our presence. Who did that second-rank traitor think made decisions in the Domain? His Majesty? He had been all for departing without any such document. It had taken all three, Buckingham, Kent and even Sussex to persuade him to get the king's signature and the Royal Seal. Agreed, they would not offer it, but it must be there. It was all too easy to see Hawkins walking out on them. A certain amount of unpleasantness had accompanied the meeting with their father, but a signature and seal had been obtained. There was a pause. Lady Buckingham nodded to the clerk, who placed on the table the necessary document. O'Neill took hold of it and handed it to Lady Hawkins. She took her time in reading.

"Thank you, my Lady, my Lords. It appears to be in order. Very well, I can now respond to the offer made by the General. Blood debt? Certainly, and I am sure we can return to it. Respect boundaries? We have responded, in a very measured way, to an entirely unprovoked incursion onto our land. Was not such respect inherent in the Treaties? Why should we now take a verbal assurance from those who have shown no such respect? What 'mechanisms', I wonder, does the Domain have in mind?"

This issue had not been considered in any depth by the Domain team. A demand for hostages was indeed expected, but had not yet been presented by Hawkins. Buckingham looked inquiringly at Pendennis, Arundel at the General. Pendennis shrugged; not his business, was the message. The General was left to attempt a response.

"In the past, my Lady, there has been a willingness to acknowledge the blood debt when our forces have transgressed across the bounds, causing loss of life. We will undertake to station a plenipotentiary here at all times, empowered to agree any settlement for such unintentional events on the spot. We could also transfer to you an agreed quantity of livestock or material in advance, to be held as an earnest of good faith."

"An agreed quantity? As security against further attacks? General, any quantity of livestock we might require would both cause your people to starve, and be more than we could feed. They would not be returned. Material? We ask you, perhaps, for so many rifles, so many bullets? And discover defects and duds too late? These are not mechanisms, General, these are either wishful thinking or downright deception."

There was a short silence. Lady Hawkins, though, had sunk back in her chair, a pallor in her face. Arundel noticed. Let the bitch die on us, and we are dealing with mere Outies with a few score brain cells between them. Spin this out at bit, get them to make an offer, adjourn to consider. Consider for just long enough to send them down the hill and back again. Each trip a nail in her coffin.

"So, what do you regard as security enough, my Lady? And what security is offered us against the rustling and intrusions that we have, until now, responded to at a purely local level?"

Hawkins straightened herself with effort.

"We do indeed have terms, my Lord. But I think that it is proper that you should know the basis on which they are made. Chief, will you oblige?"

"The attack, the intrusion, in the north is not the only hostile act of which your Domain is guilty. Paths are being cleared through the Badlands, most evidently in the south. Paths stopping just short of the Treaty Bounds. Paths often made by Westron captives taken in your so-called hunts. Captives worked or poisoned to death. Some escaped to inform us. Most paid the price of crossing Badlands in doing so."

"Colonel, will you explain to the Domain the necessary consequences of this information?"

"My Lady. You may wonder why your intrusion in the north provoked such a strong response? Because we see, not only there, but even more in the south, evidence of intention to breach the Treaties, to invade our land and kill or enslave our people. Be assured that such responses will occur wherever our people are attacked, within or without the bounds. Be assured that we have the means to cause further damage to Grounds, damage that will exceed by far what we have, with great reluctance, already inflicted."

Lady Hawkins studied the reaction across the table. Pendennis looked shocked; was he unaware of all this? Quite possibly. Buckingham: was there a touch or irritation under the poker face? Arundel was glaring. Some subordinates will get a kicking, if she judged him right. The General merely looked thoughtful. Let's hope his thoughts turn southward.

"Thank you, gentlemen. Here are our terms. First, the trivial: twenty healthy cows or forty sheep for each of our victims, to be here in fourteen days. To be brought to the ground between our stations and examined by us before acceptance. Second, as the General suggested, a plenipotentiary to remain here for the next three months, and further stays negotiated. Third, not only no incursions across the bounds, but no hostile action against any Westrons in semi-badlands bordering on either Grounds or Domain territory. Finally, we require two noble hostages, one to be first-born. We will guarantee to hold them in uncontaminated conditions.

Just a reminder, my Lords and Lady. We are aware, as you have been told, of what goes on in unassigned land. Any breach will trigger retaliation."

Another silence. These demands were what was expected. What was not, though, was the knowledge these Outies had of what went on beyond their bounds. Almost, it seemed to Arundel, as if they had located the Hunt. Be damned to them, it would happen, and on schedule. A spot of hypocrisy needed.

"These demands are well beyond the Treaties. Unassigned lands? We have as much right as you to roam. Perhaps an exchange of hostages of equivalent rank? But no matter; we will consider these terms, if only out of humanitarian concern for the Grounds, a concern that you appear not to share. Let us have an adjournment. We will notify you by flag when we are willing to respond."

"Twenty-four hours. Any delay beyond that, and these talks are at an end."

There were nods. Lady Hawkins and her team remained seated until the Domain delegation had left. The clerk remained until he was asked to leave. Alone, the Colonel opened the outer door. O'Neill and the doctor assisted Lady Hawkins to her feet. Outside, a screen of Outlanders shielded her from behind as she was near carried back down the hill.

***

The assembly in the quarters of the Point was bad-tempered. While the General attempted to brief those not present at the meeting, Arundel was swearing and pacing the room, giving some very dirty looks to Lane, who was trying to follow the General's tale. Never told me Outies had escaped. Far too close to the bounds to use them. The buggers should have been sent north, or to patches well within the Domain. Kent and Pendennis were huddled with Buckingham, getting her opinion of what had been said. Eventually, the General finished his briefing. With some shuffling, all found seats around the staff's mess table.

"So, brother, your lust for conquest and sport has led to a few short cuts. Hawkins knows your intentions. I warned you she was no fool. A little more patience, a little more discretion in the use of labour," here, she glanced at Lane, "and we could have settled this at much less cost, and you could have had your sport."

"You would accept these terms, sister? Concede, and they will know our fear. Concede, and the least little mishap," he stared at Bohun, "and they will be back for more. Even for new boundaries. Take Cotswold, and see if they can leave us the worse off by the exchange. If balloons are the best they can manage, I say knock them down now, and see what they can do. But I am all for a temporary settlement now. Just not on these terms. You saw Hawkins' condition. They will soon be leaderless, bar that fool Defoe."

"Did you ease your impatience to look at the two who spoke? Intelligent Outies, in the name of Majesty. They must have some breeding true. That O'Neill was a leader. They know things they should not. Ask Lane here: is that from just a few dying Outies crossing over?"

Lane was hesitant. Shifting Outies about was not straightforward. Use them near where they had been taken, that was so much easier. And it was few who went missing, more or less assumed dead in the Badlands. Worse, he knew that this was not the only source of information, something he had not told Arundel, at least not in clear terms.

"I fear that Lady Buckingham is right. We have never been given a free enough hand in the cities, in the RPZs. There are evaders; there are Outie refugees from our service. Some will be smuggled west. There are those that know the weakest spots in the Badlands. Even now, given the means, we can deal with further movement."

"Horses and stable doors, my Lord? And at what cost to recruitment? Short of riots, you will let them be. The supposedly retarded over there seem to be more adroit at intelligence than Truth and Justice." Contempt was in every word she spoke.

It took Sussex to bring them back to order.

"May we deal with the matter in hand? I declare an interest. They have asked for hostages, including first-born. There are only the four of us here. No one of us can cross. If two, then of necessity it will be Kent and myself." A brief smile crossed his face. "My interest in this notwithstanding, it is, surely, an unacceptable demand? Hastings, as we agreed," Hastings gasped. He had not been told of this. "But any others?"

"We have few to choose from," said Kent. "Lane? No? Pendennis? No also, my Lady? That leaves us with Bohun; we can scarcely offer them the General."

There was a buzz around the table. No first-born then. It was not contested. Arundel was satisfied.

"Good, good, offer them another if they insist, but do not name Bohun. Claim that we have to fetch from further away. Delay is to our advantage. Accept Hastings alone, and we know their weakness."

And if the worst happens, Bohun is no loss, thought Arundel, another groundling lover gone native and needing removal.

"Next," said Sussex, "A plenipotentiary here, and for how long?" There was a pause. Kent suggested Pendennis, to clear vetoes from both Arundel, who did not trust the bastard an inch, and from Buckingham, unwilling to lose talent at Dover. She intended to get him back there as soon as this charade was over. No one thought of mentioning Lane. No minor noble left at Transfer seemed adequate. So, we agree without giving a name? Yes. Someone can be sent for and take time arriving. The more delay, the better.

"The blood debt?" Sussex turned to the General. "Are these terms normal, General?"

"Sorry, my Lord, outside my experience. I have not had to deal with Outies other than in a cull or confinement. Maybe my Lord Pendennis can enlighten us?"

"Yes, they have been standard for many decades. Normally, we both know the tally of deaths. Here we know for sure of only one, but they claim for five. I am surprised they do not try for more, or for a higher price."

Pendennis looked round the room. Sussex had not yet broached the crucial issue, but he could sense its rejection. Would the Outlanders strike at once? He doubted it. They would wait for the first major incident.

"I said that I was surprised. Even more so, given that were I in their shoes, I would have looked at this delegation and upped the demand immediately. My Lord, My Lady," looking at Arundel and Buckingham, "your presence gives the matter more than routine importance. I think we can take it that this is the least important of their demands, almost a formality that would arouse suspicion if not asked."

Arundel snorted. *In their shoes*, indeed. How long had that man been in that job before I sacked him? Sixty or seventy years? Leave anyone in contact with Grounds, or Outies other than at the end of a lance or the barrel of a gun, and they went native on you. He looked around; nods, it is agreed. Sheep rather than cattle? Can be got from the Divisions either side of us? Clerk to note and act on when we are through.

"Which leaves us with no action on borders or unassigned land. General, I think there are few places where there is direct contact?"

"Indeed, my Lord. Only one Ground lies directly on the border with Outie land, that just beyond us to the north. Even then, the line of direct contact is short. Direct contact with the rest of the Domain is here and here only: on both sides it is just a narrow corridor through Badlands. Easy enough to veto incursions for as long as we wish, at the cost of a few cattle and some disgruntled farmers. Not forever, though. Some of those places are nearly clean enough to be incorporated into Grounds. That incursion in the north is one such. We should look at that sometime.

Unassigned ground is another matter. Badlands that separated us or our Grounds from the Outland have been clearing for decades. There are still many lethal patches, but others where Outies move in and out. Sterile, for the most part, but hunting grounds for that very reason. Our farmers use the fringes too. It's always been understood that casualties there are fair game, not covered by the Treaties. I am right, Lord Pendennis?"

"Yes, with a few exceptions. If they run, and leave rustled stock behind, we don't follow far. The occasional fellow puts up a futile fight. They don't raise the issue. It's the Hunts that provoke complaints, more so recently, when we have sought to surround them completely and take prisoners. Not covered by the Treaties, though, and they know it. This incident in the north? There may be more to it, but they are showing another interest now."

"Interest be damned. The Hunt will take place. We will add to the military protection. We will refuse to give any kind of guarantee for the unassigned lands. Test their nerves, not to mention their pious concern for human life. Give way this time, and it is not just this year. Forever? I don't think so."

Arundel's force hit them all. Even Buckingham did not challenge. We should see how the Outies respond. *If they reject, I will try again*, she thought. It would not take much to tip us into collapse.

They broke up for a meal. Timing was discussed. Late afternoon, Arundel suggested. Hawkins would tire. Break her, or leave the others to talk and Sussex will sugar the pill with comforting reassurances. Play on the difficulties of enforcement. Play on the tragedy of a Grounder killing attack in response to a few trivial instances.

***

In the Outlander station, there was little to discuss. They expected rejection and journeys up and down the hill. There was some astonishment that Arundel and Buckingham were present. Astonishment emphasised by Hawkins, who knew most clearly what their status was. She tried to explain. Even she, however, was unaware of the King's position as it now was. The significance of what they were about grew even greater in their minds.

Of far more concern was the state of her health. The stimulant she had taken before climbing the hill had started to wear off even while the meeting drew to a close. She lay, exhausted, on a bed. After the brief discussion that followed their return, Briggs shooed the others away. Hawkins ate a little, and sunk into what seemed more like stupor than a sleep. Two pony-riding messengers arrived for O'Neill, and were sent away with further messages. An Outlander kept watch on the hill above, waiting for a flag.

Hawkins was in deep sleep when the flag was raised. Colonel Anson tapped delicately on the door of the room. Briggs was adamant. Rousing her now would be useless. Without the stimulant, she would resemble the walking dead. Another dose now and she might die on the climb or in front of their adversaries. It was left to the colonel to ascend the hill alone, with an escort of two, to ask for a postponement to the following morning. A temporary indisposition. Nods and very polite expressions of concern, grins barely concealed. At his departure, Arundel rubbed his hands. Not long to go, by the sound of it. Ogilvie and that second Alfred must be close if not already gone. A few normal amongst an army of cretins. Soon, very soon. And then to make Defoe watch his protégés led into service before I hand him to Lane. What was that quote from the past? *The thousand-year Reich.* Whoever coined it had not contemplated a thousand-year ruler. He went to bed contented indeed.

***

Morning came, overcast and drizzling. Lady Hawkins had woken. She had even eaten a little. At Briggs' insistence, an open litter, shielded by Outlander guards, was to carry her most of the way up the hill. Only a small dose was to be given, and only on the threshold. To her dismay, but not her surprise, the Domain team were already seated, observing the assistance she required. When all were seated, it was Sussex, Sussex the emollient, who led. Added to the team, but within the limits.

"My Lady, gentlemen and lady. We have carefully considered your terms. You will not be surprised, I think, to hear that they are not acceptable to us. In the interests of tranquillity, and in the preservation of life in the Grounds, we are, however, prepared to modify our initial proposals. We accept the payment of blood debt. If we can conclude an agreement, the details can be worked out by subordinates. It is out of the question that any first-born be entrusted to you as hostages. We are prepared to offer Lord Hastings as a hostage. If you demand more, they will need to be summoned from afar. It is understood that Lord Hastings will be held at your station, and treated with the respect due to his rank.

We are prepared to offer guarantees that none of our forces will enter the Treaty-defined borders of your land. General Wilkes will so instruct all Kingsmen, Proctors and any Security forces. Subject, of course to reciprocity. Pilfering from Grounds must cease.

We cannot and will not agree to no actions in unassigned land. May I invite you to consider our position. Our farmers as well as your scavengers and robbers use that land. To be blunt, we do not trust your ability to control them. We would, of course, take action only to defend lives and property, but we cannot in conscience agree that such actions should be seen as a breach of any agreement. Claims and counter-claims: we are happy to judge their merit here when notified."

Lady Hawkins made to speak, then nodded instead to O'Neill.

"Terms, we see, that give you leave to kill and enslave under pretext of self-defence. That might work in both directions. For how long are such terms to apply? Months? Years?"

Arundel, who had been studying the team opposite, and most especially Hawkins, looked up and smiled. "As long as you wish, Mr O'Neill, as long as you wish. I will be happy with a year or two, if you can bear the abandonment of the petty thievery across the boundary of our Grounds."

Sussex added. "We would, of course, require face to face reassurance, at least once a week, that Lord Hastings and any other hostages you may hold are still alive, well and properly treated. You have a room downhill in which they could meet with people from our side. It would be inhumane to hold them for any lengthy period. Can we agree that if no breaches have occurred, he and any others will be released after three months?"

There was a pause. O'Neill and Briggs exchanged notes. Hawkins was in no state to be carried down the hill and up again. The decision had to be made here. Arundel observed every move. He whispered something to Lane, who was hard put to it not to laugh out loud.

"We can spare you time, if you would agree to withdraw and let us discuss this offer here, my Lord. It will not be above half an hour," again, O'Neill. Hawkins was manifestly suffering. Arundel nodded, with a grin, and the Domain party, clerk included, withdrew. Behind the door, He laughed out loud.

"They will agree. They are crumbling. Hawkins will be gone before the Hunt, maybe before we leave the building. Buckingham looked mystified, but

Pendennis merely thoughtful. Arundel grabbed Lane by the elbow, and led him to another room."

"We can ask Pendennis, without details, mind you, but I think that if they are in breach, their bleeding-heart morals will bind them not to use whatever they have in store. They'll likely spend days arguing about it. We need a major, undoubted breach. Not immediately, just timed to match the Hunt. It would be very convenient if Hastings died an unnatural death in their custody. A death that cancels all our obligations. A death that will ensure that the whole Court are behind us. I am sure that the visits can bring suitable snacks or sweetmeats, no? A slight delay in effect. It would not do to see a seizure while our man is with him. Maybe a bag that will last a few days, with just one special treat? No mention to others, naturally."

Even Lane was taken aback. He nodded, however, and made a mental note to ask an expert. A couple of weeks should be sufficient.

The recall was short. O'Neill agreed to the terms, with a certain degree of bluster about the unassigned lands that fooled no-one. The clerk produced two copies. There were a few minor crossings out, initialled by Sussex and O'Neill. All present signed at the base, Hawkins now with a weak, shaky hand. Hastings, looking very sulky, was led in and handed over. This time, coached by Arundel, the Domain team insisted on seeing the Outland team depart. Assisted to the door. Lady Hawkins managed to walk. The door shut firmly behind them, she was carried downhill, closely surrounded by the guards.

In the station, however, Arundel found that not all shared his euphoria. Alice gave him a look that was less than encouraging. To his remark that we could get out of this hell-hole and on with the Hunt, Pendennis dared to make a reply.

"Is it not strange, my Lord, that they accepted such terms? So readily? They are aware of our activities in the south. Is it possible that their main concern lay elsewhere? They gave us warning about the south too, indirectly. They appear ready for a fight, something unheard of for decades. Maybe for a hundred or more years."

"Bah, man. You saw the state of Hawkins. I don't know how many of those damned balloons they have, but the damage won't be mortal. I even doubt if they'd have the guts to use them. They were alarmed by our little excursion up north, that's all. Keep their beloved boundary intact. Suits me. We can deal with that later. Nothing much up there anyway, and what we have costs us an arm and a leg. Clear Cotswold, and with a few ships supplied by your works at Dover, and we have Dean in sight. As for resistance in the south, bring it on. The General here can draft in a few hundred more."

Buckingham sensed her tactical defeat. Clear Cotswold and all resources would go towards the Severn crossing. If, that is, if it is successful, and the Outies failed to deliver their unknown retaliation. Nevertheless, a marker must be put down.

"Very well. I wish you luck. You will not see me at the Hunt, Alfred, an exercise in little short of bloodlust at the best of times. Bear in mind that there are empty lands beyond the seas, lands that require not just those who can breed, but who have something between their ears. Gain a thousand or more defectives beaten into submission by Lane and his *Operatives,* and lose as many or more Grounders when the Outies respond. Never mind my colonists, Alfred, where will you find those geniuses for your military research then?"

"Empty lands? How often have we heard the refrain? None that can support healthy breeding, and you simply tell us to wait. Off you go then, and take that creature Pendennis with you. Make good use of him while you can, Sister. Clear Cotswold and the ships are mine, and more that will need building."

Very soon, the sound of a mobile was heard, carrying the two away. Kent followed shortly after. The mobiles returned to deliver the whole party to the Transfer Station. Next day, the Court departed for Windsor, and the Great Hunt. Mr Jacks was left with empty rooms, empty cellars and larders and a great deal of mess.

***

The scene at the Outlander station was very different. The outcome of the negotiations had been as expected. Ogilvie and Hawkins had judged well. Nothing, though, to laugh about. The next steps would be bloody. Even worse, though, was the state of Hawkins herself. Breathing was laboured. Her face varying from pallid to tinges of blue. She drifted in and out of consciousness, with Briggs alternately sitting by her side and getting tiny doses of broth down her. It was clear to all that she would die in the station; moving was out of the question.

Messages were sent. Anson departed for the south. Hastings was made as comfortable as possible in a small room. He found a guard outside the window. O'Neill promised him better furnishings and material to read, a great surprise to

Hastings. Long ago, the Four and others had determined not to tell lesser mortals all they knew about what was in Outie hands. He sat on the simple bed, shocked at the abrupt change in circumstances, even more so at the civility and education of O'Neill.

The following morning, he was sat down with a miscellany of Outlanders to have breakfast. Most were largely silent, eying him with curiosity. Certainly, his clothes were like nothing seen in the Outland. While they were still sitting, however, Major Briggs, as he conceived her, entered the room.

She was clearly exhausted. Sitting by Hastings, she revealed her identity.

"No need for pretence any more, Mr Hastings," he let the address pass by, "I am a doctor, and in particular the doctor for Lady Hawkins. You will have noticed that she is unwell. It is rather more than that. She is near death, Mr Hastings. A death which you will come to in turn when your dose expires. A mystery to me, Mr Hastings, but she wishes to speak to you. I will be alongside. She may not be able to say all she wishes in one go. If she indicates, you will depart, and I will recall you if necessary."

They entered the bedroom. Lady Hawkins was propped up. Her breathing rattled. Briggs sat him down on a chair so that he was as close as possible. A faint smile passed over Hawkins' face.

"We meet again, my Lord. I apologise for the changed circumstances." A pause, that seemed to Hastings to last forever.

"My Lord, I have little breath left. I have but one message for you. The Four who rule you are not gentle people. You are a hostage. Such should be treated honourably, for any accident that befell you in our care would negate the agreement we have signed."

Another, longer, pause. Briggs rose to her feet, about to send Hastings out. Hawkins waved her away.

"There is an old saying, my Lord, old beyond all reckoning: *Beware of Greeks bearing gifts.* You will be visited. It would suit my Lord Arundel to see you die in our custody. Be offered food or drink, be sure not to touch it. That is all, my Lord. And farewell."

She sank back. Briggs ushered him out of the room. At a loose end, he was free, as it seemed, to sit in the mess hall. Messengers came and went. O'Neill received many in a separate room. But around noon, Briggs emerged and called him. They entered and returned from Lady Hawkins' room. The look on their faces told all. Lady Hawkins was dead. There was a flurry of activity. Women went in to prepare the body. O'Neill approached Hastings.

"Lady Hawkins is dead. We will carry her body back to a burial place, to a church, where proper words will be said. I will accompany her for some of the way. You may not see me again." He called out, and a woman in what Hastings was coming to see as a uniform joined them. She wore two feathers.

"This is," he thought for a moment, "I guess lieutenant is the best equivalent; this is Lieutenant Jane Collins. She will command here, and is thus your guardian. I wish you luck, my Lord."

Soon after, Hastings saw the small procession descend the valley and out of sight. He retired to his room, deep in thought.

21. Damned Rabble!

As the convoy of negotiators and their hangers-on left Barlow for the east and home, Arundel was in high spirits. Sharing a mobile with Sussex, Lane and Wilkes, he joked about the Outies, the moribund rebel nobility and the pleasures of the chase. But the journey past the shattered south of Sheffield was slow and tortuous. It rained. Then the mobile carrying the four broke down, bringing the whole convoy to a halt. Occupants were removed from another vehicle to accommodate them. Problems of precedence and status reverberated down the line. Arundel and his party had moved off before a final pair of disgruntled junior nobles were crammed into a canvas-topped truck already crowded with soldiers. Eventually, the now rather soggy procession arrived at the way-station between Worksop and Retford, both blasted deserts. On the old A1, a name now understood only by the first-born, it lay in a small patch of fertility. By no means clean enough to be called a Ground, it was, nevertheless, safe enough to carry crops and permanent if mostly sterile inhabitants.

While soldiers were again put to work erecting tents for the surplus crowd, Arundel was already installed in the comfort of what was jokingly referred to by the staff as the Royal Suite. Buckingham and Pendennis were long gone south, being unburdened by a following or breakdown. Kent had been close behind them. With Lane by his side, Arundel summoned Bohun. He twisted the knife by allowing Lane to issue orders, while he sat by, notionally engrossed in papers.

"My Lord, you are to return north, taking Cornwallis with you. He will immediately arrange for all but a company of his force to start immediately for Windsor. Your Security DC will similarly be on standby to send such numbers as may be asked for by telephone. Most of his force will be required; he should plan accordingly. All large mobiles are to be requisitioned for this purpose. You will remain in Conisbrough to receive any further orders, and to report any Outie activity. Cornwallis can remain in his precious Ground. He will also report any

Outie activity to you, but on no account are you to allow anyone to cross the boundary."

Bohun was about to reply when Arundel looked up from his papers.

"By the way, I believe you have a commandant suspended; Hope, isn't it? He is here with us. A good man I believe, isn't that so, Lane?"

"Yes, indeed, my Lord. A puzzling suspension, and an unacceptable delay in dealing with the alleged offences. A very useful officer."

"So, Bohun, we have no doubts about him even if you do. There will be work enough for him further south. His suspension is hereby revoked. We will take him with us. We can deal with your local problems later." Arundel returned to his papers.

"Very good my Lords. I have one question for Lord Lane: the Barriers fall under the remit of Truth and Justice. There are many working there, and more than half of all Security forces are involved in there," a brief pause, "supervision. Am I to pass on any special instructions to the DC? Will more recruits be sent to work there?"

Lane reddened slightly. Fearing an inappropriate response on a matter so close to Lane's heart, Arundel intervened.

"The DC will be contacted when we reach Windsor. But in the meantime, active clearance is to cease. The labour will be confined to barracks and kept occupied there. I am sure they will relish the chance to improve their accommodation. And no, no more recruits will be sent north until further notice."

After all, he thought, *do what we want in the south, and Lane and Hope can get more bodies than they know what to do with.* Either that, or we stop the effort altogether. For all her obstinacy, Alice was right about little progress and much cost. Bohun dismissed, Lane was sent off to give similar instructions to other parts of the Domain in the midlands. Sent off with a bit of a frown on his face, a frown duly noted by Arundel.

The following day's journey was a lot faster. This was the Domain's trunk road, and much labour was used to keep it good condition. There was a midday break to the north of Leicester, another way station with telephones. Messages sent, it was less than an hour before the local DC and the Visitor for the substantial Ground to the south could attend in person, to be briefed by Arundel and Lane. The Visitor was relaxed and co-operative. The Ground was entirely enclosed by Domain, Domain with merely moderate capacity, but sufficient to feed the Ground and claim its recruits. He had feared new targets would be set.

There were very few Kingsmen required, just a token garrison. Rangers and Proctors between them policed the boundaries with no trouble. Certainly, most of the garrison could go south.

The DC, however, was a little less sanguine. There were unexplained movements in and out of the RPZ. Hygienist's appointments were missed, and his men were having to hunt down the missing. The bailiff was evasive. *Damned rabble*, thought Arundel. Perhaps this DC had got slack. A brief conversation with Lane, and Arundel reluctantly settled for a token fifty Security to be sent south. As they resumed their journey, Arundel quizzed Lane.

"Those problems in the RPZ, Lane. Are they out of the ordinary?"

"No, My Lord, I don't think so. These cities are a chronic problem. If it were not for the Hunt and my transfer, I would have started a crackdown in all of them. These bailiffs need clearing out. But if we put in reliable substitutes, they'd need a force permanently alongside. Proctors are useless. Most more or less refuse to enter cities. Any enforcement is down to word of mouth from the bailiff."

Another three hours and they were at Wheatley, the Domain headquarters that dealt with the Oxford Ground. Here, both the Visitor and the DC were waiting for them, summoned in advance. It was much busier than the previous stops, quite a settlement. The Ground itself lay to the west, and included much of the city, a large and high-yielding RPZ. The Domain lands were also good, and supported some small industries, shipping charcoal from the Chilterns.

The conversations here were much less satisfactory. The Visitor was subdued, but the DC was angry and worried. The same problems as at Leicester, but more of them. Stones thrown from abandoned buildings when the troopers searched for the recalcitrant. An obstreperous bailiff making excuses about bad feeling. Outrageous claims about misuse of Chosen circulating. Yes, bailiff confined to quarters. No, we cannot just remove him. We don't have enough information or manpower. Kingsmen? Here the DC turned to the Visitor.

"On standby, my Lords. Things were quiet when we left to meet you, but we have warned the bailiff that we will move in and shoot to kill if harm comes to any Security trooper. The same problems are occurring in Swindon, my Lords. They asked us for help. We had to refuse."

Arundel shot a rather evil glance at Lane. Damned rabble; double damned rabble, but why now, and how has it been allowed to build up? Lane swallowed, but remained calm.

"Tell me, either of you. There is nothing new about some Chosen being selected for reclamation, especially the dimmer ones from the RPZs. We know they suspect, but we've been careful to move them a long way off. We might have relaxed that a bit over the last year, but this trouble is brand new. Why now, I wonder?"

"We have asked ourselves the same question, my Lord. With appropriate treatment, a few that we have caught and taken out have told the same story. There were a few defectors from the works to the west, but the bailiff told us that he was dealing with it. Then, just recently, there were much worse tales around, tales about some Grounder who went walkabout and witnessed the Barriers up north. I don't know how, but he has been paraded about telling his tale. The bailiff denies it. We lack the manpower to search rigorously. If we are to bring the bailiff in for interrogation, we will need more security and a battalion of Kingsmen to keep order."

Arundel told them to wait outside. He turned an angry gaze on Lane.

"What is all this nonsense, Lane? Traitors moving from city to city? Who else is moving about without interception? If you were not so fixated on your damned reclamation, we would not have this trouble in the first place. And your eye off the ball elsewhere."

"My Lord, I have repeatedly asked for more freedom to tame the RPZs. Each time, I have been opposed by Visitors, and by my Lady Buckingham. And when an opportunity arises, as in Northernmost, a commandant is suspended, and the Visitor hands things over to the military. My Lord, the military are perhaps not as united in their dedication to your service as Truth and Justice."

Arundel simmered. Lane had indeed warned him, though it should never have reached this point in the first place. Outright revolt might kill more breeding stock than the Outies could manage. As for the military, some developed this warped sense of honour. Herding Outies was not regarded as war, but policing, and not their business, while defending the Grounds most certainly was. Alice had been at work, for sure. Always wait, keep the Grounds healthy. Jam tomorrow, never jam today.

Well, I will have to make do with Lane for now, he thought. I wonder what this Hope character is like. A subordinate with enforcement on his mind and no fancy ideas of his own, that would suit me fine. I must get the details of that case, and talk to the man. In the meantime, damn it, we will have to reinforce Oxford and Swindon. Get the Leicester men allocated here, and recruit a few more from other places in the south for Swindon. Those from the north, though, are mine, as are any soldiers. They will have had experience of the Hunt.

The Visitor and DC were recalled. Instructions were given, promises made. Containment for now, gentlemen, don't force the pace, but don't show weakness. Pass the message on to Swindon. An irritated Arundel turned to his own comfort. All but two mobiles were told to continue to Windsor. Let the Court at least be back to normal when I arrive. Lane to be sent with them, but Hope held back. I'd like a word with him as we return.

The following morning, Arundel and his smaller party completed the journey at a leisurely pace. Taking Hope along with him, he soon acquired the history of events in the north as seen through Hope's eyes. Sweet music indeed. An enforcer pure and simple; a sniffer out of treachery more single-minded than Lane. His mood lightened. Sport to be had, territory to be won, then we can deal with the soft, the over-scrupulous and the downright traitors. Let Lane be for now. He gave Hope an approving stare.

"A few more like you, Commandant, and the Domain would be better served. Be sure that I will see to it that your talents are both used and rewarded. As you are aware, there are obstacles, but they can be overcome. I think, Commandant, that you have never been present at a Hunt?"

"No, my Lord, I have not had that privilege."

"At the Hunt, Commandant, there are rare opportunities for rapid advancement. A tally of Outie scalps to your credit, most especially a tally of those who show a little fight, wins promotion and years added in the field. The only way that cannot be denied. I was minded to offer you a command in the security operation that will be needed as the Hunt advances. Dull work, Commandant, dull but necessary work, breaking captives to our will. There is an alternative. Be my guest, Commandant, as a member of the Hunt. Acquit yourself well, and the path is open. Yes? It will be so. My servants will see to your briefing and accoutrements."

***

Driving through Windsor, Arundel's comfortable mood did not last long. Certainly, preparations for the Hunt were well in train. Kingsmen were arriving, and some despatched westwards to take up positions north and south to seal off the killing ground. Pavilions were being spread and repaired, to be packed on mobiles and sent ahead of the great departure. Armourers were refurbishing the breast-plates and helmets reserved for the hunt. Hand-crafted crossbows were restrung. Young bloods were talking with stableboys and trying mounts. Only the sheer scale of the operation differentiated it from all those held previously. The environs of the Castle had surely never been so busy, nor the volume of trade in all those items that made life on the road and in camp that little bit more civilised. He had his driver go slowly through the throng, acknowledging the salutes and bows.

Even before he had arrived, though, Lane and Wilkes had been getting messages. Messages from Swindon, from Oxford, now even from Leicester. Damned cities; there were more troubles. Security teams stoned. Mobiles damaged. Even shots fired. Firearms? In the city? Not the shotguns allowed to farmers. Injuries to troopers and Security. Grounders killed, at least a dozen already. The final straw, an attack on the warehouses of the Domain at Luton. Troopers left bound and gagged. From the Castle courtyard, Arundel was rushed to a chamber where Wilkes, Lane and several commandants were struggling to make sense of the events that were unfolding. None had dared to alter his original instructions. Alter them, he must. With mounting anger, he allowed Wilkes and Lane to countermand orders where possible, and to divert the marching forces to trouble spots. Lane had about him just a hint of smugness: "*My Lord, I have repeatedly asked for more freedom to tame the RPZs. Each time, I have been opposed by Visitors, and by my Lady Buckingham.*" Well, my lad, thought Arundel, tamed they will be in good time, but not by you. Win your spurs, Hope. Lane? Good for commanding the sordid business of taming Outies. A task which will keep him away from those damned reclamations.

Things were no better the following morning. Disturbances had gone on throughout the night. Mobiles ambushed and their fuel used to make incendiaries. Two Security men killed in Oxford, and many more injured. Grounder dead? Clearly closing on a hundred. Nearly as many captured, dragged out and crammed into cells designed for the occasional deviant. Blackstone was useless as Lane's formal replacement. The man was wandering around the room, almost wringing his hands. *Why is it so rarely that I can get obedience and some brains in the same person*, thought Arundel? Wilkes took him aside.

"My Lord, Security are inadequate for this task, be there never so many of them. They are trained to arrest, to interrogate, to deal with small riots, not for combat against armed men. Pistols? Nightsticks? At least two companies of

Kingsmen are needed at each city, and at that merely for containment until the Hunt is over. A whole battalion for Oxford."

"What? Two battalions, near enough. How many are left, Wilkes? Can they not just subdue these lowlifes and let Security do their job. Clean it up and then join us? We've a few days before things get interesting. At least those at Oxford and Swindon."

"My Lord, by your own command, we read about wars before the Catastrophe. Before the development of the powerful weapons that brought it about. I read about street fighting, my Lord. Where a few in buildings and ruins held back much larger forces, even when those forces had the power to demolish whole buildings with artillery and bombs. The process took months. Only starvation can work, and that requires time and complete investment."

Again, there was no choice but to agree. Wilkes had companies moving in to the paths cleared through the Badlands. They would not be reinforced. Others would move either side of the Hunt. Smaller forces, yes, though still larger than those mustered for any previous Hunt. Security would advance alongside. Holding camps? Fewer to man them, but Outies rarely fought back.

Arundel spent the rest of the day with his stableboys, armourers and squires. A run in the tiltyard; exchanging jokes and stories of past Hunts with others in the throng. A few drinks quickly dispersed his doubts.

News the following morning was a little more reassuring. The cities were still in turmoil, but appearance of Kingsmen at crossing points, and as escorts for security had kept chaos at bay. A few Grounder casualties, and more removed for transfer to Reclamation. Leaving his commanders, Arundel strolled through the town. Heavy mobiles had started moving west, along with many carts and waggons. Provosts were shouting, waggoners swearing at the dust raised by mobiles. *All as it should be*, thought Arundel, as he walked to the stables and tournament ground, where this year's young bloods were learning, some of them from scratch, the art of riding, the art of wielding a lance and the art of using a crossbow while remaining in the saddle. Got to be sporting; pistols were your last resort if you fell and the prey were upon you. Survive, you probably would. Your squires would shoot to kill, and drag you from the field. But you would face laughter in the evening; laughter, and a few years, if any, before you had another chance. Hope was a tyro. He had ridden but once, and on a pony at that. Let's see how he is getting on. Maybe we need some reliable companions close by.

The tournament ground was crowded. There were crowds, not all usefully occupied, cheering or jeering as the chosen hunters tilted at mock Outies, or fired at targets. The foolish had chosen the most powerful beasts. Most laughter was generated when they failed to control them and took a tumble. No sign of Hope, though. He asked a tilt-master.

"Still selecting a mount, my Lord. He'll be in the stables. More sense than some out there, for a novice. He's acquired a squire, too, a lad he knew before. Both seem very pleased with each other."

Arundel headed to the stables. There, indeed, was Hope, a young man in attendance, with a riding master. All turned and saluted as he approached.

"All well, Hope? I trust Mr Hockley is seeing to your needs?"

"The commandant has more common sense than most novices, my Lord. We have tried a few mounts, and have picked Daisy here. She's biddable, and she's been in action before. The commandant has mastered her well enough."

"Very good. I was told you have acquired a squire, Hope? I presume this young man is he; introduce him, if you will."

"My Lord, this is John Gregory, freshly Chosen from the north. An ardent patriot, my Lord, who assisted us in rooting out treachery there. We met just after his selection, and he had already told me that Service in Security was what he desired. It was chance, though, a happy chance, that brought him here for training. I saw him in the street. It was easy to arrange his release. I have your Lordship to thank for the help I have received from all."

"Very good, Gregory. Delighted to hear of a youngster held in such regard by his superiors. Service as a squire is an excellent first step in Royal Service, most especially if your master wins his spurs. It can, though, be a position of some danger; have you practice with a pistol, young man?"

John shook his head. "No, my Lord. It comes later in the training."

"Hockley, when you are finished here, get a soldier to take this lad to the Armoury. The Master is to equip him and get some practice in. Here is my token. As for you, Hope, into the tilting yard with you. Practice makes, I was going to say perfect, but effective will do."

Arundel did not stop to witness any triumphs or tragedies for Hope on the field. Hunger and a desire for news drew him back to the Castle. Wilkes and Sussex were mulling over reports transcribed by an army of clerks. There was no sign of Kent.

"He pleads illness, my Lord, and has taken to his bed. But he and my Lady Buckingham have inserted their tokens. The supply of doses for the Hunt are ready to go with us. I think he will not move with us tomorrow."

No, thought Arundel, *he will stay here and plot*. I'm not leaving Sussex behind to shadow him. Either he comes, on a litter if needs be, or we get an official renunciation of authority on doctor's orders. He turned to Wilkes.

"Any developments?"

"Not of significance, my Lord. The cities appear intimidated where we show force. The hunting ground is almost ready. Troops are ready to move into advanced positions north and south to seal it. Half the numbers, I fear, but enough to make the Outies run. A few more may escape the net, but there's precious few places for them to run to, unless they are very good swimmers."

"The north?"

"Nothing. They've shut down the Barriers. The city is giving no trouble."

"A bit peculiar don't you think?" asked Sussex. "Lots of trouble where we are well equipped to deal with it, even if we have to shift forces around. None where we would be pushed to prevent even outright invasion, not a whisper. Even a touch more zealous in their duty than usual."

"Stop worrying, man. Maybe that Cornwallis fellow is more competent than we gave him credit for. We can turn our attention there when we've dealt with bigger things down here. Maybe Hope and Lane between them put the fear of God into their bailiff, and what he hears on their little network about what we do down here will add to his worries. That lot worry about their precious Ground. They'll do anything to prevent it being squeezed."

***

The Hunt. To any but the first-born, it was a ritual, an initiation into the circles of the great, a chance to shine and to earn both praise and a longer life. A ritual that was, for those originating later in the Grounds, something established in time immemorial. For those few who shared with the King an actual knowledge of its origins, it had evolved over time. Foxhunting had, of course, been an inspiration; a lordly sport with the undertow of pest control appealed to the fancy of these self-appointed rulers. But other elements soon accrued. The hunting of wild boar, of deer and the tiger hunts of an Empire gone long before their time, hunts that involved danger and required the gratifying presence of menials; these fed the imagination more powerfully.

With the near-eternal life granted to the King and those chosen with him, there was an even older, more seductive model: the Wild Hunt of mythology and fairy tale. Airborne they could not manage, but the breeding of hounds and black horses, the fascination of archaic costume and weapons, these all appealed to the increasingly disordered mind of the Sovereign. A Sovereign now influenced by the warped humour of his children's tutor. And in those early days, the means were greater, the prey far fewer in the semi-badlands lying outside the constraints of the Treaties. Hunts were frequent, kills were modest. Exercises, as Arundel came to realise, in self-indulgence alone.

Time wrought its changes. It was not long before the Four had control of the King. Not long before Outies were to be found in greater numbers in places that might in time be added to the Domain. Not long before Hunts became both more dangerous and also an increasing strain on resources. Romance had given way to something more akin to pest control. Long before the birth of any living Grounder not dosed to nobility, Arundel had sensed the need for change. The concern for human life was dangerous; to his contempt, some extended that concern to Outies, even the most hideous. Draw the new recruits in by linking participation to advancement: blood them. Hunts not at the whim of an erratic master, but annual events accompanied by the compelling blend of pomp, revelry and comradeship. Now, the prey must be driven, escape prevented, crude culls made within the chosen arena.

The final, the most recent, change had been to capture as well as kill. To break and enslave. To make good the lack of people supplied by the Grounds and those few parts of the Domain that could manage it. A little at first, passed off as an amusing experiment. More and more as Truth and Justice found the most efficient ways to break captives to a life of servitude. Now, more than ever, lay hands on that labour. Now, more than ever, prepare to take the west. Then the swap of lance for lasso, scalps for servants; servants in far greater numbers than could be extracted from the Grounds. Or from the futile hope of overseas. In the meantime, though, the ceremonial and the initiation must be maintained.

***

286

There was one last ritual to witness, the Masque, a comic performance staged by tomorrow's new hunters and their squires the evening before departure. Typically, the squires, clad in monstrous imitations of Outies would appear on stage. Some would ride on the shoulders of others, covered by a framework giving the appearance of a giant. They might carry clubs or even spears. They would prance and gibber. Some would have mock fights over a bone or a haunch of mutton. As huntsmen appeared, they would scream and run into each other. Several would fall over. They would flee to one side, pursued by the hunters, only to reappear at the other pursued still further. Hunters would make to lance several. Groaning bodies would litter the stage. A few hunters might give a comic turn, falling themselves, but rise up, hurling screaming Outies in all directions. Only horses and hounds were missing.

After Arundel and Sussex had taken their seats at the front, the lights on stage were turned up, and The Major-Domo appeared. No curtain, and it took him to raise his arms for silence. Hush fell.

"My Lords, ladies and gentlemen. Welcome to this our humble entertainment for your pleasure. In anticipation of the week's adventures, we have added a few scenes to the traditional sequence," bowing to Arundel, "which we trust will not meet with your censure."

He withdrew. Trumpets blew, in designed discordance. The stage was filled, overfilled, with a mob of Outies yammering, stumbling and fighting. A giant appeared with a sheep carcass (carefully prepared) that was torn apart, with much fighting and cursing. A single bugle note sounded, and the sound of dogs. Outies stopped. They peered around in all directions, shouting at each other. Hands were cupped to ears. Rotating Outies collided. Some left the stage to the right, only to return screaming within seconds, hotly pursued by three hunters in shiny breastplates. These dealt blows to right and left. Writhing bodies spouting blood fell to the floor. The rest fled left, pursued by the hunters. They returned from the right, followed again by the hunters. A giant toppled onto a hunter, and two others made play to rescue their comrade, leaving the giant twitching, but coming apart. The 'head' removed the mask and winked at the audience. The sequence was repeated.

So, far, so normal, thought Arundel. A few more circuits, the Outies all slain, and the hunters will bow before us. What has old Bobby thought of this time? Certainly, more Outies than usual; he's done us proud.

There was a pause. Outies returned to the stage, but no hunters followed. There were pantomime gestures of listening, Outies prowling round the stage and shushing each other. They looked sideways at each other. Then one fell upon the giant, grabbed an arm, and started chewing it. Soon all joined in, chewing or robbing the corpses of the fallen. A few sat up and fought back. Laughter from the audience.

A bugle and yapping to the right. A moment's confusion, and Outies rushed left. Hunters entered right and looked about them. Screams, yells and gunshots came from the left, and a mass of Outies entered, tripping over each other. Those in front saw the hunters and turned back, knocking over those still entering. Soon, most of the stage was a seething mass of Outies. A whistle blew to the left, and an exaggerated thumping of boots could be heard. Outies fell over each other in the effort to avoid both the left and the now impassive line of hunters to the right.

Then, to gasps from the audience, a line of Security men emerged from the left. They spread out and advanced in step towards the Outies. Thump, thump; batons swinging. In pairs, they clubbed Outies one by one, handcuffed them, and tied halters round their necks. A second rank led the dazed captives off stage in chains. Soon, only the dead remained. A Security commandant saluted the hunters and withdrew after the captives.

Hunters lined up at the back of the stage. A clear trumpet call sounded, and a first-born, red cloak billowing, made a swaggering entrance.

"Well, gentlemen, what sport have you had?" He looked around. "Not so many, gentlemen, not so many. I had expected more." An exaggerated frown.

"May it please your Lordship, this is not all." A hunter raised his voice: "Commandant, show us the day's takings, if you please."

A blast of trumpets. A procession of Outies in chains, heads bowed, escorted by Security made their way across the stage, leaving to the right, only the Commandant remaining. The procession was long (an effect achieved by sending the same players around twice more). The Commandant bowed to the first-born.

"For your service, my Lord. *Obedient* service, my Lord. In time, as many as the Kingdom wishes."

Trumpets blew. The cast, headpieces removed, crammed onto the stage. They bowed as applause reverberated around the old hall. The Major-Domo returned to the front.

"My Lords, ladies and gentlemen. I trust you enjoyed our little entertainment. A foretaste of the real thing, for which I give you the hope of Royal blessing."

Arundel was grinning broadly. Bobby could sniff the wind all right. Nice touch to have a real commandant play the part. Up to you, now, Hope my lad, up to you. Such a pity Kent absented himself. Of course, he will get to hear of it, as will Alice, in a while. But I would have loved to see him squirm.

22. A Trap Is Laid

Clearing the way for the Hunt had been a major undertaking. The Badlands had many lethal spots. Navigation had been a matter of trial and error, error involving the loss of many lives among the unchosen and Outie captives. Even the forward camps were not entirely clean and, despite their gear, the Security forces themselves were losing men to sickness.

Dusk was falling as Security sergeant Gregg ordered his squad to return over the short distance to camp, escorting the burial party disposing of those of their labouring comrades who had died during the day. One of his own too; that poor sod deserved a proper burial. A clear run for the Kingsmen now. *A narrow run, true*, he thought, *but at least this job was finished.* Trail marked; the worst patches cleared. Not without cost to his own men, nor to himself. Tomorrow, those soldiers will come, and we can pull back to safety, washing and uncontaminated gear.

A whoosh and a yell behind him. A trooper on the ground, clutching his neck. Something hissed past him. Then the crack of rifles. He dropped and peered back. All his men down except that brainless idiot Evans, staring around in amazement.

"Drop, you bloody fool," he shouted. Too late. Another crack and Evans fell. He saw movement through the scrub around him. Movement towards the camp just a hundred yards away. His captives stood in a huddle, peering this way and that. The camp stirred. More shots. Security men dropped or fell. Captives emerged from the mess tent and stared. Some with sense dropped, others retreated inside.

There was a pause. Gregg looked around him. No one near, that he could see. Then there were shouts, shouts that he could not at first make out. Then he heard, close by.

"Run, comrades, run. Run west. Run now. There is a path. Run." The shouts attracted some pistol shots from the camp. Another round of rifle fire in return. *Idiots*, thought Gregg; no hope at that distance.

The bemused gaggle of captives under his guard continued to look around in a daze. Then two started to run. A trooper stood up, pistol in hand. A whoosh, and he fell, a bolt in his chest. Then the whole group broke for it. Pistol shots brought one down, but each shot brought down a hail of bullets and bolts. Gregg lay flat. He could hear shots and shouting from the camp. A short silence, then the sound of people running through the scrub towards him. He cocked his pistol.

Four labourers came up to him, panting. They paused. Three Outies, their crooked faces betraying their origin, and one unchosen, who moved to attack him. He was about to fire, but the man was held back by an Outie. An Outie who spoke.

"You have a choice, mister. Shoot and you kill one, and you follow. Throw that pistol over here, and we will be on our way. Two *human* lives, mister."

Gregg threw the pistol. To his surprise, it was left where it fell. The four disappeared west in the increasing darkness. There were more shouts, some torches waved; The noise faded westwards, and after a period of silence and the onset of full darkness, he got to his feet, and found the pistol. Stumbling in the dark, he found the captive corpse, then those of three of his men. One missing. He called. No response. Collecting their pistols and tags, he made his way to the camp.

Someone had managed to light a few lamps. The mess tent had been turned into a crude combination of hospital and headquarters. His lieutenant sat at a table, one arm in a sling. Five other men were variously lying or sitting with bandages around them. Only two of them there were completely unharmed. Other bandaged were preparing a meal or tending the worse affected.

"You escaped, I see, sergeant. Your men? Your captives?"

"Three out of four dead, sir; No sign of Eccles, but it was dark. I retrieved their pistols and tags after it went quiet. Labour? One dead, the rest bolted."

"You are uninjured? I will add your tally to this report, then you will take it back to the Commandant, with Higgs and Michaels as escorts. Yes, now. The route is waymarked, and you will take a lamp."

A brief scribble, and a folded piece of paper was handed over. Armed with a pole-lamp the three departed. Out of sight of the camp, both men started questioning.

"You were lucky, sarge. Bloody murder here; the bastards had rifles, not to mention bows. Pistols and nightsticks? Bloody useless. Most of our lot never had the military training like us two. Rushed out to see what was happening and copped it. We dropped like stones, sarge, second nature."

"No point in firing back, either," added Michaels, "just turned themselves into targets. What's up, Sarge? Those bastards must have been watching us for days. And knew how to cross the Badlands."

"What's up? Fucked if I know. Those back at base don't know either, or we'd have had some soldiers up here with us. What's the damage, anyway?"

"Not sure, sarge, but it's heavy. It will be on that piece of paper, sarge. It's not sealed, is it?"

Gregg looked hard at the troopers in the lamplight. They'll not blab, and it scarcely matters. They lowered the lamp and unfolded the paper.

For Commandant Norris.

We were attacked in force at 9.45 this evening. A substantial force opening fire on us from three directions with rifles and crossbows. ~~13~~ 16 men killed, 8 seriously injured, 15 walking wounded (including myself). One unaccounted for, presumed dead. The object of the attack was to rescue the labour force. Of these, ~~6~~ 7 were shot dead while attempting to escape, three injured were despatched later. The remainder fled west, responding to shouts from around us. When they had gone, the attackers withdrew, as far as we can tell.

The camp is guarded as best we can. I need not explain why a renewed attack in such force will be impossible to repel.

Lt. Donald Ransome.

"Blimey, sarge. Leaving out us three there's only ten left untouched, plus those fifteen that might get off a few shots. Those were not normal Outies, sarge, were they?"

An answer would have been superfluous. Paper folded, lamp hoisted, the trio made their way north-east in the dark. Two hours later, their message was delivered to an incredulous commandant. His language became increasingly profane. No telephone. No contingency plans.

***

A few miles to the west, Chief O'Neill, six hunter companions and a squad of grinning Outlanders were shepherding their charges through the carefully marked routes in the Badlands to the small flotilla of boats waiting to cross to the Dean shore. Boats that had landed some carefully handled packages, packages carried away from the shore and concealed at intervals inland. Security? Easy game. Kingsmen would be more of a challenge.

Just a few miles further south, other boats were also busy. Guided by shielded lanterns facing west, they were beached in the shallows and quickly unloaded on the small strip of shore clear of contamination. Bigger packages here, indeed crates, manhandled with great care. Nor were they empty for the return trip. Lines of Outlanders were in turn led to the boats, which were pushed off against the rising tide.

In the dim light of lanterns, an observer would have noticed a difference between those departing and those arriving with their cargo. The latter were indeed Aeronauts, and the most able of Alfred's workers. It was Martha who commanded all. Martha who had followed Colonel Hunt to Dean. Martha who had stirred up the declining and pacific Alfred to turn his full attention to the needs of war. Aided by the colonel, who had organised a crash course in military discipline to willing but none too clever recruits.

Those departing were the old, the children, and hardest to bear, those adults whose offspring showed promise. Adults with rage in their hearts. All knew about the Hunt. Now those Hunts had an even worse significance. Not just death for the sport of Kings, but capture, torture and slavery, slavery in Badlands that no one should enter. Never before had they known where the Hunt would strike, until too late. Never before had it threatened so many, so many that could breed with at least some chance of success. Never before had there been a chance to frustrate it.

There was more. There was no way that stock could be ferried across the estuary in any numbers. They would be rounded up by the Domain, food for the nobles that treated them as quarry. Prize bulls and rams, boars and cocks had been moved west. But people first.

The following day, small parties of Outlanders moved inland, most with heavy packs on their backs. Some returned to the shore to carry a second load. One fell backwards. Those around moved rapidly away, while the fallen man struggled briefly to his feet. Spasms crossed his face; he collapsed and then lay still. The track was marked off. All moved more cautiously thereafter, bypassing the untouched corpse.

Among the now deserted huts and byres, roofs were removed. Behind walls, miniature Montgolfiers were assembled. Rockets were stacked under waterproof covers. Little piles of ceramic pots, each plugged and with a fuse protruding were stacked in many buildings. About a fifth of them had a splash of red paint.

23. Tally Ho!

The route from Windsor to the city of tents that had been set up for the Hunt was slow and twisting. Notionally within the Domain, it weaved between patches of Badlands, and in places skirted the Grounds of Oxford, Swindon and the tiny enclave of Cirencester. Domainal lands were dismal, scarcely better than semi-badland. The roads, somewhat patched up over the previous months, were slow going.

The buoyant spirit of the previous evening was dampened by drizzle. No comfortable way station to look forward to at the half way point; just tents, 'pavilions' was the preferred term, awaited the main party on the first evening. Wilkes had prudently ridden ahead on horseback, missing the masque. He arrived at the more lavishly appointed Hunt encampment a few miles north-west of Tetbury as the lumbering convoy of Court reached the halfway mark. His task was complex. Both to north and south, soldiers awaited the time to seal the Outies' escape to the estuary. Main force to be stationed around the entry at Kingscote, where it would spread north and south along the summit plateau, flanking the hunt that descended into the valleys. Security in the rear, as always; the buggers will need protection, too.

It was an operation on a scale never attempted before. As the crow flies, all three forces, north, south and central, were a mere seven miles apart. But no one could travel like a crow without a certain and painful death in prospect. Devious routes, not well marked, doubled the effective distances, routes over which no mobile could pass. Wilkes thought enviously of his studies in the Royal Archives at Arundel's request. Arundel, always hoping to find among the plethora of kit described in pre-Catastrophe manuals something that the Armoury could re-create. *Field radios, mobile phones, call in air support,* even *synchronise watches,* all beyond his reach. Co-ordination? Sunrise? The weather seemed set overcast. Eight o'clock as best you can judge, gentlemen. Reinforcements? Diverted elsewhere.

For all his internal grumbling, Wilkes felt more put upon than seriously concerned. The whole business was looking to be messy, and the moment it was finished, he would have to provide support for Security, who had stirred up hornets' nests in the cities. That fellow Cornwallis, now. Military rule up north, not those Security apes, and that Ground was running like clockwork by all the reports. Next day, he was able to greet the arrival of Arundel, the Hunt, and the myriads of hangers on that accompanied them with a degree of equanimity. The weather had brightened, and grumbling subsided to normal levels. He joined the Hunt for a lavish meal in the large tent erected. Drink was taken, drink well in excess of what the youngsters could take. Arundel was genial, ignoring the not so discreet removal of the incapable and the mopping up that preceded it. The general's sardonic view of the occasion was rudely interrupted when a soldier at the entrance gave a signal: urgent message.

Outside his own command tent, he was faced with an exhausted sergeant, still removing his outer gear, and discarding it well away from the tent. An Outie attack on the clearance camp in the north. Labour mostly escaped. Most of the Security troopers killed or injured. A message back, overnight? It might not get there in time, if at all. The company of soldiers would move on schedule. At least, they were forewarned. Even if he had any, it would take two days at least to provide reinforcements. He returned to the banquet. Arundel raised his eyebrows.

"A little local problem in the north, my Lord. Some Outies ambushed Security at the clearance. But it is finished. The troops will be there at dawn as instructed, and move later. They will face no serious threat."

Arundel grunted. "I should hope not, General. We want the quarry moving towards us, not obliging us to use bows or rifles as they attempt to swim. Make sure the flanks are covered. The stupid sods will run into the Badlands otherwise."

He looked at the now depleted banqueting scene.
"There are some who will appreciate a later start, I think. The usual signals when we depart. I will give one for your men an hour ahead."

***

Dawn broke on the seventeenth. In the north, Major Cardwell, forewarned, had taken precautions. No march in formation. Scouts ahead, peering into the wicked Badlands either side of the track. The company in loose formation, rifles at the ready. Into the Security camp, where the disconsolate survivors welcomed them. No, no time or men to cover your withdrawal, Lieutenant, and those capable will follow behind us when we move on. Prisoners, Lieutenant, prisoners. Your job, not ours, once they are disarmed.

The advance party started down the trail. As the Badlands weakened, the surroundings held more cover. At the head, troops spread out cautiously to cover the trail end, beyond which was scrub. At its entrance, though, the soldiers were close together, waiting to carry on. Suddenly there were the cracks of rifle fire ahead. All dropped, facing the Badlands around them. Just out of sight, a fire-fight developed ahead. Three Outies appeared out of the Badlands only a few yards from them. Each threw a smoking object among the soldiers before being gunned down.

The grenades exploded, two before reaching the ground, one soon after contact. Feeble explosions, at best, though shards drew blood on faces and holes in kit. There was a short silence. Then the pain, the contortions the gasps, the spasms of those nearest each explosion. Cardwell had been briefed. Agent Z.

"Space out. avoid the bodies. Anything moves, bring it down."

At least this lot have some discipline. Under cover, each waiting platoon retreated towards the camp, leapfrogging. Enough clear ground to prevent another attack like that. Those Outies must have accepted death by contamination, unless, the uneasy thought occurred, they have wriggled their way through as a few of his own scouts had learnt to do, albeit slowly. Now, though, his force was split. There was silence ahead. Then a lieutenant zig-zagged back from the trail. No Outies rose up to shoot him.

"Halted, sir. One dead, two injured. At least four Outies down."

Cardwell considered. Half of his force were now down the trail. A few of those by the camp were poisoned, but not fatally. Get them under cover. Enough clear ground. Enough rifles to prevent a rush. He turned to the Security lieutenant.

"You are in command here, Lieutenant. Anything moves around you, shoot. You'll get a yell from the trailhead if anyone's coming back, and the uniform should be enough." With most of the remaining men, he ran across the ground to the trail. At its end, his force was spread either side of the trail, facing outwards. He ordered an advance through the scrub. Soon, crossbow bolts were flying, but Outies were falling. A single rifle shot prompted a fusillade from the soldiers. A section advanced slowly to the spot. A man lay dying, his rifle cast aside as he fell. The major turned him over. Normal, indeed handsome and well built. A helmet with two feathers had rolled away. This is an Outie? He'd pass for a Grounder with no trouble. Evader? Taking the rifle, Cardwell and his party continued their advance. Slowly, cautiously, but without opposition. The ground opened up, and they reached a well-used track. A ruined house had been turned into a byre. Cattle stared at them placidly. Get the wounded behind walls and see to them. Nothing fatal. He pulled out his map. Look for the meeting place with those from the south. Spread out along it. Fire at fleeing Outies from the east. He grimaced. Well behind schedule, and no damned Security, if we catch any. He waited for action to begin.

***

As Cardwell explored his position, Arundel had given the signal to the main body, and Wilkes' men advanced from the camp without opposition, or indeed any sign of life, across the plateaux. Half an hour later, the horns sounded in the distance. The dogs could be heard. The Hunt was moving in along the valley. Soldiers took up positions to shoot at any Outies climbing the hillsides. There was no sound bar that of the Hunt. The Hunt drew closer, but still invisible. Any moment, and panicking Outies will appear, running west.

It did not happen. Ahead of the Hunt, intermittently visible, was a stampede of cattle, their bellows drowning the sound of horns and dogs. At a signal, the Hunt reined to a halt ahead of a patch of ruins. Not a single Outie had been seen. Hounds ran to and forth, baying but finding nothing. The assembled Huntsmen, many of them novices, looked around in puzzlement. Arundel was beside himself with rage. There was treachery here. The bastards knew; how?

"The scum have fled, gentlemen. But they cannot go far. There are more soldiers near the sea to bar their way. Onwards."

No sooner had he spoken, when rockets soared over them from the west. They burst in mid-air. There were a few rifle shots as well, bringing down a couple. Soldiers moved ahead of the Hunt at Wilkes' command, and those on the hillsides above fired at shadowy movements below them. At first, the rockets merely caused panic among the horses. Novices took tumbles. Then more fell, their mounts with them, vomiting and in spasm. Among the fallen was Hope. But soon it was evident that the poison was too scattered and in too small quantities. None had died, though many remained unhorsed and retching. Their mounts were scarcely better. The soldiers ahead were now exchanging fire with an enemy invisible to the huntsmen themselves.

"This is no longer a Hunt, gentlemen," shouted Arundel, "This is war. Pistols are to be used without mercy. Let us advance."

The survivors, still a substantial majority, advanced slowly behind a thin screen of soldiers. Soon they encountered a maze of overgrown ruins, the ideal refuge for the Outies. More rockets distracted the Huntsmen, now looking up and moving away from their tracks; there were collisions and more unhorsing. As they closed on the ruins, crossbow bolts found targets. Grenades, feeble enough as explosives, caused more poisoning.

The Outies, however, were few. They could be rushed from several angles. Some on the hillsides ran in the open. Arundel spurred his horse and lanced two as they fled. Resistance over, and seeing open ground beyond the contested ruins, Wilkes ordered a halt. Time to regroup and assess damage and resources. At least fifty Outies down, the injured being shot where they lay. Twenty-six of his men dead also, and a couple of the Hunt, but many more incapacitated or wounded. For the soldiers, the brief battle held few surprises for those that had encountered cornered Outies. They were angered rather than frightened by the poison, for which they had received at least some last-minute training following the Montgolfier attacks.

For the Huntsmen, the shock was awful. They had trained, briefly, to run down the fleeing, to spare those who prostrated themselves provided Security were at hand to shackle and remove them. Even those with previous Hunts under their belts had not encountered resistance of this kind. Many had lost their horses. Several hounds had perished; many were sick. The small posse of Security that had brought up the rear to deal with prisoners stood in a huddle. Many peered anxiously upwards. Wilkes approached Arundel.

"We were warned, my Lord, at the Treaty Point. Word of the Hunt has reached them, and they are prepared, much better prepared than I thought possible. There were no children or aged among them. They intended to fight, not to run. This is a military matter, my Lord, no longer a Hunt. I have yet to hear from those closing off the shore, but I anticipate that they have met resistance."

Arundel was spluttering. He managed, with an effort, to control himself.

"We are betrayed, Wilkes. This is no mere Outie plan; they've not the brains. The treachery will be punished. We will have to forego the prisoners, for now, as well as the sport. But the shore, to have and to hold, it is still possible?"

"With a pause, yes. But my forces are now much reduced. The injured and poisoned must be escorted back to camp. Any there that are able must join us. We need more ammunition, and more rifles, though there will be few enough. Your Huntsmen must take the rifles of those who have fallen. All those lacking rifles should hold back, should follow us when we advance in the morning, my Lord, the Security forces also."

"There are not so many rifles, Wilkes. But as you say, all must be assembled. On the beaches, pistols and lances may serve our purpose."

The forces were halted. A screen of soldiers guarded the west. Sussex escorted the stretchers and still retching and walking wounded back towards the camp. In the confusion of rearranging affairs, the departure of a single horseman to the east went unnoticed. As dusk fell, a stream of men and materials moved down the valley. Cooking fires were lit by the soldiers, accustomed as they were to the exigencies of combat. Huntsmen and their squires remained disconsolate and disenchanted. There were roofless ruins all about, in which men took shelter.

The night was a disturbed one. Shots rang out on the hillsides. Outies had crept up and hurled grenades. Few killed, more sickened and carried to the rear. But the soldiers were regaining confidence. They were killing more Outies. A steady advance in daylight would be unstoppable. At least, it was a dry, a balmy, midsummer night, with a gentle breeze from the west.

It was a squire who first shouted and pointed upwards. Bright against the sky, a small, flickering light passed slowly overhead. Just beyond the assembled forces, it exploded in mid-air. Then there were others. First a few, then dozens. Some passed out of sight, but others exploded, over the camp, ahead of it, behind it. The small shards falling bothered few, but then the shouts, the retching, the collapses began. Now all were up and running, looking upwards as they ran to evade the paths. It did not last long. Gradually, order was restored. There had been few deaths and only modest injuries, injuries that Wilkes knew were mostly temporary. Further, he soon realised that not all carried poison. It was clear that inducing fear and confusion was the objective. Indeed, in that confusion, Outies had crept among them and killed more. At the cost, almost always, of their own lives, but who knew how many of them there were?

300

As the night advanced, shots were heard to the west. *So*, thought Wilkes, *the companies to seal off the coast were meeting resistance.* Around midnight, he got a message from the southern wing: dug in with ruins in front of us. Boats on the estuary. A few retreated under rifle fire, but no targets now it is dark. Nothing, though, from the north.

Reassembled and reinforced, but now nervously looking upwards, the Domain's forces advanced as dawn broke. At first, it was a silent, unopposed advance over open ground. Those on the wings could see the water a mile or so ahead. But there were more ruins ahead; ruins in which Outies sheltered. Get too close, and grenades were thrown. Some had rifles. The line of advance became ragged. Some slugged it out among the ruins. Other moved quickly beyond, towards the shore. They were met by rockets from a myriad of small boats. The thought of yet more poison provoked an irregular retreat. Only the soldiers stood their ground, able to shoot at the boats and their crews. Huntsmen and the Security men retreated in confusion.

By noon, Wilkes began to feel reassured. The boats had disappeared out of range. Most of the shoreline was in his hands. Slowly, his forces were clearing the ruins. Only the north had failed to make contact. The Outie dead exceeded his own by some margin, though the number of incapacitated was too large for comfort. He attempted a triage, despatching those capable back up the valley towards the camp. It did not last long. There were shots behind him, and to the north. A few came stumbling back to report ambushes. The camp itself had been attacked, and not only by Outies. Enslaved Grounders armed only with shovels had been among their attackers. Retching, enfeebled wounded had fallen. Access to the camp was cut off. To add to the consternation, a single Montgolfier sailed eastwards at great height. The camp itself, Wilkes realised, might fall. It was vulnerable with largely unarmed servants set to prepare a now much delayed feast to mark the Hunt's return. Their position was untenable. Come night, and the advantage would lie with the Outies. He must order a retreat, a retreat along the higher and more open ground to the south, the only direction from which no attacks had come.

Arundel was angry to the point of insanity. Faced with incoherence, Wilkes left him and issued orders. Soon, the forces were moving out, a screen of soldiers protecting the bemused hunters, the security troopers and the injured. It was slow, but it was not challenged. As dusk fell, they approached the camp. The attacks there had been slight, and had been repelled. Wilkes had, of necessity, to order his tired troops to establish a perimeter, hopefully beyond the range of the infernal rockets.

The night passed without incident. By the morning of the 19th, many of the sick were again walking, though much the worse for wear. Hope was among them. Those with greater injury were loaded onto mobiles to make the slow journey back to Windsor. They needed armed protection; Messengers from further east had been attacked. Most had escaped, but some had fallen. Their news was not good. The temporary quiet in the cities had gone. Kingsmen had been fired on. Grounders had refused to surrender either to Security or to soldiers. Several hundred had been killed. Domain losses were fewer, but numbers were not enough to stamp on all provocations. At Swindon, the local commander had withdrawn across the bounds. A request had been made: either substantial reinforcements, or the attrition of cutting off supplies; which?

The ad hoc Council of War summoned by Arundel was not happy. Besides himself and Sussex there were Wilkes, a colonel from the southern, relatively unharmed pair of companies, a major who had led those with the Hunt, and Lane. Arundel was vengeful.

"They are taking more losses than us. We should attack with all we have in daylight and finish the business. There will be a permanent force on that blasted shore. Colonel, you have the force."

"The force, yes, my Lord, but not the means to supply it. Half my ammunition is already gone. Be there for more than a few days, and we will need food. To safeguard a route needs twice, maybe three times the force I command as of now." He hesitated. "My Lord, we provisioned for a Hunt, larger than usual to be sure, but not for a campaign."

Arundel glared at him. Wilkes intervened.

"Forces which we do not have here, my Lord," said Wilkes. "Nor do we have the immediate prospect of getting it, even if others follow the example of Swindon, and revert to mere containment. I have no news from the northern wing, from Cardwell."

"That is significant, brother," said Sussex. "The captives that attacked us in camp cannot have come from his entry point through the Badlands. Other entries that were being made further east must have been overrun. We will need even more forces if that is so, more than we can possibly assemble in a week, never mind today or tomorrow."

"We have enough to take a city, do we not?" This was Lane. "Threaten the death of a complete RPZ, or its enslavement. Outies are tender-hearted. Out of here with them, and a new Boundary on the estuary."

Even Arundel, sorely tempted, could see the impossibility. It was left to Sussex to ram home the idiocy.

"Lane, do you have a brain? Firstly, it will take time to muster such a force. We are no longer dealing with a bunch of scared dimwits. What do we do in the meantime, here? Suppose we do threaten, then how? Another meeting at the Point? A counter threat of more balloons and more disturbances in more cities? Second, we have already inflicted losses on Grounders that will affect recruitment to Service. Carry out that threat and things will start to break down. Our own losses are significant."

He looked around the table at his companions.

"Gentlemen, we have been defeated. Acknowledge that, or we will make matters worse. Look at this camp. Look at the mass of non-combatants that will need feeding. Look at the need to protect them as we move east. We must leave these unassigned lands and return to the acknowledged Domain. Yes, half way to Swindon. And we must start now."

All the soldiers nodded. Never before had they sustained so many casualties. Further, their men were now demoralised by the weapons used by their opponents. In any case, Kingsmen were reluctant to murder Outies by the score, still less to do the same to Grounders. Wilkes knew of the policy clashes among the Four. Lane remained silent. Arundel grunted, then placed his hands flat on the table.

"Very well. Sussex will be in charge. I will leave at once, with a platoon escort, Wilkes. Now that your men are leaving the field to Outies, I imagine you can spare that much." He left the tent. Very soon after, a convoy of five large mobiles left the camp.

If any reinforcement of the bitter decision was needed, it came as the camp was being dismantled and mobiles loaded. Major Cardwell and four of his men arrived from the north. They were unarmed. It was a sorry tale. Hearing the gunfire near the shore, they had attempted to advance in support. The company was lost in a maze of ruins. They had attempted to withdraw north as the firing ceased. One by one they were picked off. The five of them had holed up in a ruin, a few rounds each remaining. A white flag had been waved over the wall of another ruin nearby. A voice had called out to them to surrender. Surrender, and your lives are saved. Surrender and you will be returned to your forces. They had done so. They had been escorted back to the work camp. It was deserted. A few bodies of Security troopers and some Outies were all that remained. Back down the road towards their original staging post, but cutting down a side track that led to another work camp, similarly abandoned. Then escorted to within sight of the Hunt's camp, and left alone.

"There were no Outies or Grounders at that second camp, my Lord. It must have been overrun. Just a few Security killed with crossbows."

"They were giving us a message through you, Major," said Sussex. "The north is unmanned. Well, as you can see, we are retreating. It would be wise, I think, if you stayed out of sight of other troops, your men as well. Stay here and I will add you to my party."

"My Lord. There is something more to say. The Outies that took us were not like Outies. They were like Grounders. Their officer even had a touch of the noble about him. I asked him his rank, and he laughed. *What do you call me, lads? Chief O'Neill, sir.* They all said together. And they pointed to his helmet with three feathers. He said, *we are hunters not soldiers, major, but our prey usually has four legs, not two.* All had rifles, my Lord."

Sussex was jolted: O'Neill. The Chief at the Treaty Point. A man of brains. A man unaffected by any obvious deformity. How many like him? How many of our own are his equal? These and other equally disturbing thoughts ran through his mind as the Hunt convoy moved slowly east, its rear covered by a platoon of Wilkes' men.

24. Recriminations and a Defection

It was late in the evening when Arundel's convoy reached Windsor, a journey causing him to leave some behind as mobiles broke down under the demand for speed. What little news there was did little to please him. Forces in several cities had followed Swindon in withdrawing to regroup. Others were causing problems. Visitors were agitating for reinforcements and orders. The new Truth and Justice Councillor, Blackstone, was worse than useless, issuing and then countermanding orders to move Security forces to one trouble spot after another. I ought to have brought Hope with me, was the immediate thought, though the man would take at least a week to recover. That poison sometimes left victims with permanent disability.

The morning was no better. First, he discovered that Kent had left eastwards. Escorted, of course, by some officials undoubtedly loyal to himself, but clearly bent on meeting Buckingham. Yes, Buckingham had been summoned. Being alone had its advantages, of course, but these were more than offset by the lack of any forces to command. Of necessity, he must wait until Wilkes had caught up with him.

Even more disturbing though, were accounts coming in from a line of mayors and managers across both Grounds and the inhabited Domain, extending nearly to Luton. The Montgolfier that had been seen over the hunt had passed over many settlements. Canisters had been lowered and discharged, causing some panic as news of the earlier attacks had been passed on. What fell from them, though, were mere cards, many in each canister. Cards that said simply: WE CAN GO FURTHER THAN THIS. What would it be? At least seventy miles? Enough to reach Windsor itself? The balloon itself had last been seen over Badlands, Badlands sufficiently toxic to require heavy protective gear to penetrate. The news had already reached others. At the Oxford exchange point, where there was a stand-off, a large banner had been waved from the city side: "The Outies are coming, aha, aha." Oxford had not been under the flight path, though not far from it.

The castle was eerily quiet. So many were with Wilkes and Sussex; most remaining men at arms had been moved to trouble spots. For form's sake, Arundel set in motion the summons to a Council, to which the Visitors of Grounds affected were commanded to attend. As he issued orders and required service, he noticed a new, an appraising look in the eyes of those he instructed. The fate of the Hunt was known; Buckingham's return was inevitable. *Is it time to change sides?* Those eyes were asking.

To ease his feelings, he walked down to the Armoury. At the very least, he would need to be informed about stocks, and to squeeze the output of rifles, a slow and often error-prone process. Maybe he could see how far other weapons could be made effective; for certain, the Outland needed to be tamed. Recruits would be needed too.

But on the way he received another shock. On the wall of a warehouse was a set of crude images in white paint; unmistakably, cartoonish depictions of Montgolfiers. There was no writing. The paint was still drying. Cursing himself for bringing no escort to catch the perpetrators, he arrived at the Armoury in a raging temper. It was not improved by what he heard. Stocks of both weapons and ammunition were very low; vast quantities, by the Master-at-Arms' reckoning, had been commissioned for the Hunt.

"My Lord, we have also responded to calls from Visitors and commandants. Even if there are no more urgent calls, it will be weeks before we can return to the level of last month. The machinery and the men are working beyond capacity. One team became careless under pressure; there was an explosion."

"Careless! They should be whipped."

"They died, my Lord. Bar one who has lost an arm."

Even when the talk turned to other weapons, nothing was said to improve Arundel's mood. Yes, we have a few artillery pieces. But they are heavy. Move them without a powerful mobile? Very slow. Of use in demolishing fortifications, or to scatter and kill massed ranks, yes. Against dispersed and mobile snipers? Not so much. Aircraft? Yes, single or double seaters soon, but not yet, and with very limited range. We cannot keep the weight of our engines down well enough for more.

Arundel had no doubts, however, about the Armourer's loyalty. The man was as enthusiastic as he to recover as much of the military potential of the past as possible. Reluctantly, he ordered all efforts to turn to rifles, pistols and ammunition, though in truth the limitation was in machinery rather than manpower.

His return to the castle was marred by yet more fresh graffiti. Sitting down to a midday meal, he was approached by the Major-Domo.

"My Lord, may I suggest a visit to His Majesty? When Miss Forbes was relieved, she told me that my Lord Kent had spent time with him. When she mentioned the rules, he pointed to a man unknown to her, telling her that he was your representative. She was unable to follow the conversation, but His Majesty appeared very disturbed when they left."

"What man, damn it? I have authorised nobody. What is his name? He should be taken at once and locked up."

"He told her he was Lord Hill, my Lord. He was dressed appropriately for a minor noble. I checked. My Lord, there is no such person. She had no very good view of his face."

"Disturbed? What did she mean? Did she explain?"

"She said he had paroxysms, my Lord. She was not sure, but it seemed to be laughter."

Arundel considered, becoming calm for a moment. A clear deception; a clear breach. A matter to air before Council if the need arises. Even Alice cannot defend this. He stormed up to the King's room, rekindling his anger as he climbed. It was Muss Pritchard in attendance. Without a word to her, he strode to the bed, where his father appeared to be asleep. To protests from the nurse, he shook the monarch mercilessly.

"Don't pretend, Father *dear*, you are awake. What mischief has my brother told you of? What gave you such amusement? What devious little plan has he proposed to you?"

Glittering eyes looked up at him. The withered mouth turned up at the corners. There was a spasm of coughing, within which there was barely concealed laughter. Arundel felt the nurse by his side. Violently, he pushed her away.

"In the corner, and stay there, if you value your privilege."

He returned his gaze to his father. The coughing had subsided, but the malice remained. Seeing his son's arms reach out to shake him again, the King managed a few words.

"Beaten by the Outies, eh. Back here and wanting revenge on all. Remember the saying, Son, pride comes before a fall? Beaten by the Outies."

The old man coughed copiously, and was struggling for breath. The urge to smother the senile fool nearly overwhelmed Arundel. No more was to be gained here. Kent and Buckingham would be here all too soon. It would be convenient if the old man was no longer with us, and his consent no longer required. But not now, not yet. He left, giving strict instructions to the guard at the door. For safety, he added another, from his own entourage. No nobles, no clerks were to enter on any pretext. To be resisted by force if need be.

There was just one further event that day. Mid-afternoon, he was called downstairs. Two Security men held a stable boy, a boy much the worse for a vicious beating. Both he and they were liberally splashed with white paint.

"The little bastard was painting balloons, my Lord. He did not come quietly."

Treason. A rare enough crime in the Domain, and subject to the same penalty as much lesser offences: To Reclamation and the Badlands. No life to be wasted. Arundel paused. From a distance, he could see the boy preparing to spit defiance from his bloodied mouth. No time for niceties now. The boy must die, and publicly, and gagged. Security, what he had of them, were reliable. He gave his instructions.

Two hours later, Security had rounded up a crowd outside the castle gates. A crude scaffold had been set up. Bound and gagged, the boy was led out between guards. The rope was placed around his neck. Arundel stood by while the Major-Domo addressed the crowd.

"This traitor has betrayed us to the Outies. Our food, our land, our very lives are threatened. Outies are killing. Outies are threatening the Domain. From now, any such treachery merits death."

It was a terrible, a bungled killing. No drop, just a chair kicked away. The boy's legs had not been tied. There was a writhing struggle. Even Arundel had to fight to avoid vomiting. There were groans and shouts from the crowd, and the Security troopers had to draw their pistols. It was ended only when a sergeant put a bullet through the boy's brain.

A killing, a sanctioned killing. Such had not been seen by any. As the Security troopers retreated into the castle, carrying the body, the crowd slowly dispersed. A crowd not taking the intended deterrent lesson, but a crowd shocked by a breach of one of the most sacred tenets of their lives.

***

The following morning, midsummer's day, Arundel noticed a slight change of mood within the castle. Those accustomed to Court life, and to patronage, were weighing up their interests. Security in particular, no strangers to the brutality of Reclamation camps, were conscious of the hostility that might come their way were things to change. There was a further distraction as Wilkes arrived with the remains of the Hunt. There were the poisoned and the wounded to be cared for, troops to be fed, courtiers to resume their normal duties. The poisoned in particular aroused a new sense of solidarity against a barbarous foe. Wilkes himself gave Arundel a brief report and left to see to his men. It was Sussex who provided details.

"No, brother, no more attacks. We lost a few to residual poison and wounds, but the rest will recover. Wilkes left a company at our bounds. They are well armed, and in open country. We have had no reports of Outies within our Bounds. I think they will not breach the agreement."

In turn, Arundel briefed his brother on events, including news from the cities. He did not elaborate on the ill-judged execution. The forthcoming Council, when all could be assembled.

"What do you intend next, Brother?" asked Sussex.

"To return, of course, not as a Hunt, but as an army. The Outies must be crushed. Everything must be done to repair our strength. That estuary can be crossed. Take Dean and they are finished, bar the mountains in the north."

Sussex looked hard at his brother. Time out of mind, he had supported Arundel against what he had regarded as the pie-in-the-sky search for habitable lands overseas. He saw danger in his sister's obsession too; suppose there were habitable lands? Might they not be occupied, occupied by people who had no 'immortals' like themselves. People who might constitute a threat? Hence, he had supported, more reluctantly, the sacrifice of human life in Clearance at home. He had, though, listened to Dundonnell and others noting the fall in available manpower. In his view, the tribute of people and stock from the Grounds was remarkably trouble free. In a few decades, even a century, a time neither here nor there for either of them, land in the Domain would again become fertile. The Outland might follow a similar path. Even if it did, the increasing size of the fertile Domain, and its greater technological recovery would negate any threat. Arundel had tried a gamble; it had failed. Did the man realise the peril?

Recruitment from the Grounds in chaos. An Outland possessed of more power than imagined. Power stemming not from those damned balloons but from men like O'Neill. How many more were there like that?

"When do you propose such an adventure? We have lost hundreds overall, and will lose twice as many if we try direct management of the cities. We will kill Grounders, fertile Grounders, rather than recruit them. Starve them out, and you get the same result. I read the military histories in the Archives, brother. I even remember lessons in school. You must too. There were cities cut off completely that held out for a year or more. Cities where it was street by street combat. Our cities? Will you send forces into the farmland behind them? How many Grounders will be left when you have finished?"

Arundel stared at his brother. Bloody soft, as usual. Overcautious, as usual. Too bloody reasonable. But I cannot lose him, yet. Two against two, we've dealt with. Three to one and we'll slide into decadence.

"Not immediately, I acknowledge. I have already turned to the Armoury. We must recharge. Men, too. There will be training. There will be kitting out to cross the Badlands. The prize, Brother, the prize; Outies for the taking once they are subdued."

Sussex did not reply. Nothing could happen before Kent and Buckingham arrived, and the Council met. He gave a sigh and left to wash, to feed, to sleep. Arundel was left to his thoughts. As yet, he realised, Sussex had not yet heard of the sole Montgolfier and its devilish propaganda effect. Hear about it, he would, and then become even more difficult to manage. His father could no longer be relied on; given three to one, he would not assent, and Council would waver. Visitors would lobby, Dundonnell would protest. He sent messengers to summon Lane and Hope, *on a stretcher if need be.*

The two Security men duly appeared, Hope on his feet, but pale and shaking, supported by Lane. Even Lane was exhausted from the long retreat. He got them seated.

"I hope you are recovering, Commandant? And your squire, young Gregory, he is unharmed?"

"Thank you, my Lord. The doctors say I will not be permanently harmed. Master John is well. I think we may have good use of him soon."

"We have a problem, gentlemen. This setback has stirred dissension within the Domain. Security will be needed here as well as in the Grounds and at Reclamation sites. You will have had losses, Lane, but you will not have had the time or authority to assess these. As from now, you will resume command; I will dismiss Blackstone. Report to me tomorrow on the forces at our disposal, and where they are. Blackstone has been driving me mad with redeployments, so that I no longer know the position. In due time, I want a substantial, better armed force available; The Outies will be subdued, Lane; subdued and brought into our service. That means," he gave Lane a hard stare, "that reclamation work must be suspended, everywhere, and at once. Minimal supervision at sites, that is all."

Lane swallowed his temptation to protest. Fighting Outies had proved a failure. For him, reclamation was the solution. Outies were soldier's business until they were subdued. But he had already heard of the hanging, and of the graffiti.

"Very good, my Lord. But policing within the Domain, even here? It will require more men, and sharper, more potent measures to suppress dissent."

"True. We can discuss this when you have a complete picture. In the meantime, be advised that acts of treason are to be punished with death, not allocation to Reclamation. Any acts, Lane."

He turned to Hope.

"Commandant, are you able to move without Lord Lane's assistance?"

"Yes, my Lord, Gregory is waiting outside. He can provide me with help when called."

Lane was dismissed, to his deep unease. Restored to command, well and good, but Arundel appeared to have a plan that involved high risk for dubious reward. A plan that depended on the soldiers, soldiers who, to his mind, lacked the singlemindedness needed to secure the Domain's best interests.

Arundel turned to Hope.

"Commandant, I know that when you were up north, you found yourself at odds with the Visitor. Visitors go native, Commandant, and not only in the north. There will be pressure to go easy on the Grounds when we need more labour. I think, no, I trust, that you reject this approach."

"Yes, my Lord. As to the north, I think that for all its supposed merits for breeding, it wastes our resources. That Ground was riddled with treason. As you know, I was prevented from a thorough purge."

"What would be needed to impose a more direct control over Grounds, do you think? We have such in some, but they are the least productive."

"I have heard so, my Lord. But what is cause, and what effect? There are richer Grounds, Grounds that have been pampered by their Visitors. What is needed? A permanent resident, my Lord, a Security resident, to replace both the Visitor and the wretched bailiffs. Forgive me, my Lord, but there was a surrender in the face of difficulties there. Mayors, we control, and the traitors are few and easily removed. It would need better armed troopers too; rifles, my Lord, and training in their use. Those RPZs do not deliver what they might; hygienists go in fear of the bailiffs."

"Very well. Give me a few days, and I will ensure that you have a force to train and arm. We can choose our place for a demonstration, but I am minded to send you back north when you are fit. Control it, and we have our labour. Fail, and we will empty the Ground, RPZ and all. There is another matter. Young Gregory is outside? I will call him in."

Arundel shouted. A clerk was instructed, and soon returned with Gregory.

"Sit down, young man. I am sorry that your experience as the commandant's squire was less happy than it should have been. You will know that the Domain is threatened, and all patriots should be concerned to come to our aid. It is not only Outies that threaten us. There is treason within the Grounds. You have an exemplary record of reporting it. The Domain has need of you, need beyond your years and experience. I will have you gazetted as a lieutenant, Gregory. You will work under Commandant Hope, and advise him on ways to detect and eliminate such treachery within the Grounds."

John was overwhelmed. As he stuttered his grateful obedience, Hope managed to give him an encouraging grin. A clerk was summoned, orders given, and the two departed, well satisfied.

The following day was quiet. The cities had subsided into an uneasy peace after soldiers and Security had withdrawn behind the bounds. Provocative banners were withdrawn after their holders were shot at. No Outies had attempted to enter the Domain itself. The squatters in Luton had withdrawn, not, however, without loot. Fewer graffiti appeared at Windsor. To the Major-Domo's annoyance, Arundel empowered Wilkes to conscript most of the Court for military training. It was past the time of year for Selection and the deployment of the Chosen, and any attempt to impose a new levy impossible. Arundel was irritated rather than angered by interviews with the Visitors for Oxford and Swindon. Both had, as expected, pressed for negotiation with bailiffs. Given the temporary peace, he fended them off with the promise of a Council meeting. Others would no doubt be arriving soon. Only two things disturbed his increasing self-confidence. Lane had managed to get an estimate of Security losses. More than two hundred known dead, as many again injured, mostly slightly. The worrying feature, however, was the numbers unaccounted for, presumed dead. Not many, but their pistols and batons, uniforms also, would be in the hands of the city Grounders. Lane was unable to give him estimates of Grounder casualties, other than that they were many.

A conversation with Sussex was also unpleasant. His brother had been receiving reports from mayors and Proctors, all clamouring for instructions and protection prompted by the Montgolfier's message.

"What now, Brother? Dealings with any Grounds with a city are at a standstill. Soon, they will have more stock than they can feed, while going hungry themselves. You know where that will end. Starve the cities, and they will raid the farms. They are many, the farmers few. Proctors? They will vanish when the city folk descend on them. Will you send soldiers to every such Ground? For how long?"

"Soon? Not that soon. Let them sweat for a bit. We have time to assemble force. Those cities pass messages to each other all too easily. I will make an example of one. An example with 'extreme prejudice', if you remember your love of the old thrillers and spy stories. The rest will cave in fast enough. I'm thinking of the north. Security know the lie of the land, and there are those among them with scores to settle."

"You think so? Brother, they act together. Not only that, they are co-operating with Outies. Do you think the disturbances in the south were just coincidences, that they had nothing to do with the Hunt? Will you risk destroying one Ground, our best, only to have Outies damage others? There are brains over there, Brother, young brains that outsmarted us. They are still doing it. A balloon over Windsor? Maybe they cannot manage it, but fail to protect it and our rule is in peril. Sooner rather than later, we will have to negotiate with bailiffs: food for normal transfers, and evidence that the Chosen are not wasted on futile reclamation."

The brothers glared at each other. Arundel could issue orders. Sussex could countermand them. Even if overruled, there would be confusion. Security might line up behind Arundel; Kingsmen would hesitate. Only the decision of Council, confirmed by the King, would command unqualified obedience. They parted in silence.

***

By chance, it was the same squad on duty at the Treaty Point on June 23rd that had received the Outland summons back in May. A signal given, and when an Outlander appeared at the reception room, a very similar message was delivered, this time by Jane Collins, and in different, simpler writing. Its message was stark. The Outland regarded the operation of the Hunt as a breach of the Treaty in spirit, if not in the letter. There had been verbal assurances that action would be taken merely to defend lives and property. Attempts had been made to kill and enslave Outlanders. Some previously enslaved had been rescued. A much larger retaliation was now ready. A plenipotentiary was required immediately. The only terms acceptable were the recognition that the area of Cotswold attacked by the Hunt was to be recognised in perpetuity as Outland territory, reaching to the Domain boundary west of Swindon. In addition, there was to be a guarantee that the Northernmost Ground was to be free of all Domain forces bar the Visitor and his messengers.

It was the same sergeant who grappled with the telephone, and the same confusion and requests for clarification. Arundel, Sussex and Wilkes conferred. Or, rather, Arundel ranted; he pressed Wilkes for immediate assault, while knowing that the general was right to declare it impossible. In a pause, Sussex managed to speak.

"Brother, stop and consider. In practical terms, the Outlanders hold this land already. We are in no position to re-occupy it. As to the north, they ask again for what is nearly the case now. Cornwallis must have very few men, and he withdrew Security a while ago. We do not have to make public any terms we concede. Mere legalities are no defence. We may claim no breach; they attack anyway. Killings in the grounds, killings even here. How do we then respond? We are near the edge."

"As a practical matter, my Lords, we promised a plenipotentiary on hand. Is there anyone so authorised at the Point?" Wilkes asked.

"Not at the Point," replied Sussex. "A bit much to ask a noble to twiddle his thumbs there for months with just the duty force for company. But yes, Lord Steel can be there within a day, and we countersigned the original Royal authority. He will need to be briefed."

Yet another defeat, thought Arundel. As he thought it through, though, he saw the sense in Sussex' ideas. There need be no public knowledge if Steel was alone with a clerk. The duty force would have to be seen to; another little job for Lane. Another thought crossed his mind.

"Has Hastings been visited? There should have been at least one such by now."

"Yes. A Security sergeant visited him. I believe he was given some delicacies and books. He was well."

"Very well. But Steel is to insist on Hastings' presence with the Outies. He is to be released to us before any Treaty is signed. No Hastings, no deal."

Sussex looked hard at his brother, but merely nodded. He rose, and left the room to issue instructions to Steel.

***

Lord Steel was, like Hastings, a made man; one who had advanced to nobility through promotion from among the Chosen. Indeed, he and Hastings knew each other well. He had felt for Hastings as a hostage, while at the same time thinking that the man must have had a livelier experience with the Outies than he had twiddling his thumbs at Retford. Nearly all uniformed people had left to cope with the troubles down south. He was left only with a tiny band of Security, led by Sergeant Davis, who was responsible for the visits to Hastings and a small garrison of Kingsmen to service the Point and Barlow. Not the best of company, though Lieutenant Kipling was tolerable.

He had heard only rumours of the Hunt, though Davis seemed to know more. So, when he received the call from Sussex, he was astonished. A messenger was sent to the Point to announce his arrival the next day. At least, it appeared that his friend was to be freed. Otherwise, *mine not to reason why*, a slight misquotation of a remembered poem learnt in the Military Academy. Collecting Davis and his own clerk, he set off for Barlow the same day, seeing no need to jolt his kidneys by speed along the badly-maintained roads. A rather dull meal there, with Davis and Mr Jacks, who was the livelier of the two. Davis asked him some rather odd questions.

"My Lord, what is to happen if Lord Hastings is not returned? Is it not a breach of the Treaty?"

"Well, I suppose it would be. But why would he not be handed over? As far as I can see, the bigwigs thought him expendable. He was fine when you visited, was he not?"

"But if he were not there, would you be obliged to refuse their terms?"

"Again, I suppose so, though it sounds as though we are bound to fulfil them by force of circumstances. Why? I had no doubts. He is of little significance. Much like myself, Sergeant."

Davis made no further comment. Jacks entertained him slightly with stories from the formal meeting, and the squabbles among the Norman family.

"I was glad to be rid of them, my Lord. Split up as well. Lucky too, by all accounts. A while back and the lot of them would be at Reclamation."

Early next morning the small party set out for the Point. They sat in the mess room while the Kingsman sergeant signalled downhill. Very soon, a party was seen climbing the path. The sergeant recognised the two besides Hastings himself.

"My Lord, Hastings is with them, but he is dressed oddly; there is the lady who delivered the message, but also a Mr O'Neill. He was introduced as Chief, so I was told. There is no rebel, Lord, among them."

Steel and his team entered, as the others came in through the outer door. There were introductions. Of course, Jane Collins (call her lieutenant, gentlemen, it is the nearest equivalent) and Hastings had already met Davis, and Steel and Hastings were well known to each other. While Steel and O'Neill formally read each other's credentials, Hastings grinned as he spoke to Davis.

"Well met again, Sergeant. You are maybe a trifle surprised to see me."

As he spoke, he placed on the table the opened box of sweets with which he had been presented. Davis went white. He glanced at Steel who had missed the exchange entirely. As he returned O'Neill's paper, Steel glanced at Hastings. Indeed, he was dressed in Outie clothes. *Well, I suppose he took no spares with him, poor fellow*, he thought. Never mind, this business is simple. No embroidery he was told. Accept the terms, and leave with Hastings.

"Mr, oh, I beg your pardon, Chief, I am authorised to agree to the terms you have set out. My clerk has prepared two copies. It requires only our signatures, and all is concluded."

O'Neill nodded. The two documents were signed. To his amazement, Hastings also signed. Oh, well, he is, I suppose, a witness. He rose to leave. Hastings remained seated.

"Come, George, you are free. I am sure your clothes will be returned. They will be sent on when they are delivered. In the meantime, that outfit will be a sensation at a masque; truly authentic."

"George? Are you under some constraint? Is there anything to hinder his departure, Chief O'Neill?"

"None whatsoever, my Lord. He is free to join you if he so wishes."

"And I do not wish, Rupert. You saw my signature. It was not as a witness but as a delegate. I am an Outlander now. I think you will not see me again; for both our sakes, I hope not."

Steel sat down again. Indeed, he almost fell into his chair. Davis, though, was edging towards the door. Collins called out.

"My Lord, I think you will find your sergeant's presence will assist you in understanding Mr Hastings' decision."

Steel turned and sharply indicated that Davis should sit. The man was shaking. Steel turned back to Hastings, who had pulled the open box in front of him.

"Rupert, you may not know that being a hostage was thrust upon me with no notice. In the brief interval before my transfer, I heard a giggle, and the word expendable used. Well, so I am, eminently expendable. I had no illusions that if the Treaty was broken, I would be killed or imprisoned for life. And the Domain would not give a damn.

I did not think, though, that the Domain would contrive to have me die in Outlander custody, freeing my Lord Arundel to act against the Outland with no one to deny him. The sergeant here, Rupert, brought me both some books and the box of sweetmeats you see here. Don't waste them on Outies, I was told. There were two layers. We have mixed them up. Sergeant, would you do me the honour of sampling two or three of these tempting items?"

Davis went white, then green. Despite Steel's glare, he shook his head.

"No? A wise decision, Sergeant. You see, Rupert, I was advised. We shaved a small portion of each sweet. We offered those pieces to sheep, to the sheep sent us as blood debt. The top layer? No effect. The bottom layer? Some very sick sheep. None died, admitted, but they had perhaps a twentieth the amount I would have eaten in one piece."

What happened next was fast and furious. As tradition demanded, weapons had been placed on the table. Davis made a grab for his pistol; Collins moved both to grab him, and to put herself between Davis and her colleagues. But it was not murder that Davis intended. Before he could be restrained, he had shot himself. Accurately, in the head.

The Kingsman sergeant and two men burst into the room, guns at the ready. Steel signalled them to stop.

"You see, Rupert? You would not have killed him, I know. But better than most, he would know what a sentence to Reclamation would mean. Three ways to die, Rupert. He chose the cleanest, God rest his soul."

God rest his soul. Even in his shock, Steel noticed the blasphemy. That, if nothing else told him that Hastings' defection was real. O'Neill pressed a piece of paper into Steel's shaking hand. It was a signed renunciation of the Domain.

"By itself, my Lord, it might be dismissed as obtained by coercion. You are a witness to the fact that it is not. Be sure that we will respond in force to any breach of this Treaty."

The Outlanders departed. Not long after, so did Steel and the clerk. It was left to the sergeant and his men to bury the body and clean the room. They were not told what had gone on before their entry. They were told, however, not to call their superiors until given leave.

Eden and Beyond

25. On the Threshold We Stand

After the Council of War, Mark did not meet Lady Hawkins again. The following morning, he was escorted eastwards, a faster journey on ponies than that on foot in the other direction. Straight through Edale, with no sign of the Chief, and back at the Derwent House before dusk. Rhianna gave him a warm welcome. His escort dispersed to nearby houses, and he was left with her in the main hall, having handed over a parcel of letters from Chapel. He sat while she read. The place was strangely empty compared to his first visit. Indeed, he began to find the silence oppressive, and it was not eased when she summoned her husband and sat quiet while he read the letters. As darkness settled, an old man entered to light lamps and shutter windows. He saw the bearskin pinned to a wall. It seemed a lifetime since he had seen its owner brought in. Eventually, Rhianna rose to her feet.

"I've things to see to. Henry will explain a few things to you now. You'll be moving in the morning, and not in those clothes. It's good we hung onto your Grounder kit, flashy though it is." She grinned. "A marked man in sight as well as name." She left.

Henry led Mark to a smaller room. He lit no less than six lamps and placed them on a wide table. Fumbling slightly, he took out a folded paper from a drawer and opened it under the lamps. Mark recognised what it was: another map. This one, like that he had seen in Edale, was hand drawn, but in much greater detail. There were names too, some of which were familiar. Yes, there was Midhope; There was Edale, even Chapel, the last on the very edge of the map. He could see the bounds of his Ground marked off with a thick, black line.

"Got your bearings?" Henry asked. "Can you see where Jones must hide? Now look to the west."

Mark studied the map in the flickering light. Someone had painted a thin red line that passed a few miles to the west of Midhope. It weaved about both north and south. Henry pointed his finger at where the hunter had found him. It was just south of the painted line.

"You were almost in it when you crossed the moors. North or west of that line, Mark, that's Eden as we call it. Comes from the Bible if that means anything to you. The paradise before we fouled it up. Where beasts breed true, and humans might too. And around it's not much different, even down to us here at Derwent, though we get a share of the Bounty." He spat. "It's growing, Mark. It's our piece of Ground, the only really clean one. It's like your home; if anything, it's cleaner."

Trying to read that Bible had its uses, then, thought Mark. But as far as he could see, most of it was just moorland. Not that different from those on the boundary at Midhope. Not a place like Bradfield with its bustle and many fertile families. To the south and towards Chapel, he knew from experience that things were very different: Badlands all around.

"Sheep and cattle, sir. But that land cannot be good for much else, nor the land around. Do you keep people there and bring in supplies?" Mark thought about the way the Ground was managed, and what he had learnt from David and Jamie.

"A few, yes, but it is easy to contaminate. Right now, it keeps us in healthy stock. But even here in Derwent we see more fertile couples each year. Their children can breed too, and a few that are free of mental taint. Land elsewhere, though, it still holds stuff that corrupts, corrupts even healthy stock. We need to let nature take its course."

As Henry went into more details, Mark began to see the nature of the problem. He had learnt already that the Westrons had been able to corrupt Grounds, and the Peak in particular, and that had led to the Treaties. Now, though, the Domain might doubt their capacity; how much had the Montgolfiers convinced them otherwise? But this Eden could be destroyed or captured by Kingsmen on foot; it needed no pre-war weaponry or even balloons. The full significance of the Council of War hit him with more force. With a shock, he realised that this also operated in reverse. In the last resort, only his home, his Ground, was vulnerable to a focused attack. He recalled the firework he had seen at Chapel; bigger and laden with poison, enough of them could destroy it and its inhabitants: his family (if they were still there), his friends, his neighbours.

Mark spent a restless and solitary night. Only a few elders and some children were around. In the morning, though, Rhianna brought him his original clothes and letters to carry. Kitted out, and with two escorts, he started the walk north. Soon, he was past the small valley down which the hunter had led him, and not long after they reached a small hut, outside which sat two men armed with guns, and with caps bearing a single feather. One called out, and a taller woman with two feathers emerged. She approached with a smile.

"Welcome, Mr Grounder. You are on the threshold of Eden. A privilege not available to all."

There was a brief break. Mark handed over the letters, which the officer put unread in her pack. Soon, his original escorts departed south, and two more accompanied him north with the officer. The valley sides became steeper, and although he got glimpses of moorland high up, the sides were covered in luxuriant woodland. They passed a few small clearings in which cattle grazed. Cattle with calves. A few folk waved as they went by. Irresistibly, Mark's mind flew back to the march to Pickless' stint nearly a year ago and the haymakers who had waved to them as they passed. This was Ground indeed.

They were climbing. The woods thinned out as the valley turned sharply to the west, and ahead of him were a set of buildings around an open square. As at Derwent, clearly recent, and not pre-war. Alongside one was a rickety, skeletal tower. As they approached, arms at the top started moving, and Mark could make out two people at the top manipulating things he could not see. He looked around. Three similar towers could be seen on the hillsides above. One raised similar arms briefly.

Within the compound, there was much activity. In one corner, a forge was in operation. In another, a number of people were clearly learning to handle crossbows. His unusual clothes attracted some attention as they walked across the yard to one of the buildings, but they were not approached. He was led into a small room divided by a long counter, behind which two elderly men got to their feet and saluted. The officer unshouldered her pack, and placed the bundle of letters on the counter.

"Here is the Grounder for Captain O'Hanlon, and some messages he has brought. Those should be sent in immediately." She turned to Mark. "Wait here till you are called. Good luck!"

Mark sat. One man picked up the letters, knocked on an inner door and delivered them, returning to his seat. It was not a long wait, but one that tugged hard at Mark's heart. Men and women came in to talk to those behind the counter; some left, others were pointed to the door of the captain's room, spent a short time there and then left the building. All looked curiously at Mark in his unusual garb, but looks from those behind the counter prevented any talk. It was just like the Mayor's Office when he was younger, sitting or playing behind the counter at which his father regulated the business of the Ground. Eventually, the room emptied and the captain herself came to the door and summoned Mark inside.

"Welcome back, Grounder. What am I to call you, Mr Norman? Mark? Mark, very well. You are now in Eden, Mark, and like all others here you are under my command. Lord Ogilvie has explained your purpose here, I see. It is for me to tell you how it will be. Thank the Lord, we have no further incursions. Our scouts keep a close watch on the bounds by the Midhope farm and around Jones' original refuge. No sign of either Kingsmen or Jones. There were some of them hiding, not very well, on their side. I suppose they thought you might attempt to go there. No sign for a while, though. So, we are concerned to find Jones, and to do that we need you to be seen by him or your presence made known.

It's a fair hike over the hills to get to the right place. Rather than there and back each day, we'll move you nearer. You will parade about in plain sight, with companions, just as long as there is no movement from their side. If it starts, the scouts can signal faster than they can run, and you will be hustled west. We can hold them off for a bit if needed, but that's a last resort. We don't want to reveal what little strength we have. Catch up with you, and you know what has to happen."

The last words were a statement, not a question. Mark clenched his fists to avoid shaking. He stood up and left, and was shown a room that would be his, but for one night only. Up early the following morning, and a steep climb away from the compound. More towers, each in line of sight to those on either side. As they moved, the large party that was with him shrank, as pairs peeled off to relieve those at each tower. It was only two miles. A rather boggy descent in the last half led to another wooded valley. In a clearing were a set of rather makeshift tents. Two people in standard Outlander garb attended a large cauldron hung over an open fire. Others were sitting on logs, greasing weapons. The four who had remained with him talked briefly to a man with a single feather. They left him for one of the tents, while four others emerged, packs on backs but with no weapons. At a nod from the officer, they started uphill back towards the base that Mark had left.

As the man introduced himself, Mark felt a change in atmosphere. By comparison with the officers that he had met previously, Jim Smith, as he named himself, was slow of speech, and seemed to find Mark's rapid talk hard to follow. It dawned on Mark that the man could not read or write, and that while understanding his orders in a practical sense, he found them incomprehensible in terms of aim. Exposing Mark and any escort in the open seemed to him an unacceptable risk, and the opposite of all the limited training he had received. As he despatched Mark eastwards with three escorts, there was a resentful air to his orders.

The rest of the day was spent in a fruitless walk across moorland and old farmland, trying always to be conspicuous. At first, his companions stayed close by him, apparently afraid he would bolt to the Ground. They passed by a number of concealed scouts. With a lot of argument, Mark persuaded them to walk a bit apart. Jones might otherwise think he was in some way a prisoner.

The same routine was repeated, traversing different ground, on two successive days, with equal lack of success. Some areas were in line of sight of the boundary; these were avoided. At the fourth attempt, however, there was an alarm, given by a loud whistle repeated from near the boundary. His companions reacted fast. One covered him in an Outie cloak, and all retreated westwards, reversing tactics completely, using whatever cover was to hand. Mark, always kept out of sight of the boundary, had no idea what was happening. He clutched the phial hung from a chain round his neck.

He was not allowed out the following day. There were comings and goings, and rather ill-tempered mutterings among the people in the compound. Smith was not very helpful. There had been Domainers and Grounders over the boundary was all he could gather. But it seemed not to be a chase, and certainly no Outlanders had been killed or even pursued. The others were even less helpful.

It took another day of horrible boredom, not improved by a dreary, day-long drizzle, to establish what had happened. While Mark could make no sense of what was happening, a 'two-feather' man arrived in the afternoon and talked to Smith and the others. Eventually, he told Mark what was happening.

"You used to work in that farm, didn't you? Did they sometimes put cattle or sheep out beyond the boundary? Just with the farmer? Looks like they have done it again, but there was a soldier in gear with an ordinary man. That set off the alarm. Seems they did it again yesterday. Narrows our scope a bit, though they remained very close to the boundary. But the captain told me that there were other ways of luring this Jones out. It's a problem if we try for his hideaway. It's out of sight but very close to the bounds. Just one sighting, and they'd wonder why."

Mark thought hard. It made sense that animals were let out beyond the bounds in summer. Pickless would scarcely have enough fodder without. But why a Kingsman? Surely there would be new farmers there, and putting a soldier on display would certainly not entice Mark to approach, if that was the reason for their presence. Did they think Outies would rush the farmer? Didn't they always run away if seen? He shrugged inwardly.

"Yes, sir. Jones can read and write well, and he moves very cleverly. If I write a note, and make several copies, they can be tied to bushes. The scouts should know where they are, and any alarm, destroy them. If he comes across one, it will give him evidence that it is me. I can specify a meeting place, and keep waiting there. Jones cannot stay underground for ever. The captain said it was worth a try."

More frustration: the camp held no paper and no writing instruments. No need! Mark returned to the base with the officer. There was little enough there. O'Hanlon tore pages from her log book, and provided Mark with what she called a pencil, pieces of stick bound tightly round a black core of soot and some binding compound. He thought long and hard before writing; there was no scope for crossing out, still less for discarding whole pages. Eventually, he arrived at this message, approved by the captain.

For Mr Jones. This is someone you know. You have never seen my writing. You showed me a Bible and a map, and there was a shower when I was with you. I am with the Westrons. They want to help you. I will wait each night until midnight at the entrance to the woods upstream from your home, I will have a torch burning. No torch, try another night. There will be others around me. You can leave if you wish, and you will not be followed. Posted 12 June. I'll stay till 20 June if needed. After that, we may need to break into your home.

Initially, he had written his name. It was O'Hanlon who had seen the problem. Unlikely as it was that the notes would be discovered by soldiers, better not to reveal it. So, he did waste one page, but in the end got this message in using both sides. Laboriously, he made ten copies in the smallest writing he could manage. A youngster scarcely older than Mark prepared straight sticks and made a deep cut along each one. Glue, they had, and binding. Soon there were ten miniature scrolls held by wood top and bottom. Not waterproof: they could only pray for good weather. Loaded with the scrolls in an oilskin bag, Mark and two companions returned to camp in the afternoon.

The following morning, five of the scrolls were tied to bushes. Each was topped with a white rag to attract attention. All well away from the boundary and the line of sight. Scouts were left far enough away to remain unseen, but near enough to grab the scroll if the Domainers advanced. Mark was kept well out of sight, until dusk. He stationed himself then in the valley bottom where the woods began, a flaming torch waved on a pole in his hand. To no one's surprise, nothing happened, and he withdrew to the camp. The same routine the following night had the same lack of response. By the following morning, heavy rain and strong winds deterred even the scouts. It continued through the night, and Mark was not even taken to the spot.

There was a degree of despondency in the camp. O'Hanlon herself had moved forward, and there was talk of going straight to Jones' home and removing what they could, regardless of risk. Mark was strongly opposed. He did not feel confident to say what was useful, or to interpret anything they found. Keep trying, he pleaded, keep trying. If Jones had been captured and tortured, you would have seen them around his home. With reluctance, O'Hanlon agreed to three more nights. The remaining five scrolls would be fixed in the morning if the weather subsided.

It dawned bright and fair. Scouts replaced the now glutinous scrolls. The day passed slowly. As dusk fell. Mark again walked to the rendezvous, companions hiding in the bushes on either side. He waved the torch, and replenished it with others by his side. He stayed well beyond midnight. Nothing. Back at camp, Mark had trouble to get O'Hanlon to stick to her promise. But the weather held. Another day came, enlivened by one teaching him to use a crossbow. He noticed, though, that O'Hanlon stayed and that numbers in the camp were rising. Ponies with packs were being unloaded: long packets sealed in oilcloth. One was dropped, and the cloth broke. Inside, there spilled out what Mark recognised immediately as fireworks. Huge fireworks. He knew what they would contain, and at whom they would be fired; his home, his Ground. *By all that's precious*, he thought, *let us find Jones*. Let the Kingsmen not advance. The practice at Chapel came into his mind.

Again, Mark walked to the rendezvous. He waved the torch. An hour or more passed. As he bent down to light a new torch from the remains of the old, a voice, almost a whisper came from the darkness ahead of him.

"Mark? Mark Norman? It is you?"

"Yes, sir, it is."

"Are you alone?"

"No, sir, there are Westrons around me. They will welcome you, sir, not harm you. I have their word that if you go, they will not follow. We need you, sir, need you badly."

There was a silence.

"Sir, if they meant you harm, they would have rushed you already. You see that I am with them, even that they wait on my word."

Out of the dark, Jones emerged, crossbow in hand. He moved slowly towards Mark until the torchlight gave him a view of Mark's face. Mark heard the whoosh as Jones let out a sigh. Both would have hugged at that moment, had it not been for the torch and weapon in their hands. There was a shuffling as right hands were freed, and a rather formal handshake marked the reunion. Shadowy figures emerged from either side of the path, figures with a look of delight in their faces. They kept a respectful distance.

"I'm sorry to have kept you waiting, lad, truly. I saw you parading about, but then I thought the ignorant folk had caught and stripped you, and it was some kind of trap. I'd seen them all around and heard a fight a while back, though I had no idea what it was about. Stupid, it might be, but after that I was afeared they'd shoot on sight."

It was a joyous return to the camp. The Outlanders even began a marching song, though neither Mark nor Jones could grasp the words. The noise roused the whole camp, and as they entered there was a throng that parted to let the pair approach O'Hanlon. Torches were held high.

Captain O'Hanlon rose to the occasion. Walking slowly forward, she shook Jones' hand.

"My pleasure, Mr Jones, to meet a determined enemy of the King and his minions. One who has eluded his grasp for so long. One who has given us a gift of God in your pupil." She nodded towards Mark. "Sir, I am Captain O'Hanlon, at your service. We have need of you, sir, more than you can imagine."

Jones was struck dumb. Here was intelligence. Here was authority. Like no Outie he had seen, still less any of the few he had exchanged words with many years ago. He managed a mumbled thanks and stepped back a pace. Never in the last 50 or more years had he seen so many people together. Already overwhelmed by company, he almost panicked. But in the flickering torchlight, there was nothing but joy on the faces around him. Slow many may have been, but all sensed an event, an important and hopeful event too. There was a hush.

She turned to the crowd. "Comrades. It is late, and we have work to do in the morning. Mr Jones will be tired, and in the morning, we will send him to safety, where, with God's blessing, he will give us news that will save us. But let us now be glad."

Let us now be glad; the signal that all understood. The anthem that all learnt. The anthem that was reserved only for the rarest of occasions in public. The signal of a major event. A fiddle struck up. Voices were raised, only partly in tune.

And did those feet in ancient time
Walk upon England's mountains green?
And was the holy Lamb of God
On England's pleasant pastures seen?
And did the Countenance Divine
Shine forth upon our clouded hills?
And was Jerusalem builded here
Among these dark Satanic mills?
Bring me my bow of burning gold
Bring me my arrows of desire
Bring me my spear
O clouds unfold!
Bring me my chariot of fire.
I will not cease from mental fight,
Nor shall my sword sleep in my hand
Till we have built Jerusalem
In England's green and pleasant land.

26. Death and Frustration

No time was lost the following morning. Mark and Jones were moved back to the base, while messengers moved faster to bring the news to Derwent and beyond. Jones said little; he was still stunned both by the multitude of people, and by the shock of finding people like O'Hanlon among them. A short rest, and they were moved onwards to Derwent House. They were met by Chief Rhianna, who shook Jones' hand with a very slight inclination of her body. *A surreptitious bow*, thought Mark, a sign of respect that Jones himself would miss. A small crowd gathered, welcoming Mark and the escort that had brought them, but again making Jones anxious.

Rhianna soon brought them indoors, and into a small room, the same one in which he had first met O'Hanlon. Her husband joined her. Introductions were completed. Jones still looked around him in a rather dazed way. Seeing his confusion, Rhianna made a decision.

"We have news for you, for you both, but it can keep, for I doubt Mr Jones will understand one word in two unless he learns more. Mark, we will leave you two for a while. Tell Mr Jones about your time with us, and why we were anxious to see him. We will return when you call."

Mark told his tale. There were many questions, and not a few exclamations. Mark had met a rebel Lord and Lady! So, there were Outland survivors of that Great War, then, the war that he and Mark had learnt of at school. There was a patch, a very small patch, right here where animals and people bred true. How Mark had put it at risk. How the Westrons had diverted attention, and hoped to do more.

There was a tense moment. When Mark described the Montgolfier attack, knowing little more than that it had brought the Domain to the table, Jones asked,

"Where did they attack, lad? The Domain is far from the Outland in most places."

"Not Domain, sir, it had to be Ground. We had to show we could cripple their recruitment. Only a small show, sir."

"Ground! In God's name, where? Ground, where there are people? People who carry the seeds of recovery? Are we back to war, and annihilation?"

"I'm not sure, sir. I heard Worcester mentioned. They were to strike at livestock, but some people would be hit. It has given them cause to talk, and to turn them away from the north. It'll not be repeated unless they advance here, I think."

Worcester. A few miles from my old home, thought Jones. He held his head in his hands, and said nothing. Mark started to speak, but was hushed with a look and a wave of the hand. Eventually Jones raised his head.

"So, you have spared some, for now, at the expense of others, and maybe many others if your plans fail. Where do I come into this, Mark? What was it that made me worth all that effort? I'd hoped in time to pass on stuff that would help the Westrons build and recover. I thought that was why you were to find me if you could. Not to see war again."

"You showed me a map, sir, do you remember? Of where we were and places around, before the Catastrophe? There were markings on it, areas marked off. You did not know what they meant. You said there were others, maps of places you did not know. I saw other maps later, much rougher ones, sir, during my journeys with the Westrons. They showed the same area at least in part. They were made to show people which areas were most contaminated, and which the least. We think your maps may show us areas that are clean but unknown; even what kind of contamination is involved. Did you take any with you when you moved?"

Jones shook his head. "No, I did not take things I did not understand. And those maps were fragile. They were flat in those large cabinets, lots of them. All looked to be the same type. I left them be. What's in the little refuge I moved to are books and notebooks, mostly about technical stuff. I'd hoped to come across an Outlander with enough intelligence to make use of them."

Mark sighed. This was going to be much more difficult than he had imagined. He left Jones, still anguished over the deaths inflicted and the prospect of more. He found Rhianna and her husband and gave them a brief account. They returned to the room. Jones was sitting motionless. Rhianna sat opposite him.

"Mr Jones, there are a few things may help you understand. Whether Mark had run or not, they'd have found out about you, sooner or later. When those soldiers came too close, it was you they were searching for. They know nothing of what you had found in your home. If they knew, and knew where it was, they'd have gutted it, and disposed of you too. We drove them away; they were breaching the Treaties. Five of ours were killed, Mr Jones, and there's two crippled. But there's been no movement since. They've not found it yet. We had to make a response, Mr Jones, else they'd have started wondering. Probably still are, but we hope to turn their eyes elsewhere. To do that without any more killing of Grounders. So far, the Domain have talked, not fought. They may lack similar means. We don't see this as war."

Henry intervened.

"Mr Jones, have you heard of the Hunt? No? I doubt any Grounders have, except Mark here who learnt it from us. Let me tell you. The nobility assembles each year, surrounded by their servants and soldiers. They move towards the semi-Badlands, as we call them, places where folk can live, even keep cattle or grow crops, but where sterility is almost certain. Places where our people move to gain what they can, the more so if they know they are already infertile or condemned to produce monsters. Grounders may have another name for them, but they also use them for pasture.

Soldiers drive the prey, Mr Jones. They block off any escape if they can. The nobles don fancy armour, they arm themselves with lances and bows. They gallop to the chase, if chase you can call it. The prey, Mr Jones? Our people, butchered for sport. Hounds to sniff out those that hide or evade the soldiers. A poor *season* for them if the trophies number less than a hundred. They've had no such a season for ten years or more. Hundreds each year, Mr Jones, and this year they are planning on thousands. Now, they do not just kill. They have captured and enslaved; broken minds and will by torture, moved them far way. A few escaped. They were injured in body and sick in soul.

And what can we do about it, Mr Jones? Our only defence is to threaten the Grounds; their precious Grounds. Until now, we have not used that threat. Now, only because they moved into what the Treaties agree is our own land. Land that is so near that tiny patch of land that is our Ground, our hope for the future. Learn about it, and they will take it, and maybe the clues that lead them to others like it."

Mark watched Jones' face. Grounders had that respect for human life that was drummed into them from childhood. For all his years of isolation, Jones was a Grounder.

"Sir, you and I were both Chosen. Did you wonder to what service you might be called? To be a Kingsman, perhaps? To be one of the soldiers ordered to serve the Hunt? Would I have refused? How can I know? Certainly, I would not have gone over to the Outlanders. An accomplice in murder?"

Jones retreated further into himself. The Barriers he knew of. He had watched, with horror, the waste of life that took place. Horror, but a recognition that life was squandered to a purpose, perverse though it might be. Killing for sport? Gradually, his despair turned to anger.

"What do you want of me, then? I can guide you to the material I removed, though I wonder if it serves any purpose. What I left behind, I thought of destroying if I could. Mark will know where it is. Mark, you remember the ladder, the trapdoor?"

"Yes, sir. I gave Lord Ogilvie and others as much detail as I could recall."

"Well, you should know that I took steps to hide it. The ladder is gone. I hauled it up and closed the trap door. Not bolted, though; I thought they might see it from below and peer about to no purpose. Bolted, and they would start thinking. I left through an upper tunnel. I caved it in behind me, though maybe it could be dug out. I left the ground floor looking as though," he paused, looking at Rhianna, "your people had used it as a temporary shelter. The side entrance was left open."

"How tall was the ladder, Mr Jones?" asked Rhianna.

"Twenty feet, give or take. That ground floor was like a hall, and the main door is huge. They must have kept something big there. No trace when I found the place, though."

"Thank you, Mr Jones. We will move tomorrow to recover what you took away, with your guidance, unless there are signs of activity the other side. But your original home is too risky just yet. Out of sight, yes, but too close to the boundary if any venture out again. We will wait. We will need to make a ladder, though. Henry, will you see to it?

I said I had news for you. It is bad news. Mark, you should know that Lady Hawkins is dead. She died at the Treaty Point after the agreement. The exertion speeded up the end, though we all knew it was coming soon. The Domain could see she was sick, and they will hear for certain when the hostage is visited. That is not all. Lord Ogilvie is not dead, or at least not when we heard. But he is failing fast, in mind as well as body. He'll not leave Chapel. We know nothing of Lord Alfred. We are on our own now."

Jones and Mark were escorted back to the forward camp the same day. Too late to go further, they spent the night there. In the morning, Mark was left to kick his heels, while Jones was led forward to retrieve his cache. It proved a simple job. No one was seen at the boundary, and by late afternoon he returned, both he and his escort weighted down with the books and documents he had ferried from home to his second refuge.

At first sight, it was a disappointing haul. Of the Outlanders at camp, only O'Hanlon herself was literate beyond a basic level. Many of the books were technical. A quick shuffle through the pages showed little that she could understand. A few titles triggered memory of what she had seen in Manod some years back. She might not understand all, but they most likely added nothing to what the west had preserved. Jones was downcast as she read the title of each and laid them aside. Mark intervened.

"It is not like the Grounds here, sir. Old books were saved, and all who can will read them. Few enough, though. I saw a copy of that Bible you had kept hold of, and it circulates widely. They do print or copy too, much like our King's Print. They know more of history than you or I learnt in Chronicles."

"There were many more," said Jones, "Many of them were just stories. Took me time to grasp though. Grounder education left a lot out. I thought the same would be true here. There was history too, but nothing like what Mark or I were taught. I think they were kept there as a store, a secure place should others be destroyed. Perhaps the stories were to entertain those working there. There were more than fifty beds scattered among a few rooms. Almost like a garrison."

O'Hanlon paid more attention to a set of thin volumes, standard in size and covering. Numbered on the spine, their front covers bore only the faded letters **OHMS** and below them the words **Restricted: for Official Use Only. This book is not to leave the Commander's office. To be kept secure when not in use.**

"They were together in a metal cabinet," said Jones. "I forced a number open. Most had just hand-written or loose sheets in files. Ink had faded on many, and the paper was often brittle. These were the only bound volumes except the notebooks you have yet to look at."

O'Hanlon looked at the title pages. Standing Orders. Operational instructions for...routine audits. Medical matters. She glanced at the date. 2043. She recognised the significance, but it was Mark who spoke first, recalling his talks with Chief McEnery and the priest.

"That's not from the war. It's earlier. From the Catastrophe. Near the end, I think."

"A military post then; a hidden one at that, or it would have been blasted. Were there any weapons, Mr Jones, or any signs of a fight?"

"No, ma'am. Not a thing. But there are many doors, thick metal doors, that I could not open, and the huge one downstairs. No skeletons either, and I've found no graves that I could recognise. There was a kind of kitchen. The cupboards had what I took to be rotten food, long since dried out. And some tins. I opened a few that had not rusted away, but I did not dare eat anything. Get poisoned and I had no one to help."

"The door, the one you used, was it open, shut, locked, when you discovered the place?"

"Shut, not locked. It bolted from the inside only. I wondered if the main lock was at the entrance to the courtyard. That had collapsed. It puzzled me at the time that there was no sign of Outlanders."

"Easily explained, Mr Jones, at least for the time you have been there. We have discouraged anyone from going near the Bounds there. You know why, now. A few opportunists misbehave, but they are after stock let out from the Ground. Even if they had explored, they'd not have found much to interest them." O'Hanlon thought for a bit. "Strange. Just left. We don't even know if they locked up after themselves. But all those doors inside; not to be opened, Mr Jones?"

"I messed about a bit, ma'am, when I first arrived. Many had corroded into the surroundings. I battered at a few and made no impression. They have handles, all right, but no obvious keyholes. There were insets with buttons. Some of those had numbers on. Maybe all, but many were corroded too. I worked out from one of the books that they were 'combination locks.' Press buttons in the right order and the door unlocks. But all seized solid. I levered one off. There was a mechanism inside, seized up too. I think they used electric power."

O'Hanlon thought about it. An Old-timer would understand these things. And we will probably have none left, bar Defoe himself. Do we ship all this and Jones himself back to Manod? God knew what was behind those doors. Weapons? Usable still? After a while, she shrugged. The Domain would have the same problems, at least for a while. She turned to the notebooks. There were only two. One was full, the other had only ten or so pages used. The writing was not good. It looked like a diary of sorts. She turned back to the inside cover of the fully used book. There was a name, and a date: *Lt. Col. James Buchanan, Royal Engineers, 20/10/48.* She looked at the first page, barely making out the words, some of which were meaningless. There were many initials, obviously shorthand for places or people.

20 Oct. This is the last sodding straw. First the net collapsed completely ten days ago. Then the phone. Radio, zilch. Remember some bright spark mentioning carrier pigeons. Now who's laughing. Someone blasted the dam yesterday and we have f-all juice, bar the standby. Not much fuel for that, either. It'll not last long. Laptops will be out of juice too. No messages from NCHQ, Sent Sgt Williams with a message five days ago. No reply, and no Williams. Hope the poor sod hasn't copped it. More bangs to the east, I 'll be surprised if there is a single dam left standing in all the Pennines. Everything seized up till we get some proper power. Couldn't implement LMSO even if we wanted to, never mind orders. Get an EMP and we'll lose all the hard drives and back up. At least, Williams took routine data with him. Bloody miracle we've had no C&B attacks. So, back to pen and paper for what it's worth. Get the drives out of here intact, and there is the official record. If not, maybe this will find its way out somehow.

Over the page was an entry headed 21/10. More initials. *Only an Old-timer could make sense of this*, thought O'Hanlon, *and I've other things to see to.* Oh, perhaps Henry might manage; better than me, for certain. This lot needs to move. Most of it right back to Manod, unless Ogilvie's able to look at it. Send it back to Derwent with the two of them. If we get the message, then we will try for the maps, but not with Jones. He can't move fast enough if we run. Mark knows where the maps are, and, worst case, he has his phial and consent. Nobody asked Jones, and I'm not going to.

She issued instructions. Late though it was, Mark and Jones and a party set out for Derwent with the finds, and a note. Seeing them out of sight, she set out for the forward camp.

***

334

Henry and Mark sat down together the following morning to decipher Buchanan's notes. Rhianna took care of Jones by introducing him to her House. He was gradually getting accustomed to life in the Outland. It was fine weather, and as they sat outside, Jones saw many arrivals and departures. Several hunters, rifles on their shoulders, arrived from the south. Mostly, Rhianna pointed out, with no visible deformities. Some, she told him, were fathers. Fathers not always of undamaged children, but parents nevertheless. They were fed and sent on their way north, along with others, variously armed with crossbows and pikes. Strings of ponies travelled with them, carrying supplies.

"It's clean up there, Mr Jones, cleaner than anywhere else we live. But it's not a place for many crops as yet. Weather is something we cannot alter."

Indoors, Henry was struggling with Buchanan's writing, consulting Mark from time to time. After a while, they moved to the last entry in the second, incompletely filled book. The writing was even harder to read. It was dated 23 Nov.

Two more disappeared in the night. Can't blame them, though where the hell they think is any better God only knows. Probably infected anyway. Two more dead, too. Collis, Boswell and Cohen helped me carry them away. No visible action around us. No orders. We can't fulfil LMSO. All of us expect to succumb any time. Leave the place clean and tidy and head west; less bangs from there. Two sticks in my pocket; maybe some data not scrambled. Toss-up whether to destroy all hard copy. No: if anybody gets here, more likely to be our lot. God willing, they can use it. If it is the others, then we are done for anyway.

Added. Jesus, just had a large drone over. Blasted the main gate. Just explosive, thank God. Someone knows there's something here. Fired a few shots as a token gesture. Have to rely on the codes to keep this lot out of enemy hands, but just who the enemy is has become a guessing game. Out of here before another comes along. What was it that God-botherer Mills kept saying: "pray for us now and at the hour of our death." Wherever you are, Mills, pray like hell.

"Well," said Henry, "that explains no bodies. Any that died were buried or left where Jones did not find them. Makes sense they took their weapons with them. The place was abandoned. I've no idea what LMSO means, but it looks as though their last resort order was to destroy the place, and they lacked the means.

Nobody's been there since except Jones. I guess they all died. I wonder if there are more places like that, full of God knows what."

"Sticks, sir? Drone? Seems like that is a flying machine. We just learnt it as the word for male bees. The mayor used it in a sermon about laziness." The mayor? Bradfield? A wave of self-pity almost swamped Mark. He'd been bored by the mayor's preaching; being bored seemed like a delight right now.

"I can have a guess, that's all. Back then they had many kinds of flying machine. I can't remember all the kinds. It was too much like fairy tales. Sticks? No. But I think a lot of these words that make no sense are to do with *computers*. Another fairy story to me, even though those of us picked out had a month with Defoe himself trying to explain. He kept apologising that he was not a tekki as he called it. Fond of quotes from the distant past, and giggled a bit as he read them. But cried sometimes too. He said this one in a funny way: *O what we ben, and what we come to. How cud any 1 not want to be like them what had boats in the air and picters on the wind?* He even wrote it on a blackboard, spelt funny too. Just a story, he said, but the way he said it sounded more like a prophecy."

Henry paused. Mark was, after all, one of us now. Clever with it. He'd learn soon enough.

"Not all the Old-timers were like Hawkins or Ogilvie. Even Alfred can drift away in a world of his own. Of course, most died ages ago, or were killed in the war. Defoe is a hero to all, because he was the first to rebel. But he's been kept out of sight for over a hundred years, not by compulsion. I'm told he was a teacher before the Catastrophe. Name a story, ask for a poem, and he's away. So those of us who are good with books got to see him. It is done in shifts; that's when I met Rhianna. How he got a dose, and a huge one at that, nobody knows. Soon, very soon, Mark, he will be the only one. Revered, yes. Capable of leading us? No. We have to run our own affairs, us mere mortals, as he would remind us. It was not meant badly."

They returned to Buchanan's notebooks. There were daily entries. At the beginning, mostly accounts of local patrols, meeting no-one. Another messenger sent east. Dam inspected: beyond repair. Drones seen in the distance. There was one tantalising reference: *The clear areas are few, from our limited coverage. We will not get any more info: no drones left, and no fuel even if we had. No idea how much info reached HQ. Started marking up the maps before it all goes pear-shaped. No means to transmit now.* Then, a 'big bang' to the north, and the 'electrics frazzled'. The entry for November 9th seemed to be mostly swearing:

Bloody typical. Go to manual, it tells us. All seized up, NBG. Can't even access the sodding maintenance guide. Generator out. Smith tinkering for hours, no joy. Can't pull the plug. Sit here like dummies and slug it out if any hostiles approach. A couple of days later: *Brought in a civvy found wandering. Not the brightest spark, maybe PTSD? From some village I'd never heard of, strafed and blasted.* Then the final days were accounted for. The refugee had fallen sick, and died a day later. *Germ warfare. We've all been close to the poor sod. Sit it out and hope.* Then the roll-call of deaths and desertions.

Henry called Rhianna and Jones back inside. Jones had read the notebooks as best he could. They had made less sense to him than to Henry. But whatever information they held in that place, it had been obtained before Buchanan had resorted to pen and paper. Only retrieval could enlighten them further. As for the rest? Nothing that was immediately useful. The people around Defoe might make something of it. Time for decisions. The others looked to Rhianna.

"No change, then. Mr Jones, we'll take you back to Chapel, with all this material, and a note from Henry. There are those who may do more with it. If not, we'll move you right back to meet Defoe himself. We have to prepare to get the maps and anything else out when the Domain is engaged elsewhere. Mark, we'll move you back to O'Hanlon. She'll judge when it's safe to go in. There are reinforcements going north this afternoon; you'll go with them."

Jones was set to protest. Rhianna silenced him.

"Mr Jones, we need either you or Mark out of harm's way. If we are found at your refuge, O'Hanlon would try a rapid retreat, and to destroy whatever they cannot carry. Get trapped, and Mark will kill himself or be killed by us. His choice, already made. He can move faster than you if need be. You know more of what is there than him. It is the only way."

Jones was silent. After a sombre meal, lacking in further talk, two parties set off. Two escorts, not differing much from Jones himself in age, led him south to Edale and Chapel. A larger and more lively party, including Mark and two more hunters, set off north.

27. Retrieval and Reunion

There was news for Mark when he returned to O'Hanlon's base. There had been no sign of military activity from the Ground, but the farmer had been seen by himself with sheep and cattle just over the boundary. No Proctors or Kingsmen visible. At Mark's suggestion that they might be hiding, O'Hanlon laughed.

"When they were hiding, they made a hopeless job of it. Heads popping up over the walls; noisy conversations. Even a few cooking fires. We had scouts within fifty yards, and they never saw us. No, it looks like the farm has returned to normal."

"They must have found new people then," said Mark, "people they could trust. Mr Pickless would have been taken away ages ago. They must have given up thinking I would return."

"We don't think so, Mark. Most of our people are new, now, but there are a few who've been around. They reckon it's the same man as before you ran, but they can't be sure. They always kept their distance, if only because Jones was usually with him, crossbow in hand. You would be the only one who could identify him for certain."

Something leaped inside him. Pickless alive? Pickless free? How could that be? The thought of meeting again! But he saw the look on O'Hanlon's face. A troubled look.

"Mark, it is not a problem to get you near enough to be sure, but not be seen. But what then? If he is still of the same mind, we can get useful intelligence about the Ground and the forces within it, and he'd talk to you. But if it is him, why is he at liberty? Has he been turned?"

In thinking about the retrieval, O'Hanlon had thought hard about the possibility of detection. Caught in the act, and it would be hard to escape. Worse, the Domain would find the place and whatever was of value within it. She doubted that their limited supplies of gunpowder would do much to hinder a later search, and they would certainly not make any impression on the heavy doors. Who knew what lay behind them?

Any signs of movement from the Ground, and she would have to divert attention before the refuge was visible. A diversion that would involve people waiting just to the north and east. A diversion that was big enough to take all their attention and would cost many lives. A diversion that would inevitably bring the area back to the attention of the Domain, even if the refuge was not immediately discovered.

"He'd not betray us, ma'am. Seven sons; one died young, all the rest Chosen and across the bridge. He spent years shielding Mr Jones. I've never heard of any that were taken by Security come back again either."

"You call to him. If he runs, there's a bolt through his chest. Several bolts. If he grabs you, you are both dead, and we go in fast. Are you ready for that?" Mark nodded.

Later, under cover of darkness, he was guided to the boundary's edge. He sensed the presence of marksmen around him. Soon after sunrise, Pickless opened the gate that led to the moor, driving cattle before him. Him, for sure. But before he had a chance to call, the dogs looked up, and started barking. They had caught a familiar scent, but not a trail. Fearing they would also flush out the Outlanders around him Mark called rapidly, sitting up to do so. The dogs raced towards him, barking, tails flapping.

Pickless stood, astonished, for a moment. Then he walked slowly towards Mark, who rose to his feet. The figure before him, clad Outlander fashion, was Mark, but a Mark changed, a Mark older by far than the year that had passed since the stint.

"Please, sir, don't turn or run. Don't get any closer. Call the dogs to heel. We are watched, watched by Outlanders. They are armed. Are you watched too, sir, from behind?"

Pickless nodded, whistled and stood still. "No, lad. There's a Proctor who'll be sitting down to breakfast with the ladies. But you? We'd given up hoping. Jones too?"

"Jones is safe, sir, well to the west. I'd given up hope of seeing you. Still less seeing you with no guards." Mark recalled O'Hanlon's advice. "Sit, sir, facing your farm. Keep the dogs by you. I'll lie down. If the Proctor looks over the wall, he should see nothing amiss."

Pickless sat. The conversation that followed was at first fruitful. Kingsmen were withdrawn, bar a handful in the mayor's office and at the bridge. All Security forces withdrawn. Everything normal again. Normal bar their surprising freedom. Then, Pickless told him that his mother and sister had returned home.

"And my father? Muss and her sons?"

Pickless gasped. He had forgotten that Mark would not know.

"Mark, your father is dead. He was killed by Security. Not intentionally, but it was murder nonetheless. I'm sorry, Mark, I had not realised you could not know. Muss has been transferred, though I don't know where."

There was a long silence. The consequences for his family coming from his evasion had slipped out of Mark's mind in the excitement that followed. Now it returned in full force. A wave of guilt overcame him. Guilt, but also anger. Pickless heard a sob.

"He died in the Ground, Mark, not over the bridge. Not condemned to the Barriers. And his death was shocking, even to the Domain. Security have been absent ever since. No one has crossed the bridge, not even Arkell, he's just confined."

More silence. Pickless waited a while, then resumed.

"Mark, I said normal, and so it is, after a fashion. But Major Cornwallis said something about trouble elsewhere that's called their forces away. Something about war if the Outlanders come here. War, Mark?"

Mark collected himself. Something had hardened within him.

"In a way, sir, it's already started, I think. It was Kingsmen here, hunting for Jones, that started it. Now the Outlanders want to avoid bringing them back here. We are going to rescue things that Jones had found. But we don't want to offer provocation here. If we can do that without attracting attention, it may be avoided."

At that moment, there was a call from the wall. Pickless looked up to see Miss and the Proctor waving. He waved back, and they disappeared from view.

"How long do you stay out here, sir?"

"Well into the afternoon if the weather's fine, like today. Why?"

"Be sure to stay as long as possible. If you are called, give a reason to stay longer." Mark paused. "Sorry, sir, but my companions are not trustful. They are watching. Keep the dogs off them. Move back before noon, and they will shoot. I hope we meet again, sir."

With that, Mark looked closely at the wall. No sign of life. Staying low, he retreated out of sight of the wall. His companions remained, hidden.

"It's clear," he told O'Hanlon. "The whole Ground has just a handful of Kingsmen in Bradfield. Nearly all of them have been sent south. There's one Proctor at the farm. He'll not stir."

There was something in Mark's face, and in the monotone in which he delivered the message. O'Hanlon looked hard at him.

"They killed my father."

He said no more, and she did not ask for it. Rapidly, they ran back to Jones' refuge. A whistle, and a group of more than twenty emerged from the moor, several carrying sections of ladder. Into the hall. A pause while sections were lashed and pegged together. Hoisted up to the trapdoor. Mark, O'Hanlon and four others climbed up to the upper floor.

It was more or less as Mark remembered, though there were papers and books scattered on the floor. The maps were found. The topmost one was that shown to Mark, and there were many below it. There were more in other drawers. Piled on a table, though, many were fragile. Some got torn. Eventually they managed to make three heavy rolls, carefully wrapped in the threadbare blankets that Jones had salvaged and used on his own bed. The rolls were carefully lowered to the ground floor and carried away west. Mark and O'Hanlon were left on their own upstairs, moving among the unlocked rooms that Jones had worked through.

"The map was all that Jones showed you? Nothing else that he thought important, other than the stuff he carried away?"

"No, he showed me only a Bible. He will have had the same education as me. There was too much to take in, and I think he just wanted to show me how much more there was, and how different. There was so much he did not understand himself. He thought all the Outlanders were too stupid, and he had to work it out himself before trying to communicate."

O'Hanlon wandered from room to room. Only three contained any material of interest, and it was obvious that Jones had riffed rapidly through each. The training at Manod, and the conversations with Rhianna and Henry had taught her that most material of day-to-day relevance was 'digital' in those days, and would be irretrievably lost. Probably the maps, the real maps, had been kept only as, what was it, 'back-up' in the event of the kind of catastrophe that had actually happened. She found Mark in another room, riffling through papers from a filing cabinet that Jones had forced.

"I can't see anything that is of much use. The technical stuff, and the history? I think most of it is in Manod, and I guess in the Domain's libraries too, even if you Grounders never saw any of it. If they were capable of using it, we'd know by now. I was wondering if we should try to destroy anything, but I can't see the point. Smoke might attract attention, for all there's probably no one looking."

"The only thing I was looking for," replied Mark, "was any key to the symbols and shadings added to those maps. They were hand-drawn. I'd think they'd have a list or guide, and it might not have been just electric, digital or whatever. Something on the table as they were filling in the maps. But it might be a single sheet, or a little notebook. No luck, so far, but it takes a lot of time to look at each piece of paper. And some them are faded, or crumble."

"We can afford another hour, unless those outside give a warning. Jones would have recognised it if he saw it? Then are there any places it looks as though he has not searched? Near the map cabinets?"

They returned to the room in which Jones had originally sat Mark down. It seemed to be the one most thoroughly examined by Jones. All the cabinets and cupboards had been forced. Papers and books were scattered on the floor. Jones had obviously done a whirlwind inspection before leaving. Neither of them found anything helpful. It might be that there was something in what Jones had removed. After about an hour, they gave up. Down the ladder, which was disassembled behind them, and all save a few scouts walked away westwards.

***

Back at O'Hanlon's base, the three rolls were placed on a table, almost with reverence. The urge to open them was nearly overwhelming. To see what it was that they had gained, to interpret the maps as best they could. It was Mark himself who hesitated. Jones had not interpreted the scrawled lettering. They would do no better. The maps were fragile; how many times could they be rolled and unrolled before disintegrating?

"We dare not open any here. None of us will know what the maps represent just from the names. If they all look like the one I saw with Mr Jones, each is for quite a small area. Back at Chapel, the priest at least has an atlas, a book of maps at all sorts of scales. And there are more who can read too."

It was agreed. The rolls were splinted with rods, and waterproof covers made from the cut-up pieces of a tent sacrificed for the purpose. A party including

342

Mark set off for Derwent. A night spent there, then on through Edale to Chapel the following morning. By evening, the party were there, thankful for the waterproof covers, as most of their journey was a march through drizzle. Burdens left at Chief McEnery's offices, the party dispersed, leaving Mark to retire to the room he had last occupied a couple of weeks previously.

The following morning Chief McEnery and Mark carefully opened one roll. The uppermost map was not the one Mark had seen. It had the same mixture of roads, woods and towns, but with names that meant nothing to either of them. There were no divisions marked in pencil, but a large scribble across the middle: *Multi.R/M1/M2? NBG.* They tried moving it to see the next one down. It tore slightly, and they stopped.

"We need to slide them gently, and with more space than there is here. We need to find out more. Lord Ogilvie might understand them?"

"He is near death, Mark. You are lucky to be here beforehand. He is lucid, but he'll not get up from his bed."

They did their best to roll the top map up. Tears appeared, but they managed to carry it upstairs, more or less intact. Ogilvie was sat up in bed. His face was skeletal, colourless, and his breathing harsh and irregular. He managed a lop-sided smile at the sight of Mark, but did not speak. Mark broke off a part of the map, small enough to bring to within range of Ogilvie's eyes. He took it with shaking hands, which caused it to break further.

"Do you recognise this, sir?" asked Mark. "It must be from before the Catastrophe."

Ogilvie's eyes squinted at it. He gestured towards a table by the bedside. There was a magnifying glass. With his hand on Mark's, it was moved over the fragment. Ogilvie let go of Mark and lay back. The words came very slowly, and almost as a whisper.

"Ordnance Survey. Whole of Britain like this. Many maps. Hundreds of them." A long pause. "Ripon. A city. Yorkshire. Surely Badlands." Looking at the puzzled look on Mark's face, he struggled to say a few more words. "North of your home, not that far." He lay back, exhausted, and shut his eyes. Carefully gathering the pieces, they left him and returned downstairs.

"Did that mean anything to you?" asked McEnery.

"No, sir, except that each map must be of a particular place. I'd guess that your hand drawn maps were copied from something like this. The priest showed me an atlas, a book full of maps. Have you seen it?"

"Yes, seen it, but that's all. He showed it to me to point out how large the world was. Quite a shock, all those places we've never seen and never heard from after the Catastrophe. He uses it with the clever ones that he teaches to read."

"I think we should call him in. Has he been to Manod? Does he know what they have there?"

"Yes, he'll have spent time with Defoe. They show most of the clever ones what they have, in the hope they'll understand something new and pass it on. I missed out on that; too much to do here." He looked at Mark. "Did Chief Rhianna or any of the others say anything about Lord Defoe, Mark?"

"Yes, sir. I heard that he was not a very practical man. So, it would be up to us ordinary folk to make what we can of anything from the old times. Particularly now the others are near the end, or gone already."

"It's true, so Father James told me, more's the pity. Yes, I'll send someone for him. He's the best we have in Chapel."

While they waited, they looked closely at the second map down, not daring to go further. It had what was obviously sea to the right, which they assumed to be east. There was what Mark recognised as two large towns on the edge of the sea, Bridlington; Scarborough. The names meant nothing. But there were markings on this map; divisions separated by thick black lines and coded letters and numbers within each. Most had the same inscription as on the map they had already inspected, but there were others. Mark was still poring over them when the priest arrived. After a very brief welcome, there was, necessarily, a long explanation of why these might be important. To Mark's relief, the priest recognised the maps immediately.

"I have seen the like at Manod, but they were folded, and were often in pieces. Some were stuck together or backed by other paper. There were tracings of some for practical purposes; they looked different, because the sea level has risen. They had no markings on them like this."

There was no room to separate the maps, still less to open the other rolls. It did not take long to decide to move them to the church. The rolls were easy; the one unpacked was carried on the table it rested on, boards being placed on top. Father James went to summon his class. Chairs and benches were moved to the side; the remaining rolls were untied. All three laid flat on the floor. One by one, each map was lifted from the top by many hands and pulled gently across the floor. Soon, there were three rows with about thirty maps in each. Some had cracked; all were curled from the rolling. It was Lizzie who noticed that each had a number as well as a name. They ran from 20 to 120, but with some missing. It was Lizzie also who suggested dampening each very gently and weighting the edges so that they would dry flat. Father James returned with his disintegrating atlas. Gradually, names were identified, each child being assigned about six maps, and returning with the names to the priest.

The pattern unfolded. The maps extended from just a little south of themselves to somewhere just short of the northernmost part of Scotland. Scotland, a name that the children knew, but was alien to Mark. It was too risky to assemble them in the right geographical places, which would, in any case, have prevented Mark from examining them closely. Now, it was up to him to interpret. He wondered about the manuals that Jones had brought away. He asked the Chief, realising that he had not seen Jones, nor heard him mentioned.

"I should have told you. We brought him to Ogilvie, who could not say much, and showed him some of the books, including the manuals. Ogilvie was insistent; send them all with Jones himself to Manod. There are those that spend their lives trying to interpret the technical stuff they have saved. Jones left yesterday."

McEnery did not add what Ogilvie had said later: *The Librarians. Defoe took to calling them Santa's little helpers, and giggled when he did so.* A fit of coughing had prevented any explanation.

So, thought Mark, *I'm on my own.* He walked up and down each row. Down on hands and knees to inspect each. Some maps carried no markings at all. Many others had the single scrawl in the middle, as they had seen on the map of Ripon: *Multi.R/M1/M2? NBG.* The letters and numbers varied slightly among the maps, but where the whole area was indicated, the letters NBG always featured. Mark could see little pattern. It was Father James who speeded things up. With great care, he had placed little scraps of paper on the atlas map, each with the number of the sheet in the right place as best he could determine it. To write on the atlas itself was akin to sacrilege. With this guide, they found that most of the unmarked maps formed two clusters. One was the northern part of what the priest and Lizzie immediately named as North Wales, a name that meant nothing to Mark. Others were to the north-east of the area that appeared to be covered.

The priest immediately came to look at the Welsh maps. He gave a cry.

"Manod is so close to this map. We learnt to distinguish kinds of contamination by hiking on marked paths with those who knew. All that area is a mix of the totally polluted, the not so bad, semi-Badlands and a few tiny patches apparently untouched. There were hand-drawn maps in our hostels."

He turned to Mark.

"If you are right, they must not have had any information. That's why it is unmarked."

They looked for maps that covered places further east. Lizzie gave a shout.

"Mark. Come here. This is where you came from, and where we are."

It was indeed the map that Jones had shown Mark, in what seemed a distant, almost imaginary past. Yes, there was Sheffield on the edge. There was Bradfield; there was Midhope. At the bottom left was Chapel, labelled Chapel-en-le-Frith. There were the many lines and sets of letters that Mark remembered, with traces of colouring in some areas that he had not noticed. There was an animated conversation among the others that passed over Mark's head. It rose to an excited babble as they examined the maps to the west and north. The Chief left, but soon returned, holding a hand drawn map similar to the one held by the priest. A better one than that seen by Mark at Edale. They were finding connections between the lines, letters and what they knew about the level and kinds of contamination. Jones' guess had been right.

Scrabbling on the floor was becoming painful. Not only that, but the children were accidentally stepping on maps, some of which were now torn or breaking up. Father James called for order, and all moved away from the lines. The children were sent out to fetch a table. The sheet that covered their home was carefully lifted onto it. Children dismissed, the Chief and the priest pored over it, consulting the Chief's cruder map repeatedly. Mark was left rather disconsolate, and wandered up and down the remaining lines. He could see that most were free of the lines, and had the same or similar lettering as the one he had shown to Ogilvie. By contrast, a few had a mass of lines and letters.

Eventually, McEnery and Father James turned to Mark. It was the priest who explained what they had found. The different sets of letters corresponded to what they knew about contamination, but not exactly.

"The places we know that are really bad, lethal if you stay any time, they are smaller than areas that have the lettering you saw on that Ripon map. But they are within them. Things have got better. We knew that already. See your Ground? We've tried to find other areas with the same lettering. There are a few tiny patches, mostly shown with a question mark."

"What about Eden?" Mark asked. "It is on that map, surely."

"On this, yes, but the Chief's map does not extend that far. Most of Rhianna's Riding has a mass of question marks. The bits that do have lettering mostly match what we call Habitable; places where there is not much damage, but a lot of Ms. We think it means mutagens, contamination that hinders breeding true."

"I've been thinking," added the Chief. "They can't have known all this by walking over everywhere. Most of them would be killed if they tried, never mind the detail here; it would take an army anyway. They must have been mapping from the air. What if it was cloudy? Did they guess where it was not clear?"

The three set off for the Chief's office after Father James had left a note on the church door, asking no one to enter. They returned to find a white-faced young man about to set out to find them. Ogilvie had died. There had been a spasm of coughing, then a collapse. They went upstairs for a last farewell. Hawkins, now Ogilvie. Alfred, from whom nothing had been heard, could not be far behind, even if still alive. Downstairs again, they sat around a table in silence for a while. Even alive, Ogilvie could scarcely have helped them decide what to do next. Eventually McEnery spoke.

"Whatever is there in those maps of value, it will take us days, weeks even, to make sense of. We are not that far from the Domain. They are not safe. They must go west, to Manod. Defoe may be of little use, but there are those more capable. I cannot go with them; there is too much here for me to do, and too few with any brains to handle it. James?"

"I am needed here too, Chief. Others there will have the same knowledge. Mark should go with them, to safety. God help him and us if he were captured or had to die to prevent it. We will need ponies to carry the rolls, and rolling them back will be our first task. I'll write an explanation that will speed things up when they get there."

"We'll need someone with sense to lead, though. I'm pushed to spare anyone literate; all the hunters are with Rhianna or down south."

"I'd thought of that. We are due to send a few to Manod for training in any case. Lizzie is the most able. Make it clear to the party that she is in charge, and they'll obey; she's not that young. You might use your power and give her a feather, just to drive it home."

***

So it was next day that a party left for the west; six ponies, one laden with the reassembled rolls, carefully wrapped in waterproof fabric, the remainder carrying Mark, Lizzie and three escorts. The going was good, and as dusk approached, they halted for the night at a small settlement. Beds there were, and fresh mounts and guides for the next morning, when a very early start was made. There were several such stops along the way, often changing mounts and guides at midday as well as at night. Mark was amazed by the organisation, and the speed with which they travelled. Lizzie explained.

"This is one of the most important routes in all the Westland. All those to and from Manod are manned. It's as well, though that I have a feather from the Chief. Mostly, there's no one can read until we are nearly there, so a requisition would be meaningless to them."

The route was anything but straight. Even Lizzie did not recognise the names of many settlements. For the first three days, it was a depressing journey through what qualified as semi-badlands, with smaller patches that were more fertile. There were detours around the worst patches. As she told them, they were skirting a huge, evil area of very toxic Badlands just to the north. Yes, very big cities, but completely destroyed. There were semaphore towers, and once Mark saw them in action. Messages could move faster than people or goods. A few carts passed them in the opposite direction. Supplies, Lizzie told him, supplies to support the forces pouring into the east to defend Eden if need be.

The gloomy and often drizzly weather did little to lift Mark's spirits. It was not like his home, nor like Eden. Even the less clean parts of Rhianna's Riding were more cheerful. There were folk around, livestock and crops too, but all looked less than healthy or whole to Mark. For Lizzie, though, it was a big adventure; she had been scarcely ten miles beyond Chapel in all her life. The added thrill of authority, authority conferred by the feather, gave her a self-confidence that Mark found rather embarrassing, but it caused no problems with those who saw to their needs.

Things changed on the evening of the third day out. The weather cleared, and ahead of them were mountains. Mountains, as Mark discovered as they went on, larger and steeper than those close to home. No midday changes here, and fewer, far fewer, people. On both sides, the hills varied. The most toxic still mostly bare, with scars of landslides. In places, these had been cleared to reopen the road. At one such, a gang were still working. No standard kit, like that of the Kingsmen, but heavily protected by many layers, facemasks and gauntlets. Mark turned to a guide.

"It must be dangerous. How are people chosen for such work? Is it a punishment?"

The guide looked at him in horror, then turned to Lizzie, begging silently for help.

"No, Mark. Punishment is rare anyway, but at worst those convicted only go where others are already. Never to clear real Badlands by compulsion. These are volunteers. They will know already that they are sterile, or cannot have babies that are remotely normal. And they take precautions. Those clothes? Removed and buried every day, or washed in running water for a day. And never more than two days in a row."

Mark thought of tales from the Barriers. Second hand tales, as far as he was concerned, but convincing enough. He was about to pursue the topic further, to ask about those who committed murder or rape. He was prevented by the arrival of a large party outward bound from Manod. A proper war party with two hunters among them. Freshly arrived from Ireland. When Lizzie introduced Mark, he attracted much attention. Yes, Manod knew he was on the way, and they had been told a little of his significance and that of his cargo. Soon, though, they moved on, headed for the east.

It was already darkening on the twenty-seventh when they approached Manod. The landscape, rugged though it was, was much healthier than that to the east. There were large buildings along the valley. Tall chimneys smoked. At a high pass, they looked down to a mix of fertility and barrenness. But, as a guide told him, not contamination, but the relics of industry from before the catastrophe. There were caves, man-made caves, that had shielded people. One was the home, or at least the refuge, of Lord Defoe.

28. Defoe

As they descended from the pass, Mark could see that the area was well-populated. A few electric lights were switched on in some of the scattered dwellings. They passed a number of people who expressed no curiosity; such laden parties were a common sight. A question from Lizzie resulted in an escort to a well-maintained house, with many rooms. A tall woman with two feathers in her helmet greeted them.

"Janet Forbes, at your service. A librarian by trade, but I am the guest-master for those who have business with Lord Defoe. We were expecting you. We will send your cargo down to him now, and I will take you to him in the morning."

Lizzie handed over the packet of notes that Father James had composed. These were passed on to those continuing downhill. Both she and Mark were shown to small but adequately furnished bedrooms. As darkness fell, they were summoned to a lamplit meal down stairs, where they were joined by Janet. There were a few questions about their journey, and about affairs at Chapel. The death of Lord Ogilvie was news, though she had already of Lady Hawkins' passing. There was no news of Lord Alfred. Eventually, Janet turned to Mark.

"These maps you have brought. They are Ordnance Survey, we were told. Do you know what was covered? I mean geographically?"

It was Lizzie who answered, seeing Mark's hesitation.

"The northern part of England, ma'am, and I think most of Scotland. Our priest said there were maps also of this area, but they held no markings. There were others the same from elsewhere."

"But a means of identifying habitable places?"

"We think so, ma'am, but there were too many maps for us to examine. The markings matched what we know around Chapel, and around the Ground where Mark lived. Have you seen such maps?"

"Yes, though without markings, and some are older than others, and at different scales. They are all in some disrepair. They were salvaged piecemeal from houses a long time ago, often a long time after the houses were abandoned. Well, there will be many who will be keen to examine your finds in the morning."

Mark broke in.

"Excuse me, ma'am, but has Mr Jones arrived? Have you seen him?"

"Yes, indeed, he arrived two days ago. A remarkable man, but strangely ignorant. He met Lord Defoe yesterday, and my colleagues are already examining the material he brought with him."

"I am afraid you will find me the same, or worse, ma'am. He will have had the same education as me. It is what the Domain wished Grounders to know. He had time to read what was in his refuge, years in fact. We were taught only about the King's doings, and the features of our own Ground."

Janet pondered. Jones' meeting with Defoe had not gone well. It had not been one of his better days. He had persuaded Jones to recite the Declaration, then giggled and asked him if he knew who wrote it. Jones had looked baffled, and had not received an explanation. Instead, Defoe had subjected the man to a barrage of quotes from pre-Catastrophe books, gradually getting more morose. Her colleague Raymond had eventually managed to extract Jones and take him to a far more congenial assembly of librarians and their apprentices. But the man had been shocked.

There was more for her to worry about. For two centuries now, the clever, the literate, had spent time at Manod, getting at least a basic education. The very brightest stayed on. Some, like her, worked on finding ways to use the knowledge of the past. Others learnt skills that only the literate would master, and returned to their communities, always enhanced with two feathers. But whereas in the not-so-distant past, all the brightest had received Defoe's personal attention, his behaviour had led the librarians and tutors to restrict this contact to the formal. He was, after all, the hero, the founder of their society and could not be hidden away.

"Mark, has anything been said to you about Lord Defoe? Or to you, Lizzie?"

"Yes, ma'am. I gathered that he was not a practical man, as it was put to me. I expected to discuss the maps and anything else with others."

"Father James told us that he was a teacher before the Catastrophe; A teacher of literature, he said. I think it meant studying writing: poems and stories."

Janet was somewhat relieved. Lizzie had unusually arrived on her own, but bar a formal introduction, she could easily be taken in hand by others. But Mark would be required to have more, and more frequent contact.

"Mark, when you talk to him, do not be put off by his mood and manner. He is no Hawkins or Ogilvie. He has a feeling of guilt, because his life was extended so much more than others. And he will soon be the only Old-timer we have, no one to talk to who shares his knowledge of things past. Practical matters will be dealt with elsewhere."

With that, she hustled them to bed, and sat brooding a while by herself before also climbing the stairs.

***

In the morning, Mark and Lizzie were separated. He was led to a house outside the entrance to a cave, the original Manod, he was told. Sat in an empty room, he looked at the pictures adorning the walls. Relics, all of them, pictures from pre-Catastrophe times. Pictures of cities, huge and filled with soaring buildings and a multitude of mobiles. Pictures of men and women in strange clothing. Pictures of flying craft and huge ships. But also pictures of cities destroyed, roads blasted, with mobiles overturned and burning. *Pictures*, Mark thought, *from the Catastrophe or the war*. Pictures that no Grounder would ever see.

He did not wait long. Three people entered the room, and it was at once evident which was Lord Defoe, a man with an apparent age of about fifty, but one whose eyes betrayed a weariness beyond those years. A man of slight build, stooped a little and with spectacles held on his chest by strings. Beside him were two visibly younger people, man and woman, both removing two-feathered helmets as they sat beside their master. Mark stood, but was signalled to sit.

"Welcome to Manod, Master Norman. The lair of the Deceiver, indeed. I am told that you bring us news, news that may enlighten us and confound our enemies." Defoe looked at Mark.

"*How beautiful upon the mountains are the feet of him that bringeth good tidings.*"

He suppressed a giggle. Mark caught the looks exchanged between the two assistants.

"Yes, sir. We brought maps that may show you places fit to live in, and to breed in. Places like my Ground, sir. Mr Jones brought other things too, in the hope that they might help you."

"We are indeed grateful, Mark, if I may." It was the younger man who spoke. "Your companion is with our librarians now, and we will examine those maps. You will join them soon. But Lord Defoe would like to hear more about affairs in the Domain, and in your Ground. Just as you have learned, I guess, much about us that contradicts what you were taught, so we lack recent news from the other side."

The woman gave a sideways glance at Defoe. It was not going to be easy. The interview with Jones had caused confusion, and not only to Jones. Leave aside the rambling, Defoe had hinted at things that Outlanders themselves did not know, and would scarcely credit. Things that were best left in darkness. But the interview could scarcely be denied.

Initially, all went well. Defoe asked about the affairs of the Ground. About mayors and bailiffs. About the process of Choosing. About the marriage rules. The Barriers attracted questions from all three, but it dawned on Mark that in that case they might know more than him. Both the others turned to more technical questions: about electricity, about telephones, about hygiene. Mark answered as best he could. But while the technical questions were dealt with, Defoe made clear his lack of interest. He fidgeted. He fumbled about in a bag that had been over his shoulder, taking from it a number of books. He put on the spectacles, and peered at their covers. When the others had exhausted their questions, he placed a book in Mark's hands. Its cover was bare, but when Mark opened it, he gasped. *The Book of the King.* Not in the rather crude print of the copies they used in Chronicles, but in the style of the pre-Catastrophe books that were prohibited Relics. Even so, it seemed much slimmer.

"This is what you learnt from, is it not?"

"Yes, sir, exactly, but our copies were printed differently, I guess much later."

"Turn to the end."

Mark did so. It ended far earlier than the book they learnt from. Indeed, the great betrayal, the revolt of the west, was not there at all. No war, just the great Catastrophe and the beginning of the King's rule. He looked up at Defoe. The man had a wry smile on his face.

"It stops, sir. There is nothing about the war."

"And you remember the teaching of what went before?"

Unbidden, that fragment of pre-Catastrophe writing came to Mark's mind.

A tale told by an idiot, full of sound and fury, signifying nothing.

Another crooked smile. "You were well taught indeed. Can you also recite the Declaration?"

Mark did so. When he came to the item, *Who, with his royal sons and daughter, and all the company of nobles defied the Great Deceiver and his rebel traitors.* Defoe jerked slightly. A frown was followed by a tight-lipped smile.

"Well, well," Defoe muttered. "Someone saw fit to tamper with the original. Most uncanonical. Someone with brains, though; *and all the company of nobles,* nice touch."

He giggled, but both the assistants became uncomfortable. The woman spoke out.

"My Lord, Mark is bound to know these things, but I think he will be aware that they were impositions, deceits to keep him and others ignorant. May we not take him to the librarians?"

"In a moment, in a moment. I would like to ask a few other things. But," and here another giggle escaped him, "*Please don't let me detain you.*"

The two assistants looked at one another and shrugged. Stay, and there would be consequences. They could, in any case, not shield Mark for ever. They left.

Defoe's questions puzzled Mark. Describe the Choosing ceremony. What about Gods? What about the Deceiver? How had the King and nobility come to have long life but also sterility? It was that last question that drew Mark into more than mere description.

"It was not clear, sir. The Book taught us that there was some process, some treatment, that extended life, but prevented having children, that the King and first-born did this to save us from the chaos. But then there was the Catastrophe and the war, and many became sterile anyway. Except in the Grounds, of course."

"Did you ever wonder who had that treatment? And why so few? Apart from the King himself, of course."

"No, sir, not really. There was just the nobility, like the Visitor. We knew that some nobles had become rebels, like yourself, but we were told they'd all been killed in the Great War. It was a surprise to meet Lord Ogilvie and Lady Hawkins."

"And the Deceiver?"

"It was not clear, sir. My father sometimes wondered if it was a real person. We learnt that all the chaos was due to his malevolence, and that it was the King's sacrifice that had saved us. That he and the first-born preserved all the good knowledge and saved the Grounds. Which was why we owed him Service. After I had met Mr Jones, I started wondering if the Deceiver meant the God in the Bible. We were taught to reject false gods. And there was a lot of superstition that was stamped on, and dismissed as old wife's tales. Then when I first came to the Outland, I wondered if it meant you. But we never heard your name."

Defoe laughed, laughed in a way that chilled Mark. Almost a cackle. Then he went silent. Eventually, he spoke.

"Did you ever wonder who wrote the Book? Who composed the Declaration? Who declared the Deceiver to be your enemy? They were not there before the *King came into his own.*"

The last five words were said in a different tone, and it dawned on Mark that Defoe would amuse himself by quoting, quoting often with a grimace or giggle.

"And how about the Choosing ceremony, selection for Service?" Defoe persisted. "No, I suppose there was no reason for you to think about it. From time immemorial, as some would have said."

Defoe's face was hypnotising Mark. It changed from one expression to another, and another and back. A combination of a strange kind of amusement, a touch of horror and a dose of self-hatred flickered and went out, to be repeated.

"Back to that Deceiver, Mark. Did that priest at Chapel tell you anything about God?"

"A bit, sir, but it was Chief McEnery and his wife who confused me. God was three in one. There was a," Mark stumbled for the word, "creed that those in church recited. I never asked Father James about it. The Chief snorted a bit, and got a bad look from his wife. It sounded a bit like the Declaration, but not everybody had to say it."

Defoe rubbed his hands and smiled.

"A paradox, yes, a riddle? Three in one. So, what if the Deceiver is the same: imaginary, the god of Father James, and me? And if imaginary, who imagined him do you suppose?"

Mark sensed that he was being led somewhere, though to what purpose was mystifying.

"You are real enough, sir, and I can see that the King and his nobles would be pleased to ascribe evil to you. But the idea must have come first, otherwise why not your own name. It's in the Declaration, too. We could as well have been taught to hate you. As for God, the God that's in that Bible, it seems some think he is real and others do not. Mr Jones showed me that Bible, and I read bits of it when I was in Chapel. But you are not that God, he's been around for ages, even if he is invented. Far longer than you or the King."

"That God had an adversary, did he not? One who thought it," again, the slightly sing-song voice, "*better to reign in hell than serve in heaven.*"

This stumped Mark completely. Neither Father James nor Chief nor Miss McEnery had got round to the Devil or hell. But evil had been personified in the Deceiver. A dim light reached his understanding.

"If God and his enemy go back long before the King, even if not named the Deceiver, then the King might regard them both as his enemies. We learnt that the King had expelled false gods. I never really understood that, but mentioning gods in anything other than an insulting way got some patriot reporting you. Your parents got called in too. My sister got into trouble often enough; she picked it up from Father. The King was the source of all things good, and the Deceiver for all that was bad. So maybe someone rolled them into one? And gave them that name?"

"Someone? Well done. I am sorry you were not my pupil. Indeed," that tone again, "*What's in a name? That which we call a rose, by any other name would smell as sweet.*"

He looked at Mark with a grin.

"Or putrid, if the name is Deceiver."

"The King's doing then? I can see his purpose, and to include you later."

Defoe laughed out loud.

"The King? He had not the brains. But an idea could be planted in what he was pleased to call his mind. Easy enough to persuade him that it was his. And there were others clever enough to add myself to the mix by indirection. I'll warrant you never heard my name until you crossed over."

True enough, thought Mark. But why is he speaking in riddles? The ineptitude of the King was easy to understand; his father had been worth six of

Arkell, who rode high on his father's ability. So, a follower. The man knows who, but is teasing me.

Defoe tired of his game. He dismissed Mark with no further explanation.

"We will meet again, young man. Maybe you will find an answer to this and other questions. A clue: the answer is the same in each case."

The woman who had sat alongside Defoe was waiting, rather anxiously, outside the door. Beyond the cryptic comment that he would get used to Defoe, she said nothing but led him to a hall with rows of trestle tables. Many of his maps were laid out on them. Men and women were bringing books, papers and maps from elsewhere. He saw Lizzie poring over one with Janet and a man she introduced as Raymond Fisher. It included sea, but also many marked areas with different letters.

"Look, Mark. There are areas, quite large areas, with lettering similar to the land near your home. Land that could support breeding, if we are right. Areas bigger than Eden. And if we compare with the map that we know, the map that has Chapel and your home, they will have got bigger and cleaner."

"Can you get to them, though?" He pointed to one surrounded by the dreaded letters NBG.

"Not that one, yet," said Raymond, "but there are others. We have only looked at a few maps so far. There are some near enough to the sea. Indeed, the sea may meet them now, because it has risen since the maps were made. We could sail to find out."

"Mark," said Janet. "I was told you saw a bear? There have been more and more of them, and they are not swimming. There must be routes through the Badlands. We hope to find them."

Indeed, there was a buzz in the room. Some maps had been laid aside, while others were surrounded by eager men and women. Most were indeed normal in appearance, but some showed the signs of genetic damage, damage evidently not affecting their intelligence. Other maps were laid out; maps at larger scales, but bigger than those in Father James' atlas. Here, there was no compunction about marking them. Suddenly, Mark felt excluded, superfluous. These people, he realised, had learnt proper geography. They recognised the names of cities long gone, of rivers and mountains not seen for centuries. He asked for Jones, and was directed to a much smaller room. Here, he found a morose Jones sitting by himself, surrounded by a heap of books and papers, some left open. He cheered up on seeing Mark.

"Good to see you, lad." He waved at the books in front of him. "They are doing their best. All this stuff to read, to find out about real history and stuff. It's hard to take in most of it. Seems most of the stuff I brought, they knew about already. It's the handwritten stuff that excites them, but I can't understand why."

"Well, they are excited by the maps too, that's something. But I'm not much use either now. How did your meeting with Defoe go?"

"You met him too? I'd say he was a bit cracked, for all he looks fit enough. Maybe living more than the natural span does that. Better cracked like him than warped like the so-called nobility in the Domain. But there's other folk here with some brains. I'd have been with them sooner if I'd known."

"I don't think he's mad. But there's something odd about him. He spoke to me in riddles and kept laughing in a strange way. I was told he was a teacher, literature, meaning more than learning to read. But think about it, Mr Jones; why would a teacher get given near eternal life, more than two hundred years staying the same if I've understood right? More to come, too. What made him and others rebel?"

"Riddles is right, and that laugh too. I couldn't understand what he was on about, and he seemed to find that funny. As to being given whatever, maybe he taught rich kids back then, and they liked him. Mayor Ruddles was like that back home; got his kids extra teaching by dishing out credits on the sly. Worked, too, all sent off for more education. They'd end up as mayors or get to be at Court if they were Chosen. Snooty lot of patriots." Jones spat.

He relapsed into silence. Mark picked up a few of the books. Shabby and often patched, they were all obviously pre-Catastrophe. Mostly, short histories of England, or rather of Britain. There was a small atlas. There were others that seemed to be scientific. One that Jones had opened was a mere pamphlet, a guide to the City of Worcester. Jones saw Mark's attention.

"They asked me where I came from, and dug this out from some underground store. We knew where Worcester was all right, back in the day. A heap of red-hot Badlands. Nearest place that was an inhabitable town was bits of Malvern, and damned small bits at that. All farms and mills where I came from."

Mark looked at the titles of the books Jones had before him. After a while, he started paying attention to the dates of publication, remembering what Jones had told him about the Bible, and what he had read in that simple book in Chapel. They varied, though he could see that some had been reprinted. The earliest was dated 1964, but most had dates in the 2000s. The last was 2033. It was scarcely more than a booklet, full of practical advice about hygiene.

"Those librarians told me that making books had become less common, and stopped almost completely in the Catastrophe," said Jones. "Something about it all being digital. I didn't grasp the sum of it at all, but it was all electrical, and it was all destroyed. We know more about 1930 than 2030 was what he said. Didn't make much sense to me. Mr Fisher told me that later stuff was printed on bad paper, stuff not intended to keep. They've a few fragments."

"Well, sir, you had the same learning as me. You were taught about King's Years? When I was in Chapel, the Chief there gave me a book of what happened after that. We worked out that KY 1 was 2049, the way they name years here. And they think of now as 2289. That's KY 241 to us."

"That makes sense. I'd lost count of the years, but I remember it was 192 when I was Chosen and ran. A few after that before I found my home and met Pickless. Desperate, I was then. He could have turned me in, but I was past caring. Poor Pickless, he must have been taken when they came looking for me."

That gave Mark a jolt; Jones had been long gone before he had found Mr Pickless at the boundary.

"No, sir, Mr Pickless is still there. I met him. They've withdrawn nearly all the Domain forces there. There's things going on there we don't understand." Mark paused. "They killed my father, Mr Jones, killed him in the Ground."

Jones was silent. Joy over Pickless, but nothing to say to Mark. What had happened to his own family? He'd never know, but the memory of his early days in exile hit him hard. The guilt that had atrophied, but had never vanished completely. The silence was broken only when a young man came to summon them to a communal meal.

***

The afternoon that followed started a pattern. There was nothing useful that either he or Mr Jones could do. Talk over meals, the questions asked and answered on both sides, merely revealed their ignorance. Their experiences in the Ground, and their knowledge, such as it was, of life in the Domain became common currency among the librarians that ate with them. Topics of conversation now revolved around the maps and Jones' cache in a way that left them behind. Jones became even more morose. He hid away with the books that had been put before him. He had little to say even to Mark. Mark himself wandered around the settlement, occasionally looking in on those working on the maps. There, he was always welcome; he was shown the progress made in identifying potentially habitable land. But he had nothing to contribute. His novelty status had faded, while what he had brought was engaging all.

In the evenings, when he returned to the Guest House, he found Lizzie and Janet full of talk about their findings. They tried hard to include him, to keep him informed, but the place names, the distances, the kinds and levels of contamination went over his head. He would leave them to it, retiring grumpily to his room to read, reading that became fitful and inattentive. On the first morning after his interview with Defoe, a visit to the map room revealed a giant of a man he had not seen before. A man manifestly deformed of features, but with that air of intelligence that Mark had learnt to recognise. He was dressed distinctively too, in what Mark unconsciously thought of as a uniform. Janet introduced him with a malicious grin.

"Mark, may I present my Lord Admiral Nelson. He commands our ships, such as they are. My Lord Admiral, this is the Grounder, the refugee who has brought us these maps, Mark Norman." She gave an ironic bow to the giant.

A huge hand grasped Mark's.

"My Lord Defoe's little joke," he said, raising his other hand as though to cuff her. "Plain Smith's the name, or was, and I punch any sailor calls me Nelson. And Captain will be quite sufficient. These bookworms know I'd not hit them, and get away with it. And as for you, young lady, a little less cheek about our fleet, or you'll find yourself spirited away and before the mast in a flash."

Both laughed, but Janet saw the look of total bafflement on Mark's face.

"History, Mark, that's all. Nelson was a famous ship commander way back pre-Catastrophe. There were battles at sea. Defoe loves doing this, and sometimes it sticks. He calls himself Methuselah when the mood takes him. It's from the Bible. We don't oblige him though."

"I'm here to see what you have brought us, Mark. To see if there are places that we can find and study."

"And are there any, sir?"

"Oh yes, several. Most not easy though, and we've not the old charts they used. Sea's risen too. Easy enough to get wrecked. Just the crossing to what's left of Dublin is dangerous enough."

Mark left them to it, and called on Jones, to pass on the news. It did not seem to cheer the old man much.

"Isn't this what you hoped for, sir? Something that would help the Outlanders, but not mean fighting and killing?"

Jones grunted. "I suppose. I'd been thinking more of machines, of medicines, of decontaminants. I can see it was wishful thinking. I took in so much of what it was like then, Mark, before the Catastrophe, I mean. Did you know they sent men to the moon? That there were ships carrying thousands as though they were palaces? And everybody carried telephones around with them, no wires? How did they do that? Mind you, I also read that the police, Security as it is now, could find you wherever you were by your telephone, so there's that to think of. They called them mobiles too. Lots of different names for our mobiles."

The midday meal was normal enough, and Jones seemed to perk up. But while they were at table, Janet, Raymond and a few others rose, and talked together in a huddle to the woman who had been with Defoe. There were glances in Mark's direction. As the meal ended, Raymond took him aside.

"This afternoon, Mark, go for a walk. Don't be near the buildings here. Defoe wants to see you, but he is very agitated. We tell him you are out, but he is liable to come here shouting for you. We need him to be calmer before you meet him again."

Mark did as he was told. The area around Manod was, as he could see, remarkably clean, at least to the eye. But when he climbed up to the summit of the pass down which he had arrived, he could see to the north a more barren landscape out towards the horizon. As he walked, he started to wonder about the effects of living as long as Defoe, or Hawkins and Ogilvie. Or the Visitor, and the other nobles he knew lived within the Domain. All but Defoe had seemed normal, sane enough. He guessed that they were younger, even though the two in the Outland had died. But if age alone drove you mad, what about the King? What about those treated with him, if they were still alive? Even seeing some of the evil in the system he had left, he could not imagine a more malign version of Defoe having the ability to control it. He turned back towards the Guest House, and his evening meal. It passed much as the previous evening. But when Mark rose to leave, Janet asked him to sit.

"Mark, tomorrow, you will have to meet Lord Defoe again, perhaps in the morning. I think he is calmer, but we cannot be sure of his state of mind. Do not think that he will harm you physically. He has never raised a hand to anyone. He has something on his mind, something he perhaps shared with our other Old-timers, but not with us, other than in hints and indirection. We think he would have been open with Mr Jones, but found him wanting in some way. He has never asked to see Jones again. With you, it is different. He has been pestering us. Keep you from him, and we fear for his sanity."

"Will I be alone? It was when the librarians left that he became so strange, almost teasing. Then he dropped it all and sent me away. I wondered about the effect of living so long, though Lady Hawkins and Lord Ogilvie were far more understandable."

"Yes, on your own. He'll not get what he wants if any of us are around. Age only? I think not, Mark. He has always been inclined to this way of talking. You heard the change in his voice, the little laughs?" Mark nodded. "He quotes from old books. We've tracked down a few. Some very old, some from just before the Catastrophe. Certainly, quite a few from the Bible. Others, we think come from things other than books, things that are lost to us completely."

Lizzie was looking at Mark as Janet spoke. She had yet to meet Defoe; indeed, Janet had told her that she would be introduced with others when enough trainees had been gathered together. The cockiness of her treatment of Father James, and her pride in the feather, the feeling of command as they had moved west, all these had evaporated now she was among equals or betters. Certainly, she was among those wiser and better informed than herself. Mark had rather left her mind. Now, she realised that he was subject to pressures she was not asked to bear. A certain shame at her neglect took hold, and she smiled encouragingly as Mark finally turned to go upstairs.

Indeed, it was not long after breakfast the following morning that Mark was summoned from the map room. Back to the room with so many pictures, pictures that Mark could not help labelling Relics. Defoe was sat behind a table, a table strewn with books. He waved Mark to a chair facing him, and with a very different, peremptory, wave made it clear that Mark's escort should leave.

"Well, Mark, do you recall our conversation? About the Deceiver, about the Domain? And about the Book of the King?"

"Yes, sir, though I left full of questions, of things I did not understand."

"So, let us take that Book, the Book of the King. The copy I have, it stopped before the Great War, yes? Think back to your copy. Full of tales of the King's victories, full of the evils of rebellion and the wickedness of the Deceiver. We have a few such copies, copies that were," he paused, "liberated, removed by skilled people from Grounds."

"Yes, sir, it was just like that." Mark thought of Mr Arkwright, thought of David. "We even read of a plague sent from the Outland a hundred years later, though my father wondered if there was more to it."

"A wise man, then. That plague, Mark, that plague was devised to kill us. Designed by the Domain, but one that went badly wrong. But did you notice any difference, a difference in style or subject, from the time after the end of this copy, here?"

Mark thought. Chronicles had always bored him. A dull litany of dates to remember, King's victories to be celebrated. But the beginning, the part in Defoe's hands? He struggled to remember any dates other than the King's birth. He stretched out to reach the book on the table in front of him. He turned pages quickly.

"Before the War, sir, and even more before the King's reign began, it is all much vaguer. Very few dates, very few particular events. And we were discouraged from asking. Just to take in the chaos and destruction before the king established order and saved the Grounds. There was another quote from old times, sir, besides the one I gave you before." Mark flipped the pages. There it was.

"*And we are here, as on a darkling plain, swept with confused alarms of struggle and flight, where ignorant armies clash by night.* I struggled with that, sir, that's why I remembered it was there."

"Bravo! Matthew Arnold, that, from the 19th century. Boy, you should have been my pupil, not those four little Philistines. A long time before the Catastrophe. And the other? Older still. *Nothing new under the sun.* Eh?" Another laugh. "*O, what a tangled web we weave, when first we practice to deceive.*" "Lies, Mark, lies. The world before the Catastrophe was a wonderful place, mostly. We fouled it up. And paid a terrible price. It was concealed. Look at those pictures, Mark. The cities, the people."

Defoe's expression became almost sly.

"So, back to the Book. Now, *Sherlock,* what do you conclude? Do the *little grey cells* suggest anything to you?" A titter followed. Mark was completely lost, but a terrifying thought had formed slowly in his mind.

"The two parts are written by different people, sir. Things changed after the war started. At least two people, I think, because the bit I had, and this does not, could be written by anyone with the facts. It's a catalogue, like Pickless' stud book or the bit called Chronicles in that Bible. But the first part is like telling a story. A story with a moral."

He looked at Defoe. Pleasure and pain crossed the man's face.

"Hmm. Nearly right. The word that was used back then was *propaganda*. A story to justify something, or to damn it. Could be true, but usually not. Certainly not in this case. Go on, Mark."

"It's a story that likes to use quotes from other books, sir. Like yourself, sir. I was told you taught Literature, and it was all about books. Poems too. And that Declaration; it reads almost like something out of the Bible I looked at. The story ends when the war began. When you had escaped the Domain. I think you wrote that part, sir. Probably the Declaration as well?"

Mark almost flinched as he spoke. Defoe was surely confessing, confessing to a monstrous lie. Yet he had led the rebellion.

"Discovered at last, and fast at that. Yes, Mark, I wrote that part. I composed the original Declaration. I named the Domain, and caused the Grounds to be so called. Titles? Those too, though those who fled reverted to their proper names. Would you recognise the Countess of Lindisfarne and the Isles? You've met her as plain Lady Hawkins, God rest her soul. The King? The King with no name? Plain Mr Farnham. The Choosing Ceremony? Me again. You would not recognise the origin, of course; it mimics the Degree Ceremonies of Universities, with a bit of the tradition of military recruitment thrown in. *The King's Shilling.*"

Another laugh, but a deeper one, followed. Defoe's face had changed, relaxed, but somehow older. Mark waited as Defoe closed his eyes.

Oh, how could anyone understand, now. Not even those I taught after that crock of shit made himself King. That it was a joke, a come-back, a sweet revenge. Degree in Literature? Critical Theory? Deconstruction? God help us, Cultural Marxism. Fun and games, for certain, till the tide turned, and you would be out on your ear. That ego-boosting Think Tank, just when you could see the future, and it looked bad. That tycoon Farnham sizing you up across the table. A boor, but a crafty one. The drink flowing, the flattery you knew was fake, but lapped up all the same.

"So, Defoe, reality's what we choose to make it? Who's we, do you think? Might it include you?"

That Gerontology Institute; so huge, so hush hush. Tutor my children, Defoe. Demolish the past and create a new future in their minds. A new future for all, in time. And how he had loved it when I told him: "there is nothing but the text." In English, of course. "Indeed. So, you will write it, and we make sure it is the only one. Except for those who need to know otherwise." Come, build my world, Farnham was saying. Mad, of course, but the pay was great. And a snub to the dismal utilitarian STEM domination in progress. Reality turned into a joke.

Four surly teenagers, taken out of school, already entitled little brats. But they'd liked him, and their father liked the flourishes I added to his sense of grandeur. And then that next pandemic. The Institute sealed, but myself given a treatment. Not that I knew what it was. Then the Catastrophe started in earnest. And continued. And dragged on till nearly all was destroyed. But not the Institute, Oh no.

It was the kids who had let him into the truth, after they had grown up. "Hey, Deffers, do you know you are immortal? Father told us the doctors misjudged the dose. You are good for at least 300, perhaps more. We'll see you out though, roll on the next millennium." Laughter. Laughter that had changed into something more feral when they discovered that all who were dosed were rendered sterile. Not only sterile, but with sexual desire dissipated to vanishing point. Other sources of satisfaction would be needed.

Then the plan. The Grounds, the Domain, everything. The King declaring his ascendency. The new sets of pupils. Pupils mostly already sterile. Mostly, but not all, especially when they were recruited from the Grounds, but rendered sterile or damaged once in the Domain. A few realised what had happened.

Oh, he was crafty, that Farnham. They'd refined the doses. Get 50 or less, and you depended on him and on his brats for more. A cadre, that was the word, a cadre of dependents who had nothing to lose. And crafting that text had been fun. Indecent fun. Even more when the Institute was abandoned to the rising sea, and a Court set up at Windsor.

A joke that had gone sour. Few knew the whole of his role, and some of the newly ennobled confided in him. Grounders, and more of them as those in the Domain died without issue. The book burnings; the dragging-off of malcontents to clear Badlands; worst of all, the role of the Institute in contaminating land such that fertility was maintained but ability impaired. That brat Arundel, plain Alfred Farnham before, rubbing his hands at the thought of obedient servants.

The sordid, almost baby farm character of some Grounds. My reality as much as Farnham's. My guilt.

Finally, the plot. The network built up by the likes of Ogilvie and Alfred Thomas. The escape using one of the last functioning helicopters. The War. The last of the drones to destroy the Peak. The Treaties. And his elevation, insisted on by those who thought his only fault was the education of the four. And all those who knew anything of his past now gone. And now, I spill my guts to a teenager from the back of beyond.

Mark was silent, ashen-faced. Defoe's eyes remained closed, and the man was so still that only the rise and fall of his chest indicated life. *Book of the King. Declaration, Choosing. Nobility.* All he had been brought up to, and all he had rejected. All originating in the mind of the man sitting before him. And the burden of that truth on his shoulders alone.

Seeing no movement, Mark silently left the room. To the woman waiting outside the door, he said, merely, "Lord Defoe seems to have fallen asleep. Perhaps someone should be with him when he awakes."

Things Fall Apart

29. Northern Calm

It had not taken long for Bohun and Cornwallis to return to Conisbrough after the gathering at Barlow. To the Visitor's relief, nothing much seemed to be required of him. Cornwallis could gather his forces and despatch them south. There was just the DC to deal with. The initial request to prepare to despatch most of his forces southwards was rapidly followed by specific demands for at least three-quarters of the whole complement, and at once. This proved easier than either Bohun or the Visitor had expected. Cornwallis in attendance, the meeting was short and amiable.

With Hope isolated, then moved south, the DC had been finding life hard. Lane had gone, and the new Truth and Justice Commissioner, Blackstone, knew nothing and required extensive explanations for everything. While Hope's summons to the south seemed like good news to the DC, a chance, he thought, that Hope would be vindicated, he had been unable to ask him about the myriad issues that the man had handled. Landed with the task of managing the Barrier system, with its complex of rotas, shifts and transfers, operated by Hope and his predecessor, the DC's head was aching. Already, he was finding recruitment to replace the horrendous losses on site hard to accomplish. Assessment had been bending his ear about conditions, sensing an opportunity with Hope out of action. Men were used to orders, not consultation necessitated by ignorance. Now, he was told to move most of them out. But, and it was a hopeful but, it seemed that the scope of his duties was to be greatly reduced as a result.

"Can I be clear, my Lord. No work on the Barriers? Mobiles to be withdrawn? What about the Assessment staff and the medics? The labour and their security and maintenance? I presume that at least we are still absolved from any responsibility for the Ground?"

It was clear to Bohun that the DC was floundering. He had played tough only from a safe distance. Years of sitting behind a desk saying merely *make it so,* as able and ambitious subordinates had proposed and carried out the necessary tasks, had rendered him flabby. Still, he had been right behind Hope, and he was a conduit to Arundel or his minions. Bohun saw a way out.

"Deputy Commissioner, our instructions ask for numbers, not names. I think there is a need for *proper* security work down south. Here we have few problems, and the tasks for security are much reduced. What would be more natural and appropriate than that the forces despatched were to be led by their most senior officer? What few tasks remain can easily be managed by the Visitor or myself, mundane tasks indeed. Go south, go where the action is. Rewards for outstanding service might be great. Just a suggestion."

A suggestion gratefully received. The DC left to start the logistics of moving his force. The three were left to deal with the reduction in forces that followed. Skeletal indeed: a platoon of Kingsmen, about the same for Security troopers; far fewer mobiles, and most of those two-wheelers. At least, the Chosen had been dispersed to their postings, and needed no attention. The major departed to organise the departure of most of his force. He would be left only with the Ground itself and the manning of the bridge. A simpler task than that left to Bohun and the Visitor.

***

Indeed, even before being summoned south to Barlow, the major had few problems within the Ground. The Deputies appeared competent, deliveries both ways across the bridge returned to normal. Watching the Outie bounds had turned up nothing. He had a couple of meetings with the bailiff, always joined by Amelia. Mostly amiable and token exchanges, for life was indeed returning to normal. He was, however, presented with the last, trivial, component of 'Crossing the River', as he had come to think of it. Jack and Sue were waiting in the Bailiff's office. Yes, they had been testing the crossing. Relics, that was all. Yes, Mark had been among them. When he disappeared, and was named an Evader, the bailiff had ordered all the kids to stay clear. Here, Jack lowered his head. The bailiff had laughed.

"There are some that need sense beaten into them, Major. Only once, mind." He turned to Sue.

"Sue, you said something to me that bears repeating to the major; about those uphill kids."

"Yes, sir, as I told Mr Mysliborski, those kids, they weren't serious. It was business for us, Major. For them, it was just a game, a challenge. No one was talking about leaving. To be honest, we thought them not properly grown up. Spoilt. Useful, though, they found the good places."

"What about David Reynolds then? He disappeared."

"Yeah, but he was a loner. Not like the others. A bit weird to us. Couldn't swim either."

The major had shrugged. It had ceased to add anything to Mark's evasion, and there had been no more incidents. He missed a stiffening in the bailiff's expression as Sue answered. Amelia did not.

Back at Bradfield, he started to round up most of his men and send them south. After the hectic travelling, and the oppressive atmosphere around the Court at Barlow, it was a dangerously soothing experience. A quick nod to the Deputies, and he turned to the task. He needed only a handful here, and the same at the bridge. But there were ten at a time at Midhope, and more to rotate the spells of duty. There was the mayor, confined to his apartment, without his family, but needing a guard. He called for the lieutenant and briefed him. He was to command the force going south.

"To aid the Hunt, sir?" A look passed across the junior's face, quickly suppressed. *News gets around*, thought Cornwallis. *I wonder how? I only learnt at Barlow.*

"Maybe so, Lieutenant, but there are other problems there, I am told. Outlanders have become rather less prone to run when we approach, as you have witnessed here. Have you served the Hunt before?"

"No, sir, but I have served with those that have. You will pardon me, I hope, sir, but what I heard was not pleasant."

"You heard correctly. In the field, though, Kingsmen follow the rules of engagement when not ordered otherwise and overlooked. Outies run, you let them go. I can only wish you luck, and honest military duties. I am to stay here under orders. Duty, Lieutenant, duty."

And lucky for me, too, he thought. The lad might face danger from Outies as he had done. Had he been ordered to lead his force southwards in person, he would have been looking over his shoulder. Hope would be there. Accidents happen. Dismissing the lieutenant, he walked to the Proctor's Station. Phelps was present, rising smartly to attention as he entered.

"Good to see you again, Captain. Everything in order?"

"Yes, sir. To be honest, very quiet indeed. No sightings of Outies. No kids along the river, we have kept watch. Even the city is more friendly than before. Your men have even exchanged banter with the locals."

"Well, I am about to make life a little busier for you. There's a flap on down south, and most of my men will be headed there. I will still be around, and in charge, but it's back to normal duties for you. Men at the Bridge, standard patrols along the bounds. My men will be pulling out of Midhope. We may need someone there, I'll let you know. In the meantime, I want you to move Arkell down to Barlow to join his family tomorrow. I'll have talked to him later today. Is there still a guard on the Norman house?"

"Yes, sir. I've allowed a room to be used as quarters, but no damage done. We had a message from Barlow, sir. That family have been having rows, sir. Mr Jacks sounded fed up, pissed off if you'll pardon me, his words. He'd have separated them, but he had to turn them over to Proctors in North Central. Great congregation of bigwigs using all his rooms."

And I was one of them, thought Cornwallis. Well, let's make the most of our authority while we have it. He wrote some orders. Muss and her children: would Mr Jacks send them south to another Ground. Contact Heredity, find her a husband; not hard. Miss and the daughter: back to their house, and you can remove the guard. Back in the Council Hall, he went to the mayor's apartment. Already, the absence of his wives and children was making itself felt, by smell as well as by sight. Arkell himself was unshaven and unkempt.

"You are to be moved, Arkell."

He paused. Terror in the man's face. You are a bastard, the major told himself. Not as big a bastard as Mac, but still. He could summon up little sympathy for the man.

"No, Arkell, not across the bridge, and not in the hands of Security, though you richly deserve it. Things are changing, at least for a while. You're a lucky man. I am reuniting you with your family at Barlow Transfer. You'll be held there until other matters get sorted."

He took a long look at the ex-mayor.

"You'll be moved tomorrow, Arkell. I'd take what you can on your back, because no-one else will carry it for you. It might be an idea to have a wash and some clean clothes, if you have any."

That left the Picklesses. Driving a two-wheeler solo, he drove up the now familiar route. Pickless was out in the fields, Miss and Muss in the Brewhouse, watched by a solitary Kingsman, who sprung to attention as he entered.

"Am I interrupting anything, ladies?" he asked. "Anything that cannot be left for a while? I need you and your husband to hear a few things together."

"Half an hour, if you will allow it, Major," said Miss. To her surprise, the major then sent the guard away, with orders she did not hear, and himself left them on their own. Returning to the front door, he waited for the sergeant. Duties at an end, sergeant, you are to be moved south, mobiles and all. Yes, now. Yes, all of you. Report to the lieutenant for further orders. He entered the house, and sat in the dining room. The six certificates of Service on the wall seemed to him to stare at him accusingly. Pickless appeared. The Major dismissed his guard. Wait till your wives appear, Pickless, I don't want to repeat everything. Soon, all three of them sat, eying him doubtfully.

"There are to be some changes here. Kingsmen will no longer be at your property. There will be a single Proctor with a horse, simply to alert us if there are any Outie intrusions. I take it you can feed the horse? As long as I am responsible for the Division, you are on parole. I cannot answer for what will happen thereafter. However, if I can restore Mayoral authority, your good behaviour and reputation for Service in all its forms," he glanced at the certificates, "will incline me to get the charges against you dropped. There will, of course, be no Mr Jones to assist as in the past. I advise you to ask the Deputies for apprentices."

The three looked at him, astonished. Already, they had been puzzled by the failure to carry them away, their liberty, although supervised, still there.

"There have been no Outie raids, I think, since I was last here?"

"No, Major, no sign. One of your men has watched us on a few occasions when we have taken stock onto the moor. Enough in itself to keep them away, or so I would have said until your last visit. We need that grazing, Major. If not, stock need to be moved elsewhere."

"You should know that there has been trouble to the south, trouble that has involved talks with Outies. My orders are clear, Mr Pickless, the boundaries are to remain absolutely sacrosanct on either side, or worse will follow."

He paused. Stock and a lone farmer: really a breach? Certainly, a Kingsman would be regarded as such.

"I am prepared to take a risk. Just yourself, and no more than half a mile in. Any sign of Outies and you are back inside, stock or no stock. No weapon either, Pickless. There is no Jones to protect you now. If they do come, it will not be for your cattle. It will be war, an invasion."

A moment's silence. Then: "May we ask a few questions, Major?"

"By all means, Miss Pickless. Whether you get an answer is another matter."

"Mark, Mark Norman. Has there been any news?"

"No, nothing. He disappeared into the Outland. As you know, he has not turned up here, nor anywhere else that we know of. He's presumed dead or in Outie hands, possibly both."

"You said trouble, Major, trouble with Outies. Yet we are being left unprotected. You are even giving us liberty of a sort. Now you mention war, a raid in strength?"

"No full answer there, I am afraid. All I can say is that we are confident that if we offer no provocation, there will be no incursions here. The Visitor is concerned to protect this Ground. Its future does not only depend on a lack of Outie incursions. Complete tranquillity is at present its best defence when forces are needed elsewhere."

"May we ask after Mark's family, Major?"

"You may. Miss and her daughter will be returning to their home for now. No doubt a marriage will be arranged for the daughter soon, and employment for the mother. Muss and her children will move to another Division."

He looked at the increasingly baffled faces. Any more questions? No. The Major left. For the first time in a month, the Picklesses were on their own. On their own and in their own farm. Not even the promised Proctor was yet installed.

***

The following morning, Cornwallis walked to the Council Hall. The sun shone; a solitary Proctor at the entrance saluted. In the hall, a clerk was dealing with a couple of farmers. Any of his men left were out of sight. He climbed the steps to the office and knocked. The Deputies rose to greet him. Papers were arranged tidily on the table in front of them.

"Welcome back, Major," said Amelia, "a proper welcome this time. Captain Phelps told us that most of your men were to leave, and, indeed, the last of them bar three in their station, as they have called it, left as we arrived."

They had little to tell him. The Division had returned to its normal, placid state. Only the delays caused by the absence of Mr Norman had caused irritation, but between them they were mastering the daily transactions and minor difficulties of everyday life. Markham in particular had taken pride in mastering Norman's often cryptic files and ledgers. Amelia had managed the school records, the occasional visits to the city, and the hygienists' doings.

"Well done indeed. But it is a precarious tranquillity, Muss Amelia, Mr Markham, very precarious. There are doings elsewhere that have directed attention southwards. Hence the reduction in my force. When such matters are resolved, attention may return here."

He paused. Markham looked puzzled, Amelia thoughtful, her eyes sharply focused on him.

"It was events here that have provoked those doings. Your Visitor has sought to maintain the very happy and productive workings of the Division that prevailed until those events. There are other, more direct methods that the Domain uses elsewhere to obtain its needs. Methods that become more attractive the more any Ground causes difficulties. You had a taste, I think, after the evasion of Mark Norman? The city certainly had it after that Reynolds boy's disappearance.

Your Visitor will be greatly helped by continued tranquillity. A complete lack of any hint of trouble. A willingness, Mr Markham, to meet demands from the bridge with speed and in full. It will not involve people at this time of year. You will need to visit the farms and explain the necessity. Even sacrificing capacity to replenish stock should be accepted. With good fortune, it will be temporary."

He remembered Midhope.

"I have not told you. For the time being, the Pickless family are reprieved. There is no longer any guard on them. It is a very productive enterprise, as you may have gathered from Mr Norman's records. They will need more labour, later at least one apprentice. To be taken out of school if needed, but discuss the matter with Pickless as soon as possible. In fact, I think it would be desirable to grant any requests for farm work, even to bring forward the summer stint. It's not far away in any case, is it?"

Markham looked a bit doubtful even as he nodded. Dealing directly with farmers had been down to Norman. His dealings had been with stores, with transport, with, to his irritation, the warehouses at the bridge, and the Reynolds family. Altogether too friendly with the squatters for his liking. He perked up when the major turned to Amelia.

"It's not uphill, though, that is of most concern to us, it's the city. It's cities, not just yours, that get the most attention from Security. It's there that we need really good behaviour; not a squeak of disobedience or insolence. Muss Amelia, I will require you to join me in a visit to the bailiff this evening. It will mean riding behind me on a two-wheeler. I trust that will be all right?"

"There is a first time for everything, Major. Yes, I will manage. Will you send a Proctor this morning to warn him? He is often out and about when us uphill," she glanced sideways at Markham, "are sitting down to our meal or putting children to bed."

It was shortly after six that the Major drove Amelia into the city. Off the main route to the bridge, Amelia had to guide him once again to the bailiff's office. No Proctor stood at the front door. Instead, two rather large men with cudgels stood impassively outside, while a number of folk stood apart, forming what might in charity be called a queue. At the sight of the Major's uniform, some turned their backs. There were mutterings and spitting. Nothing was said as they entered. Another man stood in the dark corridor, merely nodding as they knocked and entered the bailiff's office.

It had changed. The old chairs and sofas were gone, replaced by a table on which rested a map, a hand-drawn map, of the city. Mysliborski and a young man turned from it as they entered.

"Welcome, Muss Amelia, Major." A curt nod. "Excuse me one moment. Mehmet, leave us but stay within call. Tell Jack and Michael to send any waiting home. I'll be available in the morning, not before."

The bailiff had also changed since the major had last seen him. Tired, yes, but more than that. There was an air of desperation about him. Sat again behind his antique desk, he regarded them silently. It was left to the major to open the conversation.

"Problems, Mr Mysliborski? I had hoped to find things quiet, as they are uphill. Quiet is the means of survival now, and I came to give you some explanation as to why. I hope I am not too late?"

Mysliborski remained silent. Amelia intervened.

"Stefan, if there are problems, you should tell Major Cornwallis. His forces, as you will surely have noticed, are now drastically reduced. He has kept Security off our backs for a month, for which we should all be grateful. None of those involved in last month's troubles uphill have been delivered into their hands. That is the major's doing, Stefan. What has changed so much since our last meeting?"

The bailiff looked hard at Cornwallis. The ways of the Domain, their inconsistency, only added to his caution. Muss Amelia seemed to trust him, though.

"You have been away, Major, down south of necessity, I think. Did any news of disturbance reach you there, Major? Any news of Chosen sent for slave labour? Any accounts of Security raids on cities? Of Outlanders and our own crawling to refuge, half dead from contamination? News reaches me, Major, but news impossible to keep to myself. News with messages that are hard to obey. Stay quiet, those messages say. Stay quiet while others die or are dragged into the Domain. Those outside the door, Major? Wanting action; action to draw force away from our comrades. I am having difficulties here."

Cornwallis reeled. Trouble in the cities? The summoning of forces to the south had been, as far as he knew, dedicated to the Hunt. News travelled faster between the cities, it seemed, than anything the Domain could manage or choose to reveal. He chose his words with care.

"There is indeed trouble in the south. There have been Outie attacks on a Ground. There are Outies in numbers on unassigned land, Outies that are to be removed. They are a threat. Forces have been assembled from across the Domain, many from here. We are trusted, Mr Mysliborski, despite last month's trouble. You know, I think, that other Grounds are managed more directly, most particularly in the cities. There are those that have sought to apply such methods here. Your Visitor has repelled them. Quiet, particularly quiet in a time of trouble, and they are deflected. Trouble here, and force will be applied. Force that will break any resistance, and send hundreds to the Barriers or worse."

Mysliborski stared at the major in astonishment. *The man knows less, far less, than me*, he thought. Outies to be removed? Does he think we know nothing of the Hunts? Does he think that we do not know about *Service* on the Barriers? Does he even know himself? Clearly, he does not know why the cities in the south are provoking the Domain. Indeed, he does not know anything, unless he's playing a very skilful game; surely beyond his abilities? How far can I go with him?

"Major, Major, there is no need for such a nice choice of words. *Outies to be removed.* Major, we know about the Hunts. There are always Outies to be removed from somewhere, Major, year after year. Never requiring the transfer of His Majesty's forces that we are witnessing now. Drawing your forces away to a Hunt at the other end of the Domain. A Hunt that is more than a Hunt, Major, a Hunt demanding so much labour clearing Badlands that your precious Tadgies have got slack. There are escapes back home; escapes of notionally Chosen condemned to a short and painful life. Outies with them and all, poor stupid sods. Escapees that mostly die in our care. Labour used too close to home, Major. And not only there, Major. We know that Chosen here go straight to the Barriers or elsewhere equally putrid. Eyewitness accounts, Major, accounts sent from city to city.

Breed, breed more, has been the message. Breed to serve His Majesty honourably. What are we, Major? Reproductive Priority Zones. For what? To know that many of our children will live for a few years at best and in pain to serve no useful purpose clearing land that will clear itself in time. We know, Major."

Cornwallis was struck dumb. The man knew so much. More than me. But he's been told by someone to keep things quiet and was having difficulties. But what could happen? A few hygienists evaded? No selection was due for the best part of a year. No Security would be around to seek out the recalcitrant. A raid across the Bridge? Loss of life for little gain, and potential contamination. Was some grand insurrection planned? More loss of life, and why have they held back here? He thought back to the meeting in Barlow. Nothing had been said about the Grounds, at least not directly. No hint of a changed regime, just the need to manage the Hunt.

Mysliborski saw the look on Cornwallis' face. He relented, wearily.

"Don't worry, Major. There will be no trouble here that need concern you. You have done us the favour of getting those damned Tadgies off our backs. It's known, and we are grateful. Keep the hygienists under control, Muss Amelia, that's all. There's no Security to follow complaints in any case, and the major here has few enough men. There is anger, Major. We have heard what is happening elsewhere, and a common cause arouses us. Thanks to you, though, there is no target, at least for now. Keep supplies coming across the Bridge, and there will be nothing to disturb the peace. We have a sharp way with hotheads."

Amelia could not resist a question.

"Stefan, you have told me some of these things in the past, but much of it is new; all this palaver about a Hunt. There is something I do not understand. Trouble in other cities, trouble all at once, when some of these crimes have been known to you for years, and I assume elsewhere too. It is not spontaneous, this trouble, is it? And you have been ordered to hold back. Why? If you are unable to tell us, we can at least see that it comes from your fellows, a consideration that should weigh with you and all here."

Myslyborski looked from Amelia to the major and back again. Certainly, he could tell her, but the major? In the last resort, decent though he was, he was a commissioned officer of the Crown. Would he not be bound to tell those above him, to attract attention to matters the whole operation was designed to conceal? Matters he could not explain thoroughly even to his fellow citizens, now fired up with the lust for action. Matters that he himself did not fully understand.

"It does, and it will, Muss Amelia. Major, you will understand that I cannot say more. Only that we will ensure that neither you nor the Visitor will be given any cause for anxiety, so long as things remain as they are."

It was another silent drive back to Bradfield. As they dismounted, Amelia turned to the Major.

"Major, I understand your surprise. Greater than mine, I think, as I have learnt something of city ways. The bailiff avoided a topic. You might have missed it. He mentioned the Hunt, but not the Outie attack. They will have known about it for certain. There are some strange coincidences, Major. City folk are not fools willing to die in a ditch for a lost cause. I hope that honest men do not work for a bad one. Food for thought, Major."

***

The days passed. Staying in Bradfield, Cornwallis avoided the problems faced by Bohun and the Visitor in dealing with the Barriers and other operations in the Domain. The bailiff was as good as his word; no troubles were reported from the bridge. Markham was getting an education from his visits to all the farms uphill. News from the south was sparse, though difficulties with the Hunt filtered through. It was only on 22nd June that he observed Miss and Muss

Pickless in the queue to see the deputies. Nothing notable in that; there would be quotas to arrange. Maybe they were even negotiating extra labour.

It was, however, a more significant business than he could have guessed. Indeed, there were conversations about deliveries, and requests for labour at the stint. The two women were about to ask if Muss Amelia would take a break with them, when Markham, satisfied with the arrangements, departed on yet another visit. They did not leave with him. There was a short silence. Miss Pickless broke it.

"Muss Amelia, what is your opinion of Major Cornwallis? Is he honest? As you may imagine, we are amazed to be at liberty. But we cannot help but wonder what is behind it."

"Honest? Yes, I think so. But he is a servant of the Domain. His masters, our Visitor and that Lord Bohun, have a particular view of where the Domain's interests lie. A view not held elsewhere, as far as I can see. A view that sees our Ground best left to manage its own affairs. It's not only you that have been spared. Mr Arkell is reunited with his family in the Corridor. Miss Norman and her daughter have been allowed home, and we are looking for a suitable job for her."

Miss and Muss Pickless exchanged looks. Muss nodded.

"Muss Amelia, pardon us, but are there matters that you do not discuss with the major? How much does he require of you?"

"Oh, there are plenty. The man is not interested in the details. Give him a peaceful life and he is happy. He has no idea what goes on in the city, for a start. Even less than Arkell did before. Deliver the quotas, make no trouble. That is all he wants. Most particularly now, when they are having problems elsewhere."

She looked at them. There was obviously something behind these questions.

"I am not in the same position as Mr Arkell. You know that mayors always come from another Ground? That their position and credit depend on doing just what is required? As you know, I think, I was born here. I would never be mayor. I tell the major the truth if he asks, but no more unless I think it is wise to do so. I am not beholden. Now, I think it is the other way round; their future depends on us, for a while at least."

Another look exchanged.

"Muss Amelia, we have something to tell you, something that will condemn us afresh if it is known to the major. Our husband has spoken to Mark Norman. He is alive and with the Outies. The other Evader, Mr Jones, is with them too.

There is something important in the Outland that concerns them. Something that requires no disturbance here. Even the major said that there might be war. And we would be the target."

Amelia almost jumped in surprise. Cornwallis had given her only the vaguest detail of the Outie attack on Grounds elsewhere. Was one planned here? So, now there are two threats. On the one hand, the strong arm of Security, the Tadgies as the city called them. On the other, an Outie attack that might involve poison, a return to the devastation they learnt about in Chronicles. And, certainly, if the Domain entered in force, the Outies would respond. She assured the women of her confidence. The two women left, only somewhat comforted.

She dealt with a few other cases. Closing the office, she walked down the hill to the Normans' house. The door was opened by a pale, worn-looking Miss. Ushered inside, she saw the hallway half-full of boxes and trunks. Lisa emerged from the kitchen with a cloth held absent-mindedly in her hand.

"We expect you to move us, whatever is decided," said Miss, seeing Amelia's look. "The house is too big for two, unless you intend to move a husband for Lisa in here. Even then, the space would be generous. I was told you would arrange work for me; is it that you have come for?"

Amelia nudged them into the dining room, and made them sit.

"No, I have not come about a job. That has yet to be decided. I have news of a different kind, news that you must not reveal to any. Mark is alive. He is well and living with the Outies. Mr Pickless has seen him and spoken to him. There is some strange business beyond Midhope that we do not understand, but it has involved him."

There were gasps and tears, then a torrent of questions that Amelia was completely unable to answer. It was, after all, only bittersweet news; alive, yes, but with no chance of a return home. She managed to escape, returning to her own home in thoughtful mood. Next, there must be the bailiff. The bailiff without the Major.

30. Murder Most Foul

Arundel felt the sands shifting beneath his feet. It was one thing to plan for a war, a war to reverse the Outie gains, but quite another to deal with the issues not only of the cities, but also the alarming rise of dissent within the Domain. There had been more graffiti, now not just caricature balloons, but also hanging men. The absence of any slogans, any words at all, was unsettling. Unease did not deflect him, rather it stiffened his resolve and shortened his temper. He hoped soon to find Hastings disposed of, nullifying any quibbles about treaties. Things must be in motion, irreversibly, before Buckingham's return.

He summoned Lane, Sussex and Wilkes to sort out ways and means to regain control, and to maintain his ambitions. The meeting did not go well. Lane was saying, in effect, *give us the tools, and we will finish the job.* Recruits, rifles, undercover agents from the most commendably patriotic. More hangings. Wilkes then sardonically remarked that rifles and men were needed to confront the Outies. Sussex wavered as usual. In particular, he worried not only about long-term recruitment, thus siding with Wilkes, but also in seeking to prevent the draconian approach in the Domain itself.

"Brother, either a fresh assault on Cotswold, undermanned, or subjection of the cities, either may promote another Outie attack. Any casualties, and we will have problems closer to home. Those graffiti are but a foretaste."

For once, Arundel found himself torn, and he could see that it was showing. Both sides could see this and pressed all the harder. So it was, at first, that when there was a knock on the door, and a clerk handed a sheet of paper to Arundel, he welcomed a break.

"The report from Lord Steel, my Lord. I apologise for the intrusion, but it seems urgent."

The clerk left. Arundel read what was before him. Before he could gain control of himself, he uttered a string of blasphemies the like of which had not been heard there for centuries. Blasphemies that uttered by any common person would have them seen to by Security. His face darkened. He banged the table.

"God-forsaken traitor. Pig. May he rot in the hottest fires of Hell. Vermin. By God, there will be a reckoning."

All three of his companions stared at him in amazement. Arundel himself had agreed to the terms. It should have been a formal report, no more. What could Steel have said? They sat in silence. Arundel gradually subsided, cursing himself for his outburst. Now, he would have to explain.

"That little creep Hastings has defected. He's joined the Outies, but only let Steel know once the treaty had been signed. He should be dead. Treachery, treachery everywhere."

Lane was up in a flash. "My Lords, I will see to that clerk. This must not be known." He left the room.

Wilkes leaned to pick up the message. It was snatched back by Arundel. Sussex signalled the General to leave.

There was a silence. Sussex regarded his brother's face, a face that soon turned from his. Rage had turned to sullenness. Almost, there was a shifty look there.

"So, Brother, am I to see this message? Even if the clerk is silenced, Steel himself is aware, and a long way from here. Is he to be silenced too? Who may he have talked to? Secretaries at Retford? And the staff at the Point? Will it remain hidden from Alice when she returns?"

Arundel pushed the paper towards him, his face still averted. Sussex read it while his brother sat silently. There was more than defection. An attempt to murder, an attempt that failed, a suicide as a result. Sussex passed the message back, and sat with his head in his hands. Steel had been a friend of Hastings, he knew. Both lightweights with the knack of being agreeable. Lightweights who were all too easily dismissed as expendable. His brother had indeed intended to dispose of Hastings; to what practical advantage, brother dear? As it was, either Hawkins or that crafty O'Neill had foreseen the likelihood and exposed the intention. Whatever Security did now, and he had no doubt that they would attempt suppression, the story would spread.

He looked at his brother, who showed a face full of defiance.

"Brother, you know what old Defoe would have said with that little giggle of his: *Another nice mess you've gotten me into.* Not so nice, this one. Let Security try to suppress it by more murders, and news of those will circulate.

Circulate within the Domain. Come to Council, and Alice will know. She will speak. Our father will likely side with her; at the least, any proposals will be stalled."

Arundel scowled. He looked straight at Sussex now, defiance in his eyes.

"It is the Outlands or nothing, brother. The sooner the better. If force is needed in the Domain, so be it. Do you want to see us dwindle while we wait for Alice to find us a Garden of Eden overseas? How long has she tried? A hundred and forty years?"

"At the very least, let me deal with Steel. Loose Security on him, and half the Court will be with her. His disappearance will be noted."

Arundel nodded. Sussex left him, alone in the room he had so long dominated with his presence. His mind whirled. He had, after all, a weapon at his disposal, the released doses for the Hunt. For obvious reasons, they had not been used. Cut the rations, and he had perhaps forty to offer. He went to the door and told the guard to fetch Hope as soon as he could be found.

It was not long before Lane and Hope returned together, the latter looking distinctly better. The clerk? Confined, my Lord, but we cannot be certain who else heard the message or second-hand reports of it. We are supervising the telephony room. Lord Sussex has been talking to Lord Steel. We have no authority to regulate his messages.

Arundel looked at the two sat in front of him. Both loyal, to be sure; loyalty reinforced by their position. Were the tide to turn, both would suffer. But that Lane: competent to a point, but with an agenda of his own. Hope, now there was a man with the right spirit. Simple enforcement. And no dose. He turned to Lane.

"We must have security, Lane. See to it that graffiti are removed and the perpetrators hung. Hung in public, here and anywhere else. And see to building up forces outside each city where we have withdrawn. Wilkes will be told to support you when we are ready. And reclamation is to remain halted, Lane; first things first. Go to it, man. I want a report each morning."

Lane left, concealing his displeasure. It was not the orders as such, no less was needed. But Hope was left behind. Arundel had more in mind than mere retrenchment, and he, Lane, was no longer to be a part of it.

"Commandant, I think that you have never seen His Majesty?"

"No, my Lord. I understood that it was only members of his Council, and his personal attendants who had that privilege."

"True, though there are others in Court who catch sight of him on official occasions. You will be unaware, I think, that His Majesty is a very old man, not only in appearance but also in his mental capacity. I mean old in terms of those not given a dose. Unfortunately, that has been the case for some time."

Hope looked at Arundel. An answer was clearly expected, but which one to give?

"I am sorry to hear that, my Lord. I understood that His Majesty's wishes were made known through Council. Those of us subordinate simply did as we were told. We assumed that our orders were sanctioned at the highest level. May I be pardoned if in error, my Lord, but is it the case that His Majesty is sometimes unaware of what is sanctioned in his name?"

"Regrettably, that is the case, Commandant. Or, what is worse, he may resist good advice. Of course, when a course of action is agreed by all, and especially by us, his children, his assent is given willingly. But you were at the meeting at the Treaty Point. You will be aware that we are not always in accord? What do you imagine happens then?"

Hope remained silent. He remembered the humiliation of his silencing by Lady Buckingham. He had noticed the early departure of Buckingham and Pendennis. He knew that they had, as Lane had relayed Arundel's words 'gone native' where Grounds were concerned. He knew, though, that Arundel had prevailed; the Hunt had taken place, though not with the outcome expected.

"Well, man, did you think about it?"

"We carried on according to your wishes, my Lord. It did not occur to me to question your authority." Feeling a little more was required, he added, "I was honoured by the trust you placed in me, my Lord, as we travelled south. I had hoped to restore order and obedience in the Grounds."

"Which we surely will, once we are in a position to do so. And it will be led by one ennobled, Commandant. 100 at least, and the Truth and Justice position on Council, with every prospect of further enhancement. But there is a difficulty; all our actions so far have had the Royal sanction. The unfortunate outcome of the Hunt has changed things. There are those who look to a policy of appeasement, both as regards the Outies and as regards the Service due from the Grounds."

Hope dared to look straight at Arundel. He saw an appraising look back, a direct stare. A stare that asked: *and if that sanction cannot be obtained?*

"My Lord, if His Majesty lacks the capacity, or is manifestly incapable, by what means does the Domain decide on any action to protect its interest?"

"A pertinent question, Commandant, and one which we have not had to face until now. Faced with conflicting advice, His Majesty has always declared for delay, for deferment without resolution. It has served well enough. No longer, Commandant. We can no longer be sure of his decision, and if given in Council, it will be taken as binding."

"If he is not present, my Lord? If he were to be sequestered for medical reasons? Forgive me again, but has he been absent from any meeting of his Council?"

"Oh, he has been absent often enough when we are all agreed beforehand. But you have grasped the point, Commandant. If he is absent, and may not be consulted, there must be other ways to arrive at a decision. Mere postponement will not do; His Majesty's absence must be so prolonged, and of a nature as to require decision without his sanction. Bend your mind as to how that might be achieved."

"Who has access to His Majesty, my Lord, other than his children and his personal attendants? Doctors? Does he appear in public? I would suggest that if His Majesty was declared to be suffering from an infectious and debilitating disease, there would be grounds for isolating those who came into contact with him. Yourself and any you choose excepted, of course. It would require a doctor willing to certify both those potentially infected, and those that were clear."

Hope again studied Arundel's expression. So far, so good. Arundel's face had relaxed; almost, there was a grin.

"Well done, Commandant. Such isolation, however, must be secure. Security would be involved, men who would ignore any protests from attendants. Men who would repel any attempt to gain access to those attendants, never mind His Majesty himself. Men who would, of course, be well rewarded, though not to the extent of their commander. Do you know of such men, Commandant? Men who can act as soon as tomorrow?"

"They will be found, my Lord. The attendants? A doctor? We will need the names and whereabouts. A holding place, my Lord? We can scarcely prevent Lady Buckingham, pardon me, from entering the King's apartments by force, at least not without a public affray here in the castle."

"The Armouries. They have secure spaces. I will see to it that they are to expect guests, unnamed guests of course, and to do what you tell them. Leave the doctor to me. Wait for a moment."

Arundel went to the door, and sent the guard on a mission. Soon, the Major-Domo appeared.

"Bobby, we have a medical issue concerning His Majesty's attendants. You will supply Commandant Hope here with the details of all who have had dealings with his Majesty in the last four days. Addresses, please, and details of who will be on duty tonight and tomorrow, and when their turn ends. And can you find Dr Thorndyke and send him to me directly?"

After the Major-Domo departed, there were more details to settle. At night. In full decontamination gear. Those taken to be cloaked. A closed litter for the King. An authorising letter from the doctor, with Arundel's seal. Hope left to start assembling a force. Just the doctor to deal with. Arundel set to work writing. It was not long before Thorndyke appeared. Arundel's memory had not failed him; the King's own doctor was much the same height and build as Arundel himself.

"Thank you, doctor. I fear I have bad news. Miss Greenhalgh has shown symptoms that suggest what I think is known as the white fever. She is isolated, but we will need to do the same for all who wait on His Majesty, indeed, to isolate the King himself. I would be obliged if you would sign this authorisation that I have prepared, doctor. Yes, several copies. Once you have confirmed the diagnosis, I will seal them. They are not valid without that."

"Should I not examine Miss Greenhalgh, my Lord?"

"Of course, doctor, but you will need full gear, surely? I want first to show you some places of isolation, here in the castle, but well-secured. If you will sign these now, I will show you the rooms allocated; we need your sanction and any recommendations you may have. Give my man outside instructions, and he will collect your gear and bring it here. When we return, you can see the woman, and I will affix my seal to these papers."

The doctor signed. The guard departed. Arundel led Thorndyke along many corridors and down many stairs. Through several doors that could be bolted only from the side they approached. Eventually, they entered a small, bare room with no light other than a small grill, well above reach. Another door, closed, was present on the opposite wall.

The doctor turned towards Arundel in surprise. Arundel's dagger went in. A dagger well coated with poison. Arundel did not even bother to stifle the cries. Nor did he wait until all movement had ceased. Shutting and bolting the door behind him, he returned the way they had come, not only bolting but locking several of the intermediate doors with keys kept on his belt.

The guard returned with the gear. He was despatched to tell the family and servants that their master was now quarantined. Arundel placed his seal on each of the authorisations. All was now ready.

***

Sussex had to be guarded in his telephone conversation with Steel, a Steel still shocked both by the defection of his friend and the suicide that had followed it. At least, the man had the sense to get clerks out of the room when he made his call. Witnesses? Steel himself, and the clerk that was with him. Garrison? Knew that there had been a suicide, but not why. They knew, though, that Hastings had returned to the Outland. No, they could not contact others unless through him.

"What am I to do my Lord? Should I remain here, as required by the previous treaty?"

"Yes, don't move. Certainly, do not come back to court. What about your clerk?"

"Philip? He's a man of sense. He's said nothing. But of course, we have had to explain Davis' absence. We agreed to say he was infected, and that helps us explain the garrison's isolation. It seems to have worked. He visited the Outies before, and we can blame that. I've kept myself and Philip a bit apart too."

"What's left of Security?"

"Davis was in command. We've a corporal and three men, that's all. Everyone else was sent down south."

Sussex rang off. It would not be long before those few Security men learnt the truth about Davis from their superiors. He had wondered about getting Steel to feign a breakdown in the telephone line, even to cut it. But that would undoubtedly send Security north, and he was already wondering how his brother, or Lane for that matter, might choose to deal with things. Steel had been remarkably astute, and that would protect him for a while. Hastings' defection was known only to a few. He would be thought to remain a hostage as long as no one talked.

It was not long after that Steel received another call from Lane. A call, naturally enough, to establish who knew what. The conversation went much as it had done with Sussex until the question of the garrison came up. Steel found himself at the end of a command, a command that he would have found impertinent at any other time.

"My Lord, that garrison is to remain in place. Do not relieve it. No messages other than to yourself are to be allowed. Your suggestion of infection is to be relayed to any others. We will send a force to remove them securely as soon as possible."

"There is a weekly rotation, Lane, and it includes the supply of food and other things to the Point. Go much beyond, and the garrison will start to have problems."

"Ask Corporal Tiggs to ring me. If food is needed, it will be delivered by him and a trooper alone. I hope to have a force with you in a few days."

Scarcely a demand he could refuse, thought Steel, *and then the death of Davis would be known more widely*. It turned his mind to Hastings. Security had tried to kill him, surely ordered by Lane. And not just the top, but with willing subordinates down the line. Become inconvenient, and you were disposed of. So easy to say: *we regret that the garrison had died, some cursed Outie plague to which the bastards were immune.* And could not the same reasoning be applied to himself and Philip? Maybe even to the staff at Barlow?

Although now nearly a hundred years old, Steel retained much of the youthful vitality and naivety of twenty-eight, the age at which he had received his dose. Life had been undemanding for one who had won his spurs at a Hunt, one who had enjoyed the life at Court and the camaraderie of a spell in the army. The Four had showered favours on the likes of himself and Hastings. At worst, there had been dull postings at places like Retford. Yes, Security were a bunch of unmannerly thugs, folk who dealt with the seamier side of life in the Domain; a side we could avoid, a force we could mock in the privacy of an officer's mess. The tradition of chivalry, easy to uphold when it meant little more than turning a blind eye to fleeing Outies, miserable sods unworthy of a Kingsman's sword or bullet. Now the unmannerly thugs were on his doorstep, or nearly so. Old Millsie, out at the Point with his men. As they would say to each other in the mess, salt of the earth, one of nature's gentlemen. Warn Lieutenant Kipling? What good would it do? If he tried to do anything, he'd pay the price as well. Steel did not sleep well that night. What repose he managed was broken by replays of the falling body of Davis. And those words of Hastings: *eminently disposable.*

A simple breakfast the following morning, and Steel did the usual rounds of the way station and garrison. Normally, a boring task, enlivened only with the exchange of banter with Kipling and his men, now down to a mere forty, including the five at the Point and the ten at Barlow. Today, though, Corporal Tiggs asked to accompany him, in a manner that suggested that to refuse would be to cause offence, *reportable* offence. He was being watched. He managed to shake him off only by telling him, in Kipling's presence, to brief the soldiers as to disease while he talked to the Lieutenant. Tiggs complied, with a frown.

Now, he realised, I have to tell Kipling the truth. There is no other way. At the least, Security would lack the means to overpower a forewarned force. Kipling listened, listened without any questions. Steel did not suggest any solutions, just the likely outcome. Kipling's reaction startled him.

"My Lord, I am not surprised. My last posting was on the edge of the Kentish Badlands. We were to support Clearance to make more coalfields available. There were riots beyond Security's control. I saw what those bastards did. We had to shoot Unchosen in scores before order was restored. I saw those bodies, my Lord. The signs of contamination in plenty, but that was not all. There were lashes, broken ribs, ears cut off." He paused. "My Lord, I'll not let Mills and his men fall into the hands of those bastards. But what can we do? We cannot hide them, and there is nowhere to run to."

Steel stared straight at him.

"There is a way. A way I intend to take, Lieutenant. The way taken by Lord Hastings. To cross into the Outland. If your men are willing, of course, and if they are willing to let me do the same. If not, then we will all be destroyed, discreetly, of course. You can prevent this, Lieutenant, easily enough by arresting me now, at the cost of the squad at the Point."

"I'll not do that, my Lord. But how will you evade Tiggs? Scoot off, and he will report it. You will have time enough, I guess, but can we not delay the discovery, and provide a cover?" Kipling thought hard. "My Lord, I will give you written orders for Mills. If all agree, then all should leave with you. You should telephone that all but yourself and Mills himself have died and been buried. They can make false burials easily enough. Then disappear. They'll not want to go near the place for several weeks. Knowing them, they'd send Jacks out from Transfer before risking themselves."

"Thank you, Lieutenant. I wonder if you can distract Tiggs for while? Maybe a trail and sightings of a stranger needing his dogs? I will tog up in full gear with my clerk, and depart on a diagnostic journey. I will tell Jacks and his staff that I am tending the sick and dying. They won't believe it, but they will pretend to, as they have with Hastings."

Steel rose, and the two shook hands in a very formal way. Kipling was about to wish Steel all good luck, even now suppressing the forbidden God Speed You, when Tiggs knocked and entered. He looked suspiciously at the two, but departed with Steel back to the waystation.

***

It is midnight in Windsor. Suited and visored Security forces call on several houses, waving before the bemused inhabitants the orders to remove them to quarantine. A doctor, in full protective gear accompanied by a squad of similarly covered men arrives at the King's apartment. The same orders are shown and the guard dismissed. Soon, they leave, two escorting a frightened woman, the remainder carrying the King himself. A shout from His Majesty, and the doctor acts quickly to gag him.

The exit from the castle is seen only by other kitted-up Security men. A waiting litter receives the old man, and the small procession hurries towards the Armouries. Past the guardhouse, the woman and the King are parted. She is led to a large room in which others, men, women and children have already been confined. The King is left in a small room by himself. Security guard both.

Alone with Hope in one of the Master-at-Arms' offices, Arundel removed his helmet to ease the stifling sense of confinement. He removed from his satchel a metal flask, an antique no less. A flask whose contents had once refreshed those engaged in Hunts of a less barbarous nature than those he had fostered and relished. He handed the flask to Hope, along with three thimbles.

"Very good, Hope. Here is a medicine, a preventative. Each…*each patient*, is to drink a thimbleful. It must be seen to be swallowed, Hope. Compulsion if necessary."

"Every one, my Lord?"

"Every one, Hope. All should have taken it within fifteen minutes. The door is to be locked behind you, and a guard placed. In the morning, we will arrange more suitable accommodation."

Even Hope was disturbed by the grin on Arundel's face.

"His Majesty, my Lord?"

"Oh, I think he merits a visit from his personal physician, don't you? And, by the way, no one from the Armouries is to enter this building. The Master knows this, but there may be some who have not heard. You have the quarantine declaration to show them."

Arundel replaced the doctor's helmet and walked slowly towards his confined sovereign's room. He dismissed the guard outside and entered. The King was sat in a chair, his gag still in place, his hands too feeble to reach the knot behind, the gag too tight to pull down. He had wet himself. And worse, as Arundel's nose soon told him Without a word, Arundel advanced on the old man. A quick cut, and the gag fell away. Another, much smaller flask unscrewed. The old head forced back, and a squeeze on the jaw. Up close, the King looked at his assailant through the visor. A screech of rage came forth, and he jerked his head. Poison splattered his chest. Arundel shifted to get a better grip. Feeling a thumb in his mouth, the King bit with all his strength as poison filled his mouth. Arundel recoiled, the flask falling to the floor. Glove notwithstanding, there was blood, and a glove soaked in the deadly fluid. He gripped frantically to remove the glove, his curses drowning out the croaks of the King. In a final gasp, though, it seemed to Arundel that he heard the mocking words, *beaten by Outies, beaten by Outies.* He left, nursing his injured hand and seeking water to wash away the blood and poison.

In the larger room, most had taken the medicine trustingly. All might have gone well, had one trooper not administered the dose to the very smallest child first. Symptoms of distress appeared, and others began to resist. The necessary force was applied, but there were now cries and struggles. The task was completed, but for one very young and newly promoted lieutenant, the scene was too much. His vomiting in a far corner of the room went unseen by others. Security left; the door was locked.

***

It was shortly after dawn that the way station at Retford was awoken by a hammering on the front door. The porter admitted a flustered Lieutenant Kipling. A break-in at the barracks, strangers seen running in the half-light. Dogs and Security needed, needed now. A rather bemused Tiggs was ordered to follow the Lieutenant with his men. Tranquillity restored, Steel turned to the warden.

"Mr Grayson, we have a problem concerning the garrison at the Point, since they are to be isolated. Philip and I will go to the transfer point to see what Mr Jacks can do. The remaining mobile is not to be used until we return, unless an order is received from down south."

The clerk had been quick to grasp the situation. Philip Garfield had been reared in a heavily policed Ground in the east of what was once Norfolk. Little time had been spent by the authorities in persuading Grounders of the honour and rewards of Service. His parting from parents and siblings had been far from welcome to anyone. Evasion was often contemplated, and as often rejected: where was there to run to? Even Outland was far away and unknown. Hence, Steel had no problem showing him that their lives were now at risk. The journey to Barlow was uneventful. Mr Jacks was told that they were going to investigate the situation fully kitted up, and to ferry food to the Point if necessary. It was just before noon that they reached the Point.

They were greeted with some astonishment by sergeant Mills and his squad of four. Since the dramatic events two days previously, they had had no messages other than from Philip, merely reinforcing the order given at the time. Out of the room when Hastings' defection had been formally declared, it had not taken them too long to arrive at the correct conclusion. The suicide had not been explained; Philip had discreetly removed the box of sweets left by the Outlanders, and placed it in a bag. It had returned to Retford with them.

Steel started gently.

"You all saw some strange things, right? Things that take a bit of time to get your head round? You are not the only ones. For now, the official story, the one that's known to most, is that you might be infected by something Davis caught in the Outland; something that killed him and isolated you. It might have carried Lord Hastings off as well."

He looked at them. Only the sergeant showed anything other than a kind of expectant bafflement. It was Mills who asked the obvious question.

"All well and good, sir, but how long are we to be quarantined? You'll have told those up top what actually happened?"

"Naturally, Sergeant. I could scarcely do otherwise. And for clarity, Lord Hastings did defect, and Davis tried to poison him. It was detected, and Davis took the least painful way out."

Mills looked at Steel. "I'm thinking, sir, that there are those who would want to be quite sure that those things stayed secret. We'd not say a word, would we, lads, even on the Book?"

There were nods. The soldiers sensed something wrong, but could not place it. Davis was no loss to them. Hastings? The nobs were a law unto themselves.

"That's so, Sergeant, but it's not only you. I know the truth, as does Philip here. Now think on this; suppose you were in charge of Security. Suppose that it was necessary to make sure that what happened remained unknown?"

He let the question hang. It depended on Mills. There was a long silence. The men looked to Mills for help. Eventually, the Sergeant addressed the men.

"You heard him, lads. How does it remain unknown for ever? If you wanted to make sure someone you were not sure of stayed silent, silent or you paid a price, what would you do? Especially if you were T and J?"

The penny dropped.

"Only one way there, sarge. You mean that we're for the chop, his Lordship here too."

It was Steel's opening.

"You are right. We are all dead men walking. Don't think it will be exposed. Once they have collected enough force, they will be here. Dead and buried, all of us. So sad, an infection brought by Outies. Right now, the only reason it hasn't happened is that that they don't have the means, and all but those at the top think you are infected. That keeps them off, and your comrades at Retford wouldn't do it. It would be Security goons that came."

He handed the note from Kipling to Mills. The shock on Mills' face showed plainly. He turned to Lord Steel.

"Please, sir, tell them. You must know what he has said."

"Your lieutenant has advised you to follow my example. To defect to the Outlanders. The only path to safety. Your superiors have, as they say, sold you down the river. I can assure you of this, you will be welcomed. Lord Hastings has certainly come to no harm."

The four soldiers looked imploringly at Mills.

"Unless any of you is of a mind to stop me, I'm crossing with his Lordship. If you've a mind to it, you can shoot us or bind us. I'll not fight you. Otherwise, we cross together."

There was a collective sigh. A voice uttered, "We're with you, Sarge." It was lucky, but known to the sergeant, that none had long term partners; such were rare within the Domain.

Steel was left to get things organised. A call to Jacks; two dead, Mr Jacks, and the rest sick. We will stay to help them. No one to approach. Pass the message to Retford. A flag to summon the Outlanders. It was Jane Collins that marched up the hill, two *bountifully endowed* guards with her. To her astonishment, there were seven people facing her in the reception room, and five rifles and a pistol on the table between them. She recognised Steel and his clerk, and also Mills.

"Gentlemen?"

"You see before you, Lieutenant, the whole population of the Point. We are of one mind. We wish to seek sanctuary with you."

Collins stared at them, dumbstruck. Another Lord? Kingsmen? She wished Lady Hawkins or Chief O'Neill at her side. Was this some trick of the Domain, some ploy to seek out Hastings, or to spy on their preparations. Steel saw her hesitation.

"Please, Lieutenant. I can understand that this is a surprise. Feel free to take possession of our weapons, and our ammunition." Here, he nodded, and boxes were placed on the table. "It must be quick, Lieutenant. We have covered our tracks by a tale of infection, but we are dead, dead within days if you refuse us. You witnessed Davis' death. All those on this side who know of that foul attempt on Hastings' life and its failure are as good as dead."

Collins relaxed. The Outlanders gathered up the rifles. At her command, they escorted the soldiers and Philip down the hill. Steel handed his pistol to her.

"Lieutenant, there a few things yet to do. There should be graves, empty, of course. I should answer the telephone if it rings. Tomorrow, I will give a last call, recording the deaths of all. I will leave the instrument dangling. And then join you downhill. The Domain will be happy, for now, to accept the tale of infection, and we should make it easy for them to do so. I would spare as many as possible."

"You will need some help with those graves, my Lord. And others to keep watch on that road. I will send some to help, and to look out. If any approach, you must run." She left him to himself, alone in the abandoned Point.

31. The Tangled Web

Arundel returned to his rooms, washed his hand, bandaged it, and changed his clothes in time to descend for the formal Court breakfast. The hand throbbed under the bandage, and his feeding was one-handed. *Just a stupid accident. I fell and broke a vase*, was the standard response to expressions of concern. He broke some news.

"Gentlemen, I regret to inform you that there is disease among His Majesty's staff. His Majesty has been secluded, and all staff and their families quarantined. No one other than Dr Thorndyke and a fully protected Security force under Commandant Hope are to approach them. I will report further when Thorndyke has made another inspection. In the meantime, I suggest we restrict ourselves as much as possible to our own apartments."

A shiver went around. Some diseases were no respecters of doses, be they never so large. Soon, only Sussex and a few servants remained. Sussex eyed his brother warily.

"What infection is this, Brother, and where has it come from? We have been free of all but the most trivial for decades."

"Thorndyke suspects the White Fever. He will visit all those confined later this morning, and we will get a report. As to where it comes from, I have no idea. I suggest you join Lane in the telephony room; get him to transmit the news."

Sussex departed with a single, frowning glance at his brother. Arundel returned to his own apartment. The doctor's gear upon him, he descended by a back way to meet Hope. With a Security escort, they walked to the Armouries. Arundel's pace was slow and shaky. All were dead. There was a hurried consultation. A message to the Master-at-Arms: *A fast and terrible death for most, the remainder deathly ill. Coffins, sealable coffins, to be obtained for Security. No one to approach the building.* One task remained. Fearing recognition despite the gear, Arundel sent Hope to reveal to the Master that one of those isolated was His Majesty.

"Say alive, but probably not for long, Hope. It needs to stay that way for now. Then there is one last task for you. Thorndyke's gear must be reunited with his body and destroyed. Come to my apartment to collect it; I will instruct you further."

In due course, Hope presented himself at Arundel's door. The doctor's gear discarded, his master was pale and even shaking. Instructions were given in a softer tone and keys handed over.

"There is another door to that room. Get men to leave a coffin outside it. Take just one with you, seal the body inside, then get a team to remove it for incineration. Another sad fatality, but his family will be well rewarded. When all is finished, we will arrange for your reward. 100 at first, I think, *my Lord* Hope, and the seat on Council. We will then arrange for your men to receive their rewards in turn. I was thinking of promotions and the promise of more; Credits too, of course. Will that seem appropriate?"

"For the two sergeants, my Lord, more is needed. Years added. I suggest 25 and promotion; For the rest, the hint that they may receive years in due course. I think 25 is below the threshold for nobility? At a time of their choosing, of course. Oh, there is young Gregory, my Lord. Is he too young?"

"Very well. Yes, he is too young. Just a promise for now. We have always waited until the beneficiary is at least 25. Believe me, an elderly teenager is more than we can cope with. A degree of resentment arises when the side effects of a dose become apparent. There are wild oats to be spent first. Let him win his spurs by helping you with the body."

Hope was kept very busy for the next few hours. There were not that many on whom he could rely. First, removal of most bodies from the Armoury, that of the King included, and their incineration. Then yet another to be carried through back offices in the castle when called. Satisfied, and with John Gregory in tow, he followed the tortuous route to the back room where Thorndyke's body lay.

The cold in that basement room had delayed any decay. But the doctor's body was not that of one who had died of fever. It lay contorted on the floor, the disordered uniform of an unprotected doctor upon it. A bloodstained waistcoat betrayed the fatal stab. Lips pulled back over the gaping mouth, which was covered with encrusted blood. Once again, John vomited, leaning against the wall. Impatiently, Hope opened the other door and dragged the coffin inside. Lid removed, he turned to John, still retching by the wall.

"Pull yourself together. You'll see worse than this in the Service. Take the feet, man, and let's get him in the box and nailed down."

John moved to do as he was told. But the body was stiff and bent. While Hope cursed, the boy was overtaken by another spasm and dropped his end. Hope was left to juggle and force the corpse into the coffin, add the gear, and nail down the lid. Task completed, he ordered John out of the room, went to the door from which he had drawn the coffin, and whistled. Four troopers entered and removed it. Locking and bolting both doors, he led John back up the passages to the castle rooms. Dismissing him, he sought out the Major-Domo to report yet another sad victim of the mysterious infection.

John's quarters were still the communal ones of the young, news of his promotion having failed to reach the barracks staff. Unable to face company, he tottered out into the streets, to clear his head. At the Armouries, he had at first been sure that it was indeed medicine that was being given. The child crying and twisting might not have proved otherwise, had it not been for the force used on those still to be dosed. Left to prevent entry from elsewhere, he had not witnessed the scene facing those who entered the following morning. The doctor's body, though, that was enough to strip him of any illusions. It was not just traitors that suffered.

His excursion did not last long. His uniform, that might once have provoked an evasive mixture of fear and respect, now attracted outright hostility. Folk spat in the street as they passed him. Worse, as he passed an alley, stones were thrown. One hit but did not harm. It was all he could do to avoid breaking into a run back to the castle. As it was, he passed more graffiti, balloons and hanged men both. Rounding a corner, he encountered a boy, paintbrush in hand. He halted, but the boy merely stared back, daring him to act. John walked on.

Back at barracks, he soon found that his experiences were not unique. Mildly reprimanded for venturing out alone, he discovered that orders were now for a minimum of four together outside the walls, and all to be armed. There had been hangings and arrests, but shots had been fired at crowds too. Smelling the vomit, and seeing John's condition, a sergeant ordered him to his bunk. The others now on duty, he was left to his own thoughts.

***

Lane had been ensconced in the telephony room when Arundel had made his announcement. The arrival of Sussex, and with him the news, caused something of a flurry. Sussex dismissed all but a couple of clerks. Lane had been taking calls from all over the Domain, mostly from transcripts taken down by others. Now, he was obliged both to transcribe the contents of some himself, and answer a barrage of questions from Sussex about affairs. His mood darkened when Sussex instructed the clerks that all calls other than from Security itself were to be handed to him. Soon, there were indeed calls from others. The Visitor in Northernmost called, with Bohun by his side to confirm his account. Cattle plague in the Ground and Domain. An outbreak of fever in the RPZ. All had been sealed off. *First here, now there*, thought Sussex. Some Outie plot? It seemed unlikely; Outies valued life too much. And they had what they wanted in the treaty. When the attendant clerk had completed the transcript, he handed it to Lane, who was incredulous.

"My Lord, it is not to be believed. They know very well that we would conscript more. They know that we might use the north to strike at the Outies. The bluff should be called; Court doctors should be sent, with an escort, and written orders to be admitted."

"You will not get those orders from me, Lane. I will give instructions to block travel north given to garrisons at each way station. Lord Bohun has installed a force at his southernmost way station. I think you will face mutiny if you attempt to breach the cordon when infection is advertised. For Majesty's sake, Lane, we are losing enough people already. Infection here as well. There is enough to do at Ground crossing points further south to keep you occupied."

There was a grunt from Lane, who returned to his business. Damned precautions, that was all the man was good for. His thoughts were interrupted by a call from corporal Tiggs at Retford. Almost immediately, there was a sound of shouting at the other end. Tiggs was replaced by an angry lieutenant. The clerk listening in, Lane had no choice but to hand the receiver to Sussex. Lord Steel had gone to investigate an outbreak of disease at the Treaty Point. He had found several dead, and had isolated himself there with his clerk. Jacks at the Transfer Station had confirmed that Steel had passed through in full protective gear and called back with the news.

Sussex pondered. Yet more disease, plausible enough given the report from the north. They had concealed Hastings' defection under the pretence of disease: was it now real? Was the earlier deceit known to the garrison? Steel certainly knew, as would his clerk. Steel was not a complete fool. He would know that all who had witnessed the events at the Point were at risk. The garrison left at Retford too, though Steel's disappearance would give them cover. Confirming that all travel should be prohibited, he reluctantly passed the receiver to Lane. He could not hear Tiggs' report to Lane, but the latter's face darkened. His responses to Tiggs were cryptic and brief. The call ended with a clearly enunciated message that he was to obey the lieutenant's orders until a more senior officer arrived. Lane had waved his clerk away. No record, noted Sussex.

Lane sat silent for a moment. While he had instructed the corporal to stay close to Steel, and to report on his activities, he had not revealed the cause of Davis' failure to return. But Steel had escaped; there was no other word for it. Tiggs had been deceived, and then prevented from following Steel. The damned soldiers were in on it too, that was clear. He had not the force to deal with them, and the tale of infection and the ban on movement would deter them if he had.

On the face of it, he thought, *Sussex was defending the interests of the Domain, though not in the way he knew Arundel would choose to do so.* The infection story would serve well enough for a while, but how much better would be the story of an Outie breach, a malignant raid on the Point, even on the Transfer Station. Given enough force and the right men, there could be evidence enough to support it. Go to Arundel; outflank that ambitious weasel Hope as well. Surely, with the King dead soon if not already, it was Arundel who would rule; would rule all the more securely with such a tale.

Excusing himself, he went in search of Arundel. It proved more difficult than he had expected. His Lordship was indisposed, and was not to be disturbed. It took a lot of pressure on the Major-Domo to allow even a note to be passed. Once done, however, he was swiftly summoned, much to the surprise of all.

Arundel was sat up in bed. His appearance was shocking. Pale and shivering, covered in cloaks, and with a basin on the table beside him. His left arm bandaged and held against his chest. At Lane's entry, Arundel signalled a young doctor standing beside him to leave.

"Sit down, Lane. Don't worry. I have no disease, but I have been poisoned. It is not fatal; I will recover. Another plot to be stamped on, Lane. Now tell me all."

Lane did so, while Arundel sat expressionless, only cursing under his breath at the absence of Steel. Clearly, another defection, with others as well.

"So, another traitor, another defection. Did Lord Sussex acknowledge it as such?"

"Not directly, my Lord, but I am convinced that he thinks so. I think he is minded to cover all absences with the story of disease, as with the far north, which has been sealed off by his orders."

He looked directly at Arundel.

"My Lord, while I am sure that my Lord Sussex has the welfare of the Domain at heart, I fear that he is overly concerned about any Outie attacks, and about the concerns of Groundlings and their managers. I might suggest another approach, my Lord?"

"Do go on." Arundel managed a faint expression of his grin.

"My Lord, is it not the case that we have a new, a disadvantageous, treaty with the Outies? One, nevertheless, that might incline some to oppose your Lordship's plans. Not all share your firmness of purpose, and some are afraid of an Outie retaliation. What might stiffen their resolve, my Lord? What better than a flagrant, a barbarous breach of that treaty? That disease was given out as a cover for a merciless attack on the Point and the Transfer Station. The murder or forced abduction of two nobles? Or admit the desertion of Hastings, and attribute the attack to his malign influence on the Outies? That Steel was lured to his doom?"

Arundel's grin strengthened, but a chuckle was cut short by a shooting pain up his arm. He paused to recover his composure.

"Ingenious, Lane, I grant you that. And an Outie atrocity would suit very well in Council. But there is an issue of time; not just time but sufficient men on whom we can rely. My brother and sister will be here soon, probably before the day is over. Now, we have no need to call for a Council for a few days yet, but I am wondering just how many men and to do what."

"I assume that the Point itself will be empty, my Lord. It would take few to damage it and report back. I am told that there are ten soldiers at the Transfer Station, and there are usually half a dozen staff with Mr Jacks and his family. Of course, there is Mr Grayson and his staff, and the garrison at Retford."

"It adds up, doesn't it? And Outies reaching to Retford might stretch belief just a little. A company would be needed, at least, and all reliable. Too big a risk, Lane. We need to discover who knows the whole story, or who might air suspicions in public. No deaths at Retford for certain, and we need to be selective about that Station at Barlow."

He was silent for a moment, then asked Lane to bring him pen and paper from a desk. A few lines, a signature, and he handed the order over.

"For Sussex' eyes, Lane. Get the garrison at Barlow evacuated to Retford. Leave the staff be. An easier task for you if there are no soldiers around. He is to allow you to make the call. I will think on what is to be done next. In the meantime, my Lord Lane, talk to no one. Success will be well rewarded. Now back to recruitment and training; accelerated training. Tell the guard to fetch Dr Pritchard on the way out."

Dismissing Lane, Arundel carefully removed the bandages around his hand. Already, the bitten thumb was smelling and blackened. *How long ago was it? When the last antibiotics expired; proper ones? Oh, we dealt with that plague, when was it, more than a hundred years ago. Not long after that we lost the skills and the means. Now, amputation is the only cure. Hopefully, just the thumb.*

***

It was late in the afternoon when Hope was summoned to Arundel's bedside. Propped up on pillows, he appeared to Hope better in colour, but with greatly dilated pupils. His left arm lay beneath the sheets. The vacant stare that turned on the Commandant was disconcerting, but when Arundel spoke, almost in a whisper, he lacked any hint of mental dullness or confusion. The situation at the Point was outlined, the intended remedy put forward. Those to die to be killed at the Transfer Station or at the Point itself if any remained there, killed, of course by Outie hordes driven off after fierce fighting. Not once was Lane's name mentioned.

"The question is, Hope, how many there are who need to be removed, and how? Most certainly, that damned Kingsman lieutenant, I did not get his name. Lure him to Barlow alone. He clearly conspired to help Steel defect. Jacks too, he heard Steel on the telephone. I regret it, but Tiggs and his men must go too. Honourable deaths in combat; bring the tags back. Otherwise, just establish that the rest know little for sure."

The commandant hesitated. Then, it had been *Lord* Hope; now the title was dropped. Then, there had been the promised doses, the position on Council, now yet another set of murders. The ancient words came to him, *hit man.* Tough though his chosen squad were, the events in the Armouries had shaken some. The sight of Arundel's obvious ill-health, and a creeping sense of insecurity kept him silent. What if he dies before we are dosed? If another is in power after we are done?

The dark, dilated eyes stared at him intently. "Well, man, how many can you rely on, spared from the Armouries? Those rooms must remain secure until all are removed, and the King's room for several days yet."

"Pardon me, my Lord. We had expected our reward when duty at the Armouries was complete. Some are already strained by what they have witnessed. I had presumed, my Lord, that I would fulfil any order from yourself or Council by instructing those under my authority."

Drugged though he was, Arundel recognised the challenge and restrained his anger. *But expose me*, he thought, *and you and yours are for the Barriers under any other. Sugar the pill.*

"There is no time to apply the doses; I need you to depart immediately. To travel overnight, Hope. It is a mission that I can trust to no other. But for yourself, and those you take with you, double the agreed doses on return. And before you leave, a bundle of credits to distribute as you see fit. Gazetted promotions for all; Commissioner for yourself. I will call a clerk in shortly, and you will have signed and sealed orders in your hands."

Credits and ranks, thought Arundel, *no problem, but doses?* More than he had access to from the Hunt, and Alice would not consent to more. Unless, that is, the Outie atrocity enrages all of Council. Well, *bridges and the crossing thereof.* Damn that Defoe and his circumlocutions. Amusing then, tedious intrusions now.

"Thank you, my Lord. If there are six or more that are not to return from our excursion, I will need at least twenty. At least ten rifles. Barring the King's room, it will need a replacement of all at the Armouries. I will need a few more as well. Given that it requires only guards at the entrance, could soldiers be employed at the perimeter?" He paused. "A sad matter, my Lord. I fear young Gregory has learnt too much too fast. He must not come with us."

"You want him removed?" Arundel was incredulous.

"No, no, my Lord. He is promising material. I would, however, want him away from others. I wonder if he might be transferred to your personal service. A disturbed young man in the company of his peers might say more than he ought."

A clerk was summoned; the orders signed and sealed. A small box of credits was handed to Hope. Arundel lay back, exhausted. The opiate was fading. He rang a small bell to summon a doctor. Now, he had a different problem, a discontented Lane. A new and stronger dose administered, he drifted into sleep, the sing-song voice of his teacher in his ears: *I'll think of it all tomorrow. After all, tomorrow is another day.* That voice, and the giggle that followed had, in his imagination, a tone that mocked not the speaker as usual, but the listener.

***

It was late in the evening when Buckingham, Kent, and a considerable party of Kingsmen, mariners, clerks and others less easily described entered Windsor. A party already informed of all the consequences of the failed Hunt, and thanks to a loyal clerk, a partial account of Hastings' defection. As the slow convoy of mobiles approached the castle. Lady Buckingham called a halt; she had seen the graffiti. She stepped out to investigate, Kent by her side. The balloons were understandable enough, if good cause for concern, but the hanging man?

The street was strangely empty. A single woman emerged from a side street, saw the convoy, and retreated rapidly out of sight. Impatiently, she ordered soldiers to knock on a door and bring the occupants to her. There was an altercation on the doorstep, and fearing violence, she and Kent went to the door, ordering the soldiers to stand back. Still inside, two men, a haggard woman and a badly misshapen child stared at them.

"You know who I am?"

At first, sullen looks, then a grudging, "Yes my Lady," from one of the men.

"Why is all so silent, tell me? And what is the meaning of these, these daubs on the walls?"

There was a silence. A silence that she was inclined to regard as impudence. Only a timely intervention from Kent prevented an outburst.

"There is nothing to fear. We are newly arrived, as you can see, and things appear out of the ordinary."

It was the woman who broke the silence.

"There is disease, my Lord, disease in the castle and the Armouries. We have had no orders, no details given to us, just rumours that many are confined, even that some have died. The pyres have been seen, my Lord. Burnings that are only for the diseased or contaminated. We are afraid."

"And these paintings? Has there been another Outie attack? A man hanged? Has such a thing happened?"

Another silence. Lady Buckingham's anger was nearly overwhelming. Had a Security patrol not appeared, her language might have shocked even the most hardened. As it was, one of the men spat as the patrol approached. Kent signalled them to return indoors and shut the door behind them. It was thus a Security corporal who was subject to interrogation. Yes, there had been infection, but no new cases. Yes fatal. Then the dire news, that it was His Majesty and his attendants involved.

"And His Majesty's condition?"

"We are told only that he is isolated, my Lord, strictly isolated."

Lady Buckingham turned to go, to get to the castle. Her beloved brother was behind this, for sure. But Kent held her back.

"Wait a moment, Sister." He turned again to the corporal. "These graffiti, man, these paintings; another balloon assault?"

"No, my Lord. But one flew far to the east, warning us that such was within their power. The news has provoked dissent, and we are to prevent it." He paused. "The Deceiver's doing, my Lord; some are easily led astray."

Well-schooled, thought Kent, but he persisted. "The hanging man?"

"More of the same, my Lord. My Lord Arundel had one boy hanged, caught in the act of painting. A warning. It is now the punishment for such acts. It was a shock."

"One that has failed in its aim then." Buckingham observed sourly, inclining her head towards the graffiti across the street.

"Not so, my Lady. Yes, there have been more such acts, and more hangings, but we have seen far fewer, and they are being removed."

The party returned to their mobiles. Lady Buckingham turned to her brother.

"Death? Despite all our teachings? Death rather than swelling Lane's insatiable demands for clearance? As well we learnt this before entering, Brother. An armed escort at all times. Find somewhere safe to keep the captain and our guest. In your apartments perhaps, and the less seen the better until Council is summoned."

Their entry, however, was much less threatening than expected. My Lord Arundel? Confined to bed, poisoned but recovering. Asleep and drugged. The King? Isolated in the Armouries. Sussex? With the telephones. The predominant feeling around the Court was one of relief at their arrival, although precious few were around to greet them. Settled in, they went to see Sussex, finding him paired up with Lane by the telephones. In his presence, Sussex restricted himself to the agreed accounts. Buckingham and Kent feigned surprise at Hastings' defection, but were genuinely surprised at the terms of the new treaty. Beyond that, the tales of infection, unverified or concocted. Lane stayed silent. Sussex rose.

"We as a family should assemble, I think." With the clerks as much as Lane in mind, he added, "Any calls other than those from or to Security, transcribe messages and keep them for my return."

The three assembled in their usual meeting place. Sussex was now more open.

"There is more to it, as Lane well knows. I did not want it discussed in his presence, as he has seen Alfred, but I do not know what plans were made. Steel is, I am near certain, not sick. Like Hastings, he has defected with his clerk and probably the whole squad at the Point."

"Why, in the name of all that's Royal? He went to sign this new treaty, and the mission was successful. He returned to Retford and reported to you. And then defected?"

"More strictly, he reported through a clerk to Alfred. The desertion of Hastings was revealed to Lane, Wilkes and myself. The bare fact only, until I made Alfred show me the message; me alone. Brother, Sister, our brother had planned to have Hastings die in Outie hands, and thus to void the treaty before your return. The Security sergeant visiting him in captivity delivered poisoned sweets. The ruse was detected, and the man killed himself in the presence of the Outies and Steel with his clerk. The garrison were left to bury the body, and were isolated under pretext of disease. It is not hard to see why Hastings chose to defect."

"Could it not have been claimed as a forced detention? It would have suited Alfred's purpose as well?"

"Hastings was with the Outie delegation. By Steel's account, he was free to leave and declined. There was also a signed renunciation."

Kent needed no more information.

"Poisoning presumably arranged by Lane. He may not know how that sergeant died, but he will surely guess. To maintain the fiction, that garrison, Steel, and his clerk would have to disappear. Steel realised it?"

"Just so. I was struggling, in vain, to think of ways to protect them. But it gets worse. Lane suspected something and had Steel followed, unsuccessfully, by the remaining security detail. The Kingsmen aided Steel, presumably to save their comrades at the Point. So, he must have talked, if only to the officer in command. As far as I can see, Steel has tried to protect as many as possible with calls announcing deaths and infections. Lane guesses otherwise, and he was closeted with Alfred this morning."

"Murders are planned then? Alfred has lost control. Carry out the task, and then he will worry about those who did it. This is no work for a solitary assassin. A whole platoon or more of Kingsmen, Staff at Barlow and Retford, not to mention the remaining Security force, all to be eliminated? It will be more like a war. Has Lane shown any signs of mobilising forces?"

"No, and that is strange. I have monitored nearly all calls through the clerks, and the man has scarcely left the telephony room all day. As you heard, I have ordered a ban on travel anywhere near, as well as in the far north. Disease, of course."

The conversation shifted.

"Our father? You said he was strictly isolated. We have a doctor's report? Thorndyke?"

"No, or only at second hand. He made a diagnosis of fever in one of Father's nurses, and Alfred gave his seal to isolate all, Father included. They were taken to a wing of the Armouries in the early hours. The doctor visited them later that morning. Many had died; our father was thought to be infected but alive. They are burning the bodies. I believe Thorndyke isolated himself afterwards."

"They? The Armouries men don't have gear, do they?"

"Security, I was told. But when the news came through, Lane appeared to know nothing. We assumed that Alfred had summoned what was available. I called the Master; he had been told to stay clear. Advice he was very happy to abide by. There is much fear, because everyone knows we can do little to cure."

"And since? And what is this about Alfred? Poisoned, by whom?"

"I have no further information, Sister. We can ask the Master-at-Arms. As for Alfred, he appeared this morning bandaged, and claiming an accidental injury. He has sickened since, so the Major-Domo has told me. Now it is poisoning, but how, or by whom, I have no idea. Dr Pritchard has seen him."

"He is expected to recover?"

"So the doctor said. But he is at present heavily drugged and asleep."

The three sat silent. The stories of disease sounded false, but what peril if they, or any of them, were true? Those early days, before the war, when almost all, as it seemed, had perished. Their doctors had kept them safe, but others of the first-born had perished. A giggling Defoe telling them about Sweating Sickness: singing at breakfast, dead by supper. But also, it had been the cover for the removal of those that stood in their way as the Domain was established. Their father? Almost certainly dead, dead at their brother's hand. Alfred poisoned? By whom, and to what end? For Buckingham and Kent, there was the unspoken question: Sussex' attitude had changed; changed enough? For Sussex, merely how to contain spreading disorder and violence.

Nothing more was revealed. Kent was despatched to the Armouries for more details. Sussex undertook to find Pritchard. Buckingham was left to interrogate Lane. She arrived in the telephony room to find Lane and General Wilkes shouting at each other, while clerks huddled away from the two nobles. Her arrival caused both to fall silent. She glanced at the clerks, and waved them out of the room.

"My Lords, can you give me an explanation for this unseemly behaviour?" Both Wilkes and Lane attempted to speak. She pointed to the General.

"My Lady, all forces were directed to halt movement between way stations to contain disease. An hour ago, a party of Security forces sought to pass north from Oxford. They were denied. An order from my Lord Arundel was produced. When my officer offered to telephone to confirm, he was threatened. Rifles, my Lady, were pointed at the squad at the checkpoint. We allowed the force to continue, given the order. We are not licenced to kill, and we were outnumbered. My question to Lane was simple: why was this consent not notified by telephone? My answer? A shrug and denial."

"A denial, my Lady, as a simple matter of fact. I knew, and know, nothing about such a force. The General appears to find this hard to believe."

"Are not all Security forces under your command, Lane? And rifles?"

She turned to the General.

"What sort of force, General, and commanded by whom?"

"Many were inside covered mobiles. Stevens estimated at least twenty. There was a commandant, who did not give his name, nor was one on Lord Arundel's order. Not known to Stevens."

Lady Buckingham regarded Lane. The man was angry, and understandably so, much though she despised him. Her brother could have ordered him to despatch such a force, and told him to clear its path. He had been excluded deliberately, and he was well aware of it. Big brother's little pet, slighted?

"Lord Arundel is no state to be consulted. The three of us have confirmed Lord Sussex' order for isolation and no movement between Divisions. General, you will notify all garrisons that there are to be no exceptions. I think roadblocks and reinforcements at each waystation are in order. Lane, you will notify all commandants that this force is to be detained and disarmed by Kingsmen at the next way station they reach. All calls to be transcribed, I will send the clerks back in."

She left them, and returned to the meeting room. The purpose of the heavily-armed squad was obvious enough. Its scale was monstrous. She was pondering on her brother's mind, when Sussex returned. Pritchard's account was strange. Arundel had received a wound on his left thumb. A ragged wound around which there was necrosis. The thumb had been amputated; the discarded digit was to be destroyed. Pritchard thought that the hand was saved, but was unwilling to be sure.

"I pressed him on how the injury happened, a question he had, of course, asked Alfred. He got no very coherent account. He had not been attacked, and had cut himself on a fall. But whatever he had fallen on had been disposed of. But it must have contained poison, for no wound without would show such rapid decay. And his health tells the same story."

"It would be no surprise to learn that he kept such things around him. But it is hard to imagine the situation in which he would harm himself accidentally."

"Pritchard felt the same, but was being very careful when speaking to me. He asked me a strange question: Did Arundel ever bite himself so as to draw blood? When I shook my head, he volunteered that he had thought, obviously in error, that the wound resembled a bite. As he said, he had little experience of such, other than by dogs."

"Has the thumb been destroyed?"

"For all practical purposes, yes, down a sewer. Alfred was insistent."

"Then we should look to the safety of that doctor, I think. Alfred seems inclined to dispose of anyone who knows more than he thinks wise. We must find a way to remove him from Alfred's service."

The two had to wait a while, well into the night, before Kent returned from the Armouries, a grim expression on his face. He gave his account in a very measured monotone, chronologically. He had, wisely, taken with him a squad of soldiers from the troop that had come from Dover. The Master's account was straightforward. Security had delivered sealed coffins in two batches, sixteen in all. They had been burnt in the place appointed. There remained a guard outside the room in which the King had been taken. Otherwise, he had been told to keep the building sealed until medical staff with gear came to cleanse the rooms.

"We have a name, one you will recognise, from the treaty talks. The squad that brought the victims to the place and delivered the coffins was led by Commandant Hope."

"Hope! The favoured son at the Hunt. He suffered slightly from Outie poison. Alfred was pushing him forward the whole time. Remember, Alice, you put him down firmly at the Transfer Station."

"There is more, much more, I am afraid. The Armouries do not lack all protective equipment. I kitted out with two of my men and found the guard at the supposed chamber for our father. He offered resistance. We disarmed him and relieved him of the key. He is now held by my men in close confinement."

Kent paused and looked at the others.

"The room was empty, a mere cell. There was a single chair, stained with piss and excrement. A knotted rag, cut to one side, lay beside it. There were dark stains on the chair and the floor around it. There was a left glove, stained and torn, and a tiny flask on the floor. Our father had been murdered. Held in that chair and poison forced on him. Not without a struggle, I think. There was no disease. His ashes are no doubt with all the other innocents at the base of that pyre."

Any love for their father, or from him to his children, had long since vanished. In turns a mocking onlooker, a senile obstruction and a devious plotter, his survival, potentially for hundreds of years, had been a kind of constant. Council, the Court and indeed the nobility in general, all were aware of differences among the Four. It was the King's assent, even if only for delay, that gave authority to the Domain. All had put off thinking of what was to happen if he did go before them. But the scene Kent described at last moved them to pity. To pity, but also to calculation. Tears? No. Rather, the centuries of balanced enmity asserted themselves. And Kent had, even in his horror, thought to delay the moment when other arrangements, other rules, would be needed.

"My men are reliable. I have had words, words not lacking in menace, with the Master-at-Arms. The King remains alive and confined. He will be consulted, but will not appear. His official death will await the outcome of a full Council. If needed, we will avail ourselves of witnesses to other events."

Kent and Buckingham looked at Sussex. Was there to be the usual two against two? Sussex said nothing. They dispersed, each to their own apartment.

32. Unravelling

Dawn was breaking as Hope's force approached the Leicester way station. Spirits were high. They had laughed as Hope bluffed or threatened their way through intermediate stations, where tiny squads had decided that discretion was the better part of valour, and that Arundel's seal trumped all others. One mobile driven off road in the dark had been irretrievable. The remainder were now slower than ever with the added load. In the dim light, the leading driver saw ahead of him the road blocks and the Kingsmen standing behind them. The convoy halted fifty yards from the barriers. Hope took two troopers as escort, and walked forward. He was shouted at to stop barely five yards from the block. Rifles were raised. A Kingsman captain came to the front. The altercation that followed was sharp. Arundel's order was waved; General Wilkes' and Lord Sussex' counter-order quoted. The blocks would not be removed. To emphasise the point, the captain barked an order; ten more soldiers appeared from the nearest building, rifles at the ready.

"Commandant, we have called Lord Lane himself. He knows nothing of your journey. Are you not aware that there is lethal disease, not only at Windsor, but to the north? That you and your men may either spread death to all you meet, or that you may all encounter it if you continue?"

"But, my Lord Arundel's order, Captain. Disease in the north? My Lord knows this to be false. I am commanded to investigate matters at the Treaty Point and elsewhere beyond your station. It will not go well for those who obstruct the rooting out of treason and Outie oath-breaking."

The captain stood silent with his arms folded across his chest. Hope tried his last gambit. Indicating that the two should move away from other's hearing, he spoke in a low voice.

"Captain, you may not be aware that His Majesty himself is infected, certain to die if not already dead. Lord Arundel is certain to rule. Those who have followed his orders will be rewarded. Those who did not? There is always a need for Reclamation labour."

To his astonishment, the captain laughed.

"Clearly, Commandant, you have suffered from the lack of a telephone. Lord Arundel is in no state to confirm or issue orders. The King is merely isolated. Lord Kent and Lady Buckingham are at Windsor. The order from Wilkes and Sussex? Confirmed by both, Commandant. Three out of four, the three still on their feet."

He moved back towards the roadblocks. Loud enough to be heard by those nearby, he spoke to Hope.

"I have orders for you. You and your men will leave your vehicles and hand over your arms. You will be detained here until Lord Lane decides what further action to take."

Hope stared at the captain. He turned, beckoned his men, and started to walk back to his convoy. Kingsmen raised their rifles, awaiting an order to fire. It did not come. The captain shouted at his retreating back.

"Life is precious, Commandant, even yours. You will not pass here, nor back to the south. Roadblocks and adequate forces are there now to prevent you. Any bloodshed will be on your hands. You may stew on this road forever, for there is no leaving it without surrender."

Back at his convoy, Hope got his mobiles turned around, and retreated out of sight of the waystation. They halted. Hope stood with his back to a mobile, the men sat in a semicircle around him. Short of surrender, his options were limited. A side road, to occupy some miserable Domain settlement, where there would at least be food, drink and fuel for the mobiles. To wait there until any power struggle resolved itself. Human life, he had thought as they retreated, that overrated consideration, would prevent an assault by soldiers. Little glory in that. Could not the waystation be bypassed? Reach Barlow and their mission might be fulfilled. He cursed himself for the lack of local knowledge: disused roads? Paths through Badlands? He asked for anyone with the knowledge.

"I came from Grantham Ground, sir. But we never heard much about the Domain outside. I had a mate from Leicester told me there was really bad stuff to the north and west. Security or Reclamation went fully kitted up, better stuff than we have here."

"Sir, where's this Treaty Point anyway? Are we to walk? How many days?"

"If there were roads, we've not that much fuel. We're overloaded as it is. Another one gone, and we'd be legging it."

There was a muttering. Several days marching through Badlands. For certain, that would more than cancel any benefit of years added. And then there was disease. Fine, the commandant had told them, that's all made up. But the words of the captain at the way station had spread. An awful lot of people seemed to believe it. On their way north, the small aggravations on the way had actually increased their confidence. Hope would browbeat all those smug soldiers, waving Arundel's order. They had known very well that there was a power struggle, but one in which, for certain, they were on the winning side. Now, it was dawning on them that the opposite might well be the case, and that they were up to their necks in shit if so. And then, yet again, there was disease; not all had realised that the Windsor outbreak was false, but, in any case, what about that to the north?

Hope looked at the increasingly mutinous faces in front of him.

"We can wait it out in a settlement, then. Wait for order to be restored and our rewards given."

He was faced with blank and hostile looks. Men rose to their feet, but kept their distance. Hope tried again, a certain desperation in his tone.

"You know what we have done. Surrender, and all will be exposed. You all know what it is like on the Barriers or on Reclamation. A life short and miserable. There's something else. When your fellow conscripts find that you are ex-Security, life becomes shorter and even more miserable. Take a chance, even a remote chance, to do our job, get it done, or lie low, and there are happier endings."

There was a shuffling. The men turned to a middle-aged sergeant who moved in front of the crowd.

"It's like this, *sir*. Now us lads, we were recruited to do a special job, all hush hush, all for the glory of the Domain. Disease around His Majesty; rich rewards for risking infection. All done as by your orders. Isn't that so?"

There was a murmur of assent.

"Well, it wasn't quite like that, was it, *sir*? Then ordered to come with you up north to deal with an Outie attack. Or rather to make believe there had been one. For the good of the Domain, naturally. Then we discover that those orders might not be quite in order, as it were. That there really was disease up here. Even the Commissioner had ordered us to stop."

412

Hope stared at the sergeant.

"That is rubbish, and you know it. You all had a full briefing."

"Ah, but there's rubbish that's mighty convenient to the powers that be when they're in a spot. Even to my Lord Arundel. I can hear him saying: *Sorry you were so misled, that Hope fellow went way beyond my instructions.* And twenty of us, from different units, all sent to Reclamation; a bit embarrassing for those up top. But one rogue commander, lying to save his skin, now that's a much more attractive prospect, don't you think?"

Even the sarcastic *sir* was gone. The men were now all on their feet. Some drew their pistols.

"So, we are turning around. We will surrender and explain why. How dreadfully we were misled. Come with us, and you will be both disarmed and bound. Your pistol, on the ground, now."

Hope stared at the group. His hand went to the holster, but he had scarcely put his hand on the pistol when the sergeant shot, at point blank range. The Commandant remained standing for a few seconds. Then his body slid slowly down the side of the mobile.

"Easiest this way, lads. Now there's no one to contradict us. You all saw what happened, right? Let off a shot when we were for turning around."

He ran his eyes over the group. Hardened though they were, the suddenness had shaken them.

"Think about it. Do you think he'd have come quietly? A quick death or two years or less clearing some pestilential Badland before you croak."

The sergeant removed Hope's pistol and fired a single shot. The body, with the pistol beside it, was loaded into a mobile. The convoy turned and headed back towards Leicester.

***

Rousing the castle that morning was a quiet, almost furtive affair. Courtiers and servants alike moved cautiously, inspecting their colleagues for signs of infection, inspection and interrogation at a distance. The Major-Domo had managed to chivvy servants into preparing breakfast. As more people emerged, confidence seeped back. By the time the three Royal children appeared, it became evident that no new cases had emerged overnight. Much praise was given for what was seen as Lord Arundel's prompt action the previous day. That turned thoughts to the man himself. Pritchard was sought out: much improved, was the message, but still weak and in pain. On no account to be disturbed. His Majesty? Here, Lady Buckingham thought it prudent to intervene, calling for silence.

"His Majesty is still gravely ill. There are complications due to his dose-date; he was in poor health beforehand, as is well known to most of you. Both he and his dedicated attendants will be strictly isolated. They are not to be approached."

Most of the castle's inhabitants went about their normal business. For a few, however, things were far from normal. Lane became occupied in increasing patrols in the town, and removing graffiti, while attempting to speed up the training of new recruits. It was the latter that unravelled the way in which a force had been recruited, behind his back, to execute his plan. Feigning knowledge, he established for certain that it had been Hope who had paid the visits, armed with an authority from Arundel. His anger of the previous night, furious at being bypassed, and made to look a fool in front of Wilkes, now turned to relief. Whatever had been planned, it would, by all accounts, go badly wrong. Go badly wrong under Hope's command, too. Now, Arundel's future, his plans for the Domain, would depend on him. Sink or swim together, my Lord.

There were some others at a loose end. John Gregory, assigned to Arundel's service, and kitted out to match, had had no chance to meet his new master, nor did the Major-Domo or senior staff have any use for him. Equally, the retinue that accompanied Buckingham and Kent on their return were not all those who had duties in the castle. Some wore the uniform of the Marine, the mark of those who manned the ships and docks at Dover and elsewhere. They were prohibited from leaving the castle, notionally to prevent infection, but actually because Buckingham had no desire to expose them to further hostility. They took to wandering aimlessly around the castle, until the Major-Domo lost patience, and had them herded into a room set aside for off-duty servants. John Gregory was already ensconced there. Lacking any enthusiasm for gossip, or for the few kings print books that lay scattered on tables, he was gazing out of a window when a familiar voice hailed him.

"Well, well, if it isn't John Gregory. At Court already, and in a Royal livery at that."

John turned. Before him stood Jamie. Jamie the great friend of Mark. Jamie whose patriotic spirit he had doubted. Jamie in the uniform of the Marine.

"I thought you were all for Security before we were posted. A job we all thought you would really enjoy."

The sarcasm in Jamie's voice stifled John's initial impulse to welcome someone, who if not a friend, was at least a familiar face.

"I was honoured to be chosen to serve at Court," he said, stiffly. "I am in the personal service of my Lord Arundel."

"Hmm. The one who has been poisoned." Jamie grinned. "I trust no one has made a connection." He saw the look on John's face.

"For Majesty's sake, John, a joke. I hear his Lordship is on the mend. Never mind."

Jamie had adjusted well to his selection and posting. Mark had haunted his thoughts, but with decreasing frequency. His short stay at Dover, among the mariners, had revealed a more positive side to the Domain and its service. The search for uncontaminated land overseas, for the means to breed without the constraints at home, gave those working there a sense of purpose. Had it not been for this hurried journey to Court, he would by now be embarked on his first voyage.

But look at John, he thought, *John the great patriot, John already at Court.* Not just at Court, but in the service of the most powerful noble of all. The old John, the John of the Ground, would be puffed up so much with pride as to be insufferable. But the John before him was pale, nervous and defensive, avoiding Jamie's eyes. Jamie could not resist a dig.

"Tell me, did you hear anything more about that Tadgie bastard who seemed to favour you at Conisbrough?"

That did provoke a spark, if a dim one.

"I'd mind your tongue if I were you. We are not in the seditious north now. Commandant Hope indeed showed me favour. And it was through him I was transferred to his Lordship's service."

It seemed almost cruel to tease John further. Beneath the typical pomposity, there was desperation rather than pride. Puzzled, Jamie turned away to seek the company of fellow mariners.

***

It was scarcely mid-morning when the telephony room became a Babel of shouts and temper. Lane received a call from Leicester; the clerk, following

415

instructions, attempted to transfer it to Sussex. Not before Lane had grasped the essential point: Hope was dead, and whatever mission had been planned aborted. The failure that he had anticipated, if not the death. Sussex seized the receiver, brushing Lane aside with a curse. He listened briefly and replaced the receiver. Messengers went scurrying, and all the clerks sent out. In the meantime, what was he to do with Lane? Whatever his connection with Arundel, events of the previous day made it clear that he knew little or nothing of what had happened. Sussex told him to leave.

It was not long before Buckingham and Kent joined Sussex. The way station was called, and the story repeated in more detail. Yes, Hope had been killed by his own men, killed because he had threatened them with the same when they refused to disobey instructions from the station. There was much more besides. Eventually, the receiver replaced, the three considered the events.

"The account given by those thugs does not convince me," Buckingham said. "Look at the documents carried in Hope's despatch case that the officer there opened: doses, doses of inordinate size were promised. Promotions beyond all precedent. Just for isolating the infected here, and a simulated Outie attack there? They knew very well what they were about, and it was murder, murder in both cases. On our brother's orders. Had they not been stopped they'd have been only too willing to follow those orders."

"And with a purpose," added Kent, "an Outie breach on a scale to turn the gentlest to revenge and conquest, and no father alive to impose restraint or delay."

Sussex regarded his siblings with a degree of detachment. His faith in his elder brother much shaken, he was still of a mind to preserve what was left of order. They could bring down the whole system, set some against others, and to what end?

"Think for a moment. That squad are in close confinement. Hope's documents are locked up, and few have seen them. Hope himself is gone, and Lane appears to have been excluded. There is a convincing tale of disease to account both for our father's death, when we choose to declare it, and for the missing garrison and Steel at the Point. The few who know otherwise have good reason not to say so. Alfred is strong; he is now popular because in the minds of many he saved the castle and Court from infection. Challenge him directly, and we will provoke chaos. Delay him, concentrate on retrenchment, and we may preserve the Domain."

The others glanced at each other. Both shook their heads; it was not the moment to take Sussex into their confidence.

"Very well. But the policy of the Domain has yet to be determined. Council must be summoned. There is much to explain, if not always in the most honest way. Hope's orders must be secured, here, and our brother must know we have them." Kent smiled grimly. "They are not," his voice crept to a higher pitch, "the *smoking gun*, because it is only the rewards that are mentioned, and not the killings. But they will require some explanation if made public."

Sussex nodded. Alfred had already issued a summons to Council. He could now set up a date.

***

Lane's next meeting with Arundel was in sharp contrast to the previous one, although the same process of a note and pressure on the Major-Domo was required. Arundel was visibly stronger, seated at his table rather than in his bed. His hand remained bandaged. Lane sat down opposite him, not waiting to be asked.

"As my note told you, my Lord, the mission, however intended, of Commandant Hope has failed. The man is dead. Your brothers and sister excluded me from access to any further involvement. I believe the men with him also dealt with the infection around His Majesty's person?"

Arundel remained silent.

"It is said in the Court, my Lord, that the King is sick but still lives. Does that accord with your understanding?"

"No one recovers from what ailed him, Lane. No doubt my siblings find it convenient to pretend otherwise. A sensible move for now, for now only."

"My Lord, I will speak frankly. I regret that you did not trust me to carry out the plan I put before you. Achieved or not, there would have been a degree of finesse that I fear was beyond Commandant Hope. As it is, I wonder what documents, what authorisations, have fallen into the hands of others."

"Nothing conclusive, even if embarrassing. Only talk would reveal more, and Hope's men have good reason to keep their mouths shut. Even then, I think that an excess of zeal on the commandant's part, a regrettable misinterpretation of my instructions, would render such testimony moot."

"Including all that happened in the Armouries? Of course, my Lord, I have no knowledge of these matters, as your brothers and sister acknowledge. Equally, they are aware that our earlier conversation occurred. I can see that I might be examined on its content."

"And you would say what, I wonder? Oh, not really. I can see it now. *My Lord Arundel proposed a scheme to me, and I declined to carry it out. It was thus and thus. I believed I had persuaded his Lordship of its unwisdom.* Telling testimony, no doubt. Enough to keep you from Reclamation, perhaps, but if I am brought down that is the best you can expect. Maybe a Visitor to one of the least productive Grounds? And we regret that no further doses are available. How long do you have, Lane?"

The two stared at each other across the table, Arundel drumming with fingers of his uninjured hand. Eventually, it was Arundel who backed down.

"Let us get to the point, Lane. As you have pointed out with such subtlety, we need each other. There is still the prospect of overcoming these setbacks. What is it that you require to aid me in this task?"

"Thank you, my Lord. You will understand that I have a concern for my own future after recent events. You knew, I think, that another dose would be needed soon. 200, my Lord. Today. A guarantee of my position as Commissioner for Truth and Justice, signed and sealed by yourself and kept by me. No repetition of what happened when I was replaced by Blackstone. Clear precedence over Reclamation."

"I expected no less. But 200 is more than I have at my disposal. 150? The remainder when order has been restored, and we have access to the supply. The rest will be done. I will go a little further, if opportunity arises. Grounds, Lane; I am sure that more discipline is needed. Poor Hope was a bit crass in his devotion, but he had the right idea. Now, tell me how we might proceed."

Lane looked straight at his nominal master. He said nothing. Arundel gave a sigh, and asked Lane to fetch pen and paper from a side table. He wrote silently for a while, then showed the paper to Lane. Lane nodded; Arundel rang a bell, summoned a clerk with his seal. He handed the document to Lane. The doctor was summoned, and after sight of the document, he led Lane away to the provisional dosage store, where the dosage planned for the Hunt was kept.

The process would take a few hours. Left alone, Arundel remembered that young Gregory had been left behind; as Hope had said, the boy had learnt too much too quickly. Now, his master was dead, and not in the most glamourous circumstances. Another ring, a summons, and within five minutes, John was admitted.

"Sit down, Gregory. I have some sad news. Commandant Hope has been killed. Killed in the execution of his duty by ignorant mutineers. It falls to me to be your sponsor, not just for now, as Hope and I had intended, but for the foreseeable future."

As John stammered out his thanks, there was, it seemed to Arundel, something odd about the boy's reaction. Hope was not exactly a likeable man, granted, but the boy owed all his advancement to him. Shock, yes; anything else? Not much. He shrugged; fortitude and a certain coldness were characters to be applauded.

"Have you been given any duties, Gregory?"

"No, my Lord, I am confined with those who accompanied Lady Buckingham and Lord Kent from Dover."

"That will stop. I will arrange accommodation elsewhere in a moment. You are not to be confined, but please associate only with those wearing my livery. There will be some strange stories among those newly arrived here, Gregory. The commandant's death is not widely known, but it will be shortly. Even here, there will be rumours, unpatriotic rumours, as to how he came to die. Say simply that you know otherwise, and end the conversation."

The bell was rung, and John was led away to new quarters. Arundel repressed a feeling of unease, and waited for the return of Lane. A request for a meeting with Buckingham was rejected, but with it came the announcement of timing for Council. *Better sooner than later*, he thought, as he indicated consent. Eventually, Lane reappeared, a satisfied smile on his face. They were soon into the tactics of the inevitable struggle.

***

As Kent and Buckingham retreated to their apartments, and Lane was nowhere to be found, it fell on Sussex and Wilkes to deal with the questions and reports that flooded into the castle. Although it provoked mixed feelings, the spread of news that infection had been contained thanks to Arundel's prompt action had defused much of the disaffection in the town. By Sussex' order, no more hangings had happened. Security were instructed merely to give perpetrators a beating and a dousing in their own paint. A kind of peace had been established with the cities, and transfers in both directions had resumed. As well, Sussex and Wilkes agreed, that it was not the time to move the Chosen. No Montgolfiers overflew the Domain.

The suspension of transfers to Reclamation offered another opportunity. Even the unchosen, those as yet sufficiently undamaged by Reclamation, could be directed to military or Security training. Wilkes soon left Sussex alone in the telephony room, or alone with the clerks. He had, rather too quickly, interrupted a call made by one, though on reflection, he wondered why he had bothered. A call to Retford ensured that the Transfer Station was evacuated. He asked for the Kingsman lieutenant.

"Ah, Kipling is it. Lieutenant, I believe that you have heard that your garrison at the Point have been infected? Good. And that Lord Steel investigated and isolated himself? And you have heard nothing since? Very good, Lieutenant. There is to be no access to the Transfer Station or the Point. No access. Anyone presenting orders to the contrary is to be held until you have consulted me. In due course, Lieutenant, you and I will personally inspect the Point. Yes, alone. We will certify the lack of survivors. Security? How many? Can they be moved? No mobiles. A pity. I would appreciate it, Lieutenant, if some means could be found to keep them out of reach of the telephone, but on no account are they to approach the Station or the Point. Your clerk has transcribed this? Good."

The sound of relief at the other end was satisfying. An awkwardness averted for now. He went up to Kent's apartment for a final debriefing. The door was opened by a bearded mariner, who looked at him and almost shut the door in his face. In the moment of delay, he saw Kent pushing someone through a side door; a huge, bearded man in the most outlandish clothes he had seen. The look on his brother's face was enough to deter any questions. Briefing concluded, Sussex left for his own apartment and bed. In the morning, he would head north to retrieve Hope's papers and interrogate his men.

33. In Suspense

Amelia had an immediate opportunity to visit the bailiff. Only a day after her conversation with Cornwallis, he had arrived at the mayor's office to tell them that he had been summoned to Conisbrough urgently, and would be there all day, and probably overnight. Claiming a lift to the city for a routine visit to Mysliborski, she walked from the bridge to his office. There was a short wait while a young woman went out to find him. She looked around his office. As on the previous visit, the old chairs and sofas had been replaced by tables. On one, there was a map, the one she had seen before. She could make out the obvious boundaries of contamination in its various forms, the locations of nests, and some red circles deep inside the contaminated areas. She was just tracing a much fainter line from one such spot when the bailiff returned. She gave him the news. His reaction surprised her. He gave her a long stare, saying nothing.

Uphill had always been a problem for Mysliborski. You never knew for sure what was in their minds; there were *patriots* there, those who welcomed seeing their kids chosen and those who enjoyed the credits that loyalty brought. Muss Amelia? Safe. Markham? Grumpy sod. Trustworthy? Who knew about this? Eventually, he gave a guarded response.

"I'm glad Master Norman is well, of course. Does the major know this? Or Markham?"

"No, Stefan, neither of them, and I have no intention of telling them. Oh, I know John looks down his nose at the city, but if he did find out, he'd not tell the major. The last thing we want is another excursion across the bounds. Actually, I doubt if the major himself would do such a thing; he's been told to keep things quiet. And he has barely a dozen men here anyway."

"Has the major given you any news from the south since we last met? No? There is plenty, though he may not know all of it. That precious Hunt? It's been a disaster for the Domain. The Outies pulled a fast trick, good for them. We don't have details, but the Domain were out of there with their tails between their legs.

They've had casualties. Some of ours that were on clearance there have been rescued by Outlanders. Some have joined them, others staggered back home or are on their way. Poisoned, most of them.

It's not done us any favours though. We diverted their soldiers all right, but we've suffered. Hundreds dead, Muss Amelia, and it might be a thousand by now. I'm not saying the Outies owe us; there'd have been big trouble anyway, but what may be fine for them looks different to us. Where do you think they'll turn to make up those losses? Here, of course. When they come, we'll not submit gracefully. For every one they kill, that's one less for their precious service, one less for so-called service that is little more than a death sentence. Let's see who cracks first, that's our attitude now. An old proverb, Muss Amelia: are they fool enough to kill the goose that lays the golden eggs?"

"But the major? Our Visitor? Will they not prevent this? In any case, you will wait until they try, surely? The Outies may respond, and they have killed in other Grounds."

"Cornwallis? The Visitor? even Bohun? Small fry, Muss Amelia. They'll send in the likes of that Hope bastard with ten times the force. So, no, we have not waited. Oh, we've not done anything here in the city, yet. But do you remember David Reynolds, from the family that run the warehouses? The lad who went missing and brought the damned Tadgies down on us for a week?"

"Yes, because it was strange. Even Markham thought so. The Reynolds family were left there at the bridge. We all expected them to be moved, even unchosen across the bridge. Why?"

"That lad was plain crazy. Non-swimmer he may have been, but he crossed the river somehow, and found his way to the Barriers. Talked to some without the Tadgies knowing. There was one of ours there, one whom we thought had been Chosen. He sent David back here. We moved him quick down south, where he'd not be recognised. But he told us what went on there, thanks to our lad. Know how long you live there, Muss Amelia? Two years average, few make it to four. To no good purpose either, by his account. We've that account written down and circulated, and he's given witness in many cities now."

"We all knew that life was brutal at the Barriers, Stefan, even if we had no details, just rumours. What was new?"

"Deceit, that was new. Half those there had been Chosen, not punished for anything. And with little to show for all the labour. Then we've had reports from the south. The Domain was clever in the beginning. They'd send people far away from home. The poor sods wouldn't even know where they were. Our Henry at the Barriers being local was a slip-up, but now they've got sloppier, as I told you and the major. That Hunt? They trapped locals who knew where they were and escaped. Now, we are all ready for defiance."

"Not waited, though; what do you mean?"

"We brought David back here last week, knowing the Tadgies were gone. He went to the Barriers, Muss Amelia, and a dozen lads and lasses with him. He knew the safe way there. No labour going on, a couple of dozy troopers asleep in their beds. We took out the whole lot yesterday. They are here now. Most are wrecks. But only possible now, before the Domain turns its attention back here. Major off to Conisbrough this morning? I can guess why. We'll soon see how they react. I expect a visit from the major tomorrow. Then we'll find out."

***

Mysliborski was right. Roused by one of his men in the middle of the night, there had been a call for the major from Bohun. The Barrier labour had vanished that morning. No fight, no casualties. They could only have gone south. Any reports? Come here tomorrow. Cornwallis got dressed, and went to the Proctor's Station. A sergeant was on duty. Anything unusual along the river or elsewhere?

"No, sir, or not really. A patrol found a bunch of city kids by the river and gave chase, but they dodged away and were into ruins faster than us. We were going to send a message to the bailiff in the morning."

"Very well, Sergeant. Tell Captain Phelps to double patrols all along the river, and south of Stocksbridge. Take in anyone you find."

Come morning, he drove to the bridge with Muss Amelia, then thankfully transferred to a four-wheeler and driver for the journey to Conisbrough. He found a mixed bunch of people in the Visitor's office, awaiting his arrival. Apart from the Visitor, an assistant and Bohun, there was a Senior from Land Assessment, his own lieutenant Hardy, a Security sergeant he did not know, a Ranger lieutenant and Dr Macdonald, the one, he remembered, who had reported on Hope's treatment of Norman.

The account he received from the Senior and the Security man was astonishing. Everything was as normal under the circumstances the evening before, but empty the following morning, bar one dead worker left wrapped up in blankets. How many? 160! Where had they gone? Shrugs. Was there no guard? Never necessary, Major, nowhere to run to, and the workers knew that individual escapes resulted in collective punishments. Dr MacDonald interrupted.

"There were two left behind in the shack for the seriously ill, Major. 'Heaven's Gate' they call it; it's apart from the others. They knew nothing. One may be dead already, but I'd like transport to bring the other back here. There were more there that were very ill. They've gone. They must have been carried. I was going to ask that they be moved back here today."

Like the Proctors, the Rangers had nothing to report. Some of them had also been sent south, and patrols were less frequent, but no alarm had been triggered, and the dogs had picked up no trails. So, where had they gone? The road east was exposed, with Badlands on either side. They'd have been seen when the doctor, sergeant and senior had driven east to report, especially if they were carrying the sick. In most directions, there were lethal Badlands that the workers would have known all too well. They must have gone south. Was there a route?

"There might be, Major," said the senior. "There is woodland downstream, relatively clean. We've had an eye on it as more promising than the patches to the north where Commandant Hope insisted that we worked on. We never studied it thoroughly. Like the Royal Forest by the river, it could have been assigned to the Ground. It was you, my Lord," she turned to the Visitor, "who told us that expansion was not policy."

Cornwallis looked at the Visitor and Bohun. Both had remained silent. All three of them knew that this event would bring Security back with a vengeance once it was known. Only the apparent setback for the Hunt, and troubles in the southern cities would delay a response. Or, of course, a delay before the Court was aware.

"With your consent, my Lords, I suggest we employ all Security and Ranger personnel in searching the east bank of the river north of the city. The Proctors are already engaged on the west bank, to no avail as yet. My men should patrol the road south from here, and block any traffic; news of this might spark further defections. All telephone calls outside should be made only from the Visitor's Office here."

There were nods. The juniors departed, with the exception of the Security sergeant, held back by Cornwallis' glance.

"Sergeant, I take it that you were in command at the work camp? And you had how many men?"

"Four, sir, including myself."

"Was there a duty rota, sergeant? Was the camp patrolled at night? That night?"

The sergeant reddened. "That night, no, sir."

"And why not, sergeant? I take it there was a duty rota?"

The sergeant nodded, but did not reply. The major let the indiscipline go by.

"A dereliction of duty, then. Is there a record, or standing orders?"

The sergeant cracked.

"Lieutenant Hockey is in command, sir. He told me to go easy on ourselves since there was no real work to be done. It would have meant twelve hours in every twenty-four. There seemed no point, sir."

"This matter will be taken further, sergeant. In the meantime, you are to return to the camp with any troopers who came here with you. It may be that some of these lost souls will return to the camp. Immediately. You will be relieved when I say so."

The sergeant left. Cornwallis turned to the Visitor.

"My Lord, your authority is paramount. I ask that you send your assistant accompanied by two of my men to arrest Lieutenant Hockey and hold him here; a charge of dereliction of duty. And send a messenger to the bridge to put all Security forces under the command of the most senior Ranger."

The assistant left. The three were left to consider the possibilities. For now, news of this breakout would not travel. New recruits were not being sent north; work on the Barriers had been suspended, and no reports were required. The Ground was intact, and with it the healthy breeding potential that they all valued. All depended on what happened elsewhere. At the moment, Arundel or Security were in no position to send forces north, but the breakout would provoke a reaction, as would their failure to report it. Worse, of all Grounds, this was the most vulnerable to an Outie assault. Outies had poison; who knew how much? Their fate was in other hands.

**

Cornwallis spent the night at Conisbrough. The few squads deployed in the Domain had reported no trouble at mines or workings. To save on the increasingly severe transport problems, it was arranged that he would return to the bridge with a heavy mobile of supplies: food for the Grounders, especially

425

those in the city. Calls to Bradfield yielded nothing of note. No strangers had been found. Deposited at the bridge, he required a Proctor to guide him to the bailiff's office. Of course, the man was not there. His arrival at the front door had provoked a flurry of activity on the street, with several engaging him in conversation, and arguing about where the bailiff might be found. After some disappeared to search, he was ushered into the office. The table that had replaced the old sofas was bare.

The young man who had been dismissed at the previous meeting, Mehmet, was very solicitous. Refreshments? No thank you. Eventually, he disappeared, and the major was left on his own. A prowl around the office revealed nothing of interest at first. Then he noticed a very faded picture in a frame, an engraving of some sort. It displayed a military man on horseback in a uniform that appeared to him to be wildly theatrical; metal armour, a lance, and the appearance of wings behind; huge, stylised wings. Clearly, pre-Catastrophe, but like nothing he had learnt of in training. There was faded writing below, unintelligible. A prohibited Relic, he wondered. He did not remember seeing it before. More like the gear the nobles used for their Hunts, though they had never sprouted wings.

He was still examining it when the bailiff returned. Although he turned to greet Mysliborski, it was obvious that the bailiff had seen what had engaged him. There was a frown, then a shrug.

"Claimed to be an ancestor, Major, from times long gone, so my grandfather always said. I've never really believed it, mind, though there were soldiers like that. Brave fellows, by all accounts."

He looked at the major.

"It's not been on display for a while, Major. Any damned Tadgie in here and it would have been confiscated, and I would be out on my ear. Mehmet ought to have put it away. It was back up there to give me courage, now those bastards aren't around."

Cornwallis recognised the challenge. *What are you going to do about it, Major?* But it struck a chord. His own name had been embellished by his father, though without the concrete, if spurious, support of a picture. A good name, Son. There was a general, he was told, though not a successful one, then a studier of birds. He'd had to get his mouth round the word, ornithologist.

"We should all have respect for our ancestors, Mysliborski. I've not seen it. But if Truth and Justice are around. I'd make sure it's tucked away. I don't know the details of the Relic rules as regards pictures, but at a guess, they'd take it and you too, as you say."

The bailiff gave a sigh. He went to his chair behind the antique desk.

"So, why the summons, Major?"

"The Barriers, Mysliborski, the Barriers. The whole labour force vanished. They weren't on the road. They aren't in the King's Forest. The Proctors have seen no trace uphill. But they told me some of your lads were up river, and led them a dance. I think it was a distraction. I think those poor sods are with you, unless you've already moved them south."

There was a silence. The bailiff's face was stony.

"I am going to explain a few things, Mysliborski. Right now, nobody beyond Conisbrough knows this has happened. Recruitment and reporting have been halted for some time. The Visitor intends to keep it that way. There's enough trouble down south to delay any interest, so long as this is not known. The few Security men left are either back on the Barriers or around Conisbrough. They cannot telephone, and my men are guarding the road south. No traffic allowed except for food from the south, and I'm not sure we'll see much of that. It'll be a few weeks before attention turns back here."

"And when it does, Major? An empty camp not reported for weeks. No recaptures. Oh, they'll be all over us no doubt. There will be killings. Bring enough force and they'll finish us in the end, or starve us out. But what about you, Major, you and your beloved Visitor, not to mention Bohun? That Hope bastard, he'd take great delight treating you the way he treated poor old Norman."

"Just so. That is why I said what I did. We are all in the same boat. If anything, we are in worse trouble than you, since none of us can breed. Surrender, and they'd show mercy to some. No such choice for us, and no capacity to resist either. Why? Because we think this Division is the future, your city included.

We are not alone here, simply on one side of an argument around the Court. An argument we have been losing until now, Mysliborski. There are those who would move everything of value south to save on supply. There are those who would waste yet more lives on the Barriers. It is little short of a miracle that this has not happened already. What is happening down south may change things. We made our decision, a gamble, if you like. Here I am. Are we on the same side?"

Ever so slowly, a grin spread over the bailiff's face. He came from behind the desk and, as the major rose to meet him, there was a very formal handshake.

"Yes, Major, I think so. Let us not disgrace our ancestors, mythical though they may be. Yes, Major, we have the refugees. 160 there were, but five poor sods died getting here, and another two went last night. There's more than forty in a bad way, but we've not trusted the hygienists. All are scarred, and there'll be none that are fertile, even those there only for a few weeks. It'll not be long before we have a food problem too. We scrape by as it is, and we've stashed a fair bit in hideouts in the south. Places the bastards won't reach without so much protective gear they'll fall over."

"We can hope that it does not come to that. Hygienists? Leave that to me and Muss Amelia to sort out the trusted. I'll get a real doctor and her staff in here as well. They have more experience of real damage and how to treat it. I'll think about food. There's some to spare at Conisbrough since nearly all the forces went south. While there's so much on down south, we can make-believe a crop failure or cattle disease to cancel shipments. I'll side-line Markham, though I don't think he will be a problem. Go talk to Reynolds, though. Now's the time to show him his son."

***

Back in Bradfield, Cornwallis was kept busy. It was easy enough to persuade the Visitor to release more supplies to the bridge, and to send Dr Macdonald and a few assistants to see to the refugees. By the time he had contacted Reynolds at the bridge, he had already been reunited with his son; there were going to be no problems there.

Uphill, though, was more of a problem, as were the hygienists as a body. Some of the teachers too. Status and security for incomers, like the mayor, had depended on reliable loyalty to the Domain, all the more so if you were yourself sterile. And what about the notionally patriotic families like the Gregorys; it was the chosen son who had sent Hope on the rampage. It would not be long before changes in supply chains and requisitions were noticed. The orders would change for Markham, too. He had expected more demands to be met. Now, such demands must be diverted to the city, or indeed kept at home. Not that there was any easy way for anyone to communicate outside the Ground.

Cornwallis bided his time before acting. First on the list was Phelps. He looked at the file. An incomer, as expected, but fertile and married to locals. All the children too young to be chosen. Phelps, he knew, had no love for Security. What about his men? The conversation was guarded at first. No, the Proctors had found nothing out of the ordinary, along the river or elsewhere. Service at the bridge? Not popular, but there had been no problems.

"Captain, you know that my forces are much reduced, and Security has withdrawn. The Visitor is anxious to keep it that way, as am I. There are problems elsewhere in the Domain, Captain, that mean that this situation may be sustained for a while, perhaps for good. Any reports from here that we might be in any way a problem, and that situation might change for the worse. I know that anything out of the ordinary, you would report it to me. How about your force as a whole? Are there any that might see an advantage in, let us say, an independent report to the Domain behind your back? I know that Security might pay handsomely for such information. I don't mean mere Credits."

"You mean patriots, sir? Before this spring, I could give you some names. After last month's doings, there'll be none. That Hope, sir, he had contempt for all of us. We noticed."

"Nobody tempted to slip down to the Corridor, then? Your one-time mayor, Arkell is there. And it's known, I think."

The captain looked puzzled.

"No, sir. But what would they report? Things have been dead quiet for weeks, except for your asking us to patrol the river the other day. That turned up nothing but a few squatter kids, and they scarpered."

"Captain, you or your men will certainly notice a few things. Even if your duties in the city are confined to the bridge, you will encounter some odd traffic, and see some folk who look unwell; contaminated men and women. There will be fewer hygienist's visits there too. It is the Visitor's wish that these matters are known only in the Division. And by the way, I think it would be as well to talk of city folk, not squatters. We need to work together to keep the peace. I am still worried about Mr Arkell, though. A man in his position has much to gain by zealous assistance to the Domain."

Phelps was still confused, but picked up one message.

"I can bar any traffic to the Corridor, if that is what you wish, sir. Mr Jacks is a friend, and would let me know of any arrivals, and keep them away from Mr

Arkell. I can pick the squads for the Station that gives access, though any of us would obey that order."

"An excellent idea; all traffic. We will see about livestock and their minders, But I think the farmers nearby have already had sheep requisitioned? There should be no more requests for a while. Oh, one other thing: keep kids well clear of the city. I'll put it out that there is an infection. There are indeed the sick there now."

Conversation with Muss Amelia the following day was more straightforward. She had already heard of the major's talk with the bailiff. For now, they were secure, but not forever. Who were the patriots, the ones most likely to reveal anything that smelt of disloyalty, and who stood to gain by doing so?

"I'd have said Muss Norman for a start, but you have had her transferred. There's the Gregory family too. Incomers with their electrical expertise. There are a few others too, but they are not likely to hear anything odd. It's the hygienists and teachers you need to think about. Most are incomers and they had the strongest training elsewhere. Many are ambitious for promotion and transfer, and more than you might think are sterile themselves. I've heard a few fancying being brought to Court."

"Hygienists in the city? They're the ones most likely to see things we would rather they did not. I've asked for doctors and staff to come over, and we can impose a quarantine. There is disease, even if it's not infectious. And the teachers there?"

"I think we should close all the schools early. Bring forward the stint, uphill and down. Infection is a good spur, Major. It frightens everybody. It will keep the hygienists out, odd though that might seem; they'd call in doctors anyway. Get the teachers out in the fields. Stefan will find plenty for the city children to do; there are patches clearing that can be prepared for use. Uphill, well, you can justify the change by using the demands made by the Domain. John has been preparing them for that anyway. I'll keep the hygienists as a whole busy uphill. Most of them are safe, though there is no need to tell them everything. What about the Proctors?"

"I've seen Phelps. He has no love for Security. They will look to block the route to the corridor. The more I think of it, the more sense it makes to use an infection in the city to account for any break in routine. We can take over normal stock transfers at the city bounds. What happens to it after that is for us to determine. The Visitor will find it handy too."

Amelia regarded the major carefully.

"Major, we know that however good we are with all this, it is not forever; the end is not in our hands. If things go badly elsewhere, Security, and soldiers like yourself will be here in force. The Division will be cleared out. There will be banishments to the Barriers or to similar death traps. The Outlanders may retaliate if there is any incursion here or elsewhere. This must be their easiest target. There will be deaths. There are those particularly vulnerable. May I transfer Miss and Lisa Norman to the Pickless farm? At the least, they will be welcomed by the Outlanders, and can escape west. In the hands of the Domain, they are dead."

The major nodded. He noted that she had referred neither to her own prospects, nor to his. These were evident. Later that day, he had a long telephone conversation with the Visitor. The notices were duly posted. Cattle murrain among the farms, an undiagnosed but infectious disease in the city. Entry and exit sealed at the bridge, at the corridor and on the trunk road south from Conisbrough. Only later did Bohun ring him back. The quarantine messages had been delivered, but had been received by Security, and not by the usual clerks.

"Your contact, my Lord, Songbird was it?"

"Nothing, Major. It took ages to dictate the message to the man at the other end. Not a clerk. And he would not answer any questions either. But there was a later message relayed from Lord Sussex. We were to block and arrest any Security detail approaching our way station. Where they think we get the men to do such a thing, I have no idea, but we would block anyway. There's something strange going on down there; it is not just our doings that are concerning them."

***

Cornwallis found himself in a strange mood of suspense the following morning. The routines of the Ground, though somewhat altered, rumbled on without his intervention. The round of visits, visits to the Proctors, to the mayor's office were amiable and trivial. To Muss Amelia's raised eyebrows, he returned a shrug: nothing new to pass on. A calm that could not last, but one out of their hands. He drove down to the city. Mysliborski's office had changed in one detail. The table, cleared rapidly before his previous entry, now had the well-worn and heavily marked street map seen by Amelia. Two young women were with the bailiff.

"Welcome, Major. As a military man, we would welcome your assessment of our defences. Come and see."

It took the major a while to grasp the multitude of symbols, lines and different coloured spots that adorned the map. In his transitory visits, he had formed only a distinction between the clear north and contaminated south. The reality was more complex, a mosaic of clear patches, some minute, and others indicating different levels and kinds of contamination. Within the larger clear areas to the north, the locations of nests were marked. To the south, the numerous tiny patches free from contamination were linked to the clear north by twisting lines not confined to old streets, but often traversing buildings or what might remain of them.

"Generations of work, Major, to find those patches, and ways to reach them at minimum cost. Lives shortened to clear a few pathways. And no signs on the ground. Each has a team that learns the knowledge; each little spot has supplies laid down, weapons and all. And in the north? We've more nests than the hygienists know of. Nests approached by ginnels round the back, with fronts that look like they've not been touched since the Catastrophe. Bar a few firing points, of course."

Cornwallis was impressed. Even Kingsmen would find this daunting. Security would be hopeless. But there was a major flaw.

"You'd hold them off for certain, Mysliborski, even without firearms. But suppose they sit round the edge and starve you out? you need food brought in, don't you, food in exchange for children, I know. They'd grub up the gardens and dig up the warrens to speed things up."

"True enough, Major. But would they go through with it? You put your finger on it: they need our children. RPZ." The bailiff spat. "It's not only here that's ready. Find half a dozen cities the same, and they'd come to terms. There's more; come with me, Major."

The bailiff led him down a corridor, and unlocked another room. On racks were ten Security uniforms, the full protective ones. Some had holes. On a table were the same number of pistols and small boxes with ammunition.

"Our share from the troubles down south, Major. Not all their losses were retrieved. Our folk are better supplied down there, mind, because that's where the fighting has been. Never mind the bullets, the uniforms alone will cause them a lot of confusion. Wonderful thing, the Metro, Major."

They returned to the office. Cornwallis was both impressed and shaken. He imagined the carnage had Hope and others prevailed at Court or Council. Add a few rifles to the mix, and even a blockade would be hard to maintain. The conversation switched to other matters. The refugees? Here, the bailiff showed his rage.

"Fifteen more dead, poor sods, for all that lady doctor can do. A saint, that one. And five more likely in the next few weeks. There's few will have a normal life. I talked to each one, Major. More than half of them Chosen, and sent there from all over. That news went back down the line, you can be sure."

"That reminds me. The Reynolds boy?"

"He's with his family, as you know. He'll do, but what with his experiences up there, then being shunted around to tell his story, I'm told he's a bit strange in the head. But we've got him a partner. There was quite a queue, with him being seen as a hero. He got to choose, now the hygienists are off our back. Early days, Major, but we hope he wasn't damaged. If all works out, I reckon there'd be a statue of him downtown."

The major returned to Bradfield. There had been a call from Conisbrough. He rang back. The news was dramatic.

"Songbird was back, briefly. Major, Hope is dead, killed by his own men while trying to pass Leicester. Lord Arundel has been poisoned, but is recovering. There is infection, and the King has been isolated. The call was interrupted. All we could hear was some shouting."

The telephone was passed from the Visitor to Bohun.

"The message was strange, Major. Our man would have had others in the room. The news about Hope was straightforward. The rest had an air about it. He kept on saying *it is said that*. There is something false about the infection there. Who licenced Hope, and who ordered him stopped? Who poisoned Arundel?"

"Is the King not ill then? Is he held hostage?"

"I don't know. There is another possibility, Major. He may be dead."

Cornwallis put the telephone down. Chaos in the south bought them time, sure enough. But, like the city, the whole Northern Division, Ground and Domain combined were not self-sustaining. They'd last a while, but not forever.

The right faction must win, and win soon, or they would be faced with starvation or surrender. Still, there was one piece of news he could pass on.

"I have news for you, Muss Amelia. Commandant Hope is dead. He was killed by his own men when he refused to obey an order from above."

A grim smile lit up her face.

"I may pass this news to the Normans and Picklesses?"

The Major nodded.

34. Rent Asunder

The morning after his difficult interview with Lane, Arundel felt well enough to appear in public. Still pale and haggard, and with his left hand bandaged, he nevertheless radiated a degree of bonhomie and determination. To those congratulating him on both his recovery and his prompt action in the face of disease, his message was simple: *Rearmament, gentlemen, rearmament and recruitment; those Outies will get their deserts.* He made an early visit to the Armouries. Young Gregory was always by his side, to the sardonic amusement of Jamie and those of his companions to whom he had revealed the connection. His visit, though, was not to his father or those nominally caring for him, but to the Master-at-Arms. In Gregory's hearing, the talk was about rifles, about ammunition, about gear for use in Badlands.

The King's room, indeed, the whole building, was heavily guarded. Only a few were around to notice that those on duty now bore Buckingham or Kent livery. Even fewer noticed over the following days that no doctor visited. John, who knew with near certainty that the King was dead, dared to ask Arundel about the guards. Arundel laughed.

"Well observed. I think you know that my father is dead. It would be remarkable for him to be the sole survivor of such a deadly fever. Certainly, my brothers and sister know it too, and many others will have guessed. It suits us all to pretend otherwise, so why should I worry about who guards an empty tomb? The truth is a weapon, Gregory. We shall see who needs to use it first. In the meantime, the fiction will be maintained."

John probed no further. The sight of Thorndyke's body, the room where the attendants were poisoned, both were lodged in his mind. But Arundel's aims, the suppression of Outies, and the bringing of order to the Grounds, these he was conditioned to approve. There were more visits, Arundel being unable to contain his impatience. On one such visit, John was sent out of earshot while an angry conversation took place between his master, Wilkes, Lane and the Master-at-

Arms. It ended with the departure of a very angry Wilkes, while the Master-at-Arms shrugged and went about his business. Lane also departed, with a smile of satisfaction. Almost as if to himself, Arundel had muttered as he and John returned to the castle.

"Damned military mind. Do we need all these separate forces? Properly armed, Security meets all our needs. Wilkes is an old woman."

Back at the castle, John was present when Dr Pritchard came to change Arundel's dressing. As he completed his task, Pritchard spoke to his patient. The doctor appeared frightened, and spoke with a stutter.

"M-my Lord, all is g-going well. I have instructed a n-nurse to attend to your bandages. M-my Lord Kent has a servant with an, an infected leg. N-no danger to others, m-my Lord, but all m-my skills are needed to save the man's leg, possibly his l-life."

Arundel's face darkened. "I require your presence, doctor. Indeed, I am about to order a room to be made available for you. You will stay. Others can deal with a damned servant. If he exists."

"M-my Lord, Lady Buckingham, she, she said that she was sure her brother would consent willingly, knowing the n-need. She said so in front of others."

Arundel made to bang his fist, remembering his injury just in time. A gruff 'get out' were his only words. John was himself dismissed soon after the doctor's departure. *The wretch has spoken to Alice*, he thought, *spoken too much*. A point, Sister dear, but that is all.

John did not immediately understand this exchange. Why was the doctor so nervous, and Arundel so angry? Then a connection hit him: doctor's uniform. The body in the basement room had been so clothed. Dr Thorndyke had been declared dead from disease. His body? Hope was dead, too, though not, it seemed, for doing anything that angered Arundel. A certain unease became stronger in John's mind.

***

For others in the castle, the following days, as June turned to July, returned to something like normal. No new infections, and only the diminished numbers available to prepare for the forthcoming Council causing grumbling, most especially from the Major-Domo and his senior stewards. Lane and Wilkes were rarely seen, and never together; their new recruits, accustomed to the leisurely pace and comfort of Court were now subject to regular drills, the discomfort of barracks life and the enthusiastic hectoring of sergeants.

One by one, members of Council not already resident arrived at Windsor. Thanks to regular patrols by Security, and to a real improvement in the feeling of those outside the walls, their eyes were not sullied by any graffiti. There were many more in these parties, for Kent had summoned Visitors and younger nobles to attend from all parts except the Northernmost. It was not long before he noticed Lane working assiduously to cultivate some. A casual conversation with the Major-Domo established that many private dinners were delivered to Arundel's apartments.

***

Sussex had a fast but very uncomfortable journey north. Arriving at the Leicester way station on the evening of June 28th, he took possession of Hope's documents. He said as little as possible to the Kingsman captain who had halted and then arrested Hope's squad. The prisoners had, of necessity, been left together, and the stories of the few he questioned were remarkably similar. The commandant had asked us to deal with infection among His Majesty's attendants. We administered a medicine, but it did not work. We sealed the coffins, and the Armouries took them for cremation. We were offered both doses and other rewards in recognition of the danger. We set off north to simulate an Outie attack at the Point. No, we had no further instructions; we thought that all there had died of disease.

Sussex had no time to press them further. He ordered the two sergeants to be sent south under heavy guard. Evening though it was, he continued north, going more and more slowly as darkness fell. He reached Retford only just before midnight, and after a brief talk with Kipling, was about to go to bed. Grayson detained him.

"My Lord, when Lord Steel returned with the Treaty, he passed me this bag; as you can see, its clasp is held with his seal. It was to be delivered unopened to you. Had you not arrived, I would have sent it south with a courier, once travel restrictions were lifted."

Under a flickering lamp in his room, Sussex looked at the contents. There was a rather crumpled box, tied around with string. There was a note. *This box contains sweetmeats sent to Hastings in captivity. Some at least are poisoned.*

Davis killed himself rather than eat any. Steel. Even though he mocked himself, Sussex went to wash his hands after replacing both in the bag.

Early the following morning, he spoke to all at the now very overcrowded station. Both Jacks and Grayson appeared honestly convinced that all absences other than that of Hastings were indeed the result of infection. The soldiers volunteered little; Lieutenant Kipling merely nodded agreement as the two wardens spoke. Things were rather different when he spoke to corporal Tiggs alone.

"Corporal, I believe you were ordered to keep Lord Steel under observation. Why was that?"

"I do not know, sir. I was not to hinder him, but to report on his activities to Lord Lane."

"Did you not ask why? Or even wonder?"

The corporal's face was stony. "Not my place to ask why, sir." Sussex waited.

"Naturally, sir, I presumed that Lord Lane had his reasons for wanting to know. Lord Steel went to some trouble to prevent me staying by his side, and he was aided by Lieutenant Kipling. And I was denied the use of a mobile to follow him when I discovered he had left for the Point or the Transfer Station. I passed that information on."

"Your sergeant, Davis. He was in good health when he left for the Point with Lord Steel?"

"Yes, sir."

"Did you not think it strange, if he was infected, that Lord Steel and his clerk felt able to return here?"

Even as he spoke, Sussex realised that that question might occur to others. Sooner or later, the truth of Davis' death would be known. Later, for preference. Tiggs volunteered that Steel and his clerk had kept themselves a little apart for a day. Those two had returned, but not Davis. The corporal had indeed found it strange. But he recalled, silently, a laughing remark by his sergeant to the effect that he was supposed to return with the hostage. *I don't think I'll be bringing that one back.* And, indeed, Lord Hastings had not returned either.

Sussex pondered. He had no reason to think the corporal guilty of any misdeeds. Transferring him south would require explanation, and his arrival at Windsor would provoke questions. Summoning Grayson and one of his clerks, he made Tiggs repeat his instructions from Lane, under oath on *The Book of the*

King, and sign the record made by the clerk. To Grayson, he gave instructions that neither Tiggs nor any of his men were to have access to the telephone.

His visit to the Point with Kipling was a brief one. Leaving Retford with full kit stowed, they drove right past Jack's Station and on. The kit was ignored. The buildings were empty and intact. There were graves, graves enough to account for the garrison, for Davis, and one other, presumably the clerk. The place was lacking any weapons or ammunition. As they inspected the graves, a flicker of movement on the hillside above caught his attention. But all remained still as he stared upwards. Outies were watching. He turned to the lieutenant.

"I think you know the truth of the matter, Lieutenant, or at least part of it. There was no disease here. All who were here, including your men, are in the Outland. Except, of course, for Davis. I am just guessing, Lieutenant, but I suspect that your men would not have fled had Lord Steel not conveyed some message from you."

Sussex construed the lieutenant's silence as an admission. He hastened to reassure.

"If so, you did right. You will not be aware that a Security force was headed north to make sure that the tale of disease was unchallenged; securely unchallenged. Or maybe a tale of assault by Outies. It was intercepted, and any travel north of Leicester is now prohibited. We have, however, to maintain the fiction for a while. We will dig yet another grave, Lieutenant, the grave of the late Lord Steel, whose body we found in the mess-room. With our report, no further deaths are to be expected."

Remaining silent, Kipling nevertheless assisted in digging and infilling a final grave. The job completed, they were about to leave, when he turned to Sussex.

"My Lord, might it be to our advantage for those in the Outland to know how these matters are to be regarded within the Domain? Should any of our side be seen among them, it might lead to the conclusion that they had been kidnapped or suborned. It would certainly refute the story of disease."

Sussex nodded. Returning inside, he raised a flag, memories decades old revived. It was not long before Jane Collins and an escort were facing him across the table. Introductions completed, he spoke briefly.

"I am sorry to summon you. However, it is the case that all who were stationed here have died. A plague that we have not identified. Their graves are outside. I trust that this infection has not been transferred?"

"Thank you, my Lord. We have had no infections among us." No mention of those with us, Sussex noted.

"I am glad. Such an outbreak, so close to your land, has naturally aroused fear of an accidental or deliberate infection from the west. Or even worse, some might assume an attack, contrary to our recent treaty. It is important that no actions on your side, nothing seen or heard, might encourage doubts about these unhappy events. We have no wish to disturb the peace."

Collins regarded him carefully. The ruling of the Domain was not a matter to which she had given much thought, nor had her education or training prepared her. The name, though, Sussex, did resonate; one of the supreme four, the near-mythical Royal Family. His message was plain enough; the attempted murder of Hastings was to be concealed, as were his and the later defections. The Outland was being asked to accept the deceit to maintain the peace. Not for her to decide, but it was clear to her that the Domain was not of one mind. The truth was inconvenient to some if not all.

"We also wish to keep the peace, my Lord. Our Chiefs will be informed. Will a flag be raised when you feel able to occupy the Point again?"

Sussex nodded. Collins departed, and soon afterwards Sussex and Kipling returned to their mobile and headed south, then east towards Retford. Jacks was ordered to reoccupy his Station; Kipling arranged a garrison to accompany him. The Point was to remain unvisited. A call to Conisbrough, a short night's sleep, and Sussex and his escort headed south, the bag and numerous papers held close.

***

Come July 1st and the castle was restored to something like its normal activity, with arrivals from all over the Domain. A revived Arundel, still bandaged, was moving through the public spaces, greeting new arrivals with enthusiasm. Several became engaged in private conversations. Sussex was nowhere to be seen, while Kent and Buckingham seemed rather reclusive. Juniors, though were mingling. Many found old friends from the Grounds from which they had been taken. Stories were swapped. Many were wild in the extreme, but there were some that recurred. Two in particular found their way to their masters' apartments.

As Jamie reported to Kent, several of those in service in various Divisions reported that their masters were in high spirits. Several sneered at his Marine livery.

"The tide has turned, and you'll be stranded. The Outies are the target; rich rewards for those who win their spurs."

But from those that wore loyalty less obviously on their sleeves, Kent and Buckingham picked up a more worrying tale. While never explicitly stated, there were many, and not only those already ennobled, who anticipated not mere reward, but enhanced longevity in return for loyalty. A gift which no one of the four was entitled to authorise. Even the very junior seemed to hint at joys to come.

"Alfred has already committed the doses released for the Hunt," said Kent. "In fact, he has probably committed more than is there. I inquired; Lane alone has already received 150."

"150 for that little creep? High stakes indeed, and he cannot afford to lose. The guard is as it should be?" asked Buckingham.

"Yes, though Alfred has placed more on those kept apart for the Hunt. It will not take much to exhaust those stocks after what he has used on Lane. He will disappoint, even anger many, but too late for them to obtain any satisfaction."

"Unless, of course, he expects to have sole control. At least, we have the means to prevent it."

In the other direction, the stories were less clear. The Marine juniors seemed to know that their masters had some person with them. Never seen, or only glimpses of strange attire as the person concerned was shielded while in transit from mobile to tent, or, eventually, to Kent's apartments. Neither Arundel nor Lane could make anything of it. Arundel was dismissive.

"Maybe Alice has acquired some ranting prophet in rags, to play on superstition. Or some escapee from Reclamation to give testimony to our brutal ways." A laugh. "I think, though, that we have enough to sway the Council?"

"Yes, my Lord. But we have promised more than we can deliver, the more so if we cannot control the central store."

"*Sufficient unto the day,*" said Arundel in that sing-song voice. *Why the hell,* he thought, *can I not get that old fraud's voice out of my head.*

At noon, Sussex arrived, together with two prisoners who were hurried away to cells guarded by his own men; these were the sergeants he had despatched and then collected as he passed by Oxford. Publicly, he made known the slaughter caused by disease at the Treaty Point, and the need for the continued ban on movement north. Settled into his apartments, it was not long before he summoned Wilkes. A Wilkes already disposed to a stubborn opposition to what he saw as the transfer of military capability to Security, and a reluctance to face the growing power of the Outies. Sussex was smooth.

"It would appear, Wilkes, that my Lord Arundel will seek to persuade Council to prepare an immediate assault on the Outlands. Territory to be held, servants for the Domain to be conscripted. A major undertaking indeed, Wilkes. You are prepared?"

"No, my Lord. I have not even received weapons enough to replace losses at the Hunt. And the Master-at-Arms has been told to deliver half their production to Security. Rifles for police, not soldiers. My Lord, you witnessed the Outie strength at the Hunt. And there was that strange incident in the north, if you remember; Outies standing up to fight, even to attack. And there are those balloons, my Lord, until we can overrun their launching sites."

"Are you saying that it cannot be done?"

"No, my Lord. In time, anything is possible. The Master may at last develop flying machines that are not death traps for those that use them. Double the size of my forces; give us time to train. Use specialists or the unchosen to make paths through the Badlands."

He paused. Memories of his browsing in the archives returned.

"My Lord, the danger to the Domain is damage to the Grounds, damage that will cripple us for generations. At the Catastrophe, and before, attacks by air were commonplace. Civilians were killed in large numbers. They were trained to take cover, to watch for hostile aircraft and sound the alarm. We should establish such a system before we attack. Easy enough to spot those balloons. It is time, my Lord. Give me time, and anything may be achieved."

"Thank you. Be sure to argue in Council as you have with me. The Grounds are our lifeblood."

There was one more task to perform before he met Kent and Buckingham. Down in the cells were the two sergeants from Hope's band of desperadoes, each in a separate cell. Sussex had one brought up, noisily, past the cell of the other. At first, the man stuck rigidly to the agreed story. Sussex probed.

"Such a simple task, sergeant. A spot of lying about Outies, granted, but a simple job of vandalism at the Point. Worth 50 years, 50 years for a sergeant with no distinction to his record? Quite a reward. I'm inclined to think that rather more was involved. There were others able to deny that simple story. Were there any, any shall we say, instructions regarding those?"

The sergeant said nothing.

"Back to that night at the Armouries. All, that is all, apparently, with the exception of His Majesty, dead within 36 hours, most in less than eight. A bit surprising, sergeant. His Majesty, with all respect to his status, was not a well man beforehand. And for such a virulent disease, spread so rapidly among attendants, to affect none of those responsible for their isolation. Some might find that hard to believe."

"We were well-protected, sir. I had no sight of the King himself."

"Sergeant, you will be aware that any rewards are out of the question; rather, it is the issue of punishment for the little escapade up north. Certainly, your refusal to co-operate with Commandant Hope counts in your favour, late in coming though it was. There are degrees of hardship when assigned to Reclamation, sergeant. Identities can also be concealed. I think you can imagine just how a Tadgie sergeant would be regarded by his fellow unfortunates."

The sergeant remained silent.

"I will leave you to think about it, sergeant. An account that answers all our concerns might persuade us to think of consequences less severe."

Unlike the sergeants, Sussex had memories of modes of interrogation, fictional and real, from those distant days before the Catastrophe. He summoned a guard. The sergeant was bound and gagged. Sussex led him back personally to the cells. As they passed the cell of the other, Sussex spoke.

"Thank you, sergeant. Your help is appreciated. Those who speak as you have done will merit clemency."

A trick, a cheap one; it would have failed back then. It worked. The other, not the brightest of men, soon revealed the intended killing of all who might question the tale of Outie attack. The commandant had said there were traitors to be dealt with. Sussex sighed; It was not only in the Outland that brains were in short supply.

"Traitors including your own comrades at the way station, I think, sergeant. Did it not occur to you that those that planned such an atrocity might later think that those doing the deed should suffer the same fate? Did you really think that such remarkable rewards would be forthcoming? You were taken for a fool. Luckily for you, that, at least, is wholly believable. It will be taken into account."

Despite the breakdown in the man's composure that followed, answers as to events in the Armouries were less satisfactory. It seemed that he had believed the tale of disease, and had been guarding the building rather than administering medicine. Good enough. Sussex procured a clerk. A statement was signed and witnessed. As he left Sussex ordered the guard doubled. All bar himself were to be barred. Yes, by force if needed, and an alarm sounded. Now, he could talk to his brother and sister. Talk to get any precipitate action delayed.

The meeting was less than satisfactory to him. Certainly, the others agreed, these witnesses were to be welcomed. The statement of Tiggs too; all added up to a deliberate attempt to stage an Outie atrocity. The warrants issued to Hope, the discovery that Lane had received a massive dose and the evident irritation of Wilkes all provided evidence in Sussex' eyes in favour of delay, delay that could be argued for without any outright condemnation of their brother. Hope could carry the guilt. To Sussex, the next step was clear; the three of them should confront him privately. Surely, he would back down, his ambitions delayed rather than extinguished? A united front would be maintained in Council, and the King's absence would not matter. To his amazement, neither was willing to follow that path.

"We will not face our brother other than in Council. All should hear your witnesses, including Wilkes. All should know about Lane's dose. All know that the supply is limited."

As she spoke, Lady Buckingham glanced at Kent. There was a scarcely perceptible shaking of heads. It is still not the time. She turned back to Sussex.

"Delay is not enough, brother. We must end this plan to milk the Outland once and for all. Give Wilkes even double the force, and the losses will be too great to bear. How many more of those damned balloons are there? How much Agent Z do they have? How many could they kill in the Grounds? Outies no longer run. Now they fight, and they have a fair number of our weapons. What might they do in the north, even without balloons?"

Unwilling to approach Alfred alone, Sussex had no choice but to agree. No doubt, the case for delay would be strong, and might convince many. But Alfred would fight against abandonment, and there was no King to give that final yes or no. Open division without that means of resolution. The military against Truth and Justice. He left with an increasing sense not merely of missing something in his brother's and sister's approach, but of being excluded.

Left alone, Alice turned to George. They had already discussed their plans for Council. The witnesses were prepared, the surprise complete. But even that might not sway enough. The weapon of last resort, the weapon that removed their own power as well as Alfred's: It must be ready.

"You have the team ready? To act before Council concludes? Before Alfred moves?"

"They are ready. I have only to arrange the signal from the meeting."

"You have enough to make sure?"

Kent nodded. "You remember Defoe, Sister, recalling that tale he both loved and hated. The story that had him weeping and laughing at the same time. The one he said so crudely we had turned arse over tit. What was the quote he poked us with, again and again just before he fled? *When she was tempted, she resisted. "I pass the test, I will diminish and go into the west, and remain Galadriel." Not you, I think.* I did not understand then. He was right, wasn't he? Now, well, the name and direction may be wrong, but that is all."

They hugged.

***

The following day passed in apparent calm. Only the Major-Domo was seen to be rushing about. The Council would be a problem. Not merely the Councillors and their staff, but Visitors, nobles acting as intermediaries, senior officers from both the military and Truth and Justice, all with clerks. Traditional refreshments would need to be brought in, not laid out beforehand.

But it was only servants so occupied. Retinues, allowed out now that infection was no longer feared and the mood of the town restored, wandered easily through the streets. For many, it was their first view of the centre of power, seemingly better endowed than their backwater postings. To the inhabitants, the numbers of those with credits to burn was a pleasant surprise. Stocks of numerous items ran out. Parents, grandparents, the elderly more generally, were robbed of their treasures on the promise that equivalents would be purchased later more cheaply. The grumbling associated with the forced recruitment to soldiering or policing declined.

Somehow, doubts about the King's survival also circulated. It was noticed that it was those associated with Arundel who were the biggest spenders. Towards evening, new graffiti appeared, crude images of Arundel with a crown on his head. Unseen by most, a few depicted ships sinking. Security patrols were cheered rather than hindered whereas a few parties in Marine uniforms were hassled. As darkness fell, it was noticed that those who came with Kent or Buckingham had disappeared. Around the castle, illustrations from the *Book* lay around; illustrations of the kind Jamie had possessed, depicting Outies in their most misshapen and aggressive form. Arundel, safe in his apartments, was well pleased with Lane's work.

"When we have gained Council, Lane, when the policy is set, then we hear that His Majesty has died. And we move to succession. Both by precedence, and by acclamation. There are those outside ready to demand it? The messenger on hand?"

"All primed, my Lord."

"Any reaction, Lane, any counter moves?"

"None that I can see, my Lord. Certainly, none outside the walls. I am told that Lord Sussex holds prisoners. I assume they are from Hope's misguided foray." Lane looked straight at Arundel as he spoke.

"Sussex? Hope? The papers say nothing conclusive. Testimony from a few thugs who had not the sense to keep their mouths shut. My brother will argue merely for delay; he will accept being overruled, and flap about trying to protect Grounds. We can suggest he involves himself in *Civil Defence.*" Arundel gave a snort. "What about the others?"

"They have isolated themselves, my Lord. Their retinue bars all approaches to their apartments. There seem to be many, but they have not strayed since nightfall."

35. Downfall

The start of Council had been scheduled for ten o'clock. Long before, the old chapel filled up. The same table around which Councillors sat was moved closer to the dais; another was added to its end. Behind each side, rows of chairs, benches even, had replaced the space and the tables that held the usual refreshments. The Major-Domo was rapidly losing patience. There were squabbles over seating. The more self-important Councillors complained about their clerk's sitting alongside rather than behind. Lane was an early arrival. A clutch of Councillors sat close to him, and competition for seats behind him was intense and bad-tempered. Wilkes arrived later, ostentatiously sitting apart. He was joined by Dundonnell, the reclusive Commissioner for Reclamation. The remainder were obliged to fill the gap. Notably, Wilkes kept an empty seat beside him, brushing away all comers.

It took the striking of the clock, and the furious ringing of a bell by the Major-Domo to get all in place. The Four entered. Contrary to precedent, several armed men in livery accompanied all but Sussex, men who placed themselves impassively behind their patrons. The throne remained empty. In the very brief meeting beforehand, it had been agreed that the Major-Domo would explain the King's absence. Arundel would chair. A matter of surprise, as he had anticipated an objection. The price seemed trivial: a new Councillor for Maritime Affairs.

The room fell silent. The Major-Domo announced, baldly, that the King was, as was well-known, unable to attend.

"His Majesty has therefore graciously ordered that any decision arrived at by this Council should be regarded as his wish, and duly executed. In his absence, his heirs have agreed that my Lord Arundel will take the chair."

Arundel rose. "Before we commence, gentlemen, my sister, the Lady Buckingham, has brought to my attention the fact that Maritime Affairs has lacked a representative here on Council. She wishes such a post to be created and filled. The name of Captain Henshaw has been proposed."

There was a murmur. Captain. Not a Lord. No enhancement, then, something almost unheard of. A name known only to very few. Councillors looked anxiously at Arundel. Did he want assent or rejection? Arundel made it easy.

"We should welcome this proposal, gentlemen. Such an *important* post should not be left unfilled."

There was a vague, but unanimous sign of consent. Ushers at the back made a path for a tall, well-built man in Marine uniform. A man visibly in late middle age at best, white of beard and grey of hair, approached the empty seat next to Wilkes; he bowed towards the dais and sat down. Arundel resumed.

"My Lords, my Lords and gentleman," there was a snigger from somewhere near Lane, and a number of grins from those around him. "You know why this Council has been called; you know why we have invited so many to attend our deliberations. You will know of the murderous attack on our Grounds by Outies. You will know that the Hunt was sabotaged, that Outies not only used the coward's weapon of poison, but that they were aided and abetted by disturbances in our cities, affecting the source of our labour and the means by which we preserve the Domain.

We were forced, how I hate that word, but it fits, forced to accede to a treaty with that rabble, a treaty we have good reason to think has already been broken at the Treaty Point itself under pretence of a plague. Broken or not, that treaty imperils our existence. In two ways, my Lords. Collusion in the Grounds and among some who manage them threatens our ability to acquire Service. Even without such traitorous behaviour, the supply does not meet the demand. Our numbers are declining. There are Outies, my Lords, Outies that can breed, but who can be rendered obedient to our will. Thousands, my Lords, no, tens, even hundreds of thousands for the taking. Land that is nearly ripe for the status of Grounds. The Outies have resisted. We have suffered, but we have the measure of their strength. Balloons? Of limited use, my Lords. A device which depends on surprise. Prepared, and they are of little effect.

It is my wish that we move, move now, to stamp out all resistance. To destroy at source the origins of these clumsy weapons. To seize both territory and inhabitants. Then to impose a much stricter discipline on the Grounds, and especially the cities, cities whose inhabitants have colluded with Outies. To this end, I hope to have the endorsement of you all for the detailed proposals that will be put before you."

Sussex was already standing before he had finished. Arundel gave way with an ironic bow.

"My Lords, Captain, indeed all who are here. The Outlanders are indeed a potential threat. As yet, though, they have abided by the terms of our treaties. There have been no incursions into the land of the Domain. Engagements in no man's land, as at the Hunt? They were not covered in writing, at our insistence. We might hope, in due time, to expand the bounds of the Domain. That time is not now. You know the fate of the Hunt, but perhaps not the full extent of our losses. With the trouble in the cities, we have lost more than a thousand. And not just men, weapons too. We have, at best, a fragile truce with several cities. My brother has suggested that we turn on them after an assault on the Outland. Do you think that truce will hold when we are engaged with the Outland? My Lord General, would you inform Council of our strength and capability relative to the situation before the Hunt?"

Wilkes rose. "Certainly, my Lord. Our numbers are well down. We have indeed conscripted more, though not yet enough to replace the loss. But numbers alone are not the problem. We are used to a weak opponent, one who runs unless cornered. That is no longer the case, my Lords. Not only do they fight, but they have discipline. They have clever leaders, my Lords. They have some of our weapons. In any area with ruins or other cover, they have a tactical advantage with their poison."

There was a slight stir. Faces turned to Arundel, who remained impassive. Sussex pressed further.

"General, can you tell us of your needs in any campaign where such resistance is likely?"

"Certainly, more rifles and ammunition, my Lord, a lot more. More than the Armouries can deliver within a year, possibly more. More heavy kit to cross Badlands, more labour to clear paths. Much more training. My Lords, these timings depend on the full production of the Armouries. But half their production is now dedicated to Security."

Another stir. Arundel retained his composure, but Lane was visibly angered. He made to speak, but was waved down by Arundel.

"My Lords," he said, "The General is, no doubt, well-intentioned. But Kingsmen alone were not as effective as I would have expected in the unfortunate engagement at the Hunt. We are better informed now. Certainly, I have diverted weapons production to Security. They are, I believe, more accustomed to dealing with the recalcitrant, and it will fall to them to manage our newly acquired assets. And to bring greater pressure to bear on those Groundlings who defy us. They do not fear the cities.

Of course, I am not suggesting an attack tomorrow, but it must be months, and few of them, rather than years before we move. Years in which our strength will decay, and that of the Outies increase. They are treaty-breakers, My Lords. Wait, and they will attack us."

It was Wilkes' turn to anger.

"It is not their balloons alone that threaten us. There is a clear passage to our best Ground in the north, as we have discovered. They can overrun, poison or contaminate on foot. Attack in one place, and they will retaliate in another. Defend the north while we regain Cotswold or anywhere to the south, and we will need three, no, four times our present strength. Reverse it and the situation is the same. And the north is quarantined and at present undefended. So far, the Outies have abided by the treaty there. Fear the cities? Yes, my Lords, we fear them with good reason, but can find the means to restore order. Many pistols were lost, many of our men killed in the *fearless* assaults by those under Lord Lane's command. Discipline, my Lords, discipline and training. And time."

Lane rose to his feet, face showing his indignation. Arundel was again attempting to restrain him when Sussex started speaking. The interruption provoked gasps.

"My Lords, as the General has told you, the Outlanders have not broken the treaty in the north. In a place where, now, they could walk in and remove all who live there. Nor have they broken it elsewhere. No Outlander has set foot in Ground or Domain." He paused, just long enough for Arundel to rise.

"However," he shouted, before Arundel could speak. "However, my Lords, it is the case that some forces of the Domain, our forces, attempted to make believe that there was an Outlander breach, an attack on the Treaty Point. An attempt made by Security forces under the command of a Commandant Hope. Hope is dead, my Lords, killed by his own men when he refused to surrender at Leicester. His journey was authorised by my brother, Lord Arundel." He turned and picked up a satchel. "The orders, endorsed, were retrieved from his effects. They are open to inspection."

The silence was total. Eyes turned to Arundel. Unflustered, he rose to his feet.

"By all means, let my orders to Hope be read by all. You will find no reference in them to 'make believe' that an Outie attack had occurred. They were to establish for certain what had happened to account for the disappearance of a whole garrison, together with Lord Steel and his clerk. Disease, we were told, by those more inclined to protect their own interests than those of the Domain. Lord Hastings had already disappeared. There was good reason to doubt, to wonder what part the Outies might have played."

Sussex signalled. The confessor sergeant was brought in. Rather than examine him, Sussex read out his statement. He turned to the man.

"Sergeant, you made this statement, before witnesses. Is it a true statement?"

The sergeant nodded; requested to speak up, a mumbled 'Yes, my Lord' was heard. There were mutterings around the hall. The sergeant was removed. Eyes turned to Arundel. Only to those close to him on the dais was a tic in his left eye visible.

"I gave no such orders. You will find none in the documents my brother has with him. If, if and only if that statement is true, I can only assume that Hope acted on his own, in a misguided attempt to fulfil what he assumed would find favour. The commandant was indeed robust in his approach to security. My Lords, it would seem that I misjudged him, for which I am sorry. He has, in any case, paid the direst penalty for his presumption."

Sussex surveyed the assembly below him. Most would follow Alfred; many would have received promises. He must be indirect.

"My Lords, as you heard, the sergeants accompanying Commandant Hope were to be rewarded with fifty years each for their part."

That fact had not been overlooked by those assembled, many promised and more hoping for such rewards. He rammed the point home.

"Fifty years? For a simple routine inspection of potential plague at the Treaty Point? An inspection that could as well be carried out locally? The issue is this. The General has put before you the reasons, sound, practical reasons, why any attack on the Outland without careful, long-term preparation puts the whole Domain at risk. There was one circumstance, and one only, that might outweigh such reasons. A breach of the treaty by Outies, a significant and bloody breach. Hope had intended to provide us with its appearance, a breach sufficient to stir our hearts with anger."

He paused. *Avoid his brother, but Lane? By implication, not by name. Yet.*

"My Lords, this was not a device confined to one wayward commandant, nor was it confined to his ill-fated journey. An earlier attempt was made, from our side, to cause Lord Hastings to die in Outie custody. A breach indeed; a justification for war. It was made known to us by Lord Steel, and also to the Outland. We judged it right to conceal this. But after Lord Steel's return from the Point with the treaty, he was watched by Security, and not on the instructions of Hope. I have sworn testimony as to the orders given. Had he not died already from disease, I might think that his end, by other means, might have followed soon after. It was, perhaps, not just one commandant who presumed to interpret the interest of the Domain in their own way? My Lords, it seems that there are those who wished to create an atmosphere that called for revenge."

In the rows behind, there was now a susurration: whispers, glances at both Lane and Arundel. Councillors, though, remained silent. Never before had they had to vote or to speak, to decide which of the four to back. Speak out, and dismissal might follow; some remembered the fate of Pendennis not long before. Kent and Buckingham sat silent, their faces giving no clue to their opinions. Arundel rose slowly. A few paces, and he stood directly before the throne.

"For Majesty's sake. These sworn statements from ignorant men, these well-intentioned but foolish subterfuges apparently devised by overzealous Security? So what? My brother has shielded you from the full truth, the full danger that the Outlands present. Hastings did not return when the Treaty was signed, as we demanded. Disease? No, defection, my Lords, defection to the Outlands. Whether willing or coerced we cannot tell. Steel said it was willingly. Steel is dead; or is he? The garrison?"

Sussex stood and shouted.

"Overzealous? Foolish? Who promised Hope 200, and has already given Lane 150? And yes, dead. All buried bar Steel himself, buried by me and Lieutenant Kipling."

There was a shocked silence. Such doses were unheard-of. Arundel moved towards his brother, towering over him, his guards close behind. Kent signalled his to move towards Sussex. They faced each other, barely a yard apart. A pause, and Arundel turned to the front.

"Oh, really? You were prepared to bury a plague-ridden corpse? I wonder what is in those graves? Sheep carcases perhaps? Heather? Rocks? It is easy enough to find out, Brother. More likely a new bunch of traitors or captives is with the Outies. It is what comes with treating with monsters, spawn of the Deceiver. They must be…"

A fierce ringing drowned his voice. Buckingham had moved and grabbed the bell that the Major-Domo had put aside. Guards bunched behind their principals, hands on hilts or holsters. She ceased the ringing, and broke the silence that followed.

"My Lords, there are other voices to be heard, other facts to lay before you." She faced Arundel directly. A pause; *she can have nothing of note, nothing to sway opinion other than her own,* was his thought. He gave a mocking bow and returned to his seat. Sussex followed suit. The guards retreated to the rear.

"My Lords, you have heard two arguments. One," she bowed towards Arundel, "that looks to replenish our realm by conquest; that reckons that rewards will outweigh losses, great though they may be. The other," she nodded at Sussex, then turned to look at Wilkes, "gives reasons to doubt; reasons to think that we risk too much." She paused, and looked round the room.

"My Lords, there is one thing in common between these arguments. That for our survival we depend on the capacity of the Domain, the Grounds and whatever we may, sooner or later, acquire from the Outlands, or from the failing task of Reclamation. I have a different argument to put before you. You have welcomed the new Commissioner, Captain Henshaw. It is appropriate that I introduce him before I ask him to speak. The captain is our most experienced mariner. A year ago, he set out on a voyage, one of many to discover new land, uncontaminated land."

There was a snort from Arundel.

"Yet another such. 140 years of failure; a greater waste of resources than anything ascribed to Reclamation. Mud and contamination are all there is to show for it. Nothing better than the grubbier parts of our Domain."

There was some laughter. But Lady Buckingham merely smiled. A smile that stilled the room.

"A year ago, my Lords, he set sail in our best, our largest ship. He did not return; rather, he did not return until three weeks ago. We had given him up, him and all his crew. He had made for the north, where the seas are treacherous. Another failure to be used against our efforts to find more land, land that we could use. But, as you can see, he has returned. Captain, give us an account of your voyage. Your voyage and what you found at its end."

The captain rose, an impressive figure with a look of authority in his eyes.

"My Lady, my Lords. It is as my Lady has said. It may be that not all have received instruction on the geography of the seas and lands to our east, lands diminished by the rising sea. Again, and again, we have encountered land half submerged, land polluted beyond repair. At best, a few places little different than the poorest in the Domain, as my Lord Arundel has said. No signs of human life. But the old maps show different land to the north. Land rocky and high. A few had attempted to find it; they did not return. Land that was previously called Sweden, or Norway."

There was a murmur. Not all had been given access to the archives; many, indeed, had only the vaguest notion of what lay overseas or how far away it was. Most had come to regard a posting to Marine as just one step up from Reclamation.

"There were favourable winds. We did find a rocky coast, a dangerous coast with many islands. There were many signs of contamination. But as we ventured north the damage decreased. There were forests that appeared untouched. No sign of human life. Then the weather changed; strong winds that threatened to drive us onto rocks. We could find sheltered anchorage. We went ashore. There was water, there were deer to hunt. Territory for the taking, as we thought."

Another loud intervention from Arundel.

"Territory that claims the lives of how many in wrecks, Captain. The chances, man, one in five, one in ten?" There was laughter from those around Lane. "I wonder who might take those odds for a patch of rocky ground. Ground devoid of places to farm, in any case requiring clearance. Yes, Captain, I also know my geography. Regions so harsh that their escape from attack might be attributed to lack of targets."

The captain did not flinch. He remained silent until the hubbub died away.

"After a few days, we were visited, visited by hunters, my Lords. People; not just people, as we soon discovered. Fertile people, folk as prolific as those in our most productive Grounds. People without disfigurement."

A shockwave went through the room. It had never been said that, for sure, only the Domain and the Outland had sustained human life through the Catastrophe, but the lack of any evidence to the contrary had somehow percolated through the collective mind, so that it was almost taken as established fact: the Domain was the last, best hope of humanity. Lady Buckingham forestalled Arundel.

"Captain, these people, these hunters, were they not hostile? You were taking their deer."

"Quite the contrary, my Lady. We could not understand their language, but we were treated almost like, like the highest of nobility." Almost, but held back in time, he had said *like Gods.* "They fingered our clothes. They knew what guns were, though they had none. The first left us and returned with others. A party of my men were led inland, led to a settlement. A primitive place indeed, but one with children. Healthy children, though grievously short of food.

I had a choice, my Lords. Weather allowing it, we could stock up and return before the summer was over, before the storms worsened and the winds always against us. We had, indeed, started such preparations. Even without language, those hunters saw our intent. They begged, my Lords, begged on their knees that we would stay. I put it to the crew; would they stay a winter, a winter and a spring."

He regarded the assembly. All bar Buckingham were men. Men like his own, mostly without partners.

"It did not take much persuasion, my Lords. Those that visited the settlement, and there were many such visits, found good reason to stay. In hope, I should add; I enforced a strict discipline."

A small burst of laughter, quickly stilled as Arundel rose again.

"Good reason, Captain? A good reason for open war with a bunch of savages. Did those poor innocents know that your men were sterile, or would father monsters?"

"I made sure, as best I could, that they were aware. With your consent, I would like to defer that matter. I promise it will be fully answered. But there is a question, my Lord, that you have not asked; why they begged us to stay. I can tell you. They were starving. Not visibly, but slowly. They could grow little and harvest less from the wild. Their hunters travelled further each year to find game. Winter, winter and spring, were harsh beyond our reckoning. We had guns, rifles. They knew of their power, though legend had exaggerated their effects.

My Lords, staying with them, I made some effort to learn their language and their history. The Catastrophe hit hard. The towns and cities were destroyed, and remain lethal. There was a huge one to the north; Red hot and barren. There were but few survivors, with less than us in resources. They had no means of preserving what we have preserved. No paper, no writing, no reading. No machinery, no electricity. The past recalled only by stories passed from one generation to the next."

Arundel rose and turned towards his sister.

"So, my Lady, this is the big surprise, the telling argument for sustaining the Domain overseas? The reason why we should abandon the riches on our doorstep for scraps of land with starving inhabitants. Land that is dangerous to reach; land unsuited for any useful production?"

He turned to the captain, down at the far end of the Councillors' table.

"I suppose, Captain, that we should commend you on your adventurous spirit and navigational skills. They will be put to much better use when we sail in the Severn Sea, sail in force to reclaim the Outland for our own. The savages, for that is what they have become, can wait, if indeed they survive."

There was a murmur of approval around the room. Lane looked inquiringly at Arundel: *is it time? A shake of the head.* Eyes turned again to Buckingham.

"My Lords, the captain's account is not yet complete. Continue, please."

"It was not just our guns, or the ship, or the books, nor any other product of our," a pause, "civilisation, that attracted the greatest interest. It was our protective kits, the kits we wear to cross the semi-badlands in search of better land. My Lords, they tell us of empty lands to the east, better land, land that was depopulated by disease. Large areas that were uncontaminated. Land inaccessible to them now because of the Badlands in between. Land that some had died while finding it, tracking through Badlands. Badlands that would sterilise those whom it did not kill. Land through which paths could be cleared, land through which Grounders and they themselves could pass with impunity if kitted out."

"There is one more matter, Captain. Time, I think to produce an ambassador, a spokesman if you will."

The captain nodded. A boy behind him squeezed to the main door, and returned with a veritable giant of a man, a giant clearly normal, and not the product of some mutagen. A man clad mainly in leather and wool. He stood calmly by the captain.

"My Lords, may I introduce Mr Bengt Bengtsson, from the village of Kullavik. Mr Bengtsson agreed to accompany us back here. Five of my men remain there, armed, to assist in their hunts. I regret that he has learnt little of our language. I have learnt a little of his, and I will endeavour to translate."

"Mr Bengtsson, tell us your age. *Säg oss din ålder.*"

"*Jag är fyrtionio år gammal.*" The captain raised both hands five times, the last with one finger turned down. A nod. "Forty-nine, my Lords. You are married? *Du är gift?*" A nod. "You have children? *Du har barn?*" Four fingers held up. "Grandchildren? *Barnbarn?*" There was a pause, and the man looked sad. It took some exchanges and signs before the captain could turn to the assembly.

"He had six, but three died very young. He hopes for more."

Arundel grew impatient.

"So, he is fertile, or so he says. A man may brag or be cuckolded."

Something about Arundel's words were understood by Bengtsson, who turned to the captain. A conversation inaudible to most ended when the captain turned back to the assembly.

"My Lord, if fertile and willing partners are provided, he is happy to prove the truth of his words."

There was an outbreak of laughter. Bengtsson grinned. Arundel sat, fuming. The next part of the conversation became complicated. The captain managed to make it clear that Bengtsson's folk were happy to co-operate. That they understood that new lands gained would be open to all who were fertile.

"Are they that foolish, or think that we are more so?" said Arundel. "They are not of our stock; they do not speak our language. They gain this passage to *Paradise* with our help, then keep it for themselves. If not, do they not see an end to themselves, absorbed into our realm? Will there not be war, a much harder war to fight than for the Outland?"

It was Kent who answered.

"The captain talked to others when he was there. We have, with difficulty, had further conversations with Mr Bengtsson. My Lords, they already face an end. Their numbers have fallen. The captain arrived in an unusually kind year. And, yes, there are birth defects, but due to small numbers and inbreeding. Those dealing with our smallest Grounds will recognise the problem, and its solution by transfers. They have nowhere to transfer to. Unlike ourselves, they have retained hope that there were others luckier than themselves. The captain's arrival justified that hope."

There was a muttered conversation between the captain and Bengtsson. Eventually, the stranger rose.

"What the Lord says, this is true. With you, live. Without, die." The thumbs down made the meaning clear.

Arundel was quick to grasp the admission.

"So, my Lords, there is land. Rather, we should say, perhaps there is land. Land imagined in the garbled stories of an illiterate savage. Land that requires major reclamation work to find and to colonise. Land that is hard to reach. Land that will cost lives simply in crossing the sea."

He looked around the hall.

"Land that, if it exists, in due time can be reached when it is empty. Land that requires us to have the people, the ships, the gear in sufficient quantities. Quantities we can find only when the Outland is ours, when the Grounds yield their dues of Service. My Lords, this is no substitute for action now, on our own land, with no watery grave to block us."

When it is empty. The captain started to rise, but Wilkes pulled him down, and nodded to Dundonnell. Dundonnell, frequently regarded as the dimmest of Councillors, the most given to hand-wringing protests about the human cost of clearance, protests that were routinely dismissed. Shaking, he got to his feet. Arundel gave a contemptuous shrug, and sat down.

"My Lords, my Lady. We have the means. Reclamation has stopped. The labour is unused. It could scarcely be worse used than it has been under the administration of Truth and Justice. There are thousands who would risk any death at sea in preference to their present labours. Labours that have already rendered most unfit for military service. And Truth and Justice? They have protective equipment enough." His look was turned to Lane.

Lane started to rise, but Arundel gave him a look and a signal. Lane turned to two beside him, who pushed their way through the crowd to the doors. Unseen by most, Lady Buckingham nodded at Jamie who left through a side door. There was a murmuring in the crowd, and a look of terror on all Councillors' faces, all that is except Lane, the captain and Wilkes. They could see a vote being needed. A vote that would mark the losers out for demotion or worse. It was not even clear which option Sussex would support. A brave soul rose to ask for the only way out.

"My Lords, my Lady. We know that the King is confined by illness. But may the choices not be put to him? Never before have we had to act without his assent, or by the assurance that his children are all of one mind?"

There were nods all around the Councillors' table. Arundel rose.

"His Majesty is not confined. He is dead, killed by the plague that took those who attended him. We must make a decision without his guidance and consent."

A silence. Some knew, many suspected, but more still were taken by surprise. Glances at the dais, however, left no doubt that all the Four had known. Kent made to rise, but was forestalled by Lane.

"My lords, it is sad news indeed. The King is dead. Is the Domain then leaderless, left at the mercy of mere opinions? Opinions of mere servants like ourselves, accustomed to obey, not to decide? My Lords, I believe not. Times past, when none could live beyond the natural span, Kings died. What followed? His firstborn son became King at the moment of his father's passing. As it was said: *The King is dead. Long live the King.* My Lord Arundel's modesty has been too great. My Lords, we have a King, King Alfred of Arundel."

"King Alfred! King Alfred!" Shouts from those around Lane gained in volume. Many rose to their feet. The west door swung open to admit yet more into the crowded hall. More councillors rose to their feet. Soon only those around Wilkes remained seated. Arundel once more moved to place himself in front of the throne.

As he raised his hand to still the shouting, a blast shook the building. Glass from the ancient, much patched windows rained down with dust. In the confusion, more guards in the liveries of Kent and Buckingham appeared on the dais. A squad of Marines lined up just below it. As the debris settled, cries and shots could be heard outside. A scuffle on stage pushed Arundel to one side. Pistols were drawn. Even as those below dusted themselves or held handkerchiefs to bleeding faces, the tableau above caught the attention of all. In the silence, Lady Buckingham stepped to the edge of the dais.

"My Lords, gentlemen. I believe that many of you have been promised great rewards in return for this Enterprise of the Outlands. Not just years, I suspect, but decades, even centuries. My Lord Lane has already received his. Rewards that a King Alfred, freshly acclaimed, would distribute to his loyal subjects."

She looked around the hall.

"My Lords, gentlemen, there was never enough supply to meet all those promises. Too late, many of you would discover that truth. There needed to be an end to this corruption, this playing on the fear of death and decrepitude. Now, there is none. That explosion? The store of what remains. There are no such rewards, not now nor in the future."

Arundel was stunned. *The fools. What have they done? Their power is as much diminished as mine.* He looked around. Most might still want the assurance of a King, rewards or no. But he had been outwitted; there were far more of those with arms behind his sister than he could muster. In his silence, Kent stepped forward.

"The King is dead. But our father was not the son of a King before him. His rule, as you were all taught, rested on his foresight in protecting himself and others during the Catastrophe and on his power to reward those loyal to his rule. There were other forms of rule. The King is dead, certainly. Of what? No one living remains to tell us, not even his doctor. His body is reduced to ashes. His supposed confinement was overseen by that same Commandant Hope whose attempt to fool us into reacting to an Outie atrocity was, fortunately, prevented.

Our father, even in declining health, was a man of caution. Councillors will recall that when there was discord among us, he would command delay; delay and prudence. Delay and prudence that angered some to a degree that provoked that commandant's despicable deception."

He paused, and looked pointedly at Lane.

"The King is dead. Was not that death remarkably convenient for those thirsty for a quick if bloody solution to our problems?"

Arundel could not let this pass. Lane was not to be trusted, but Lane knew nothing of the King's death.

"A slur, a monstrous slur, on those who struggled to contain the plague around His Majesty. And on those who risked all to remove the bodies to avoid spread. What evidence of anything else is there? Nothing at all."

He was about to continue, when there was a struggle behind him. A young man in the uniform of a Security lieutenant broke free from his companions behind Arundel and ran almost into Kent's arms, falling as he ran. Pistols were raised. A short, a stunned silence followed as Kent helped John Gregory to his feet. He stared into the eyes of a boy distraught, a boy driven over the edge.

"My Lord," said in whisper, "the doctor, he was killed; stabbed and poisoned. I saw his body. Here, in the castle." The boy shuddered. "Others too in the Armouries, I saw it."

"The King?"

"I never saw him, my Lord."

"Can you say so, out loud?" John nodded. Kent stepped forward.

"What evidence, My Lords? Listen well."

John started.

"The doctor attending the King was murdered. I was used by Commandant Hope to assist in carrying the body away. And the King's attendants were not sick, they were—"

A shot was fired. As John fell, there was an exchange of fire on the dais. As the smoke cleared, several bodies lay on the floor. Among them was that of Arundel, who had fired the fatal shot. As Kent bent over his dying brother, he heard the whispered words in the sing-song voice of their tutor: "*and the meek shall inherit the earth.* And you are welcome to it, brother." Eyes filmed over; breath ceased. And other words echoed in Kent's head: *and the subsequent proceedings interested him no more.* He was pushed aside by two of Arundel's men, and before anyone else could react, Arundel's escort left the hall through the side door, bearing the body of their master.

The silence that followed was short-lived. Those outside still pressed forward, unaware of what had happened. Shouts of 'King Alfred' changed to 'Treachery! Murder!' as news of what had happened filtered back. Shots in the air from Kent's men and the Marines silenced the crowd, who were pushed back by Lane and a phalanx of supporters and several nobles making a rapid departure. They were not opposed. Sussex signalled, and the doors shut behind them. The hubbub outside faded away; two shots were heard before silence descended on the interior. Lady Buckingham spoke.

"For those who did not hear, this poor boy," she glanced down at John Gregory's body, "told us the truth. The King, our father, was murdered, murdered with all his attendants. There was no disease. There was a conspiracy. It has been exposed. Those responsible will be brought to justice.

The King is dead, my Lords, gentlemen. The Domain lives. His Council is here. His surviving children are here. As before, what the Council decides, and the three of us consent to, that will be the law. Will Council now affirm that this is the case?"

She looked down on the diminished crowd. Four Councillors had left with Lane, along with many of those in attendance. The rest remained, clearly minded to assent. Only old Dundonnell rose to his feet.

"My Lady, I am sure that all of us assent with willing heart. But should we not have, I would say a King, but Sovereign would be the better title?"

There were nods and grunts of approval. Buckingham grinned, and shook her head. *Damn Defoe*, she thought, as the words *brown nosing* forced their way through her mind.

"All in good time, my Lord. Let us first restore order in the Domain, root out disloyalty and restore tranquillity. While we are all united, there is no need of a final arbiter. Those that could plot against one Sovereign can as easily do so against another, but not against the will of us all, openly arrived at. We are all agreed, My Lords, Gentleman?"

There was no dissent. Kent banged the gavel used by his father. Buckingham spoke the traditional, comforting words that had previously come from the throne.

"As it is proposed, so it shall be."

Formally, the meeting was at an end. Kent and Buckingham left with some of their retainers. Sussex motioned Marines to remove John Gregory's body and the two others left on the dais. Most dispersed to their quarters, while a few left the castle under the watchful eyes of Wilkes' men, who had deployed to defend the entrances against any more rushes. Only in the telephony room was there a fight, as Sussex entered to find a Security sergeant menacing the operators. Disarmed, he was sent to join the two already under guard on Sussex' orders.

***

As he left, Lane's mind was hard at work. The coup had failed; his master was dead, almost certainly; Buckingham held the castle. Those around him were confused. Many, recruited to acclaim Arundel, had not witnessed the shooting on the dais. Cries of *King Alfred* and *Death to Outies* were still to be heard. As he headed for the Town Hall, he noted that there was no pursuit. A battle had been lost, but not a war. Those inside would be as uncertain as most of those around him.

The town was in the hands of Security. Reluctance to kill, the reluctance he despised, would stall any immediate response from Buckingham or Wilkes. The Town Hall was taken over, clerks hustled away from the Council Chamber and the telephones. The mayor, Lord Mayor here, was nowhere to be found. From behind a cordon of Security troopers, the message spread to the crowd outside: Lord Arundel was wounded only, not dead; Buckingham would spare the Outies, but force good subjects to risk their lives in a mad venture overseas. Soon shouts of *Treachery, Revenge,* were added to the clamour. Safe for the moment.

Lane regarded the gathering of Visitors, nobles and Councillors who had left with him, along with the Security officers on whom he could rely. Rather fewer

462

than those who had clustered behind him in the chapel were here, he noted. No doses, and the stakes were higher. Plenty, used to obedience in return for reward, would sit on the fence. Even those assembled were worried, uncertain, looking for a lead. He raised his voice.

"My Lords, I will be frank. The Domain, our Domain, is threatened as never before. You all know of our manpower problems, of our declining resources. Let us consider the consequences."

He picked out the Visitor of Luton.

"My Lord Carmichael, have you not faced increasing demands for service, demands that provoke a rebellious spirit in your Ground?"

"That's so, Lane. But that demand has come from the needs of Reclamation among others, a need with which you are strongly associated."

There was a murmur among the Visitors present. Lane merely smiled. He turned to Lord Richards, comfortably placed at Court, and notable for his elaborate retinue, and his enthusiasm for the Hunt.

"My Lord, have you not noticed restrictions on recruitment to your service? To a certain decline in the facilities to which you rightly feel entitled?"

There was some nervous laughter. Richards was often mocked as a dandy, but all had felt the increasing constriction in the levels of service they received. There was a sense of a slow deterioration, one felt most acutely by those with the greatest life expectancy.

"True enough, but nothing to match the impositions since the Hunt, Lane," Richards drawled. "That damned Wilkes has removed half my servants. To no good purpose as far as I can see. No doses to come, we hear, though you have ensured your own future. We no longer have eternity in which to plan for future comfort. If not jam today, then at least tomorrow, not a century hence."

"Indeed. And why is there to be no jam tomorrow, as you put it? My Lords, I admit that I thought that reclamation was the means to solve our problems. Slow it might be, but better than hare-brained schemes to find territory overseas, chased with no results for more than a century. My Lord Arundel had a better plan. You heard it. Subdue the Outland. Subdue those capable of breeding, but of breeding mere servants. Expand our Grounds. A plan that was to have been started with the Hunt."

He paused, and looked around. All knew of the disaster that was Cotswold, and the penalties that had followed, even the shameful concessions to the Outlanders.

"It failed. Why did it fail? Treason, my Lords. The troubles in the cities? The supposed infection in the north? Coincidences or conspiracy? An Outland suddenly full of fight, an Outland that has claimed a piece of no-mans-land bigger than many Grounds. An Outland that gains in strength while we decline. An Outland that must be subdued, bent to our will. Then no heavy demands on your Ground, my Lord, no stinting in the amenities of Court."

"All well and good, Lane, but how will this be achieved. There are no Kingsmen here. And few from those Grounds or Divisions that have seen those damned balloons overhead. The Domain is powerless to move in any direction, unless you are proposing to attack the castle. There are no doses to reward those who risk their lives. There must be a resolution."

"Certainly not to attack the castle, my Lord. I hold no suspicion of Lord Wilkes' patriotism, merely of his judgment. Even my Lord Sussex, I believe, has been motivated by a misplaced sense of caution. Too many have reacted to Outie success by seeking to avoid provocation. The lure, the spurious lure, of avoiding conflict by turning overseas has now seduced many. It is events in the north, and at the Treaty Point that cause me to suspect collusion and treachery.

It is to the north that we must turn, turn with force. It is undefended, my Lords, scarcely a hundred men with arms throughout. At the Treaty Point, there will be evidence enough of Outie brutality. We will expose the fiction of infection; there is none, believe me, either there or in the north generally. Then into the Ground and into Outie territory. Territory easy to access without the obstruction of Badlands to block our path."

"You mean war, Lane. The Outies will respond. It is everything that those in the castle have sought to avoid."

"And when evidence of Outie atrocities reaches Windsor? When the duplicity of those in the north is exposed? When more balloons spread their poison, poison that we are forewarned of? Poison limited in quantity and with only the crudest means of delivery? How do you think Wilkes will respond? The Castle will have no choice. And if the Outies show no fight? Then we expose the caution for the cowardice that it is."

The conversation that followed satisfied Lane. Nobles quizzed him and the other officers about forces, about weapons, about likely responses to his move north. Even if not wholly convinced that Lane would achieve his ends, they were reassured to find that little was required of them other than to keep the townsfolk happy with the turn of events, and to create an atmosphere that discouraged

Kingsmen from dominating the town. The issue of what happened after all went as planned, of who might rule and how was carefully avoided. Lord Richards was sent to tell the crowd that the Domain would clear the north and subdue the Outies. There were cheers without. The remainder dispersed, now under the obligation to find lodgings in the town. The accompanying Security trooper for each discouraged any objections to such billeting.

Security commandants started to recall patrols, to assemble the necessary fleet of mobiles. Weapons, though, were a problem. Pistols aplenty, but rifles few, despite Arundel's instructions to the Armouries. More could be acquired on the way, but that thought prompted another. Telephoning the commandant at Oxford, Lane was tersely rebuffed by a clerk: *No messages from the mayor's office to be allowed, sir, by Lord Sussex' command.* The same message from Leicester. Soon, it became evident that he had been isolated. Too late, perhaps, he grabbed a clerk from the mayor's telephony room, and used his knowledge to cut the castle's connections.

His thoughts then turned to the Armouries themselves. Probably not much in stock, but certainly more ammunition and some explosives. He assembled a troop of forty, and marched boldly to the main gates, to be greeted not by the Master, but by Arundel's bodyguard captain. A man in a state of nerves that forces would be sent to arrest them.

"Yes, my Lord, Lord Arundel is dead. He lived but seconds after being shot. His body lies awaiting instructions for burial. And we await orders, my Lord, in fear of retribution."

"You have no reason to fear, Captain. I am now in command of the forces to carry out his Lordship's plan, to root out treachery in the north, and to subdue the Outies. You are to join us, Captain, if you will. But we came here also to equip ourselves for the fight. Rifles, Captain, rifles and ammunition, mobiles and fuel. Do you control the Armouries?"

"Only in part, my Lord. The Master opened the gates, and retreated to his office with a handful of Kingsmen. He has all the keys. He awaits orders. Coercion would mean bloodshed."

Lane collected three troopers and walked to the Master's office. Kingsmen at the door raised their rifles. A message, and he was admitted. The Master was slumped in a chair. Entitled though he was, he had not attended the Council. The disputes over allocation of weapons, the obvious tension between Lane and Wilkes, and his conviction that he had been an unwitting party to mass murder had left him drained and bewildered. Fearing violence, he had dismissed his workers when Arundel's men had arrived with their master's corpse. He knew very well what Lane would demand. Was it to be first come, first served? Or, rather, was Lane to get what he wanted with or without bloodshed. Wearily, before Lane could open his mouth, he placed on the desk in front of him, two sets of massive keys.

"Do me a favour, my Lord. Point your pistol at my head, summon the soldiers from the door."

They entered, and were struck silent.

"You see how it is. There is to be no bloodshed. You will surrender your weapons to Lord Lane. He will, no doubt, hold you here until he has what he requires. You are outnumbered, and there is no point in resistance. My Lord, I trust that this will suffice. You should place me with them when you have what you need."

Grateful for what he could remove, Lane found the haul of weapons was paltry. Nearly all reserves had been sent to arm Wilkes' and his own new recruits. With the aid of Arundel's men, all that could be moved was placed in the Armouries' mobiles. Arundel's body was carried to the cremation site and left burning. No corpse, and where needed the story of his survival could be sustained. The whole party left in the loaded mobiles.

An hour later, Sussex arrived at the gate to find it open, the buildings empty, the stores ransacked. Only a furious knocking revealed the captives. The foe was that much stronger. He returned unmolested to the castle. A few of those unconvinced by Lane's evangelism in the mayor's office had already told those within of his intentions.

36. The Battle of Barlow

Sussex' message north to Bohun on June 30th had been straightforward. Take control at Retford; you are expected. Prevent access to the Transfer Station and the Point. Bohun relayed the message to the Visitor and Cornwallis as soon as he could get hold of them.

"It is not just Hastings, but Steel also," said the Visitor. "The Outlander nobility must have near doubled even if its old-timers have survived. Not to mention a body of trained men and their weapons. Do they know of our deception, our tale of plague?"

"Yes," said Bohun. "Sussex met them before he left the Point. They will not flaunt the defectors in our face so long as the new treaty holds. Or so he says. There was only some female lieutenant to talk to."

"Up to us then. Expose the truth of defections, or have Security make believe an Outie attack, and Court and Council will be for war and all that will follow."

Bohun turned to Cornwallis.

"Major, we need you to take command there. That Kipling fellow and his men sound reliable, and it is the largest force we have. No one should pass without reference to us, and certainly no armed body. Those graves will not survive inspection."

"Very good, my Lord. I see no point in removing any soldiers from here, but I will take demolition gear. If we are outnumbered, it will be possible to delay any advance."

The consequences of failure were left unspoken. Cornwallis left to busy himself with assembling the gear for demolition, and in finding as his driver the most experienced in their use. Others, he ordered to place charges at bridges and causeways between the boundary station and Retford. It was the following morning that they set out in a heavily-laden mobile, driven with great caution. He was greeted with relief by Kipling.

"Your men, Lieutenant; are they aware of the truth of what has happened to their comrades?"

"Yes, sir. I said nothing at first, but Lord Sussex and I returned without weapons or tags. My mistake, I should have told Mills to leave them behind. They'd put two and two together, and they know they'll be for the chop if Security get their way. And they could see from my face that Mills wasn't dead. Security comes, we fight."

"It may not come to that, Lieutenant. If we face a rogue batch of Security, we simply fight. Worst case, we retreat to the Outland. They appear to welcome visitors. Security would need a large force to deal with professionals like us. An armed force with Court sanction, we stall. If there are Kingsmen there, they'll not lightly fire on comrades. There is still an official quarantine. But a request to allow an unarmed party, perhaps with doctors in kit, to be taken to inspect the point? Those graves, Lieutenant. I guess they are easily found? Other than Davis', they would be found empty?"

"Yes, sir, or to contain merely rocks or cut heather. There is another thing, sir. Corporal Tiggs; I think he is honest enough, but what he might say under questioning might arouse more suspicion."

"Tiggs? Can you spare a driver and a mobile? On my orders, then, he and his men are to go north for duties at the mines. If he's any sense, he'll not be banking on any confession or collusion to save him. Hope would have murdered him for certain. But those graves, Lieutenant, they must disappear. We need a pyre, the normal way of dealing with infected corpses, a pyre with enough circumstantial evidence to pass muster. Tomorrow, we will see to that with the aid of your men at Barlow."

The rest of the day was spent organising defences. Men were despatched to lay charges. A two-wheeler was sent south, to give advanced warning of any force moving north. The last task was to brief Grayson and his staff. Well aware himself of what might happen, the man had not confided in his staff, but a diffuse sense of threat had taken hold.

"There may be fighting, gentlemen. Fighting against those who are not merciful. No place for the unarmed. First shots, and you are in mobiles headed north. A small pack each; I suggest you think of its contents now. The road will be destroyed behind you."

The following morning, the two officers travelled to the Transfer Station. To Jacks' consternation, his own graveyard was dug into, and skeletons removed.

With the troop at the Station, they continued to the Point. Soon, a huge blaze was seen by those in the Outlander's post, but no flags summoned them. Enough scrap metal and a couple of defective rifles from store had been added to leave the molten remains of what might be weapons and tags. The few skeletal remains were well-calcined.

"Lane will not believe, but Court doctors will with our testimony in their hands. Leave two men here in case the Outies signal."

It was late evening before they returned to Barlow. There was an interview with Jacks. When ordered, you will evacuate northwards into the Ground. No questions, no argument, just move, as far and as fast as possible. Yes, the Arkells as well.

The return to Retford the following morning was delayed. The mobile would not start, and they stood around as Jacks' mechanic fussed over engine and fuel. The journey was further delayed by repeated stops as the engine overheated, and it was dusk again when they reached Retford. Grayson rushed to meet them, his face a picture of dismay.

"The King is dead, Major. They say it is murder. Lord Arundel also. Fighting in the castle. Lane has disappeared. Will he be coming for us, Major?"

A coherent account needed a call to Bohun. The debate, the explosion, and the shootings on the dais. Arundel dead? Yes, but his body was removed by his men. There will be claims to the contrary.

"And now?" asked the Major.

"It is not clear. The line was cut later. As far as we can tell, Buckingham and Wilkes had control of the castle, or most of it. We heard shooting in the telephony room when Songbird was calling, and he was cut off. It was Sussex himself who called later. But Lane left with a body of nobles and a few Councillors. Arundel's men have retreated to the Armouries. I think Sussex was going to negotiate with them."

"Is there still killing?" For all his military experience, Cornwallis was shocked.

"No, or at least not to Sussex' knowledge when he called. The man is in a funk, though. The town is seething. There are far more Security there than soldiers, and somehow the message that we will all starve if the Outies are not dealt with has spread. Even that Buckingham intends to round people up and force them overseas. And the idea that Arundel's actions saved the town from disease still circulates. Sussex is trying to mediate. And the castle is full of

469

Councillors, Visitors and nobles running around like headless chickens. All used to obeying orders."

"The explosion? Is it true that there are now no doses?"

"So he said. The storage rooms were destroyed completely. I don't know about the supply for the Hunt, but it sounds as though most was used on Lane. It was an elaborate plan. Buckingham and Kent must have prepared for years while they searched for new Grounds. Not a word to us, Major, not even to Sussex."

"No doses, no King." The Major felt the need for formality. "Do we have a government, my Lord? To whom do you answer?"

"In theory, to the three who are left. But the line has gone dead since Sussex called. We can reach Leicester and Oxford, but they have also lost the line to Windsor. We assume that Lane has cut them and is moving north. We have no idea with what force, but he can recruit many at Oxford. Few soldiers left there, but many Security."

"And Leicester? The Visitor there, Cadogan?"

"As good as nothing there. There was little trouble, and forces withdrawn for the Hunt never returned. The Visitor? Down at Windsor with the rest of them. Captain Faulkner? In a funk. If Lane approaches with any force, he will certainly not try to block him. At best, he will seal himself off with his few Kingsmen and hope they are not attacked, merely bypassed. I can't be sure he won't hand over weapons and mobiles; Lane is quite capable of inventing an order from Cadogan, to save the captain's face."

"That will not happen here, my Lord. The soldiers will resist, but there are barely forty of them. Faced with odds, they will fight a retreat, not northwards, but towards Barlow and then the Point. They will all defect. Kipling will have mined the roads to delay pursuit. I have arranged for all civilians to move north or into the Ground at the first sign of fighting."

"Which gives Lane a clear path north, where we have even less with which to fight. And you would do what, Major?"

The question hit Cornwallis. *And you would do what, Major?* No order, not even a suggestion. Any more, he realised, than he could have ordered Kipling, who had simply told him what would happen. Until Lane was dealt with, there was no government, no authority, no Domain. What do I command? Why, just myself. A wry 'Well, Major?' from the receiver ended his brief, unspoken soliloquy.

"There would be little point in my returning north single-handed, my Lord. It may be that Wilkes or Buckingham will be on Lane's tail. Any delay works to our advantage. Get the message that Retford is under attack, or find the line cut, and get as much of the road destroyed as possible as soon as Grayson is safely with you. Those escorting the civilians will blow charges behind them. Destroy what fuel you cannot move back to Conisbrough. Most of all, tell the bailiff in Sheffield. They are ready for a fight, my Lord, more prepared than you can imagine. You could take refuge there if Conisbrough is threatened."

There was the sound of laughter.

"Indeed, Major. We are contemplating something even more radical, an even greater reversal of the natural order, as I am sure the late Lord Arundel would see it. Major, we think Lane will go towards the Treaty Point, not towards Conisbrough. Create yet again the semblance of an Outie attack, and then move north into the Ground. Hold it hostage, as it were; all know how Buckingham values it. Raid the Outland from there, provoke another attack by balloons, win over the fearful down south. Isolate the city from the rear. He knows the difficulty of a direct assault across the bridge.

We have a different idea, Major. We should all defect to the Outland. No, not by moving, unless driven by defeat, but by working with them to repel Lane. As you discovered back in May, Major, they are disciplined. They have come by some of our weapons and men. Steel at least has military training. Maybe they even have some of those poison grenades and rockets up north."

Another silence. Before Cornwallis could compose his thoughts, Bohun expanded on his notion.

"You will remember your, shall we say, little excursions into the Outland in May? That brought down so much trouble on our heads? You must have noticed that the Outland you crossed was little blighted. Indeed, if it were not for the Treaties and the desire for a quiet life, we could have extended the Ground several miles west. A fact that we took trouble to conceal from Council, and most particularly from Arundel. Easy enough; none of them really know what natural moorland looks like. Any number of Outies could safely cross to the Ground, as we could cross to them. And of course, the Treaty Point itself gives access each way, narrow though it may be."

Already, the tactician in Cornwallis was at work, despite the strategic revolution put before him. Lure a few of Lane's forces north. Make a retreat towards the Station, with apparent reluctance. Then a counter attack from both west and north. The mere appearance of Outies, Outies perhaps with the poison that had demoralised Security at the Hunt, might induce panic.

"It could work, my Lord, and at the least, some could escape west rather than ending up on the Barriers or worse. But how are the Outies to be warned, never mind persuaded? If Lane attacks, as he surely will, and they have no warning, there will be Montgolfiers all over the south and even more trouble in the cities."

"Just so. That must be Lane's hope. Ditherers at Court, even among your fellow soldiers, will be full of patriotic fury. So, the warning, hopefully the alliance: That is your job, Major. And it must be done soon. As long as we have the telephone, any Outie can talk direct to us here from the Point if they need confirmation."

***

It was a very large, but uncoordinated convoy that departed from Windsor on the morning of the 4th. Around 150 veteran Security troopers were accompanied by about 60 new recruits, Arundel's retinue, and a handful of civilian enthusiasts. Lane's commandants attempted to keep the flock together, frequently frustrated by breakdowns and even one collision. No attempt was made to hinder them, and the few townsfolk who saw them leave cheered as mobiles assembled.

The journey to Oxford was easy. Outside the way station, the mobiles in front encountered a single mobile and six Kingsmen. Their lieutenant ordered the column to halt, to be greeted with laughter and the brandishing of weapons. As Lane hectored the lieutenant, and invited his men to defect, kitted troopers moved to cut the soldiers off. Turning to withdraw, he faced them, lined up across the road. Surrender was the only option, and the convoy continued, taking with it both mobile and weapons. The men, stolidly refusing to change sides, were left unarmed and bootless by the road. At the way station itself, resistance was more determined. The Kingsman captain managed to destroy two fuel dumps before retreating to the Station itself, and rifle fire with no casualties deterred any assault.

Lane ordered an overnight halt, the unconquered way station notwithstanding. A visit to the city crossing point recruited more Security, and while Kingsmen were forced aside, the small supply of weapons and ammunition was sequestered. Even more valuable, though, were the supplies of fuel. A roll-call before they headed towards Leicester on 5th July yielded 350 men with arms, of which half had rifles. Soon, the convoy was stretched out over several miles of road, and a trail of broken-down vehicles, the occupants of which had been transferred to others, marked its passage. They were far from Leicester by sunset, and camped out on the road while stragglers caught up.

There was no early start the following morning. Several mobiles had insufficient fuel to reach Leicester. Fuel was shifted, some mobiles loaded even more heavily, while others were abandoned. The atmosphere, though, was of cheerful, confident chaos. Never before had Security men seen such an army, even at Hunts. Arundel's black and white banners streamed from poles strapped to the vehicles. Now, they were the bosses, free of the condescension of soldiers. It was with open mockery, therefore, that they greeted the arrival of a fast mobile from the south, carrying no less than a full colonel with a message, rather an order, from Windsor. Forced to leave his mobile at the tail end, he was obliged to walk through the line to reach Lane. Lane, sitting one leg over the other in a camp chair, did not rise to greet him. The colonel handed over a paper, a paper conspicuously carrying the seals of Buckingham, Kent and Sussex. Lane put it to one side, on a small table, beside his pistol.

"Let me guess, Colonel. I am to stop my advance and return to Windsor? And all those seals. My, the old guard have been busy."

There were titters among the watching crowd. The colonel stood impassive.

"The problem is, my dear Colonel, that I have other orders, orders from my Lord Arundel, perhaps I should rather say, from King Alfred. They take precedence, I think. Indeed, I believe they empower me to command you to join us."

"Lord Arundel? You know very well that he is dead, as is his late Majesty. Authority rests with his surviving children whose seals are here. There is no King."

"So certain, Colonel? What if I were to tell you that we have His Majesty, his Lordship if you will be pedantic. And no, he is far too sick to receive a visitor. Sick from a shot fired by a traitor, Colonel. We are about the Domain's business, Colonel. When we have cleared out the nest of traitors in the north, when we have taught the Outies that obedience is better than defiance, then we will return to Windsor; to Windsor where there will be a reckoning with Outie-lovers."

The colonel turned to go. Men moved to prevent him, but Lane waved them away.

"We value human life, and I would not have an unwilling man pressed into our cause. You are free to go, as is your driver. But not your arms, Colonel, nor your mobile. It is quite a walk back to Oxford, but no doubt the exercise will do you good."

The colonel reached for his holster. Whether to disarm or defy remained unknown, for Lane calmly raised his pistol and shot. The colonel fell.

"A lesson, gentlemen: pride comes before a fall, literally in this case. Body in the ditch, please."

As he spoke, he lit a match, and holding the unread paper, set it alight. The seals melted, dripping wax, before he threw it to the ground and stamped it out. Soon, the convoy resumed its journey, leaving behind a driver lacking not only his vehicle and his weapons, but his belt and shoes too.

These theatricals raised morale even further, and it was in high spirits that the head of the convoy approached the Leicester Way Station. It was met by a handful of Security men in a state of confusion. They had been bundled out of the station itself with no explanation. When Lane approached it, shots were fired. He retreated out of range. He turned to one of the expelled.

"How many are in there, and what else, fuel for example?"

"Just thirty, sir. But the magazine and spares are inside. And those taken when Commandant Hope was killed. They are prisoners. The fuel? It's over there. He pointed to a long shed some fifty yards away. What is happening, sir? We have no orders, and cannot telephone to the Ground exchange point."

"How many of you at the Exchange? Fifty? They have mobiles and fuel?"

A single mobile was despatched to collect them. While they waited, Lane sent a commandant forward to the Station with a white flag. He returned empty-handed.

"No joy, sir. They will fire on anyone that approaches. But they will not hinder us at the fuel store, though it is in range. They know what we are about, sir."

Lane paused, and consulted with his commandants. They could storm the building, but at a cost. Those familiar with the urban warfare of the cities shook their heads.

"We would lose at least fifty, sir. They'll be better shots than us. If they are really determined, they'll blow the place up as we enter. Or we spend ages, and wait till nightfall. But they are used to the hand-to-hand stuff. And we'd have injured too. Leave them behind and they'd be taken. Not good for morale."

Much as he would have liked a victory, Lane accepted the advice. There were, after all, no mobiles inside the Station. But he gained a point. Told that they would be fired on otherwise, the Kingsmen released Hope's gang. The party from the crossing point arrived. Fuel was loaded, surplus mobiles disabled, and the convoy moved out. Lane had, however, forgotten one thing, the telephone, and Captain Faulkner had recovered some spirit. A full account was soon in the hands of Cornwallis and Bohun, a second choice when Windsor remained cut off.

There was another overnight stop on the road, a bare five miles from Retford. The attack would be tricky, for there were Badlands on either side of the road, land that could be crossed only in kit, and in daylight sufficient to steer from the hotspots. The otherwise narrow front on the road gave an advantage to the defence. Morale was boosted by the arrival of straggling contingents of Security from outlying settlements in the Domain. News had spread. The evening tally recorded 486 men, and 216 rifles. A force larger than any had seen, bar the last, ignominious Hunt. Ten to one at least: victory, surely, so long as the men don't panic under fire. Commandants were consulted, the battle plan drawn up. Best shots down the road, kitted squads in the Badlands on either side.

Soon after dawn on the 7th, the whole convoy moved slowly forward, two mobiles well ahead of the rest. It was not long before they saw a two-wheeler turn in front of them and race north. A few minutes after it had disappeared from view, there was an explosion to the north, and a cloud of smoke rose from behind a gentle rise. Two squads of troopers kitted up and advanced either side of the road, while a larger force moved along it, the two mobiles providing cover.

The damage to the road was slight, easily repaired in time, but enough to stop all but the most robust mobiles for now. More forces were brought up, and the advance continued on foot. Others behind started to repair the damage. The Station was in plain view. At two hundred yards, there was a burst of fire from it. Those on the road dropped. Those on either side advanced a little further, the hummocky Badlands and a few ruins providing some cover. But fire was desultory. Neither side now had targets. A lucky shot brought down one kitted trooper to the west; the remainder stayed firmly behind cover. A whistle blew and those on the road retreated rapidly, a few shots from the Station failing to find targets.

Lane consulted his commandants. The only way west for mobiles and those lacking kit was through the Station itself. A frontal attack in daylight would be costly, perhaps even a failure. At night, they could get closer. A few had primitive grenades. Get them moving, get them in the open, and numbers would tell.

It was so carefully planned. As dusk fell, a small convoy of mobiles, heaved across the damaged road, were backed slowly towards the Station. They were fired on, but the drivers were shielded. A few troopers fell, but most were covered. On either side, kitted men advanced, those on the east moving to the north to attack any retreat there. Those to the west moved to cover the road to Barlow and the Point. Darkness complete, the mobiles moved again, attracting fire. Men crept towards the outer buildings. Grenades were thrown, and a confused firefight started.

It was too easy. A few defenders fell. Others drove away rapidly through firing both northwards and to the west. The main Security forces piled into the compound to find it empty. Fuel tanks breached, the telephone system destroyed, the pantries bare or contaminated. Then shots to north and west told that the flanks were engaging. The forces moving out on each road, necessarily on foot, met their kitted comrades in disarray. Hearing mobiles departing the Station, they had moved onto or alongside the road only to be shot down from behind. They dived for cover, and the single mobiles that had drawn them out passed by their crouching forms. Forces moving along each road encountered no one beyond. The Kingsmen had retreated out of sight.

By midnight, all was again quiet. The Station was theirs, and the roads clear for at least a mile each way. By dawn, Lane had managed to clear damaged mobiles off the road, and bring up the remainder to the Station. Twenty dead, all but four killed in the ambushes on the roads. Kits, holed or not, to be stripped, weapons, ammunition and tags retrieved. Fourteen wounded, though only two seriously. Four Kingsmen dead among the buildings, one on the west road. All but one with no weapon; comrades had removed them as they escaped.

"A high price, but not a crippling one," Lane said to his commandants. "I'll warrant we caused more damage to them, given how few they are."

"They tricked us well, though, and in advance. Had we rushed the place in daylight we'd have carried it with fewer losses. They guessed our strategy easily enough."

Lane frowned. Morale had taken a beating, despite the objective being achieved. As the force prepared to move west, there was a further blow. Shots were heard to the north. Two mobiles sped up the road, skidding to a halt at the sight of a body ahead. Men on either side rose from the ditches as they stopped. Just ahead was a crater, easily filled, but a temporary obstruction.

"Popped up out of the ditch beyond the crater, sir, shot and then scarpered. Didn't get any."

"How many?"

"We saw five, sir. But there was more movement in the ditches."

It took one of the commandants to point to the significance of the incident.

"We don't know how many of them moved up here or went west, sir. We can't leave our back exposed. A detachment must hold this road and the Station, and hold it securely."

Lane cursed inwardly. But before moving, he had to assign a further twenty, with the wounded, to hold the Station. They needed supplies and fuel too, to send messages by mobile. All in all, both he and the main force headed westwards in no high spirits. Spirits further dampened by a steady rain that stalled some mobiles. For several miles, there were no obstructions and no resistance. Kitted troops went ahead on either side. When they reached another crater, it was small, almost token, and filling it caused little delay. By evening, they had managed fifteen miles. Ruins increased, but no fire came from them, and most were in heavily contaminated land. The rain cleared by nightfall, and the mood improved. The darkness passed peacefully.

Progress was rapid the following morning, to the extent that Lane was tempted to move directly by mobile rather than at the pace of the troopers on his flanks. Around noon, though, there was some excitement. Fire came from a roadside ruin. But when troopers moved to surround it, a mobile shot out from cover and sped away west. The pattern repeated itself; there would be shots or a mobile ahead, but a rapid retreat when flanking troopers closed in. By dusk, they were scarcely three miles from Barlow, and passed the worst of the contaminated edges of Sheffield. Lane began to wonder whether there were fewer forces opposing him than had seemed likely, or whether they were all behind him. If the latter, the garrison would hold them up for long enough for him to do the business.

The assault on Barlow the following morning was an anti-climax. The buildings remained silent as they approached. They were, indeed, completely empty, barracks and all. There were no mobiles, no fuel, no food. Scouts moving west and north, however, found cratered roads and sporadic fire. They withdrew without loss. To the south, they encountered only some frightened Proctors.

There had been no incursions into their Ground, but news of the disturbances had reached them. They were only too willing to sit tight, and to continue the block on any movement.

Lane summoned his staff. The buildings were defensible, and the forces happy to find a measure of comfort within them. So, what next? He knew from Hope's reports that fuel was scarce in the Ground, and non-existent at the Point. The craters made by his retreating foes were more substantial than those on the great highway to the east.

"Footwork from now on, gentlemen, at least until we have driven this remnant into the Outland or scurrying back to the Ground. We have fuel only for a few vehicles now. Simultaneous, or one after the other? Gain the Point, create the evidence, and doubters from the south can be given an escorted tour. But in the north, once we have crossed into the Ground, there is a wide front on which our numbers can deploy. Into the Outland; a clear, victorious incursion that will provoke retaliation, with no need for us to cater for simple-minded visitors from the Court."

One of those sent south for the Hunt and the troubled cities spoke up.

"Both, sir, if I may suggest it, but most to the north. They have split their forces, and there can be scarcely twenty between us and the Point. With kit, and forty or so of us, they will be continually outflanked and retreating. We need go no further than the Point itself. Northwards, though, we can't trust those damned Groundlings. That city; it was too damned quiet, so we heard, and those buggers gave us enough trouble down south. We'll have to protect the right flank. We would still have 200 or more to move forward."

Lane nodded. Night was no good, because flankers in the Badlands needed to see their paths. Dawn, then, with a small force to hold the Station and care for any casualties. Forces allocated, sentries posted, the force settled down. The evening became livelier, however, when someone discovered a cellarful of beer barrels, undisturbed. By the time Lane was aware, it was certainly too late to assert discipline. *Hopefully*, he thought, *there can hardly be enough to sozzle the lot.*

The shock was complete. At midnight, rockets burst over the compound. Sentries outside and on the roads fell, silently taken with bolts. A few managed to fire. There was chaos in the Station as men rose and grabbed their weapons. In the faint moonlight, strange apparitions appeared to the east, dodging on and off the road. Those with pistols advanced on them to be met with grenades that disintegrated overhead. Troopers contaminated dropped, while their comrades at the Station spent as much time looking upwards as in front. A fresh wave, and many retreated indoors. Bodies, and the twitching and vomiting injured littered the open ground.

There was a pause. Lane managed to instil some order. No-one had penetrated the compound itself, and riflemen brought down a few shadowy figures seen moving around. The Kingsman's barracks, across the road, was still his, but a messenger crossing to assess their state was shot down. His body lay on the road. In the Warden's house, there was consternation. Poison. Crossbows. Outies with Kingsmen? City scum too, maybe. Lane did his best to rally those around him.

"Daylight, gentlemen, daylight. We have the rifles. There is little shelter out there, and our range is greater than their fireworks. Hold firm. The fools have done our work for us. Some Outie corpses, with luck, some captives and their Kingsman friends, and we have what we need. Treason and Outie aggression. Windsor will not allow this to go unpunished. We will see them off, and return with our prizes."

His voice retained enough authority to still the looks of fear on many faces. The brighter among the officers, however, doubted his words. Their numerical advantage had gone; the enemy had them as good as surrounded. Make a dash for the south, into another Ground, get to where the rear-guard would not be outflanked? The compound was also burdened with the injured and those recovering from lesser doses of poison. But nothing was said, there was nothing that could be said, until daylight revealed more.

The revelation was not comforting. As a little light appeared in the sky, a loud explosion to the east, followed by others, told them that the road had gone. Mobiles were now redundant. Minutes later, an explosion in the barracks was followed by shouts and shooting. Men erupted in a bunch towards the road and the main compound. A barrage of rifle fire engulfed them, despite the frantic attempts to give covering fire at targets near impossible to find. No one made the journey. In full daylight, the diminished force inside the beleaguered Station could see no sign of their opponents, bar a single movement past a window in the barracks across the road. That provoked a fusillade, but for all they knew, the bullets smashed harmlessly in the walls.

The two commandants left standing observed their leader with concern. Their foe had rifles; who knew how many? We have to move, but they just sit tight under cover. Lane stared into the hostile surroundings with eyes that seemed barely focused. Only the south offered any chance, if a costly one. The suggestion prompted a snarl.

"With our tails between our legs? With no captives, no deformed corpses, to back our claim? No, we must claim the Point. Hold out there, and we will be vindicated."

There was a shout from a window by the main gate.

"A white flag, a party approaching, sir."

The three rushed to the entrance. Fifty yards away stood a party of Kingsmen, rifles held downwards. No Outlanders. At their head, not only a major, but a man in Outie gear, complete with a three-feathered helmet. Only Lane recognised Cornwallis and Lord Hastings. Approaching closer, Hastings shouted.

"You are completely surrounded, Lane. Try to leave, and you will be eliminated. Stay, and we will wait patiently. The Domain is aware of your schemes. The Outland will not be provoked. There will be no war. Surrender. Surrender to the authorities of the Domain. Your safety is protected."

Hastings raised his voice still further; Lane's companions should hear.

"Reclamation is reformed. Do not fear exposure to the lethal contamination. Do not fear a lifetime of servitude. The Domain will be forgiving to those who have been misled."

"Trust your word, the word of a traitor, of Outie scum? Fire, men, traitors for the taking."

Lane's voice was cut off. No shots were fired from the Station. Those outside heard shouting, and a single shot inside. A commandant emerged hands raised.

"Time, please. An hour to consider?"

Hastings nodded, and his party withdrew to the barracks. Inside, a commandant stood over a bleeding Lane, from whom he had wrested the pistol that had been aimed at the party outside. It took less than half an hour for the commandant to reappear. The party emerged from the barracks.

"Into the hands of Kingsmen, not Outlanders, and taken east into the Domain? We will surrender. Otherwise, we will die or starve here."

A glance from Cornwallis towards Hastings, and a nod.

"Accepted. My men will be here. You will emerge in single file and leave your weapons as instructed. You will wait until we have secured the station, and we have assessed the wounded. Any resistance within, and lives are forfeit. There will be a march to the east, and you will repair the road as we move. Those too injured to travel will follow you in mobiles when that job is done. Just one thing more: you, Commandant, will remain here with us. You will not be handed over to Outlanders."

Rather less than 200 lined up and left their weapons. Kingsmen and Outlanders watched impassively as the disarmed men were assembled on the road. Other soldiers emerged from the station and gave the all-clear. Outies and others moved in. A Kingsman approached Cornwallis and whispered in his ear. Soon, a mobile led a bedraggled procession in the direction of the first crater. In all there were a mere twenty Kingsmen guarding the prisoners; a similar number, strengthened by city folk, went ahead to confront the Retford garrison.

The commandant was led inside. In the courtyard, he saw Outies attending to the sick and wounded. Their distorted features, features he associated with every kind of depravity, contrasted with the obvious kindness of their behaviour. He was led into an office and given a chair. Cornwallis and Hastings faced him. More disconcerting, though was an Outie, a woman visibly deformed, who sat beside them, pen and paper at the ready.

"Miss Evans, Commandant. Our conversation must be recorded."

She gave the commandant a lop-sided but patently sardonic grin.

"My pleasure to meet you in such happy circumstances, *sir*."

"Did you not wonder, Commandant, that we did not question the absence of your leader in the procession outside? He was slightly injured, I think, when you or others prevented him from firing on us. We discovered him, hung from a beam in the stables. Suicide, we wonder?"

The commandant looked down at his feet.

"He went mad, sir, I think. He led us to think we were facing just a handful of soldiers. Not an army, not Outies. He was convinced we could take the Point, even after what happened in the night."

"Manners, Commandant. Outlanders from now on. Or Westrons would show a deep and well-deserved respect. The stable door was not bolted. Well, let suicide, 'while the balance of his mind was disturbed', be the verdict. Nobody can doubt that he was unbalanced."

Bit by bit, the journey north was recorded. Truth be told, the commandant could add little to what either Cornwallis or those stationed further south could determine for themselves. The murder of the colonel sent to stop them was perhaps the most revealing. It was Miss Evans who showed the greatest revulsion. With the body counts made around Barlow, more than a third of the nearly 500 who had set out were dead. Another forty or so lay injured, and several might not recover. There remained only the garrison at Retford. It would not be hard to obtain their surrender.

Inquisition over, Hastings signalled to the guard by the door.

"You were indeed facing an army, Commandant. In fact, three armies besides the handful of Kingsmen. Armies that will remain together until the affairs of the Domain and the Outland are settled to their satisfaction. A message that you will deliver when we take you south."

There was a short pause, a knock, and three people entered the room. Two Outlanders in what the commandant could see was a kind of uniform, Outlanders with feathers in their helmets and no trace of deformity. The man, tall, bearded and straight, gave off a perceptible air of nobility.

"Chief O'Neill, Commandant. I can claim at least a little credit for your masters' discomfiture in Cotswold. A fraction of my force came here to round up your little gang of policemen."

"Captain O'Hanlon," the woman introduced herself. "Yet another Outlander army, Commandant, from the north." She grinned at Cornwallis. "The major here can attest to our military skills."

The commandant's mouth nearly fell open. Not at the revelation of Outlander strength, but at the notion that a woman would command soldiers. He stuttered.

"You…you came through the Ground? You were not opposed?"

"Not at all. We were garlanded, Commandant. We are their army now. Had you not fallen into our trap, you would have had to fight every inch of the way to the Outland. Be glad you were spared that."

The third person was much less impressive. Short, balding, middle-aged, his clothes resembled those of any of the many city dwellers the commandant had seen in the course of enforcement duties. The man grinned broadly.

"Mr Mysliborski, the Bailiff of Sheffield, Commandant. City folk have waited decades for something like this. Did you see figures on the road to your east? Wrapped up to be scarcely human? We know how to cross Badlands. Think yourself lucky that your precious Lord Lane did not lead you north to take the Ground from the east."

He placed on the table a standard Security pistol.

"Much more where that came from, Commandant. And from every city where your thugs were too cocky for their own good. Evens the score on the streets."

The three left. The commandant was locked in a first-floor room, a pot being provided. There was a window. When he opened it and leaned out, a huge Outie with a crossbow grinned up at him. He withdrew.

As evening came, there were sounds of celebration outside. A meal was brought to him. And then there was singing. The tune and the words were unknown to him, but the intensity was obvious. He caught the last words as the song ended: ...*in England's green and pleasant land.* The silence that followed was profound.

37. Brave New World

The rest of July saw the Outland in a state of frenetic activity. At Manod and the nearby ports, if they could be thus dignified, the fleet for the great northern adventure was assembled and fitted out. Beached vessels long abandoned were repaired, the tiny shipbuilding enterprise enhanced. Volunteers, not only from the Outland, were trained by Captain Smith and his mariners. Stock moving from the east were corralled, and the business of finding uncontaminated forage became a pressing concern.

At Chapel, to which Lizzie had soon returned armed with maps, parties of the sterile or genetically damaged were forcing paths to the north, waymarking routes to cleaner ground. Encounters with bears moving the other way necessitated the presence of hunters among them. The settlement was enlarged with holding pens for stock on their way west. Some would remain until the paths encountered clean land.

The call had gone out beyond the west. Very soon, the inhabitants of Bradfield were confronted with a stream of city dwellers passing west. City dwellers who, to say the least, had no sense of inferiority with respect to the rather staid and originally loyal Grounders. As time passed, the accents of these rather uncouth travellers changed. Mysliborski had put the word out along the Metro. Some farmers, and even more of their stock joined the trek westwards. Among them were Mark's mother and sister. The happy reunion at Manod was followed by the family decision to join the expedition.

The great upheaval had not happened without an anxious debate beforehand. The risks were obvious; a storm, and the overloaded ships and their occupants, human and animal would be lost. Why not explore, take time, risk less on a single voyage, await the building of more ships and the training of more mariners? The Domain had shown no sign of aggression; Lane's *Raid,* the word already used by all in tones that copied Defoe's giggling reference, had been dealt with. His further references to *The First Fleet,* prompted by his sight of some villainous-looking city volunteers, passed over the heads of those who heard him. It was O'Neill, paying a rare visit, and Hastings, wearing his Outland helmet with three feathers, who had driven the decision. Both knew that the intentions of the surviving three, the *Triumvirate* in Defoe's mocking tone, were far from clear, and their control uncertain.

"We are sure," argued O'Neill, "sure as can be, that there is land for the taking. The maps are clear. We are not sure of the Domain. Lane's force were amateurs, mere thugs with guns. Their soldiers are trained and better equipped. Arundel may be dead, but there will many who think as he did. There will be struggles in the Domain. The soldiers will obey whoever is on top. We have peace for now, but there will be many who resent the loss of Service, of the comfort provided by the levies on Grounds and cities. The more so since we have heard that there are no longer doses to reward the faithful."

"There is more," added Hastings. "The north is undefended, save for Mysliborski blocking the crossing. He can be bypassed. The road to Eden would be wide open, and the Ground taken if not destroyed. Time is on their side if they are minded to follow Arundel's path. On their side, at least, if we have no sanctuary, no place they cannot reach."

***

Long before the fleet's departure in early August, the librarians had pored over the printed and handwritten material rescued from Jones' hideaway. Jones himself was of little use, and sank further into a depression which no one could alleviate. Before she had returned to Chapel, Lizzie tried to cheer him up before her departure for Chapel, but the unrewarding task was neglected as the librarians became first excited and then anxious. The handwritten log, and other notes scrawled on the manuals that Jones had retrieved had drawn attention to the sealed space behind the vast and corroded door in Jones' refuge. The entries and the notes were cryptic. A manual identified the space, but gave no clue as to its contents. There were no instructions on opening it, merely an elaborate protocol for its destruction, a protocol concluding with a password to be sent direct from the highest authority. The scribbled note in the margin asked the pertinent question:

What the hell? Not weapons, or we would surely be given access in the last resort. And if not for us, for whom?

The manual gave further instructions. Five minutes to evacuate after the final code. Get your stuff outside, be a hundred yards clear. Another note:

Not a big bang then. No poisons released, nothing nuclear.

A few cryptic entries in Buchanan's log became clearer.

No orders for the big one. And no electrics. Does the code operate without them?

Two days before the final entry:

No message, no phone, no code. We cannot destroy it; our puny charges would scarcely make a dent, and might bugger up the release for whoever is supposed to open it.

Although no further description was given, it was easy to see that whatever was behind that door must not fall into enemy hands, but equally was not for the garrison's use. Only higher, perhaps the highest authorities could access it rather than ensure its destruction. Whatever it was had never been used, even in the chaotic last days of the Catastrophe. It was Lizzie who pointed out that the notes excluded anything directly dangerous or contaminating. Raymond added that it would not have been mere arms or even drones, things that would be left to the commander on the spot, not to an order from afar. The matter remained a puzzle, though someone joked that it might contain supplies of good liquor for the nobility.

The problem was forgotten until Lord Hastings arrived at Manod. After the battle at Barlow, O'Neill had held onto Steel and sent Hastings west to be questioned by Defoe and his staff. As expected, the first session with Defoe had been confusing to both Hastings and the staff who sat with him. Promoted and dosed long after the Great War, Hastings had no clear idea of Defoe's previous role. Defoe got bored very quickly; as he remarked afterwards, "No wiser than that Jones fellow. They were certainly not selecting for brains when they dished out doses."

Hastings was more useful when questioned about the numbers of the nobility and the strength of the Kingsmen. And among the librarians, more useful still.

486

Clever he was not, but his memory was good. The subject of doses came up. He recalled the award and the treatment in great detail. To start with, the information merely confirmed what the Old-timers had told them.

"Who made the decision to dose you?"

"Oh, the Family, of course. We knew that they all had to agree. There was only one secure holding room. You waited in an anteroom, and a doctor and assistants looked after you. Lord Sussex looked in to congratulate me afterwards. I was a bit curious, and asked him if it was made afresh, or was what was left after the Catastrophe."

"What did he say?"

"Oh, that it was all made before the war. No prospect of making any more; the equipment was, he said, hi-tech. What was left was abandoned with the Institute and the move to Windsor. A millennium, if we are lucky, before we reach that level again was what he said."

"It was the only supply? What would happen if it ran out or was destroyed?"

"I asked that too, though not directly. They kept the whole thing very secret, and that area was heavily guarded. That was clever, now I think about it. They gave small repeat doses to the guards and doctors, so they always had something to lose. Lord Sussex did say something strange though. I can't recall the exact words, but when he said there was plenty left, he added that this was the only supply as far as he knew. I did not think about it at the time."

"As far as he knew? Did they not have complete control?" asked Fisher.

"We certainly all thought so. Of course, the order was signed by the King himself, but it was common knowledge that all of his children had to agree."

"And if they did not?"

The question revived all Hastings' anger at his attempted poisoning and the divisions that it had revealed. There was bitterness in his tone.

"We all knew that there were disagreements and bargaining. I was surprised myself to get a dose. I worked out that it was probably a trade-off: let x get a dose, and we'll approve of y. After all, he's harmless. Harmless and expendable. That's how it went."

Fisher could see that Defoe had to be asked. They marched back to the old man's room. He was sat with a book open in his lap. He was giggling, and scarcely looked up when they entered. It was the *Book of the King,* open at the page holding the Declaration.

"What a clever boy I was, don't you think?" he said in a half-mocking, half irritated manner, as he waved them to chairs. "What can I do for you, my Lord?"

Raymond had the task of getting Defoe to focus.

"My Lord, it is true, is it not, that you received a dose on the direct order of the King? And before the Catastrophe?"

"Yes, yes, you know that very well. And no doubt more details from that Norman boy."

"Did his children have any say in the matter?"

"Well, they knew after the event, and that my dose was larger than intended. They wished me well of it, but I think the King, Farnham as was, would have made his own mind up." His irritation swelled up. "What is all this about? Its ancient history. And from what I'm told, there are none left now."

"They were made before the war, even before the Catastrophe, is it not so? And when did the children start to control the doses, my Lord? Were there not others who were first-born, who received doses before that?"

"Oh, yes, that surrender to his children. A terrible mistake. A few other families got the same treatment before the Catastrophe. Men and women who already had children and acquired doses for their brats. They were the first-born. It led to assassinations and more. Farnham wised up quickly, and parents were not treated thereafter. But he'd lost most of his grip already. One of the reasons I decided to abandon ship. A bunch of young hooligans in charge, squabbling among themselves."

"But they did not kill their father, did they? Did he take any precautions, or was he too incapable?"

"Not that incapable. He was no intellectual." A giggle. "He used me for the creative ideas. The Four would have been at each other's throats if he went. I think access to the doses needed some key or password that needed his input. And he said once that he had another insurance policy, whatever he meant by that. He was shrewd enough when it came to money or power."

Hastings was merely baffled, but Fisher frowned.

"Could there have been supplies elsewhere? All the eggs in one basket would have been a risk. Might he have kept supplies hidden, hidden somewhere his children knew nothing about?"

"Certainly, he could, but he never said so. By the time I left, he hated all of them, though the real venom was for Arundel. But where is this leading? From everything we have heard, the doses were always given by the four. I think those dosed earlier were mostly disposed of. There were no new nobles springing out of thin air afterwards. The whole thing was very formal and public."

Fisher and Hastings withdrew.

"He's right, Fisher, as far as I know. We swap stories of our initiation, and it's the same for all. Isn't it what your own Old-timers told you?"

Fisher nodded, and went his own way. He said little to his colleagues, and over the next few days he directed attention to other, more technical issues. His mood changed, and the enthusiasm that had driven earlier investigations seemed to fade. The fleet on its way, the minds of all at Manod bent towards its fate and the construction of yet more ships. When he announced his need to follow an inquiry in the east, it scarcely registered with his colleagues.

***

It had taken time, and no little ingenuity to assemble the gathering in the Chief's house in Chapel. Fisher sat in the chair once occupied by Ogilvie. Around the table sat O'Neill, lured by a series of cryptic messages, Chief McEnery, naturally enough, and Rhianna, summoned from the depleted Riding of Derwent. Had Ogilvie been present, he would have deplored the absence of a scribe.

The others waited on Fisher to speak. The Chief of librarians so far from his seclusion, his almost troglodyte existence at Manod, had aroused their interest no less than the obscure way in which his summons had been couched. He did not waste time.

"Chief Evans, I take it that Mr Jones' refuge remains untouched by the Domain?"

Rhianna nodded.

"Untouched and unknown, even to those in the north like Major Cornwallis."

"As well for all of us. That refuge holds, I believe, a weapon of terrible power. The power that has sustained the Domain. The power to confer eternal, if sterile life. To who knows how many. I believe it is a cache of doses, doses concealed by the King before his children came to control him. Who controls those doses controls thousands, tens of thousands. They become Kings."

The shock was followed by a barrage of questions. He laid out the evidence. No, he could not be certain, how could he? What other explanation made more sense?

"Would not its contents spoil if the store is opened by force?" asked McEnery. "It is hard to believe that such a treatment could survive for as long as it has in the Domain."

"I do not know, Chief. Those who open it would soon find out. The Domain has, perhaps we should say had, stocks that have lasted that long. We know nothing of the way in which they kept them."

"Clearly, the Domain, or at least those Royal children, know nothing of it. At present, they are in no position to take possession if they learn. Sussex may suspect its existence, from what Hastings has told you." O'Neill paused. "Would they recognise it if they did find it?"

"Again, I have no idea. If the container is in the same form as their own, almost certainly yes. Otherwise?" Fisher shrugged.

The three newly-informed looked at each other. Rhianna broke the silence.

"It is not the Domain we need fear, Mr Fisher, but ourselves. Which of us would not grasp not only immortality, but the power to award it as we willed? To award it in measured doses that ensured loyalty and obedience? To create a new Domain and all that goes with it? A new Hunt in the lands of the east?"

At those last words, O'Neill shuddered. He alone had witnessed at first hand the barbarism, the corruption of the soul that had conceived such a thing. Had Arundel once had a soul, an iota of decency or mercy?

"We must destroy it. In the hands of the Domain, it is a threat, though given that they have destroyed their own supply, they might do the same again if the right faction finds it. For us, it is fatal."

He turned to Fisher.

"Do we have any idea of its size and strength?"

Fisher shook his head.

"Captain O'Hanlon will have seen it, or at least its front," said Rhianna. "And it would be her job to destroy it. At the very least, the whole building can be reduced to rubble. It requires all the gunpowder we can collect. Give her the means, and the job will be done."

***

Two weeks later, Pickless and his wives found the stream of emigrants through his yard and onwards blocked, under the request of an Outlander captain. Only an hour or two, sir, he was told, and I think you will know when it is possible for them to resume their march. His farm was thus the temporary resting place for about twenty city dwellers from far south, speaking in accents he barely understood. The Proctor guard had long been discontinued.

Miss and Muss were in the yard with refreshments when a huge explosion to the north-west shook the buildings and caused Muss to drop her tray. A cloud of smoke rose in the air as the rumbles died away. An Outlander soon appeared, giving a thumbs up. The migrants resumed their journey. As they passed the smoking rocks that had been Jones' home for decades, they found charred and torn sheets of paper scattered in the heather and along the trail. One passer-by picked up one sheet at random. There was handwriting on it, and he was literate enough to make out some letters and words.

NBG. No bloody goo…
LMSO. …ast man standing orde…

He cast it away. It fluttered briefly in the breeze and landed in the heather. Rain soon turned the scattered papers to mush.

***

It was growing dark, and the late October rain beat down on the convoy of mobiles disgorging its passengers at the Barlow Station. Staff held large umbrellas over Buckingham and Kent, while others assisted clerks, caterers and a small contingent of Kingsmen. The last vehicle, considerably behind the others, contained Pendennis and his clerks. Mr Jacks once again felt put upon; yet another assembly of the mighty, though not on the scale he had had to deal with in June. Never mind the repairs and clearing up after the battle.

A roaring fire, and a dose of strong spirits gradually restored the travellers, who had been both cold and silent for most of their slow journey from Retford.

"When will those oh-so-happy northerners join us, do you suppose?" asked Kent.

"Jacks says tomorrow morning. He did not know how many. The idea is to move to the Point the same day."

"And how do we regard them?" asked Buckingham, of no one in particular. "Are they of a piece with us, or a part of the Outlander delegation?"

It was a pertinent question, to which there was no answer. The rout at Barlow had indeed averted war with the Outland. Kingsmen had later retaken Retford with ease, and the demoralised remnants of Lane's expedition taken south. As intended, the captive commandant and the transcript of his interrogation had made clear to Wilkes the extent and effectiveness of Outlander and city folk forces. The colonel commanding the soldiers sent north to pursue Lane had been told, politely, to advance no further than Retford. The fictitious quarantine had saved face, and subsequent telephone conversations with the north had been anodyne and remarkably uninformative. De facto, the North was independent. As far as those in the south could see, the threat of starvation had disappeared. Certainly, the north had asked for no more supplies.

Neither Buckingham nor Wilkes had been disposed to challenge this prolonged isolation. The Domain had been in turmoil, with Sussex attempting to negotiate with those nobles and Security units that had cheered Lane's forces as they left for the north. Rumours of Arundel's survival still circulated, as did the more frightening notion that Buckingham intended to conscript for service overseas. Gradually, a semblance of order had been restored. It had been Bohun and Cornwallis who had dealings with the Outlanders, not Windsor. Until now, no meeting, no new treaty, had been agreed between the Outland and the nominal rulers of the Domain. Now, though, the Outland had asked for a meeting, a meeting at the highest level, a meeting at which representatives of the north must be present.

"Let us see who appears tomorrow. I'll warrant it is not just the authorities."

"They are surely beginning to feel the pinch? We'd normally be moving people out and food in. We've sent some, but not the usual amounts. They have not asked for more."

"There was movement behind us today, my Lady," said Pendennis. "You were well ahead when a party crossed the road. They stopped to talk. City folk they were, wrapped up in what passes for gear, crossing Badlands. Quite a gang, men, women and children. No fear of us; indeed, they seemed amused. I asked how they found their way. One bold fellow laughed and told me to *buy a ticket for the Metro and you'll find out.* They have paths."

"I guess we knew that from the way each city kept in touch. Does this mean they are evacuating those they can't feed? I doubt other cities can do much to help."

"No, quite the opposite. They were moving north, and in some numbers. To Newfoundland, one said, and laughed. They were very jolly. Come selection and choosing to the south, I think we will have difficulties, though where the hell they are going, I don't know. The north can't feed them all."

The puzzle remained unsolved. It was mid-morning the following day before the northerners arrived, the leaders on horseback. There was quite a party, including several in Outlander garb. Of the six riders, two were women, one an Outlander with three feathers in a leather helmet, the other soberly dressed, but wearing around her neck the standard Mayor's chain of office. The Visitor's introductions left no doubt about the nature of the delegation.

"My Lady, my Lords, allow me to introduce the delegation from our Pennine Realm. Following the custom of the west, we have three Ridings. Captain O'Hanlon speaks for the Riding of Derwentdale, Muss Franklin, now Mayor of the Riding of Bradfield, Mr Myslibonski, Bailiff of the City and Riding of Sheffield. You know Major Cornwallis, who commands our forces, and of course Lord Bohun, who now manages the as yet sterile grounds to the east." He paused. "The notional territory of the Domain."

Lady Buckingham retained her composure.

"Well, well. Realm; a nice word; Defoe could not have done better. And your role, my Lord? A faithful servant of the Domain, as I recall."

"I have the honour, my Lady, to preside over our new found Realm with the consent of my colleagues here. There is no title. My service to the Domain has indeed ended, less bloodily than that of the late Lord Lane."

"And the Outland? What have they to say about this Realm of yours?"

O'Hanlon spoke up.

"The Outland is no Domain. When we have acted as one, there has been no compulsion. When we meet at the Point, there will truly be three parties to any agreement. There will be another from my Riding at the Point tomorrow."

There were no more questions. In the afternoon, all would head to the Point. Separated for a meal, the Domain contingent absorbed the shock.

"A secession? Even, in fact, yet another extension of the Outland at our expense. The Queen of Grounds lost. Can we let this go? Will others not follow?"

"How can we stop it? We can reclaim the sterile Domain by force easily enough, but to what purpose? One of the most desolate, maintained only to service the Ground and provide a little coal. Not to mention Lane and his obsession with clearance. Attack from there, and we face not just the city, but

Outlanders as well. Grounders? Any sign that we will take possession and they will skip west. Not to mention more balloons and harassment in the south. We have better things to do with our lives and theirs. More to the point, why have they summoned us?"

***

With mobiles, it was the Domain party that arrived first at the Treaty Point. There had been changes. Alongside the buildings were substantial tents, well equipped to house many. The Kingsmen manning it through the summer and autumn had been fraternising with Outlanders, and indeed with their own comrades who had crossed over with sergeant Mills. Neither Jacks nor Kipling had rebuked them. Settled in the buildings rather than tents, there was, nevertheless, the uncomfortable feeling among the delegation that they were guests. Uniforms notwithstanding, it was not clear to whom the soldiers answered.

The party from the north were not far behind them, and settled happily into the tents. As night fell, there was singing from the lamp-lit tents, but a silence descended on the buildings. The delegation from the Domain had much to think about.

Early morning walks brought Kent and Cornwallis together by chance. They contemplated the remains of the pyre made by the major and Kipling in the summer.

"An unnecessary precaution, as it turned out;" said Cornwallis, "I wonder, my Lord, if it would have been sufficient?"

"If Lane had time here, no. There would have been a report of Outie butchery. Had we arrived before he had a chance to tamper with things, then maybe. For that, at least, we have something to thank you for, Major."

Kent paused; the change that had taken place, the direct challenge to the Domain, was still unassimilated.

"My apologies. Maybe I should talk of General or Chief?"

Cornwallis grinned.

"None needed, my Lord. No title has been bestowed on me, merely the acknowledgement as commander. Commander in name only, for there must be agreement among us for any action."

"Tell me then, Major, who may we expect to come up the hill to talk to us later this morning. Are there still nobles in the Outland?"

"Not for me to say, my Lord, but I believe only one Old-timer still lives, Lord Defoe, and he will not be present. You will be aware that there are new recruits to the Westron nobility. They may be present. We will see."

There was no malice in Cornwallis' reply, but the mild irony struck home. They parted to their respective quarters, where the sounds of breakfast preparation were becoming louder. An hour or so later, the northern delegation entered the Point building and a flag was raised, summoning the Outlanders. The meeting room had been altered. Instead of the long table, there was an approximation to a triangle. With clerks and a token set of soldiers, the room was already more crowded than usual when the Outlanders entered.

Only three principals. O'Neill, now known to all, Lord Steel, now arrayed in Outlander gear, and a woman, unknown to the Domain, introduced as Chief Evans of the Derwentdale Riding. All three laid aside helmets with three feathers. Buckingham picked up the duplication.

"A Riding," she paused on the word, "a district, I presume, represented in two delegations. Under whose authority is this Riding?"

Rhianna glanced at O'Hanlon, then spoke.

"Neither or both, my Lady, which is why there are two of us, and why we have asked for this meeting. Chief O'Neill is best placed to explain."

O'Neill regarded those around the table. The two first-born, the Royalty, facing him had not supported the assault, the provocation, offered by the Lane Raid, a name transmitted to him from Manod. But its prevention had depended on those in the north, not on the Domain's rulers. He knew, in outline only, that they had discovered land overseas. A fact that might inhibit aggression, but would also increase their demands on Grounds and cities.

"We must thank you, my Lady, for abiding by our recent Treaty in the face of those determined to provoke conflict. However, that provocation has had the effects that you see here, a Realm that combines a part of our West with the northernmost part of your Domain. A new Treaty is required to acknowledge that Realm, free to determine its own future. A Realm from which any movement to the Domain, or to the Outland, is by free choice by those involved."

Expected, and hard to deny, though the implications for Service, and for a source of fertility were severe. But there was something in O'Neill's face that showed that there was more to come, more and even less palatable.

"Of course, movement from the Domain and its Grounds should also be free and unconstrained. At the very least, from your cities, your Reproductive Priority Zones."

His voice hardened on the last three words. Buckingham and Kent were silent. It was Pendennis who broke the tension.

"A demand that you have already pre-empted, I think, O'Neill. We have seen city dwellers moving north, north through routes cleared and marked for some time. The Ground here cannot support so many. Even before now, we had to send food and materials to sustain it. To what end?"

O'Neill turned to an Outlander standing behind him, a massive, bearded man, visibly disfigured.

"My Lord Admiral," he said, earning a mock punch from the giant, "please tell our guests of your recent adventures."

Buckingham flinched inwardly. *Guests.* In our own station. Would that we had anyone with half the skill, the power this Outlander has. Brother, here is your dumb Outie servant; as well you are no longer with us.

"*Captain* Smith, may it please you, a mariner by trade. It is common knowledge, is it not, that all land much to the north of here was desolate. Badlands of the worst kind. Badlands that would take centuries to heal."

He turned his head towards Cornwallis.

"A long time ago, the major here was involved in trying to catch an evader from your Service, a young man, Mark Norman. Luckily for us all, he escaped your forces and found refuge with us. In his travels, he came upon information, information from before the War, from the end of the Catastrophe. Maps, maps that showed areas far to the north that remained uninhabited. Diseased, no doubt, in the past, but not polluted. Areas with the quality of this Ground to our north."

Smith had been briefed. No Jones, nor his refuge. What might be retrieved from the rubble? No names, no locations: They also had land to occupy, but, by all accounts, land more dangerous to reach and harder to farm. Let them brave the passage from the south to unknown locations if they dare, but do not tempt them to think to march west to Manod.

"We have found some of those areas. We are occupying them. Occupying them with people who breed true, untainted. There are few enough such folk in the Outland as you know it, but many in the cities."

"And young Mr Norman, together with his mother and sister are now among them," added O'Neill. "There is room for thousands, tens of thousands. They are larger than when they were mapped. There are more to reach when paths are cleared. No need any longer for us to scrape existence in every tiny patch of semi-badland. And no need for city dwellers to sacrifice their sons and daughters to sterile service. Several hundred have already moved. In the spring, it will be thousands in our larger fleet. With livestock from the Ground. Livestock that will no longer be going south."

Before any in the Domain party could overcome their surprise, Amelia, with a nod from Rhianna, spoke out.

"Do not think to starve us. Our Ground, and the Derwentdale Riding can expand, no, have already expanded beyond what you can have imagined. Land between us? Supposedly poisoned? It has been clear for many decades. Your Visitor," she gave him a grin, "knew this very well, as did Chief Evans. It suited all to abide by treaties, to keep your precious Ground free of poaching, to remove any need for military action from the Domain and to shield from view an expanding Ground of the Outlander's own. Only the Norman boy's flight and the Domain's response put all at risk."

"Another matter for your consideration," said Mysliborski. "There are fewer of us in the city than in the summer, but we are better prepared and better armed. The crossing from the Domain is narrow. We will certainly have help from our friends if an attempt is made to force it. Perhaps chemical help."

Cornwallis added the final touch.

"You have seen how we dealt with Lane. Try to advance along this narrow corridor, try to do the same to advance into the Ground, and you will discover foes not only ahead, but behind and on both sides. Conisbrough? You are welcome to it. Advance north and you will have only the inconvenience of extensive road repair and the absence of any supplies."

The Domain party were struck silent. O'Neill proposed an adjournment, and both Outlanders and those from the north retired to the tents. When they were out of earshot, Buckingham gave a bitter laugh.

"A mirror image, by Majesty. Here we are, poised to recruit the fertile and their stock and seed to our own Newfoundland, only to find that they have been taken from us. It will not be only from the north. Those cities, our RPZs, will be drained and drained. A pity we did not bring Wilkes with us."

"Wilkes? To what purpose?" asked Kent. "That Cornwallis fellow laid out the position fair and square. We would win, in the end. Narrow the crossing might be, but the city could be bypassed, and the Ground occupied. We could at least hinder movements north across this corridor. Or apply pressure elsewhere. But at what cost?"

"Retaliation elsewhere," said Pendennis. "Those damned balloons would strike our Grounds again. Advance through Cotswold? Wilkes would demand three times the force we possess and a year or more to produce enough weapons and ammunition. The same here in the north. The cities would resist again; that means yet more recruitment. It would be ourselves who ended up starving."

"Not only that," added Kent. "Move into the Ground, and the people will move west. We could move others in, but we would have to maintain a border force or advance deeper into Outie lands. As our brother would have wished. He would not have counted the cost, but it is greater than he could have conceived."

***

It was a melancholy party that made its way back from the Point towards Windsor. Terms had been agreed, as they had to be. Assured that the Domain would launch no assault, would not interfere with recruitment from the cities accessible to the west, both the north, the Pennine Realm as they must now call it, and the Outland had been happy to deal with the practicalities of trade, the supply of electricity and the exchange of food, goods and livestock.

Pressed briefly, perhaps unwisely, by Pendennis, on the problems for the Domain in peopling its own Newfoundland, O'Neill had merely shrugged. It was not his problem. He was happy to restore Conisbrough and its desolate surroundings to the Domain, with any who wished to remain there. The bridge across which so many journeys had brought them to this place was now to mark a new frontier. His final demand met no opposition: no Hunts, ever again. As Kent said later, no doses and there would be few that would miss it in any case.

There was one bright spot, most especially for Lady Buckingham. Paused at Retford, they were joined by a solitary Bohun. A Bohun who wished to join them in their journey south, and had followed them soon after their departure.

"My Lady," he said, "what is left in the Northernmost Division, at Conisbrough, is now merely a transit place; it is little more than a way station. No work for me there, no need to maintain the place as the means of protecting the supply of Service from the Ground, nor to support that murderous work at the Barriers. No need to liaise with the Court or yourself. There is, likewise, no useful work I can do for the new Realm, nothing that others cannot do as well or better."

Buckingham was at first taken aback.

"You are defecting, my Lord? Defecting for a second time. How do your new compatriots regard your departure?"

"All agreed, my Lady. They have no use for Conisbrough. I am but a shadowy figure in their eyes, unknown in person to those in the Ground or the city. The Visitor they know and trust, now."

"And with us? The need for the subterfuge, the deflection of attention from the north, they have gone, like it or not."

"You have new Ground in prospect overseas, I heard. Another volunteer, another recruit, might be welcome? I have about forty years left, I think, years I am happy to spend in establishing it."

***

The augmented party returned to Windsor. While the months that had followed Barlow had been turbulent, the three had managed to establish a degree of order. Not without resistance, the Security Corps had been dismantled. A force more akin to the Proctors of the Grounds had been assigned to man the crossing points to Grounds and cities. A force answerable to Pendennis, and not to Truth and Justice, a Commission that had been wound up. Instead, a new force, the Constabulary, had been set up to maintain order within the Domain. The title, of course, stemmed from Defoe's erratic educational programme those centuries ago. At Windsor itself, the centre of what was left of resistance to the new reality, Kent had arranged a public bonfire of the black uniforms that symbolised the old regime.

Reclamation had ceased, other than the maintenance of tracks and the monitoring of natural improvement. The problem of those Security troopers and civilians captured as disturbances were quelled was easily solved. Now, faced with the prospect of residual reclamation work at home, or transport overseas to conduct clearance fully kitted out, the volunteers for the latter were numerous. They were joined by hygienists and a few others expelled by newly assertive Grounds.

Even if they had so wished it to continue, the era of coercion in the cities or the Grounds was over. Those finding themselves sterile might volunteer for

Service; that would be all. Wilkes was firm when the issue was raised on their return.

"My Lady, the men will not enter the cities or any Ground uninvited. Come selection and Choosing, we are at their mercy."

Buckingham and Kent had looked at each other at that. There was a grim, an ironic, sense of achievement that was shared silently. The future, as they had seen, was with the fertile—the fertile and mortal. It had arrived in a manner not of their choosing. Indeed, there were changes that overshadowed their private triumph overseas. There was discomfort ahead. No more the luxury of Court. Short commons for many in the years to come. She whispered to her brother as Wilkes left them, whispered nevertheless in the mocking tones of Defoe:

"*We'll think of it all tomorrow. Tomorrow. After all, tomorrow is another day.*"

Kent grinned and made no reply.